CN

THE
BURNING
ROAD

Also by Ann Benson

THE PLAGUE TALES

THE
BURNING
ROAD

A NOVEL

ANN BENSON

Delacorte Press

Published by
Delacorte Press
Random House, Inc.
1540 Broadway
New York, New York 10036

Library of Congress Cataloging in Publication Data
Benson, Ann.
    The burning road / by Ann Benson.
        p.   cm.
    ISBN 0-385-33289-0
    I. Title.
PS3552.E547659B87   1999
813'.54—dc21   98-27783
                                                    CIP

Designed by Lynn Newmark

Manufactured in the United States of America
Published simultaneously in Canada

April 1999

10   9   8   7   6   5   4   3   2   1

BVG

The author cherishes her memories of
Al Prives and Linda Cohen Horn
and dedicates this book to them.

ACKNOWLEDGMENTS

Meryl Glassman did thorough and excellent background research in French, work that enabled me to bring the fourteenth century characters alive more fully and accurately. The wonderful people at Delacorte Press, especially my precious editor Jackie Cantor, made this sometimes difficult project feel easy. Jennifer Robinson, Peter Miller, and DeLin Cormeny of PMA Literary and Film Management made it all possible in the first place. The support of friends and family contributed immeasurably to my joy in the entire process. My thanks to everyone who helped along the way.

THE
BURNING
ROAD

1358

When had Alejandro Canches last read the language on the papyrus before him? It would not come clear to his sleepy mind. *In Spain,* he thought; *no, France, when I was first here.*

Ah, yes, he remembered, *it was in England. The letter from my father, left behind when we fled.*

He struggled to reach back into the memory of that time, to push aside the veil of the years, for nestled dormant beneath the bitter wisdom of manhood was the sweet eagerness of the boy he had once been, the one who had studied these letters by candlelight under the careful scrutiny of his family. He had found pleasure in the task, while other boys his age complained. *Of what use is all this studying?* they would say. *Soon we shall all be forced to speak Spanish anyway.*

If we are not killed before then, he recalled thinking at the time.

The first page was done, its symbols unlocked, the words finally revealed. He felt the pride of that small boy, and the hunger for praise that never died. He ached to the depths of his immortal soul to do more, but his mortal body seemed determined to forbid him that joy. Would he awaken later in a cold pool of his own spittle, with the letters smeared to ruin beneath his cheek? Or would the candle burn down while he snored with his chin on his chest, and spread its wax upon the leaves? He could not allow either.

He carefully turned back the papyrus pages and read to himself again what he had translated. The symbols, applied with aching precision in the purest gold, ran right to left on the page.

ABRAHAM THE JEW, PRINCE, PRIEST, LEVITE, ASTROLOGER, AND PHILOSOPHER, TO THE NATION OF THE JEWS, BY THE WRATH OF GOD DISPERSED AMONG THE GAULS, SENDETH HEALTH.

In these pages, the apothecary had claimed, there were great secrets. And it was only because he was in desperate straits, the rogue had further said, that he would consider parting with such a treasure. So the young woman who called Alejandro Canches her *père* had reached into the pocket of her skirt on a trip to the apothecary shop and extracted the gold coin he insisted she always carry, should they somehow be separated, and boldly exchanged the coin for the book. Alejandro had sent her out for herbs, and she had returned with leaves of a different sort. She had known what it would mean to him.

He glanced across the small dark cottage in which they made their home of the moment, and smiled at her sleeping form. "I have taught you well, then," he said quietly.

Straw crinkled as the young woman shifted. Her soft voice drifted through the darkness, affectionate but chiding.

"Père? Are you still awake?"

"Aye, child," he said, "your book will not let me go."

"I am no longer a child, Père. You must call me by my name, or 'daughter,' if that pleases you. But not 'child.' And it is *your* book, but I begin to regret buying it for you. Now you must go to bed and give your eyes some peace."

"My eyes do not lack peace. They have far too much peace. They are hungry for the words on these pages. And you must never regret this acquisition."

She rose up on one elbow and rubbed the sleep from her face. "I shall if you will not heed your own warning that too much use will ruin the eyes."

He peered through the semidarkness at the young woman who had grown up so fine and lovely under his care, so straight and strong and fair. Only the barest hints of child-flesh remained on her face and fingers, and soon, he knew, that too would melt away, along with her innocence. But the rosy blush of girlhood still lingered on her cheeks, and Alejandro wished silently that it would remain just a little longer.

She has become a woman, he admitted to himself. This notion was accompanied by a familiar twinge that he had yet to define to his own satisfaction, though he often thought "helpless joy" to be as close a description of it as he would ever find. It had lurked in his heart since the day, a decade before, when he'd suddenly found himself with this child to raise, and had grown as he discovered that despite his considerable learning, he was no better prepared than an unlettered man for the task. Although some men seemed to know just what to do and when to do it, he himself was not a man who did the work of mothering with natural grace. He thought it God's cruel trick that the Black Death had claimed so many mothers—it was they who had labored alongside the physicians to bring comfort to their dying husbands and children, and then because of their proximity had died themselves in terrible numbers. And though he abhorred the dearth of mothers and physicians, Alejandro wished that more priests had been taken. Those who had survived were the ones who had locked themselves away for the sake of self-preservation while their brothers perished in service. He considered them a thoroughly scurrilous lot.

He had done his solitary best for the girl, without a wife, for he would not sully the memory of the woman he had loved in England by marrying for mere convenience. And Kate had never complained of her lack of mothering. She had reached the threshold of womanhood with unusual grace and now stood ready to cross it. As the motherless ward of a renegade Jew, she had, through some unfathomable miracle, become a creature worthy of awe.

The lovely creature spoke. "Please, Père, I beg you to heed your own wisdom. Go to sleep. Otherwise I shall have to do your reading for you when you are an old man."

This brought a smile to his lips. "May God in His wisdom grant that I shall live long enough to know such a worry. And that you shall still be with me when I do." He closed the manuscript carefully. "But you are right. I should go to sleep. Suddenly the straw seems terribly inviting."

He moved the tome aside so it would not be splattered with wax, then placed one hand behind the candle flame and drew in a breath to blow it out.

There was a knock on the door.

Their heads turned in tandem toward the unfamiliar sound, and Kate's voice came through the darkness in a frightened whisper. "Père? Who—?"

"Shhh, child . . . be silent," he whispered back. He sat frozen in the chair, the light of the candle still flickering before him.

The knock came again, then a man's firm, strong voice. "I beg you, I am in need of a healer . . . the apothecary sent me."

Alejandro shot an alarmed glance at Kate, who sat trembling on her straw bed with the wool cover pulled up protectively around her neck. He leaned closer and said in an urgent whisper, "How does he know I am a healer?"

"He . . . he thinks that *I* am the healer!"

"What? What nonsense is this?"

"I had to tell the apothecary *something,* Père!" she whispered back, her voice almost desperate. "The man was inordinately curious and would not let the inquiry go! And it is not nonsense. You yourself have trained me in the healing arts. And so to satisfy him I told him that *I*—"

"Midwife!" the urgent plea came from beyond the door. "Please! I implore you to open up! Your help is sorely needed!"

Alejandro wanted simply to shoot a look of fatherly consternation at her, to shake a scolding finger in her face, to tell her she must never behave so foolishly again, and be done with it. But there was a stranger at the door. "Why did you not tell me this before?" he asked.

She hastened to explain. "It did not seem necessary, Père—when the apothecary asked why I wanted such herbs as you sent me for, I told him that *I* was learning the healing arts! *That* was why he showed me the book. I swear, I said nothing of you."

He saw fright in her eyes, and understood that she was frightened of him. It was a woeful realization, one that filled him with shame. She had been trying to protect him from discovery and please him with the gift of the book. His anger melted. "All right. What's done is done," he said. "Now I must think how to answer."

Kate tossed the cover aside and rose up from her pallet, shivering in her thin shift. She found her shawl in the darkness and wrapped it tightly about her shoulders. "Why do anything at all?" she whispered. "Why not just ignore him—the door is strong enough. Eventually he will give up and move on."

Another knock came, more insistent. They huddled closer together.

"There is nowhere else for him to go, if he is being pursued."

"Then we must open the door and turn him away!" she answered, her words barely audible.

"He may not be so easily repelled."

"I will tell him I cannot help. Surely he will not insist!"

The knock was louder this time, the voice pleadingly urgent. "Midwife—I beg you, open the door! I mean you no harm . . . I have brought an injured man!"

"A moment, sir!" Kate called back. And with her words, all possibilities of hiding were eliminated.

She ignored the astonished look on Alejandro's face. "He has the speech of an educated man. He cannot be a ruffian."

"That is no guarantee that he will not harm us. Or betray us. A peasant is not likely to know that we are sought. An educated man might."

Their words were rushed and panicky. "But why a ruse—why not just capture us and be done with it?"

An injury—work for his hands. All his physician's healing instincts rose up, overwhelming his better judgment. Often of late his hands seemed to tremble in need of the work of healing. And it was entirely possible that the man had come solely because he *was* in need of help.

Alejandro's heart almost sang with the thought.

He nodded his head toward the door and whispered, "God grant that we shall not regret doing this."

There came more pounding, then pleading. *"Midwife!"*

"Lie down on your pallet, Père," she whispered urgently, "and do not show yourself just yet. Let me speak for us."

"I cannot allow you to face this man alone—"

"Be calm, I beseech you! A midwife is expected, and that is what we shall present. Pretend to be infirm—if I need your help or advice, I will say that I need to tend to you. If I kneel beside you we can whisper to each other without his hearing what is said."

"Aye," he answered quietly. "When did you become so brave and clever?" He hugged her to him for a few moments, cherishing the warmth she gave, missing terribly the small child she had once been. "May God protect us," he said, and reluctantly he went to his bed.

Staring back at her through the flickering light of the upheld candle was not the devil she had expected, but the frightened, uncertain face of a man she had not seen before, either in the nearby village of Meaux or in their recent travels north of Paris. Kate felt certain she would have remembered a man of such distinctive appearance—but he was not familiar.

The silhouette of her unwanted caller nearly filled the doorway and she could feel his need to enter, but she stood her ground and barred the path through some miracle of courage. One glance in the candlelight told her that the man was younger than Père but older than herself, with intelligent, quick eyes and a high brow. And though his clothing did not speak of poverty, it was disheveled and dirty, as was his hair. He appeared to have been involved in a skirmish.

She returned his hard look with one equally firm. "Sir, the apothecary has made too much of my skills, and I do not—"

But he would not be refused, and pushed her aside. On the travois he dragged over the threshold were two forms—a heavy burden for even the strongest man.

"Help me with these wounded!" he ordered.

She ignored his demand and kept her eyes fixed steadily on him as he bent to his companions, one of whom began to groan and writhe. "Karle . . ." the fallen soldier called out in his pain. "Help me, Karle . . . I am run through, I fear."

The stranger beckoned urgently with his hand. "Bring the light—I cannot see him!"

Kate held up her candle with one hand as the stranger pulled aside the blanket covering both men, and when the horror of what lay beneath it met her eyes she gasped out a quick and desperate prayer. Both men wore torn, filthy woolen garments that were soaked through with blood. On first glance she could not tell if both were bleeding or, if it was only one, from whom the blood originated.

"Dear God in heaven," she cried, "has there been a battle?" And then, with deeper fear in her voice, she looked with dismay at the man who had been called Karle and asked, "Are there English nearby?"

The stranger gave her a suspicious look and said, "Midwife, though I would swear you are far too young to bear that title, it was not the dogs of England who did this to these good men, but the forces of Charles of Navarre, their own countryman!"

As relief washed through her, she heard her own name called low from Alejandro's straw pallet. The stranger Karle quickly turned his head in the direction of the sound. His hand went straight to a knife strapped to his belt.

"It is my father," she explained quickly. "He is ailing!" And before Karle could protest, she rushed to Alejandro's side and kneeled down next to him.

"Be careful," Alejandro whispered to her, "there is danger here. . . ."

"What shall I do? He *says* there are no English."

"We can never know when Edward's agents may be at hand."

One of the injured men began to wail. Kate turned to go back to him, but Alejandro grasped her by the shawl and held her at his side. "Wait!" he said in a low voice. "Do nothing, but watch what he does."

"Midwife!" Karle called. "What keeps you? You must come *now*!"

She turned to face him and said, "My father—"

But the cries of the maimed—the pain of their wounds, the agony of knowing that they had been cut down by the swords of their own countrymen—overwhelmed the sound of her words. Finally Alejandro could stand it no more. Muttering curses, he threw off his cover and rose up from the pallet. He went straight to where the two men lay and knelt down beside them. "Give me light!" he said. Kate thrust the candle up so its light would be cast where he needed it.

Karle stared down at the physician, then glanced back at the daughter. "You make too light of your skills," he said. "You seem to have worked a miracle on your ailing father. *Midwife*." The title was spoken with an unmistakable sneer. "But perhaps I should be addressing your father as such, and not yourself."

Alejandro cut off his examination of the groaning warriors and stood up abruptly. He held out a bloody hand, which Kate knew from years of assisting him to mean that her *père* wanted a cloth. Alejandro took the one she found and wiped the blood from his hands, and then came nose-to-nose with the younger man. "Address me as you like," he warned, "but you will not speak to my daughter in such a tone."

They stood with their eyes locked in a combative gaze and took each other's measure. Neither seemed to find the other lacking, but it was the intruder who stepped back first. "I meant no disrespect," Guillaume Karle said, "neither to you nor her. Nor is it my intent to harm either of you. I came here seeking help, expecting only a midwife. Your circumstances are of no interest to me. I need to stay out of sight, for I am known to all around here, and as you can see, the night has brought— *difficulty*." He gestured toward his fallen comrades. "I will be grateful for anything that you or your daughter can do for these two." He swallowed hard. "Now you have looked at them," he said. "What say you?"

Alejandro's defensive posture relaxed a bit. He put the bloody rag down on the table and took Karle by the elbow, then led him out of the injured men's earshot. "One will live; I will have to take his arm, but he will live."

"You possess the skills to do this?"

Slowly, warily, Alejandro nodded. "I am a physician."

The look he received back from Karle was one of genuine surprise. "You have hidden yourself well, then, sir. It is said there are no physicians hereabout."

"Not well enough, I think, since you seem to have found me. But had you not, you would have found the skills to take the arm yourself, had the need to do so arisen. Of this I can assure you."

Karle's expression was full of doubt. "I cannot say that I would have it in me. What of the other?"

Alejandro sighed and shook his head slowly from side to side. "Are you a merciful man?" he asked.

As if insulted, Karle raised his chin and said, "To a fault."

"Then you must show the other your best mercy by dispatching him quickly. He shall not survive more than a few hours, and those, I promise you, will be agony. I have laudanum enough to quiet the one whose arm must come off, but not enough to ease the pain of the other. It will best be eased with the sharp thrust of a sword."

Karle glanced nervously over Alejandro's shoulder in the direction of his two prone warriors; Kate was comforting both as best she could by gently wiping the sweat off their brows and cleansing their faces with cool water.

"You have no poison?" he asked quietly.

Alejandro studied Karle's eyes again. He recognized in them the same expression he had often seen in his own reflection, the fear and uncertainty of a man on the run. He decided he had nothing to lose by speaking frankly.

"I am trained in the healing arts, and I have sworn an oath to do no harm. I have broken that oath more times than I care to recall, but I am not of a mind to do it again right now. And I have no skills with poison. Such things are the business of the apothecary. Or the alchemist. Practitioners of a different cloth than I."

"I meant no offense—"

"I took none. Now, this man is your comrade, is he not?"

Karle looked down with stricken pity, and the image of the man's falling rushed undesired through his memory. "Aye. A worthy one."

"Then be as worthy a comrade to him, and dispatch him."

Reluctant horror spread slowly over Karle's face. "I have killed many soldiers in battle," he said, "but never one of my own. I have seen it done, but I do not know if I have the will to do it myself."

Alejandro put a hand gently on Karle's chest, just above his heart. Karle stiffened, but did not move away. "Angle the sword horizontally so it will slip between these ribs," he said, demonstrating the exact location with his fingers, "then give one quick thrust."

Karle winced as if he could feel the sword between his own ribs.

"It is no different in method than slaying a boar or other such beast," Alejandro said sympathetically. "Though it will seem far more abhorrent to you. But if the dying one is sent swiftly to meet his God, we can concentrate our efforts on the one who may yet live." He stared directly into Karle's eyes. "I think we must do this quickly, eh?"

The amber-haired man knew Alejandro was right, and nodded.

They lifted the man who could be saved off the travois and placed him on the long table in the center of the dark cottage. Alejandro handed the bloody rag to Karle and whispered, "Place this around the sword to soak up the blood before you thrust. There will be blood enough when we take this one's arm. Now hurry, or we will lose them both."

The physician turned away. Guillaume Karle stood over his mortally wounded comrade, a rag in one hand, his sword in the other. Tears filled his eyes as he placed the tip of the sword on the man's chest. He crossed himself, then pressed down with all his might. The dying man arched his back upward and let out a sharp breath, but did not cry out. He fell back limp, and blood began to ooze out of his open mouth.

Alejandro gave Karle a sympathetic nod and said, "You have shown courage. And the man died well and honorably. Now move him aside and come here; your help is needed."

Karle was too stunned even to consider protesting and did as he was bidden, then came back to the table, where Kate and Alejandro were busy at work. They had already cut away the cloth of the warrior's sleeve to expose the mangled, soon-to-be-removed appendage, and had slowed the bleeding by tying a torn strip of the sleeve cloth tightly around the upper arm. Blood no longer spurted, but instead oozed; still, the man's skin was ghastly white.

The physician said, "There is little time—I have already dosed him with laudanum, but its effects will not last long. He *will* feel something of what we do, so you must lean on his chest with all your weight to keep him still." He touched the handle of a wooden spoon gently on the lips of his patient, who took it between his teeth almost instinctively and bit down. "Scream if you like," he told the frightened warrior, "but keep the stick in your mouth and no one will hear it outside these walls. I will do this as quickly as I can." He touched the man's sweaty forehead briefly. "God be with you."

Karle held the man down but turned away, for he could not stomach the look of raw terror on his comrade's face. He let his eyes wander; they came to rest on the tools laid out on the edge of the table, a sight no more appealing. More than once he had seen similar tools used to draw and quarter a man with slow and deliberate cruelty. But the physician's motions were mercifully swift and far more practiced than Karle expected, and remarkably the soldier did not writhe. Instead he lost consciousness, for which blessing Karle whispered a heartfelt prayer of thanks.

"We are done," Alejandro said. He touched Karle on the shoulder. "You need not hold him down anymore." He went to the hearth and pulled an iron out of the coals. He pressed the glowing tip against the oozing stump of the upper arm. The hiss was quickly followed by a loathsome stench, and all three turned their heads away. When the cautery was complete, Alejandro poured wine over the blackened stump and wrapped it in clean cloth bandages.

His work finished, he sat down on a bench and buried his face in his hands. He breathed deeply a few times, then looked up at the other two. "The air in here is foul," he said.

He went to the door and opened it a crack, then looked outside. "The shadows are still," he reported. He beckoned with his hand to Kate and Karle. "Come out into the air. It will clear your senses."

But Karle was reluctant to leave his comrade on the table, so Alejandro reassured him. "He will not move, for his body has suffered a grave insult."

The daughter followed the father out into the night air and stood beside him. Alejandro placed a consoling arm around her shoulder. Through the darkness, the stunned Karle watched as comforting was passed between them. The night was now velvety black and he could just make out their silhouettes; he was surprised to see that the young woman was a shade taller than the man he had heard her call Père. He watched as the physician stroked her hair in a soothing, fatherly manner, and tried to calm her as she wept against his shoulder.

And though the night's events had left him in a state where cogent thought felt almost unnatural, he found himself momentarily disturbed by how unalike the two seemed.

As the light of day filtered into the small cottage, Guillaume Karle sat on a bench and watched as his unconscious companion's chest slowly rose and fell. What remained of the man's left arm was wrapped in a bloody bandage, but the color of the seepage was not the bright red the physician had warned him to watch for; instead, it was the pale, dullish color that indicated all was going as well as could be expected.

He glanced over at his two benefactors and allowed himself, now that the need for urgency had passed, a moment of curiosity. The physician lay on a straw pallet, apparently sleeping, but with one eye half-open. Karle had the sense that the man was well used to incomplete repose. Beyond him lay the maiden Kate on her own pallet. The physician was a lean, angular man, dark and olive-complected, with softly curling locks the color of coal. He was oddly handsome, with long limbs and finely shaped hands. And while Kate too was long and well-shaped, she was fair and pink, almost Nordic in her coloration, with eyes that had sparkled blue even in the light of the candle the night before.

As if he knew he were being watched, the physician stirred and opened his eyes fully. He rose up on one elbow and met Karle's gaze. "What of your man?" he inquired immediately.

"Quiet," Karle replied. "He sleeps. I have kept him from moving as you said I should."

"Well done," Alejandro said as he rose from the bed. He took a quick look at the bandage on the stump, then said, "Good. There is no fresh bleeding. This bodes well."

He took a basin down from a cupboard and filled it with water from a large pitcher that sat on the edge of the hearth, then stripped off his shirt and began to wash himself, first his face, then the upper part of his body, and finally, with painstaking attention, his hands. Though Alejandro angled his body so his chest could not fully be seen, Karle caught a quick glimpse of what he thought might be a scar. The Frenchman gave a moment's thought to inquiring about it, but decided to leave it be.

But the physician made no attempt to contain his own curiosity. As he dressed himself, he said, "I have heard of no battles hereabout. How came these men to be wounded? And contrary to what you may have heard, it is rumored that there *is* a physician in the next town. Why did you not seek his services before those of a midwife?"

"Which question would you have me answer first?" Karle asked warily.

"Whichever you like," Alejandro replied with similar wariness. "But answer them both."

Karle looked him straight in the eye. "As you wish," he said, "but when I am through with the telling, I will likewise want some answers from you."

"No doubt," Alejandro said. "We shall see if you get them. Right now you are far more in my debt than I in yours." He glanced at the sleeping, one-armed man. "You will pay by speaking. Start by telling me your name."

The amber-haired man hesitated a moment, then said, "You heard my man speak my name last night."

"He called you Karle," Alejandro recalled.

"*Guillaume* Karle," he said, and nodded his head. "There are many who would pay handsomely for knowledge of my whereabouts." He grinned bitterly and said, "But here I am, as you say, in *your* debt. Now permit me the honor of knowing to whom I am speaking, and why you are hiding as well."

Karle's quick and accurate appraisal of their situation caught the physician by surprise. He raised one eyebrow and said, "In due time. How were these men wounded?"

Karle drew in a breath. "They rode with me against the oppression of the nobility. They caught their wounds in the battle to claim their rightful portion of the soil of France."

Alejandro saw a zealot's fire in the eyes of the young man, and in his brow, the tight weariness that was the fire's inevitable toll. "What remains of France to be portioned?" he asked. "All is gone to the Free Companies, is it not?"

"They have taken all that is gold or silver," Karle said indignantly. "But France herself, the good earth of France, is there still and will always be there. We want only that share of land that will allow each man to live decently. And freedom from the excessive taxation the nobility forces upon us to finance their despicable wars."

"Ah," Alejandro said, "I see. Simple requests, then."

Karle gave him a caustic look. "But one must be hiding in a cabinet not to know of these things. How is it that you do not?"

Alejandro's mouth curled in the faintest smile. "We shall speak of my circumstances when yours are more fully explained."

Karle took in a breath and continued. "We rose up against the royal palace at Meaux last night. Against Charles of Navarre. He was far better prepared than we thought he might be, and many more than these two were wounded. Those who could, scattered."

Alejandro considered the walk from Meaux. He had done it many times. Unburdened and in daylight, it took well more than an hour. But this man had dragged two wounded companions behind him with only the moon to guide his steps. His opinion of the intruder improved.

"Some may escape to their own homes," Karle went on. "They will take what wounded they can. But some who are hurt will have been left. God alone knows what will happen to the bodies of those who fell in the battle. We could not stay behind to gather them up."

"Who will see to this one?" Alejandro pointed to the dead man on the travois. "He will shortly be unpleasant company."

The ghastly remains were beginning to bloat as putrefaction took hold of his inner organs. "I suppose it shall be upon me to see to him," Karle said with resignation.

"He cannot be buried near this cottage," Alejandro said quickly.

Karle sighed. "I will take him into the forest to bury him, then." He looked up at the one-armed man still sleeping on the table and added grimly, "Along with Jean's arm."

They heard a stirring behind them as Kate sat up. "There is a clearing in the wood to the north," she said. "There are many berries there, but I saw no signs of anyone having passed through recently. It is not holy ground, but it seems otherwise fit for a burial."

"There is no holy ground left in all of France, I fear," Karle said. "But I thank you for telling me of this place."

She nodded in the direction of the corpse. "All brave men deserve a good end, do they not?"

Alejandro watched Guillaume Karle's eyes digest the sight of Kate, then reluctantly break away. When the two men faced each other again, Karle's skin was flushed, as if he had been caught in an indecent thought.

"Perhaps, if you are of a mind to do so, your *père* will allow you to show me this clearing," he said quietly.

She answered too eagerly for the physician's liking. "I shall be glad to."

"We shall all go together," Alejandro said.

"What of my man?" Karle said.

"We will see to his needs before leaving," the physician said. "Clean him, give him water and the little bit of laudanum I have left. And if he is made fast to the table, I am not concerned to leave him alone."

Not nearly as concerned as I am to have you alone with Kate, he thought.

2007

Janie Crowe was out in her backyard trimming shrubs to the soaring strains of Maria Callas when the tiny phone in her pocket began to vibrate. She'd been waiting for the call, but the music's distraction was so complete that the sensation made her jump a little, and when she yanked off her earphones a few hairs got caught in one of the pads. Wincing, she untangled the captive strands as the bird-squawk of the too-warm spring day assaulted her freshly uncovered ears. She looked up at the treetops and snarled, "Be quiet!" There was a moment of silence from the canopy before they started in again.

But these birds, who daily decorated her precious flowers with their odious droppings, *did* have one rather endearing habit: they ate the huge, disease-laden mosquitoes that had migrated north all the way into her area of western Massachusetts. With their food supply so plentiful, and with legislated improvements in air quality, the birds had managed a nice comeback from near demise a few years earlier.

She set the earphones down with regret. Maria Callas, unfortunately, would not be making a comeback anytime in the foreseeable future, no matter how carefully the atmosphere was rebalanced or how many mosquitoes they fed her.

Be a great project to bring her back, though, Janie thought for a brief moment. *She's buried in Paris. . . .*

But mere mortals such as herself could not get visas to Paris. And no more digging, her lawyer had insisted. Digging is trouble.

Janie pulled the insistent phone out of her pocket and whispered a wish that the call would be from the lawyer in question, and that he would, for a change, be the bearer of glad tidings. She flipped open the phone and said, "On," in the flat tone she'd trained the device to recognize, and then added a friendlier "Hello." The familiar but rather tired-sounding voice of attorney Tom Macalester came over the airwaves, and Janie thought, *finally.*

"You're outside . . ." he said after they'd exchanged greetings. "Birds."

"I am. Taming some shrubs that think they've been moved to Florida. They like this hot weather, a lot more than I do—I wilt, they get happy." She lowered herself into a lawn chair with a quiet *oomph.* "However, I'm getting the distinct impression from the sound of your voice that *you* aren't happy about something," she said when she got settled. "You sound—dismayed."

"And I was so determined to put on a good front."

On the computer-phone inside the house, she knew she would see him frowning. On the cellular, she could hear it in his voice. "Maybe that stuff works on juries, Tom, but I know you too well."

"Oh, really?" he said sarcastically. "Then why is it I'm always wishing we knew each other just a little better?"

With a jaded-sounding chuckle, she said, "There's only one way we could know each other better than we already do."

He laughed. "Your place or mine?"

"Okay, now you sound more like yourself."

"Good." He paused and took a breath, and when he spoke again, his tone of voice was far more serious. "I heard from the reinstatement committee. About your application."

Janie had been right. He was unhappy, and therefore in very short order she was as well. She'd been a neurologist of some accomplishment before the Outbreaks—when the rogue disease DR SAM (an acronym for drug-resistant *Staphylococcus aureus mexicalis,* coined by a clever journalist who'd later drunk himself to death) had dropped its load of misery on an unprepared world.

How could they have known or prepared? It was so much worse than anyone could have imagined. She half listened to Tom recite the legal minutiae of her quest for reinstatement to the life she'd once known. A scene from the previous day flashed through her mind as the same reasons for denial she'd heard before were repeated again in Tom's most empathetic voice. No matter how sweetly he delivered the news, each time it became more hateful to her. So she pushed it into the back of her mind with the memory of the victim and police vehicles crowded around a Dumpster in the supermarket parking lot, the green biosafe suits, the green cordoning tape, and then, as she drove by slowly with the window rolled down, one cop's comment into a cell phone:

"Tell someone to turn off the counters."

She knew which counters he'd meant. They'd been turned off once before. It was one small step in the progression of events that led to the dramatic changes in her life. She'd been a good mother, a loving wife, a satisfied human being with a lot still on her horizon. But it had all been taken away from her—first her family, by the disease itself, and then her profession, in the forced medical realignment of the early post-Outbreak era. And then came the fateful trip to London, the one that was supposed to set her on the right road to a new and rewarding career in forensic archaeology. It had been the biggest fiasco of her life. Now, with the help of the accomplished lawyer who'd been her longtime friend, she was desperately trying to get back what little she could of the life she'd known before.

It was beginning to seem like the process itself would consume her.

Tom's voice resurfaced in her consciousness. "A lot of those professional and employment rights were suspended during the first wave," Tom explained, "and the cases with potential to set precedent still haven't worked their way through the courts. But no one's pulling out of the class-action suit yet, so I'd advise you to stay in. We'll keep trying for an individual reinstatement of your license. Whichever comes first, we don't care. The ultimate goal is to get you back in practice, however we have to do it."

"Jesus, Tom, we have a Bill of Rights, a Constitution. . . ."

"I know. Everyone knows. Don't ask me how we all forgot those things."

"Isn't that why we elect representatives, to stay on top of this stuff?"

"Your representative already said she couldn't do a thing for you. And it's a well-established precedent that in times of national emergency, the government has a broad mandate to do what's necessary to 'maintain order,' whatever that means."

"The emergency's over. The scanners are gone, the isolation wards have been dismantled . . ."

"I know." He paused for a contemplative moment that seemed more weighted than it ought to have been. "At least they mostly have." Then he added, "But I still wouldn't be looking for those rights to be restored anytime soon."

"Why not, for God's sake?"

"I've had this discussion more often than I'd like," he said in a resigned tone of voice. "It never comes out any better. Word is that there's pretty strong resistance to putting things back the way they were before—especially among the powers-that-be. They like things restricted. Remember what happened when they tried to get Big Dattie dismantled?"

It had been an almost laughable exercise in futility, when a coalition of concerned civil liberties groups pooled their talents and resources and sued for the destruction of the universal genetic database that had grown slowly over the years before the DNA code of ethics was established and reached its full flower during the first Outbreak. It was out there on some monstrous server, with its insidious and dangerous data, a constant reminder that nothing was truly private anymore. On balance, the proponents of keeping it intact had argued, it's more beneficial than harmful. And the disease counters, they claimed, were absolutely necessary. Opponents had reacted with a flurry of flag-waving and proprivacy rhetoric, with which Janie actually found herself in tentative agreement. And diseases could be counted in other, less invasive, ways they'd put forth. Janie recalled her stunned disbelief at how quickly the Supreme Court had reached its decision in that case, and the surprising stab of fear she'd felt on hearing that they'd found the database a necessary evil, and had let it stand.

"You must hear all this stuff hot off the presses," she said.

"Most of it never makes it to the presses."

He'd become an expert in medical law many years before, long in advance of the abrupt rise in demand for his specialty in the wake of all the confusing changes the Outbreaks had wrought. He'd lawyered his way through the first wave as a champion to the isolated, the quarantined, the shunned. Tom's practice had boomed in the calmer aftermath, and he'd tucked a lot of potential alliances away in some mental back pocket, into which Janie knew he would have no fear of reaching should it become necessary. He maintained skirting contact with groups who were looking for the Outbreaks' DR SAM, the beastly disease, to slouch toward the United States for reincarnation, despite the vehement and continued pooh-poohing of those who ought to have known better. It would do as it would, despite the best intentions of the medical establishment, and continued efforts to eradicate it. First time around, after a protracted reign of terror, it had finally departed of its own whimsical accord, leaving in its wake a plethora of bewildered and mortified health professionals.

Not to mention dead ones.

"So," she said wearily, "what do you think I should do?"

"Right now? Absolutely nothing."

"Tom, I—"

"I know," he interrupted her, "it's against your religion to be patient. Unfortunately, your options are pretty slim. Patience is still the best one."

He'd already told her that she should expect her application for reinstatement to neurology to be denied, so this phone call was really only a confirmation. Still, it was frustrating. "Good Lord," she said. It sounded too much like whining to her. "Everything in my life is on hold. I don't know how I'm going to stay patient for much longer."

"What else can you do, Janie? Pestering these people isn't going to help. They're up to their necks in applications. In fact, I'd wait about six months before you reapply."

"I don't want to wait that long. Not unless I absolutely have to."

"Well, I think you do absolutely have to, unless your current circumstances change dramatically. The only way we're going to get you back in business right now is if you have some unique specialty—like repairing optic nerves or reversing certain kinds of brain damage—or something equally impossible."

"Twenty years of training and practice aren't enough?"

"Apparently not. Forgive me, I know this sounds awful. But according to government figures, there are more nonspecialized neurologists than necessary for current population levels. If a few more of you had croaked during the Outbreaks, then it would be a different story, maybe. Now, if you were willing to do infectious diseases . . ."

"Don't go there, Tom. . . ."

"I'm only saying that it's a wide-open specialty and a quick retrain, so if you really want to practice medicine, it's something to con—"

"No. Not now, not ever."

"Your talent could be used there, Janie."

A guilty pause. "I know. But I just can't."

"Okay, then you're going to have to be content with doing research at the foundation for a little while longer. Until a few of the old guys die off. Or things lighten up. Then we'll try again."

She sighed in deep disappointment. "This stinks."

"I know. But at least you're working."

"If you can call it that. I hate my job. It's like being someone's secretary. All I do is detail work."

He managed a little laugh. "Well, you could always do forensic archaeology."

"This from the guy who doesn't want me to dig." She closed her eyes
and rubbed her tightening forehead. "Any news from Immigration?"

"Sorry, no," Tom said. "Do you want me to call Bruce and tell him?"

"No. I was going to call tomorrow, anyway. If it were good news, I'd
call today. But bad news can wait."

She took off her gardening gloves and dropped them into her tool bin,
but before going into her house Janie stood in the garage next to the
venerable but beat-looking Volvo she'd bought shiny and new a thousand
years before. In the oddly comforting presence of the familiar car, she
rubbed her palm for a moment, daydreaming of easier times. She could
no longer find the tiny implant in the flesh pad below her thumb; not
even the slightest lump remained. The actual chip, as promised by the
immigration officer in Boston—*You won't even know it's there in a day or
two,* he'd said—had been sucked up as a nutrient by the surrounding
cells, but not until its electronic data had been absorbed into her flesh. It
was a legally mandated physical insult, approaching universal application,
necessitated by the artful work of some criminal genius who'd hacked
into the appropriate server and, with a few well-placed lines of code,
dispatched cornea and palm print identification to the heaven reserved
for archaic, useless technologies.

But as time passed, she'd allowed her personal distaste for electronic
intrusion to wear down, because it was incredibly convenient to have an
instant identity, and as long as she maintained a good credit rating she
could do almost anything she needed to do with a simple swipe of the
hand. But she'd felt none of the first-library-card pride that accompanied
the issuance of her Social Security number and driver's license, back in
the paper days. Instead, after they'd blown the chip into her palm, she'd
stared in quiet horror at the little red mark and longed painfully for the
twentieth century.

It was the final straw in her problem-ridden reentry from England to
the United States, which was highlighted by the visa rejection of the man
she intended to marry when they were settled on her side of the big pond,
because someone in London thought he needed a talking-to about a
certain bio-incident that had occurred in the institute where he did his
research.

But it had been a mishap in the course of Janie's research on London
soil samples that had brought about the near catastrophe, a project that

had nothing to do with Bruce except that he worked in the facility where the chemical analysis of the samples was to be performed. He'd been something of an innocent bystander, caught up in the intrigue when he began to care about Janie, the woman at the center of it, and he quickly became the one who helped her when she found herself in trouble. Accompanied by her assistant, and all dressed up in burglar's garb on a dark night, she'd stolen a small sample of soil from a certain piece of property, against the wishes of the property's caretaker. And in the dirt they dug up, there had been a small piece of decaying fabric, on whose fibers was embedded a sporified bacterium, an archaic bacterium whose present-day form was rather substantially mutated. At first, no one recognized it for what it was. It had been reborn in a lab accident, and revealed itself to be *Yersinia pestis.* . . .

. . . the causative agent of bubonic plague. It promptly picked up a passing plasmid and became a monster.

With a frantic effort, she and Bruce and her assistant, Caroline, had managed to contain *Y. pestis* when it started to reproduce, at a rate that promised to make up for its six-hundred-year interment. To their eternal horror, a few people had succumbed to it, though in consideration of this particular bacterium's history it was a miraculously low number. Caroline had become so ill herself that she nearly died.

And through the skill and cleverness of Bruce's efforts, Janie had somehow escaped scrutiny for the incident, though in truth she'd been far more heavily involved than he had been.

The memory of it all put her in a momentary daze as scenes of yore drifted in and out; she tried to will them all back into the underlayer of her consciousness, but they kept clawing their way back to the surface. She let her glance drift over to the corner of the garage where the research tools she'd brought back with her were now stored, in their well-traveled canvas bag, and wondered if they were beginning to rust inside it.

Get rid of them, she told herself. But she'd tried before, and couldn't seem to do it. They were a direct connection to something she wasn't ready to break away from, and they'd turned out to be a fortunate distraction in the reentry process, enabling her to slip through an even more unusual item that might otherwise have attracted attention.

Too bad I couldn't have wrapped Bruce in laundry and tucked him into my suitcase next to the journal. . . .

. . . the journal that held the secrets of an ancient physician, whose determination and skill had shown Janie the light when all seemed impossibly dark.

She sighed, and shook her head from side to side. *It would be so much easier if I could just be doing some work that means something again. . . .*

A unique specialty, Tom had said.

Is there anything unique left in this world? she wondered dismally. She left the daydream and went into the house.

There were reams of "government figures" in the universal genetic database, including, after years of laborious data entry, the complete genome of nearly every U.S. citizen, and when Janie sat before a computer as she did now, considering a trip inside, she always ended up feeling confused and overwhelmed.

Get over it, her supervisor at the New Alchemy Foundation had told her. *It's just part of your job.*

It was, and she was familiar with the techniques involved in collecting, sorting, and evaluating data, but the database into which she was about to make an entry could be a scary, forbidding place, if only for its size. Her feelings about its existence changed from day to day. One minute it seemed a wonderland, ripe for exploration, the next a wasteland to be trudged through in protective mind-gear. And every time she went inside it Janie felt like a trespasser, an outsider, someone who had no right to be there. It was a sentiment encouraged by the opening screen of the operating system, which did not say WELCOME TO BIG DATTIE, COME RIGHT IN, but rather:

STOP! YOU HAVE REQUESTED ENTRY INTO A SECURE DATABASE. PLEASE FOLLOW ALL SUBSEQUENT ON-SCREEN INSTRUCTIONS EXACTLY. FAILURE TO DO SO MAY RESULT IN IMMEDIATE DISCONNECTION AND REVOCATION OF FUTURE ENTRY PRIVILEGES. THIS VISIT WILL BE RECORDED IN ITS ENTIRETY.

Someday, she thought, *I'll be brave enough to waltz in there and just float around looking at stuff, with no particular place to go . . .* but this would not be the day. Janie did precisely as she was instructed, nothing more or less, initializing the required commands with cold precision. She placed her right hand with its invisible but always detectable electronic code on the flat surface of the computer screen and waited for the sensor to process it. And somewhere, deep in the bowels of Big Dattie, she envisioned certain tickers going up one notch, the ones having to do with overeducated middle-aged white females of mid to high income who worked for the New Alchemy Foundation and were searching for information from the particular computer she happened to be using. Someone would find this information germane, at some time. But Janie didn't want to meet that person. Ever.

The screen came up yellow—too happy a background color for the stern text being displayed. She was prompted by a beep to choose a route into the database, so she touched an entry point on the screen and waited, engaging in silent self-amusement as her search was directed down this demographic data path and that. *Speeding south on Boy Boulevard, cutting over onto Route 13, turning left on White Street.* It would have been so much more efficient just to type in the name of the boy in question, Abraham Prives, but there was something about being so direct that Janie found unsavory, almost assaultive.

Because if someone just entered her name into the database and got all the information she was about to request, it would absolutely frost her. Of course, someone surely had, perhaps many people had, for reasons she would find disturbing. But she didn't wish to dwell on that.

C'est la vie, she forced herself to think. *But just once, if I could just let myself be a bad girl . . .*

Abraham Prives—the name flashed on successive screens as his data file was compiled. How cold and impersonal it all looked as it stacked itself electronically. Janie touched the screen when a photographic image of him came up, to pause the progress. She saw a still photo of a sweet-looking boy who might have been ten or eleven when he'd smiled for the camera. The large brown eyes hinted at intelligence, but there was a certain reticence in them. Janie wondered if Abraham was perhaps a bit shy.

Yet he was not so shy that he wouldn't play a team sport. Janie was reviewing his file in the first place because he'd had an accident while playing soccer, a simple collision with another player that somehow resulted in Abraham lying flat and immobile in a hospital bed at Jameson Memorial Hospital, with two vertebrae shattered into splinters like a dropped crystal wineglass. The shards of bone had caused hideous damage to his spinal column. It was a puzzling and incongruous injury, considering the common nature of the accident itself, and that abnormality had prompted someone from the Jameson Trauma receiving area to contact the New Alchemy Foundation, where Janie worked as a research associate.

The file would be transferred to her data dump at the foundation, where she would later retrieve and examine it in unhurried detail. But before doing so and closing out of Big Dattie's operating system, she took a brief cruise through the information on Abraham, in the hope of forming a more complete idea about him. The database told her that he was in the ninety-fourth intelligence percentile, fully immunized, that his father had died in the Outbreaks but his mother had survived. He played sports and studied Russian in school. A nice, well-rounded, post-Outbreak thirteen-year-old.

He'd broken a bone before—his wrist, the previous year. It had been a messy break, one that confounded his orthopedist and then took an inordinately long time to heal. The orthopedist had tested him for osteogenesis imperfecta, a long shot—but that rare bone disorder usually surfaced shortly after birth, and Abraham's results were, as expected, negative.

The boy had been back on the soccer field for only a month when the spinal tragedy struck.

He went down like a sack of potatoes and he couldn't move anything, the coach had told her when she contacted him. *I just don't understand. . . .*

Janie did understand, especially the sack of potatoes part. *The bad news is . . .* she thought as she pressed the screen icon that would transfer the file to her computer.

On her list of Abraham Prives things-to-do was to speak with the person at Jameson who'd initially called the foundation. But when she'd asked around at the hospital for the person's name, no one at Jameson seemed to know him. She decided her supervisor must have remembered it incorrectly, and was annoyed with him, not an unusual state in their strained relationship. But it didn't matter in the long run who'd called— just that the call had been made. She was not in the business of shooting messengers.

Before closing out of Big Dattie, she looked at the messengers of doom—the disease counters—and experienced a great longing to shoot *them.* It was pretty much what she expected—tuberculosis was down slightly, pneumonia up just a tad, HIV, as always, insidiously rising. But when she moved down the list to DR SAM, Big Dattie advised her that the counter for that particular disease was temporarily disabled.

It always came down to money. That much hadn't changed, and probably never would.

"Look, it's an interesting case, and I understand your eagerness to take it on, but I don't have the budget," Chester Malin said.

"Then why did you send me over there?"

"Somebody called, remember? What was I going to do, just ignore it? We have to look at these potential candidates. But we don't have to decide to take them."

Janie often wondered how this man had become a supervisor. Now he crossed his arms over his ample belly and tipped his chair back so it balanced on two legs. As always, the sleeves of his shirt were rolled up, revealing hairy forearms, one of which sported a tattoo of crossed guns. Monkey Man, his coworkers had nicknamed him behind his back, a moniker he unknowingly encouraged by scratching his dry scalp with one hand when he was thinking about something.

And though he'd come on to her on more than one occasion, he was a charter member of Janie's personal Last Man on Earth Club.

She tried to ignore his oddities—there was too much convincing to be done. "Oh, come on, Chet—someone thought this case would fit the profile. And I had a call yesterday from Northern Hospital in Boston that I haven't followed up on yet, but it sounds similar. These kids both have such clear spinal involvement that we almost have to include them in our project—or someone's going to ask why we didn't. We might get accused of trying to skew the results. And two cases—doesn't that seem a little odd? What if we have an emerging disease here? Think what that would mean for this place. The reputation enhancement would be just incred—"

"It's not an emerging disease," he said sharply. "From what I saw in the viewer, it's just a particularly nasty broken back. Maybe his soccer coach is trying to cover his own ass for letting the kid get in a dangerous situation."

"I called a couple of people who saw it happen—the coach gave me their names. And they confirmed what he told me—that it wasn't a rough collision, or anything out of the ordinary. Apparently it was the kind of thing where the kids usually get up and brush themselves off and keep playing. Which is what the other player did. But not the Prives boy. I just wonder why."

"Well, I hate to tell you this, but you're not going to find out. It'll cost too much money."

"For an opportunity like this there must be some contingency funding—and we're already giving expensive care to the current project participants—one more certainly isn't going to be noticed."

"Are you kidding?" he said. "Those are eagles roosting upstairs, not chickadees. They notice everything."

She frowned. "So you don't think they'll go for it?"

"No. I don't."

"And you won't support me."

"Not unless you can give me a much better reason to, no."

As Janie was leaving his office in a huff, Chet opened up the personnel program on his computer. He tapped in a few words and closed it again.

She hadn't seen her former academic advisor in a few months, and Janie was surprised when she called John Sandhaus to find that he'd moved from his spacious house on the outskirts of town to the residence apartment in one of the dormitories at the nearby university.

"Hey," he said with a smile when she came in the door, "it's great to see you."

"Yeah," Janie said, hugging him. "We need to be more careful about staying in touch."

"You're right," he said. "My life just keeps going by faster and faster, it seems."

"I know the feeling." She gestured around his apartment. "But this is all new for you."

"I'm getting used to it," he said. "I think I might actually like it. Cathy does, at least. I was looking out the window one day last fall, watching the leaves come down," he said, "and it hit me like a ton of bricks: I've probably spent six months of my life raking leaves. And it was in that exact moment that I realized I couldn't rake another one. Ever. Falling leaves became the symbol of my entrapment in the rigid behaviors of modern society. And I, the human *schmuck*, was spending a lot of time trying to make nature behave. So we moved. And now we have a built-in supply of baby-sitters, guaranteed to self-renew every September."

"And a steady flow of beer-sodden adolescents, also guaranteed to self-renew. Problem is, you won't be able to spank them."

"Yeah? Watch me. But it's been okay so far. We're liking it. I probably wouldn't have taken a spot in one of the new dorms—too sterile. This one's nice, though. Reminds me of an apartment building I used to live in when we were in Cambridge. And the rent is right, that's for sure."

"You got a decent price on your own house, I hope. . . ."

Mezzo, mezzo, he motioned with one hand. "Reasonably good. The market's still pretty flooded. Frankly, I was just glad we were able to sell it."

"I'm never going to move again. They'll have to scrape me off the kitchen floor of my house."

"Well, you have a lot of memories tied up in it. For us, it wasn't so bad."

"You were very lucky."

"Yes, we were." A moment of silence passed. "Come on," John said to break it, "I'll show you around."

After the tour they sat down at a table in the dining area off the kitchen and continued to exchange the details of the last few months.

"That girl who worked for you in England . . ." John said.

"Caroline."

"Yeah. How's she doing now?"

"Much better. In fact, she just got married a couple of months ago."

"No kidding! That's great." He paused briefly. "I remember you were telling me she had this English cop who was hot for her. That the guy?"

"The very one. He's now a lieutenant in the western Massachusetts division of Biopol."

"Whoa," John said. "That's impressive. But what I wanted to know was about her, uh—"

"Condition," Janie said with a smile. "She's getting better all the time. Her toe is pretty well healed. It flares up every now and then—I don't precisely know why, and she doesn't want to go to any other doctor about it. . . ."

"Understandable."

"Yeah, I guess. But she's doing pretty well. She was determined to walk down the aisle without a limp, and by God, she did it. Took a lot of effort on her part. And I'm not sure her psyche is ever going to be completely healed. Fortunately, Michael's very understanding." She paused for a second. "For a biocop. She was the last person I'd match up with someone so official. But they're truly in love, from all appearances . . ."

"Hey, that's all that matters, right? Even cops can fall in love. I sometimes forget that there are real humans inside those suits. Glad we're not seeing too many of them lately."

A question flashed through Janie's mind when John said that: *Or are we seeing more of them?* It seemed that way sometimes.

"It was a tough thing, what she went through," John continued. "You too."

"Yeah, it was. I think we're both still going through it, in some ways."

"Just try to remember, it could have been worse. A *lot* worse. Hey, what about that guy *you* met over there? Are you still trying to get him out?"

She lowered her gaze as if she were contemplating the handle of her coffee mug. "Yeah, I am, but it's a frustrating process. I'm making my lawyer awfully rich."

"Tom?"

"Yeah."

"What does he say about the chances?"

"Not very good, unfortunately. What makes it hardest to take is that Bruce is a U.S. citizen. He's been a resident of England for twenty years, but he's still got his U.S. passport."

"What was the problem, then?"

"He set off all these bells and whistles when they scanned his passport."

"And you didn't."

"No. Amazingly enough, I didn't."

"The luck of the long-legged, I guess. Well, you never know, things may change and he'll be able to get in."

"I'm not holding my breath."

John smirked. "None of us are, these days. Now, you said when you called that you wanted to pick my brain."

Janie sat up straight; her expression brightened. "And your computer's, if you don't mind."

"I charge a million bucks to touch a computer."

"I don't mean you should actually touch it yourself, John, I mean, God forbid you should slime yourself . . . I just need to know where to go for something, that's all."

"What could I possibly know about where to go on a computer that you don't?"

"I need to find out what sort of grant money is out there. You always seem to have such great sources, and I've been out of that loop for a while . . . you're really sort of the Grant King, aren't you? Or have you been losing your touch?"

"Oh, come on, Janie."

"No, really. You always know how to get money. You're like a money magnet."

"What do you need money for?"

"This kid was referred to the foundation's spinal regeneration study, but my supervisor is giving me a hard time about bringing him in. And there might be another similar case in Boston that I'd want to include. The foundation apparently doesn't have the money."

John gave her a curious look. "Sure it does. With that endowment? If it were a profit company, you couldn't afford the stock." He stirred his coffee and tapped the spoon on the edge of the cup. "They just don't want to spend it. I hope you're not surprised by that."

"I guess I'm not, really . . . disappointed, of course, but probably not surprised."

"Good. My high opinion of you would be lowered if you were."

"But there's another reason . . ."

She explained what Tom had said about her relicensing. "The more I learn about this boy, the more I think there's something unique there."

"But he broke a bone . . . that's not neurological."

"His spine is heavily traumatized. That *is* neurological. Look, I know it's not your field, so you might not see it the way I do. But trust me, there's something unique there. Maybe unique enough to get me relicensed, if I poke around enough."

"Is it that important to you?"

"I hate what I'm doing now. It's meaningless. I feel like I'm some kind of milkmaid; all I do is move buckets of information from one place to another so they can make it look like their drugs are effective."

"Well, are they?"

"Maybe. A couple are promising. And now they've got so much money and staff tied up in making something work, they've got to keep everything going. Otherwise the investments they've already made will just go down the tubes. Which is another reason there should be money available to bring this kid in."

"You never know why these organizations do what they do. They have a board of directors, just like other big companies. That's really what they all are, big companies that claim they aren't going to make a profit. The government lets them get away with it for some reason. Too much politics, not enough science."

"I hate to think of it that way. Makes me feel like such a—whore, almost. But I suppose it's true. I mean, I took the position with the foundation because I really wanted to get back to work. I needed to work, to keep my mind off . . . things, but also because it seemed like there was a conscience there. At least it did at the time. Now I guess I wonder."

John chuckled ironically. "That's what I thought when I first started here—and now I find myself looking the other way all the time. The Ivory Tower—I wouldn't be just another corporate hack schmoozing my way to the golden handshake. But I am. The only real difference is that I have tenure. So what are you gonna do? That's the way the world works these days." He shrugged and smiled. "We can only do what we can, right?"

"Right. So *you* can look through some grant lists for me." She smiled.

It was always in the evening, when he was asleep in England and she was awake and lonely in Massachusetts, that Janie most fervently wished Bruce had managed to make it into the country. She'd spent only a few quiet evenings with him in London the year before; except for the very beginning, their entire association over there had been one difficulty after another. But she'd acquired a taste for such evenings rather quickly, and now her mind conjured up this safe and appealing image of the two of them spending comfortable time together, like a pair of childhood sweethearts who'd been a couple for years, who knew and forgave each other's foibles. In reality, there was a lot of uncharted territory between them, and much still to discover.

And though Tom was relatively certain that Janie would not have to go through anything further in connection with the "problem" she'd had in England, for Bruce the dangers still persisted. He still lived there and was still under investigation, though he hadn't been charged with anything, and probably wouldn't ever be—the British biocops who had him in their sights had found no way to make anything more damning than sleeping with a Yank stick to him yet. But they knew of his involvement in a certain difficult affair, and they were making his life as miserable as possible to compensate for their own ineptitude.

Janie found herself wallowing in the strange and unfamiliar miasma of self-pity as she watched the sun set over her beloved garden. *Shake it off,* she told herself. *You're tougher than that.* And it was true—she was resilient and resourceful. It was just that, lately, the self-preservation skills didn't seem quite so sharp anymore when she called on them.

She was beginning to think she was perhaps a little depressed. *No wonder—I hate my work, and the man I love is on the other side of a very big ocean.* She took a cleansing breath and turned her attention to the item on her lap. Though it was no worse for its ocean crossing wrapped in her sweaty T-shirt, the journal was obviously ancient and very fragile. From the cracks in its leather binding when it came into her hands, and by the worn condition of its parchment leaves, Janie was certain that it had been a working book, one that had been handled regularly, perhaps as often as daily, by a long series of owners throughout its history. Each one had left an unmistakable mark on the journal—writings, translations, a scratch here, a smudge there, the occasional dog-eared corner— from the photograph of the last owner before herself all the way back to the faded and spidery scrawl of the man for whom this journal had originally been bound.

Was it expensive, she wondered, when his father gave it to him, more than six hundred years before? And what coin of which realm had he used to purchase it? The proud parent of Alejandro Canches had probably gone to a bookbinder to have the journal made, so that when the son went off to be educated he might have a permanent place to document the blossoming of his intellect. Sometime during the boy's medical studies in Montpelier, his entries had switched from Hebrew to French. It was these later writings that Janie had painstakingly deciphered, word by word, through correspondence with an Internet group of Francophiles who reveled in *la langue française ancienne*. She had never shown the book itself to anyone but Caroline.

But no matter how many times she turned the pages and read the words, there were questions that could not be answered. Now that she had time on her hands, and a reason to seek distraction, she turned to it more and more. It was beginning to make her nuts.

"Why did you suddenly drop out of sight there?" she wondered aloud.

Half of everyone had died in London in the year 1348.

"Or did you run, like I did?" she asked again of the ancient physician.

But if he'd run, why would he have left something of such importance to himself behind? She couldn't envision him as the kind of man who would abandon something so precious.

"Well, you died sometime, so rest in peace."

The old wooden Adirondack rocker made a thin but rhythmic creaking as she moved slowly back and forth with the book open before her. *I left Bruce behind, and he was important to me.*

But these were different times.

Weren't they?

In different times, there would have been other materials that might be used for the task at hand, but now Kate had to sacrifice something so that it might be accomplished. She watched with pained dismay as Alejandro tore up one of her two remaining shifts and used the long white strips to tie the injured man securely to the table.

"We shall buy you another," he reassured her.

"No doubt the Free Companies have left the weavers undisturbed that they may see to the making of women's finery," she said almost bitterly. "Another one shall not be easily had, Père."

"I know," he said with a half-smile of apology. "Had I a shirt to spare, I would have used it instead."

"Why not the dead man's clothes?"

Karle protested. "Would you send him to meet his God naked? Since the time of Adam, men have been covered before God."

She sighed heavily. "It would have been better if we had the means to make some rope. Surely a proper vine grows somewhere nearby and has escaped the burnings." She glanced at the semiconscious man who was now firmly secured to the boards of the table with the torn strips of her former finery. "In the meantime, I suppose my shift has gone to good purpose."

"Aye," Alejandro said. "He must not roll or he may bleed red again." He leaned over and spoke gently into his patient's ear, though he thought it unlikely that the man could hear him. "We shall return soon enough. You will be safe here. Try not to cry out."

He hoped they would find the man alive when they came back. He did not speak of his doubts.

When they set out just before dawn with the body of Karle's unnamed soldier on the travois, the light was still thin, and as the forest deepened around them they had to step carefully. After a time, long beams of light began to ease their way. Small hidden beasts stirred in the bramble as the intruders progressed over the little-used path. Each time the caravan breached some sacred avian territory, the air would fill with the caws of protesting birds. But none of the offended came down from the heights of the treetops to ward them off. Their gruesome, bloating cargo was sufficient deterrent.

"A curse on your horse," Karle said as he struggled forward. "He is a miserable, intractable beast. Were he mine, I would beat him with a sturdy branch for such behavior."

"He has never liked the smell of death," Alejandro explained. "That is why he balked. And I have suffered from the ill effects of a balking beast quite enough in my life. I do not wish to do so again." The sight of the donkey rising up in protest filled his memory, accompanied by the scream of the young Spanish girl as the moldering cadaver in the donkey's cart tumbled to the ground—the beginning of his tortuous flight through all of Europa, with its painful ending in London. He shoved it away and adjusted his grip on the wood poles of the travois. "Must we *carry* this thing?" he said. "Can it not as easily be dragged?"

"Aye, and we will leave a trail across the forest floor that even a nobleman could follow," the Frenchman Karle answered. "May it please God that Navarre does not ride out in search of me before we return for Jean. It was dark when I erased our tracks last night, and I was rushing to escape. I cannot be sure they are well enough hidden." He glanced backward nervously and surveyed the trail their footfalls left in the sticks and leaves. "We will need a pardoner of extraordinary skill to erase the sin of our footprints on *this* forest floor."

"A cut branch will do better than any pardoner, I think, and will surely come cheaper," Alejandro said.

"There's a bit of truth, God knows," Karle panted. "And here's another: I must rest for a moment."

After a few minutes, the unlikely trio resumed their pressing mission of mercy. In one hand Kate carried Alejandro's small spade, a pitiful thing compared to the sturdy iron shovel the blacksmith Carlos Alderón had forged for him so long ago in Spain. *Would that I had a pardoner back then to ease the consequences of that "sin,"* he thought. But what pardoner would buy back the sins of a Jew? And at what exorbitant price?

A fly landed lazily on his nose. He blew upward and it lifted off in search of another sweaty victim to bother, finally settling on the corpse. *Yet what sin was it to be seeking knowledge?* he wondered.

His steady, trudging footsteps lulled him into remembrance.

Almost ten years ago. The thought filled him with terrible remorse and he sank deeper into melancholy with each plodding step through the forest. Chaotic years of pestilence and turmoil and flight, of forced wandering through the whole of Europa, the last few years spent trying to elude the warring forces of Edward Plantagenet and a slew of that English king's own cousins, all French royalty, none of whom seemed to understand that the true ruler of Europa was a pestilence so foul that its own Creator must surely quake in its presence. For a long decade Alejandro had watched the plague subside, return, subside, return, running hither and yon through France, England, Spain, Bohemia, and anywhere else its carrier rats could hide, sending to their graves in bruised and putrid condition nearly half the citizens of those "enlightened" societies. For one-tenth of a century he and the girl had fled from one "safe" place to another, hiding their identities, only to find that no place was really ever safe enough. Always, to see the golden child with the Moorish-looking man would raise someone's eyebrow. Who did she resemble, the little beauty? *Surely,* their incredulous looks would accuse, *she cannot be your daughter. And I have seen that face, or one so like it, before . . .*

They had spent the first cold winter hiding outside Calais, moving from one abandoned cottage to the next, always just a pace or two ahead of those who sought him for the handsome bounty his head would earn. He heard whisperings of a *ghetto* in Strasbourgh, and they rode there in a state of hopeful anticipation.

On that winter afternoon they found not the expected safe haven, but *confutatis, maledictus.* Jews milled about the town square with their bundled possessions, surrounded by ready archers, having been herded there from Basel and Friedberg by frenzied Christians who shouted rabid, nonsensical accusations of poisoned wells. How he had admired the courageous Christian deputies of Strasbourgh who repeatedly said they could find no complaint with "their" Jews; he had prayed to whichever God would listen for that wisdom to prevail. But on the afternoon of Friday the thirteenth, he watched in horror as an angry mob dragged the sympathetic deputies of Strasbourgh out of the council hall and replaced them with sympathizers. On St. Valentine's morn, the Jews were given their choice: baptism or burning. Perhaps a thousand had come forward to receive the sacrament of St. John. The rest, some said fifteen thousand, were burned, many choosing self-immolation within the *ghetto* over slow roasting with their kin on the common platforms.

He could almost feel their ashes drifting down around him, and the snickering of his balking horse seemed to fill his ears. The mud of the rutted roads seemed to fly up fresh in his face, blinding him, bringing tears to his eyes. Alejandro felt himself sinking into the horror, crying out for mercy, praying for deliverance. . . .

He was surprised when he was rescued from his own abyss by Kate's gentle voice.

"Père . . ."

She had seen this expression on his face a thousand times before, the glazed look of pain he seemed unable to hide. It came upon him often, unannounced, like the shadow of a mountain, and took away all of his light.

"Père, we are here."

He seemed momentarily confused. "*Wha*—where?"

"The clearing."

"Ah, yes," he said in an unsteady voice. "So soon, then?"

It was not lost on their companion, this quiet, practiced ritual of salvation. The Frenchman Karle read their expressions, and suspected that the daughter had rescued the father many times before. *She has brought him back from some awful memory,* he observed to himself as he lowered his ends of the poles. Almost mechanically, Alejandro did the same.

"Hardly soon enough," the young Frenchman said as he flailed his arms about to rid them of the stiffness. "Would you punish yourself further?"

The physician took another moment to recover himself as Karle watched him carefully. He shook his head to clear it out and rubbed his face briskly. "No," he said quietly, "this much punishment will do for now." He reached out and took the spade from Kate, then pressed its tip into the soil, testing the firmness. "It seems soft enough here," he said. "I will loosen the dirt, if you will scoop it away."

Karle nodded and got down on his knees. After every few thrusts Alejandro made into the soil, Karle used his bare hands to shove aside what had been loosened. Kate lent her hands to the task, and before long the hole was too deep to scoop from its edge. Karle stepped down into it and continued removing the dirt. They stopped digging when the rim of the hole was as high as his chest.

"This will suffice, I think," Karle said.

It should be fully a man's height deep, Alejandro thought to himself, *or the animals will come.* But he had seen far shallower graves, mass graves where hundreds of plague victims had been covered by what seemed like a mere shovelful of dirt, and this hole seemed almost a royal crypt in comparison. He extended a hand to Karle to help him climb out, and together they rolled the body into the grave, along with the severed arm of the other man.

When the dirt had been tamped in place again, both men stood silent at the graveside. Kate was surprised that the Frenchman Karle, so eager to see his dead comrade properly buried, had so little interest in seeing to the man's eternal soul. From Alejandro, such disdain was only to expected: he openly despised all Christian ritual. But soon it came clear to her, for the Jew and the Frenchman were staring at each other, preoccupied with their mutual mistrust. Prayers for the dead man were forgotten.

Ah, Père, she thought sadly, *when shall you lose your bitterness, if ever?* He was terribly slow, she knew, to accept any newcomer into his confidence, and until he felt safe he would keep his deepest thoughts to himself.

But the Frenchman was not so cautious or shy. "Well, it is done, then," Karle said as he stood before them. "I could not have done this alone, and I am more grateful than I can say for your help. You do not know me at all, and yet you came to my aid. Perhaps this indicates some kinship of which we are not aware." He stepped out of the clearing and broke three long, leafy branches off a nearby tree. "Compliant green pardoners for the trespass of our feet, and very cheaply had. We will drag these behind us as we walk out again, and I dare any noble to discover the sins of our footsteps." He handed a branch to each of the others. "And perhaps on our way out of these woods, we new kin can uncover our similarities. Perhaps we shall explain to each other why it is that we are all hiding."

But Alejandro and Kate said little as the trio walked out of the forest. Guillaume Karle did not give them opportunity.

"The battle was a complete travesty," he said. "Once a mercenary from Firenze told me of a word they use there—*fiasco*—to describe when everything goes wrong. Well, nothing more could possibly have gone wrong in this battle. We were outnumbered, outarmed, and Navarre's men were far more dedicated than we expected, though it seems uncanny that such a fiend could inspire loyalty of that sort." He let out a pained sigh. "We rose against his forces yesterday afternoon, as we had heard that he intended to confiscate a goodly cache of wool from a farmer who had wisely stored it away. The man stood to make a decent *sou* when he sold it, a profit his cleverness surely merited! But Navarre would have it sent to the weavers to make winter tunics for his followers . . . it is not enough that he has taken every sack of wheat and every length of sausage between here and Bohemia; now he must have the means by which these poor souls cover their backs against the coming cold! And of all the great good fortune, the queen and all her ladies were in the castle at Meaux. Feasting on delicacies, while all around them peasants starve to death."

Food! Kate felt her stomach stir. She daydreamed as the Frenchman talked, of the golden loaves that Alejandro had always, in their earlier travels, pulled from some secret hiding place in his pack—a habit he had acquired from a well-admired but long-dead comrade. *And I, the little fool, thought it was magic! Now I know it was wisdom.* She glanced at Alejandro and saw the unsettled look on his lean face. *No doubt he dreams of those same magic loaves as he listens to this Frenchman's complaints.*

Karle kept walking and talking, dragging his branch behind him, every now and then looking back. "We stood our ground, and were gaining; victory seemed but a thrust away." Then anger crept into his voice. "But out of nowhere came two knights returned from crusade. The ill luck of it cannot be believed! Cousins, one English, one French. But both sworn to uphold a lady in distress, no matter how disgustingly royal the knave she makes her bed with."

His bitterness seemed almost unholy in its depth. "They were too much for us; they came with horses and swords and bows, and we could not stand against them with our pitiful sticks and knives. By now that wool is on its way to Navarre's weavers. No doubt it was passed directly over the bodies of those who died to protect it."

He seemed not to require refreshment, but thrived on his own words. "They treat the peasants as little more than animals, yet they expect them to produce, produce, produce! But there is not a plow to be had in all of France, thanks to the plundering of the Free Companies . . . and even if there were, what nags they have not commandeered are too decrepit to pull the plows. And should there by some miracle be horses and plows, there is no seed. It has all been eaten. . . ."

They had heard these grumblings of discontent in their travels, but had, of necessity, stayed low, ignoring the growing chaos. Yet Guillaume Karle related the dire condition of France with evocative passion and heart. And as Kate listened to the recounting of his efforts on behalf of the downtrodden peasantry, she began to understand that Karle had taken the burdens of King Jean's lowest subjects onto his own shoulders and was as much a fugitive as they.

Substantial shoulders they were; she could not help but notice. He was a well-built, handsome man of unusual stature for a Frenchman. He was fair like her own people, and she found herself staring at him as the words poured out of his mouth. His step was firm and purposeful, and his gray eyes sparkled with the fire of excitement. He seemed to have found his way past the horrors of the previous night's *coup de grâce*, and was already plotting anew.

Before the sun had reached its full height, familiar landmarks began to come into view. They stopped in a small grove of trees when the cottage was perhaps only a hundred paces away.

"I see no sign that anything is amiss," Alejandro said as he peered through the branches, "but the quiet itself is bothersome."

"Compared to the din of battle, it is a blessing," Karle said. He started to rise.

Alejandro caught him by the wrist. "Wait."

"What of Jean? Should he not be attended to?" Karle said. He tried to pull his arm free.

Alejandro gripped it more firmly. "Were he going to die of his wounds, he would already be dead. Be patient. Trouble is not always so quick to reveal itself. What the eyes cannot see, the heart can sometimes feel. And right now, my heart distrusts the peace that my eyes see."

Reluctantly, Karle crouched down again. He stared for a few moments through the branches. "Neither my heart nor my eyes report anything to me."

Alejandro grunted cynically as he peered through the trees. He turned back to Karle and said, "Your heart is young. When it is of an age with mine, you will know that it may be broken at any moment. I had a dear companion once who was a skilled warrior. He told me many times that such serenity as lies before us now can be disrupted in an instant."

They stayed where they were, silently watching the cottage for several minutes.

"There is no one there," Karle finally said. "Let us see to the injured man. I will take him back to his family, then I will try to see to the ones we left behind."

Once again Alejandro put a stop to his youthful enthusiasm. "Wait here. I will go ahead to see that there are no unwelcome visitors. I think perhaps you may be more hunted than I at the moment." He rose slowly from his crouch. "I shall come back for you if it is safe to come forward."

There was a brief silence. "And if it is not?" Karle said.

"Then I shall call out like a bird of prey." He nodded toward Kate. "And you shall take the hand of my daughter and fly off. She knows where she will find me again." He smiled at the young woman and touched her cheek with fatherly affection. "All will be well, I am certain of it." He stood and started for the clearing, but stopped before stepping out of the shadows.

"But . . ." he said, his voice a bit hesitant. He reached into one pocket and took out a small sack, which he placed in Kate's hand. Coins clinked against each other, and Kate put the sack into the pocket of her skirt with a small nod.

Alejandro gazed at his daughter for a long moment, then turned back to Karle and said, "I make you this promise: If God sees fit to separate us, we will be rejoined. And when we are, she had better have no complaints."

In every place they'd hidden themselves in the years since England, it seemed they could not get away from windows. Often the first thing each would ask the other when observing a dwelling that appeared to be abandoned was *Are there too many ways to see inside?* The Jew physician and his adopted Christian daughter had become far more skillful than they'd wanted at shutting out the eyes of the world using parchment, or woven fabric, or sometimes planks of wood. He had taught her, comforted her, and chastised her in the thin light of torches and candles. Their craving for daylight was constant and sometimes nearly desperate, but their understanding of the darkness had thus become nearly perfect.

But now it was he who wished to see inside, to spy upon his own home to see what might have transpired within during their morning's absence. There was only one window through which he might do so, and that had been as carefully covered as all the rest they had encountered in their travels, so he could see nothing at all. Alejandro cursed his own proficiency and wished for once that he had made a poor job of doing something.

He slunk between the trees and slipped into the stable, where he found his willful horse still in the stall, complacently nibbling at the pile of long grass that had been set in front of him the day before. A quick glance at the water trough told him that it was in need of refilling, but a trip to the stream with a bucket was out of the question until a safer moment. He greeted the huge stallion with a few gentle strokes on the nose. The horse snorted softly, as if he somehow knew better than to betray his master's presence by whinnying. The physician whispered a few reassuring words to his mount and slipped back outside again.

He stayed close to the wall and crept around the back of the cottage, keeping to the shaded side. When he reached the point where the side met the front wall, he crouched down and peered cautiously around the corner. There was no horse tethered outside, but in the soft dry dirt he saw the marks of hooves—too many to be from just one horse; he deduced that a riding party of some sort must have been here. But the dust had already settled, so they must have long since departed.

We might have been here, he thought uncomfortably, *but for burying the dead man. But have they left someone behind, someone waiting inside to surprise me?* There were no footprints leading up to the door, but they might have been pardoned with a leafy branch just as his own had in leaving the forest. A chilling fear gripped at his belly, though there was no clear cause for it. The door looked just the same as it always did, and exactly as it had been when they left before dawn, but someone could easily have opened it and then closed it in the same position. *Why did I not leave a stick, or a rock, or some other such device hidden on the door as I usually do, so I would know upon return whether it had been disturbed?*

He need not have questioned himself, for answer was maddeningly simple: because he was himself so disturbed by the sudden appearance of the Frenchman and his eyes for Kate that he had not thought clearly. He knew it was an expensive oversight, and he cursed himself.

He sidled along the front wall and knocked tentatively on the wood planking of the door, then stood back, waiting for some sound from within. But he heard only the occasional moan of pain from the man who still lay tied to the table. Alejandro waited for a few moments, a brief bit of time that seemed eternal as he stood with his back pressed against the stonework, but no one appeared. So the physician boldly—*foolishly,* he thought—reached around the stones and into the recess. With one quick push, he shoved the heavy door open. It creaked slowly inward and finally came to a stop.

He was all indecision. He half-expected to be greeted by some smirking knight, pleasured in anticipation of the fine ransom he would collect when he harvested the fugitives. And there might be a good price on the head of Karle, as well, even better perhaps than the one on his own. Add then the purse for the royal daughter, and it would be a fortunate fellow indeed who collected such a bounty.

But, God be praised, no grinning captor awaited him. All that greeted him were the grunted supplications of the one-armed fellow, who despite his other misfortunes was lucky enough to yet breathe. He had soiled himself in the absence of caretakers who might have helped him relieve himself in a more dignified manner, and the bandages sealing his arm wound were soaked pink with ooze. Closed up as it had been, the small house stank of the man's various exudations. But he was alive, and well enough to moan. *This bodes well,* Alejandro thought with some relief.

He entered cautiously, looking first behind the door, and when he found no one lurking there to dismember him he closed the door again. He poked through the ashes of the hearth with the iron and found a glowing coal, with which he lit a candle. As his eyes adjusted to the dimness of the light, he took a quick look around. *It looks undisturbed,* he thought, *but too undisturbed for my liking.* The book he had been studying was still on the hearth near his pallet where he had set it the night before. He reached under the straw and poked around until his fingers found the hidden metal ring. With a great heave, he pulled upward, and raised the wood panel on which the pile of straw lay. He looked into the cellar below, and saw his treasured leather saddlebag still there. He reached down and picked it up by the handle, and was satisfied by its weight that the contents had not been removed. He dropped it with a thud and let the cover to the secret cellar fall shut again. He smiled with relief and thought that when they were resettled he would buy Kate all the shifts still left in France if she so desired.

For now they would have to move on again. He had no doubt that those who pursued the rebel Guillaume Karle would be fierce and dogged in that pursuit. The man was, Alejandro thought, either incredibly brave or insanely foolish. He had led an attack against a castle sheltering royal women and children. It was an act that would not go unavenged.

"But surely," Alejandro had maintained on their trek out of the woods, "you must have realized that word would reach the knights, wherever they might be . . . ladies were in danger, and such a situation is never taken lightly, even by an enemy. Any knight worth his armor would have come to their aid, be he French or English or even Bohemian! Such is the obligation of knighthood."

"And how would a physician know of such things?" Karle had demanded.

"I am a learned man" was all he had dared say, but he added the silent thought, *a learned man promised knighthood by the king of England himself, along with the hand of the Princess Isabella's companion. . . .*

The injured man pulled him back from his unrealized dreams with a cry of pain, and Alejandro turned his attention to the poor fellow on the table before him. The man was sweating, but a hand to the forehead did not reveal a true fever. He is sweating from the pain, Alejandro realized, not from fever. He ladled a small amount of water into the man's mouth, then used his own sleeve to wipe away the rivulets that dribbled down the side of his face. "I am sorry I have nothing more to relieve you," he said gently to the man.

The anguished man finally managed to speak words. "I feel no pain in what remains," he croaked, "but what was once there, and is no more, seems to be on fire. It is as if my arm burns in hell, but is still attached."

He had heard this before from those who had lost limbs, that the phantom limb had taken on a life of its own, and now ruled the remaining body with its desperate need to be remembered. "We have laid it to rest. I am sorry that we had to take it, but had I left it attached your entire body would be on its way to eternity."

"If Navarre finds us," the man panted fearfully, "he will happily take my other arm." He tried to lift his head to look around. "And where is Karle? He must not be captured, or our cause is lost!"

Alejandro wiped the man's brow. "He waits in safety with my daughter not far away. When I have done with you, I will signal them to return. I can work more quickly without him standing over my shoulder. He is a distracting fellow." His words seemed to put his suffering patient at ease, so he continued to speak as he tended to him. "But surely this Navarre will do you no harm now; it would be a grave sin not to show pity on one so maimed, especially after all our good work to save you. God would surely punish any man for such a transgression."

"God looks the other way when Navarre is at work."

"God never looks away, my friend. He sees all. Now God will look at your wound by making me reveal it."

He began to unwind the bandage on the stump. *Would a life without arms be worse than death?* Alejandro wondered with a shudder, and was silently grateful that he would probably never know.

But in the silence he thought he heard the faint sound of hooves in the distance. He stopped what he was doing for a moment and listened. The sound seemed to disappear for a moment, but it returned again to become more distinct, closer-sounding. The patient looked toward the wood door of the cottage and began to mutter in fear. The poor man had soiled himself again, Alejandro realized, before he was even cleaned from the last time. He hastily rewound the same dressing, cursing his luck as he did so, for he had touched this dressing with his own hands, which were still fouled from the burial of the other man's corpse.

But that will not matter if these riders do not pass, he thought, his heart pounding. *Perhaps they will not see this place at all, but will continue on, no wiser to its presence.* He had chosen it for its concealment, and it had seemed somehow safer than the other choices; with so many dead in the wars and gone from the plague, there were hundreds of cottages empty and for the taking. But Karle had found them easily enough, and though he had tried to hide his path, some traces of it must have remained. *A curse on all that walks, flies, swims, or slithers,* he thought angrily. *Why could I not have chosen better?*

He began to untie his whimpering patient, but the sound of riders approaching now seemed dangerously close. He drew a knife out of his boot and cut away the strips he had torn from Kate's shift. The linen seemed to have turned to oak in his absence, and the knife unaccountably dull. With the patient still partly tied to the table, he rushed to the window. He ripped off the covering parchment, then cupped his hands around his mouth and called out like the hawk he would have loved to be at that moment. He grabbed the metal ring in the straw and yanked it upward—confirming his notion that there was room for two in the hiding space.

It was not space that proved to be the mightier enemy, but time. The hooves were as loud as thunder, and he could hear the snorting of lathered horses. Would God agree, when his judgment came, that he had an obligation to save himself, if not for himself, then for Kate? For all those whose suffering he might ease in the time that remained to him?

It was not a question he had time to pose to himself. He whispered desperately, "Forgive me, fellow, I am sorry to the depths of my soul . . . I beg you not to give us away. For my daughter's sake. God be with you." Then he slipped into the dirt cellar alongside his saddlebag and lay down. He let the plank fall over him, straw and all. And before his eyes were adjusted to the darkness, the approaching horses had come to rest outside the stone cottage. He heard the sound of the door opening, and of masculine voices speaking in French. His bladder seemed suddenly so full that it would burst, and he begged whichever God might be listening for the blessing of one more chance to empty it standing up.

Sitting on a chair next to the bed in Abraham Prives's room at Jameson Memorial Hospital was a woman who anyone could easily see was the boy's mother, if not by the resemblance then by the drawn look on her face. Janie raised her hand to tap on the open door, but held it back for a moment when she realized that Mrs. Prives was clutching her son's hand and talking quietly to him, an event she thought ought not to be interrupted.

He can probably hear everything, Janie mused sadly as she watched from a distance, although she wouldn't know for sure unless she had the chance to test the boy's hearing. Meanwhile, the mother would wait—for some sign that he heard her, for any indication that the boy she'd known was going to return. She was in excellent company, Janie knew, because somewhere in the world there was always a parent waiting for a child to come back from something.

It was outside this very hospital that Janie had stood herself, years before, at a hastily erected fence, a chilling effect of martial law that neither she nor anyone who'd stood with her had ever experienced prior to the Outbreak of DR SAM that occasioned it. There had been no domestic wars or civil uprisings during her lifetime, but the fence itself seemed a foreign invader. The hated barrier had done its dirty job and had long since been removed, but the sight of it would always be indelibly planted in Janie's memory. She and hundreds of others had begged and pleaded for passage through it, only to be held at bay by the ready guns of cops who were just as frightened as the people in the throng they were supposed to be containing. Many of the contained and the containers had kin inside that hospital—or friends, or associates who had suddenly fallen to the rogue bacteria. DR SAM had changed everything, everywhere, for just about everyone, and though conditions had eased and life had become more normal, it would never be entirely the same again.

She stood outside the Prives child's door and waited for the scene inside to change, rubbing her palm absentmindedly at the injection point as memories of those dark days resurfaced. Her senses betrayed her with psycho-trickery, making it all seem real again: the cold metal links, endlessly intertwined, the dank metallic smell they left on her fingers, the flashing lights of the ambulance caravans that threaded slowly down State Route 9 to the hospital, heading for the temporary crematorium, which had not yet been dismantled. On wet days, Janie sometimes thought she could smell the soot of the bodies that had been burned so the scourge that took them down would not be spread. But it had spread, and in some places, it still existed. It would never be corralled completely. Just suppressed.

Among those bodies was that of her only child, who would not come back no matter how long Janie waited.

She let a few more seconds pass and then knocked lightly. The mother turned in her direction.

Janie said tentatively, "Mrs. Prives?"

A hopeful nod.

"I'm Jane Crowe, from the New Alchemy Foundation. We, uh—"

Mrs. Prives, a slightly pear-shaped woman with graying hair and thick bifocals, stood very quickly and made a nervous gesture of smoothing her skirt. "Oh, yes," came the thin voice.

Janie remained at the door, not knowing what to do. Mrs. Prives motioned with her hand. "Please. Come in."

"I don't want to interrupt anything—"

A faint smile came over the woman's face. "I've got kids. So I'm used to it." She turned back toward her son. "Abe's not—awake, I don't think, so you're probably not bothering him."

Janie returned the smile as she came to the bedside. "You never know. I hope I am bothering him. I also hope we'll know soon whether I am or not."

Mrs. Prives glanced at her son, then back at Janie again. "That would certainly be a step forward. Do you have any new—I mean, is there anything more you can tell me?"

Janie knew what she wanted to ask. It saddened her that people often felt so apologetic about requesting information. How had that reticence become so terribly widespread, so pathetically universal? She often felt it herself, and hated it, because the framework supporting that reluctance to ask questions could only be fear. "I'm trying to work it out so we can move him to the foundation's patient care center. I'll be frank with you, though, I'm running into some difficulties. There are some financial issues to be resolved yet."

Bitterness crept onto the mother's face. "There always are."

"I know. I'm sorry, especially if I got your hopes up for no good reason. But if it's any consolation, you're not alone—we're also trying to bring in another boy with a problem similar to Abraham's—"

Mrs. Prives interrupted her. "Similar how?"

"The same kind of bone shattering."

"The people here told me it was very rare to have a break like that."

"Well, it is, we all think."

"You think?"

Janie hesitated, wanting to phrase her answer with as much clarity and as little discouragement as possible. "There hasn't really been a lot of 'thinking' done on it, that's how unusual it is. I'm trying to get a permit now to do a system-wide search to see if there are other similar cases."

"Is it difficult to get one?"

"Unfortunately, or fortunately, depending on your point of view, yes, it's difficult. But not impossible. The foundation has a good success rate for getting database search permits."

"Is this other boy local?"

"Boston."

"Oh. Not really, then."

Janie was quiet for a moment. "No, I suppose not." And as she silently crossed her fingers that the permit application she'd already filed would be granted, she thought, *In a case like this, the same hemisphere would almost seem local.*

She got so involved in making phone inquiries on Abraham's behalf that she almost forgot her afternoon appointment. But eventually there came an undistracted moment during which Janie took a quick look at her planner, and there it was—a meeting she'd arranged a few days earlier, and almost forgotten.

It was denial, she realized. She grabbed her purse and ran out the door. The dark-paneled, brass-trimmed elevator she rode down on still looked like it belonged in the commercial bank that had once occupied the building, only to be gobbled up when its CEO and most of the board of directors bowed low to DR SAM and could not rise again. It was a classic case of mid-Outbreak consolidation, a corporate big fish displaying supremacy on the food chain by gobbling up a corporate little fish, with most of the benefit predictably falling into the laps of a few pushy but fortunate stockholders, who had the foresight to make hay while the plague raged.

Her timing was luckier than it usually was—the bus that went to the university was just coming curbside as she skipped down the granite stairs. Janie passed her right hand over the entry sensor and boarded as soon as the door *whooshed* open, wishing she could justify the gas to make this trip by car. It would certainly take less time. Somewhere in Big Dattie the ticker on her bus rides along this route would go up one notch, as soon as the day's ridership data were dumped into the system. But being single, childless, and without an aging family member to support put her into the lowest fuel allotment category, and she was using way too much of her annual gallonage on questionable little jaunts. So the ticker would continue to go up now and then. She made herself stop thinking about it.

If they would just ease up immigration, maybe there would be enough workers so gas production could get back to normal, she thought wishfully as the bus pulled out onto the street again.

Maybe Bruce could get in if he agreed to work for a refinery. . . .

She *hmphed* at the ironic realization that her transoceanic lover, should he ever be successful in getting back into the United States, would make more money as a laborer in an oil field than he would in a hospital working as a physician.

The National Hebrew Book Depository was a quick walk from the end of the bus route, down a slate pathway into the lush woods at the far southern end of the university campus. Tucked away harmoniously among the trees, it was a stunning contemporary building, one that managed to give the deceptive impression of being little more than a cabin in the woods, because its sprawl had been so artfully mitigated in good design. Janie knew from her research into the place that the depository boasted nearly unbelievable security, at the nearly obnoxious insistence of the curator she was going to see today. The rough-hewn exterior planking hid a bomb-, bullet-, and fire-resistant steel and concrete frame that protected the building's precious contents from the malicious mischief that such a politically charged establishment was bound to attract.

The curator, Myra Ross, was a compact, gray-haired sixtyish woman whose petite stature seemed incongruous with her immense personality. The first time they'd met, a couple of weeks before at the opening of an exhibit, the tiny woman had looked up at tall, lanky, still dark-haired Janie with undisguised envy, and then promptly tamed her with wit and charm and immense intelligence. Janie found that envy amusing, in view of the energy-per-cubic-inch that the curator seemed to possess, a vitality she considered impossible for herself.

She greeted Janie on this day with a firm handshake in the reception area outside her office, and as she led Janie into her private lair she said, "I must tell you, Dr. Crowe, there is seldom so much *intrigue* surrounding a potential donation. I usually know the pieces that people contact me about. But you have me completely stumped and, I might add, fascinated." She gestured toward a well-padded chair, into which Janie settled.

In a quick glance around, Janie saw that the walls of the curator's office were covered with an impressive array of award certificates and diplomas, all mixed in among photographs of the woman herself, beaming in the presence of a stunning assortment of celebrity contributors.

"You've met Barbra Streisand?" Janie said in awe.

"On several occasions. She's been an outstanding supporter of the depository."

"What's she like?"

"Oh, she's lovely," Myra said. "A lady. Unlike some of our contributors. 'Here's the check, now go away,' some of them have the nerve to say. They don't want to be involved, really. But Barbra actually came here for the private opening party. It was a thrill, let me tell you. And she is still a beautiful lady. We should all look so good."

"Not in this life," Janie said with an ironic smile.

"Yes, well . . . we all have our burdens. But you, may I say, have no reason to complain. Now, why don't you tell me a little bit more about this book of yours. As I said, I'm intrigued."

Janie drew in a long breath. "I think it's actually more of a journal than a book," she said. "It was kept by a Jewish physician in the fourteenth century. It was passed down through a series of people who used it for what it was—which I think was essentially a health care manual. All of them wrote in it, but he was the first. And the most prolific." She paused. "In all honesty, I would have been very surprised if you'd heard of this journal before now. It hasn't ever been circulated, at least not that I'm aware of. It was in the same place for more than six hundred years, a little house outside London. There was a bit of what you might call 'intrigue' about the way it came into my hands. That's why I've been somewhat secretive about it."

"I wish you would tell me how you acquired it, Dr. Crowe. I assure you I'll keep anything you tell me in the strictest confidence."

"I understand," Janie said quietly, "and I don't doubt that you would. But there are some potential—illegalities, I guess you could say, about the way it came into my hands. I'm not sure it's wise for you to know about them. At least, not any more than is absolutely necessary." She shifted uncomfortably in her chair. "I feel at this time, though, that the book ought to be someplace safer than where it is now. So I'm beginning an investigation into where that ought to be. You're my first stop."

Myra Ross gave Janie an unexpectedly stern look, the rough equivalent of a shaken index finger pointing straight at her nose. "You must tell me if it's stolen. Because if it is, of course you'll understand, we can't possibly—"

"No. I didn't steal it. And I don't think anyone else did, either. As I said, it was lost to the world for a very long time. Until the—well, let me just say that the journal's last owner is dead—he was burned in the fire that destroyed that house."

It was a true statement, if somewhat stretched. "He had no heirs. I rescued the book when it happened. Otherwise it would've burned. That would have been a terrible loss, believe me."

"If it's what you claim it is, that would certainly be true." Myra leaned back and regarded Janie silently for a few moments, taking her measure. "So. You might want to place your journal here. Forgive me for being blunt, but I assume then that you want us to give you something back. That's usually how it works."

"What I want is a guarantee of access to the journal, whenever I want. And your promise that if you buy it from me, it won't ever be sold to anyone else."

"Well, I can promise you access only when the depository is open, unless you make the necessary arrangements ahead of time. We would try our best to accommodate you, if you place it here. But you understand that there are security considerations."

"Yes. Of course. That's what I meant, anyway."

"And as far as selling it is concerned, any cloud on your ownership would pass on to us if we bought it from you, so we wouldn't be able to turn around and sell it again. But your claim of ownership isn't likely to raise the same sort of questions that ours might—so maybe it wouldn't be a good idea for us to own it. There are lots of other possibilities. The first one that comes to mind is an arrangement that many institutions like ours favor—a 'permanent' loan under contract. That way the book would always belong to you. We would keep it here and display it, but it would still be your asset. You can borrow against it, if you need to raise money, remove it for personal use when you want to, and so on. Surely you've seen placards in museums that say something like 'On loan from the collection of thus-and-such.' "

"I have. But I wouldn't want my name posted."

"Then it could say 'Anonymous collection' if that's what you'd prefer."

"That would be my preference, yes."

"It wouldn't be a problem. It's very standard practice to use that sort of notation. Now, if that arrangement is satisfactory to you, and you decide to choose us as the book's new home, we'd have an appraisal done right away so we could be sure it would be properly insured. How much insurance are you carrying on it now?"

"None, I'm ashamed to say. At least not beyond my normal home-owner's insurance."

With a pointed stare, the curator said, "How do you sleep at night, Dr. Crowe?"

Janie looked down guiltily. "I don't know. Some nights, I don't, to be honest. That's part of why I'm here."

"Well, then, let's do what we can to remedy that, shall we? Bring this treasure in for me to see. The sooner the better. And be careful."

The time difference was something Janie hadn't gotten used to. She was still at work, and Bruce was getting ready for bed. They'd prearranged the call, but she was a few minutes late, so when she logged on there he was, smiling almost eagerly back at her from the computer screen, a vision in plaid flannel.

"Nice pajamas," she said. "Are they new?"

"Yeah. You like them?"

"I do."

"Harrods was having a sale. I picked you up a little something too. From the lingerie department."

"Ooh, show me!"

"Nope. It'll have to wait until I see you in person."

"Which will, I'm pleased to report, be next month."

"Really? Oh, my God, that's great! Where are we going?"

"You'll never guess. Iceland."

His excitement toned down a little. "You're right. That wouldn't be someplace I'd guess."

"The travel agent says it's actually quite a wonderful place."

"Janie, it's a great big rock. In the middle of nowhere."

"Do we care? We're going to be busy. And she's going to send me a booklet, so when we're not busy we'll know what else to do."

"How long can you get away for?"

"Five days, maybe six."

"Then we won't need any booklets."

She laughed. "That was my thinking too. The agent's going to get the final itinerary to me in the next couple of days."

"Good. You'll beam it over. . . ."

"Of course, as soon as I have it." She paused for a moment. "God, I miss you. I know it doesn't come through over the airwaves, but I hope you know it and feel it. I *want* you to feel it."

"I do," he said. "I miss you, too."

"I'm sorry I was late calling."

"That's okay; I wasn't really sleepy, anyway. Been tossing and turning for a couple of nights now. Can't seem to get settled—I have all this unspent energy."

She snickered naughtily. "Is there something wrong with your right hand?"

"Ha ha. I'm a lefty, remember?"

"Oh, yeah. It's been so long I forgot. Anyway, I apologize. I had an important appointment." After a moment's pause, she said, "I went out to the Hebrew Book Depository this afternoon."

Bruce's expression darkened slightly. "What for?"

"I'm thinking about taking the journal there."

"Oh, for God's sake, here we go again . . . you promised me you wouldn't obsess over it anymore."

"I'm not obsessing. I'm just—being careful. I'm worried—what if something happened to it? I would never forgive myself."

"Janie—what could happen? You have smoke alarms . . . you tell me it's a very safe neighborhood. . . ."

"It is, but there have been some break-ins not far from here. I'm afraid—"

"And of course a thief is going to be looking for a moldy old journal, when all your jewelry is in the house. Come on. I don't think you need to worry about its being stolen."

"Maybe not. But I do."

"Well, I think it's completely unnecessary. But do what you want. I just think there are lots of other more important things to put your energy into right now."

There was a sudden lull in the conversation.

"Speaking of which, is there any news?" Bruce finally said.

With a sigh, Janie said, "There is. Tom told me my application for reinstatement has been denied again."

"I'm sorry," Bruce said quietly. He waited a long moment before asking his next question. "What did he say about the other thing?"

"He hasn't heard anything yet."

"Did they give him any idea when they might make a decision?"

"No."

"Well, that's a big drag."

Janie agreed with a nod. "I was really hoping we'd have a better idea of when by now." She borrowed Tom's words from the previous day's conversation: "I guess we'll just have to be patient for a little while longer."

"I guess. It's just hard . . . but my God, we'll see each other next month. It feels like it's been forever since I've really seen you. In person, I mean."

She gave a sad smile. "That's because it has."

It took a while to come down from the session with Bruce, so Janie stayed a little later at work to take care of some of the stupid mind-numbing details that comprised her job. She filled out observation logs, posted data, and saw to her correspondence, most of it electronic.

She opened her mail utility to the usual funny little man in a U.S. Post Office uniform who came onto the screen and waved a handful of letters, the indicator that there were messages waiting. After doing a little tap dance, he expressed his readiness to serve all her mail needs.

Make that male needs, Janie thought, and you've got a deal. . . .

She composed and queued everything and sent it out. Then she picked up the waiting correspondence.

As usual, most of it was junk. There was a brief love note that Bruce had sent before she'd spoken with him, and an invitation to attend a seminar on technology in medicine being sponsored by the medical school where she'd done her studies. A slew of unsolicited advertisements, which she gleefully disintegrated. Then there was a strange, short message:

Who are you?

Janie stared at the cryptic little communication, which was signed *Wargirl*. It had a needling effect on her psyche, and it intrigued her, though she wasn't quite sure why.

She studied the electronic details of the transmission. By its lack of flagging, it was a personal message, not a come-on advertisement or any other kind of disguised enticement. But that was about all she could glean, because the date and time of relay had been blocked out and there was no visible return address. The message was marked as being reply-primed, so Janie could answer if she wanted to. She just wouldn't know where the reply was going.

Why go to the bother of making it invisibly reply-primed? It was a complicated process, designed to make it inconvenient for crank e-mailers.

So this either was not a crank or it was a very determined crank.

"Okay, I'll play," she whispered aloud. Who wants to know? she wrote back.

Wargirl. The nickname sounded young. *Kids*, she thought. *Smart kids. Too smart.*

Then she made a few quick phone calls, the last of which was to John Sandhaus.

"I did find something that looks like it's worth pursuing, but not through the Ednet," he told her. "There's a site one of my students told me about. You outline your proposal and they match you up to a list of funders for the kind of work you're interested in doing. Slide you through the whole process in a couple of days."

"Sounds too easy," Janie said skeptically.

"Well, of course. And there's the catch. They charge a one-percent fee if you actually get the money. Nothing if you don't."

"I suppose it's worth a shot, then, especially if it's only a contingency fee. If they wanted money up front, I wouldn't even consider it."

"Hey, I wouldn't either. Why don't you drop by and I'll help you fill out the form?"

"You're actually volunteering to touch a computer?"

"Who said anything about my touching it? You're the one who's gonna do the filling in. I'm just gonna stand behind you and bark instructions. It's worth a shot, I think, and hey, what have you got to lose?"

Potentially, some privacy—not that Janie actually thought she had much left. GetGrant wasn't satisfied with her e-mail address and a description of the proposed work, which she entered in what was probably excessive detail. They also wanted to know everything else about her, nearly down to her shoe size.

"Doesn't it bother you," John asked, "to give out all this information about yourself?"

As she typed in the last few bits of information, Janie said to him, "I'm already so out there in everyone's database that it almost doesn't matter anymore. Sending this stuff out one more time isn't going to make much of a difference in my life.

I don't think, she added to herself.

The sound of the hooves reached the thicket where Kate and Karle crouched waiting. They listened, horrified, as the *clop clop clop* steadily increased in volume, mixing incongruously with the sweet chirping of small birds overhead.

And then the hooves seemed nearly thunderous, their sound overpowering everything but Alejandro's unmistakable signal. The birdcall cut through the buzzing of the insects and stilled the birds for the briefest of moments, until the muted choir fluttered upward and let loose a cacophony of caws, loud enough to awaken the poor soul who had just that morning been buried. Kate moaned, "Oh, Père . . ." as Guillaume Karle grabbed her by the hand and tried to pull her away.

She resisted and tried to wrench her hand from his grip, and finally he was forced to drag her, but when the snorting and neighing of the horses began to seem like it was but a few paces away, she realized that there was no choice but to run. So she followed, and they stumbled wildly through the thicket, always moving away from the cottage, staying out of the clearings and off the paths, pounding through the thorny underbrush until their garments were shredded and small rivulets of blood seeped from the scratches on their arms and ankles. They ran until they were panting so badly that neither one could hope to speak. Finally Kate pulled hard on Karle's sleeve to stop him, for she could not go farther without resting, even if only briefly. The vehemence of her yanking surprised him, and he came so abruptly to a halt that she slammed into him. They teetered, gasping and unbalanced, in each other's arms for a few moments before regaining equilibrium. Then they dropped to their knees, clutching at each other, and sucked in great gulps of warm, pine-scented air on the forest floor.

The man who leapt down off his horse in a cloud of dust would be king of France if all went according to his plan, or, as he was so fond of bellowing when frustrated by the limitations of his power, "if only my mother had been a man!" But his mother, the daughter of Louis X, had been shunted off to the mountain domain of Navarre, of which Charles could now properly call himself king, a kingdom far too insignificant and remote to satisfy his lofty ambitions.

He was a smallish man but fearsome nonetheless, and there seemed about him always to be an air of depravity, as if he were harboring some unhatched scheme that could come to no good. When he first heard himself called Charles the Bad, the young King of Navarre was said to have smiled. *Let them think me bad,* he'd roared in delight, *let them fear me!* It would only help him to accomplish his intended purposes. He could do nothing if the rest of the nobility thought him weak and vulnerable.

He threw open the door and strode into the small stone cottage, sword drawn and ready, his bearing appropriately regal, without first allowing the young knight who accompanied him to determine if the place was empty. After a quick, disparaging glance at the wounded man on the table, Charles of Navarre made a cursory search of the rest of the small space, poking and prodding here and there with the tip of his weapon, until he satisfied himself that the one-armed man was alone in the dwelling.

He came tableside and stood over the frightened man, sneering down at him. "Well, well, well, look at this," he called back to his companion. "It seems that Karle has left me something to do. And he has already started the work for me. I am to be chastised for thinking him ungenerous." He poked at the oozing stump with the tip of the sword, and the injured man screamed out in pain. "Though I will admit that I would have preferred a *whole* peasant to torture into revealing his whereabouts."

"Pig," the man hissed defiantly.

Navarre poked again, and the man blubbered in agony. The diminutive nobleman leaned over the wounded soldier and sniffed the air. "You stink of fear, *Monsieur Jacques.* You wear it in your pants, I think." He smiled evilly. "You need not fear me; I am a man of great pity and compassion. Tell me what you know, and I will see to your comfort."

"I know nothing . . ." he moaned.

"Oh, come now! Do you think me stupid? Even *les Jacques* do not go into battle without an escape plan. Or was the son-of-a-whore Karle so full of arrogance like the rest of his Picardy brethren that he thought he would have no need for such a plan?"

Alejandro could hear the man's sobs through the straw-covered planking. "Nothing . . ."

"Eh? Nothing?" he heard Navarre say. "Nothing at all? Well, here is something to know. You shall no longer have the pleasure of scratching your own ass."

Alejandro heard the sword *whoosh* through the air, then the smashing of the bone as it sliced through the man's remaining arm. The fine metal weapon rang like a bell as it reverberated against the wood of the table. His patient let out a long and bloodcurdling scream, and then fell silent.

Charles of Navarre pulled the sleeve off the severed arm and used it to wipe the blood off his sword. Then he thrust sharp weapon violently downward into the straw pallet and cursed so profanely that Alejandro, hearing the muffled words from his subterranean hiding place, thought surely the man's chances of entering the Christian heaven had been significantly diminished by that one utterance.

The tip of the sword stuck in the planking. Alejandro searched frantically for something to grab, so that when Navarre pulled up on his sword, the planking would not come with it. Bits of dirt filtered down through the cracks in the planking and drifted into his eyes. He squeezed them shut, and groped about in the darkness. He found a knothole and thrust his thumb into it, then pulled downward with all his strength, just before the nobleman pulled up on the sword. Mercifully, the weapon came free, just in time for Alejandro to stifle a dusty sneeze.

Overhead, Navarre examined the tip of his sword for damage, and when satisfied that the blade was intact slid it into the ornate scabbard strapped to his belt. His dark face wore a look of complete disgust. "Once again, the scoundrel has gotten away," he said to the knight. "And he will not return here, mark my words. This place is no longer safe for him. Nor will he go back to Meaux, for his forces have been scattered into the wind! Why can they not stand and fight, as true knights? Why must they slip away like cowards and hide?"

"Sire, they have not the proper training and temperament, and they do not know the courtesies of proper battle—they are ill-equipped and afraid. . . ."

"And yet they can do such damage as they have done nevertheless! I am shamed before my peers by the uncanny success of their rebellious insouciance."

"Sire," the knight protested, "what success do you speak of? The *Jacques* were *ruined* at Meaux! Surely they can no longer hope to gather sufficient numbers to rise up—"

"They nearly took the castle before we 'ruined' them, if that is what you wish to call it! They were nearly pounding on the door when we 'ruined' them! And were it not for the unexpected arrival of the Captal de Buch and Count Phoebus, they might have come through that door, and engaged in a lovely little soiree with three hundred ladies and children! And I would have been shamed before all of France! Not a man among the nobility would have stood with me had they taken hostages."

"Yes, but happily, Sire—"

"Do not speak to me of happiness, for I shall know none until I see Guillaume Karle dead. He shall be declared king of the *Jacques* when I get my hands on him, and then summarily deposed, and his crowned head shall tumble at my feet, where I shall take great pleasure in stomping on it."

He slammed his gloved hand down on the table where the mutilated man lay, the last of his life seeping out of him. "We will likely get nothing more out of this one."

The knight watched in terse silence as his king paced around the small cottage with nervous, almost explosive energy. It was painful to watch, so intense was Navarre's agitation. He let out a small breath of relief when the king finally stopped and stood in one place.

Navarre's eyes settled on the one object that seemed out of place—a massive brass-covered book lying beside the hearth. He knelt down beside it and opened the cover, then motioned for the knight to come near.

"What do you make of this?" he asked suspiciously.

"Sire, what should I make of it? It is some heathen script. I am not learned in such writings."

Charles of Navarre turned another page. "I have seen such writings before. This is the hand of a Jew."

The knight seemed puzzled. "Can there be any still about?"

"None that I know of," Navarre answered. "But it seems that Karle has managed to find one. And he has come to him for comfort. Such an association is fitting for the sort of man he has become—a lover of plowmen and beggars and charwomen. It is only fitting that he should also become a lover of Jews."

But the book held no answers to the whereabouts of his quarry, so

Charles of Navarre left it where it lay. Finally, after kicking the severed arm and then spitting on the dying soldier, he stomped out of the cottage and headed to his horse. He got up onto the animal's back in one graceful motion, then pulled on the reins and galloped off.

The young knight watched in dismay, knowing he would be chastised by Charles's military advisors for allowing him to ride off without their presence. And he would be further vilified by the nobles who had allied themselves with Charles for allowing the leader to risk searching Karle's supposed hiding place without protection. He hurried out of the cottage, leaving the door open after him, and struggled up onto his own mount. He followed at a slow trot, keeping the dust of his liege's rough ride before him on the road, and allowed the king of Navarre his distance. Let the others vilify him if they would—he was simply not man enough to keep the impetuous Charles from doing the mad things he often did when inspired by indignation. They would reach his stronghold far too soon for the knight's liking, even were they to travel at a snail's pace.

Only when there had been silence for a good long time did Alejandro dare to lift up the planked cover to his dark earthen cave, and when he finally emerged into the light again, he saw quickly that it was too late to do anything for the poor wretch who lay still tied to the table. What was left of the poor soul now resembled a tree trunk more than a man. The arm that Charles of Navarre had so handily removed was under the table covered with dust, and was beginning to serve as a landing place for buzzing flies. The armless warrior was bled white and lay almost motionless, but somehow he still drew breath.

We cling, when all hope is lost, to the illusion of hope, Alejandro mused sadly. *What horror floats through his mind?* he wondered as he stood over the wreck of a soldier who might once have shown great valor, a man who had managed to live through what the Frenchman Karle had described as a very bloody battle.

May it please God that I never know such horror. He set aside his Hippocratic vows once again and pulled out the knife that he kept always in his boot, the fine one his father had given him so long ago in Spain. "I commend you to your God," he whispered to the near corpse, then quickly thrust the knife into the man's heart. The life flowed out of him, even before Alejandro could wipe the knife clean and restore it to his boot.

"To Paris, then," he said aloud, surprising himself with the sound of his own voice. And if God was good, and Guillaume Karle was a man of

his word, he would find Kate there, in the place they had so frequently
visited when she was a child and still begging to learn anything he could
find to put before her. He pulled the saddlebag out of the cellar and laid it
on the floor. In it was his fortune—the gold of his family, the gold from
the pope, the gold of King Edward, hardly touched in a decade of running. Enough gold to cover the streets of Paris in delicate, finely woven
ladies' shifts—if only such shifts could be found. He stuffed what little
food he had into the bag, and then stood to leave. As he took one last
look around, he saw the heavy manuscript still beside the hearth.

He would not leave another book behind, as he had done when fleeing
England. Such secrets as this book might hold must not fall into the
wrong hands.

Karle was surprised, but not unhappy, when Kate named Paris as the
location of the rendezvous.

"But why there?" he asked. "I surmise that you and your *père* are as
much on the run as I. It would seem a dangerous place to meet."

"It is," she acceded. "But in these times, we could not be certain that
any other meeting place would survive. How many burned villages and
ravaged castles have you encountered in the countryside? Many. Could
the same happen to Paris? Never. It shall always stand. And I shall always
be able to find my way there. All roads lead to Paris, Père says."

"All roads lead to Rome, or so says the *legend*."

"Ah, but that was said many centuries ago. When Rome still had its
glory. In these modern times, it is Paris that is the center of the world. Or
so those who would stake their claim to pieces of it would say. And I
know some parts of that city very well."

"And how did you come by this familiarity with Paris?" Guillaume
Karle asked.

"We spent much time there when I was a girl."

"I was not aware that you are not still a girl," he observed sternly. "Yet
I fear you will find Paris much changed from your last visit there."

"I am seventeen," she said, her chin raised, "and the mistress of Père's
household."

"Hmm," Karle said through his nose. "Such household as it now is."

She scowled and shook a finger at him. "We had household enough to
serve you and your men. And now, thanks to your imposition, *if* I find
Père we shall be forced to find a new home."

Appropriately chastised, Karle did not respond. They rested by the
edge of a stream as their horses took their fill of water—horses liberated

from the stables of a local squire by Karle while Kate, pressed into unwilling service as an accomplice in his thievery, stood watch outside. He had been nervous during the deed, for he could not help but wonder what she would have done had they been caught at the theft—how she might have stood against an outraged groom. Would she have strangled him with her white hands, her long, fine fingers? Or kicked him in the manhood with her delicate foot?

Unlikely, he thought. *At best she would have screamed out a warning.* But they had not been discovered and now Karle kept a vigilant eye on the ill-gotten beasts, for the animals were unfamiliar and therefore unpredictable. He waited patiently until the horses had drunk their fill and were secured to a tree before seeing to his own refreshment.

He dipped his cupped hands in the water of the clear, fast-running stream and began to bring the liquid to his mouth, but Kate put a hand on his arm and stopped him. "Wash only. Before we drink, the water must be strained through a cloth."

He let the water drip through his fingers. "This is a bit of nonsense," he said.

"Not nonsense at all. Great wisdom."

"*Curious* wisdom," he said. "And *not* local," he added suspiciously.

"There are tiny beasts who live in all waters," Kate told him. "Père says so. He says that many people who suffer from difficulties of the bowel do so because they are not careful about the water they drink."

Karle gave her an incredulous look. "And has he seen these beasts, or only dreamed of them?"

"He knows that they are there."

"How does he come by such knowledge?"

"Père studies all that he sees. He studies some things he can only imagine by thinking deeply about them. He is a very learned man, as he told you. He has served a pope, studied under the best professors, and attended to the health of m—uh—many important people." She stammered over her last few words, and looked away briefly to recover her confidence.

But if her remarks made Karle curious, he was careful not to show it, and when she had regained her composure she showed him a square of finely woven silk. "We each carry one of these to purify what we drink. If we can, we even boil the water."

"In God's name, why do you do that? It takes away the vitality of it."

She made a thin smile. "Do you know of any beast, large or small, who can survive a boiling?"

"*Hmph,*" he grunted. "No."

Curiosity began to taunt him and he found himself with an abundance of unspoken questions. These were terribly bold claims—to serve a pope, to know of invisible small beasts in the water—this *père* of hers seemed no ordinary man. But he decided to delay his inquiries until a time when he had more of her confidence, for he knew she would be more truthful if she trusted him. He considered how he might hasten the winning of it. *Show interest,* he thought suddenly. *Women—girls—cannot resist this, and respond with wagging tongues.* He was pleased with his own cunning. "And has this cured you of your bowel afflictions?"

"I cannot say," she said proudly, "for I do not suffer any."

Karle looked at her with raised eyebrows. He knew almost no one who escaped occasional bouts of dysentery or diarrhea, especially in these times of war, when streams and rivers often ran red with blood, and all the wells were suspect. "And all of your water is dripped through this—cloth?"

"Yes," she said, handing it to him. "See how finely it is woven; Père said it came from the very end of the earth, from the place called Nippon, where it is as common as our coarsest wool. It is very precious, and I should be loath to lose it. All of the impure beasts are caught in its threads. I boil the cloth itself as often as the opportunity presents itself."

"Remarkable," Karle said. He had no need to feign interest in her chatter—it was wild enough to be fascinating. He handed the filmy cloth back to her. "I have never seen such a wonder before."

"Père knows many things that no one else knows," she said.

"He seems an unusual man, indeed."

Kate sighed and wiped at one of her eyes. "More than you can understand. He is a most excellent physician." She looked Karle directly in the eye, and challenged him with a story she knew he would find hard to believe. "He saved me from the plague when I was but seven. And then he saved himself when he was afflicted."

It was a stunning revelation. Karle stared at her in abject disbelief and whispered, "You have lived through plague?"

She set the silk down in her lap and slowly unwrapped her shawl. She exposed her long white neck to his eager eyes, and pointed to a series of small scars that were surrounded by a slightly discolored area, the unmistakable scars of the buboes that every plague victim suffered.

Alejandro had a scar on his chest—*I saw it when he washed himself,* Karle thought. "But—*how?*" he said.

"He gave me a foul-tasting medicine, and watched over me, and after a fortnight I was cured."

These claims were almost too much for him to believe. Yet she bore the scars; that much was undeniable. He reached out tentatively in the direction of her neck, wondering if she would allow him to touch her, but she did not stop his hand. He felt the hardness of one of the scars with his own fingertips. "Forgive me this intimacy," he said as he drew his hand away, "but I find this very difficult to accept. I have never heard of one gone to buboes who lived to tell of it. Some lived, of course, but not after the buboes appeared."

" 'Tis rare, I know," she said, "and in some, Père says it is simply the will of God that keeps the sufferer alive. Some seem to muster defenses against the pest. Their bodies fight, as well as if they wielded swords. He does not understand why."

"He cannot understand *everything*."

"You must not underestimate him. I was so afflicted that I would not have been among those who lived. My sickness was grave, very grave." She looked away pensively for a moment, then glanced back at him. "I remember little of it, only that Père was constantly at my side, as was . . ." She paused, and released a tightly held breath. "For me, it was the medicine that did it. You see, he had learned of a cure."

The great conviction in her voice gave curious credence to the nearly impossible story she told. And though he was certain that Kate was upset by the separation from her supposed father, Karle did not think her insane. "You do not seem to be suffering from the typical weaknesses of female temperament that lead to delusion," he observed. "I daresay you believe what you are telling me to be true."

She gave him a defiant look, tinged with wariness. "What gain might I realize by telling you lies?" she asked.

"I cannot say," Karle answered. *But such a fantastic story!* He wanted to ask more, but reluctantly held his tongue. *I must not frighten or badger her into silence,* he warned himself, *for it seems there is much to be learned from her.* For a moment, he satisfied himself by simply looking at her, this cream-skinned, golden-haired, impossibly curved girl-woman into whose company he had suddenly been thrust. He found himself thinking, *Rarely does nature work such marvels as this.* He turned his eyes away from her, and back to the horses again.

"I am terribly hungry," she said. "Now that we are finally at rest, my stomach screams for me to fill it. Have you any food?"

"Not a morsel," he said. They had run through an orchard, but he had not thought it wise to stop until they were certain that they were not being pursued. The fruit had been left behind with great regret.

"Have you a weapon to hunt?" she asked.

"Only my sword."

"Then we shall have to make do with this." She lifted her skirt and pulled a knife out of the edge of her stocking. It was small and slender, but the blade nearly gleamed and Karle imagined that it was very sharp.

"You are full of surprises, maiden," Karle said.

"Père has always told me that I must be prepared to leave in the space of a breath. He says I must always expect that which is unexpected."

"Is there nothing but wisdom pouring out of this man's mouth? Does he say nothing stupid or inane? Ever?"

She chuckled lightly. "He is a man of few words. Most are gems. But let us not speak of that now. I will skin what you can catch," she said, and then taking from her skirt pocket a small piece of glass for fire-starting, she added, "And roast it, as well."

"I lack practice in hunting, I fear," he said. "This sword has swung at the necks of more men lately than beasts."

"And before you carried a sword, did you not carry a bow?"

"Not since my boyhood," he confessed unhappily. "I was indentured to an accountant who was in the service of a Picard nobleman. Before I took to this rebellion, I worked more at the figures than in the woods. I was provided with much learning, on account, my master said, of my superior intelligence. I know some bits of French and Latin letters, and I am most clever at the ledgers."

"No doubt your modesty also served to convince him of your worth," Kate said wryly.

"I did the work as well as any man."

"I doubt not that you did," Kate said, "and more cheaply, I am sure. Much to your master's benefit."

"Indeed," Karle said. "It is always the lords and ladies who benefit from the labors of their underlings. I saved my pennies, and often went to him with an offer to buy out the remainder of my servitude. It was fortunate that I was not married and obligated to the support of a wife and young ones. But still, I wanted to advance myself. In preparation for a time when I might have a family of my own. Always he refused me my freedom."

Kate heard great bitterness and regret in his voice and she felt sympathy for his plight. "You have been ill-used by his refusal, it seems to me," she said gently. "But right at this moment we need to slay us some food. If you have forgotten those skills, you must say so."

His silence spoke more clearly than any words he might have said, and with a sigh of resignation, Kate rose up from her rest to do what needed to be done. "I shall make a blind trap, and if God is watching over us, we shall have a rabbit. I am especially fond of a well-roasted doe. I do not like it when I find little ones inside her still, but we need not eat them. Although if we are hungry enough, I am sure you will find them quite tasty. . . ."

He was glad when she slipped off into the bushes and thus ceased her discourse on the delights of eating fetal rabbits, but he kept an eye on her as she went about her business. He listened as she rustled about, cutting small branches, and watched with great curiosity as she easily formed them into a bucket-shaped trap. Then with a *shhh* and a wave, she motioned him to back away. He stepped out of sight in the brush, and a few moments later he heard her thrashing about, creating an unholy noise. Soon a fat rabbit bounded out of the underbrush, directly into her tangle of twigs. She was on it in a second, and its throat was slit. "A jack," she said as she examined its underside. "Pity. Well, it will fill our bellies nevertheless."

Karle stared in dumbfounded astonishment as the golden-haired goddess-maiden, the young woman he was supposed to be protecting, lit a fire and prepared the food that she, by her own clever efforts, had caught and killed. She had the unlucky beast skinned, gutted, and impaled on a sharpened green stick before Karle could even salivate. "The fur is so soft," she said, stroking the still-warm pelt against her cheek as its former wearer sizzled over the flame. "A pity it cannot be saved for gloves. But where would it be stored? We are too much on the move." She wrapped the feet and the viscera inside the pelt and tossed them far across the stream. "*Monsieur le Renard* will enjoy them after we have departed from here," she said with a smile.

Soon the intoxicating aroma of the roasting meat filled the air, and Karle worried aloud that it would bring unwanted attention to them. "We should take this feast away from here to eat it," he said. "The smell is such that we are likely to attract inquiry."

She nodded, and poked at the meat with her knife. "It seems well enough done," she said, and pulled the spit off the fire. The meat still sizzled as she climbed onto her horse with the stick in hand. "Are we to fear bears or nobles?" she asked.

"Both would be equally unwelcome," he answered. "And truth be told, maiden, I would eat the rabbit raw were it not cooked."

"Père says meat must always be well cooked because there are—"

"Tiny beasts living within the beasts?" he asked mockingly.

"Aye," she said with all seriousness. "How did you know? Especially within the small furry creatures. I am forbidden entirely to eat rats. He says I must starve first. You see, by eating the larger beast, we risk taking in the smaller ones—"

He interrupted her again. "Larger beasts will always eat smaller beasts," he said. "Regardless of what poisons they hold. And seldom do they have the luxury of cooking them first. It is the will of God. No one need have great learning to understand this." He turned and rode off to find a more secluded spot in which they might enjoy the rabbit's tender flesh, as he was certain God intended for them to do, tiny beasts or no.

"Surely," Karle said as the drippings from the juicy meat ran down his chin, "this is what God must eat. That is why He is God. Because He has eaten food this delicious."

Kate tossed away a denuded bone and licked the fat that clung to her fingers. "One wishes that whatever God rules small things would have seen fit to make rabbits a bit larger. I could eat another."

"Or two," Karle agreed.

"And now I must see to some womanly things," she said, rising up.

What could she mean? What womanly things? "Where are you going?" he asked.

"To the pond nearby," she said, pointing west.

"There is a pond? How do you know this?"

She laughed. "The geese. Can you not hear them? Perhaps if we are very fortunate, we shall catch one to roast."

He listened for a moment and became aware of the dull honking sounds. Of course he had heard them in the background, but in his hunger he had given no thought to what they obviously meant, that there would be some body of water nearby. He tossed aside the bone he had been gnawing and stood up. "I will go with you."

She blushed a bit and said, "I desire some privacy, sir."

Karle was flustered. "But I am to watch over you. I promised your *père*."

"I will return quite whole and sound, I assure you. I only wish to clean myself. In decent privacy."

"I will stay near you. I will turn away."

She gave him a look of great displeasure. "As you wish," she said, "but do please honor me. A woman needs her peace now and then."

He was about to say, *You are yet a girl,* but she had already turned and was walking in the direction she'd pointed, and as he followed with his eyes, he could not fail to notice that she moved in a distinctly ungirlish manner. Before there was too much distance between them, he untethered the horses and pulled them along, pursuing her through the long grass.

They came through a thicket of brush to the edge of a small pond, and in the fading light they could see steam rising from the surface of the still water. It was a beautiful sight, and Kate made a small sigh as she looked at it. "Père says air loses its heat more quickly than the water, and that it wants the heat, so it pulls it up from the water. This is why he enjoys bathing at this time of day. As do I."

"You are going to bathe?" he said in surprise. "You said only that you wished to clean yourself."

"How better to do it than bathing?"

He seemed flustered. "But will this not be harmful to your health?"

"I assure you," she replied to his stare, "I shall be all the more healthy for it. Now, you promised me privacy, or have you forgotten?"

Without another word he turned away, and soon heard the rustle of cloth as she removed her filthy skirt and shift. Then came the soft splash of her feet entering the water. Before long he heard the sounds of swimming, and he thought, *She is fully immersed, so now I may look.* Just as he began to turn his head, something large and gray and wet came whizzing by; he ducked, and the wiggling object narrowly missed him. The flat, roundish fish landed with a flopping thud in the grass and began to thrash about.

"Breakfast," she said in a sweet, laughing voice, with her curiously English accent. "While I finish bathing, see that *Monsieur le Poisson* does not flop back into the water. Or you shall have to catch your own *petit déjeuner.*"

Kate's hair, from which she had earlier wrung all the water, was now drying in the warmth of the small fire they had built. They were secreted in a small clearing surrounded by very tall trees, so the smoke from their fire would dissipate among the branches before being noticed, should anyone be watching from a castle wall. She was wrapped in only her shawl while her other garments hung on a nearby branch, drying from a hasty but sorely needed laundering in the waters of the pond. "May God grant that we are not interrupted in the night, or I shall have to flee on horseback with only my hair and shawl to cover me."

Karle imagined such a scene with a touch of silent pleasure and whispered to himself, "May God forbid it."

They had come across a lone apple tree not far from the pond, and had gathered as many fruits as could be bundled into her wet clothing. By the time they settled on their sleeping spot, their hands and faces were sticky with the juice of the tart fruits, and their stomachs bulging. Kate cut one in half with her knife and skillfully hollowed out the centers, creating two small cups from which they could drink. Water dripped from the filled silk cloth into one of those apple cups, and when it was full, Kate handed it to Karle, who drank thirstily.

"Père has told me that I must never pass by fresh water without having my fill. Though with my stomach so full of apples, there hardly even seems room for water."

Karle said nothing for a moment. He set his apple-cup back under the dripping silk, then looked directly into her eyes and said firmly, "He is not your *père*. He cannot be. Kin cannot be so unalike as you and he."

She squirmed uncomfortably and pulled the large shawl closer around herself. She looked away, suddenly unwilling to meet his glance. "How can you say this?" she said. "You know nothing of us."

"Where is your *mère*?" he asked.

She seemed caught off-guard by the question, but answered after a moment's hesitation, "She is dead."

"How?"

Her voice, when she answered, was flat and dry. "Of the plague," she said.

And by the distant, hurt look on Kate's face, Karle knew she was telling him the truth. Yet he did not doubt that she had also spoken the truth when she claimed that this man had cured her, and himself, of plague. *So why not the mother?*

It was as if she had heard his thought. "It was before he perfected the cure. But she lived a fortnight before she passed over," she hastened to add. "A whole fortnight!"

For a moment, it seemed to him that she glowed with a cherished memory, and then the warmth of it faded from her face. She had avoided responding to his original challenge, so he repeated it. "I say again he is not your *père*."

She glared at him over the glow of the fire. Her face was caught in its ghoulish orange light, and it was filled with something like hatred. He was surprised by how much it stung him. He tried desperately to see beyond the mask she wore, but she would not let him through it. Finally, when he could no longer stand the silent void, he filled it, foolishly, with accusations. "There is not a drop of his dark blood flowing in your fair body. And the daughters of mere physicians are not educated as you have been. You sound English, you look English, you even speak the vile language. Your French is of the sort spoken at Court. And you have said that you can read. *Women do not read*, unless they are very wellborn, indeed!"

"Père taught me. And I assure you, he is *not* wellborn."

"But he is an educated man. And his French is tinged with the sound of Spanish, and with the Christian name Alejandro, it seems only natural that he must be of that heritage."

Her eyes were locked on his; then she suddenly lowered her head and looked away, as if she could no longer bear the weight of his scrutiny. But when her eyes met his again, her expression was pure defiance.

"You are a shrewd man to notice all these things."

"I am an honorable man, trying to understand the nature of a maiden whose well-being has been placed in my care. I mean to keep my word to this man who gave you into my care, whoever he might be to you, and I will be far better able to do it if I have some knowledge of your circumstances." He poked at the embers with a stick to release some of their heat into the cooling air. "And I will admit," he said in a quiet tone, "I am curious. You seem an unusual pair."

Kate watched as he rearranged the charred bits of wood to bring forth their full warmth. His movements were assured but careful, and he managed to do what was needed without releasing a swarm of glowing sparks that might give away their position. When she finally answered, there was still an edge of bitterness in her voice, but it was softer. "You are right— he is not my true father," she told him. "But the man who spilled his seed between the unwilling thighs of my lady mother, may she rest in peace, was no more a father to me than a rat might be to a lily. Yes, I am wellborn, but in the home of the man who sired me, I was dust under the feather bed—and just as quickly swept aside. Père has done everything for me that the truest father would, and more! And he did it all only because he cherishes me. He was obligated by nothing more than the goodness and mercy in his own heart. I am a blessed woman to have been fostered by such a father as he."

She turned away from him and lay down in the pine needles, an unmistakable sign that their discussion was finished. He noticed that her shawl, though large, was made of thin fabric, and though it provided well enough for modesty, it could not be giving her much warmth. Her garments were still damp, and Guillaume Karle began to worry that she might take a chill. *Alive and well* was the challenge the man she called Père had given him. For all her bravery and skill, she was in truth just a maiden on the run, alone with a man she barely knew, hoping to regain the family she had lost, which family consisted solely of one enigmatic man who was not her true father.

She bears a great deal for one of such tender age, he thought with great sympathy. *But too many secrets.* He spoke gently to her. "I apologize if my inquiries have caused you distress. I was merely curious. Your circumstances seem . . . unique."

"Oh, they are different, indeed," she sighed. "That much is surely true." She shivered again in the night air.

"The air grows colder," he said. "By now the heat of the pond is leaping out into the air in great white clouds." He laughed a little, hoping she would find amusement in his comment. But she remained quiet.

"And you are shivering," he said, drawing closer to her.

"It seems I am always cold," she answered with a small, muffled sniff. "I can never find enough warmth." Then she began to weep in earnest.

Quietly, Karle moved himself next to her and lay down. And though her body stiffened a bit, she did not push him away when he pressed his belly up against her back, sidling against her with an uncanny fit. He wrapped his arms around the front of her and gave her his warmth, and after a while he could feel her relax and drift into sleep. He lay awake, breathing slowly through her smoke-scented hair, and listened to his own heart as it pounded madly against her back.

When Janie came into the research unit in the morning, the Monkey Man handed her a printed page, accompanied by a glare that clearly said, *Explain.*

She gave him the most innocent look she could conjure, then scanned silently through the words, trying to hide her excitement, as if the subject matter of the page were a complete mystery to her. As her eyes moved down the page her feigned surprise turned genuine. "Oh, my God, Chet—they granted my request for a system-wide search."

"So I read," he said. "I didn't even know you'd applied for it." His face was the very image of disapproval. "I thought we discussed this yesterday."

"We did. But I didn't think we'd actually come to any conclusion. And I figured it couldn't hurt to go ahead with the application anyway, just in case. We don't actually have to use it, if we don't want to. But if we do, then—"

"I guess you don't have as much experience in this sort of thing as I thought you did," he said disdainfully. "They keep track of this stuff, you know. So if you apply for a search, and they give it to you, and then you don't use it, there'll be this cute little notation on our request history file. It'll say 'squandered the time of search request approval personnel with unused request,' or something like that. Jesus, Janie, you don't put those people through a request approval process and then say 'never mind.'"

She wondered who "those people" might be but didn't ask, because in the long run it was unimportant. "Well, there is still a chance that—"

"That what? Money would drift down from the aerie? I distinctly recall telling you that the likelihood of that happening was slim."

He had. She couldn't deny it. She could only hope to deflect his anger. "I'm on the trail of some grant money," she said. "Obviously I don't know if I'll get it. But I still think you should take this upstairs. What's the worst that could happen?"

"Whatever it is, it'll happen to me, not you. They might just fire my stupid ass for bringing it to them in the first place."

And such a hairy stupid ass it probably is, although I hope never to find out. "They're not going to fire you. And they might actually say yes."

"Look, Janie, what they're going to tell me upstairs about this Prives kid is no. It's too risky. If we bring him in, and he doesn't respond in the same way the others do, it'll lower our success rate. And that just means the patent on whatever drug or protocol comes out of this will be worth less when we try to license it out. I don't have to tell you what that means for everyone around here."

Shrinking endowment, budget cutbacks, potential layoffs, institutional agita. Doctors and technicians who would be giving serious thought to working on assembly lines, herself perhaps among them. She sighed aloud. "No, you don't."

But what if they were successful? The payoff might be enormous. Janie gave Chet a little smile of challenge and said, "Have you given any thought to what would happen if the protocol actually worked for this particular kid? Who knows how many others there are out there like him."

"You're talking about a very rare kind of trauma. Very rare. How many more could there be?"

"I don't know. But I will know after I make the search."

"You're not going to make that search."

"B-but"—she stammered—"you just said we shouldn't make it look like we were squandering a search permit."

"Use the permit," he said, "but go in and bring out something really horseshit. Find out how many angels can dance on the head of a pin. Then don't do anything like this again without asking me first."

She allowed a few tense seconds to pass. "You don't know what I'll find if I do that search, Chet. You can't possibly know."

"Maybe not, but I don't particularly care right now. I have a good solid study going and it doesn't need an infusion of hopeless cases to fuck it up. And what I do know is that I'm going to end up looking like a fool because the people upstairs will think I sanctioned this. I don't want them thinking I would go for something like this—it's a tremendous long shot."

"So was Xeroxing," she said, "once upon a time. But maybe I should be going elsewhere for support. Then think of all the explaining you'll have to do upstairs if I come up with something that works and you passed on it."

Scowling, Chet said, "If it didn't have to be your ID, I'd do this myself and be done with it. Now go in there and find out how many of the popes have been Catholic. Then give me a nice, neat report on it. And don't go snooping around on your own anymore. You'll make us all look bad."

Janie managed, against all odds, to close the door to her cubicle office without ripping it off the hinges in anger and disgust. She spent the next few minutes muttering curses under her breath, gender-based epithets that could not be said aloud in the workplace without resulting in well-founded charges of harassment. All of her considerable vitriol was aimed at Chet Malin, and when it had finally dissipated enough for her to go about her business, she indulged in a few moments of compulsive desk-neatening to clear her head of the leftover fuzz that such institutional encounters always seemed to create.

Asshole, she thought. He must have done something for someone to get this job.

And then she thought, *There but for the grace of God go I.* She tossed his negativity out of her consciousness. It landed at her feet with a compliant thud.

"Fuck you, Chet," she said aloud. "Here I go. Catch me if you can."

She nimbled up her fingers with a few quick flexes, then entered Big Dattie, but as the doors to information opened before her she heard Tom Macalester's stern but affectionate warning inside her head.

No more digging.

"What are you, my guardian angel?" she whispered. She could almost see him grinning from the head of some huge pin, and tried to push the image out of her mind.

Big Dattie's own warning came up, then the yellow screen, and finally she was allowed to enter her search criteria. Dozens of pages came up. She scrolled through the list and saw the name Abraham Prives, as she'd expected, and also the name of the boy from Boston. But the information was still too vague, so she asked Big Dattie to report only those cases where the injury had been described as shattering or splintering.

She expected it to take a few seconds for the data to run through the filters, because when Big Dattie found very few or no hits for a request, it assumed an error and rechecked itself automatically, resulting in a slight delay. But the results were almost instant, and Janie found herself staring in slight surprise at a list of thirty-odd names.

She backtracked and expanded the age a year in each direction. The computer gave her back a list of over a hundred names.

Sort the results, she told the machine. *Find the correlations. List by date of injury.*

"Well, well, well . . ." she whispered as she read through the final product. "Look what we have here."

When Janie called Tom Macalester to ask for a meeting, he said, "It's too nice for offices today. Let's meet in the square. I have something I need to talk to you about too."

"You first," Janie said when they met an hour later.

"I thought it was ladies first."

"You're misinformed. It's 'ladies get to decide.' "

"Okay. You may not like this, but hear me out before you start shrieking."

"I shriek?"

"Sometimes. This might be one of those occasions. I've been giving Bruce's immigration problems some consideration," Tom said, "and I feel like I'm hitting a wall. I think it's the wall everyone hits in situations like this, so it's not totally alarming, and I think in the long run everything will work out. But I'm not very adept at immigration, and I don't have any good ideas about how to scale this wall. I don't know if you ought to be standing by your man with me as an advocate."

He wouldn't look her in the eye. She wondered why. Was he lying, or hiding something from her that he thought she might not want to hear? Maybe masking some private thoughts about her situation that she wouldn't appreciate? Tom was usually so direct. Janie found his behavior almost unnerving.

Whatever it was that was bothering him, she'd always trusted him and saw no reason not to trust him now. "I have great faith in you," she said quietly.

Back came the eye contact. It always seemed so intense to her.

"I know," he said. "I appreciate that. And normally I'm flattered, it's just—well, Bruce isn't, I mean, you're really my client, and—I have to be honest—immigration law really isn't my thing. I've gotten specialized in medical law and bioethics to the point where I guess I really don't feel the same level of confidence working in other areas. I think you might do better with someone who knows a little more about it than I do."

He was right—she did want to shriek. But he was so reasonable and thoughtful in what he'd said and so obviously troubled by what he viewed as his failure that Janie almost felt sorry for him. She could see self-disappointment reflected in his posture and his carriage. For the first time, she noticed a few worry lines in his forehead.

Janie took hold of her longtime friend's hand and gave it a light squeeze as they headed toward a group of benches. She patted it, then let go. "You're my lawyer, Tom. And I have every confidence that you'll consult whomever you need to consult. I really don't want to deal with anyone else, especially now when so much seems to be—askew." She looked at him and smiled. "And I guess I've grown accustomed to your face, or something like that."

He gave her a funny little grin, then shook his head and sighed. "Ever the cliché queen."

"Sorry."

"It's okay. I forgive you. But I'm serious about this. Immigration is beyond my field of expertise, at least at this level. And all of a sudden I've got some other time obligations that really aren't negotiable, and I feel like I'm taking on too much."

Janie gave him a curious look. "Such as?"

"I've been approached for some consulting work by a bioethics think tank. For some reason they seem to feel they need a lawyer in their midst. I think there are some biopatent issues that they need advice on."

"Tom, this is great—"

He smiled broadly. "I know. It's the kind of law I really love, where I feel completely at home. But it will take some time, at least until I settle into the rhythm of it. So my point is that I shouldn't be taking your money if I can't give you your money's worth."

"Now, there's an old-fashioned attitude."

"Hey, they don't call me Tom-osaurus Rex for nothing." He pointed toward a vendor's cart. "Want a hot dog?"

"*Ugh*. No thanks. Do you have any idea what's in those things?"

"Yeah. All sorts of shit. Literally."

"And you still eat them?"

"With relish, yuk, yuk."

"Jesus, Tom, and you ride me for using clichés. Your jokes get lamer every year."

"Along with the rest of me, my dear."

"Yeah, it's one long downward slide, this life. Listen, I appreciate your candor, both about your situation and mine. But I don't want to change lawyers now. If you have to, get someone else to do the actual work, and I'll pay the bill, but I don't want to have to talk to anyone else directly. You're the only lawyer I've ever been able to stomach. So be my buffer. That's what I want."

"Okay."

He smiled, but Janie thought it was tinged with sadness.

"If you're sure," he added.

"I am."

The smile drifted away and a brief expression of uncertainty came over Tom's face; for a moment Janie was inclined to ask him if something else was bothering him. But just as quickly he seemed to shake it off and the familiar man she'd known since their late childhood returned.

"So," he said, "I'm done pissing and moaning about my fears of professional inadequacy. What is it you wanted to piss and moan about?"

"Nothing, actually. There's something rather exciting I need to show you."

He smiled, then glanced around almost furtively and leaned closer. "Here? I mean, I'm thrilled, but it's public. . . ."

Janie couldn't help but chuckle. "Give it a rest, will you? The other day you said something about having a unique specialty. Would working on a unique problem have the same kind of effect, even if it wasn't necessarily my specialty?"

"It would depend on the problem, but yes, it might. Have you got something?"

"I think so. It's possible that I may have stumbled onto a new syndrome." She handed him the list of names. "These kids are all suffering from the same supposedly 'very rare' problem of splintered bones. I discovered it on a trip into Big Dattie—and don't worry, I had a permit."

"Well, that's good, at least."

"I didn't dig illegally. I'm trying not to do that anymore—on my lawyer's advice."

"I'm absolutely positive that your lawyer appreciates that."

"Except it might cut into his income."

"He'll live."

"With or without me, I'm sure. Anyway, I found this pattern. Not just broken bones, shattered bones. The similarity of the shattering problem is just too coincidental to be overlooked. I sorted them by date—take a look at this." She handed him a chart showing the pattern of incidents. "There's a very sudden increase in frequency."

The chart showed a dramatic spike. "And in all of the cases I've read so far, one really striking similarity is that the injuries alone couldn't account for the severity of the problem."

"So what are you saying?"

"That there has to be some inherent weakness there. Something that causes a vulnerability to sudden, unexplained breakage. Maybe genetic. But it could also be disease-based. And I don't see any indication from these kids' records that anyone else is looking into it. So—that would make it unique, right?"

"I suppose. You'd need to hook up with someone who specializes in this type of skeletal problem."

"How hard do you think that's going to be? I'll just yank someone off an oil rig."

She expected him to laugh, but instead Tom frowned. "Janie, I think you're reaching on this one. I don't think it's a bad idea to look into this . . . pattern, though I want to be sure you keep me very well informed of what you're doing—but using it as a means of getting relicensed, I don't know. It's a stretch."

Her face turned pensive. Then determined. "Maybe it is. But goddamn it, I have to stretch. What I'm doing for work means absolutely nothing to me. And whether it leads to my getting relicensed, here's a chance to do some good for a lot of other people. That's why I got into medicine in the first place. I seem to have forgotten it somewhere along the line. I don't want to walk away from this."

Caroline Porter Rosow sat in a chair at her kitchen table with her leg extended and her foot raised up to rest on a plastic drape that covered Janie's lap. She turned her foot slightly so Janie could get a better look at the stub of the partially removed little toe, still tender almost a year later. Janie, wearing bio-impermeable gloves, moved what was left of the toe from side to side with her own fingers.

As she examined the appendage, she chatted, partly to distract Caroline from the discomfort of her probings and partly because there was news to convey. After their troubling experience abroad, they were far more than friends, and there were few if any secrets between them. "Well, it looks like I'm going to have sex again in my life."

"You didn't buy one of those—*things*, did you?"

"No, smartass. The travel agent says there are plenty of visas available for Iceland. Bruce and I are going to meet there—next month."

"Janie, this is great. . . ."

"I know. I'm excited. But Bruce was a little disappointed when he heard it was going to be Iceland."

"Well, their chief attraction is volcanoes . . . so don't forget to pack an umbrella. A really big one, and fireproof. This wouldn't happen to be the same travel agent that set up the London trip, would it?"

Janie wiggled another of Caroline's toes, a bit more forcefully than she'd moved the others, then the stub again. "The very one."

"Uh-oh . . ."

"Nothing can possibly happen there. It's rock, remember? I won't be able to dig anything up." She manipulated the entire front of Caroline's foot. "That doesn't hurt, does it?"

"Just a little bit." She winced slightly and shifted in her chair, as if changing the position of her backside would make any difference in her foot. "God, it's about time you two got together. How long has it been now?"

"Four months. Since Mexico. And I don't have to tell you that Iceland could only be an improvement." Now Janie moved the toe up and down. "Does this hurt more than it did last week?"

"No." Then she winced. "I lied. Yes. But it hurts mainly when it rains. And when you move it. Not ordinarily, though."

"Did it hurt when it rained before you were sick?"

"Sometimes."

"Ah. Well, that might explain it, then. The miraculous phenomenon of phantom pain." She separated the remains of the little toe from the one next to it and looked at the flesh between the two. "It's a little red in here. That doesn't make me happy. How do your shoes feel?"

"As nasty as ever. They all still hurt."

"Even with the foam filler?"

"It doesn't make that much of a difference. It helps, but I can still feel everything. God, I would kill to be able to wear a nice pair of high heels again."

"I'm afraid your fuck-me-pump days are over, babe. Sorry. At least you didn't lose the foot . . . and you can always wear fishnet stockings, if the mood strikes you." She patted the side of Caroline's foot affectionately and let go. "Let me see your hand now."

Caroline held out her freckled left hand, conspicuously presenting her wedding band. She extended her fingers tauntingly and laughed. Janie slapped the back of the hand lightly, then took it in her own and brought it closer for a good look.

"Okay, I'm jealous," Janie said. "Are you happy? Your guy gets in, and mine doesn't. Yours marries you. Mine says he'll marry me if he ever gets here. But do I have a ring yet? No."

Caroline laughed lightly and shook her head. "Oh, my, are we ever self-absorbed . . . you really do need a different job."

"I guess I do," Janie said with an ironic chuckle. She turned Caroline's hand over and examined the palm, and saw nothing unexpected—the bruises were all gone, and all that remained were faint scars where one or two buboes had been. "It looks really good. You've been taking good care of your hands. I was afraid your body would overreact when they injected your ID sensor because your immune system was so whacked out from plague. But it didn't—everything looks fine."

Caroline drew her hand away suddenly. "That was almost a year ago. How come you didn't tell me you were worried about this before now?"

After the briefest pause, Janie said, "I didn't want to concern you. I told you what to watch for, didn't I?"

"Yeah, but not what it might mean."

"Well, nothing happened, so don't worry."

"I worry about everything. You know that."

"God help us when you have kids." She lowered her voice, so Caroline's husband, Michael, wouldn't overhear. "Speaking of which, did you get your period?"

Caroline made an uncertain face and shook her head no.

"Wow. Well, maybe . . . how late are you?"

"Just a day."

"Well, I'll keep my fingers crossed for you."

"Thanks."

Caroline had been so ill with plague in London, so racked with infection, that Janie thought there would be terrible implications for all of her body systems, and in truth Caroline's kidneys were not what they once were. *When you get pregnant,* she'd told her, *you'll never get out of the bathroom.*

But she hadn't gotten pregnant, not in eight months of doing the deed every day, sometimes twice, depending on her cycle, and using no birth control. It was not a good sign.

A severe fall, they'd explained to the immigration agent at Logan Airport. *Scraped her hand.* It explained the bruising, the bandages, the limp, and the extremely shell-shocked mental state in which Caroline had made her appearance at the immigration office in Boston. *She had a little concussion,* Janie explained for her. *She's still a bit dazed.* And though her strange condition had raised a few eyebrows, Caroline did not set off any of the biosensors, because they'd made sure she was contagion-free before trying to leave Britain. The breath Janie held as Caroline passed through the readers was one of her life's longest, and without question, the most happily expelled.

"Now, about your foot. I am not entirely happy with that toe. It looks a little tender to me."

"It is a little tender."

"You wear socks all the time?"

"Except when I'm wearing sandals."

"You really shouldn't leave that toe exposed. If you scrape it or bang it into something, it could be a problem. Are you replacing your socks regularly?"

"Yes."

"Washing them in hot water with lots of bleach?"

"Of course."

"Washing the new ones before you wear them?"

Silence.

"Caroline, it's important."

"I know. But sometimes I forget."

"Try not to, please. A lot of them are imported. They don't go through the same kind of inspections U.S. goods go through."

"That's why I can afford to buy them. But, okay, I'll be more careful."

As Caroline pulled a clean cotton sock over her damaged foot, Janie removed her gloves and stowed them in a plastic bag. She would dispose of them in the foundation's biosafe refuse room the next day. As she washed her hands in the kitchen sink, she said, "So, your prince is apparently still charming. . . ."

"Yeah, but he complains about us not having any royalty here."

"What—he never heard of the Kennedys?"

"Too Irish for him."

"Oh, poor baby. Is he still trying to get you to make Yorkshire pudding?"

"I think he may be giving up on that one. I tried to make it again last week, but I just can't use all that fat, not without gagging, anyway. So it was dry. He looked pretty disappointed."

"Still doesn't want you to work?"

"No," Caroline said. "And to tell you the truth, I'm not unhappy to be staying home."

"It probably grows on you," she said as she wiped her hands on a paper towel. "I imagine it would, I mean. I don't really remember how it felt—the last time I wasn't working or in school was when Betsy was a little baby." She tossed the towel in the wastebasket. "And that was only for a few weeks."

There was a conspicuous silence. Caroline saw the conflicted look on Janie's face and said sympathetically, "Staying home's not for everyone. You had a practice."

"And I hope to again," she said.

"How is that looking?"

"Well, until a little while ago, not too good."

"Oh? Is there news?"

"Actually, there is. I found something I think might be unique enough to qualify me for a reapplication." Once again, she explained what she'd discovered. With each additional recitation, she was more and more convinced that it was worth pursuing. "Thing is, though, I'm going to need some help. With a data search. As I review what I've already found I see a couple of things that just scream for another look."

"And those would be . . . ?"

"Well, for starters, why did this thing pop up all of a sudden? Wouldn't there have been at least a few incidences prior to this sudden surge?"

"Maybe there were and no one caught them."

"Maybe. It also might have happened B.D."

"Oh," Caroline said, "things did actually happen before the database, didn't they? Sometimes I forget."

"Yes, and contrary to our rose-colored view of those good old days, it wasn't all pleasant." She let out a long breath. "It's possible that there were a few cases of whatever this is, and no one connected them. Or maybe someone connected them and was working on something and then didn't make it through the Outbreaks."

"A reasonable assumption."

"I'm bothered by how quickly this seems to have showed up, because I have a suspicion that it's a genetic problem. At least that there's a genetic propensity."

"What makes you think that?"

Janie took a copy of the list of names out of her purse and handed it to Caroline. "Take a look at it. Tell me if you notice anything."

Caroline took the list and started reciting names. "David Aaronson, Elliot Bernstein, Michael Cohen . . ." She looked up and shrugged.

"These boys are all Jewish."

Caroline was quiet for a moment. "And if that's the case, just who do you think you're going to get to help you?"

"Your prince, my dear. Your lovely half-Jewish prince."

Michael Rosow, former British biocop and pursuer of international biocriminals—one of whom now happened to be his wife—son of a Jewish father and a Christian mother, did not like the idea one little bit when Janie presented it to him.

"My king will not be pleased," he said adamantly.

"Your king barely knows he's king. He wouldn't know a database if one rose up out of Loch Ness and swallowed him. And you don't really give a damn if he does or doesn't, anyway. You aren't going back there anytime soon. So tell me what really bothers you about doing it."

He waited a moment before answering. "I'm afraid I'll get caught, that's all."

Janie had no snappy comeback for that response. "I understand that. And I'd be surprised if you weren't uneasy about it. But if we could figure out a way for you to get in there without getting caught, would you do it?"

"I don't know."

"Maybe we could borrow an identity."

Michael gave her a very direct and castigating look. "Shall we just cut off someone's hand, then?"

Janie winced as she recalled the nauseating episode in London that gave rise to Michael's question. "No. I don't think so."

"Right," Michael said. "You'll want to wait at least a year between, of course. Only proper."

Eventually, with adequate prodding on Janie's part that even she would have agreed bordered on nagging, Michael let it slip that once someone was into a computer and had established an identity, he could use the specialized infrared device that was standard equipment on biocop palmbooks to get into the database anonymously. The database would record the entry as having been made by the person whose sensor had activated the computer initially, and there would be no trace left of the true interloper.

"How can I get one?"

"You have to be kidding," he said. "I got one only because I'm a lieutenant. Anyone below that rank isn't allowed to use one."

So, she thought, *he can do it.* It was only an unknowing accomplice she needed now.

On the way home from their house, Janie stopped outside one of the nicer-looking local watering holes, one she'd often noticed but never entered. On this particular evening there was no line outside, so she ran a comb quickly through her hair, straightened her clothing, and went inside.

The computer bar was all glass and chrome, with low lighting, Early Meat Market as Janie expected it would be, perhaps a bit more elegant by virtue of its lofty patronage. She entered at the height of happy hour, when throngs of young nouveau riche techno-elite milled about and dropped credits, the new electronic dollars, on overpriced drinks at a rate that would alarm a Rockefeller, all while attempting to make a little cyber-time. They would sit at their numbered terminals and exchange anonymous witticisms with attractive customers at other terminals. And although she was quite comfortable with her own techno-savvy and not in the least bit threatened by the brilliance oozing all around her, Janie couldn't help but feel terribly out of place—she was a good twenty years older than any other woman in the establishment.

So she sat at one end of the bar, anonymously nursing a glass of Pinot Noir while the play progressed all around her. She watched intently, observing the actions of these smooth cyber-youths, her eyes tuned for the one detail that would spark an idea.

And eventually she was rewarded, not by the unanticipated detail but by a pattern that emerged gradually, somewhere in the middle of her third glass of wine, which she brazenly allowed herself because she was taking the bus home that night—alone but, for a change, not unhappy. She'd noticed that people made contact on their terminals after logging on, and if someone showed an interest he or she would get up and leave the terminal in operative mode to pursue real human contact. The computer would maintain the operative mode for an additional five minutes. So they *could* get in—and the person who'd been on the terminal would have an alibi. No one would get blamed.

She tossed down the last of her wine in one determined belt and left the bar, never having traded a phrase with anyone.

"Tomorrow night I want to take you out, just you and me," she said to Caroline on the phone later, when a bit of the haze had worn off.

"What's the occasion?"

"There isn't one. Yet. But I'm working on it." She explained her plan.

Reluctantly Caroline agreed to help, and made the offer Janie had hoped she would make.

"Caroline, this is great—you don't know how I appreciate your help with this."

Caroline sighed and said, "I just hope this works out better than the last time we got dressed up to get you something someone didn't want you to have."

A lejandro's horse was skittish all afternoon, for the smell of death could not be escaped. The roads were littered with the bloating bodies of those men who had succumbed in their attempt to escape the wrath of Charles of Navarre. Soon Alejandro came upon a section of the road where the bodies were all charred, as if some generous benefactor had come along and sacrificed the oil required to sustain the burning of a corpse, at least long enough to keep the animals at bay.

He had seen such horrors a decade ago on the route to England as they rode past Paris and headed for Calais. France had been horribly ravaged by the Plague Maiden, who seemed to plant her kiss on every other forehead she encountered in her journey of terror across Europa. Back then the wars were new and oil still plentiful, far more plentiful than men with the strength to dig graves. So bodies had been burned where they lay and he could still see the pyres in his mind. He had written of one such road in his long lost book of wisdom.

Who, if anyone, was reading it now? Who had discovered the secrets of his life, the intimacies of the soul that he'd laid bare on its parchment? He would never know unless he returned to England, which seemed an impossibility.

Now as he rode he was coming upon flaming bodies before the fires had gone out, and he found himself whispering one prayer after another, almost continually, for the souls of these dead. So he guided the unhappy horse into the brush and went through the woods in a parallel route, for he did not want to leave the tiniest hint of his journey.

They stopped at every watering place along the route to Paris, and when the water seemed good Alejandro strained it through his cloth and took his fill. In one spot the water seemed particularly sweet and fine, so he filtered it into his water bag and drank until he thought he would burst.

When they came upon a drinking spot only a short distance after the last one, he himself had no need but he urged the horse forward. It was an ooze more than a spring, with no clear shore, and it lacked the ripples of fish or frogs or insects. The animal seemed completely uninterested.

"What, my friend, are you so sure of your next drink that you can afford to pass this one by? Surely you are smarter than the man who rides you." He jumped down off the horse, took him by the reins, and led him to the edge of the water. But the animal would not drink.

"So it is true, then, what they say about a horse who is led to water." He stroked the animal's neck. "I had believed it a witch's tale."

He knelt down beside the water and ran his fingers through it, and as he did so his nostrils began to tingle at a familiar smell. Sulfur. The same smell he had known outside Mother Sarah's cottage near London.

He leaned closer, sniffed harder. It had to be—and he had thought never to find the stuff again! He ran back to the horse and grabbed his water bag. After taking a long drink of the filtered water, he poured out the rest. And without using his Nipponese cloth, he filled the bag with the yellowish magic liquid that seeped up out of the ground.

He would have to obtain another water bag. But no matter. This could not be passed by.

"We should be in Paris by now," Kate said unhappily.

"It is not far."

"But we ride and ride, and we never seem to get there . . . I do not understand this route you have chosen. Père will be worried."

It was not the first time she had protested their indirect route, and just as he had before, Guillaume Karle did his best to put her off. And when she would not be ignored, he responded to her complaints with a cryptic explanation. "Your *père* said only to present you alive and well. He did not specify a route. Or a time."

"I am becoming less well with every league we travel. And why must we stop at these farmhouses so often? You disappear inside and leave me outside for all the world to see."

His reasons were always good enough to soothe her, but never enough to silence her completely. And so she waited in perturbed agitation outside cottage after cottage, fuming impatiently while Karle slipped inside to deliver news, or receive messages, or formulate new schemes to advance his rebellion. Sometimes he returned with food, but more often he would leave behind a bit of what little they had.

He came out from one house with a half-loaf of bread. He broke it in two and handed a piece to Kate. Though far from fresh, she took it eagerly and tore off a chunk with her teeth. "Were we in Paris," she said with something like a sneer, "we might have jam for our bread. We might even have bread with some regularity."

"Soon enough we shall be there, and you can spread such delights as you can find on your bread. But even Paris wants delights these days." Then he gave her a look of frank disapproval and chided her. "You sound like a princess with your concern for such things."

She could not keep herself from reddening. "I care not for delights," she said, her voice full of hurt, "even jam. But sometimes merely the thought of a good thing can bring a sense of its pleasure—I am hurting no one with my little dreams. The one delight I truly desire is that of rejoining Père."

"Soon enough," Karle said again.

The continued postponement began to wear on her. "Perhaps I shall leave your company and ride directly to Paris," she said on the third day of their travels. "Then you can be about your important business, and I, mine." She sat proudly on her horse, expecting thanks for her announcement that he would soon be free of his obligation to care for her.

Instead of expressing gratitude, in a voice of disbelief Karle said, "Are you mad? A maiden alone is easy prey for an errant knight. And there are plenty about." He chuckled cynically. "And though I will admit you wield it well enough, your little knife is no match for a sword."

"No true knight would behave poorly against me!"

Karle's horse pranced nervously in response to his unfamiliar rider, all the more so because of the rider's agitation. "But the deeds of the false ones cannot be anticipated," Karle told her, his tone hard and unreassuring. "How is it that you are so sheltered from the truth of these times? Has your *père* kept *you* locked in a cabinet as well?"

She looked away in shame. She could not explain the reasons for the isolation in which she and Alejandro had lived.

"Let me tell you how knights, even the truest, behave these days," he continued. "They run wild all through France, without patronage. There are no lords to pay them, for those lords grow fat as hostages at Edward's generous table. And should a lord be foolishly inclined to give up the luxury of life in the English Court and return to the chaos of France, his vassals have not the means to buy his freedom! Knights now crave the comfort of *any* allegiance, and to find it they join the Free Companies. Everything not lashed down has been stolen by these 'heroes,' including women, whom they use for their pleasure and then discard."

"This cannot be true! They cannot *all* be such fiends as you describe. . . ."

"Forgive me," he said sarcastically. "I exaggerate. One or two have come to our cause. A few who serve God before king will not join in the desecration of France. But you will not be safe from the others. Not alone." His hard blue eyes bore down on her, full of condemnation. "How can you not know this?"

What could she tell him to excuse her ignorance? She had come by it honestly enough. She groped for a plausible answer. "I have devoted myself to—um—st-study . . ." she stammered, "of midwifery."

"A fine bit of good it does to know midwifery if you are dead on the side of the road, ravaged by some supposedly 'noble' knight. You must try to stay alive, so you can put your skills to proper use," he said. "If your claims are true, you would be of great help in our cause." He dared her with his eyes. "Come with me now, and you shall see."

He heeled the horse in the flanks and rode off. And against all that made sense to her, she followed.

But this time she did not wait outside. They were greeted at the door of a small, decrepit stone house by a cheerless woman with stick-thin arms and a belly swollen by pregnancy, and by the hollowness of the woman's cheeks, Kate could see that the babe within had taken what it could get, and left the mother with little sustenance for herself.

May God grant that I shall never know such want myself, she prayed silently as she gawked at the woman. The desperate prayer seemed so loud that she wondered if anyone had heard it.

The woman stared back at Kate with great suspicion, but when Karle vouched for her they were invited to enter.

The house was bare except for the most rudimentary furnishings. It was dim, for there were no candles to be seen anywhere, and chilly, for the hearth was cold. The air was foul with the musty-dank smell of sickness.

"*Bonjour, madame,*" Kate said with quiet politeness and a nod of her head.

The thin woman made a small curtsy, surprising Kate. Then she smiled hopefully at Karle, who returned her salutation with a little incline of his head, and the question "What of your husband?"

The *madame* gestured toward a pallet of matted straw before the cold hearth. The husband lay on it, unmoving, silent, thin as a branch, pale as the moon. "He rises only to empty himself," the woman said. "Thank God he can still do that much, for I have not the strength to lift him anymore. Everything he takes in still comes out of him as dirty water," she whispered sadly. "Though he eats almost nothing."

"What of the little one?" Karle asked, looking around.

The woman extended her hand in the direction of a shadowy corner; there they saw a small boy, who stared out from the darkness with the hollow, vacant eyes of one who thinks of nothing but food.

"This one's not taken sick, thank God, but he's no bigger than he was two summers ago. And he says nothing anymore," she added with a pained look. "I fear he's become addled."

Kate looked around, but saw no other children. "Are there any others?"

With an agonized sob, she clutched at her breast and said, "Gone! By the hand of the plague itself!"

Kate and Karle stared at each other. "There is plague about?" Karle whispered.

Through her tears the woman managed to say, "Now and again it visits, and always it takes someone with it before it slinks back into its hole."

Kate came forward and put a hand on the woman's shoulder. She meant it as a comfort, but the woman shivered slightly, and Kate thought the bones might be protruding from the skin underneath the ragged dress. "When did your child die?"

"At the last turn of the moon."

"And you buried him?"

"As best I could . . . I dug a shallow hole on the edge of the west field and laid him in it, then covered him in rocks. I pray the animals have not gotten to him."

As well you ought, Kate thought. "*Madame,* are there often rats about?"

The swollen-eyed woman stared at her. "You need make such an inquiry?"

"I ask because there are physicians who think that rats may be the source of plague."

"Then we shall all die, for we have been forced to eat them."

Her gorge rose. "And your son who died? Did he eat a rat?"

"He may have; I cannot say for sure. He was of an age where he could hunt on his own. And we reached the point where we did not always share what we caught with each other." She crossed herself quickly. "May God save us from that sin. The boy might have caught one, and in his hunger, eaten it before he ever brought it home. But I do not know."

Without the benefit of the cooking pot's cleansing of the flesh, Kate thought. "No one is to eat rats," she said firmly, "ever again. To do so is almost sure death."

"We are sure to die anyway."

Kate had no reply for that hopeless remark. She was appalled by the desperation she saw, and gave the last of their apples to the woman. She was suddenly ashamed of her own glowing health, embarrassed by the flesh on her bones. "Have you no bread at all?" she asked.

"How are we to make bread? They've taken the plow—so there is no wheat, and therefore no flour. And my husband cannot till the soil; he cannot stand up long enough to turn one row. We cannot even grow a turnip. And all of our livestock have been claimed by Navarre!" She turned her head to one side and spat viciously in the dust of her floor.

Then she began to weep and the little boy came out of the corner to cling to her skirt. "How have we come to this state?" she sobbed. "We had so much to give praise for! And now it is all gone!"

Guillaume Karle leaned closer to Kate and whispered, "Is there nothing you can do for this man? *Midwife?*"

She gave Karle a look of dreadful uncertainty, then went to the bedside of the sallow-looking peasant. She took in what information she could without touching him, for to do so might bring the man's sickness upon her. *The cholera,* she concluded from her brief observation. Alejandro had often described the symptoms to her; he had spoken with bittersweet fondness of his old soldier comrade who feared war's cholera to the very depth of his soul, only to give that great soul to the plague instead.

She turned back to Karle. "There is little that can be done," she whispered. "But I dare not leave them with no hope at all." She looked at the woman and said, "You must gather what fuel you can, for all your husband's water must be boiled before he drinks it. He must drink as much as possible. By the look of his skin, he is quite dry." Then she turned to the child. "Do you know the dandelion?" she asked him.

He nodded dully.

"Then you must harvest as much of it as you can find, for it will help your *père* to recover. Bring the leaves to your *maman* and she will make a tea for him."

She turned back to the woman again. "The tea made from dandelion leaves may help his stomach; perhaps then he will be able to keep some nourishment inside him." She reached out and placed a hand on the woman's swollen belly. "You must dry the leaves that are left from making the tea, then grind them and take them as a powder. There is a magic in them that will strengthen both you and your child."

The woman, who appeared to be at least twice the age of the girl who now served as her advisor, gave Guillaume a suspicious look. He passed the look directly on to Kate.

She understood their hesitation and said firmly, "These are things my *père* taught me." Then she lowered her eyes and whispered to Karle, "When he spoke to me through the door of my cabinet."

Karle could not help but smile, though he tried to hide it from the sickly woman. "This is good advice," he told the woman, "and you should heed it."

"But she is such a young one—" the woman began to say.

"But her *père* is a physician. And though she *is* young, this midwife has acquired much wisdom from him."

This seemed to satisfy the woman, so she fortified the child with a hug and sent him out to gather the required leaves. "There may be wood enough for a fire, perhaps," she said as she wrapped a tattered shawl around her thin shoulders. "Behind the house."

They followed her out and brought back enough wood to get the fire going. Then Karle bade the woman farewell. "I will pray daily for your husband's recovery."

They left the house and its pathetic occupants, and remounted their horses. "Why did she curtsy to me?" Kate said curiously.

"Because it has been so long since she has seen healthy flesh like yours, she must take you for some kind of goddess." He smiled cynically. "Or at the very least, a princess."

She stared at him for a disconcerting moment, and when she realized he was joking, regained herself. The desire to move onward came over her with great and sudden urgency. She looked up into the sky for the sun, and then pointed.

"West," she said, and turned her horse.

"Where are you going?" Karle called as he followed her.

"To the west field," she cried back.

They found the grave quite easily. Some of the rocks had been shoved aside, but whatever beast had tried to dislodge them had not managed to finish the job. Still, Kate was grateful to see that much of her work had been done already by something with claws.

As she dug at the remaining rocks with her small hands, Karle watched in curious awe. When he tried to come closer she waved him off. "Stay back—then no one will be able to accuse you of participating."

"But this is punishable by death—*you* must stop!"

Rocks flying as she tossed them away, she said, "I cannot. This is of great import."

"But *why?* What can a maiden want—"

"Right now my deeds are those of a midwife, not a maiden. So stand guard. . . ."

The pile beside her had grown considerably, and she began to wonder if the woman had been right in saying that the grave was shallow, when she came upon what she thought was the rotted flesh of a thigh. She shoved away a few more rocks until she found the arm that rested against the thigh of the dead child, at its end a withered hand. And as Karle watched in horror, she reached into her stocking and pulled out her knife, then severed the hand from the body at the wrist joint. She tore off a strip of her shawl and wrapped the blackened appendage in it. And after a hasty restoration of the cairn, she stood, swooning, and retched in dry revulsion.

When their gazes came together, Karle saw the briefest flash of the driven animal in her eyes. "You are mad," he hissed.

But then she was the maiden again, and fully aware of the nature of her deed. "Do not say it too loudly, Karle," she whispered as she regained herself. "God will hear you. You must believe me when I tell you that it is a bit of good fortune that we found this, for we may need it." She held it out at arm's length. "But the greater fortune is that it no longer smells."

Alejandro watched from the small window of his attic room on Rue des Rosiers as an old woman in a simple gray frock and white apron greeted the day with a broom in one hand and a bucket in the other. First she swept the stones clear of the night's droppings, shoving them decisively away from her stoop, muttering as she banished the cursed brown piles to the gutter. Then she emptied her bucket of water over those same stones and swept them yet again, with vigor enough to ensure that nothing offensive would survive her rough treatment. He had watched her do the same thing the day before, and the day before that as well.

Had the citizens of London only been so fastidious, he mused regretfully, *perhaps more would have lived . . .* but plenty of Parisians had died in the first wave of the Black Death, despite the relative cleanliness of the city, so he could not fault the filth of London entirely for the devastation that had occurred there. Many claimed the English were a different sort of people than the French, more savage, nearly barbaric, some even said. And in truth, he could not recall ever seeing an Englishwoman attack the ever-present ordure on the London cobblestones with as much ferocity as this elderly Parisian *dame* now demonstrated. But he would not agree with the notion, widely held among the French, that the English were a slothful people, for they attacked many other things with great ferocity.

The French, for example. As often as possible. He smiled to himself in his attic aerie.

The old woman was now busily undoing the shutters that kept her rounds and crocks of cheese safe from those who would liberate them, *sans sou,* in the night. Food was dear with the shortages of war, and a generous portion of cheese had become a great luxury, to be enjoyed only by the very rich or the very cunning. Released from the night's entrapment, the pungent, curdy odor wafted upward and across the street; it was all the enticement Alejandro needed to leave the cobwebs and dank straw of his temporary hideaway to search for something with which to fill his growling stomach.

A huge wooden sign hung over the tiny shop, fashioned in the shape of a wedge and painted yellow, with the word *fromages* carved into the surface. Bits of soot and dirt clung to the hollowed-out letters, for it was beyond the reach of the old woman to clean them. He thought momentarily of offering to do the work for her. It would be a great kindness, and even after all he had been through Alejandro was still a kind man.

But he was not fool enough to make the offer, for such a kindness would implant him in her memory. Since arriving in Paris, Alejandro had taken care to avoid doing the same thing twice, lest he attract the notice of someone with nothing more to do than watch the comings and goings of the inhabitants of that particular *arrondissement.* Beyond Abraham's book it was all that he himself had to do, and he was amazed by how much he noticed when he had the time to observe: the sultry young woman who invited gentlemen up her dark stairway over and over again, all day and into the night; the rough boys who played at sticks and often made each other bleed in their otherwise good-natured contests; the shy young widow draped in black, pulling along a sniffling child and carrying a basket that always seemed so terribly empty. These people were all familiar to him now, and he had been in their environs only a few days. How long would it be before one of them noticed him, and wondered?

The day before he had heard the sweet voice of a little girl—she had cried out, "Père!" and the sound of it had robbed him of his breath. He'd whirled around just in time to see the happy homecoming of a lucky *père* returning from somewhere with things that his little one needed, not the least of which was his heart and its abundant affection. He swept a laughing child up into his arms and covered her rosy little face with fatherly kisses as Alejandro watched, feeling painful envy.

He does not know how quickly it will pass, how soon she will be a woman and no longer in need of him.

He would rotate his visits to various shops, never lingering too long in one place, and he never stood in the same location for more than a few minutes. But he always watched, wherever he might be standing, for it was on this street, in this group of small shops and markets, among the last few Jews of Paris, that Kate would come looking for him.

He was not yet worried that she had not arrived, for he himself had had the advantage of riding, and she was traveling on foot. Or had they somehow managed to acquire horses? Was it still "they"? The physician worried belatedly, with a terrible sense of impotence, if the Frenchman Karle was as trustworthy as he had judged him to be or if he would take the gold that had been given for her care and abandon her. She had more gold of her own tucked into another secret pocket of her skirt, one with a button so the coins could never slip out accidentally. He had taught her that she must never allow herself to lack an item that could be readily exchanged for the necessities of survival. One gold coin could buy her a journey halfway across Europa, if she spent it right, and he had raised her to be frugal. She would make a good wife, he thought with pride, despite her vagabond upbringing. Should the day come when she might marry, she would manage her husband's affairs and household with care and teach her children well.

May God grant that the world will once again come to sanity, and that such simple joys will someday be hers.

He found himself somehow standing before the cheeses, and heard the gray-frocked old woman ask him his preference in a voice more firm than he would have thought from her. He pointed out his modest choice from among the temptations and paid her price in small coins. After thanking her with a smile and a nod, he quickly crossed the street and headed for the *boulangerie,* where he bought a long golden loaf of still-warm *pain.* He spoke not one word from the time he left the room to the time he returned with his food.

He sat down at the window again, and watched.

Kate was quiet and sober as they rode, and barely spoke until they stopped at the next stream. "The tale that woman told—it shames me to know that such things happen! To steal a man's wealth is dishonorable enough," she said as the water dripped through her silk. "But to rob him of the means to provide for his family is quite another thing entirely. Surely this is the *most* grievous of thefts."

"They have stolen everything from these peasants," he said cynically. "*Jacques Bonhomme*, the good peasant. The worst sin among these unfortunates is the sin of unprivileged birth."

"We are all born in sin," she said. "But it is no sin to be born poor. The only sin lies in doing nothing to improve one's lot."

"The lords of France have made it impossible for their subjects to do that."

"Then I too should rise up, had I been treated so," Kate said, "or I should not be able to face my God. I cannot understand why He has not allowed you to prevail." She shook her head in bewilderment. "This failure of your army must be part of some plan, some greater design, for your cause must surely be just in God's eyes. We cannot always know why He works as He does."

Her remark seemed to make Guillaume Karle angry. "It was not the work of God, it was luck, pure bad luck! But for the chance arrival of her champions, we might now be holding the wife of the king's son and negotiating with her head."

Kate gave him a hard look. "Surely you would never consider taking the lady's head."

"And why not? Shall it be left on her neck simply because she is born royal? Should she be spared the same treatment that her husband's subjects have suffered, often for the most trivial reasons? If her head could buy a thousand plows, would it not seem a reasonable thing for her to part with it?"

The young woman whose capture would buy a thousand plows and more put an uneasy hand on her neck and said, "Perhaps to you this seems a fair exchange. But I assure you, the lady would till all the fields in France with her own hands to save her neck."

Karle snickered. "Perhaps to see such a sight it might be worth sparing her life. Now that she is under the protection of Navarre, I shall not have the opportunity to decide. For the moment. But we shall see if another opportunity presents itself."

Alejandro's only real distraction from increasing worry was his work on the precious book Kate had bought for him, and even that did not bring perfect respite. One minute the pages captured him with their promise of revelation, and the next his gaze was drawn to the busy street below, his heart pulled by the hope of reunion. He sat hunched over the ancient tome in the light of his one window, looking out at ever shortening intervals to scan the street with a furrowed brow. His eyes would dart anxiously from one young woman to another, driven by the dream that the next girl he saw would be the one he sought.

He felt dulled by the disappointment of looking at stranger after stranger and never seeing what he longed to see. Still, his work of words moved forward almost of its own volition, and it soon became his one joy. Line by line, he pried the meaning from the symbols, and the words they formed began to burn themselves into his memory. But this too added to his worries: of what use would this freed and then memorized wisdom be to those Jews dispersed by the will of God in Gaul, if the things they needed to know remained locked inside his head? *And what if* . . . he thought with a shudder, *what if I should die before these words can be shared?* Once unlocked, they should be preserved. Of that there could be no doubt.

He had bought a quill and inkstone, but he had nothing on which to write his translations as he made them except the pages themselves.

A sacrilege! his conscience admonished him. *To mar such beauty with your own scribblings! It belongs to those unfortunate Jews for whose benefit it was intended.*

Then his reason cried indignantly, *Am I not one of them myself?*

His reason finally triumphed. *But for my efforts, it would be lost to them for all time.*

So, he thought, allowing himself a brief moment of amusement, *this argument is settled, and happily it has gone in my favor.* And as the sun neared its peak in the sky, he realized that he still had not spoken one audible word that day.

"Dear God," he prayed aloud, "please grant me at least someone to argue with, that I may be spared the ignominy of doing so with only myself."

With painstaking care, he began to write the translations on the facing leaves. The Hebrew was archaic, of a style that a poorly educated Jew would not be able to read. French, he decided, would be best, for surely French would always be the most important language in the world, and there would always be a Jew who would understand it.

How had the apothecary obtained this treasure? Surely not from Abraham himself, for the book was very old. Alejandro had no doubt that the manuscript's shrewd author was long gone and dwelling peacefully with the shades of his ancestors. Had the wretched man who sold it to Kate for a gold crown stolen it from some charred satchel, or had it first been sold to him, perhaps for a handful of pennies, by some widowed mother desperate to feed her children?

He sighed in the distressing realization that he would never know the intricacies of its journey into his own hands. He knew only that it had been well worth the gold crown exchanged for it, and more. *Ah, Abraham,* he mused, *may God grant you peace, for you have left a work that merits the sweetest reward. And it was brought out of hiding by a Christian girl, who somehow had the wisdom to know what it was.* This, he knew, would be a surprise to the ancient and long-dead priest, should he be watching from his seat at the side of the prophets.

Yet the revelations of this Levite were not entirely sweet, for after his initial, benign greeting Abraham had issued a string of stern admonishments against misuse of his wisdom. *Maranatha!* he wrote, a word Alejandro could not translate, though the physician-cum-scribe found himself greatly impressed by its sound. It was peppered repeatedly on the page among the harsh warnings, but try as he might he could not decipher its meaning from the words around it.

Woe shall be to anyone who casts his eyes upon these leaves and is not a Sacrificer or a Scribe. Maranatha!

This worried him. Surely at present he could consider himself a scribe, he thought, but what, exactly, was a sacrificer? Was it wise for him to proceed without this knowledge? What woe might come to him by way of this ancient text?

In truth, what woe has not already befallen me, that I should fear any other woe? he thought.

His eyes were beginning to smart, so he rubbed them for a moment to ease the strain. He thought of Kate, and of how she had offered his own advice back to him—take care not to ruin your eyes with too much reading. He ran his fingers through his hair to push it away from his face. A single strand came loose and floated down. It settled in the thin space between two of the papyrus pages. He tried for a moment to get it out, but his fingers were too thick.

It will come to nothing, he finally decided, and left it there. He placed the book carefully in his bag, and with one last look out the window set out to find someone who might reveal its secret word to him. And though he considered them all to be parasitic charlatans, he thought it likely that a priest could tell him. *They know the names of all their enemies,* he remembered. Surely one would know this word. He could ask without engendering too much interest, if he asked discreetly. He could claim to be a scholar of some sort—*Ah, there is a thought! Perhaps there is a scholar I might ask!* He would find no lack of them at the university, only a short walk away. Surely there he could engage in an intellectual inquiry without seeming at all conspicuous. *Perhaps I will even find someone to argue with.* . . .

Kate would come sooner or later, he knew it in his heart, and neither his worry nor his will could change the moment of her arrival. He would not be gone long, probably only a few hours, and she would wait if she came to their meeting place while he was absent. He knew he need not watch for her every moment. It was only his great longing to rejoin her that made him want to do so.

The expression on Caroline Rosow's face when she glanced around the computer bar was an incongruous mix of curiosity and disdain. "This isn't what I expected," she said.

Janie leaned closer to her and said, "What did you expect?"

"I'm not exactly sure. But not this. This is—*sad.*"

"Among other things," Janie said. Then she added quietly, "I'm glad you're here. I was afraid you might have changed your mind."

"I almost did. Michael was in a state when he got home, and I wasn't sure he was going to settle in for the night. If he went out again he'd miss the palmbook."

Janie frowned and said, "Did something happen to him at work today?"

"Not to him, specifically. But something did happen." She was quiet for a moment before saying, "They brought one in today. That hasn't happened in a while. He came home very upset, saying he'd forgotten how gruesome they could be. Apparently, the guy hadn't sought any medical treatment." She sighed heavily and flexed her fingers. "He said the man's fingers and toes were pretty much gone by the time he died."

"Ugh," Janie groaned. She wondered if Michael had been privy to the victim she'd seen near the supermarket, and kept it to himself. "Where was he from?"

"Kendall."

"God, that's close."

"I know. But Michael said this particular victim was from a community where they eschew medical treatment except under the most dire circumstances."

"DR SAM isn't dire?"

"Maybe it came on quickly."

"It always does."

But even someone stupid enough to let himself die for his irrational beliefs evoked sympathy. *Hail Mary . . .* she felt herself beginning, when she heard the door open. She cast a quick look backward.

"Oh," she said quietly as the prayer slipped away, "this looks like a good one, maybe."

Janie stepped back into the anonymity of a shadow and observed as the little drama, one that was repeated innumerable times each day all over the world by people of every shape and size and color, unfolded before her in uniquely American style. Caroline, dressed to kill, perfectly made-up and seductively coifed, flashed a smile at the entering young man as he passed. His step hesitated slightly and he smiled back, then looked her up and down appreciatively. He continued on, and made his way with obvious determination to an available terminal.

Caroline did the same. Janie noticed she was limping a little, then looked down at her friend's feet. She gasped when she saw that they were encased in a pair of old but great-looking high heels.

"Shit," Janie muttered under her breath. "Caroline, what are you doing?"

But Caroline wasn't focusing on her feet, as Janie would have liked. The young redhead was quick and efficient in logging on to her terminal once she was settled in front of it, and it wasn't three minutes before she scratched her ear, the prearranged signal that she'd been contacted by someone at another terminal. Then a little smirk told Janie that it was the guy she'd exchanged glances with at the door.

Janie watched as Caroline said something soft in what she assumed was a sexy voice, though the bar was too noisy for her to hear. But predictably enough, across the room, the young man rose up from his own terminal and strolled casually toward her, wearing a victorious grin on his face and carrying a bottle of wine in one hand. He pulled up a chair and sat down next to Caroline, then extended his hand in greeting.

"No, don't take it," Janie whispered.

But Caroline did. Janie gasped. There could be traces.

Good Lord, Crowe, you're being paranoid. . . .

She closed her eyes for a moment and tried to shake off her growing sense of trouble, and when she opened them again Caroline and her catch were interacting quite successfully. The young man was unusual-looking, extremely tall and quite thin, but handsome in a funny way, someone Janie found attractive herself. He appeared to be in his late twenties or early thirties, and had a halo of tight strawberry-blond curls and a ridiculous-looking beard, a goatee of the type that had gone out of style shortly after the turn of the century.

"Now just keep him occupied for a few minutes," Janie whispered.

She slipped off her shadowed stool and walked across the bar to the now-abandoned terminal. She sat down a few feet away and pulled Michael's purloined Biopol palmbook out of her purse. With the flick of a thumbnail, she opened it and logged in using the number Caroline had given her, a number that would allow her access to just about any database she wanted, a number without which she would be the target of immediate arrest. She aimed the infrared broadcaster in the direction of the abandoned terminal, and in a few moments had the palmbook blended electronically into its signal.

She looked at the timer on the screen. It would be only three minutes until the terminal went into hibernation mode. "It'll have to do," she whispered with quiet determination. She tapped the keys carefully and deliberately, for the palmbook would not respond to her voice. But in just a few seconds, the palmbook screen showed the familiar yellow warning page for Big Dattie.

She'd memorized the necessary commands and entered them as if she were trying to disarm a nuclear bomb before the timer went off. Biting her lip as her fingers flew, she probed deeper and deeper into the database until she had the material she needed.

The screen was filled with file names. There were so many—she wondered if the palmbook's memory would hold them all. But she cast that worry aside, because she would do what she could with what she got from the database. There were no other options, no other viable plans. Whatever came out of this illegal incursion would have to suffice.

The timer ticked downward, and finally, when there were fewer than ten seconds left, the last of the files crossed over the airwaves and settled into the palmbook.

Six seconds remained when she closed the cover on the little unit.

"He was cute," Caroline said.

"Unusual-looking," Janie said.

"And he seemed like a really nice guy. He was a computer major, but now he's one of the assistant basketball coaches at the university."

"Funny. That doesn't fit with his image. The height, maybe, but he looked very smart. . . ."

"Oh, he is, I think," Caroline said. "I liked him. A lot."

As Janie dumped the stolen data files from the palmbook into her own laptop, she gave her friend a chiding smirk. "That will be all now, Mrs. Rosow. You had a nice little interlude, but you're a proper married lady again."

A sultry smile came over Caroline's still-red lips. Mae West–style, she pouffed her hair with one hand while perching the other seductively on her hip. "And how should a proper married lady act?"

As she closed the cover on her computer, Janie sighed and said, "I don't remember very well. But probably not like that."

Through the miracle of caffeine, Janie was still awake at two A.M. as the data she had stolen were sorted and arranged and developed in her own biostatistics program. It would have been easier and faster to use Big Dattie's own filtering mechanisms, but there was something very powerful about having the raw data, unsullied by someone else's notion of how they ought to be interpreted. The numbers and lists and DNA codes spoke to her in a language all their own, saying *There's something in here. You just have to look.*

Janie waited for the compiler to do its job. She loved being surprised by what the data had to say. It gave her a kind of gambling high, a sense of anticipation that was hard to come by in any other way. Such work always brought to the surface some ancient wrathful goddess that lurked deep inside her psyche, waiting after millennia of suppression for the moment when her creative fury could be unleashed in pursuit of some evasive truth.

She was tweaking the answers out with forbidden digging, and they were emerging pattern by reticent pattern, but at a certain point she found herself stymied. None of the boys' parents seemed to show any sign of abnormal breakage or a repeated history of fractures as their sons had.

She glanced at the wall clock. Bruce would be awake in London and in the middle of his morning routine.

She called him directly on the telephone, bypassing the conference mode of the computer. He listened, as always, with patience and consideration to her musings over the dilemma at hand. "I thought it was genetic," she told him. "But now I'm not so sure. The parents are all pretty normal. Maybe it's environmental."

"Did you manage to get the demographic information in the download? Where they all live, what their activities are?"

"Yes. I'm amazed at what I got out of there in such a short time."

"Post them on a map," Bruce said. "You might see something there."

It was an extremely logical suggestion. "That's a great idea," she said. "I knew there was a reason why I love you."

"We make a good team, even if we are transatlantic."

Janie sighed, wishing she could embrace him through the phone, needing badly to be touched all of a sudden. She could hear water running in the background. "Are you shaving?"

"Yeah."

"I wish I could smell that stuff you use. . . ."

"I wish you could smell it too."

"Iceland," she whispered.

"I can't wait," he replied.

When she'd called Tom at home the next morning local time after a night of thin sleep, Janie heard the same water-running, blade-scraping noises, and found herself wondering what *his* morning routine was like.

But when he sat down at the table in the diner where they met for breakfast, the scent of his shaving lotion was very real, and it smelled wonderful.

Janie gave him a big smile of greeting, trying to hide the slight blush that was rising unbidden on her cheeks, prompted by a scent that her nose was apparently more hungry for than she'd realized. *Think of him as a priest,* she told herself. *That ought to shut down those leftover urges pretty quickly.*

She took a deep breath and confessed what she could. "Bless me, Father, for I have sinned."

"Oy, Janie, I hate it when you start a conversation that way. Okay, what did you do this time?"

"I went digging again. Not in the ground, though."

"Well, that's a relief, at least. . . ."

"Maybe not. I, uh, *borrowed* some data from Big Dattie."

"Janie! What the hell—" He leaned forward over the table and lowered his voice. "I'm not sure I want to hear this!"

"You told me to tell you everything I did—"

"Everything that related to your application for reinstatement."

"Well, this is related to that, at least indirectly."

"You can't include information gained illegally on an application for reinstatement. My expectation was that it would all be legal."

She was quiet for a moment, smarting from his castigation. "If everything I did was legal, why would I need you?"

Tom took a long and lawyerly breath. Janie could almost hear him counting to ten. He sat up again and composed himself, and when he finally spoke, his words came out measured and controlled.

"You don't, unless you care about how the rest of your life goes. If you're happy with your current professional situation, you don't need me. If you're satisfied with phone sex to London, then you don't need me either, although as I've told you, you could probably get better immigration results with someone else. If you are absolutely certain that there will never be repercussions from what happened in London . . ."

He paused for a moment and stewed, while Janie sat in chastised silence. "You know what the number one item on the lawyer list of questions not to ask the client is?" he said finally.

"Not really."

"Sorry. I'm going to tell you anyway. It's 'Did you do it?' And I'll tell you why. We don't really want to know. That way, if someone asks 'Mr. Lawyer, is your client guilty?' we can say something other than 'No comment,' something like 'I have no personal knowledge. . . .' "

"Tom."

"That way if someone from Biopol wants to know all about your little unauthorized excursion into their database, which as I'm sure you know carries a rather stiff penalty, I can truthfully say I have no personal knowledge of it." He paused, fuming, and gathered his thoughts. "I can't believe Caroline went along with this."

"She didn't seem to think it was particularly risky."

"Of course it's risky. Everything with those assholes is a risk."

She waited a minute for the unexpectedly emotional dust to settle and said, "I'm sorry. It just never occurred to me that I should be keeping something from you. We've never had secrets before."

"Did you and Harry have secrets when you were married?"

"Well, of course, a few."

"There you go," he said, as if it were the last word.

For a moment Janie was sorely tempted to remind Tom that some of the secrets she'd kept from Harry before he died were things that she'd shared with Tom himself, bittersweet youthful indiscretions, some of which she'd sooner forget, events Tom knew about because he'd been there too. A hastily extinguished joint, a beer bottle tossed away just in the nick of time. A begging session with a cop who'd caught Janie and Tom parking on a deserted farm road, rounding third base and headed in a heat for home plate, back when there were still farms in the community where they'd grown up together and people who would be offended if they came across the two of them in that condition. The humiliation of being made to get out of the car, only partly clothed, while the cop ran his flashlight up and down their young bodies, shaming them completely. A blanket on a beach in Wellfleet, with the mist coming in, and the only other person for miles around a lone and rather preoccupied surfer, where they'd touched each other's secret places with youthful delight and awe.

But it didn't seem like a good idea at the moment to dredge up the past. "Well, anyway, now you know."

"I do," he said unhappily. "And I don't like it. Be careful when you're poking around in there. *Please.* You never know who's going to be watching."

She wasn't sure precisely what he meant. But she agreed to do what he asked. "I'll be careful. I promise."

As soon as she'd gotten her more pressing work obligations out of the way, Janie opened a data program on her foundation computer. She said all the necessary magic words, and a map festooned with red dots appeared on the screen, each mark showing the hometown of one of her "subjects."

She blinked when she first looked at it. The map showed the entire United States but the dots were all clustered in the Northeast, with a small number of exceptions. One or two were on the West Coast in greater Los Angeles, and a handful were from the Chicago area. There was only one Midwestern dot, in St. Paul, Minnesota.

But they were all urban families, and mostly Easterners. The vast majority were bunched up between New York City and her own area of western Massachusetts.

Their surnames were all Jewish-sounding. None of the parents had the problem that their sons seemed to be evidencing—it appeared to have sprung up within the younger generation.

It was time to start talking to some of them.

The phone buzzed on her belt, surprising her out of her concentration.

She answered it quickly, listened for a few moments, then put her program on hibernation. She was wanted for an audience with the Monkey Man.

"I'm still looking for that report on Catholic popes," he said.

"I've been a little busy, Chet."

"With what?"

"With the work I'm supposed to be doing, what do you think?"

"Just checking," he said. "I wouldn't want you to do something stupid."

She scowled at him. "Chet, everything I do in this job is stupid."

Malin seemed shocked that she would stand up to him, and for a moment he was flustered into speechlessness. "Well," he finally said, "just watch out. Unauthorized stupid activities can get you in a lot of trouble."

"I'll try to remember that."

Not having the sanction of her employer was incredibly frustrating. The work she'd discovered was something Janie knew she could sink her teeth into, something that was looking more intriguing all the time. She decided to start contacting the families herself, thinking that just maybe a conversation would spark the necessary moment of recognition and lead her down the road to an idea. Like all good physicians, practicing or not, she knew that the best place to start treating any patient was with a complete history. And there were lots of questions she could ask that couldn't be answered in a data evaluation.

It would certainly justify a trip to visit Abraham Prives, perhaps not in Chet Malin's beady little eyes . . . but she wasn't going to let him hold her under his thumb.

When she got to Jameson Memorial she entered by her usual route, the emergency entrance, because there were tissue tests there waiting to be retrieved and it was the shortest route to the Prives boy's room. It was, as always, the scene of much scurrying and bustling. There were cubicles off to both sides of a long hallway that led to the hospital's main building, each with its own sealable door and opaque drape. Janie glanced from side to side as she proceeded apace down the corridor, and saw kids with air casts, old people with IV lines, a man who looked to be some sort of construction worker with his hand wrapped in a bloody bandage, the usual assortment of maladies.

And then there were the green-suited cops holding down—

She stopped. It was not the usual fare, she realized as she stared into the cubicle. Certainly there were reasons for people to be convulsing on the floor of an ER cubicle. But the biocops put a whole different light on it.

One of the green men saw her, reached up, and with a good yank closed the opaque drape.

She ran down the remainder of the corridor, and it wasn't until she was in the elevator with the door closing that she allowed herself to breathe.

If that was DR SAM, that room will be closed off until they can tear it down to the studs, she thought as she rode upward. *Oh, please,* she prayed silently, *let it not be that.*

When she got off the elevator at Abraham's floor, she sat down in a chair in the waiting area and panted until she'd regained herself. Then soberly, quietly, she went to the boy's room.

Mrs. Prives was precisely where Janie had seen her the first time, sitting in a chair by the edge of the bed, talking to her unresponsive son.

"I wish I had more to tell you" was all she could say to the woman's instant flurry of questions. "I haven't found any funding yet, but I haven't given up the search. It takes time."

"Everything seems to take time."

"I know. It's got to be difficult for you." She paused for a moment. "What are Abraham's doctors telling you?"

"That there isn't much that can be done for him right now, at least not until the swelling goes down."

"Well, they're probably right about that. No one will be able to do much of anything until then. That's the real culprit in all of this—the spine just gets too big for the space it's supposed to be in. And in Abraham's case, the space has been compromised. So wait-and-see is the best course of action."

"So why are you here, then," the woman said bitterly, "if there's nothing more to be done?"

"I didn't say there was nothing more to be done, just that right now doing nothing is appropriate. And the reason I'm here is that I'd like to ask you some questions. Of course this is all voluntary. You can tell me to go away if you want to."

"No," the mother said wearily, "I don't want you to go away. Forgive me if I was snippy with you. I'm snippy with just about everyone these days."

"I can understand why." Janie took in a preparatory breath, then related the gist of her findings without revealing how surprisingly large the number of other victims had turned out to be. Then she began with the questions. "I saw from the database that you've lived here in town for five years."

The mother nodded. "I have family in the area. And the school system is good. With my husband gone I didn't really want to stay where we were."

"Which was where?"

"High Falls, New York. It's this little podunk town in the Hudson River Valley. My husband was teaching at Vassar and it was a pretty easy commute, just over the river. It was gorgeous there."

Janie said, "I know the area. There are some beautiful spots out that way. Was Abraham born while you lived there?"

"Actually, he was born in Manhattan. We moved up to High Falls when he was about two years old." She glanced over at her son. "It was a bit tough at first, I remember; I was used to everything being so close and handy. But after I learned my way around, I grew to love it. I got used to the slower pace, found other kids for Abraham to play with. It got to feel like paradise after a while."

Janie pulled a notepad out of her pocket and wrote *High Falls, New York* on the top sheet. "Were there any unusual environmental incidents or issues you remember from the time that you lived there?"

Mrs. Prives's brow tightened slightly as she concentrated. "Not that I recall. My husband might have remembered something—he used to read the papers a lot more than I did, and he paid attention to that sort of thing. I was too busy raising my kids to keep track of everything that was going on around us."

"But nothing major sticks out in your mind, nothing about the water or a pollution site?"

"Oh, we drank bottled water, of course, but we didn't have to. They tested the water all the time there. It was very hard—I remember I had to add this stuff to our laundry to keep it from being stained—but it wasn't polluted."

Hard water, Janie scribbled. But she didn't think it would mean much of anything. Water with high mineral content could be found in just about every state in the country. And it didn't cause broken bones—in fact, it was often instrumental in preventing them.

"Now, I saw in Abraham's record that he's been fully immunized. Has he had any unusual diseases, anything that might not have shown up on his database file?"

"Not that I remember. He's always been so healthy, that's why this is so hard to take." She glanced at her son. "He was incredibly active. Loved to hike and swim and—"

She paused for a moment, her forehead creased with the search for a memory. "I do recall one thing," she finally said. "Once when Abraham was at camp, he went swimming in a pond that had some sort of beaver bacteria in it, they found out later. So all the boys at camp got an injection of some antibiotic to prevent them from getting a stomach infection. I remember because they had to call me for permission. He hates injections. I was tempted to drive out there—it's just on this side of the state border."

A small fire was lit inside Janie's imagination. *It might be nothing,* she told herself. "How old was he at the time?"

"Six, I think. Yes, six. It was his first time at camp. Thank God he got to go, because the camp had to close for a couple of years after the Outbreaks—the owners died and none of their other family members wanted to run the place. They found someone after a couple of summers, though."

"Did Abraham go back then?"

"Oh, yes. He went every year that he could. It's a religious camp for boys who are studying Hebrew. Not that we're all that religious, really, it's just that he was going to be bar mitzvahed this fall." She looked at him again and sighed sadly. "But I think it's going to be delayed a bit."

Janie asked her some inconsequential questions, just to be polite. She jotted down a few more things before asking the question that really mattered to her.

"Oh, by the way, I might want to contact the people at the camp to see if they can tell me which antibiotic was used. Would you mind if I used your name as a reference?"

"No, not at all, not if it might help," Mrs. Prives said. "It was Camp Meir. After Golda. It's in this little town just on the border, called Burning Road."

She sat with the ancient book on her lap and rocked back and forth in the cool night air. *Burning Road,* she thought to herself, almost incredulously.

. . . and often the bodies did not find repose in the ground, for there was not adequate room nor adequate gravediggers, and those that were set out on the sides of the roads for collection had to be burned where they lay . . . indeed, it seemed some days as if the roads themselves were burning.

"I know how you feel," she said to her long-dead colleague, the plague physician who had penned those words in his elegant hand. *There were burning roads back then, even. Everywhere I turn, I seem to find another one.*

Beside her on the swing was a newspaper. A small story on page two told of three small outbreaks of drug-resistant *Staphylococcus aureus mexicalis*. Dr. Janie shuddered as she read of these new cases of DR SAM.

Sometime in the middle of the night Janie was awakened from a nightmare, one in which she'd been weaving her way between funeral pyres, and her first thought was a sense of gladness that she'd been snapped out of it. But that notion changed when she realized that what had brought her out of one hell was the door opening to another—a closer, much more real hell. It was the cold sound of tinkling shards of glass falling in a crystalline shower on her kitchen floor. As icy fingers of terror walked down her spine, she reached instinctively for the light switch. But the door to the hallway was open, which was why the noise had been loud enough to awaken her.

They'll see the light, she realized. She sat up in bed, pulled the covers up to her neck, and stared into the darkness for a scared moment, wishing with every cell in her body that she could reach over and wake someone up.

More sounds, ill-defined but nevertheless frightening, drifted through the house from the kitchen area, which faced away from the street and into the woods. Shaking, she picked up the handset of the bedside phone and dialed 911, only to realize when nothing happened that there was no dial tone.

Where is my cellular phone? In the kitchen, charging from the wall socket because she'd forgotten to leave it out in the light and the battery had gone completely dry. It was in the corner of the counter, out of sight, because Janie thought the charging unit was ugly. She wanted it out of sight, and now it was very out of reach.

So Janie got out of the bed with excruciating care and tiptoed as noiselessly as possible over the rug-covered floor. She went into her bathroom and closed the door, whispering a silent prayer of thanks to the hinge god that it didn't squeak when she pushed it. The thin nightdress she wore seemed woefully inadequate in the night air so she wrapped a bath towel around her shivering shoulders.

She waited, trembling, with only a locked wood door between herself and the unknown intruder. She pressed one ear up against the wall that connected the bathroom to the hallway and listened, hearing the unmistakable sounds of rummaging. It was only when she had heard nothing for a full fifteen minutes that she dared to open the door again.

* * *

When she got her hands on the cell phone, she tried to speak Caroline's name but her voice was so shaky that the unit wouldn't recognize it, so she had to look up the number in her paper address book and dial it with her finger. Then she dialed Tom.

Only then did she turn on the kitchen light and survey the mess. Drawers were emptied, chairs tipped, her desk rummaged through—and there, where she'd left her notebook computer before retiring, was a blank expanse of desk. They'd taken it.

But what on earth for? They're so cheap now. . . .

And then she realized—there was information inside it, information she'd acquired in marginally legal ways. For a moment she panicked, but then she remembered that she couldn't be connected to that acquisition except through a permit, which made part of what she had legal. And she'd copied all the data on a removable disk to take it to her office. That disk was in her purse, hung by habit from a hook on the inside of the coat closet door, which the thief had, for some unfathomable reason, overlooked.

She rushed into the living room—more mayhem—and let her eyes go directly to the bookshelf.

There, in its proper place, was Alejandro's journal. She ran to it, pulled it off the shelf, and hugged it to her chest.

Everyone arrived at once—Michael, Tom, and the police cruisers. The presence of officials and friends did little to eliminate the horrible, nauseating sense of violation that overtook her as she slowly realized what had happened. She sat on a chair in her living room, the towel still wrapped around her shoulders, and rocked back and forth with the journal clutched to her heart, while Tom kept one warm hand on her shoulder.

Within the hour it was determined that whoever had done the deed was familiar enough with investigative technique to leave virtually no workable evidence. "I wish I could say we'll get this bastard, but I doubt very much that we will," Michael said. "Bloke must've been wearing a wet suit. There's no hair, no dander, no footprints, nothing. A total bust on usable clues. Only thing might help us catch him is the loot. Do you have any idea of what's missing?"

"Just the computer," Janie said. "As far as I can tell." She looked up and saw Michael's worried look. "He didn't even bother to go into the bedroom. Thank God, because I don't know what I would have done. I keep my jewelry there, not that it's exactly the crown jewels."

"But you'd think a thief would at least look there, anyway," Tom said.

"He didn't take my silverware, either. It was my grandmother's, and it's in a silver chest right on my sideboard. It's probably worth a fortune."

Michael sighed and sat down on the couch. "Then all they wanted was the computer."

"And to scare me," Janie said. "Bad."

The police investigators milled around for a bit longer, but there was little more to be gained, and as the first little light of dawn crept through the treetops Janie watched their van pull out of her driveway.

"Caroline says you're to come home with me straightaway," Michael said firmly. "So perhaps you'll want to gather a few things . . ."

"No, I'll be okay," Janie said. She nodded toward the window. "It's stark-raving morning already. I'm going to go into my office at the foundation in a little while, after I get myself cleaned up. I don't think I could sleep right now, anyway. I'm way too wired."

"I'll make you some breakfast, if you want," Tom said, "and I can drop you off at the foundation when I go in."

She gave him a grateful smile. "You might be my hero right now. I can't tell you how I appreciate this." She turned to Michael. "But tell Caroline I love her more than ever for the invitation. And tell her I'll be okay."

Tom made himself very much at home in her big kitchen, and while Janie was vainly trying to shower off the slimy sense of having been invaded he put together a fabulous Mexican omelet, with toast and fruit salad. And by the time she'd finished eating it she was feeling half normal.

But she was not feeling safe, not by a long shot. While Tom was straightening up the kitchen, she went to the living room and got the journal down from the shelf where she'd replaced it earlier. Then she went to the hallway closet and took the data disk out of her purse. She tucked the disk inside the back cover of the journal and stuffed it all into a large manila envelope.

"Can you put this in your office safe for me?"

"Sure. What—"

"Items of supreme personal importance. Just until I can get a safe of my own."

"Scared you, didn't he?"

"Oh, yeah."

They rode in silence to the downtown area, Tom driving, Janie in the passenger seat. After promising to check in on her later, he gave her a quick peck on the cheek and an encouraging smile, and as she walked up the steps into the foundation's main entry, Janie could almost feel him still watching her. She wanted to turn and wave, but fought the surprisingly strong urge; she didn't turn around until she'd heard the whine of his engine pulling away from the curb. She knew his eyes would no longer be on her, but rather on the road ahead, and that it was safe for her to put her eyes on him. She did, with a growing sense of wonder and curiosity.

Why had she called him last night, when Michael was a more than adequate champion and far more official?

It seemed like the natural thing to do, she told herself. Besides, he was her lawyer.

The elevator doors opened in front of her, and she stepped inside, surrounded once again by gleaming polished brass. When she got to her office, it seemed safe enough, at a time when safety was the overriding need, so Janie sat down at the computer and started dully going through a series of day-starting tasks. She checked everything she needed to check, and found to her great relief that she had no appointments. And there were only interoffice missives to be read.

But there was always e-mail. The little mailman was wonderfully familiar, a welcome sight on the computer screen, waving another handful of letters. The first was from Caroline: *Call me if you need anything—there's a sale on notebooks at Computer Heaven if you want to replace yours. I can pick you up later if you want to go. Michael got me plenty of gas.*

One from her auto mechanic: *Time for an oil change.*

One from Bruce: *Love you, miss you, talk to you later, bye.* He didn't know about her rough night. She didn't look forward to telling him: he would go through a predictable round of self-deprecation for not being there when she needed him.

And one more. *Do not be afraid,* it said. It was signed *Wargirl.*

All through the morning Charles of Navarre watched from a high tower in the Château de Coucy as a steady stream of nobles were admitted through the stout gate into the courtyard. They had all come to see him in the hopes of forming an alliance, for the chaos throughout France had reached disastrous proportions and required containment. And though the nobles now seeking his leadership had managed rather soundly to subdue the peasants who rose against them at Meaux, the king of Navarre knew that the favorable outcome of that contest had not been assured before it began. Had the insurrectionists solidified their numbers under able leadership, they might have won. The rebellious *Jacquerie* had come too close to victory for any French noble to breathe easily, and all of those who had escaped with their holdings intact now agreed that the final blow must be delivered quickly and decisively if they were to retain their right to rule and tax.

The day was clear and blue with a fine soft breeze, and the sun was so bright that Charles needed to shade his eyes against it. As he looked out over the impressive and favorably placed holdings of his host, Charles was envious, for when looking at the lush countryside no one need wonder how the brave and damnably handsome Baron de Coucy had inherited such wealth. But how, in the midst of indescribable deprivation and poverty, could *les pauvres misérables* who worked Coucy's estate be further taxed? Even Charles the Bad, the most despised despot in all of France, understood that blood could not be gotten from a stone.

Still, he and the rest of his kind had tried to squeeze it out of them. He could not really fault the unprivileged for rising up, nor the *bourgeoisie* for supporting them, nor some members of his own class for their apparent unwillingness to stomp them down. Rebellion could easily be justified in such distressing times.

Nevertheless, it is not to be tolerated, not now, not ever. It was his sacred duty, Charles believed, to seize power and suppress the uprising, to unite those French nobles who had survived the mayhem under his own strong rule. It was a right, perhaps even an obligation, passed directly from God through his grandfather, the great Louis himself. He welcomed the challenge, for the small kingdom of Navarre was not realm enough to contain his ambitions, and tucked into the foothills of the Pyrenees it was too far from the centers of power and wealth to suit him.

The Dauphin be damned, he thought as the parade of nobles continued, *and may his pitiful Valois father grow fat and stupid as a captive in the Court of the idiot Edward. May Jean de Valois never leave that damp and miserable island.*

Guillaume Karle stared at the sight before him. "No!" he cried as he jumped down from his horse. "Not again!"

Kate remained astride her mount, gripping the reins with white knuckles. She squeezed her eyes tightly shut and began a desperate prayer. "Hail Mary, full of grace, the Lord is with thee . . ."

Karle raised an angry voice over her soft murmurings. "The vicious bastard!" he shouted. "He means to slaughter every one of us!" He clenched his fist and shook it in the air. "Satan himself could not have imparted a crueler torture!"

". . . now and at the hour of our death," Kate concluded. She crossed herself with one shaking hand and wiped a tear from her cheek. Then she whispered, "Amen."

Before them was the body of a scrawny peasant man, tied upright to a tree, with the hands bound behind and ankles lashed to its base. The head, through some miracle still attached, drooped forward on the chest, and the wide-open, unseeing eyes stared vacantly down at the victim's own entrails, which had been pulled out to a distance of at least three paces from the rest of him. The exposed guts lay on the ground, a pool of blood at the end of their length where they had been gnawed by some hungry animal.

"A wolf has already been here," Karle said stiffly as he came closer to the grisly find. "They are growing bolder every day because the people weaken from hunger. They are cunning enough to smell it in us."

Or had a weasel or a fox come in the night to dine on this poor fellow? Kate could not help but wonder how long before losing consciousness this man had watched as animals of the forest growled at each other over the prize of his glistening guts, their eyes glowing like coals in the dark.

She finally found the courage to dismount just as Guillaume Karle turned away from the pitiful sight and retched.

"This is the handiwork of Navarre," he said bitterly as he wiped his mouth. He spat into the dirt. "But how can he have been in all these places?"

"This may have been done by one of his supporters."

"Then he is passing on his cruelest tricks to them!"

They had seen another gruesome casualty of Navarre's campaign of reprisal barely an hour before, propped up against a rotting rain barrel, his severed head placed neatly in his lap. The day before they had buried three others, one crucified, one roasted, another with his eyes gouged and tongue cut out. Each new grave they dug with their pitiful sticks and rocks was more shallow than the one before it, and it was becoming quite plain to them that their continued journey might consist of nothing but laborious burials. Together they removed the man from the tree trunk and laid him gently down on the ground. With the tip of one boot, Karle guided the man's innards along until they rested on his belly. He did not attempt to shove them back inside.

"Why in God's name must they mutilate these poor folk so?" Kate wondered aloud. "Why not just kill them, and be done with it?"

"That is a question that even God may not answer," Karle said. "Navarre has turned his knights into a company of slaughterers." He gave her a forlorn and weary look. "Shall we bury this one, as well?"

"Have you the strength? I do not, of that I am certain."

"But we cannot simply leave him here," Karle said.

"If we bury every mutilated body we come across, we shall never reach Paris!"

He knew she was right. He sat down wearily on a fallen log. "How are we to resist this? It seems so hopeless."

She was quiet for a moment, then sat down beside him. "You must fight this fire with a fire of your own," she said.

Karle gave her a tired look. "I do not understand. We are little candles, blown out with one small puff. Navarre is a blazing torch, and difficult to extinguish."

She reached out tentatively and rested her hand on his shoulder, hoping it would comfort him. "I understand that. But it is only logical to fight him as he has fought you. The best way to answer one attack is with another of a similar nature." She thought for a moment, then said, "I will tell you something Père told me."

Karle groaned. "Now is hardly the time for another of your 'Père' tales," he said wearily.

"You must hear this one before you judge it useless. You recall that he cured me of plague?"

"Aye. Your plague tale. I am yet deciding if I think it true."

Her expression hardened. "You would be wise not to doubt it. And there is a great lesson to be learned, one that might profit you if you are clever enough to comprehend it. You see, he told me that he used the dust of the dead to cure me—the dried and powdered flesh of those who had died before me of the same illness. That was why I took the hand of that child who died of plague, to have the flesh for drying! It was a secret given him by a very accomplished midwife, the same one who delivered my mother of me."

He let out a long, frustrated breath and buried his face in his hands. "While I am sure *you* consider these gems of midwifery germane to my situation, I still do not understand—"

She cut off his protest. "*Think*, Karle. Consider the logic of it. What could be more clever than to use plague to battle plague? And so must you plague this Navarre."

"Shall we attack him with disease?" he said sarcastically.

"That is not so stupid a notion as you might think. But that is not what I meant." Her eyes flashed with undisguised excitement and unmaidenly determination. "You must become to him the same scourge that he is to you. He is organized, he has weapons, and he leads his forces in a military fashion. You must do the same."

"We cannot possibly answer him in kind!"

"But you can answer him in the same *nature*, to the extent that it is possible, instead of scattering like rats before an army of dogs."

He thought about what she was saying for a long, quiet moment. In the stillness they could hear the low buzzing of flies as they swarmed around the peasant's corpse, lighting now and then to lay their eggs in the wet wound. A nearby crow shrieked out a sharp summons to his distant brethren, an invitation to the waiting feast.

"Unite your followers," she urged him. "Have them meet in one place at one time and bid them bring everything that can possibly be called a weapon. Find anything that will serve as a standard, and hold it high in front of their assemblage! Then they will think themselves soldiers. And they will begin to act as if they were!"

It was something he had not considered. They were *Jacques,* not soldiers. "These men are simple peasants, and know nothing of these things."

"Then teach them!" she added quickly. "Even peasants can learn the ways of soldiering if properly instructed."

"But who—how?"

"Do not underestimate yourself, Karle. Or the men who would follow you. This enemy of yours will not be expecting such an action. It will give you an advantage you have not enjoyed before."

Even at Meaux, though their numbers were great they had been undone by their own sloppiness. But they had almost succeeded! Would they have known victory if they had marched as a true army, in lines, with leaders, employing strategies of war?

Karle surprised himself by thinking, *It might have been possible.* It was marvelously simple, and all too obvious. Why had he not considered it before? *The numbers of dead from that failure . . .* and even more were perishing in the cruel retribution that now followed on its heels. Might they have lived?

"You are completely right," he said with quiet excitement. He studied her young face, searching for the source of her surprising breadth of knowledge. "How have you come to understand these warrior notions, still a maid as you are?"

She took on a look of cynical sadness. "When I was a little girl, the men who frequented our household spoke of little else than warring. They mostly ignored my interruptions, for my questions were bothersome and the things I had to say were of no interest to them. But I seldom had a choice about listening when *they* spoke. And all they talked of was war, and weapons, and strategy, and soldiering. Perhaps a bit of their wisdom leapt out and settled in me."

"It would seem that it did. And through you, perhaps it shall leap to me." He stood up and brushed his hands together. "And now I will use my newfound wisdom to say that we should, as you have urged, get to Paris," he said. "There are men there who will help me formulate such a strategy."

Kate made no attempt to hide her glee. "At last!" she cried.

"It is the only logical thing to do. You have convinced me that there is nothing more I can accomplish by myself. I must seek the aid and counsel of Etienne Marcel."

"Who?"

He stared dumbfounded at her. *"Marcel.* How can such a *brilliante* as yourself not know the name of the provost of Paris?"

She shrugged, looking slightly amused. "Père deplores all politics. He did not speak of such things while he had me locked in the cabinet."

"Then I shall speak to you of these affairs as we ride. You must not be ignorant."

He cupped his hands together and offered them toward her. She understood and put her foot in his hands, and he boosted her up onto her horse. Then he remounted his own and settled himself onto the animal's back. "And when we meet your *père* in Paris, I shall be sure to tell him that you must be allowed to see more of the world."

She glanced back once more at the dead peasant. "I think perhaps I have seen more of it than I care to already," she said as they rode off.

Alejandro walked west on Rue des Rosiers, heading toward Rue Vieux du Temple. He scanned each doorway as he passed, looking for traces of the welcoming *mezuzahs* that had once adorned them. All had been removed. He saw only faint outlines of the symbols that had once been there, for the soot had been scrubbed away, or the wood whitewashed if such a luxury could be afforded. He wondered what had gone through the minds of the Jewish housewives of Paris as they labored to remove the marks when their presence had become a condemnation of those who dwelled within. Had they come out onto the street all at once, and bemoaned their fate together? Or had they slunk out one at a time in private grief to do the deed? It didn't matter, he supposed; the symbols were gone. No Jew in Paris wanted to be known as such, for it could bring only misery.

But the traces of their presence could still be found if one knew how to look. He had discovered this section of Paris many years before through discreet inquiries after he and Kate had fled the burning holocaust at Strasbourgh, and trusted that if the need arose he could lose himself among the people who lived there, at least for a time. Now and again he would smell, or hear, or simply sense something that put him in mind of his past. It made his heart ache with loneliness sometimes to encounter those reminders, but still he sought them out.

He turned south on Old Temple Street and then west again along the river, and marveled at the striking difference between the relative cleanliness of the Seine and the deplorable filth of the Thames. He remembered his first impression of the river when he had arrived in London: bodies floating in the fetid waters, the stench that rose clear up to the planks of the high bridge, and oarsmen with their mouths and noses covered in cloth. And the English went about their business in spite of it all, as if they were not living on the banks of a cesspool. In Paris, one could cross the Seine on many bridges without feeling the need to retch, for the citizens of Paris would not tolerate such abuse of their beautiful river.

Still, only a desperate man would drink these waters, he thought.

There was little more than foot traffic on the bridge, for horses had become terribly precious. He had paid handsomely to stable his own mount on the northern outskirts of the city, and promised even more to the groom when he returned, more than the groom could hope to get by selling the horse. The nobility were keeping to themselves or had escaped the city altogether, and there were few carriages to be seen. He crossed paths with an occasional mule-drawn cart, but most of the traffic he encountered was on foot.

He stopped when he reached the island and stared up at the Cathedral de Notre Dame de Paris, allowing the huge edifice to impose all of its Christian might on him for a moment. Slipping through the power of the place was its sheer beauty, and he was torn between his admiration of its magnificence and his understanding of what it represented. He supposed by now it must finally be finished; the papal guards who had accompanied him on his ride through France a decade earlier had spoken of it and bemoaned the fact that they would not have a chance to see it. But their descriptions of it, with one tower done and the other only partly finished, lingered clearly in his mind. With a few glances back and forth, he compared the two peaks and judged that they were largely alike. He wondered briefly how skilled laborers had been found in the wake of the plague's devastation of the populace. *Most likely those with known skills were forced to work, like it or not,* he thought. Christian priests had a way of convincing their believers to do the work of God, he knew. They had many ways.

And here he would find priests, most certainly. While other churches went priestless, this crown jewel of French Christendom would be overrun with them. He did not envy the parishioners.

He crossed the large open square, sidestepping the ever-present pigeons, and wondered briefly why they had not been caught and eaten yet. The shape of each cobblestone pressed into his feet through the well-softened soles of his leather boots, and the cathedral loomed larger with every step he took toward it. A chill rushed through him as he stepped into its shadow, and he felt weighted and burdened, as if the hands of the Christian God had reached down from His heaven and pressed on his shoulders. The stones suddenly turned cold under his feet, and he stopped.

The sound of voices in uniform chant drifted out from the open door of the enormous church. Alejandro stood very still and listened. Despite his distrust of anything Christian, he allowed the captivating, harmonious tones to fill his soul. Why was their music so damnably beautiful, when all else was simply damnable? His beloved Adele had often confessed her sins under its spell, and once, as he had waited for her to finish, he had felt himself mesmerized by the haunting sounds.

But now he had no penitent to await, and he could not let the music overtake him, for his mind was not free to wallow in such sensual luxury at the moment. There was a word to be unraveled.

"*Maranatha,*" he said cautiously to the first priest who passed by him. "What does it mean?"

But the priest, a man far scruffier than he would have expected to find in such a cathedral, only stared at him, and kept walking. The next one smiled at least, and said, "God will know, my son, but I surely do not." Alejandro was grateful for the man's kindness, but disappointed by his lack of knowledge. The third simply shook his head and shrugged, leaving the physician no wiser for the brief encounters.

So it must be the university, then, he thought with mild frustration, and though the notion of going there excited him, he had hoped it would not come to that, for it would keep him away from Rue des Rosiers longer than he would have liked. He glanced up at the sun; it was still high enough to allow for a brief sojourn across the Seine. He stepped out of the shadows of Notre Dame and headed over the bridge to *la rive gauche.*

It amazed him that learning could still persist in such times, but all around him he saw unmistakable signs of it. Though there were certainly fewer than there might have been in peace, he saw many young men wearing the simple robes of new scholarship. And some actually carried books! He had heard whispers of books called *incunabula,* with pages reproduced by cut blocks of wood, inked with fat and soot, and then joined together, but such wonders, he had thought, existed only in the Orient. Could this be what these young men carried? *How marvelous if it were true!* They sat at small tables and leaned on stone walls, drinking the cheapest wine the cafes would sell, and traded opinions with the urgent certainty of unsullied youth, though how even youth could remain untouched by pestilence, war, and famine was beyond his understanding. Then he recalled the heady glory of his own student days, and it all came clear to him. He had felt immortal then, unshakable. He had had no sense of what lay ahead.

He approached a beautiful mansion, so modern and new in the midst of the small ancient houses all around it, and stopped for a moment to admire it. He was drawn by the sturdiness of stonework, and intrigued by the details of appointment that could be seen here and there on the elegant manse. He saw glass—*glass*—in all the windows. In this *maison*, the residents would know the blessing of light without the scourge of wind.

When he'd seen enough of the new house, he headed toward the Place de la Sorbonne. There he found himself surrounded by the sweet sounds of Latin, for it was only through this ancient and eternal language that the scholars of Europa who gathered in Paris could speak with one another. Of all the tongues he spoke, it was by far his favorite, for it flowed off the lips as softly as a kiss and landed welcome on the ears of the recipient. And it was only because of his fluency in Latin that he had been able to master the difficult and bothersome language of the English people, who borrowed words so freely. Why this English was gaining favor, he did not understand; everyone agreed it was poorly suited to polite use. It was simply too ugly. Kate spoke it well enough, but shades of it colored her French and he had often warned her to be careful of its influence.

Would the English have a word or phrase that meant the same as the mysterious *Maranatha*? Probably not. *The lack of depth will be its eventual downfall,* he thought. But Latin surely would.

He passed a clutch of robed scholars and slowed his pace. He looked back at the group, some of whom had their backs to him. There were two soldiers not far away, both of whom looked bored and out of place; Alejandro thought it likely that neither could understand what was being said by the pedants nearby. Nor would they care.

So why not just ask? He would be in no danger if he addressed them in Latin. They might simply think him one of their own, albeit poorly dressed, perhaps a traveling teacher. Then he could return to the Rue des Rosiers with the mystery solved and disappear into its familiar safety while he waited for Kate.

And so he approached them. He apologized for the interruption if it was unwelcome, and bid them all good health. And though he was received politely, he could feel the eyes of these men burning into him. Their curiosity felt like the point of a sharp blade prodding him in his most private places. *But I am here,* he thought, shoving his uncertainty aside, *and I will ask.*

"Maranatha," he said. He pronounced each unfamiliar syllable carefully. And then in Latin, he added, "I have come across this word in a manuscript, and I do not understand what it means. I had hoped that one among you might shed some illumination on it."

To his surprise, the answer came in French, and before he saw the face of the speaker, he recognized the voice.

"*Il veut dire 'Venez, mon dieu,'*" said Guy de Chauliac. "Roughly speaking, 'Come, O Lord.' It is Aramaic. I have had to acquire a good deal of it in my studies. And may I say *bienvenu à Paris*, colleague. It has been far too long since we last met."

Guy de Chauliac had only to snap his fingers and nod in Alejandro's direction, and the two bored soldiers, obviously the French dignitary's own personal guards, were on him. They grabbed him from behind, and though he struggled mightily, he was no match for two strong men, and he was quickly contained. Still, he fought back like an animal, to which the elegant de Chauliac reacted with a look of disgust and a wave of his hand. This resulted in the Jew receiving a hearty smack on the back of his head, and he went down onto his hands and knees, straddling his precious bag of possessions. He grabbed hold of it and tried to crawl away between the legs of his captors, but he was caught by the back of the shirt and beaten down again.

And then he felt himself being dragged through the streets by the two rough Gauls as the princely de Chauliac led the way, carrying in his long arms all that Alejandro owned in the world. As he was hauled through the piles of horse dung and over the rough cobblestones like a common criminal, the crowds parted to let the party pass, and the people of Paris stared down at him. It was no wonder: shrieking protests like a madman, bloody from his beating, and smeared with the familiar odious brown, he was not a pleasant sight. His shame was outdone only by his anger.

De Chauliac looked down his nose from the top of a flight of stairs as Alejandro was tossed down their full length by his ruffian escorts and into a clammy crypt, where he jolted to a stop on the damp stone floor. The air *oofed* out of him, and he lay there, stunned by the fall and his sudden ill turn of fortune.

Gradually his breath returned, and he sat up on his elbows to look around. His vision was blurry and his head ached from its earlier thumping, but bit by bit it cleared and seeing returned. He was grateful for the slivers of light that came from a narrow window near the ceiling: the imprisonment that began his journey from Spain a decade before had been terrifyingly lightless. His eyes settled on a long stone rectangle, simply adorned with one plain cross on its lid. *A burial vault. So I am in a tomb, then.* After a silent apology to whoever might be resting inside, he grabbed one edge and tried to stand, but found to his great unhappiness that one of his ankles would not cooperate. He sat back down, wincing, and examined the balky joint with his hands. He pressed all around it with his fingers and judged with great relief that it was not broken. But it was beginning to swell, and Alejandro knew that it needed to be bound.

He removed his shirt, and was about to tear away one of the sleeves to use as a binding, when the door opened at the top of the stairs. He looked up and saw the silhouettes of his captors heading down the stairs and toward him. He hastened to put his shirt back on, and just as he finished he was grabbed at both elbows and yanked to his feet.

Limping pathetically, he was led through the crypt and up a different flight of stairs. When he came back into the daylight again, he found himself in the courtyard of the fine mansion he had, a short while before, stopped to admire. He wondered as he bumped over the stones why his spine had not tingled as he'd passed it earlier, considering who the occupant had turned out to be.

That noble *hôtelier* awaited him in a large wood-paneled room, handsomely furnished and richly draped with ornate hangings. Alejandro was deposited roughly on a beautiful woven rug in front of the patrician doctor, who sat in a high-backed chair and leered at him with visible malevolence, silently demanding a decade's worth of explanations.

He will not believe what I have been through. He will think me mad.

So he said nothing, but looked around and saw to his amazement that the room was full of books. As he stood there, recovering what grace he could, Alejandro scanned the shelves and tried to estimate the number. There must have been hundreds of them, and though he had heard wild stories of a library in Córdoba with more books than a man could count in a week, not since his days as a student at the University of Montpelier had he seen so many volumes in one place as here. King Edward's library at Windsor Castle was not half as large.

"You are plainly taken with the contents of my shelves, Physician," de Chauliac noted. "This does not surprise me. There are many fine volumes here. I have collected them with great care."

Alejandro just stared at him. He had not even the faintest notion of what he should say. So he smiled derisively and said, "Greetings, *Monsieur de*—ah, pardon! I mean Dr. de Chauliac . . . it has indeed been a very long time. We are both older now, but I am compelled to observe that you have aged well, and you look to be in splendid health!"

"*Merci,* Dr. Canches. I recall from your brief studies with me that you had fine skills of observation." Of course de Chauliac would have discovered his true name. Spanish soldiers would have told him when they arrived in Avignon to arrest him, only to find him already gone.

"And what of your patron, His Holiness Pope Clement? How does he fare?"

Ah, it is so kind of you to ask, but you must have been living in a cave, he imagined de Chauliac responding. Instead the Frenchman said, "I regret to tell you that my holy patron was felled by a strike of lightning after he sent you to England. Alas, I tried, but I could not save him. His very blood was boiled by the force of it. It was, shall we say, an unfortunate— and rather unattractive—event."

An irony too rich to be believed, Alejandro thought. "Such a tragedy— especially after your skillful protection of his health."

But as he stood in the man's library, surrounded by his impressive collection of wisdom, Alejandro could not help but feel a small admiration for the pope's former physician. Despite the evil turn that de Chauliac and the now deceased Clement had done to him in shipping him off to England, he had learned much in the short time he had studied under this teacher.

You must use all of your skills to isolate them from the contagion, de Chauliac had said in preparing him for the journey, *for I believe that it may be passed through the air from one victim to another, and we never see the means of it! God has willed that the plague's vehicle shall be visible only to Himself for the present. We can only imagine it. But it is there, sure as there were seven days in the Creation. It is there, and one day, God willing, we shall be able to see it.*

Like Alejandro knew there were tiny beasts in the water, de Chauliac had hinted at tiny beasts in the air.

"It was rats," the Jew blurted out.

De Chauliac raised one eyebrow and leaned forward in his chair. *"Pardon?"*

"Rats," Alejandro said again.

De Chauliac's hard blue eyes darted quickly into the corners of the room. "I assure you, there are no rats here. In the kitchen, perhaps, but that is well away, in the cellar." His voice took on a slightly hurt tone, surprising his listener. "I had thought you would be more impressed by my collection."

"No!" Alejandro said. "I mean yes! Your library is—" He hesitated, looking for the proper word. "Magnificent! I have not seen the likes of it in a very long time."

A satisfied smile spread slowly across de Chauliac's face, but then, seemingly outside his control, his brow took on the creases and lines of uncertainty. "Why, then, do you speak of rats?"

"The contagion!" he answered excitedly. "Of the plague. It is carried by rats, I am certain of it!"

De Chauliac stared at him for a moment, then let out a series of small chuckles, which grew steadily until they had become full, mocking laughter. Soon he was gripping his sides; even the guards at the door were losing their stiff composure.

"I am *certain* of it!" Alejandro repeated, nearly shouting, and the laughter ceased.

De Chauliac stood, lifting his patrician bones slowly off the chair until he reached his full magnificence. He moved forward until his face was only a few inches from Alejandro's. The tall French physician spoke in low, even tones, saying, "While you are a guest in my home, *monsieur,* you shall not raise your voice. I do not think it good behavior."

Alejandro remained still and silent. On hearing the word *guest,* he was reminded that he was a prisoner in this library until de Chauliac thought to move him back to the abysmal crypt, and decided that he would not raise his voice again.

"My apologies, *monsieur,*" he said with proper contrition. "I do not mean to besmirch your hospitality. It was only my great eagerness to share this knowledge with you that caused me to shout."

De Chauliac's eyes were still locked on his, Alejandro saw in them something he could not quite fathom. Was it—*but no.* It could not be. He had thought, for the briefest moment, that he had seen the look of something akin to sadness in those blue eyes. As if de Chauliac somehow felt—*betrayed.*

The Frenchman turned away suddenly and picked up a pile of neatly folded clothes from a nearby table. "Here," he said, thrusting the clothing toward Alejandro, "we shall discuss this crazed theory of yours further at dinner." He shook a finger at Alejandro's soiled breeches. "But first you will clean yourself. You stink."

And he glided majestically out of the room, leaving Alejandro alone with his guards and a wealth of books. But he had no opportunity to enjoy the volumes. Almost immediately his guards led him away and through a series of long halls and twisting passages to a small chamber on the top floor of the mansion, which seemed to have an almost endless number of rooms. He made an effort to memorize the route, but realized when they shut the stout wood door behind him that an escape attempt could be blocked at any one of a dozen points along its progress. There was a window with clear glass that was large enough to fit his body through, but when he opened the wood-encased panes and looked downward it seemed a dizzying height, far too great to survive an unprotected jump. The street below was busy with traffic, and if he did not break both his legs he was sure to be captured, and what then?

No. He would wait, and he would try to gather intelligence before deciding what to do.

If he opened the framed glass window and stuck his head out, he could just barely see the river. Across it lay the relative safety of the Rue des Rosiers, in the Marais. Was Kate there now, waiting in vain for him to see her? If so, there was only himself to blame. He had been curious about a strange new word whose meaning, when finally discovered, seemed insignificant compared to the woe it had caused him. *Woe be to anyone . . .* he recalled from the manuscript with a shudder. This Abraham, it seemed, was something of a prophet.

God curse my curiosity, he thought dismally, *for it is eternally my undoing.* Had he not been curious about why Carlos Alderón had died, he would not have dissected his body, an act that ultimately brought about his forced flight from Spain. Had he not curiously inquired about a medical practice in Avignon, he would not have been conscripted by de Chauliac, then the agent of the clever and manipulative Pope Clement VI, to go to England as the protector of the royal family's health. And once there, had he not sought a greater understanding of an English midwife's claim of a cure for plague, he would not have had to escape to France.

But then Kate would not have survived it. Nor would I.

And in view of that conclusion, his woes seemed a worthwhile trade. He sat down on a small chair and tried to compose his thoughts, and in that state of relative stillness the odors of what he had been dragged through revealed themselves. There was a pitcher of water on a small table, and a cloth beside it. He followed de Chauliac's bidding and cleaned himself, then put on the fresh clothing he had been given, his mind retracing all the while the events of the day, especially their final exchange of words. And despite his unhappiness, he realized with an unexpected but welcome start of pleasure that for the first time in many days his speech had been directed at someone other than himself; earlier the priests, then the students, and finally his erstwhile teacher. Now he found that something de Chauliac had said was stuck in his mind like a sinew of beef between two teeth. No matter how he poked and prodded, it would not go away. Something about tiny beasts in the air? It nagged at him, and he knew that he would have to pry it out for further examination.

For despite the difficulty of his situation, he was once again curious.

Camp Meir, Janie entered into the search engine. She was curious, and she thought the search might lead someplace where a few answers might be lurking.

The first hit was an on-line brochure advertising the place to the families of prospective campers. She went through each page carefully, visiting all the links, backpaging when needed. There were beautiful pictures of idyllic grounds, and photos of the insides of the cabins that she was sure were exaggerated in their cleanliness, for there were no cobwebs or horseflies, and no wet towels left on unmade bunks. Parents would like these pristine photos, but their kids would know better. There were detailed menus of the meals the camp served, followed by glowing resumes of the directors and supervisory staff. Wholesome-looking counselors in matching Israel-blue T-shirts and khaki shorts smiled out from a group shot in which they all had their arms linked together. And there were toothy photos of healthy-looking young boys with clean faces and golden tans, not a torn shirt among them. Happy campers, all.

In the second Internet site, Camp Meir was high on an alphabetical list of summer camps where Hebrew was taught, and was linked back to the site she'd just visited. The third site was simply a directory of New York State summer camps, so she whizzed through it.

But the last was far more interesting—it was the personal home page of a fourteen-year-old boy who had, among other activities he'd once enjoyed, attended Camp Meir. He wanted to hear from other camp alums. On the home page of the site was a photograph of the boy, smiling from his wheelchair.

She bookmarked it, then printed it and stuck it in her purse.

Mrs. Prives was still sitting at her son's bedside, wearing the same tired-looking outfit Janie had seen on her each time she'd visited the room. She wondered if the poor woman had left the bedside for more than a bathroom visit, or if she had anyone—friend, family, neighbor—who could bring her some fresh clothing from home. If not, Janie decided, she would volunteer herself to make a clothes run.

She was about to greet Mrs. Prives and voice the offer when the woman turned and faced her, and Janie was surprised by the dramatic, almost striking change in the look on her face. "There's been an improvement in his condition," the mother said excitedly. "He's been waking up off and on." Her smile was almost pathetically hopeful.

Janie waited for a few seconds before saying anything. A change in consciousness, while a positive sign, didn't necessarily mean much in terms of a spinal injury. But she held back that damning pronouncement and tried to make her own smile seem sincere. "That's wonderful," she said quietly. She went back to the door and looked out into the hallway—there was no one in sight, so she closed the door. Then she returned to Abraham's bedside and gave the mother a permission-seeking glance. The mother nodded almost eagerly.

She did a quick examination of the boy, searching for even the smallest indication that his condition truly had improved. But he was essentially the same, as far as she could tell from the cursory once-over. Then she scraped a few skin cells from one of his arms and dropped the swab into a plastic bag, which she sealed carefully. She eyed the computerized file attached to the foot of his bed with aching frustration, because her ID chip was not among those that would open its viewer. Even if Mrs. Prives gave permission for her to look at it, her lack of official status would make it nearly impossible to convince hospital administrators that she was worthy of a peek. And Chet would be of no help. He would thwart her, if anything.

But she let it go, because in truth Janie doubted that the electronic file would show much of anything beyond what she already knew. And she didn't have the heart to tell this hopeful mother that achieving consciousness was not going to be Abraham's most difficult challenge. *Not only is he paralyzed,* she thought, *but if he's conscious, he'll be aware of it too.* Still, it was an obvious joy to his mother, who surely deserved to have her weighty vigil lightened, if only for a brief time.

So Janie kept her thoughts to herself and turned to another matter. "That camp Abraham went to, where he had the injection for that beaver thing—I'd like to look into that a little further, if that's all right with you."

"Why?"

"From what you've told me I think he might have been exposed to something called *Giardia*. It's an organism that can cause disease, and it's spread by contact with any water source the spores live in. The symptoms can sometimes be hard to detect," she lied, "but there can be"—she glanced suggestively toward Abraham—"aftereffects. Years later, sometimes."

Mrs. Prives's smile faded. "Oh, dear, I had no idea . . . no one said anything at the time."

"Well, it's not widely known, and to tell you the truth we weren't paying a lot of mind to things like *Giardia* during the worst of the Outbreaks. DR SAM had our complete attention. But I wondered if you might have kept any records from that time."

"I didn't keep anything. Last time we moved I threw out everything that wasn't absolutely necessary." She made a thin smile. "You get tired of carting it all around after a while, and after the Outbreaks, well, all those papers seemed sort of unimportant, if you know what I mean."

"I do," Janie said with a nod.

"But I don't remember seeing anything like that when I did the last purge."

"Would you mind if I contacted the camp and asked for Abraham's records?"

"No. Not at all." For a moment, Mrs. Prives paused, her expression both pensive and troubled. Then she looked directly into Janie's eyes. "You don't suppose . . ." She couldn't seem to finish the question.

That his stay at that camp might have had something to do with his current situation? You betcha. I just don't know what yet. But again, she lied. "I doubt it. And I don't want to speculate. Though I do think it's worth looking into. I'll need a letter of authorization." She reached into her bag and took out a piece of paper and a pen. "I brought one with me, on the off-chance that—"

Mrs. Prives grabbed the letter and pen and scrawled her signature at the bottom of the letter without even reading it. "Anything you think will help." She handed the letter back, a bitter look on her face. "Have you heard anything yet . . . about the funding?"

"No. I'm sorry. I'm still on it, though. And I'll keep on it until I run out of options. We're not even close to that point yet."

"Good. I want to thank you for your perseverance."

"Let's just hope it pays off." She paused briefly. "So what have they told you here, about Abraham's waking up?"

"They haven't told me anything."

Janie gave her a look that said *Then how*—

"Dr. Crowe. I'm his mother. A mother knows her child."

Janie couldn't disagree.

She was brittle from lack of sleep and confused by the night's events, and she should have just gone home for lunch and stayed home for a nap so that when she woke up again, her mind would actually be working and she could make some sense out of the crazy maelstrom that suddenly seemed to be swirling all around her.

Please, let me just go to sleep, and when I open my eyes again, let it be Christmas, with all these problems solved. An unwanted Christmas melody drifted through her brain, with unfamiliar words—

It's beginning to feel a lot like London. . . .

Her stomach started to knot. *Oh, please, no. Not London. Let it feel like anything but London. . . .*

. . . with its compudocs and biocops and smiling friendly people who would turn you in for sneezing without a hankie, but only after an impeccably polite offer of tea. It had seemed so genteel when she'd first arrived, so civilized and orderly, but by the time she escaped, she was clicking her heels and screaming, *There's no place like home, there's no place like home. . . .*

But today even the notion of home didn't hold its customary appeal, for reasons Janie didn't have to think about. She did what her sleep-deprived mind told her to do, and walked to a nearby diner for a caffeine hit and maybe a bite of lunch.

On an ordinary day she would seat herself at the most hidden corner table she could find, flip open her laptop in front of her, and proceed to digest both her sandwich and the local Net news at the same time. She would skip from international news to national news to science news to sports news, and then if she had time, she'd guiltily survey the *People* magazine site. It was a predictable, familiar daily routine, disrupted by her sudden and painful lack of hardware.

And every time John Sandhaus had ranted about computers having too much power and predicted the eventual rise of the technochallenged, declaring them in advance the new Bolsheviks, every time he'd hurled something at his own computer and prayed for the overthrow of the big databases that seemed suddenly to know everything about everyone, Janie would shake a finger in his face and say, *Bite your tongue, neanderthal. How would we live without computers?*

Here she was, answering her own question with the purchase of a newspaper.

But the sad fact was that the "newspaper" machine was nothing more than an Internet terminal with printing capabilities, and one that allowed her to pay with her ID sensor, at that. She flattened her hand against the credit receptor on the machine and pressed a button, then stood back and watched while it inscribed, on regulation newsprint, a copy of the local gazette that had been updated within the hour. She knew that some of the newer machines even folded them.

But not this one. She folded the paper herself, enjoying the comfortable, familiar crinkly sounds the newsprint made as she forced it into obedience. With the still-warm paper tucked under one arm, she picked up a sandwich and coffee from the deli counter and wove her way through the landscape of tables until she found one that was suitably remote. She sat down stiffly, feeling suddenly old and tired.

Then she put the paper down on the table so the top half showed and read the boldface headline:

HEALTH OFFICIALS FEAR NEW OUTBREAK

It took her breath away. This was the second such report she'd seen in as many days. But DR SAM had been so much a part of their lives that it was seldom deemed newsworthy. It was reported in the mainstream press only when it hit hard and fast.

She set down her coffee cup. *So this must be serious.*

"Administrators of the town's only elementary school were forced to close the building until further notice. . . ."

Oh, no, not children, please not any more children.

It was a thousand miles away. But the victim Caroline had told her about lived no more than twenty miles away. Outbreak miles could be very, very short, depending on how the carrier traveled.

There must be some good news in this thing, she thought unhappily. She turned the paper over and read the next offering.

POPULAR ASSISTANT COACH DIES IN BICYCLE MISHAP

And the subheadline, just below it:

Unexplained accident prompts call for investigation from university officials.

There was a photograph. It might have been two or three years old;

there was no goatee and the hair was longer. But it was unquestionably the man Caroline had enticed into leaving his computer terminal a few nights before.

The adrenaline surge was almost overpowering. Though Janie's stomach was long empty of the breakfast Tom had made her eat earlier, it seemed suddenly to want to toss back out the very memory of that meal. Nausea flooded through her, and a veneer of cold clammy sweat appeared on her skin. The newspaper slipped from her hands and fluttered noisily to the floor.

People all around her stared momentarily, and she met their prying eyes with an almost menacing look that said *Not your business.* When she felt unwatched again, she closed her eyes and pressed one hand against her forehead. She forced herself to pick up the paper and read the accompanying article, though she was terrified of what the text might reveal.

. . . an experienced cyclist with a perfect safety record . . . on his way home from work on the bicycle path . . . his usual route . . . deserted stretch . . . no obvious cause for going into the ditch . . . helmet saved him from head injury, but his neck was broken, and he apparently died instantly.

She reached into her purse and pulled out her cell phone. She spoke the name Caroline, unsure of whether it would recognize her trembling voice, but it did. She picked up after two rings.

"We have to tell Michael," Caroline said on hearing the news.

"I know," Janie said. She dreaded his reaction.

She wouldn't come to the station, but insisted on meeting him in the square, where no one else could hear them.

"Dear God," he said when he read the story. "I don't understand."

"What's to understand? The man is dead, all of a sudden. And we were with him just a few days ago."

"It could be nothing more than a crazy coincidence," Michael said as he tried, with little success, to refold the paper.

"Michael, please. You're a cop. You know this sort of stuff never turns out to be a coincidence. My house gets broken into and they take nothing but my computer. Which just happens to have some interesting, *stolen* data on it. Then this guy, who happens to have had a part in the acquisition of those data—"

"He wasn't aware of that, so he couldn't possibly have told anyone—"

"He didn't have to. The sign-on ID on the terminal at the computer bar was his. I mean, I was concerned about someone thinking it was him if the entry got discovered, but I was worried about an official investigation. It never occurred to me to think that something like this might happen . . . and we were so careful to set it up so he couldn't even be charged. All I wanted to do was get these data, and now . . . oh, God."

"Janie, there's nothing terribly odd about a bicycle accident, people die in them all the time, and a broken neck is often the cause."

"Michael, why are you here?" Janie said abruptly.

He seemed confused by her question. "Because you called me. You asked me to meet you."

"No. I mean why are you here in this country?"

"What does that have to do with anything?"

"I'll tell you what—you're here because when people were suddenly dying of plague in London, and Caroline's DNA showed up under the fingernails of one of the victims, you didn't buy it as just a coincidence."

He stared at her for a moment.

"Because like most people with half a brain, you believe that true coincidence is a very rare thing. But I haven't even told you everything yet. This morning I had a bizarre e-mail message, with no return address. It was the second one I've had from someone by the same nickname— Wargirl. The first one was just a 'Hi, who are you' e-mail, and I thought it was a random transmission, or maybe a kid playing with the computer buttons. But this one said 'Do not be afraid.' " She paused for a moment. "It came at a time when I *was* afraid, apparently with good reason. I don't think it was a fluke."

Michael didn't openly agree with her hypothesis, but he had no reasonable counterargument with which to refute it, either. "I can look into the investigation and see what the inside word is. It's not always the same as what you read in the paper."

She gave him a cynical look. "No. You're kidding. You've completely shattered my faith in the news media."

He said, "Sorry, luv. I'm not thinking quite straight." Then with a pointed stare, he added, "You took me a little by surprise with all this."

He should be screaming at her. He was being unbelievably kind about their theft of his device. So with true contrition in her heart, Janie said, "Michael, I'm sorry, I know now that this was—"

"Forget it," he said abruptly. "I probably would've done the same in your shoes. Now—this message—what was the nickname again? I'll see if I can dig up anything on it."

"Wargirl," Janie said with relief, "just like it sounds."

* * *

When she stepped through the door into the reception area of Tom's law firm later that afternoon, the stress lines in her forehead were so visible that Tom's secretary asked Janie if she was feeling all right. She answered yes, not really meaning it, and offered a limp explanation.

"I didn't sleep too well last night, that's all."

And because she knew the basics of Janie's legal circumstances, the woman nodded sympathetically and said, "Oh, I'm sorry. This must be a very difficult time for you. But things will be better soon, I'm sure of it. Mr. Macalester is working very hard on your case."

Cases, Janie thought to herself, *and it looks like there might be another.* "I know he is. I have complete faith in him. Listen, I don't have an appointment, but I don't need more than a couple of minutes. I gave Tom something to hold in the safe for me. I just wanted to get it back if I could, please."

"Why don't you have a seat—let me just check and see what he's up to."

She was as wired as a lioness, and she would rather have paced around to work some of the energy off, but Janie did as she was told and sat. The overstuffed chair was so comfortable and welcoming that when Tom came out of his office to greet her a few minutes later, she was already close to dozing. He roused her with a gentle touch on the arm.

"Hey, sleepyhead."

Janie came awake quickly and sat up. She rubbed her eyes and ran her fingers through her hair. "Whoa. I guess I should've expected that to happen."

"Don't worry about it." He smiled warmly and patted her on the shoulder. "Even Superwoman needs to sleep every now and then. Monica said you wanted to get your things out of the safe."

"Right. I did. Not things, though. Just thing. I put two items in that envelope. I'd like to leave one of them here. But I'll probably be back for it pretty soon. I have to make some arrangements first."

"That's fine. Come on back to the inner sanctum."

Janie rose up and followed Tom through the quietly decorated office. She'd been there so many times before that it was as familiar to her as her own workplace, and far more welcoming. The private space in which he practiced his profession was as spare as Tom himself—nothing extraneous, nothing without meaning or function. The furnishings were all expensive and carefully chosen, but unshowy, evidence of the success of Tom's quiet but often brilliant work on behalf of his clients.

He went directly to a wood cabinet behind his desk and opened it with an ornate brass key. Janie saw a gray metal safe built into the cabinet's wood framework.

"Turn around," he told her, "or someone might torture you for the combination."

"Hey, if it would wake me up . . ."

He laughed and pressed a series of buttons on the panel, and the outer door popped open. He did the same on the inner door.

"That must be quite a safe," Janie said, listening, her back still turned. "What do you have in there, top secrets?"

"Only yours," he said. "None of my other clients are anywhere near as interesting as you." He poked around inside the safe and pulled out the envelope she'd given him, then turned around and handed it to her. "I can get you a cup of coffee, if you want. Maybe it would perk you up."

As if she hadn't heard him, she took the envelope with two hands, holding it in front of her while she felt the contents with her fingers. She set the envelope on her lap, undid the clasp, and carefully withdrew the journal. She opened the back cover of the old book with great reverence. Tom watched, fascinated, as she withdrew a twenty-first-century data disk from inside the leaves of the fourteenth-century journal.

"Should I be guessing which one of those things you're going to take with you?"

"The disk," she told him, "but only long enough to make a copy of it. Then I'm going to bring it back. The journal I'm going to leave here, maybe for a few more days, if you don't mind."

"I don't mind at all. And I can probably copy that disk right now if you want. Then you can take the copy with you and put the original back in the safe."

In her frazzled state, it hadn't even occurred to her to ask for such a simple thing. "That would be great—it would save me some trouble."

Tom tapped the intercom button. His secretary appeared in the doorway a few moments later. "Take this disk, please, and make us a copy, would you?"

"Of course."

That settled, he offered the coffee again.

"Thanks, but I think I'll just take the disk and go. I'm so tired I can barely think straight. It's been a crazy day."

"Night, you mean."

"No, I meant day—some things happened today. . . ."

Her hesitation prompted Tom to say, "Anything you want to talk about?"

"Yeah. Some things I'm going to *need* to talk to you about. But not right now. I have to let it all settle in first. Tomorrow, maybe."

Monica came back with two disks. Janie put one in the envelope, the other in her purse, then handed the envelope to Tom, who secured it in the safe again.

"Okay," she said, "That's that, I guess. I think I'd better go home now, before I collapse. I haven't exactly been looking forward to it, but I think I'd better." She made a dark little chuckle. "After all, I do live there, I suppose."

"I'll drive you. I'm through for the day anyway."

"Are you sure?"

"Yeah. I am. I'm ready to get out of here. I need some quiet to concentrate, and I can do that in my home office better than here."

"You're too good to me, Tom. Thanks. I'm afraid I'd fall asleep on the bus."

"Nope. Not gonna let that happen."

It didn't feel like home when she got there. It felt spoiled and violated, corrupted even. Janie knew the feeling would pass in time, but at the moment time was not passing quickly enough. She opened the door with a key and went inside cautiously with Tom close behind.

She was greeted by the remains of the mess, but it wasn't too terrible; much of what had been overturned or tossed around had been righted and repositioned by the well-meaning cops Michael had brought with him in the middle of the night. To bring it back to her own standard, Janie knew, would require some time alone with buckets and brushes and scrubbers. And Maria Callas. *Hey, maybe an exorcist . . .*

And just down the hall, there was a bed, her bed, with clean, cool sheets and fluffy pillows and a silk-covered down comforter.

She picked up the phone, and the dial tone told her that the phone company had kept its promise. She looked around, decided it was all too much to contemplate, and turned toward Tom with a discouraged look on her face. "You know what? I'm just going to bed. I can't even think of doing anything else right now."

He pulled a chair out from the kitchen table and sat down. "I'll stay till you're asleep."

"Do you have the time? What about that work?"

"I've got my briefcase in the car. So it's fine."

"You just keep saving my life all the time. I'm always wondering what I did to deserve it." She yawned and rubbed her forehead. "I'd offer to make you something to eat but I don't think I'd do too well."

"Forget it. I'm not hungry right now. I'll get something later, after I leave."

"Okay. Well, good night, I guess." And after the briefest hesitation, she turned and headed down the hallway.

"Janie . . ."

"What?"

There was a moment of silence, then Tom said, "Leave the door open. So I can look in on you. That way I'll know when to go."

Tom was moments from leaving when the phone began to ring. Though it was not his own, the universal urge to answer overtook him. He picked it up before the second ring.

"Dr. Crowe's residence," he said tentatively.

There was a brief pause, and then the surprised voice of a man came over the line. "Who is this?"

"This is Dr. Crowe's attorney."

"Tom?"

"Yes . . ."

"This is Bruce."

"Oh. Hello."

Another brief pause. "Is Janie there?"

"She is. But she's asleep."

Bruce seemed to struggle for words momentarily. "It's—what—seven o'clock there? Or did I figure it wrong?"

"No, you figured right. Seven-oh-eight, to be precise. Janie had a little bit of a problem last night."

Bruce's alarm came through the phone from across the Atlantic. "What kind of a problem?"

"Someone broke in here."

"Oh, my God, is she all right?"

"She's fine. She managed to hide in the bathroom—the guy never made it that far. She's exhausted, though—it happened a little after two and the cops were here until after dawn. She'll be fine after a good night's sleep, but she's a little shaken."

"Well, what did—who—"

"They don't know yet. Michael Rosow got here right away, but they didn't find a lot of evidence and he doesn't seem to think they're going to catch anyone. And all they took was her computer, anyway. I guess it was pretty quick. It probably felt like hours to her, though."

Bruce digested that information quietly for a few moments. "You're sure she's all right?"

"As all right as she can be under the circumstances. I drove her home from my office this afternoon. I was . . . uh, just about to leave."

"Before you go, could you leave her a note for me?"

"Sure."

"Just tell her I called. No—wait. Tell her I love her too."

Tom dutifully scribbled the words *Bruce called* on a pad of paper, then added *I love you.* He put it on the counter in plain view and left.

With the sentries newly charged by the provost to increase their vigilance, it was becoming an increasingly trying task to get through the walls of Paris. One by one, the gates to the city had been closed over the previous few days, and all who attempted to enter were now dependent on the good graces of the rough men who guarded them. But Karle made quiet inquiries and found out which ones were secret sympathizers, and successfully prevailed upon one man to let them through. They left their horses with him, with the promise of payment for their care, and the agreement that he should keep the animals for himself if they did not return within a certain period of time. Either way, the man would profit, and he was only too happy to oblige them.

Kate told him the location of the prearranged meeting place. "But why would he want to meet you there?" Karle asked. "It is an area peopled by Jews."

And after a moment of confusing uncertainty over how to explain, Kate answered, "Because no one will think to look there."

He still did not know what they were fleeing. "Now you must tell me who would be looking."

She simply smiled and said, "I will leave that to Père."

Her smile, he had found lately, had become an unexpected bit of pleasure. It took him away, albeit briefly, from the bad news and the strife and the misery. *I will miss the sound of her voice when she is gone,* he realized. *And her uncanny cleverness.* But he kept these thoughts to himself, for he knew it would be far better for him if she *were* gone. As his tasks of insurrection became more difficult, her continued presence would become more of a distraction, and no longer the occasional joy it had quietly grown to be. There would be dangers, and he could not take the time to protect a woman from harm when there was a rebellion to be seen to.

A girl, I mean. In either case, a female, and therefore trouble.

But after a period of waiting during which the shadows lengthened considerably, he began to wonder if she would be taken off his hands after all.

"Are you certain this is the correct place?"

"Without a doubt."

"How long ago were you last here?"

"Many years, but it has not changed much." She pointed to the yellow wedge-shaped symbol above the *fromagerie.* "The sign is exactly as it was when we came here before."

In view of her certainty he chose not to question her further, and remained quiet for a time. But as the day edged toward a close he grew visibly impatient and felt compelled to press his inquiry. "What will happen if he is delayed? We cannot wait here through the night."

"You need not wait. You have fulfilled your obligation. But give back my coins, please." She held out her hand.

The dismissal surprised him. "How can you so lightly offend me, after what we have been through together? Did you think I would steal your coins and leave you helpless?"

His anger caught her off-guard. "I . . . I'm sorry . . . I meant no disrespect—but I would *not* be helpless."

He wondered if it was fear that made her behave with such false bravado. *Is she trying to hide it? Perhaps I should be gentler with her.* "It is possible that your *père* did not get through the walls before the gates were closed."

"It is unlikely that he would allow himself to be delayed as we were. In any case, he would find a way. He is a very clever man."

"So you have said."

"It is true. And he has made me a clever maiden."

"Nevertheless, I shall wait with you to be sure he comes."

"As you like," she said.

They did not speak again until the sun had disappeared behind the tallest building on the street.

"I must go to Marcel," Karle finally said.

"Then go," she said. And very quietly, she added, "With my thanks for your escort. And your company." She held out her hand again for the bag of coins.

He did not know what to do—it was growing dark, and she had no accommodations, and she was a young woman alone, and—

—and he did not wish her to be gone just yet.

"I am loath to leave you here," he said. "It seems an unmanly thing to do, in view of my promise to care for you. Come with me to the provost's house. He will give us shelter for the night—then we will return here tomorrow. Soon it will be too dark to see your *père* even if he does arrive. And he would not want you to be alone out here, I am sure of it."

Behind the firm resolve on her face, he saw a worried maiden who was as undecided as he of what to do next.

"Please," he said.

"All right," she finally said, "but I will hold you to your promise. To return tomorrow."

Relief flooded through him, but he did not allow her to see it. "I will not fail you," he said solemnly. Then he took her hand and led her toward the river.

"Ah, Dr. Canches," de Chauliac said as his freshly garbed prisoner limped into the candlelit *salle à dîner,* "sit down." He gestured toward a chair across the table from where he himself sat. "You must rest your leg."

The guards stayed outside the door as the physician hobbled to the chair.

"Have you determined the nature of your injury?" his teacher asked.

"I do not believe that there are any broken bones," the younger man answered. "It will heal in a few days, at most."

"Ah, this is very good news. But of course, I shall wish to examine you myself. While you are in my care, I do not wish any harm to befall you. I shall do so after we dine."

"You may suit yourself, de Chauliac, but you will find my bones quite intact."

"I have found the Jews to be a weak-boned lot, I must say. In my time at Montpelier, I observed that among the old, especially, there is much breakage of the limbs."

"We are not so easily broken as you might think."

"Ah," de Chauliac said, "I remember your defiant spirit well, and fondly. You are especially fine company when you are disturbed." He waved a hand and a servant appeared with a flask. Their goblets were filled with a dark and aromatic liquid. De Chauliac raised his in salute, and said, "I propose a toast, to many scintillating conversations." He smiled broadly. "And to the return of the Prodigal Son."

"I have heard this parable of your Christ," he said, "but I do not understand."

"Ah, yes," de Chauliac said. "As you did not understand 'Marana-tha.'"

Alejandro squirmed in his chair, which had proven itself to be far less comfortable than it looked at first glance. *He toys with me,* he thought. *And he enjoys it.*

"I shall explain," de Chauliac continued. "The son takes his portion of his father's wealth and runs off to a faraway land, where he squanders it. When he returns in poverty, the father rejoices and makes him welcome again, forgiving the wayward son his profligate ways."

His discomfort growing, the younger physician said, "Forgiveness is a fine thing, especially between father and son. But I have not squandered my father's wealth. Nor have I any sons, so I am not certain what you mean by this tale."

De Chauliac stared at him through the candle-glow and said, "But we hear from England that you have what one might call a daughter."

A cold stab of fear shot through him.

De Chauliac saw it on his face, and smiled almost wickedly. "But this story is not about sons or daughters, rather it is about a gift that was not wisely used. You see, you were given a gift in Avignon, by myself, by His Holiness the Pope, and you squandered *that* gift." He set down his goblet and nodded to the servant, who brought out a plate of meat and set it on the table between the two men.

De Chauliac sniffed the steam that rose from the offering. "Lovely," he said. He closed his eyes momentarily and enjoyed the aroma of onions and spices. "But we shall not continue to speak of these things just now. They are too distressing, and will upset our digestion. Such delights as I set before you this evening are hard to come by these days, very hard indeed." He picked up a knife and cut off a small chunk of meat, which he then stabbed with the tip of the knife and stuck into his mouth. "Please," he said as he chewed, "Eat. Though you look well enough, one could say that you are a bit thin."

Alejandro ate the meat in silence, his eyes glued distrustfully to his captor, thinking, *It is as if he has planned for my return.*

"Now you must tell me of your travels, Physician. After your flight from Canterbury, we heard far less of you than we would have liked."

We? Who, precisely, was "we"? Almost unconsciously, he gripped the knife tighter, causing the veins on the back of his hand to bulge blue. He thought momentarily of leaping across the table and slitting the throat of the dangerous, arrogant man who held him prisoner.

Not wishing to alarm his captor, he laid the implement on the table, but kept his hand near it as the idea of putting an end to de Chauliac swirled tumultuously around in his mind. It would only take the blink of an eye. But the guards would be upon him in an instant, and there could be no gain in it.

Moreover, it would be the act of an animal. Unlike the scoundrel bishop in Spain, the Frenchman de Chauliac possessed an intellect worthy of preservation. *And I am tired to my bones of all this death,* he admitted to himself. *There will have to be another way.*

He slipped his hand off the knife and sighed. "My travels are a long and sad story," he said. "You will be poorly entertained."

But de Chauliac smiled and said, "I think not. Unless you have changed since we last spoke. But I see signs that some qualities persist. You are still a man of inquiry. Why else would you be carrying such a manuscript as you had when I 'found' you?"

The Jew's face took on a stark look of alarm as he remembered the book.

"Do not fear," de Chauliac said. "You must realize that I, of all people, would have great respect for such a piece. I will treat it with care."

Alejandro relaxed a bit.

"Begin after Canterbury," de Chauliac said. "I have been told what happened before then. Had you been in any court in Europa, you would have heard many troubadours singing of your endeavors. You have become something of a legend, you know."

Karle waited until it was full dark, when all the citizens of Paris, those at least with food, would be at their dinners. "Even in such evil times as these, those who patrol the streets will stop and partake of a little something," he told Kate. "Paris retains *some* civilization."

Nevertheless, he was not fool enough to walk right up to the main door of Pillar House, where Marcel lived since beginning his term as provost; there was no sense in tempting trouble to find them. They went instead to the door near the kitchen and looked in through the window. There they saw a maid standing over the hot hearth, busily stirring the contents of an iron pot.

Tap, tap, tap on the glass. The maid turned her head not toward the window, but toward the door instead. A look of anticipation came over her face.

"She must have a lover," Karle whispered to Kate. "I think we have just stumbled upon their secret signal."

Happily, they had, for the young girl quickly wiped her hands on her apron and smoothed her hair.

"Make ready your knife," Karle told Kate.

"Karle!" she whispered in horror. "She is just a girl! She is not even as old as I am—"

"You will do her no harm," he said, "I only want you to scare her. I cannot hold a knife against her and reason with her at the same time. I want her to lead us to Marcel."

"You do not *know* this Marcel?"

"I have never met the man. But we are brothers in the spirit of rebellion."

And before Kate had a chance to argue further, the girl was rushing to the kitchen door. She pulled it open, looked back inside once, then stepped quickly outside, anticipating an embrace.

Before she could protest, Karle got hold of her and placed a hand over her mouth. "The knife!" he said, and Kate pulled it from her stocking, then nervously shoved the blade under the maid's nose. The girl's eyes widened in terror, but Kate could not help but wonder if she would notice how badly the hand that held the knife, her own, was shaking.

"Is Marcel in the *maison*?" Karle demanded in a rough whisper.

The wide-eyed girl nodded her head yes while Karle's hand was still clamped to her mouth.

His words came fast and urgent. "Then you will take us to him. I mean no one here any harm, but I must not be seen by anyone beyond this household and I will do what is necessary to protect myself. I will take my hand off your mouth, but if you scream, I *will* harm you. Do not doubt it."

In stunned silence, Kate did as Karle had asked her to, and pressed the tip of the knife into the small of the girl's back. Karle took his hand off the servant's mouth and grabbed the knife, then clasping both her small hands behind her back, he shoved her forward. "Lead the way," he said.

She led them up a dark and narrow flight of stairs into the torchlit *maison*. They followed her toward the salon, and when they crossed the threshold they saw, from behind, a man sitting in a chair. He was bent to some parchment, reading by the light of several candles.

"*Monsieur le Provoste,*" the maid said timidly.

"*Oui*" was Marcel's absent response.

"There are, uh, *guests* here to see you."

Etienne Marcel put down the letter and turned his head, and when he saw that the maid was held captive, he rose up abruptly. He faced the party square on and put one hand on the short sword at his belt. "Let go of her," he said. "Only a coward hides behind a girl."

"I am no coward, sir, but a man who means you well. Yet I did not know what sort of reception I might get from you, so I thought it wise to ensure a gentle one. No one shall come to harm." He let go of the maid's hand, at which point the frightened girl rushed away from him and into the safe embrace of her employer.

Karle held his arms open and showed the knife. He waved it in Kate's direction, and she came up behind him. She took the small weapon and tucked it into her stocking again.

"You are Marcel, I presume," Karle said.

Etienne Marcel, still ready to draw out the sword, nodded in affirmation. "And yourself, sir?"

"I am Guillaume Karle."

Marcel took his hand off the scabbard and thrust it eagerly forward in greeting. "*Mon dieu!*" he said, pumping Karle's arm up and down. "You are the *last* person I expected to see here!" He turned to the confused maid. "Don't just stand there, bring wine, and plenty of it!" She ran off to do his bidding.

Marcel motioned them toward chairs and said, "At last! God has decided that we should meet."

How could Alejandro describe that time, even to someone with the keen intelligence of de Chauliac? All the things he had seen and the places he had been; hell on earth—or might it have been heaven? Some wild combination of both in a life he would never have dreamed possible. . . .

Sensing Alejandro's reticence, de Chauliac prodded him with a question that was certain to elicit a response. "Why did you risk bringing the child with you?"

It snapped him out of his melancholy. "Because both she and her nurse begged me to. Both feared Isabella's wrath, I think with good reason." He looked into his captor's eyes. "You were right to warn me about Isabella. I should have been more vigilant."

De Chauliac made a cynical chuckling sound. "Even Adam failed to recognize the serpent."

At this comment, Alejandro made a small, wry smile, but it quickly faded as he continued his narration. "For a time after leaving England we moved constantly; it seemed everywhere I looked there were English soldiers. I know they had many other reasons for being in France, but all I could think was that they were waiting for me. I could not allow Kate—the girl—to speak, for she would give herself away. She was a very talkative child, and charming, and it sorrowed me greatly to keep her so still."

"You are quite fond of her, then."

He sighed. "As if she were my own child. I despair of ever passing on my own spirit through a child, so she is very precious to me."

Under the influence of the wine, de Chauliac was far less acidic, almost sympathetic. "But you are yet a young man," he said, "at least much younger than I, and surely, if any of us live through this terrible time, we shall have the opportunity to spill our seed successfully. And I see no lack of heavy wombs in Paris, though God alone knows how many of those shall come to live births. But life goes on, Physician, as it always has and, God willing, always will. And though many would say that the Jews ought to perish once and for all, I do not agree. There is a place in this world for everyone and everything. Why, God saw fit to preserve a breeding pair of every animal through Noah. I sincerely doubt that it is in His plan to eliminate the Jews entirely."

The amity that was forming between them vanished when Alejandro heard these words. *So we are animals to him. But he does not mean to have me killed.* It brought him a temporary feeling of relief. *But what then,* he wondered as the relief passed, *does he plan for me?*

"And if any Jews were to go forth and multiply, I would want them to be Jews such as yourself."

"Jews who do not look or act like Jews?"

"Men of intellect, reason, and wisdom, men who understand the world and how it ought to be."

"The world ought to be better," Alejandro said.

"You are right, colleague. It seems that we are all, Christians and Jews alike, dancing in the hands of Satan as he stares down at us in evil glee. In time, I have faith that this will change." He smiled. "But continue with your tale."

After another moment's hesitation, Alejandro went on. "After the first winter, we went to Strasbourgh."

"Oh," de Chauliac said with a sad shake of his head, "it was a pity what happened there."

"A harsher word is called for, I think. *Aberration* might do. But what-ever one calls that tragedy, the result was that we could not stay. We came to Paris for a time, and lived in the Marais among other Jews."

"You were here, in Paris?"

He nodded. "And then after a time we fled north again."

"Where did you go?"

"One would be hard-pressed to name a place we did *not* go," he said with a sigh. "We could hardly ride into a village and announce ourselves. '*Attendez!* Here we are, a fugitive Jew, despised and hunted by the princess of England, and the illicit daughter of King Edward, kidnapped from her cruel father's Court at her own request.' Who would welcome such a pair, for any reason other than to ransom us?"

"Then how did you live? No one would take you in, surely."

"There was never any lack of abandoned houses. We always chose the most isolated, and we would stay only until we thought we might have been noticed. Then we would move on to the next one, carrying with us what we had, which as you know from your current possession of it, has not amounted to much."

De Chauliac *hmphed.* "Nor was it precisely meager. You still have your gold, some of it given to you by my sainted patron, no doubt. You Jews are a frugal lot."

"We are, when it serves us to be."

"And you did not practice medicine in all that time? There are some fine tools in your bag."

He sighed in frustration. "Only very little."

De Chauliac sat back in his chair. "So you see? You *did* squander your gift."

"I passed my gifts on to the child by teaching her all that I learned myself," he protested. "She has become a fine healer. And when help was sorely needed, I always gave it. But every time we made ourselves known, we were forced to move on. The risk of capture was much too great."

"I think perhaps you are too worried, at least now." He sat forward and folded his hands together in front of his face. "Let me tell you what I have heard through my spies. For the first year you were actively hunted, especially while Clement was alive. The pontiff was naturally quite 'disap-pointed' when he heard who you really were; and though he was what some would call a Jew lover, he felt that by sending you to England he had humiliated himself. I tried my best to defend you, of course, by pointing out that you were successful in your mission. No more of the English royals died from plague. Still, he was not satisfied."

"So we *were* in danger, then."

"For a time. But after Clement's death, there was only Isabella who truly carried a grudge against you—her father was far too preoccupied with the affairs of state. She was able to keep the hunt going for a few years after that, but as Edward got more involved in resuming the war, his interest in pleasing her waned."

"It seemed quite healthy when I was there."

"Oh, I believe it was. He doted on her shamelessly. But now, in truth, he is only interested in seeing Isabella married."

"She is yet a spinster? But she must be twenty-six or twenty-seven by now."

De Chauliac laughed. "Why should this surprise you? Even a royal shrew is still a shrew. She did manage to impose the continuation of the hunt for you on her brother Edward, who has been in France more often than her father. He has turned into a fearsome warrior—he is called the Black Prince now for the armor he favors. He questioned me himself about you on one of his journeys here. But his interest seemed ingenuine. It was my feeling that he pursued you only because of his sister's insistence. They are fond of each other, for some reason."

"I know. And I find it curious."

"Indeed. Now he has given you up altogether."

De Chauliac saw the look of relief on Alejandro's face. Disliking it, he added, "However, their brother Lionel is not so preoccupied with war. He is here in Paris now, with his entire household. I have been called upon to minister to his family on occasion. I have fallen out of favor with the clergy, somehow, but my services seem still to have some value to the royals."

He saw a look of worry welling up again and laughed lightly. "Do not fear. Lionel does not remember you. I have questioned him already, much to his great irritation. His servants came and went from time to time toward the end of your stay at Windsor, and some of them may have seen you, but Lionel was at Eltham with Gaddesdon during most of the scourge. And he did not bring his servants along on this journey."

"Hmm," Alejandro said, "the inimitable Master Gaddesdon."

"An idiot," de Chauliac observed blandly. "One fails to understand Edward's faith in him."

Bring us proof, Gaddesdon had said when Alejandro had begged him for an audience with King Edward. *Then you shall have our ear.* "He did not believe me either about the rats."

De Chauliac flicked away the dot of meat on his fingertip and leaned forward. "Ah, yes, the rats," he said. "Please forgive my earlier mockery.

At first thought, it seemed a silly theory. But I am always willing to listen. You have my ear now."

"A gift not to be squandered," Alejandro said.

Nearly all of Paris was out on the streets to find what little cool air there was, with the notable exceptions of Etienne Marcel and Guillaume Karle, who remained inside and suffered in the steamy heat, for they had secrets that could not wait for cooler weather to be shared.

Kate suffered with them, and was forced to warn them constantly to keep their voices low, for they were whispering at the top of their lungs and the windows were wide open.

How quickly these two have found their common ground, she thought. *They have only just made acquaintance, yet they argue with the plain talk of old cronies.*

"Navarre is just another noble," Karle insisted, "although he calls himself king. He would be king of all France, I think, and we shall all suffer for it. He is no better than what we have now, nor substantially different."

"I beg to disagree, my comrade, he is a far sight better than our current monarch. Stronger, at least."

"I have seen the evidence of his strength. May God spare us all."

Marcel frowned. "He can serve us well. He can lead us against his own kind, and we would do far better with him than we would without him."

"He is a vicious rogue, and not to be trusted!"

"He can be trusted to look after his own interests, and all we need do to ensure our own success is to make sure that our interests are aligned with his."

"But how can our interests *ever* be concurrent? He will make himself our new master, and he will be a far crueler one than the weakling who now pretends to the throne. And he will do nothing to stop the wars, for they serve his purpose! Everyone is at war with everyone else: Jean against Edward, Navarre against the Dauphin, peasants against nobles, nobles against each other! France is in a state of anarchy such as has never been seen before. We must rise up while we have the chance, and take control!"

"These are pretty notions, Karle, but ill-considered," Marcel insisted. "Now think of this: If we promise to support Navarre's uprising against the Dauphin, then the nobility will all be engaged in a battle to the death among themselves, and we will be armed and in close proximity to them! When the battles are over, we shall *still* be armed, and their numbers will be reduced. They will be weak, and we can strike the fatal blow."

Karle had heard the same plan from Kate. And though he despised the idea of furthering Navarre's cause in order to secure his own, it seemed a sure way to put himself and his men in a good position to rise up against Navarre.

"I must admit," he said, "that it could work."

"Then, happily, we are in agreement!" Marcel cried. He motioned to the serving girl, Marie, who, having received the profuse apologies of Karle and Kate after their rough introduction, stood by ready to do her work. "Let us drink to the success of one noble over another—may they slay each other down to the last knight, and leave France to the rest of us!"

The girl came forward and poured the two goblets full. Marcel made a toast: "To the downfall of all the nobility."

Karle tapped his goblet against Marcel's. "And to our success in seeing Navarre himself eventually among those who fall, for my head will roll in the dust by my own hand before I call him king."

Marcel rose up halfway in his seat and shook a finger in Karle's face. "We shall use him as needed, and you are a fool if you cannot see the wisdom of it!"

Their conflicting words met in a midair tangle. They agreed, then they disagreed, they insulted, then soothed. They drank, then drank some more. *How very French,* Kate thought as she watched them go at each other with words and goblets. They toasted and cursed each other in the same breath. Theories of revolt were tossed back and forth like hot coals, each new lob eliciting a stronger response. Finally, Kate could no longer hold her tongue.

"Gentlemen!" she cried. "You slash at each other from the same side of the battle line! Marcel is right, and Karle is right. But I think perhaps Karle is a bit *more* right."

"You see?" Karle slurred. "Even a woman understands this."

Through half-slit eyes, Marcel peered at her. "Eh? What is this nonsense your wench offers?"

"His *wench* has seen the handiwork of Navarre," she said. "And were I a peasant, I would sooner follow the devil straight into hell than bend myself to the whim of Charles of Navarre."

Marcel gave her a curious, drunken look. "But you *are* a peasant. And a lovely one, I think."

Karle winked at Kate and raised his goblet drunkenly. "A toast to the beauty of the *peasant* wench!"

She did not know whether she ought to feel grateful or insulted. But she was red with embarrassment.

They toasted her, and then the pitch of the argument rose again as its

intelligence diminished. Finally, when Kate could stand it no more, she
threw up her hands and interceded.

"*Messieurs!*" she hissed. "It is no longer yourselves but the wine that
speaks for you! And very little of import is being said."

Marcel stared drunkenly at her. "Beautiful and audacious," he said. He
peered through hazy eyes at Karle and said, "Where did you say you
found her?"

Karle reached out and took hold of her arm, then pulled her toward
him. She struggled briefly against his embrace, but landed in his lap.
"This is no wench," he said with fuzzy pride. "This is a midwife. And she
has been put in my care by her own *père.*"

Horror flooded through her. Would Karle now drunkenly give her
away, after protecting her only moments ago?

But Marcel burst into laughter. He slapped his hand down on the table
and slurred, "*Mais oui,* of course, but under the veil of this wine I mis-
took her for the recent results of a midwife's effort. She looks still a babe
herself. She is fresh, and pink, and plump like a newborn, no?"

Kate's cheeks burned with shame and resentment. How dare these
drunken sots treat her skills so lightly, and speak of her as if she were not
there to hear it? She glared at the two of them. Karle failed to notice, for
his eyes were beginning to cross.

Then Marcel laughed and said, "And now it is time for this drunken
fool to retire to his soft bed." He made a halfhearted attempt to rise, then
thought better of it and plopped back into his wooden chair again. He
slowly slumped forward and rested his head on his own arm. His lids
fluttered shut, and in a few seconds he was snoring.

The serving girl quietly came forward and took the goblets away, returning with a pair of lit candles. She stared back and forth between the
two men in frank disapproval of their besotted state and shook her head
in disgust. "Follow me," she said to Kate. "Bring your 'gentleman.' "

"He is not *my* gentleman," Kate said as she slid off his lap and out of
his grasp. With considerable effort, she dragged and shoved the limp-
limbed Karle to his feet. "At the moment, he seems more a sack of flour,
and just as cooperative."

"I am no one's sack of flour," he protested drunkenly.

"Least of all mine," Kate said. She supported him on one shoulder,
trying not to breathe the odors of unwashed travel and strong red wine,
as the servant led the way up a narrow flight of stairs.

At the top of the stairs they were shown to a tiny chamber with one
straw bed pushed up against the window and a chamber pot in one
corner. There was barely enough room for a person to stand next to it.

And when the maid saw the look of dismay on Kate's face, she said, "It is all there is. Except the master's room."

Which the master will probably not enter tonight unless he is carried there. And this girl was too small to do it. *So his ample bed will be occupied by a servant while I sweat next to this drunken pig.*

"Please help me get him on the bed," she pleaded, and together the two young women managed somehow to arrange the imposing figure of Guillaume Karle lengthwise on the straw. Kate stepped over him on the mat and threw open the shutters on the small window. "Can you bring me a bowl of water and a cloth, please? I will not lie down next to this dog without cleansing him first, for I should surely rise up with fleas."

Marie returned a few minutes later with the requested items. She gave them to Kate, then bowed backward out of the room wearing an ironic smile of sisterhood. *"Bonne chance, mademoiselle."*

Left alone with her inglorious hero, Kate struggled to strip him of all his clothing, raising his arms and legs as needed and pulling the garments off bit by tedious bit. The boots were the most difficult, for the leather was old and had molded itself to the shape of his leg. She stood at one end of the pallet and tugged, grunting as she strained to free his feet, which must be sore and blistered after so much travel. Her own were— and her shoes did not fit nearly so tightly as Karle's. The breeches required unlacing, and as she was pulling the cords out of the guide holes, Karle drunkenly tried to roll away, so she was forced to hold him flat with one hand while the other did the work. His hair became tangled in some frayed threads of his tunic as she pulled it over his head—the tattered garment would require significant mending were he to wear it much longer. The clothes were soiled and sweaty and smelled quite rank, so she stuffed everything into a corner near the window. He lay on the straw, naked and helpless, unaware of the fine service that was about to be done for him by a young woman, who in a different turn of fate . . .

She looked him over in the candlelight, cautiously admiring his strong body, while a blush rose up on her cheeks. The night seemed suddenly to have grown inexplicably warm, so she dipped her fingers into the pitcher of water and patted a few drops onto her own forehead to cool herself. But it had little effect.

If Père could see her now . . . what would he say? She wondered if Alejandro would chide her for first rendering this poor man naked, and then gazing upon him when he had not the means to cover himself.

He would understand, in view of the improvement in Karle's condition, especially his cleanliness, because Père is so enamored of cleanliness. . . .

A shaft of moonbeams streamed in, so she blew out the candles and set them aside, allowing Karle a small bit of modesty. She poured some water into the bowl and wet the cloth, then squeezed out the excess, and slowly began to wipe away the accumulated grit from the man's damp flesh.

He groaned in his stupor, and she thought for a moment that the feel of the wet cloth was disturbing to him. But in the moonlight she saw that though his eyes were closed, his lips were open in a most inviting smile. *The cool of the water feels good on his skin,* she surmised, and she looked forward to washing herself when she had finished with him. She rinsed the rag in the bowl and started working on him anew, but as she worked her way down his chest, a slight movement caught her attention.

Bon dieu, she thought, *so this is what they mean when they talk about . . .* She sat back on her haunches, staring at Guillaume Karle's rising appendage in wary admiration. Her curiosity burned, making itself known by a rush of warmth in a part of her that had never spoken before. She looked at his face; he was lost to the world, stuporously drunk. Very slowly she reached out, her fingers trembling slightly, and touched him in his private place.

She let her fingers rest upon him for a moment, and then suddenly, that part of him moved again, ever so minutely, and with a small gasp she pulled her hand away and clutched it to her own chest.

But the feel of his skin was still on her fingertips, and she held the hand out for a moment and examined it in the candlelight. It looked the same, and she was sure that it was her own familiar hand. Nevertheless, it felt somehow different.

Slightly shaken, she rinsed the dirty rag as best she could, then tossed the used water from the bowl out the window. She refilled the bowl from the pitcher, and then quietly removed her own clothing and washed herself, looking back over her shoulder every now and then at her sodden *gentilhomme.* She pulled on her light shift and lay down, and as the straw rustled beneath her, Guillaume Karle reached out, as if it were the most natural thing for him to do, and put his hand on her arm. He opened his eyes just a slit. "Was I dreaming," he murmured hazily, "or were your hands upon me just now?"

She hesitated a moment, then said, "You stank, so I washed you. They gave us only this one bed."

He seemed confused and wrinkled his brow.

The hand he had placed on her arm was warm and the touch was tender, and quite against her will Kate felt herself warming to him. But she recovered her self-control and said, in a low but stern voice, "We have no choice but to bed together. I will trust you to be honorable. If you are not I will be forced to pour the remaining water over you."

"But I," he slurred, "I could have sworn—"

She reached out and put a finger on his lips to *shush* him. "You are drunk, Karle," she whispered. "Go back to sleep now."

He closed his eyes again and began to drift away. "Ah. yes. You are right." His words ran together so she could barely understand him. "I am drunk."

But the last few words he sighed out before slipping away were unmistakable. "And you are beautiful."

Alejandro belched, which somewhat relieved his discomfort, and worried for a guilty moment that Kate might be going hungry somewhere in the streets of Paris while he himself was stuffed near to bursting in this handsome mansion.

Where is she now? Is this rogue Karle seeing that she is well cared for?

He wondered also if de Chauliac felt any embarrassment over the richness of his table when so many French peasants were starving in the countryside, but decided it was not in the man's nature to concern himself with such things. *But he will want to be complimented.* "I thank you for your hospitality," he said, the words bitter on his tongue. "I have not seen a meal the likes of this since my time in Edward's Court."

"I am much flattered, Physician, for Edward is a notable host." Then he raised an eyebrow and said, "But surely you could have afforded to live well."

And now, by virtue of your possession of my fortune, I may not, but you surely shall. "It was not a matter of cost," the Jew said. "I did not wish to attract notice with ostentatious behavior."

"Eating well can hardly be considered ostentatious. Do not forget that you are in France. Everyone here eats as well as possible. Some better than others, of course."

Alejandro wondered if de Chauliac had any real notion of the starvation that was occurring in the French countryside. Anger welled up inside him toward his arrogant captor, but through some miracle of will he managed to keep it in check. He remained outwardly calm, though inside he was all turmoil and uncertainty. All he could think of was escape and reunion with Kate. And if he could not reclaim his gold, so be it. He would still survive.

But what of Abraham's book? Surely de Chauliac would understand its value and treat it with due reverence, but in the Frenchman's possession its critical message would not reach the intended audience.

Perhaps he would give it back. . . .

No. It would be ridiculous to ask. De Chauliac would never consent. *Yet he cannot unlock its secrets without the help of a Jew. And I am the only Jew he has.*

He was arguing with himself again, in the presence of another human being, and that would not do.

"The manuscript I brought . . ." he began, choosing his words carefully.

"Ah, yes," de Chauliac said. He sat back expectantly and waited for Alejandro to continue.

"It is a piece of some value to me."

"It is a handsome volume, I will admit." He made a curious face. "But it seems no more valuable than any other. Wherein lies its importance?"

Again, de Chauliac was toying with him, for enough had been translated to reveal the nature of its secrets.

But he would hear me say it. "It contains messages of wisdom for my people."

"Messages from your God?"

"No."

De Chauliac's questions suddenly took on the tone of an interrogation. "Then from whom?"

Alejandro was silent.

"From whom, I ask again."

"I do not know from whom!" he nearly shouted. "I only know the man's name is Abraham, and that he claims to be a priest and Levite."

"There are symbols of alchemy on those pages, colleague. Is this Abraham a practitioner of that art?"

"I have not deciphered enough of the text to know the answer to that."

De Chauliac was quiet and contemplative for the next few moments. Alejandro watched as the elegant Frenchman sat motionless in his carved chair and stared off into some thought-filled distance, seemingly oblivious of his guest's presence.

Then the elder physician rose up from the table and began to pace around the room. Still he was quiet, apparently lost in his own considerations. Finally he glanced in Alejandro's direction and spoke. "Tomorrow I shall invite some guests to dine with me. Among them will be a man who is familiar with the craft of alchemy."

Alejandro gave de Chauliac a frosty stare. *Tomorrow?* he thought. *No, not tomorrow, for tomorrow I shall be gone, even if it costs me a broken leg.* "As you wish," he said with a solemn nod. "I shall look forward to it."

*   *   *

When he was returned to his small room that night by a fresh pair of guards, Alejandro saw to his great unhappiness that the window had been fitted with wooden bars. It was a hasty job, none too carefully done, and the carpenter had left small bits of wood on the floor below. He reached down and picked up one of the chunks and twirled it between his fingers for a moment.

So he will keep me here, he thought to himself as the wood rolled against the skin of his thumb. *I will not be turned over to any other authorities.*

And then he bitterly laughed aloud. *There are no other authorities right now.*

He tried to look out, but his head would not fit between the bars. *At least he could have given me that much,* he thought unhappily. *A view of the river. Something to hope for.*

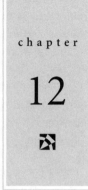
Birds. Sunlight through the blinds. The smell of coffee.

Tom must've programmed the coffeepot yesterday before he left, Janie thought. Her gratitude was immense. She surprised herself by thinking, *Too bad he isn't here to make breakfast again.*

But then the wonderful aroma of pancakes caught her attention. *He did stay,* she thought; the notion was unexpectedly pleasing to her. Perhaps he'd slept on the couch. She slipped a robe over her nightgown, tied the belt loosely, and following the trail of scents, headed for the kitchen.

There was a plate of pancakes on the counter, with a pat of butter sliding down the side of the golden pile. Next to it was a mug of coffee, with a saucer placed over it. And next to the mug was the note.

Bruce called—I love you.

She held it out in front of her, fully arm's-length, and stared at it.

She heard noises coming from the living room, and turned her head in that direction.

"Tom?" she said.

No answer. Still clutching the note, she headed into the large, high-ceilinged room, anticipating a warm good morning.

But it was not Tom, familiar friend and advocate. Instead it was a total stranger, a young woman, perhaps in her early twenties, a person Janie could not remember having seen anywhere before, certainly not in her own home. The girl was humming to herself as she bent and rose, picking up the remnants of the thief's work from the day before. She was long-limbed and rather bony, with massively curly dark-blond hair tied into a bandana and an apron wrapped around her waist. She was benign-looking and busy, and could have been a housekeeper or maid engrossed in her tasks.

But she was still an intruder. Janie gasped and swore, and, still clutching the note, ran back into the kitchen in search of something sharp and menacing.

The young woman dropped the things she'd gathered up and ran after her.

"Wait . . ." she called out.

As the stranger stepped into the kitchen, she was greeted by a bright, shiny carving knife, gripped firmly in Janie's right hand, held high and ready.

"*Get out,*" Janie hissed.

"No, wait, This isn't what you think—"

"You didn't get enough last time?" She flashed the knife.

"No, Dr. Crowe, wait a minute—I'm not a thief, if you'll just put—"

Janie made a quick stabbing motion with the knife in the air, this time with more menace. The young woman cringed backward.

"Who *are* you?"

There was a nervous pause. "I asked you that question once."

"No, you didn't. I've never met you before."

"Not in person, no. Now, please. Put down the knife."

"No. Not until you give me one hell of an explanation for what you're doing here." Her voice was trembling with fear, but she stood her ground firmly. "And if you're lucky I'll decide not to use this."

The girl backed away a little farther, holding one hand out protectively. "Do not be afraid," she said quietly.

"What?" Janie demanded.

"I said, do not be afraid."

The e-mail. This must be the person who had sent her the e-mail. "Oh, my God." Janie and the young woman locked eyes, and after a few moments, she slowly lowered the knife and set it down on the counter. She kept one hand on the hilt, and stared at the young stranger with the unspoken message: *Don't do anything stupid.*

The girl released a long-held and relieved-sounding breath. She displayed her empty hands and said, "I'm unarmed. Not even a nail file."

It still did not explain her presence. "Keep talking," Janie said.

"I will," she said. "Just—relax. Please. My name is Kristina Warger."

She stepped forward tentatively and extended her hand. "I've been look-ing forward to meeting you."

Janie wasn't quite ready to put her hand out to this unknown person, so she stepped back and pulled her robe tighter around herself.

Warger. Very clever.

"Wargirl," she said.

Kristina smiled softly. "That would be me."

"*What* are you doing in my kitchen?"

As if she was surprised by Janie's question, Kristina gestured toward the plate and mug and said, in complete innocence, "I was making your breakfast. I thought you'd be hungry." Then she tilted her head in the direction of the living room. "And I thought I would clean up a little. But I was just about to wake you up because there are things I don't know where to put, and the pancakes were going to get—"

"Stop. Just *stop.*" An image of waking up to find this stranger standing over her flooded Janie's forebrain. It was no comfort that Kristina Warger seemed so—young. "I need to know how you got in here," she said.

"I tried the door. It was unlocked."

Unlocked? Janie thought. That was impossible. Tom was too careful to have left it unlocked.

She paused for a moment, her eyes narrowed in suspicion. "Did Tom send you?" she asked.

"Tom who?"

She'd awakened with almost ravenous hunger, but Janie was so stunned by the morning's events that she could only pick at the pancakes, tasty though they were. Tom's note, with its seductive ambiguity, was momen-tarily set aside in the question and answer session that followed her initial encounter with Kristina Warger.

"Camp Meir," Kristina finally told her. "That's why I'm here. You struck a nerve with your inquiries. It required a—*response.*"

"But—did someone send you, or is this your own thing . . . ?"

"Oh, I was sent." She sipped her own coffee, then smiled.

"By whom?"

"Do you really want to know?"

"Of course!"

"Well, I'm sorry—I can't reveal who sent me just yet. I'm going to need to find out a few things first. From you."

Janie glared angrily at her bold and presumptuous visitor. *So auda-*

cious, she thought. But so much like Betsy! "If you know about my inquiries into the camp, then you must be keeping a pretty close eye on me already."

"Not really. You found us, actually. You accepted a cookie from the Web site. We just tracked it."

"I'm sure lots of people visit that site."

"You're the only one without a kid."

Janie took a moment to let the sting of that remark dissipate, then said, "Oh, come on—I'm sure other people without a good reason have stumbled onto it."

"Stumbled, peeked, and left. You hung out on a couple of sites for quite a while. Printed one, even."

Janie felt her blood pressure rising. "So you've been looking at my computer activities—I'm going to assume then that you know an awful lot about me already."

"Some. What can be learned in that way. Computers do have their limits, you know. I'm still interested in knowing how you discovered Camp Meir in the first place."

"Discovered it? I didn't *discover* it. I was told about it. I just checked into it because I'm doing some work for a boy who once went there."

There was a quick flash of recognition on Kristina's face, and for a moment Janie expected to hear her speak the name Abraham Prives. But she was disappointed. Kristina simply said, "You printed the one with the boy in a wheelchair. We know from your resume—"

"Wait a minute—you keep saying 'we'—who is *we?*"

Kristina Warger was apparently unaccustomed to interruptions, and seemed not to like them. "In a minute," she said in a perturbed tone of voice. "I don't want to lose my train of thought. As I was saying, we know from your resume and from other work of yours we've reviewed that you're a very bright woman. You're also a thorough and observant scientist. Your work in neurosurgery was nothing short of brilliant. By the way, we all think it's a shame about your relicensing problem."

Janie stared in disbelief as the young woman continued her detailed recitation. "And your research work on the soil in London—well, what can I say, it was just magnificent. So impressive."

"I haven't published that work yet."

For a moment, Kristina seemed not to know what to say. "Well, anyway, I've seen it. I didn't realize it hadn't been published."

"It's on the hard drive of my computer. The one that was stolen. And on my computer at work. My attorney also has a print copy."

"Well, it's not important how—"

"Oh, yes it is. To me, anyway."

Kristina forced a smile and went on, apparently unfazed by Janie's continued challenges. "It's not important how we know the quality of your work. But we do. So naturally we assumed, when you looked at Camp Meir on the Net, that you put two and two together and came up with fifty-three. Or some other cardinal number."

"You could say that."

Janie took a long hard look at the young woman in front of her. She could not help but dwell for a moment on the realization that in about a month, her own daughter Betsy would have turned twenty had she not contracted DR SAM.

This one's not much older than that. Janie closed her eyes for a moment and tried to imagine Betsy sitting at a stranger's kitchen table after having made herself quite comfortable without invitation; it was not a vision that came together neatly. Betsy had been a spirited child, but she'd never had the chance to discover her own power. She could not have done this.

And where did this young woman, a creature of such tender years, come up with her audacity? Living through the Outbreaks had made some young people daring, even hard—weird cults had grown up among groups of adolescent DR SAM survivors. But was this girl hard?

No. Daring, yes, tough, maybe. But Janie didn't get hardness. There seemed even to be a bit of vulnerability there, some approval-seeking.

"Now, maybe you'd better explain this *we.*"

For a moment, Kristina Warger looked confused. "Um, *we* . . . ?" she said.

"Yeah, *we.* You just said *we* know this and *we* know that and *we* assumed the other thing. I asked you who *we* are."

"Uh . . ."

"Don't you remember?"

Janie saw Kristina's eyes move back and forth rapidly as she searched her memory. It was as if, during Janie's momentary silence, the girl had drifted off somewhere.

Then the light of recall flashed on her face. "Oh! Yes. *We.*" Recovered from her short lapse, she drew in a breath, as if preparing for a diatribe. But her explanation was short and so mechanically delivered that it appeared to her attentive listener to have been very carefully crafted, and then memorized.

"We are an agency comprised of concerned citizen volunteers, and we investigate cases of what we think might be illegal genetic manipulation."

Simple enough, Janie thought. "A government agency?"

Kristina seemed almost offended by that question. "Oh, no," she said quickly. "Private. Completely independent. Volunteers, like I said."

"How are you funded?"

The girl waited for a moment before speaking, as if deciding what she ought to say. There seemed to be no script for this particular inquiry. "We have our ways" was what she put forth, quite tentatively. "But that shouldn't concern you, at least not for the moment."

"Well, it does, whether *you* think it should or not, just like I'm concerned about how you've seen my London paper. But more concerned about why you're here in the first place. It can't be to compliment me on my scientific acumen. And I don't believe anyone from Camp Meir sent you."

"Not exactly, no."

"Then there's got to be something you want from me."

"Oh, there is."

"And that would be?"

"We want you to do something for us."

What a surprise. "Which is?"

"A little investigation."

"I'm not an investigator—but there are plenty of people out there who are. Why don't you contact one of them?"

"Because we don't trust any of them."

"And you trust me?"

"Yes. You've been—recommended."

"If you don't mind my asking, by whom?"

"Right now, I don't think it would be good for me to reveal that."

She was playing cat and mouse with a kid. Could anything be more ridiculous? "Oh, for God's sake, this is—"

Kristina overrode Janie's protests with a forceful elaboration. "We have some people flagged in our own database as possible victims of genetic manipulation." As Janie stopped speaking, Kristina lowered her voice. "You've stumbled across some of them. And you have the skills to help us figure out what's going on."

"But I'm not a geneticist."

"That's all right. I know a lot about genetics. And we have people who can help you deal with the information you get inside—"

"By inside, I presume you mean inside Big Dattie."

Kristina nodded. And then she took a small, folded piece of paper from one of her pockets. She unfolded it methodically and glanced at what was written before continuing. "Abraham Prives," she said. "Your instincts on him were perfect. So we felt it was a good idea to look into you. And when we looked deeper, we liked what we saw."

Janie gestured in the direction of the living room. "You could have been a little gentler."

"How have we been ungentle?"

"Last night—the break-in."

Her response was measured and very serious. "That wasn't us. That's why I'm here this morning. We didn't think it was wise to wait any longer."

At first Janie refused to believe that Kristina and her group had had nothing to do with the break-in, but the girl was insistent. And despite her initial shock and anger, Janie found herself being drawn in, almost against her will, certainly against all common sense.

"Then who could it have been?"

"That's what we don't know, and precisely what we want to find out. It's just too much of a coincidence that you should be looking into it, and then the computer you used to do that snooping was the only thing in your house to be stolen," Kristina said. Then she leaned forward, and with a look of intense concentration on her face, she stared into Janie's eyes.

It seemed almost a challenge.

It was. "We know you have the skills, the motivation, the tenacity to do this," Kristina said, "to find out who's trying to protect Camp Meir and why. But I should warn you—there may be some danger in it. If you decide you want to help us, and we hope you do, you should probably put your affairs in order."

It seemed a little extreme. "Will someone try to hurt me?" Janie asked.

"Probably not physically. But you should make hard copies of everything, and get all your most precious possessions to a safe place. Just in case."

"When do I need to let you know?"

"As soon as possible."

"How can I get in touch with you?"

"We'll be in touch with you."

And with that promise, Kristina left. She got into a tiny little car that she'd left parked in the driveway overnight, and drove off.

From her kitchen door, Janie watched the car pull away and wondered where she was going.

Then she sat down at the kitchen table to collect her thoughts. The note from Bruce, written by Tom, was still there. She picked it up and stared at it, hoping it would speak to her. But it remained stoically silent and confounding.

It wasn't their customary call time, but she badly needed a fix. She was relieved to find Bruce still in his office in London.

"You won't believe what's happened in the last twenty-four hours."

Bruce listened, without interrupting, while she related the whole thing over the phone. From the excited tone in her rendition, it was plain that she expected him to share her fascination with the whole thing. But his reaction was far from encouraging.

"I know you're not going to appreciate this," he said quietly, "but I don't like the sound of this at all. Twice in two days you've had strangers in your house. Someone is 'looking into' *you*. Janie—I'm worried about you—this is bizarre stuff, and I guess I would expect you to be a little more hesitant. It sounds like you're ready to jump right in. Maybe you should hold off—maybe you should just get a visa to anywhere you can and get the hell out of there. Quit your job and just leave. Go anywhere."

"Bruce, what are you saying? I can't just leave—I mean, I would love to quit my job, but the rest of my life . . . I couldn't just walk out."

"Why not?"

"Because—because I have responsibilities, that's why."

"What could be so important that you'd allow yourself to be put in danger?"

The dignity of having something meaningful to do flashed into her brain. *The adrenaline of doing it. Abraham Prives. And maybe a lot of other little boys.*

But she didn't say any of those things aloud. "First of all, I don't know that I'm really in any danger."

"A man is dead, and your house was broken into. A charming stranger shows up—who happens to be about the same age as your departed child, which of course will pull on your heartstrings—and tries to convince you to do something that reeks of illegality. That's danger."

"I'll be all right, I can take care of myself—"

"And what about us? If you get into trouble, if you have problems, those things happen to both of us. We may never be able to work it all out so we can be together . . . is that what you want?"

She thought her concern for their eventual reunion was a given, something he knew she would always pursue. How could he think it wasn't important to her? It chafed at her that he'd even brought it up.

"No, of course not," she said after a pause. "But what about my responsibility to myself? I think this might be something I want to do. It feels—important."

"I know. You hate your job. I understand that. But you know it's just temporary, until things get back to normal."

"Which is not likely to happen anytime soon."

"Janie, please, don't do this."

"Bruce—please don't ask me *not* to. It's going to stick in my craw. It already is."

She heard him sigh. She was almost glad she couldn't see him.

"Did Tom leave you the note I asked him to?"

"He did."

"Well, I meant it. I love you, and I just want what's best for both of us."

After they disconnected, she crumpled up the note and tossed it in the recycling bin. It was time to settle some affairs.

Her first call was to the Hebrew Book Depository. Myra Ross was only too happy to hear from her. "I'll keep my schedule clear," the curator said. "Call me as soon as you have the journal back." Then she added, in an excited tone of voice, "This is wonderful. Just wonderful. I'll look forward to hearing from you."

She expended precious gas on a drive to Tom's office, after calling to be sure he would be there. She took with her a pouch of personal items, mostly from her jewelry box: the engagement ring that her now-deceased husband had given her, some inexpensive but very precious pieces of jewelry that her mother had left behind when she too fell to DR SAM. Her grandmother's silver service. A small paper envelope full of Betsy's baby teeth and a lock of the little girl's golden hair. Another data disk, this one with digital copies of her entire photo album and home video collection, which chronicled her life before things went bad.

"I'm gonna need a bigger safe if you keep bringing things in here," Tom told her when she arrived. "Maybe you should just move in."

"Hey, if I thought I could fit in that safe, I might consider it. Listen, Tom, is my will up-to-date?"

"Of course. We did it three months ago."

"Oh. Right. I forgot."

Concern crept onto Tom's face. "Well, you have had a lot on your mind lately, but you're not usually forgetful, especially about things like that, so I guess I have to say I'm wondering . . ."

His comment made her think of Kristina Warger, with her temporary memory lapse.

Maybe it was something contagious.

"And you have copies of my insurance policies?"

His expression darkened even further. "Is there something I should know that you're not telling me? You talked yesterday about needing to tell me some things. I have time right now."

She looked at him for a brief moment, and wondered if she should tell him about her morning encounter. She'd trusted him with everything; why not this? "No," she finally said, though it made her feel sad somehow to utter the word. "It turned out to be nothing. It was just fatigue. My imagination gets out of hand sometimes." She smiled. "You know that. It's just that the other night scared me. I don't want to lose the things that are important to me. Sometimes I think they're all I'm going to have when I get older. *If* I get older."

"Are you being just a bit alarmist, maybe?"

"No," she said firmly. "I don't think so."

Janie left her car parked near Tom's office and took a cab. The fare was expensive, but seemed almost trivial in view of her sudden sense that everything in her life, including the journal, was exposed and up for grabs. She was very happy when the cab pulled up right outside the door of the book depository, leaving her only a few steps to traverse with her precious cargo.

A car with dark-tinted windows pulled into the parking lot as she was alighting from the cab, then slid neatly into a space between two other cars. She stood there and watched, expecting the driver to get out. But no one did. She remained on the spot for a second with the padded envelope clutched to her chest.

It's nothing. She managed to convince herself that it was only heightened sensitivity, a natural state of mind in view of her last few days, and it was bound to give way to unnecessary paranoia. But as she negotiated the short distance to the safety of the depository's front door, her steps were swift. She checked in immediately at the security desk and was sent directly to the reception area where Mrs. Ross would be waiting for her.

"Let's go into one of the workrooms, shall we?" the curator said when she appeared.

Janie nodded and walked obediently down a long hallway at Myra's side. Her eyes darted all around, into every doorway they passed.

"Are you okay?" Myra asked. "You seem a little rattled by something."

It shows, then. "I'm okay," Janie said. She made a conscious effort to calm herself. "I was just nervous bringing the journal here."

Myra glanced at the tightly clutched package in Janie's arms and smiled with almost maternal reassurance. "That's understandable," she said.

After a few steps more, she stopped and gestured toward a room off to the right. "Here we are."

She led Janie into a large room. The light pouring in from a bank of skylights overhead was bright but indirect, without clearly defined rays. There was minimal furniture in the room, all of it functional. She laid her package down on the central table and pushed it slowly in Myra's direction.

"We use this space for restoration and repair projects," Myra said. "It's wonderfully equipped." Then with a look of excitement that Janie thought was limited to small children, Myra pulled the unadorned envelope toward her and undid the clasp. "Plain brown wrapper," she said with a little laugh. "You'd think it was a report of some sort, or something equally numbing. Not a treasure."

Myra found a pair of latex gloves in a drawer beneath the counter and put them on, arranging each finger just so in what appeared to Janie to be a practiced ritual of examination, something the curator might do for any new item that came in. She slid the journal carefully out of its brown sleeve and placed it flat on the table directly in front of her, then opened the cover carefully and looked at the first page.

"Oh, my," she said quietly.

Janie thought she saw the film of tears in the curator's eyes. "I thought I was the only one who got misty over stuff like this," she said.

"Oh, I'm hopeless," Myra said. "I get terribly emotional over rare items. I will tell you, though, it's been a while since I actually cried over a new piece." She sniffed lightly. "If this is what you claim it is, and at first glance it looks very real, then this"—she swept her hand through the air over the journal as if she were blessing it—"is nothing short of magnificent."

She let her gaze fall onto the page again. "Alejandro Canches," she said aloud. "Spanish. That was a relatively common surname. But it's an unusual first name for a Jew of that century."

"I know very little about that period in history, only what I've read since I acquired the journal," Janie told her. "I've been trying to understand the context of the times, but it's difficult . . . and most of the journal isn't about his life in Spain, it's about his studies in France and his later journeys. That part I've been able to translate for myself. I got a lot of help from scholars of archaic French I found on the EdNet. It's the stuff at the very beginning, the stuff in Hebrew, that's really got me stumped."

She paused, for a brief moment, hoping Myra would say *Oh, don't worry, dear, I can read it.* But the curator remained quiet.

"Can you tell me what it says?" she finally said.

Myra scanned the Hebrew text briefly, and then sighed. There was a hint of frustration in it. "I can't. Not without a huge amount of effort, anyway. It's not going to be impossible to get it translated, but I have to tell you that there aren't tons of people who will be able to do it. But there are some people I can contact."

"That would be wonderful," Janie said. "Really wonderful."

"It might take time."

"I understand."

Myra spent a few moments examining the outer binding. She turned the journal on its end and looked at the spine, then flipped it over and looked at the back. "Hmm," she said as she righted it again, "Something is rather odd here. Probably not something you'd notice, but . . ."

Janie almost chuckled. "There are lots of things I don't notice. What specifically do you mean?"

"Well, I think it's been rearranged. The pages, I mean. In fact, I'm almost certain it has been, unless it's a forgery, which even from this quick glance I don't think it is." She turned to the back of the book and looked at the most recent, English language entries for a quick moment. "The Hebrew should have been back here. We start our books on the right side." She turned back to the beginning again and studied the lettering for a moment. "These pages aren't in the order I'd expect to find them in. So this journal has been taken apart and rebound at some point in time."

She opened a drawer and pulled out a metal pointer. She ran the tip of it along a barely visible seam in the leather. "Look. Right here. It's been resewn."

"My goodness . . ."

"Oh, it doesn't diminish the book's worth or value, it's just strange, that's all. I guess it must have offended someone's sense of order terribly to have that Hebrew at the back. It would have to have been a non-Jew who did it."

"I can't say for sure," Janie said tentatively, "but I don't think any of the people who had it after Alejandro were Jews. Best I can figure, they were all English and, oddly enough, until the very last one before me they were all women."

While carefully turning a parchment page, Myra gave Janie a suspicious look. "There must be a story behind this."

Janie sighed and stayed quiet for a moment. "You can read it for yourself. But I will tell you that Alejandro Canches was basically a fugitive. He studied medicine in France."

"Montpelier, no doubt."

"Yes! How did you *know*?"

"It would have been just about the only place that would let him attend."

"Oh," Janie said, rather humbly, "I didn't think of that."

"You'd have no reason to. Anyway, go on."

"He had to run clear across Europe because he killed a bishop."

"Oh, dear . . . not a good thing for a Jew to do." Then a little smile snuck onto Myra's face. "But I'd venture a guess that he probably had a good reason."

"He did. And in his later writings, at least, he comes across as a very thoughtful and serious man. He doesn't strike me as the kind of man would do such a thing lightly."

With a slightly pensive look, Myra said, "No one does such things lightly. No one sane, that is. But you're speaking of him in the present tense. As if he were still alive."

Janie's expression turned wistful. "For me, he is. Very much alive. Which is part of why I feel so compelled to make sure he stays alive in here." She touched the cover of the journal. "And in here." She touched her chest above the heart. After a brief silence, she said, "You know, he probably just turned the book around and started all over again in French at the beginning. Nobody would have seen the Hebrew at the back if he did."

"Probably not," Myra agreed, "not unless they were specifically looking for it." She turned another page with almost excruciating care. "His handwriting is gorgeous. So elegant."

"I have a feeling that everything about him was elegant."

Myra smiled. "You say this journal dates from when?"

"The worst year of the Black Death, 1348."

"Then you may be romanticizing him just a bit. He was probably not the swashbuckling hero you'd imagine him to be. He probably did a lot of things to survive that wouldn't have sat well with you. But those were his times. We have it easier now."

Janie gazed reflectively at the journal, then looked up at Myra. "Do we? Somehow living in a time like that appeals to me. We're all so—suppressed now, by our government, our circumstances . . ."

"My dear," Myra said, "forgive me, but you don't begin to know what suppression is. And I hope you never learn." She picked up the journal and slipped it carefully back into the envelope. "Look, I'm going to have to take a better look at this beauty—and there are a couple of people whose brains I want to pick, but they're usually pretty available so it probably won't be more than a couple of days before I can get back to you with more information. The translations may take a bit longer. But in the meantime, I'm going to put an insurance binder on it for two hundred fifty thousand dollars."

Janie almost gasped. "Wow," she said.

The look of surprise on Janie's face made Myra chuckle. "What did you think a manuscript of this sort would be worth?"

"I had no idea. But not that much. Maybe I should have a couple of my thug friends come in and steal it."

Myra paused and gave her a pointed look. "They would probably not enjoy the reaction of our security system."

"I'm sorry, that was a stupid thing to say, even in jest." She laughed, a bit nervously. "I guess I'm a little unsettled by that figure. This other information—what exactly are you talking about?"

"Oh, there can be so many variables on an item like this—where the parchment was made, maybe who the original binder was, what types of ink were used, that sort of thing."

"Not stuff I would lose sleep wondering about," Janie said.

"There are people who do, believe it or not."

"Oh, I believe you. Now, if you could just show me what Alejandro looked like . . ."

"I'm afraid that's not our bailiwick here," Myra said. "You'll have to get someone else to do that."

W here cool moonbeams had poured through the open window the night before, the hot light of the sun now streamed
in. It burned the skin of Kate's exposed arm, enough to
wake her. She opened her eyes and peered up through the window, and
saw that the sun was already high in the sky. And though she had slept
long, she awoke still feeling sleepy. She sat up very slowly and looked
around.

Karle's clothing was no longer stuffed into the corner, and she wondered how he had found the wherewithal to put it all on again, in view of
its rank condition. She stood carefully, adjusting herself slowly to the
vertical state, and slipped her blouse and skirt over her thin white shift.
The once white garment was now gray with grime and spotted from
travel. *A good scrubbing and a few hours of hanging in the sun would do it
wonders* was her wishful thought as she smoothed her hair with her
fingers. But the time to do such things seemed a luxury, never mind the
heated water, the basin, and the soap.

There was a bit of water left from the night before in the pitcher; it was
tepid, but when she splashed it on her face some of her lingering sleepi-
ness went away. Her stomach growled out a hungry order to find sustenance, which she obeyed by going downstairs to the main floor.

At the table in the comfortable salon she saw both Etienne Marcel and
Guillaume Karle bent intently over what looked to be maps. They were

hard at the business of revolt, she assumed, but looked more to be men of numbers, for both were freshly shaved and neat-haired, and looked to be about the king's business, not rebels against it. And to her great surprise, Karle was attired in clean garments. *Likely borrowed from Marcel.* The notion struck her not without amusement; the two were of a height, but Marcel was a good deal more portly, a rounder, older man and far more worn. Karle was lean and well muscled, and she admitted to herself with vague irritation, rather shapely. *Well, no matter if the garments hang on him,* she thought with relief. *At least they will not smell.*

"*Bonjour,*" she said quietly, and they looked up at her.

"Ah! *Mademoiselle!*" Marcel said with a wry grin. He rose slightly from his chair and nodded politely in her direction. "You slept so soundly, Marie was frightened that you might have gone to meet your God. I am relieved to see that you have not. In anticipation of this we saved you some of the morning's bread. Go down to the kitchen, and you shall find her there. She will feed you." And then he looked back down at his work, an act of cursory dismissal.

She turned her gaze to Guillaume Karle, who nodded like Marcel had with appropriate courtesy. But his expression revealed the barest hint of a grin, as if there was some undefined intimacy to be accounted for. Suddenly uncomfortable, she gave back a thin smile and retreated to the kitchen.

The kitchen smelled slightly of lye, and Kate had to pick her way through Guillaume Karle's wet, hanging clothes to find the servant Marie, who promptly and indignantly said, "He meant to wear them again in this house. I would not allow it."

"This is great wisdom," Kate said. She took hold of one shirtsleeve and brought it to her nose. Beyond the harsh smell of the soap, she detected the scent of lavender. Karle would certainly not care if his clothes were scented; Kate wondered if the servant had added it to the washwater with the idea that it would please his companion, namely herself. Did they give the appearance of association? *That* kind of association? She dared not ask. "You have worked miracles," she said. "And though the 'gentleman' may not notice your skill, *I* have. *Merci.* Now *Monsieur* Marcel brazenly assured me I would find some bread in your keeping," she said.

The servant nodded and pulled a small loaf out of a basket.

Kate accepted it eagerly. She ran the loaf under her nose and drew in its savory aroma. "How have you come by such fine wheat?"

"*Monsieur* has his allies," the servant answered with a shrug. "I do not ask who they are. I simply take what *madame* gives me to run the *maison.*"

"And is *madame* about the house at present?"

"*Mais non, mademoiselle. Monsieur* has sent her away for her own protection. To the south, to stay with her *maman.*"

"You did not accompany her?"

The girl's eyes twinkled coquettishly. "Of course not. Who would look after the needs of *Monsieur le Provoste?*"

Who indeed? Kate wondered. The bread in her hands was still slightly warm; she broke off a small chunk and popped it into her mouth. It was not the coarse, grainy bread of the peasantry, but a golden loaf made expertly of fine, light flour, a difficult and expensive acquisition even in times of peace. Her amazement only increased when the servant reached into a cupboard and retrieved a beautiful ripe plum. She handed it over with a grin, and Kate whispered softly, "*Mon dieu.* How lovely."

She sat on a stool in the cool cellar kitchen and ate her treasures with the relish of one familiar with such delights, but long deprived of their pleasure. Then after a long drink of water and an effusive expression of gratitude to her benefactress, she went back upstairs to join the men.

She found them scheming quite vigorously, having apparently come to some understanding over the previous night's drunken differences. She overheard Marcel's words as she came within earshot.

"There is a distinct lack of clarity about the alliances."

She watched the provost's finger move on the map. "Everyone is scattered," he continued, "both our allies and our enemies. Navarre is here, at the Château de Coucy, where the baron has made him welcome."

I know this name of Coucy, she realized. She searched her mind with great thoroughness. Where had it been said?

In my father's Court. She stepped closer.

And when she did, Marcel reacted with disapproval. He said nothing, but glared at Karle, as if silently demanding that Karle do something about her presence.

Kate did not wait for Karle to react, but moved closer still and stood behind him. She peered over his shoulder with interest.

Marcel's eyes narrowed suspiciously. "She reads maps?" he said pointedly to Karle.

Guillaume Karle began to look nervous, and stood up. "Please excuse me for a moment, *Monsieur le Provoste.*" He took Kate by the arm and led her to another, smaller room, where they could speak privately.

"I beg you to indulge me," he said. "I must confer with Marcel while I have the chance. I do not mean to leave you alone, or besmirch your cleverness, but I'm afraid I must."

"And what am I to do with myself while you attend to these important matters?"

Karle did not have an instant response, but after a moment's thought, said, "Perhaps the maid has marketing to do. You could accompany her."

She considered the unseemly possibility that Karle had told Marcel she was *his* maid, and realized with great unhappiness that the provost was indeed treating her as if he thought that to be the case. The notion stung her with unexpected sharpness, but she kept it to herself. "What of returning to Rue des Rosiers?" she asked quietly.

"We shall go this afternoon, as soon as I am finished with Marcel."

Angry, hurt, and a bit bewildered, she agreed to leave him alone with Marcel. "Very well," she sniffed. "I shall see if the maid wants company." She turned away from him abruptly and headed toward the kitchen in a huff. Her soiled shift would get its due, after all.

It was not until after the shift had been washed and dried and was back on her body again that Guillaume Karle finally came to escort her to Rue des Rosiers.

She gathered her few possessions together and said good-bye to Marie, who had proved herself to be an amiable companion in their short time together. Marcel was otherwise occupied, so she could not thank him personally—nor was she exactly eager to do so, for there was something about him that made her spine tingle, and not in a pleasant manner. She wondered if Karle felt the same, but did not ask. Soon, when she was reunited with Père, it would not matter.

"I shall trust you to express my gratitude to him when you return," she said to Karle as they descended the stairs.

"You may count on me, *mademoiselle*," he said gallantly. "I shall not fail you."

"So you have promised, but you nearly failed me this afternoon," she said. "I had begun to believe that you would not be able to tear yourself away from your rebel comrade."

"We are not rebels at the moment. Only schemers to rebellion." But his expression was filled with hope and excitement. "Marcel believes that if we ally ourselves temporarily with Navarre, the king's forces may be defeated."

"But—Navarre is a monster! Do you think it possible to trust him?"

"I do not know. But I think it necessary for me to give it a good deal of thought."

She could hear the uncertainty in his voice, and thought to herself that he was right to be hesitant. But he had been led into consideration of this strange alliance by a shrewd statesman, a politician with great persuasive skills, for whom he was probably no match in diplomacy.

Perhaps I should try to dissuade him from this path. It can lead nowhere good.

"Karle, I was thinking . . ." she started to say.

"What?"

"Oh . . . nothing. It is not important." For soon, when she rejoined Père, it would be no concern of hers at all. Very quietly, she said, "I just wanted to say that I wish you good fortune in this endeavor. And I thank you for coming for me." Then she turned their discourse in a different direction. "And it was not a minute too soon! Marie is a pleasant companion, but her chatter—*madame* this and *monsieur* that! One fears the poor thing knows naught beyond that which she has seen within those walls. I should *die* were that to be my lot."

"Then be grateful that God has not ordained such a life for you, and that you know something beyond servitude. But consider this: Marie has a decent home, a belly that is regularly full, and a *sou* or two to call her own. Few outside the walls of Paris can claim that. Few inside, for that matter. And Marcel has made certain that she enjoys a certain amount of liberty, in keeping with his philosophy. Often there are people of great influence in his home. Perhaps he wishes to set a proper example by showing them how one ought to treat a servant."

He admires this Marcel overly much, she thought suddenly, her concern renewed. *It colors his thinking.* "Still, he keeps her a servant."

"That is true. Her liberty is restricted. And you, lady, enjoy a greater gift of liberty than she."

Such liberty as it is. But she felt briefly shamed, for she knew he spoke the truth. "I *am* grateful for what God has given me. But He has been whimsical in His gifts. He gives, He takes, He toys with me, I think."

"You are no more or less God's plaything than any other mortal soul on this earth."

She slowed her pace, then came to a halt and stared at him. "Oh, yes, Karle, I am. God has played most enthusiastically with me. And with Père. More than you can ever know."

He stared back at her, his eyes burning with curiosity. "I beseech you to tell me how."

His interest seemed so genuine; she was tempted to reveal it all to him. It would be such a relief to be able to speak freely of her life; to confide the complete truth to someone other than Alejandro was a blessing she had not known since her earliest childhood. But it was not a decision that was entirely hers. *Père will want to speak to this notion,* she thought. "I . . . *do* want to, Karle, but I must speak with my *père* first."

He was curious to the point of distraction, but even more than that, Karle was realizing his own unhappiness that Alejandro would soon reclaim Kate, her company, her devotion, her full and loving attention. Her mere presence at his side had become a comfort to him, and for the briefest moment he wished with all his heart to shake off the responsibilities that had fallen to him, to return to simple manhood, to leave the bloodshed behind. To once again be ordinary, and live an ordinary life, with all its trials and pains and momentary joys. *Here, at my side, though she is barely more than a girl, is one whose company would make an ordinary life noble! Truly, this is fortune!*

But soon she would be gone. With every step toward the meeting place the thought of her impending departure from his side became more troubling to him. Rue des Rosiers was only a short distance away when he finally found the courage to take her by the arm and draw her to a stop. "I know you are impatient to proceed, but I would speak to you of a certain matter before we arrive at the meeting place," he said. "It would please me greatly to know that I might find you again when all of this madness is over." Then quietly, he added, "If you would agree, that is, to be found."

Their eyes met momentarily and then Kate looked away. Even in the dim light her cheeks glowed red. "I should also be pleased," she whispered.

"What might your *père* say to the notion of you staying with me?"

Surprise took over her expression. "Only myself?"

"No," Karle explained quickly. "I meant both of you, of course."

She was filled with strange and unfamiliar emotions: hope, excitement, anticipation. But it was all colored by the reality of their plight. "I have no idea what he should say to such a plan. If you mean to make us soldiers in your cause, he is likely not to agree. But he must speak for himself, as he no doubt will if you propose this."

Karle took hold of one of her hands. In contrast to his own, it was small and delicate. With far more confidence than he felt, he said, "And *you* have no objection to my speaking to him on this matter?"

"No, Karle, I . . . I . . . think I would welcome it."

He pressed his inquiry to where he had hoped it would finally lead. "And were you to speak for yourself, what should your answer be?"

"It would be yes."

The undisguised happiness on his face surprised her.

"But I must consider what Père wants," she quickly added.

"A physician would be very useful in our cause."

"He wants no part of war, I assure you."

"A midwife, then? I have seen what you can do."

She gave him a small smile. "There is much for me yet to learn. But I would try to make myself useful."

"I have seen how useful you can be," he said. "But were you only to stand beside me, with no purpose other than the comfort of your presence, you would be the most worthy and welcome comrade."

And they walked on, their affection finally, if clumsily, declared.

In the small room to which de Chauliac had relegated him, Alejandro passed his first full day of captivity in comfortable solitude. Outside the door stood the ever-present guards, two stalwart soldiers who never said one word between them, but silently and stoically kept vigil. Alejandro had no doubt that should he attempt anything untoward, they would break their silence and fall upon him in an instant. But while he was well behaved, they left him alone.

The attic room was by no means unpleasant. There was air enough, and light, and the ceilings were freshly whitewashed, so when light came in through the window it bounced off the sloped surfaces and gave the small space a pleasing, warm glow. His captor had been good enough to provide him with a wonderful diversion—a recently acquired manuscript of a Greek tragedy, a rare and precious thing, for which Alejandro felt the most conflicted gratitude. He wondered at de Chauliac's eagerness to see to his contentment, amply demonstrated by his tender of the valuable Greek book. And though the younger physician's Greek was old and ill-used, for his father had disapproved of its acquisition, he recalled enough to find the small book thoroughly engrossing. But however compelling, the book's entertainment did little to dispel the constant and gnawing worry that he had made a bad choice in putting Kate into the keeping of Guillaume Karle.

I will kill him with my own hands if she suffers in any way, he thought. *He himself will suffer like no Christian has ever suffered before.*

He heard the soft rustle of robes and approaching footsteps, and looked up to see de Chauliac standing in the doorway of his small room.

"Good day, colleague," the stately Frenchman said with a nod of his head. "How are you faring on this lovely afternoon?"

The physician regarded his host with cool resentment. "Well enough, considering my captivity."

"I would have you think of yourself as a guest in my home." He made a thin-lipped smile. "One without the means to leave just yet."

"Your hospitality is remarkable, colleague, more so in view of the times. But I don't suppose I need to tell you that I would sooner be miserable in freedom than your pampered captive."

"Perhaps you would do well to consider that you might be my *miserable* captive," de Chauliac said with a wry smile.

He stood slowly and faced his keeper. "I am not fool enough to have missed that possibility."

De Chauliac laughed. "I do not consider you any sort of fool, my friend."

"You flatter me unnecessarily, de Chauliac. You need not be insincere. We are not friends. If that is what you consider us to be, then you define friendship far more loosely than I. Friends do not keep each other in chains."

"Please, Alejandro," the captor said, "you are *not* in chains."

"But I am unlikely to be leaving you anytime soon."

"I simply cannot allow you to leave without first enjoying the full benefits of your visit." He joined Alejandro at the window. "You see, I have much planned for you. There are many things we need to speak about, and I have craved such an opportunity for a very long time. Many years, in fact. And you must not think that your stay here will be unfruitful. Tomorrow we shall enjoy the company of some illustrious guests. I have arranged an evening's entertainment for us as I told you I would. I think you will find the company both delightful and inspiring."

"I prefer to choose my own company," Alejandro replied frostily. "And does it not concern you that my true identity may be discovered? Someone may take me away—and then you shall have no one to toy with."

De Chauliac stared at him with eyes of blue ice, and when he spoke his voice was measured and controlled. "I assure you, colleague, I am not toying with you. Just yet. Be certain that you shall know it when I do."

Alejandro flung back his own daggers. "While I wait for that, perhaps you would be good enough to return my manuscript to me. There is much work yet for me to do on it. And though I am delighted with the Greek, I feel as though I might accomplish something more useful in this time. Until you have decided what you will do with me, that is."

De Chauliac was quiet, nearly expressionless; Alejandro tried desperately to read his captor's emotions. He saw tamped-down anger, certainly, and doubt over what ought to be done. But there was something more, something less expected. De Chauliac looked hurt. After a few moments of silence, his host finally said, "I suppose it would be acceptable for you to have it back, if it will keep you profitably occupied."

Alejandro curtly nodded his thanks.

"Until tomorrow, then," the Frenchman said as he departed.

Alejandro turned wordlessly away from him and stared out the window. *Tomorrow?* he thought. *Tomorrow I will not be here.*

Kate fought off confused tears until they had almost reached Pillar House again, but as she and Karle rounded the last corner she was finally overtaken by them. He had intended to lead her toward the front door, but when he saw the glow of light coming from the salon window he decided instead to take her in through the kitchen.

The servant Marie opened the door for them. "What is this, you are back?"

Kate's tears poured out of her. With an effusion of sisterly clucking, Marie drew the weeping *mademoiselle* inside. Glaring at Karle, she led Kate away to a stool, where she made her sit. The servant stared at the Frenchman with a look of terrible accusation on her face, then cooed at Kate, "What has he done to you, this beast of a man?"

Though he tried to protest his innocence in the matter, Marie promptly banished him from the kitchen. "Go join your men," she said angrily. "They are upstairs, planning even more cunning ways to make women shed tears." Flustered, Karle obeyed her by disappearing hastily.

"Here," Marie said, "drink this." She handed Kate a goblet of strong red wine. "It will soothe the nerves. And your nerves just now seem in great need of soothing. Now tell me, has this oaf mistreated you?"

Kate hitched and sobbed pitifully. "Karle has done nothing to upset me. He has been nothing but kind and conscientious. We were to meet my *père* at a prearranged meeting place, where I was to be reunited with him. But when we came to the place where we were supposed to find him, Père was not there." She began to bawl. "And I am not completely unhappy, as I thought I would be! I am so confused! I fear that something terrible has befallen him, but I . . . I . . . ."

"Oh, hush," Marie said soothingly. "Do not speak such unholy thoughts. I am sure that he is only delayed."

"I wish I could be sure of that! Surely by now he should have found me. We made no plan beyond this meeting. But now," she wept, "I find myself wanting to stay with Karle!" She wiped away her tears. "I do not know what I ought to do. These things are so confusing."

Marie put an arm around Kate's shoulder and tried to calm her. "And upsetting—you are torn between your father and your lover, as all women are at one time or another."

"He is not my lover, but . . . but . . ."

"But you wish him to be."

"Yes! No! I do not know! Oh, how can one not know one's own heart?"

"When *does* one know one's own heart? You must simply bide your time until it reveals itself to you."

Kate gave Marie a pathetically unhappy look. "And what am I to do until then? I have no home, I cannot find my *père*, this Karle is so new to me . . ."

"Why, of course you shall stay here in *Monsieur* Marcel's house. He is a generous man and would not see you put out. And I will not allow it! He has much to occupy him these days, and with *madame* so far away, your company would be a blessing to me."

Kate attempted to protest, but the servant would not hear of it. "You shall be no bother. I daresay you might actually be helpful. After all, there are now two gentlemen in the house, and two gentlemen always seem to require the work of a hundred ladies, don't you agree? They will not admit it, though."

Kate did not admit that she had no basis on which to make such a comparison, but she did not disagree.

"I know not the habits of the younger one, but perhaps you can see to his needs as I see to those of *Monsieur* Marcel," Marie said with a teasing wink. "No doubt your gentleman would have preferred your hand in the washing of his disgusting garments this morning instead of mine." Then she giggled and said, "So would I."

"But what will he think if I begin to serve him in that manner? Will he think me his—*woman*? I cannot be sure that that is what I wish to be."

"He will think how much he would miss it if you stop, and try doubly hard to please you. Now, dry your eyes and take heart, for your confusion will soon come to an end. This I promise you."

They passed what little remained of the *après-midi* in household chores and the preparation of a simple late meal. And when the gentlemen retired to the salon for another round of strategic arguing, Marie helped Kate wash her long hair. As it dried, Kate taught the servant how to play at cards, which instruction delighted the young woman, who had never enjoyed such games before.

"You have a quick aptitude," Kate observed.

"A useless one, then," Marie said. "Only those of noble station have time for such folly. Did *Monsieur* Karle teach you?" she asked, in all sincerity.

Kate answered truthfully, saying only what she could. "My mother once served a highborn lady in England," she said. *If only I could say just how highborn!* "There were many fine things she learned and thus taught me."

"I have noticed that you have fine ways about you," Marie said. "I wondered how you acquired them."

"There is much to be learned by observation," Kate offered, hoping it would suffice.

Marie laughed. "One wishes some fine wealth would come from observation."

"Do not envy the wealthy," Kate said. "They are not always the happiest of people."

"I should very much like to test this notion myself," the servant said as she laid down a card and triumphantly captured the hand. "I have little doubt that I could prove you wrong."

Suddenly the summoning bell interrupted their play. Marie immediately set down her cards and hurried up the narrow stairs. After a few moments she returned to the kitchen with a look of excitement on her face. "*Monsieur le Provoste* needs a message to be sent. He would not send me alone, but he says since there are two of us, we will be safe. That is, if you wish to accompany me. It could wait until morning, but I would like a bit of air. It is but a short walk."

The look of concern on Guillaume Karle's face when she left the house lingered deliciously in Kate's mind as she and Marie headed toward their destination. His obvious worry was strangely satisfying to her; she might have felt slighted had he not exhibited some discomfort at having her out of his sight, however momentarily.

The amber-haired Frenchman had occupied her thoughts almost exclusively since their earlier exchange of—what should she call it—endearments? *No; too strong a word yet.* Devotion? *He is devoted to his cause far more than he will ever be to me, or to anyone,* she thought. It would have to be a softer word. *Admiration,* she decided, would best describe what had been expressed between them.

She wondered what Alejandro would think of her admiration for Karle—he had already trusted the Frenchman enough to put her in his care, but that was an act of near desperation against a wager that should have gone the other way. Given time, would he think him brave, and intelligent, and spirited, as she herself did? Even he could not deny that it was only natural for her to attach herself to a strong man who would look after her. It was prudent and sensible.

How long would it be before passion overtook her sensibility?

These thoughts engaged her so completely that she barely heard any of what the chatty Marie had to say as they progressed on their route. It was too dark to take in the wonders of the city, now tarnished by anarchy but still thoroughly marvelous; and before she knew it, they were inside a cobblestoned courtyard, standing in front of a massive wooden door.

"Bonsoir," Marie said to the servant who answered their knock. "We bring a message for your master." She handed a small folded parchment to the man. "We are to bring back a reply, if possible."

The manservant said, "Wait here, please."

"Will you not invite us in?" Marie asked boldly.

The servant seemed slightly distressed by the question and looked back into the house over his shoulder. His reticence piqued Kate's curiosity and she tried, without attracting too much notice, to peer around him while he was engaged in an exchange with Marie. But there was little she could see, for most of the house was dark. *Even the rich do not waste candles these days,* she thought. Behind the servant was a large reception area that gave way to what she thought were several other rooms or passageways. Most were dark and unoccupied, except one, which glowed with soft illumination. *The salon,* she decided by her brief glimpse of its furnishings. Two guards stood stoic vigil outside the lit room. They stared straight ahead and paid no attention to the curious visitors leering from the door.

She heard no sound from the glowing room, no conversation or movement, and it occurred to her that someone in that room might be reading or studying something. Kate found herself drawn to the soft light like a moth, and strained to catch a glimpse beyond the manservant in the doorway. Marie was still trying to convince the entrenched valet to let them cross the threshold—without much luck. But it was not for lack of trying that they were not allowed to enter.

"I think perhaps you should wait here," the manservant finally said. "I have heard enough persuasion." He said it with an odd smile, then closed the door and disappeared with the message.

As she stared at the sturdy wood planks that now filled her view, Kate considered the irony of it: *I am a king's daughter. A servant has just closed a door in my face.*

She did not have long to ponder that absurdity, for in a short while the door opened again. When she looked beyond the servant this time, she saw that the previously illuminated room was now dark and the guards were gone.

Very suddenly, she thought. *Why?*

There would be no answer. The servant handed Marie the same parchment, refolded once again. "Give this to Marcel," he said.

"*Très bien, monsieur,*" Marie said. "*Bonsoir, et merci.*"

And with a small curtsy, she turned. Kate lingered a brief moment longer, hoping for another look inside. Finally Marie took her by the arm and pulled her along.

From his small barred window, Alejandro looked out to the street below. He peered intently into the velvety Paris darkness, hoping for some sight of the unexpected visitors that had been the cause of his sudden upstairs banishment. He spoke aloud, to stay in the habit of it, and did not care if his guards thought him odd. *Let them. They despise me already for being a Jew; let them also think me insane.* "Tomorrow," he whispered aloud, "he will put me on display to his chosen guests, yet tonight he does not wish these strangers to see me here."

He heard the creaking of the heavy gate, and the footsteps of the departing visitors. He saw two figures emerge from the courtyard door, and understood why the steps had sounded so light. *They are women,* he realized when he saw their shapes. *One very tall, like my Kate.* His heart ached with the thought of her.

The visitors disappeared into the darkness, and as they faded from his vision he felt a desperate wish for the simplest contact with them, for even the smallest exchange of words so that he might prove to himself that he was not dreaming his hated isolation. To change places with one or the other of them, even for a moment, would be the most wonderful blessing he could imagine.

Right now, he mused sadly, *I would even consider being a woman, should freedom come with such a condition.*

* * *

They came into the house through the servants' door to the kitchen, as Kate and Karle had done the night before. *"Monsieur* said he would have many gentlemen about tonight," Marie told Kate. "They are discussing their war again. He does not wish to be interrupted. Nor have I any wish to be disturbed by their silly demands for service. Do *this,* Marie! Then do *that,* Marie! So we shall not let them know we are back just yet, eh?"

Karle will be among them, Kate thought. She surprised herself with a sharp pang of disappointment that she would not have him to herself.

The expected din of male voices floated down the cellar stairs as Kate and Marie passed time again at cards. The words were garbled by distance and walls and were therefore unintelligible, but the excitement of the discussion was clear and its urgency unmistakable.

"They love this war," Marie said with a sad shake of her head.

"Only those who have not seen it firsthand," Kate countered. "This war is too cruel to be imagined." A quick silent recollection of some of the horrors she and Karle had witnessed in their journey to Paris flashed through her mind, numbing her. The remembered atrocities came back too vividly and weighed heavily on her soul. She felt her spirit sink, and fatigue settled onto her like a cloak of wet wool. "Suddenly I am very tired," she said. "I would like to go to bed."

"Shall you sleep upstairs again?" Marie asked, one eyebrow arched in curiosity.

Kate sat quietly for a moment, then folded her hand of cards. "Is there another room?"

"No, but a pallet could be laid here in the kitchen for you, if you like. Sometimes I sleep here myself, although it remains unknown where I shall be tonight." She winked and laughed. "In any case, you are welcome. But it would not have the comforts of the straw bed."

Comfort was something she needed desperately this night, whatever its shape. "Then I think I shall go upstairs."

"Comfort it is, then," Marie said. *"Monsieur* would not mind if you took some wine before going to bed. He himself almost always does so. He says that it improves his—how shall one describe it? His *temperament.* Perhaps it will improve your . . . repose."

"If so, then it would be a most welcome potion."

Marie quickly found the goblet and flagon and poured out a good dose of the dark red stuff for Kate. Then she splashed a few sips into a smaller mug, which she raised in toast. "May you find great and gentle comfort in your bed tonight."

Indeed, Kate thought, and downed her wine.

* * *

The gathered leaders of Paris stilled their voices and watched as she passed quickly and quietly by them, her head bowed and her eyes lowered. It was something the men of King Edward's Court had never done. But then she had been an annoying child, not the lissome, golden-haired object of desire she had grown into. She could feel the eyes of the unfamiliar men burning into her as she quietly rounded the staircase and padded up the stairs. And one by one, she felt the burn fade away as their unspoken fantasies dissipated, unfulfilled, and each of the salon's occupants turned his attention back to the cause at hand. Their voices rose again, and their utterances were filled with the words of war. Though the tone was now more muted, it was certainly no less enthusiastic.

But as she disappeared into the small upstairs hallway, the presence of Karle's gaze still lingered. She felt it like a hand on her back and it stayed with her as she shed her outer garments and lay down on the straw. And as the wine drew her into sleep, she imagined that hand warm and firm on the small of her back, even in her dreams.

She awoke later to find him kneeling at her side in the darkness, his real hand where she'd imagined it to be, the fingers working soft circles into the flesh of her waist. She opened her eyes and saw him looking at her, his face full of uncertainty.

How could he think I might not want him? she wondered dreamily. She took hold of his hand and brought it to her lips, and kissed it gently. The palm was rough and callused from sword and rein. And then she drew him to her. He came willingly, a great and gentle comforter, and wrapped himself around her. They declared their mutual affection, quite unsensibly.

Alejandro awoke with a jolt of fear from a disturbing dream, and struggled desperately to throw off the haze of terror that had overtaken him. But the cold fingers of fear would not be loosed, and gripped his belly with unshakable resolve. The thought that his nightly terrors, finally conquered after so many years, might return, filled him with a haunting, overwhelming dread. "Ah, Carlos Alderón," he whispered into the night air, "have you come back again? Please," he begged the shade who had haunted him for such a long time, "leave me to enjoy what little peace I have."

But as he searched his brain for the memory of the night's dream, he realized that it was not the ghost of the blacksmith who had marched angrily through his sleep. It was Kate, not her ghost, but the living image of the girl herself, who had made the macabre visit to his psyche. And unlike his former dreams of Carlos Alderón, in this new midnight ride it was not the shrouded blacksmith who gave chase, but Alejandro himself, and the prey, to his horror, was his daughter. But she would not be caught, and instead slipped past him at a seemingly impossible speed. He called her name aloud and reached out to grab her, but his hand came up short of her skirts, and she sped away, out of his reach, beyond his control, a woman quite apart.

With the journal safely stashed at the depository and her personal treasures seen to, Janie felt a bit less vulnerable. Thus freed, she set out on a new journey, the one Kristina Warger had so temptingly laid out before her.

Her first step was to contact the new owners of Camp Meir.

"We took it over from the previous owners two years after the first Outbreak," Jason Davis told her when she called. "We went there as kids ourselves, my brother and I."

"Is your brother also involved in the operation of the place?" Janie asked.

"He probably would be, if he were still with us. It was my wife and I who bought it."

She should have known better. "I'm sorry. I guess I didn't do my homework very well."

"We've all lost someone, Dr. Crowe. I'm not offended. Anyway, my mother and father thought it was a terribly important thing for us to go there, that it helped to shape us as young men, so I used some of the money from their estate toward the purchase. The price was very good at the time. It seemed a shame that no one was keeping it going, and I thought it was a fitting memorial to them. Have you ever gotten out there?"

"I haven't," Janie said. "I'd like to, though. I've been a little loose with my allotment of fuel lately. I'm trying to be careful."

"Oh. Well, unfortunately, the buses don't go out that way yet."

"Maybe that's not so unfortunate. But your Web site is very well done, and I think I got a pretty good idea of what the camp is all about."

"The physical camp, yes. It's a good representation of what the place looks like, what the facilities are—but the thing that made it really special, the thing you can't see in the pictures, was the sense of spirituality we came away with. Not religion, necessarily. The program never really focused on religion. It was something more subtle than that. Maybe—community. Something we don't seem to have much of in this world anymore. And it's grown there, believe it or not." He brought forward a fond memory and shared it with her. "My mother always said that when I went to Meir I was already a nice boy, but when I came back, I was nicer."

"Well, that's a pretty significant thing in a teenage boy," Janie said.

"Don't I know it," Davis said. "I have a teenage boy. He can be a real terror."

Of course, that teenage son would have been a camper. . . .

She figured backward. "How old is your son, Mr. Davis?"

"He's seventeen now. Though he likes to think he's thirty. I keep trying to tell him not to grow up too fast."

"Did he attend the camp before you took it over?"

"He did."

"Was he there during the summer when there was the *Giardia* scare?"

Davis seemed to hesitate slightly before answering. "That was before we owned it." He cleared his throat. "My wife and I were having some difficulties that year. She took our children up to Maine that whole summer to stay with her family. It seemed like the right thing to do at the time."

You may never know how right. "Well, kids are very adaptable."

"They are. DR SAM sort of put everything back in focus for us, and we were able to work out our differences. We're still together, I'm happy to say."

"That's really nice to hear."

"Anyway, my son went back to the camp after we bought it. I'm not sure he appreciated it the way we did. He was too busy being a boy of the new millennium. But enough of *my* fascinating story. You said you were interested in some of the old records."

It was something of a relief, finally, to get to the matter she'd contacted him about, not that she found Outbreak nostalgia disturbing—it had become almost a part of the new etiquette to trade stories, almost as a greeting. "Yes, but from before your ownership, during the summer when there was the *Giardia* scare. I'm involved in the care of one of your former campers, a young man by the name of Abraham Prives. He had an unfortunate accident and I'm—working with his mother."

"What happened to him?"

"He collided with another boy while playing soccer and suffered a severe spinal break."

There was complete silence on the other end of the conversation. Janie thought for a moment that they'd been thrown off the network. "Mr. Davis? Are you still there?"

"Yes," he said, after a moment of hesitation. "I am." His tone was quieter, almost pensive. "I'm just shocked, that's all. It's every parent's worst nightmare." He seemed to recover a bit, and added, "But I'm afraid I'm going to have to disappoint you, Dr. Crowe. The records from that time are very incomplete. They were kept on paper, you see, and while no one was taking care of the place, there was quite a lot of vandalism. One of the file cabinets was nearly destroyed by some squatters. We did manage to evict them eventually, but not before they had a chance to do some pretty substantial damage to the place."

She felt her stomach sink on hearing this news. "I don't understand why people behave that way."

"Neither do I."

After a long sigh, she said, "It would be extremely helpful to have a list of the boys who were treated for *Giardia*. Failing that, a list of the general population that summer would do."

"I don't know if we have either, to be quite honest with you."

"Do you have any record of who it was that made the determination of a potential *Giardia* problem?"

"I would assume it was someone from a public health agency. But I really don't know."

"And what township is the camp located in? Maybe someone involved in the local government would remember."

"The town of Burning Road. But if you don't get anywhere with them, you might try the county."

What little faith she might have had in local government was completely shattered by the time Janie finished dealing with officials from the town of Burning Road and the county in which it was seated. They would not give her anything until she filed a request using Freedom of Information Act forms.

"I want employment records showing who was working in the health department at the time, not the psychosexual history of the mayor," she said to the clerk in charge; later, she considered in a moment of regret that it might have been an unnecessarily aggressive thing to say.

But what can you do when confronted with morons, psychopaths, and mental defectives? she thought with some bitterness. And when she spoke with Kristina Warger later that night to report on the results of her first task in their joint quest, Janie felt compelled to say, "You know, some of what I did today is stuff that doesn't really require me, specifically. Why is it that *I* need to do these things, and not you, or someone else from your group?"

"Because right now we don't have anyone but me available. We're not exactly a big group. And you have more credibility than I do. You're more mature, probably a lot more adept at social things. And I remind all these people of their own children," she said. "They won't talk to me the same way they'll talk to you."

"*I'm* talking to you."

"But you're smart enough and curious enough to look beyond my youth. Most people aren't."

Indeed, Kristina's youth was part of what Janie found fascinating about her. Somewhat bemused, she said, "Which aren't they? Smart, or curious?"

"Oh, lots of people are smart. But curious . . . it's a quality you don't see enough of. People don't seem to ask questions anymore."

Anymore? Janie wanted to ask, sarcastically, if the youthful Kristina had come to this astute conclusion through a prolonged period of observation, if it was a tidbit of wisdom gathered over the span of her life. But she reserved the question for another occasion, when she might have a better handle on the girl's unusual quirks.

For the moment, she simply agreed. "I think that's a result of people getting unsavory answers for the last few years. There are lots of things we all just don't want to know. So why ask? It's completely understandable."

"And completely tragic. But there's another reason why we need you. Some of us have rather high profiles. Don't misunderstand me—you're not exactly unknown. But it would be very difficult for some of my colleagues to look into these things without raising a few eyebrows."

Colleagues? Janie wondered when young girls had started to have "colleagues." "I guess this wasn't what I expected when I signed on. I mean, I actually did take care of some loose ends in my life, but if this is what this project is going to be about, I don't think I'm going to face much in the way of danger."

"The night is young, Dr. Crowe, very young. Please don't be fooled. Now, we're going to have to take a different tack, I think. We have the list of boys who have this problem. But we don't have the camp's records, so we can't make a comparison to see if there's any overlap."

"What about that other Web site—the one about the camper who wanted to hear from other campers. Maybe he *has* heard from some. He'd have an e-mail list, maybe."

There was a momentary pause. "We could contact him, I suppose. But we'd prefer not to involve any of the children themselves in this process unless it's absolutely necessary."

"Why?"

Kristina Warger used a quiet voice when she said, "They don't react well when you tell them to put their affairs in order. But if we have to do it, we have to do it, that's all."

Michael Rosow missed the days in England when he would get up and go to work dressed in a three-piece pinstripe with the standard issue black umbrella hooked over his right arm, in the time before guns became mandatory. *Damned inconvenient,* he remembered thinking when he'd been forced to switch his umbrella to the left side to accommodate the firearm. And he'd just gotten accustomed once again to wearing a suit as one of the privileges of lieutenancy when DR SAM first emerged from Mexico, and he, along with every "expendable" British cop of any rank, was reassigned to Biopol. "Just for the duration," they'd been assured, but the duration had turned out, as they all expected it would, to be forever. Because with each little resurgence of DR SAM, the fear of the general Outbreaks happening all over again came back. Michael no longer believed that the fear would ever really dissipate among those who'd been through it.

He'd been surprised, when he transferred to U.S. Biopol, to discover that reassignment had been "voluntary" in the United States. "We had a good union," one cop had told him. "We also have a Bill of Rights," another said. "So we couldn't be forced into anything. At least at first."

You also had the slowest governmental response to the Outbreaks, and the highest death rate in the civilized world, he recalled thinking at the time.

He hated the weird, crinkly, blindingly green self-contained garments known as biosuits. And when the bullets in his sidearm were replaced by chemical pellets, he hated that even more, though he would be the first to admit that the "no blood" policy was sensible, if cumbersome to enact. But he loved the other toys associated with being a biocop with an undeniable passion, and relished using them. It had been on the screen of a bioimager that he'd first seen Caroline, and his obsession with her had been born.

So when he went to the chief investigator in the death of the assistant basketball coach and fished for details, he expected to be told about the findings of the victim's postmortem bodyprint, the contents of the bag of evidence that had been sucked up at the scene, the computerized analysis of the scene photos.

"My wife knows someone who knows the deceased," he said to his colleague, who questioned why Michael was interested. "Word is, the gent was a thoroughly decent chap. Bit of a flirt, but that's not worth getting killed for, what?"

"We'd all be dead if it was," the investigator said. "Look, I was just about to go over to the lab. The guy's going to be printed in a little while."

"That hasn't been done yet?"

The other cop glanced around nervously. "They're a little backed up," he confided. "Had a few cases come in from the outlying areas. They don't have the same kind of equipment we do."

Michael didn't ask what sort of cases the man was referring to; he almost didn't want to know.

"Hey," the other cop said suddenly, "you want to come along, see for yourself?"

"Smashing idea."

They rode over together in a Biopol van equipped with all the latest toys, and as the other cop drove, Michael examined the investigative paraphernalia with enthusiastic glee, comparing it to what he'd had in his previous post. It was all bigger, shinier, mightier, and newer than what he'd had in England.

"It's the American way, I guess, all these goodies," he said to his van-mate. "But let me tell you, in jolly old England our weaponeers are bloody top-notch. I'll just have a look-see at your little water pistols here."

He opened the weapons cache, expecting to find the usual assortment of sidearms and rifles, and a few empty slots where the chemical rifles rested in Outbreak times. But in this van those slots were filled. He stared at the weapons for a moment, recalling the last time he'd used one in England, on a hapless guard in a laboratory incident, a man who'd died unnecessarily because he happened to be in the wrong place at the wrong time. In his forebrain he could see the man clutching the back of his neck where the bullet had hit, and crumpling within seconds to the ground, his body already reacting to the poison. They were little different from the dart guns of feral tribes, but their toxic payload was delivered with guaranteed force and unfailing accuracy. And at the height of DR SAM's reign, troubling frequency.

He hadn't seen them in the near-year since he'd left England. But here they were again. He closed the cabinet and went forward to the passenger seat.

"I see you're carrying chemical rifles."

"Yep," the other cop said quietly. "They refitted all these units again a couple of days ago."

Why had he not been told? "Anyone say why?"

"No. And I didn't ask." They came to a stoplight and he looked away from the road, directly into Michael's eyes. "Tell you the truth, Lieutenant, I don't want to know. I'll just do what they tell me to do if the time comes. But until then, quite frankly, I don't want to think about it."

The light changed; they drove on in silence for the rest of the route to the forensic facility.

The silence continued as he watched the deceased's stiff body being hoisted onto the horizontal bodyprinter. Technicians seated the corpse on the lower bed of sensors with care and precision. They inserted the probes in all the appropriate places, then brought down the upper module of sensors, with its tens of thousands of receptors, each one as fluid in placement as the undulating spines of a sea urchin. There was a flash, and then another, as light and electricity were fed into the minuscule receptors, which radioed back the separate tiny images to a central computer for reorganization into a complete three-dimensional image.

"Well, it was a clean print," Michael's colleague said when the technician handed him a readout and a disk a short while later, "but on a quick glance, I'd have to say the results are pretty slim."

He handed Michael a single sheet of paper that was barely a third full. "Shame. Just when the basketball team was finally getting good again too."

Michael had expected three, maybe four sheets of data. "This is all they got?"

"Hey, it's right there, you saw them do the print. It was a solid read."

Michael frowned at the slim offering of evidence. "What about at the scene? Did you have any better luck?"

The cop shrugged. "We sucked up everything that was there. We got basically nothing."

"Bloody hell."

"My sentiments exactly. This case gets weirder by the minute." After a thoughtful pause, he said, "You know, if I didn't know better I'd say that someone got there ahead of us and sucked up all the evidence before we could. We shoulda gotten five hundred human positives from the sucker. This was a public bicycle path—how many people do you suppose biked or ran on that path and dripped a little sweat while they were at it? Christ, the President jogged on that path. I heard he sweats like a pig. But we got borscht."

"What about questioning his friends and family?"

"We did, and according to everyone I talked to, he was the all-American boy. Highly regarded at work, well liked in his apartment complex. He wasn't some right-wing nut or a pedophile, none of the things you'd look for in someone who died funny."

"Nothing collected from the exterior body search?"

"Nothing but his own signatures. No pubic hairs, no perfume residue, no dander under the fingernails. I'll tell you one thing I know about this victim, though, and it's not for public consumption."

"No, of course not," Michael said.

"Because the basketball program has an image to protect."

"Indeed. I'd never breathe a word of it."

The investigator leaned closer and whispered, "There wasn't a trace of female DNA anywhere on his person. This guy had to be a complete loser with women. Either that, or someone cleaned him up real good."

He rode back to the station in a rather contemplative state, and went immediately to his own vehicle for the drive home. There was no record of his palmbook having entered Big Dattie, for which he was grateful. Janie had done the dirty deed correctly.

Michael asked Caroline later if she'd touched the man in any way.

"We shook hands."

"*Hmm,*" he said quietly. "There wasn't one molecule of trace tissue."

Children don't react well to being told to put their affairs in order, Kristina had said, so in consideration of this rather obvious bit of wisdom, Janie refrained from acting on her first impulse, which was to contact the wheelchair-bound boy on the Internet and ask for a list of those camp alumni who'd gotten in touch with him. Instead she tried Mrs. Prives, who was as cheerfully cooperative as possible, if still somewhat distracted.

She listed what names she could remember. "I have some of the addresses at home," she told Janie, "but I keep in touch only with a couple of the other families. Abraham might have a few, but I don't know where he would keep them."

"It's all right," Janie said. The names alone would be enough. "This is a big help."

Get a new computer, she ordered herself as she looked at the short list. She could start on the desktop machine in her office, which had all the necessary sorting, collating, and evaluation capabilities, but it would be terribly frustrating to continue it there, attached as she would be by an electronic umbilicus to the foundation's servers. But the foundation's computers did have a few unique capabilities, high among them the ability to "watch" for something to fall "outside the limits of expected and tolerable variability." The first time Janie had seen that phrase, she'd fallen in love with it and made it her own. It became her new goal to find someplace "outside the limits," and it often made her sad to think how very inside she'd become in the course of solving her life's dilemmas, despite a clear and conscious opposite intent. She had been in the outside state when she'd noticed the Camp Meir boys and recognized the significance of their situation.

When she completed her manual checklist, she was able to see that without exception, all of the Camp Meir boys were on the general list of bone-shattered boys.

Well, she thought, *if there was ever really any doubt, it's been laid to rest now.*

Kristina would want to see this.

Long time no see, she e-mailed Wargirl.

Kristina showed up at Janie's home that night, just as Janie was making her own dinner of brown rice, tofu, and broccoli, though after a brief, earlier conversation with Michael she had little appetite.

Kristina, in contrast, looked positively starved. "Grab a chair," Janie told her, "there's plenty for both of us."

"Thanks," Kristina said. "I could eat twenty-four hours a day."

Janie regarded Kristina's thin frame. "Right," she said cynically.

"I can't seem to gain any weight, though."

"I know someone else like that. You both annoy the hell out of me."

"You should try having my metabolism for a day or two before you say that."

Janie had noticed that Kristina was a fidgety young woman, one with a temperament that might once have been described as "spirited" or even "nervous." She had a level of energy that seemed enviable on the surface.

But Janie wondered, as she watched Kristina eat, looking way too much like what Betsy might have looked like at that same table, how Kristina's mother had coped with a child so full of the devil as this one obviously was.

Joyfully, she decided.

"So," she said, after casting off the Betsy-spell, "we have the beginnings of a list. Abraham's mother gave me some names. I found them all on the bone-trauma list I got out of Big Dattie. Which leads me to another thought. I think you're right that we shouldn't contact the boy on the Web site. But maybe we should try his mother or father."

It was easy enough to get the phone number—he'd posted his parents' names on his site, which she'd printed and kept. And those parents, when given the *Giardia* scare story, had more names. By the time Janie was through talking with them, she had a third of the names on the list checked off.

"Well, that pretty much settles it," Kristina said as they went over the results of their evening's efforts. "I'm just surprised no one else has seen this."

"No one had a reason to look."

"So now we move to the next phase, I guess," Kristina said.

"Which would be?"

"We have to make complete files on all these boys. Then maybe when we sort the data, we'll be able to see some sort of pattern. If we can't find anyone official to tell us anything, we'll just have to see it for ourselves."

Janie looked around with a helpless expression. "I miss my computer. I'm going to have to get out and buy another one before we can do any more of this."

"Oh, goodness, I forgot," Kristina said. She got up quickly from the table. "Wait right here."

She returned from her tiny car a few moments later carrying a securely taped box that was suspicious in its absence of exterior markings. She set it down carefully on the kitchen counter.

"Is that for me?" Janie asked with mild surprise as she watched Kristina pull tape off the box.

Kristina smiled and nodded, then started pulling wads and wads of bubble wrap out of the box. And just when it began to seem that the box had to have been packed with nothing but stuffing, Janie saw her gently lift a notebook computer out. The young girl carried the small computer reverently to the table and placed it in front of her hostess.

"Dr. Crowe, meet Virtual Memorial. A little present from *us.*"

* * *

"The picture is pretty good," one of the watchers said.

"Are you sure this is the right time to give her that unit?" the other asked. "I worry that it might be too soon."

"I worry that if we don't give it to her now, we'll lose the perfect opportunity. She's like a mother hen with no eggs—if you give her an unfamiliar one, she'll sit on it just to keep herself occupied."

"Does it bother you, though, to be using someone from the outside? It does me."

"No. Not at all. In fact, I think it's wise—it creates a certain amount of insulation. I don't like having Kristina so exposed. But what does bother me, an awful lot, is that this particular woman *is* outside. She should be in here with us."

"So there must be others all across the country, then," Janie said to Kristina, "others just like me."

"And some of them," Kristina said, "the ones who are in the right places, are looking after other boys on the list, just like you are with Abraham. We have a lot of supporters across the country, mostly in positions similar to yours, where they have access to patients, the Mednet, computer systems . . . but they aren't official caregivers. Lab technicians, midlevel administrators, research people who can look in and touch base and ask questions, but don't leave unexpected footprints. But they'll be different from you in one regard."

"What's that?"

"You'll be telling them what to do."

Janie was quick to react. "No. I can't. I'm not the boss type."

Kristina stifled a little laugh. "That's not what we've heard."

"What you've *heard*?"

"Dr. Crowe. Please don't pretend you don't understand why we enlisted you. It was because we watched you and liked what we saw."

Janie spent a few silent and uncomfortable moments deciding how she ought to react. "I think you're confusing boss with bossy," she finally continued. "Bossy I'll give you. But not *boss*. I've made it through a lot of years without holding any kind of administrative position and I intend to make it through the rest of my natural life in that state. It's just not my style to oversee other people. Too much interaction, of a kind I especially dislike."

"I think you're underestimating yourself. You'd be very good at it."

"I don't think so. And another thing—it would be very difficult for me to get away right now because—"

"Don't worry about that. You won't be doing any traveling at all," Kristina said, as if the matter were settled, as if Janie's opinion or preference carried absolutely no weight.

"I'm going to Iceland, quite soon, as a matter of fact."

"We're aware of that, but that's not the kind of travel I mean. You won't have to travel for this work. And no one seems to think that your trip will disrupt the work you're doing for us. It probably won't ever be so time-sensitive that a few days' delay will screw things up. Unless, of course, something urgent comes up in the meantime."

"And then what?"

"And then we'll figure out what to do."

"I'm going to be away for five days."

"That shouldn't be a problem. However, if you get very involved with all this and you want to postpone that trip, no one would object."

Janie gave it a moment's thought, and then felt slightly perturbed at herself for having done it. "I haven't seen my man in four months."

"We know. And you should see him. You'll feel better if you do, perform better. And as far as the boss thing is concerned, your only interaction with the others out there will be electronic. You're the central clearinghouse for everything they gather. That's what we mean by 'boss'—you'll be telling your contacts if you need more data or if the data they've sent don't make any sense. Just like you do now for the foundation. Except now you'll be able to do everything from right here," Kristina went on, "and the only person you'll have to interact with is me." She patted the little computer, then let her hand rest on its closed top. "And Virtual Memorial, here."

"Okay," Janie said. "You've made me feel a little better. But now I'm wondering why this little guy has a name."

"Because he's unique—one of a kind, really. He has special capabilities that members of our group have designed specifically for the work at hand. Programs that are written just for this project, specialized communications devices, things you won't find in your ordinary drugstore-type computer. As records come in from the various sources, they'll automatically drop into the correct programs without your having to think about it. You'll just keep an eye on the process."

Hmph. Janie said, "But I like to think."

"And you will. You'll see what's missing, what's still needed. And when we've got everything entered, it has the evaluation programming too. And it's got a secure communications port that no one will be able to break into."

"From what I understand, that's not really possible anymore."

"It is if you have your own satellite."

Janie stared. "Don't tell me."

Kristina nodded and grinned. "We launched it last year. And it's been running perfectly since the day we put it into operation. Now, the units we've provided to you and everyone else are the only ones that can connect to our satellite."

"You guys must have a mountain of money to be able to do this work."

"Not really. But we are very judicious with the money we have."

"Where does it come from?"

"Various sources. But I can't be more specific than that."

"You must have someone or something major behind you."

"I can only tell you that we have some generous supporters who really believe in the work we're doing."

Janie found these deliberately vague answers to be terribly unsatisfying. They did little more than evoke an unwanted sense of suspicion in her. "They must," she said.

"They do. And we're hoping you'll believe in the work, as well."

"That's something I can't say one way or the other right now—I'm going to have to do some more of it first, I think."

"In time it's our guess that you'll hop onboard for the whole ride, as quickly as everyone else seems to," Kristina said. Her expression was almost challenging again. "But in the meantime, there are some things about this machine that I probably should explain. The first and most important thing is that we don't want it falling into the wrong hands."

"I feel stupid asking why, but why?"

"Because some of the information you gather may be a little bit 'sensitive.'"

"I'm beginning to feel like this entire project is going to turn out to be 'sensitive.'"

"It might. But that won't become clear until we go a little further with it."

"So I'm going to have to keep my eye on Junior, here."

"We wish you would," Kristina said. "Now, you should also back up the files every day. You can send all the files up to the satellite, and it will store them for you. But if you don't send in an updated file to replace one that's been entered within three days of the last update, it will dump those unattended files."

"Oh, dear," Janie said. "That's rather ungracious of it. Even house-guests usually get a week."

"If we were going to allow longer storage, we would have needed a fancier satellite. We decided it would be a good idea to use a nice little unit. The FCC believes that our satellite belongs to a conservation advocacy organization and that its intended use is the tracking of environmental data. That's how we got the space allotment. So we bought a standard small tracking satellite and then gutted everything that it came with. Then we had our nerd-in-residence build it some entirely new innards."

"You have a dedicated nerd?"

A proud young smile preceded Kristina's answer. "We do."

Janie shook her head. "I'm very impressed." It was all very well thought out. Someone in this organization had both vision and will, Janie realized suddenly, to have set all this in place. This person was probably a terrific fund-raiser, to boot. And it was almost always the same story with entities or occurrences of this scope: One human being was the driving force behind it. Others might follow, some close enough to look like they were part of the leadership, but there was always just one leader.

Janie couldn't help but wonder who it might be. *Probably someone I've never even heard of, someone with quiet power and the balls to use it.* She knew she would either worship or hate that leader if she ever met him. Or her.

"What next, then, now you've shown me where the leash is?"

"I guess you walk the dog."

When Alejandro opened his eyes again in the morning, he saw Abraham's manuscript lying on a table near the window, and at its side, ink and quill. To add to his surprise, there was a tray of inviting morning refreshments—a beautiful red apple, a slab of cheese, a loaf of crusty golden bread. Next to the porcelain basin were a pitcher of water and a clean white cloth.

Did I sleep so soundly that I was unaware of someone's entry? It disturbed him to think that he had. And he realized with considerable chagrin that the treatment he was receiving as de Chauliac's prisoner was equal in quality to the attention he had been given as King Edward's guest at Windsor Castle. *He means to have me grow used to it,* Alejandro thought. *He wants me complacent.*

An easy task, he thought unhappily. *I have become so resigned to the harsh uncertainty of living on the run that the simplest kindness undoes me entirely.* His life had been harsh, sometimes almost unbearably harsh. But through it all, he had raised a child, against all the rules of nature, who would have him see to his own self-preservation before that of another man's offspring. That he still had all his own teeth was a wonder to him, for a man with less will might be dipping his crusty bread in water before downing it and eyeing that wonderful apple with little more than wistful memories of the pleasure of chewing it. He was still strong and prepared to do what was necessary to survive. And though he was not the man he had once been, the strength lost had departed from his soul, not his body.

But who can blame me for allowing myself a moment of enjoyment? It was bad enough to spend so much of the night in unconscious, futile pursuit of reunion with the ones he loved, or running from the closing reach of some long-dead giant with vindictive intent, but then to open one's eyes on the cold dirt of a hovel floor as he had done morning after cold morning—he could only believe that it was the stinging joke of the Christian God, who must have been staring down from heaven and laughing at the predicament of this wretched wandering Jew, pulling on the strings of fate, taking divine pleasure when he jumped and jerked like a puppet. To awaken in a clean bed, without mice scampering so close to his ear that he could hear the rustling of the straw and feel the tiny wind of their passage, their highways only a finger's breadth from his very flesh—what luxury! He sat up on his elbow and looked around at his comfortable surroundings. *If I am to be a prisoner, let it be under conditions such as these!*

He cleaned himself, then filled his belly, chewing gratefully with intact teeth, and turned his attention to the manuscript. The papyrus began to fill with his beautifully rendered writings. Abraham's words crossed the ages with miraculously fresh wisdom. When done with patience and careful thought, which he applied to it now, the deciphering went smoothly, and soon he found himself nearly smiling at his own cleverness.

Then he stumbled upon a passage that defied sense.

Take care of your bones, it read, *not to let them break. There are those among you who lack*—but what was this word? Enshrouded as it was in archaic symbols, he could not make its meaning out. *Bones of back,* was the literal meaning. In the context of the passage, it could only mean *spine.* Why such a detailed and specific admonition, when no other issues of personal health were addressed so minutely? And what had de Chauliac said that now tickled his brain when he read these words?

He left a space to accommodate the word when he would finally glean its meaning. *Which I will,* he assured himself. He was just tackling the first few words of the next passage when he heard a knock on the door.

There was no handle on the inside—de Chauliac had had it removed by the same clumsy carpenter who had filled the open window with bars, so the knock was a mere courtesy. His ever-present guards controlled all passage and after a few seconds one of them entered, his gaze downcast.

It made Alejandro angry, the way they refused to meet his eyes with their own. *Why do they never look at me straight on, any of them? Am I simply an object to be escorted here and there, at the will of their master?* It was discretion, perhaps, that led them to do it . . . surely in a household of such elegance, even the guards would be expected to behave in a discreet manner.

And then a stabbing realization hit him: *They fear me. But not because I can harm them.*

The guard offered up an armful of clothing, but still kept his eyes directed elsewhere. "For tonight's entertainment," he mumbled.

Alejandro stood motionless, silently challenging the man to look at his face. He wondered bitterly, *What do they think they will find—some exotic beast, with vile and unthinkable habits?* His resentment grew with every passing second. *Do you fear that you will enter and find me with my manhood stiff in my hand, a look of ungodly pleasure on my face? Or shall I bare my teeth and show you the fangs your priests say all Jews have, dripping with the blood of Christian infants?* He reached out and yanked the clothing away, and the guard quickly left.

He inspected the offerings in a cloud of discontent. De Chauliac had presented him a handsome suit of apparel, and an insulting notion entered his mind: *One's toys must always be displayed in the best possible state.* There was a fine blue linen tunic, and a pair of elegant black breeches of a length to reach just below the knee. He held them up to himself; they looked to be a perfect fit. He wondered briefly if de Chauliac had sent a tailor in to measure him as he slept in the night.

But never mind, he thought with a smile, *for when I escape, I will be most admirably attired.*

Charles of Navarre accepted the proffered letter from Baron de Coucy's page and then dismissed him with a quick wave of his hand. The red seal was one that he now recognized at a glance, for he had seen it on countless correspondences of late. *Another communication from my "ally" in Paris.* To think of the horses they had worn down with their daily letters! It was a sinful waste, but necessary.

He read Marcel's words with eager interest.

Guillaume Karle arrived here last night, as you predicted he would. I find him to be an especially intelligent man, if slightly overzealous, but this passion is well directed toward insurrection and can serve us well. To my surprise he is accompanied by a young maid, who I suspect is a great comfort to him by the fine look of her, and what man could be blamed for treating himself to the attentions of a woman in times such as these? We must have our pleasures, after all.

I am happy to report that he does not allow her to distract him from the cause of rebellion, his devotion to which seems unequaled among his fellows. It is my carefully considered opinion that with the proper persuasion, he could be quite successful in gathering an army of peasants to assist in our cause.

But I regret to tell you, although I suspect you will not find this declaration surprising, that he detests you with as much passion as he loves the notion of freedom. And if what he has told me of your escapades in the countryside is true, then I cannot honestly say that I find fault in him for feeling as he does. Perhaps, dear sir, it is time for you to reconsider the ferocity of your raids on the peasantry. Make trouble, certainly, for this is only to be expected. But do not slay them with such obvious enthusiasm. You must convince those nobles who support you to amend their behavior likewise.

And I beseech you to reconsider your pursuit of Karle himself, for it will not do us any good to have him dead or in chains. It will benefit us greatly, at least for the moment, to bring him to our side against those who would deny you your claim. If you are fighting both him and the supporters of the king, your forces will be unnecessarily divided.

Of course such a respite must be reconsidered from time to time, and if after you have claimed your rightful place you find him too much of a threat, you should do what is needed to ensure your position.

There were other bits of news, but none of it nearly as important. "I am pleased," he told the Baron de Coucy later, "with the doings of Marcel."

But he does not do these things out of any loyalty to me, Navarre thought. *He does them because he thinks that when all is said and done, he will still rule Paris.*

Such arrogance from a man of his *bourgeois* birth was not to be permitted. *When I am king of all France, perhaps I will let him keep it. If it pleases me.*

The light of the sun had never seemed more benevolent, nor any pallet of straw so much a comfort.

Kate turned her head toward Guillaume Karle, who still slept. She traced the outline of his jaw with her finger, and on feeling her delicate touch he opened his eyes. The corners of his mouth curled in a little smile, and he pulled her close to him.

Contentment flooded through her, and she thought, *Could there be more joy than that which I know right now?*

"What a sweet night it was," he whispered softly. "The sun came far too quickly for my liking."

"And here I was, just thinking how beautiful its light is today." She laughed softly. "It would seem we are already at odds, and over a matter we cannot hope to influence."

He kissed her lightly on the forehead and said, "A matter that will take care of itself, regardless of our thinking on it. The sun will leave and return again, without concern for either of our wishes." And then his smile faded. "There are other matters that will not resolve themselves so easily, I think."

As soon as those words left his lips, Kate found herself acutely aware of the passing of time, of the tragic and inevitable death of each precious moment. The night was already gone, the day marching inexorably forward. They would emerge from their straw womb and go about the lives they had known before, their doings on this day oddly unaffected by what had passed between them in the night. There was a rebellion to be seen to, a father to be found. No night of first love would grab those two hanging swords, put there by God Himself, out of the air above them, and then fling them away.

And when Père was found, she knew that he would not fail to recognize the difference in her. She felt it herself, with terrible and confusing keenness. Could she keep such a change from showing on her face? *Not with the help of the Blessed Virgin herself.* He would know with one look that she was no longer entirely his daughter.

He cannot think that I will eternally be his child. He must know that it cannot be.

When Karle got up on one elbow as if to rise, Kate clutched at his arm.

Please not yet, she thought desperately. "Must you leave my side so soon?"

He lay back down again and pulled her close to him and whispered into her ear. "Were it only mine to choose, I would never leave your side. But one cannot slay dragons while languishing in the arms of the lady one wishes to protect."

"The dragons will wait."

"But they must still be slain."

She pulled him closer. "They will wait."

*   *   *

And now the rays of that beautiful sun were lengthening again as it made its way toward yet another *rendezvous* with the horizon. A heavy silence hung between Kate and Karle as they progressed once more toward Rue des Rosiers, and Kate found herself having to almost force each leg to move forward, for her steps were weighted with confusion and regret. *What strange new body has my soul occupied?* she wondered to herself. *In one day, it has acquired a will of its own, one quite foreign to me.*

But what luscious disobedience, what sweet shame! She was unusually aware of her own womanly parts as she walked, for the first time used as God had intended. *As God intended!* she repeated in her mind.

Why, then, was it a matter of shame?

She was filled with questions she had never thought to ask before. When a man and woman lie together, did the homunculus always pass from him to her, and plant a child? *Surely not,* she reasoned, *or women would always be with child! But what if it did?* Where did those homunculi go, if not welcomed into the female womb? Is there a special place in the hereafter for the unused contribution of a man to fatherhood? It seemed only sensible that there must be. And what should a lady do if her lover wishes to know her, but her menses are upon her?

She yearned, briefly, for a reunion with her departed mother, or even her old nurse, or the midwife Mother Sarah, any one of whom would have an answer for this question and would deliver it with a kindly wink and the glint of understanding in her eye. Père had said, in their infrequent and strained discussions of womanly matters, in his sweetly bungling attempt to be both mother and father to her, that the Jews had strict laws governing the activities between a man and a woman in their bed. "In this the Christians are more sensible," he had reluctantly admitted. "They hold no restriction but that the man and woman must be wedded before their God."

She keenly felt the sting of that one sacred restriction, in light of her own blatant disregard of it. And suddenly she felt unaccountably fearful. Would she burn in hell for this? *Please God, no! Have I not suffered enough by Your whimsy?*

Where was the fairness in it? How many women had her true father bedded, while being wed to only one of them? No one had kept an actual count, to the undeserved benefit of his reputation. He made only the most transparent attempts to hide his infidelities. And had her own mother not been Edward's lover, albeit unwillingly, without benefit of marriage?

She was certain that her lady mother was nestled in the arms of God Himself, being consoled by angels with promises of an eternal life less tragic than her earthly one. Any other fate for one so poorly used was simply unimaginable. *God makes allowances,* she assured herself, *despite what the priests would have us believe.*

But Père had taken the Lady Throxwood to his bed; the outcome had not been good.

I shall have to pray for forgiveness, she thought.

But what delicious sin! She would pay the pardoner, without complaint, if only it could be made all right.

And as they returned again to Marcel's house, having not found Alejandro, Kate felt strangely relieved.

De Chauliac's servants scurried about the house in frenzied preparation for the night's festivities. Alejandro sat at one end of the table in the Frenchman's study, watching the madness swirl around him. Abraham's manuscript was open before him. De Chauliac himself sat at the other end with a volume of medical lore in his hands, but his eyes could not seem to keep to the pages. They looked instead over his long nose and sternly judged the progress of the preparations. By the look on his face, the Jew guessed that his captor found the progress wanting, and wondered why de Chauliac had no mistress to see to such needs. And why was he himself required to be a witness to it? *I would have you present during my studies,* the French physician had explained when he'd had Alejandro brought out of his small room earlier. *The need to discuss some point may arise.*

Then summon one of your students, Alejandro had said. *Surely they all clamor for the privilege of studying at your feet.*

Indeed they do, but I much prefer the company of equals during my reading, de Chauliac had countered.

"You are fretting, Frenchman, not reading. Why then must you have my company?"

"Because I would have it. *Spaniard.*" He smiled caustically. "Although it seems worth little at the moment."

Because I will not satisfy you with conversation. Except for his recent complaint, Alejandro had spoken not a word unless first addressed by his host, though he ached for a decent discussion of something, *anything,* that would take his mind off his present difficulties. The puzzling word he had found earlier was still undeciphered, and there was so much more in his manuscript that begged clarification, yet he would not allow himself the simple pleasure of engaging in repartee, because to do so would give the same to his captor, and he would not be party to anything so repulsive as de Chauliac's pleasure.

As the shadows lengthened and the evening's activities grew nearer, those who would provide the entertainment began to arrive. First came musicians and a fool, and then an exotic-looking woman with dark hair and a swarthy complexion, not unlike his own, who de Chauliac vowed would thrill him with her dancing. "She rotates her belly in a most enticing manner," he said with a naughty, almost boyish smile. "She is glad to have employment in these lean times, so she will do her best to please her audience."

Alejandro followed her with his eyes as she crossed the vestibule. A small grin worked its way through his reticence and he said, "And how shall the ladies take to this entertainment?"

De Chauliac laughed. "There will be none tonight. Most have been sent away until Paris is itself again."

Alejandro thought of Kate, who must now be somewhere in Paris. He prayed silently, though it galled him to do so, that she was still with Karle. "Is it really so dangerous for women here now?" he asked.

"Only for noblewomen," de Chauliac replied. "Those of the lower classes still come and go as they please." He glanced out the window, judging the time. "I think perhaps it is time for you to return to your room now," he said. "Though I do not wish to give up our inspiring discussions. You should rest for a while, and then prepare yourself."

For what? he wondered as the guards led him away.

Perhaps an hour later, de Chauliac himself appeared to escort Alejandro downstairs again. "You look quite handsome, Physician," he said. "But then, you cut a noble figure when I sent you off to England in all that finery. You have not lost your dash with the passing of the years. I must say, one would never suspect you are a Jew."

As you yourself did not, he thought. But he kept his sentiment to himself, for it would only agitate his keeper, and he wanted him as placid as possible. It would not serve his purposes to have de Chauliac angry tonight.

As if he could read Alejandro's thoughts of escape, the Frenchman said, "I will now do you the kindness of warning you. Do not try to take advantage of my occupation with my guests by attempting to run from here. There will be many guards posted tonight. You may move about the house as does any other guest, but you will be watched. Carefully. Do I make myself clear?"

"You do," Alejandro said.

"Now, as to the matter of presenting you to the other guests, I will introduce you as Dr. Hernandez."

Are there any Jews among you? he remembered hearing de Chauliac say years before. This elegant fiend looked little different than he had in the papal palace in Avignon, where he had addressed all the physicians of Avignon who had somehow contrived to escape the plague's clutches. *If so, step forward.* He had not, declaring himself instead to be his companion, the Spaniard Hernandez, who had been stolen from him only the day before by the dreaded plague. Still numb from the bitter loss, he remembered watching the other Jews with terrible envy when they were dismissed, judged to be unfit for the work of His Holiness Pope Clement VI. He remembered wishing with all his heart and soul that he had let his foot do what it had ached to do. One step, leading to an entirely different path.

De Chauliac failed to notice his distraction, and kept on with his warnings. "I have faith that you will not embarrass me, because such folly will not come to any good. I would advise you just to enjoy the company, for you shall not know the likes of it again soon."

"And if anyone asks of our association?"

"We shall say, quite truthfully, that you are simply a former student of mine, now a physician of some importance in your own land." He made a sugary smile and said, "Perhaps we shall say that you have returned to Paris for a visit to your mentor. It is not entirely untrue."

Not if one adds, under extreme protest.

"Nothing more need be said. But do not doubt that you will know great discomfort if I am shamed in any way by your actions."

The admonishment issued, de Chauliac turned and led the way. Alejandro followed, plotting madly.

The entire house was awash with the light of torches and candles, and the air was filled with music, not the strange and haunting sounds that filled the churches of the Christian God, but lilts of a more lively and secular tempo. The entire manse smelled of the rare spices and exotic herbs de Chauliac's cooks had used with the intention of pleasuring the palates of his guests. A pair of liveried menservants stood at the entry door, and all throughout the house Alejandro saw more, far more than would be needed to keep him prisoner. Positioned conveniently at all possible

sorties, they stood motionless and grim, just as de Chauliac had promised
they would. Every time he looked, he found their eyes upon him, watching, waiting with their instructions for him to do something foolish.

One by one the luminous celebrants entered the sybaritic realm de
Chauliac had arranged for them, and Alejandro was presented to each
one according to the scheme his host had concocted earlier. When six
gentlemen were already deep in conversation, a short and portly man, far
less impressively attired than the others, stepped through the door. Alejandro was surprised to see that it was to this man that de Chauliac gave
the most attention.

The greeting was almost overbearingly solicitous. "Ah, *Monsieur
Flamel,*" de Chauliac oozed, "How delighted I am that you have come! I
was beginning to fear that you would not be with us this evening."

As he handed his cloak to a servant, Nicholas Flamel said, "*Je regrette,
Monsieur le Docteur,* my tardiness. It was unavoidable. My wife, you see,
does not take kindly to being left alone." The little man made an exaggerated, unpracticed bow, and Alejandro was reminded of his own clumsy
first efforts in Edward's court, and of how Kate, then barely seven, had
subsequently taken it upon herself to teach him the fine points of courtly
behavior.

She was my only friend for a time, he reminisced.

Flamel elaborated on his explanation, though Alejandro was sure, by
the look on de Chauliac's face, that the host could have done without it.
"I was forced to see to her demands before she would allow me to make
my exit."

"I understand her anger at the loss of your inspiring company. We
shall be certain to send you home with your arms full of sweets to make
amends. One hopes that such a gesture will ameliorate her loss."

"Only if I feed them to her morsel by morsel," Flamel said with a
chuckle.

Another unnecessary tidbit, but de Chauliac remained engaged. For
some reason Alejandro could not determine, he seemed to want the
strange little man's attention. "Then permit me to encourage you to do
so," de Chauliac said with a wink. "One hopes you will find some pleasure in such activity yourself." He took Flamel by the arm and drew him
toward Alejandro. "And now I would have you meet another colleague of
mine, the honorable Dr. Hernandez, a man whom I hold in nearly as
much esteem as I do yourself, for he too is especially learned and wise.
But how could he not be? He was once my pupil."

"At the university?" Flamel inquired unexpectedly.

And before de Chauliac could change the dangerous and unanticipated direction of the discourse, Alejandro said, "In Avignon. During the first year of the pestilence."

Flamel's f~~ lit ~p with curiosity. "Were you one of those sent out, then, by His Ho. ?ope Clement, may he rest in peace?"

And as de Chauliac looked on in speechless horror, Alejandro smiled and said, "Aye. I was among them."

"How very marvelous! And to which court were you sent?" Flamel asked.

He saw the color drain from de Chauliac's face, and smiled inwardly. *Your games will not always go as you wish, my friend,* he thought. "I did a good deal of roving from place to place. I was, one might truthfully say, rather ' ne to wandering."

' . artful answer, de Chauliac seemed to recover some of his com-
p~su~. "I am most eager for you to see a manuscript that Dr. Hernandez has brought with him," he said to Flamel, "for it contains symbols of alchemy in the language of the Jews, and is sure to fascinate you."

Flamel's red face nearly exploded with excitement. He foamed as he spoke. "Then the surprise you wrote of in your invitation is at last revealed!" He smiled broadly. "Truly, sir, at first I did not understand the reason for your kindness. This is more than I hoped for!" And then, for a moment, he took on a pensive look, which changed quickly into one of great excitement. "Dear God," he said, *"Monsieur* de Chauliac . . . dare I hope . . . is this the manuscript of one called Abraham?"

Feigning innocence, de Chauliac looked at Alejandro and grinned. His eyebrows raised, he said, "Colleague?"

Alejandro's heart dropped into his stomach. "It is," he finally answered.

"Praise be to all the saints!" Flamel almost cried. "I have heard of this book and sought it for years!"

De Chauliac glowed almost victoriously. "And tonight you shall see it," he said, "when my other guests are gone. It requires one's complete attention. If you can contain yourself until after we have dined and seen our entertainment, we shall look upon it together."

"You had best prepare a wagonload of sweets for my wife, then," he said almost giddily.

"It shall be arranged," de Chauliac said.

More gentlemen arrived, but de Chauliac did not make such a point of introductions. Still, he was in his most charming and gracious glory as the house filled with revelers and the mirth increased. Alejandro found himself unwillingly caught up in the festivities, and was almost beginning to enjoy himself when a slight young man, who might more reasonably have been called a boy, came through the door.

He was dressed in the attire of a page or a valet, and stood looking around with a piece of parchment in his hand, clearly wanting to deliver it. He seemed terribly out of place, far more so than even the groveling Flamel, and very nervous.

And then Alejandro thought his eyes were betraying him: emblazoned on the page's mantle was the symbol of the house of Plantagenet. His senses rose to full alert when this page questioned the guards in French that was clearly influenced by another language.

English!

De Chauliac came forward and extended his open hand. "Am I to assume that this message is for me?"

"If you are, as my patron calls him, 'The Illustrious and Magnificent Monsieur le Docteur de Chauliac,' then it would be for you, indeed."

De Chauliac beamed. "And from your mantle, I judge that you are sent by the illustrious and magnificent Prince Lionel, young page."

Alejandro felt himself trembling; he looked around for someplace to hide. But where would he go? There were guards and other guests who would all observe whatever attempt he made to secret himself away. All would make note of his behavior; all would find it strange and curious.

Lionel! The younger brother of Isabella!

But then the boy spoke again. "Geoffrey Chaucer, at your service, O, illustrious and magnificent physician. I am instructed to bid you the most hearty and enthusiastic good evening from that notable prince."

The older half-brother of Kate!

"And might I inquire, young Chaucer, why your prince does not deliver this well-said greeting himself, as I have invited him to do?"

"My prince begs your indulgence, sir. He regrets that he cannot be here tonight," the page said.

Alejandro's horror began to drain away, but with agonizing slowness.

"And yesterday he promised his presence!" de Chauliac said, pouting with disappointment. "I am most grievously offended!"

The page went down on one knee and played out his prince's apology in abject drama. "Have pity on him, sir! He has taken to his bed with an episode of gout. He is suffering much pain and vows not to rise again tonight."

"Oh, dear," de Chauliac said sternly. "You must tell me, young man, if his keepers are mistreating him."

"Gracious no, sir," the page said. "I daresay that the Dauphin has done himself proud in seeing to Prince Lionel's confinement. And that of the rest of us, who are not royals, and therefore far less deserving of luxury. But we all find the arrangements to be most satisfactory."

De Chauliac motioned for the page Chaucer to rise. He was clearly pleased with the length to which Lionel had gone in instructing the page to beg for forgiveness. "Good," he said. "I am greatly relieved. But then we French have refined the art of treating our captives with tenderness and affection, have we not?" And though de Chauliac did not turn his eyes away from Lionel's page, Alejandro knew that the comment was directed at none other than himself.

Chaucer seemed only too happy to agree with him. "Indeed, sir, the French seem very . . . *affectionate.*"

De Chauliac laughed. "The Dauphin has charged me with seeing to Prince Lionel's health and vigor while he is a guest on our soil. Apparently, I have failed, and I am sincerely sorry. Oh!" he said dramatically. "The shame of it! We cannot send the good prince back to his doting father with his vitality sapped by our profligate French ways, can we? No, no. This must be corrected."

"If you know of some cure for gout, good physician," the page said, "then give it over to my lord's benefit."

"Cure? Ah, well. There is none, I am sad to say. But one may take precautions. I shall visit your prince again quite soon and reissue the precautions I have already given him. Advice he has clearly, and I hasten to add, *imprudently* ignored in favor of having his pleasures as he will. You must tell him that though I love him well, he is a most aggravating patient, and you must convey my annoyance. As well, of course, as my most sincere wishes for a speedy recovery from his affliction."

The young man nodded and said, "I shall do so, my lord, straight-away." Then he bowed and turned toward the door.

De Chauliac reached out and took him by the arm. "But there is a place set for him at the table, and it will go empty now. With so much want in the world, God will not look kindly upon me for failing to fill it." He regarded the page for a moment. "You seem an affable lad. You must stay and take your liege's place."

Chaucer seemed flustered by this offer. "But he expects me to return."

"Then he shall be disappointed, as I am that my table lacks his fair and dear presence," de Chauliac said. "It seems a reasonable exchange."

"I am unqualified to fill the chair of a prince, sir. Of that there can be absolutely no doubt. And what of the guards who escorted me here? They have instructions to see me safely back."

But de Chauliac would not be denied. He put an arm around the young man's shoulder and said, "We shall feed them well while they wait. I shall see to Lionel's satisfaction on the matter personally. Now tell me again, for I have already forgotten, what is your name?"

"Geoffrey, sir."

"Have you a surname, young Geoffrey?"

"Yes, sir. Chaucer."

"Aha!" de Chauliac said. "I have heard your name in Lionel's household. You have made a marked impression on your prince, young Chaucer—he speaks highly of you! He tells me that you often amuse him with tales of great imagination. In *English,* he says. You must be clever indeed." And as if he could not help himself, he shot a sly, sarcastic glance in Alejandro's direction.

"Do you speak English, sir?" the page inquired with excitement.

Alejandro looked quickly at de Chauliac, who seemed to be enjoying his discomfort greatly. But the Frenchman made no attempt to change the subject, so Alejandro answered, "A bit."

"Then I am doubly glad to make your acquaintance," Chaucer said, pumping Alejandro's hand. He slipped into English. "I have had no one to talk to."

He struggled, but the words came back to him, harsh and guttural. "An affliction I understand only too well myself."

"How did you acquire it?"

And though the Jew was liking the young man more and more with each passing moment, he hesitated to answer. "In my travels I have run across an Englishman or two," he finally said. "It has been forced upon my ears, and I have taken it up, albeit against my own choosing. It is a talent of mine, somewhat unwanted."

"Everyone seems to have an opinion of our language. Tell me," he said, "what is yours?"

It was a dangerous subject, but would this curious fellow Chaucer make more of Alejandro's refusal to answer than his unlikely knowledge of English? There was a risk that he would. "I find it difficult," Alejandro reluctantly said. "And confusing. It is unlike any other language I have learned. I often find it lacking in words for proper expression."

"In time it shall be more worthy," Chaucer said.

Alejandro could not help but smile. *Too bad he is not a Jew,* he thought cynically. *One hopes the English royals will learn to appreciate him.* "Do you mean, my young friend, to improve it all by yourself?"

"If need be," young Chaucer said with a grin.

*   *   *

There were still two seats empty at the huge oak table when all present were seated; de Chauliac ignored them pointedly and went about the business of seeing to the comfort of his prompt guests. Alejandro was pleased to find himself seated next to the friendly young page, but a bit unhappy to discover the overly inquisitive Nicholas Flamel on his other side.

But soon they were far too distracted for him to notice his table-mates, for the dark young woman entered the dining hall, followed closely by the musicians, who accompanied her sensuous glide toward the table with a reedy, almost oriental air. She swayed in time to the dark thrumming of the drums; with each step forward, one hip was thrust out invitingly, the other angled back, a teasing position meant to tantalize de Chauliac's guests, an intent the dark woman accomplished with great facility.

And then to Alejandro's surprise, she placed a bare foot up on one of the empty wooden chairs and nimbly hoisted herself to the tabletop. Her toes were encircled with rings of gold and silver, and she wore voluminous pantaloons of the filmiest, most transparent fabric Alejandro had ever seen. *Like a virgin's veil,* he thought, an incongruous comparison.

"Once I saw a woman of Romanie dance for King Edward," Adele had told him. "She was dripping with ornaments of silver and gold, chains and charms that jingled as she moved, and her plump breasts were contained only in circles of cloth of gold, held together by the thinnest of strings tied at her back." Adele had drawn rounded shapes in the air with her hands as she described it, and he had felt his heart speed up. "And yet," Adele had said with girlish giggles, "this dancer covered her face like a shy maiden! One could almost see the king's manhood rise beneath his tunic."

"And the queen did not object?" he had asked.

"The queen arranged it," his lover had replied with a blush. "It was a gift, for the anniversary of her husband's birth. Royal ladies are accustomed to such exotic displays. And everyone wishes to be the first to show them some new and exciting thing, so they see these things often!"

Far more often than the Jews of Aragon, he had thought at the time.

Chaucer tapped his arm lightly and said, "In court I saw such a woman dance, from Romanie, I think." Alejandro wondered if the youth had been reading his thoughts.

And as if summoned, the dancer was suddenly before them, her knees slightly bent, her thinly covered womanly parts less than an arm's length in front of their faces. She raised one foot, balancing easily on the other, and touched one toe to the tip of Alejandro's nose, even as her hips still worked their rhythmic magic. He blushed full crimson before her foot met the tabletop again. The room came alive with cheering and applause, and out of the corner of his eye he could see de Chauliac's wicked grin of satisfaction. Had this sultry *demoiselle* been instructed to entice him specifically? He thought it likely that she had. She smiled seductively and parted her lips, and showed her pink tongue, to the great appreciation of the gathered men, who whistled and pounded on the table and called for him to meet her challenge. And then she lowered herself and leaned forward, her breasts fairly bobbing in front of his face.

In an act of self-defense, he grabbed the page at his side and thrust the youth upward until his face was buried in the woman's cleavage. Shouts of encouragement and lewd suggestions rose up, and wild laughter. The music swirled, the air grew hotter, the din of voices nearly unbearable, and Chaucer had one knee on the table, ready to hoist himself up to join his would-be paramour. And then it all came to a sudden stop as de Chauliac stood, his eyes fixed toward the door to the dining hall. Everyone else's eyes followed.

The last of his guests had finally arrived. There in the door, somewhat breathless from their hurried pace, stood Etienne Marcel and Guillaume Karle.

Janie was operating in mental overdrive by the time Kristina left her alone with Virtual Memorial. It felt almost like having a new pet. There were things to learn, personality traits to be uncovered, and she found herself feeling wide awake and alive, though by this time of night, she generally started to tire. A glance at the clock told her that it was the middle of the night in London, too late to call Bruce. And she couldn't be sure if the edge of difficulty in their last call had worn off yet. Despite her affection for him, she knew only too well that Bruce could be preachy, and the last thing she wanted in a moment when she was so engaged in something new was to be lectured about it.

But she did need a good physical laundering, a complete body purge, to get out all the impurities that had settled in from too little sleep, too much stress, too many things to think about. A run or a fast walk would do it.

I have to talk to Michael and Caroline anyway.

It was a moonlit night, and most of the route was well illuminated; Janie was halfway down the first block on her way to their house when she realized that Virtual Memorial was still sitting on her kitchen counter.

I should take it with me.

But there's no data on it yet. It's probably all right to leave it behind.

The memory of what had happened to her last laptop rose up and

snarled in her face. She stopped, turned around, and went back to retrieve it.

I guess I walk the dog. She put the small unit into a lightweight, padded
nylon backpack and set out again.

Part of her route took her over the bike path where the coach's accident had occurred. It was a route she traveled regularly, and she thought
she knew it well. But when she left the street and entered the wooded cut-
through, a sudden cold isolation came over her, not the type of solitude
she loved and often even craved, but instead the visceral, compelling kind
that urges the body to keep moving at all costs. She did as the adrenaline
bid her, taking care not to trip on any of the treacherous obstacles she
knew she might encounter, for they were plentiful in a time when one
could not dig up a weed without first getting the proper permit. Exposed
roots, low branches, creeping vines, they were out there in little armies,
ready to reach out and grab her by the ankle. She stepped high and quick.

She came at last to the bike path itself, and when her feet touched the
pavement, Janie silently blessed the unknown government official who'd
had the foresight, against what was probably staunch environmental op-
position, to stamp APPROVED on the plan for this path. After the dark and
grabby woods even the hard pavement seemed friendly, but as she moved
into a stretch of the path where the addition of one strategically placed
lightbulb would have been wise, the cold feeling began to return again.
One foot steadily in front of the other, she panted her way past the
shadowed inlets—they were perfect places to hide, but she'd never noticed them before.

Had it been dark and shadowy, as it was now, when the young coach
tumbled and died? Was his mind on something so absorbing that he
didn't notice a rock or a stick or even a turtle—or perhaps a person?

Bike and all, someone could dash out of the darkness to trip or push
or otherwise overwhelm a rider, then give a quick snap to the neck,
arrange the body so it would look like an accident, and . . . off again. It
would take only a few seconds.

When she arrived at the end of their lot, sweating and shivering at the
same time, she saw Michael and Caroline on their porch swing, rocking
back and forth in the quiet of the evening. There was a certain ease they
had with each other, a comfort Janie could feel even through the darkness. But their enjoyment of each other would be tempered, she knew, as
it would on many subsequent evenings, by the question of why Caroline
had seen fit to take Michael's police palmbook, an act that had had
terrible ramifications.

It was loyalty, Michael, Janie wanted to say. *She feels loyal to me because*

I saved her life. But that was an explanation that would be better and more believable coming from Caroline herself. In time, Janie had no doubt that Caroline would get there. In the meantime, they looked as if they were doing all right.

When these thoughts had completed their circuit through her brain, she left the velvety shadows and stepped out into the light of the street-lamp.

"Hey," Caroline said warmly when she saw Janie, "come sit with us." She patted the seat of the swing.

As Janie sat down, she said, "Thanks." She nodded a greeting at Michael. "I was wondering . . . I wanted to, uh, ask . . ." She stopped for a moment and fixed her gaze downward. After a few seconds of internal penance, she looked up again. "Sorry," she said. "I should've called. But I'm not liking telephones much lately," Janie said. "Especially when there are things to talk about that I don't want other people to overhear."

Michael knew what Janie wanted without having to hear it. The coach's death would be the subject of their conversations until they worked it into the lore of their relationship, until it became an implied undercurrent and open discussion was no longer necessary. He allowed her a few moments to get settled, then elaborated on the small bits of information he'd given her earlier.

"They haven't officially listed it as a suspicious death. They probably won't because there isn't any evidence to lead them to a suspect or a conviction. But that in and of itself makes the death suspicious. There should at least be something there to look at."

Janie wondered in that moment if she ought to be telling Kristina about the coach's death. *She probably already knows,* she thought. But what if she didn't? Was it important for her—for them—to know? But if she did tell Kristina, Caroline, perhaps even Michael, might be implicated. It was one thing for her to put herself in the middle of a tornado, but quite another for her friends to be similarly exposed.

"It's so odd that there were no traces," Janie said. "Are they sure? There wasn't the littlest bit of evidence?"

"Nothing."

"Well, it means they won't come looking for Caroline, or you, or me, but it also means they probably won't figure out who did it to him, if someone did."

"Maybe it was really just an accident."

He gave her a surprised stare. "There's a change of tune. You were convinced this was foul play a couple of days ago."

"I don't know what I think now," she said after a moment.

Michael and Caroline didn't know about Kristina and the work Janie had taken on with her. Kristina didn't know about Janie's little fishing trip for boy data with Caroline; she'd tracked Janie down through her inquiry into the camp. Or so she'd said. For some reason she couldn't define, Janie believed her.

Which could only mean that some other person, or entity, or "agency," even, was keeping an eye on the Camp Meir boys. Not necessarily on the camp itself—although that remained to be seen. The dead man had to have been a message—and Janie had no reason to think it was being directed at Michael or Caroline. But if Kristina and her "agency" had found her through the camp, wouldn't the others, who were rapidly taking on the persona of the "bad guys" in her mind, also find her that way?

If they hadn't already, perhaps they wouldn't. Maybe Camp Meir's Web site was too close a link for anyone to risk exposing himself with an electronic monitoring of it.

None of these thoughts could be voiced aloud, or written down. *I'm the only one who knows everything,* Janie suddenly realized. *I'd better take good care of myself.*

She turned to Michael. "Do you think you could you give me a ride home?"

The meeting between Kristina and the man who oversaw what she did was almost like a debriefing.

"I'm beginning to feel like some sort of secret government operative," she said to him.

"Which you would know about, of course," he said with a laugh.

"Well, I've read a lot."

"I know. I'm just teasing you—trying to keep things light. But it does seem like this whole project has become very clandestine all of a sudden."

"Well, it is, don't you think?"

"I suppose so. And the sooner the whole deal is out in the open, the better I'll feel. You know, your work has been really exceptional, Kristina. You did an excellent job tonight. You were clear and concise in your explanations, and very firm with our new 'leader' about what her obligations will be."

"Well, you know, I've had plenty of time to prepare."

"Time obviously well spent. It's funny, though. I thought she might react with a little more . . . hesitation. I think I was expecting her to shrink up a little more. Back away, maybe."

"I think she might actually feel challenged."

"I wonder. It would be nice to know what she's really thinking about all this."

"I'm happy to tell you, that's about the only thing we don't know. The machine is working really beautifully. The transmissions are coming through crystal-clear. She took it with her when she went to visit her friends and we picked up everything. It was brilliant of you to suggest adding the transmitter."

"You know what, it seemed ridiculous not to. Funny, though, to use a transmitter of that sort nowadays. It's an old-fashioned thing, really. But it works."

Janie rose early enough to beat the birds the next morning, and though she knew he wouldn't be home, she called Bruce. She didn't really want to speak with him, but only to check in, touch base, do whatever it was she needed to do to keep the relationship rolling while she so rudely ignored his advice to bolt out of her increasingly complicated life, for at least a while. The message she left was brief, but she hoped her affection for him would come through and he would understand that she loved him, her recent rogue behavior notwithstanding.

And promptly thereafter, with a cup of fully leaded coffee in her hand, she launched into rogue mode with a vengeance.

She activated Virtual Memorial and put it in host status, then invited whatever guest files might be roosting on the satellite to come on down. Forty-three of them did, and posted themselves with all their information in the data collection program. V.M. then spent the next few minutes comparing the names and IDs to the list she'd obtained from Big Dattie and reviewing each submission for completeness.

The operatives—Janie didn't quite know what else to call them—had done a remarkably good job of getting information. Sadly, almost all of the boys whose data had been submitted were hospitalized, hence the ease of obtaining the data. In her mind's eye Janie envisioned an innocent-looking lab technician or social worker or administrative assistant coming to the bedside of a young boy, who would be lying flat on his back, secured in air casts just as Abraham Prives was. A mother or father, or perhaps if the child was fortunate, both, would be sitting at the bedside, face drawn and pale, hands wringing desperately. The operative would whisper a few apologies for the interruption, which the distraught parent or parents would forgive, for after all, wasn't all this witch-doctoring for the good of the child? And with the loved ones looking on, oblivious, the

operative would quietly run a cell collection swab down the child's arm
and discreetly tuck it into a plastic bag; next stop, the DNA evaluation lab
if the facility had one.

It was easy for her to pick out the files that had been sent by operatives
who in their routine lives were administrators, for those files contained
the complete bodyprints of the patients. Techs wouldn't have access to
that level of information, unless, of course, they were bodyprinting techs.
There seemed to be one operative in Manhattan—they were all anonymous to her—who had access to lots of information. The files that came
from there were almost perfectly complete.

For each file with incomplete data, she relayed a note to the sender that
more was required, listed precisely what blanks needed still to be filled,
and requested notification if such information could not be obtained for
some reason. Janie knew that for some of these boys, they would simply
not be able to get bodyprints.

But we can do what we need to do without them, maybe . . .

She smiled to herself as she shut down V.M. She'd thought *we.*

The tone of voice in Myra Ross's message was nearly frantic.

Dear God, she thought as she played it back again, *please don't let
anything have happened to that journal.*

But despite her pleading, Myra refused to tell her anything over the
phone when Janie returned the call. "You simply have to come here," she
insisted. "There's something I have to show you."

And Janie couldn't budge her. "You have to come."

"But I can't get away right now, I'm in the middle of something."

"Come as soon as you can, then."

And the curiosity was killing her. "All right, I can be there in about an
hour."

"I'll tell the guard to expect you," Myra said.

By the time Janie reached the museum, Myra's excitement had fully
infected her. The curator led her immediately to the same workroom
they'd been in before.

"I want you to take a look at this," she said.

To Janie's surprise, there were two books on the table. One was the
journal. The other was larger and obviously older, with what looked to be
a brass cover, tarnished with age and dented from handling. It appeared
to be a manuscript of some sort, and it had a presence nearly as compelling as the journal, though Janie didn't know precisely why. She only

knew that she was as quickly caught up in its spell as she had been with the journal. She reached out instinctively to touch it.

In midreach, she heard Myra groan. Janie drew back her hand, feeling the phantom sting of some imaginary ruler on her trespassing knuckles.

"Oh, God, I'm sorry."

After letting out her tightly held breath, Myra said, "It's okay. Actually, it's a completely understandable reaction. I'd want to touch it if I were you, but we have to refrain from any unnecessary contact with this manuscript, it's just too old and fragile to be handled." Then with forgiving hands, she motioned Janie to come closer. "But this is what I wanted you to see—so take a look. Tell me what you notice."

She opened it with exquisite care to a particular page. Janie looked, intently, her eyebrows furrowed in a search for something that might be significant. The two tomes were very different in appearance and materials: Alejandro's was leatherbound, its pages mostly parchment. Scratchy, technical-looking drawings littered the text to illustrate what was written. The other one had beautifully rendered ornate drawings, below which there was text in what Janie took to be Hebrew. On the leaf-facing, there was handwriting, in faded ink, done by some European scribe, if one judged by the look of it.

"The pages," she said, "they're so thin. They almost look like they should be crumbling."

"We treated them with a preservative. But that's not what I want you to notice."

It was beginning to feel like some sort of test. *C-minus,* Janie graded herself. "I give up," she finally said to Myra. "What am I supposed to be seeing here?"

"I thought you'd see it in a second," the curator said, her expression almost pained.

"I'm sorry, I must be a complete idiot. It's probably just because I'm tired, I've had a busy day, but I just don't know what—"

"The handwriting. There's the same handwriting in both of these books."

Janie stared in awe at the other manuscript. Though the inscriptions had almost disappeared through time, she finally saw it. *"Alejandro's?"* she whispered.

"We believe so."

Janie felt her knees weaken. "Sweet Jesus," she said.

* * *

A few minutes later she was sipping a small glass of water and sitting on a stool as Myra Ross explained what she'd learned so far.

"I didn't notice it until I put the newer one under a microscope. And then I kept thinking to myself, *Where have I seen this before?* So we took close digital images from both of them and went through a pretty detailed enhancement procedure we've developed for this type of thing. In ancient writings the variables of material are so great that it's difficult to identify handwriting itself. But there were a number of words that were common to both books, so we enlarged them dramatically and overlaid them on the computer. They were nearly identical. We assume this fellow Canches wrote in both of these manuscripts." She sighed dreamily, then glanced over at the two books. Then she looked back at Janie and said, "I don't mind telling you it was a thrilling moment for me when I discovered this."

"It's thrilling for me, so I can understand," Janie said. "I might have also said 'explosive, mind-shattering, beyond belief.' "

"All appropriate words. But that's not all. It gets even wilder. These two books are from entirely different time periods. We know that yours originated in the 1300s, but we haven't pinned down a definitive date for the other one. It's quite a bit older, though, perhaps by as much as several centuries. But we can't tell just how much older. We've been through the whole thing, several times over, and there isn't a date anywhere in the original text. The dating processes we have give a range, but not a terribly narrow one."

"Then how could the handwriting possibly be the same?"

"Alejandro's writing in the older one is not original text. It was added well after the book was first produced. We've come to the conclusion that your Dr. Canches was one of the translators of the earlier book."

"There was more than one translator?"

"There were several. We had a medieval handwriting analyst look at the Abraham manuscript when we first acquired it. It was also clear from the language used in the translation—Canches's French was Court French, which is an archaic version of what is spoken today, a little like Old English. That's why you've been able to get help in translating your journal. He might have learned it in an academic setting, or maybe in a noble household. At a certain point, the handwriting changes, and when it does, the French changes too. It becomes Provençal, which is more like Spanish than French, really. People who used it were of the lower classes, at least at the time—I really don't know much about its use today—or they came from smaller cities or towns in the southern sections of France.

We think Canches was the first of several who ultimately had a hand in it. He apparently recognized its value and put some time into it."

"I know he loved learning, just for itself—but I wonder what would have made this book valuable to him."

"That's hard to say, specifically. But if I were a Jew of the time, I would have appreciated anything that made my way a little easier. And this book is essentially a very long letter of instruction from the author, a man named Abraham, to the Jews who lived in Europe." Her eyes twinkled with excitement. "He gives them advice on how they ought to live for the first part of the book, but the bulk of it is really an alchemy manual. There are all sorts of detailed recipes for turning ordinary metals into gold. I would guess that this Abraham wanted to be sure that his people had the financial resources to survive. So he gives them a bunch of recipes for how to make their own gold. It's remarkably fascinating."

"But that stuff is all nonsense."

"Nonsense to us, but at that time there were plenty of people who believed fervently that it could be done. It was a medieval and early Renaissance obsession, really. These days we obsess over trying to figure out a way to 'beam people up.' Back then it was transmutation of metals. It's quite possible that your Dr. Canches himself believed it could be done."

"I don't think so," Janie said adamantly. "Alejandro was a scientist, a very good one."

Myra Ross's eyes sparkled. "A *medieval* scientist. He probably believed the world was flat, if he gave it any thought at all. And that babies were made when little tiny humans—they called them homunculi—swam from the father to the mother during intercourse. So it wouldn't be unnatural for him to give an alchemy manual serious attention. Alchemists were the first practitioners, in Europe, anyway, of anything even remotely like the chemistry we know today. And it was all bound up in religious ritual—"

The curator stopped speaking when she saw the unhappy look on Janie's face. "What's the matter?" she asked.

"I feel a little disappointed."

"Good heavens, why? You're trying to make him into a hero again. Forget it. This is so much more exciting."

"From reading his journal I had this notion that he was brilliant."

Myra sighed and shook her head. "Hebrew, French, Latin, Spanish, not to mention English, which was a very fledgling language at the time. I'd say he was brilliant. The translation work that followed his was nowhere near as accurate. He did a good chunk of the beginning, then he seems to have stopped working on it rather abruptly. Although I will tell you, he made a couple of mistakes. But if I had to bet, I'd say he made those errors deliberately. They were simple words, and he'd gotten them right in other places."

"He wasn't careless like that."

"Maybe he was doing this under some coercion and didn't want the book's truth to fall into the wrong hands."

"Now that sounds more like him," Janie said.

Myra smiled and then glanced down at the manuscript. "Mistakes and all, though, it's fascinating, what it says." She carefully turned back the pages and read the salutation aloud. "Abraham the Jew, Priest, Levite, Astrologer, and Philosopher, to the Nation of the Jews, by the wrath of God dispersed among the Gauls, sendeth health." She beamed with satisfaction. "He wrote it on the back side of the leaves. Papyrus, so they literally are leaves. That's why they're in such fragile condition. Leaves are *supposed* to decompose."

Janie shook her head in disbelief. "This is too much."

"I agree. This fellow got around."

"Whether he wanted to or not," Janie said. With something akin to longing, she glanced back and forth between the two tomes. "I've been fascinated with Alejandro Canches since I first saw his journal." With a look of intensity on her face, she said, "Do you know he understood antibodies in the fourteenth century, and used that understanding to figure out a cure for plague? Plague! If someone in authority had listened to him, if they'd just done a few simple things, it might have shortened the course of the Black Death and saved millions of lives. But they probably all thought he was crazy." She stared vacantly down at her feet, then looked up again with a troubled expression. "Crazy or not, sometimes I feel almost like I love this man. Across all those centuries. Not romantic love, just this deep miraculous wonder, something like what you feel for a child."

Myra's expression warmed. "Then I declare you an official honorary Jewish Mother," she said. "Now you can legally say, 'And this is my son, the doctor . . .'"

Janie finally laughed and said, "I'm honored. Truly. So, tell me, as one Jewish mother to another, what does this all mean?"

"It means your little book is worth a lot more than I originally thought. And I'm not just talking about money."

*   *   *

The news of the journal's potential value wasn't particularly troubling—but it was another recent check-in to Janie's Brain Hotel, and it would be wanting room service soon.

And when Janie herself checked in with Virtual Memorial that afternoon, she found another surprise. An evaluation she'd set in motion that morning was complete, and the results beckoned.

She knew that the second she opened that file, it would own her.

"I lied the other day," she said to Tom. "I do need to talk."

"Well, you know what? I think you should take a hike."

Whoa. She tucked a loose strand of hair behind her ear and bit her own lip, and was grateful that Tom couldn't see her nervous little gestures. "Uh . . . did I forget to pay my bill?"

His laugh was belly-deep and it refreshed her to hear it. "No. That was just another one of my lame attempts at humor," he said. "Not my thing, I guess, though I'll probably never stop trying to be funny. I had some time blocked out for a hike this afternoon. And the weather is cooperating. But my regular partner canceled. I'd still like to go, I just don't want to go by myself. You can hike and talk at the same time, right?"

His regular partner. It had an ominous sound, but she didn't ask. "Today, I don't know. I'm not making any promises. But I'll certainly give it a shot."

"The number-one thing most hikers do wrong is take too much stuff." He tugged playfully on her shoulder strap as she stepped up on a ledge in front of him. "This would be easier if your backpack were lighter."

"It's not heavy," Janie protested. "And I didn't bring anything extraneous."

They made their way methodically up a long, sloped rock surface, more than a hill, less than a mountain, treacherous as a lion's den. Tom had described it on the way there as an "intermediate trail." But partway up the going became a little difficult and Janie had to struggle for a handhold. She looked back over her shoulder and scowled at Tom, who was close behind, laughing as quietly as he could under his breath. She saw the amusement on his face and experienced a momentary urge to plant her cleated foot in the middle of it.

"You think this is funny?" she said. "I don't. I distinctly remember you saying *hike.*"

Once she was on solid ground at the top of the formation, Janie sat down in front of a boulder and, leaning back, let her weary arms and legs relax. She took a long pull from her water bottle. She poured a little water over her face and wiped it off on the sleeve of her shirt, and while she was in the neighborhood lifted up one arm for a quick sniff.

"Phew," she said, her nose wrinkled, "between the sweat and the insect repellent, I am truly gross and disgusting."

"It's a basic human right to be that way every now and then. So here we are, exercising our rights."

He had such a young-looking grin on his face that Janie forgot for a moment that he was as middle-aged as she. With a bandana tied around his head, she envisioned the full shock of hair he'd once had, though any discerning observer could have seen even in his youth that it would someday go thinner on him. "This is how humans are supposed to live," he proclaimed to the rocks as he thumped enthusiastically on his chest with closed fists. "Sweat and dirt and muscle aches."

"*Ugh.*" Janie laughed. "Not *this* human. Show me to the nearest Jacuzzi."

"Later, woman. You have to earn it today." He pulled out his own water bottle and indulged in a hearty drink, then wiped his face with boyish disregard on the sleeve of his T-shirt. "So," he said matter-of-factly, "talk."

"Sure you don't want to torture me a little more first?"

"No. You look tortured enough."

"Well, that's appropriate, I think."

Tom waited a moment, then said, "It's all getting to you, isn't it?"

A hawk circling overhead caught Janie's attention. She shielded her eyes and looked upward, watching as it glided with no visible effort in search of its next meal, which it would not have to pay for or cook. She sighed with envy and looked back at her dear and trusted companion. "Yeah, it's getting to me, all right. Bruce told me a couple of days ago that he thought I should just chuck it all and run away to any place that will have me. Maybe he was right."

Tom flicked a mosquito off his arm and let out an ironic little *hmph.* "Bolivia will have you," he said. "So will Madagascar. And even someone as inept at immigration law as I seem to be could probably get you into certain central African countries. Or India, if you're really desperate."

"Too bad I don't want to go to any of those places."

"Actually, I'm rather glad you don't."

Their eyes met and held.

"I'd miss you."

Eons of silence went by. Then Janie found her voice again.

"I think I'd miss you too."

The moment suddenly needed adjustment, and Tom, as always, found a way to tune it with a touch of self-deprecation. "I mean, what would you do with all your money if you didn't have to give it to me?"

"Probably give it to my new lawyer."

He laughed, and it sounded completely genuine. "Well, at least it would stay within the profession. I suppose that's something to be grateful for." He neatly changed the subject, saving them both. "Now, you dragged me all the way up here to talk. . . ."

Eyebrows raised, she said, "We seem to have different recollections of who did the dragging." Then she sighed and looked away, eventually letting her gaze fix itself on the distant horizon. "It feels like it's all closing in on me again."

He reached out and put one hand on her shoulder, and after the slightest hesitation, massaged it lightly. "Your legal problems are all going to resolve themselves in time. Just be patient, is all I can tell you."

"I wish my problems were only legal."

"My warranty doesn't cover any other kind."

"I don't need a lawyer right now, Tom, I need a friend."

All hints of humor dropped from Tom's voice. "Janie. You know you've got that. You don't even need to ask."

"I know. I didn't mean to imply that I didn't. Sorry. How good a friend do you feel like being today?"

The smart-aleck in him resurfaced. "As good as you want."

"Top-secret-type good?"

"Damn. And I thought maybe I was finally gonna get somewhere with you."

She couldn't help but smile at him. "Well, maybe not top secret. I don't really know what to make of all this." She opened her backpack and pulled out Virtual Memorial, and while holding it on her lap told him about the enigmatic Kristina and her bolder-than-brass entry into Janie's life. She outlined the intriguing challenge presented by this young woman who was way too much like Betsy for Janie's comfort.

"It's like *Mission: Impossible.*"

"And it all happens right here on V.M., my new pet. I'm not supposed to leave him alone."

"Why not? Does he chew the furniture?"

"No, thank God, and so far he seems to be paper-trained." She flipped open the cover and the screen flashed to life. "Probably because it could cause a lot of trouble if he fell into the wrong hands."

He considered it all for a few moments. "Is this why you've been

asking about your will and your insurance and bringing in all your valuables to my safe?"

"Yes. Kristina told me it would be a good idea to 'set my affairs in
order.' "

"Wow." Tom gazed out over the rocks below for a moment, then
turned back to Janie and said, "To borrow a phrase from our youth, this
is heavy."

"Yeah. That's what I think too. Tonight I'm going to run through the
first evaluation of the collected data. I have no idea what I'm going to
find, but I'm hoping some connections will start to appear."

"Janie," Tom said after a minute of reflection, "does any of this bother
you at all?"

"Of course it does. I'd be an idiot not to be scared. That seems to be
my natural state these days. These little reports of DR SAM are frightening the hell out of me."

"Well, that's not unique to you. I'm scared of that too."

"God, Tom, what would we do if it came back again?"

"I don't know."

Janie was quiet for a minute. "But you know what?" she finally
said. Afraid or not, I can't wait to go home and start looking at the
data."

Tom took hold of her hand and gave it a brief, encouraging squeeze.
"But still you say this is all making you crazy. I don't think that's what it
is. I think you feel alive for the first time in ages, and you don't know
what to do with all that positive energy."

"But I feel so—conflicted . . . for so many reasons . . ."

"Foremost of which is that you're trying so hard to have this nice,
normal life. That may not be what the Cosmic Troll has in mind for
you."

"Well, just for once I wish he would crawl out from under that bridge
in a better mood."

"Not your call, my dear."

"We could argue about that."

Tom gave her a wry little smile and said, "We probably wouldn't get
anywhere if we did."

She took in a long breath, then let it out slowly and deliberately. "So
what do you think I should do, O Wise One?"

"Do you want the lawyer answer or the friend answer?"

"We're in friend mode, aren't we?"

"Then I think you should do this—investigation, I guess it is—with everything you've got. You won't be happy with yourself unless you do. And I don't believe you should even think about going anywhere else until you're satisfied that you've finished with it." He stood up and brushed the dirt off the seat of his pants. "Except," he said, pointing toward the next crop of rocks, "up."

"What about Iceland?"

He wouldn't look her in the eye. "Well, of course, you shouldn't pass that by."

He left her at her door with a gentle kiss, which Janie revisited in her mind several times before deciding it was really just a friendly kiss after all and nothing to get excited about. Then she got into the shower and scrubbed her skin until it glowed red and all the grit and sweat and chemicals of the mountain excursion went screaming down the drain like a tribe of banished cooties.

The little mailman on her computer was smiling and waving letters when she checked.

All the ads were marked as required, so she dumped them without so much as a glance and proceeded to the stuff that mattered to her. The personal messages were ordered by diminishing size. From Bruce: *I love you, please don't misunderstand what I'm saying, I think you're wonderful,* and other expressions of apologetic misery. From Caroline: *Everything okay? We're worried about you. Call me as soon as you can.* From Wargirl: *Later.*

She assumed it meant that Kristina would be coming over later that evening. With her hair still wrapped in a white towel, Janie opened the evaluation program and started to do what she'd hungered to do earlier.

But as the sorted data unfolded before her, she found herself feeling disappointed. She had run them through filters for age, place of birth, height, weight, heritage, inoculations, medical history, all the basics. And the sorry truth was that nothing she saw was terribly striking. The most visible common denominator was still the summer camp.

It was both annoying and frustrating. "Okay, be that way," she said to the computer, as if it had some personal responsibility for the data that had been entered into it. "But now how about you tell me something I don't already know?" She opened the command window for genetic evaluation. "Here," she said, touching the screen, "that oughta keep you busy while I get dressed."

Her phone calls were done, her hair was dry, and a quick dinner was digesting in her stomach when she came back to check on V.M.'s progress a little while later. The little notebook computer was about 80 percent finished with the monumental task she'd assigned him. There were still a number of boys left to go, but there on the screen in front of her Janie thought she saw, finally, something unexpected.

"I think I may have been saved from my own foolishness by these newcomers," Chaucer whispered to Alejandro when he was back in his seat again.

But the Jew at his side did not respond, for his attention was completely focused on Guillaume Karle, who had taken the seat directly opposite him at the table, and now stared, white-faced, directly into his eyes.

Their concentration on each other was not lost on de Chauliac, who watched the proceedings like an eagle from his high-backed chair at the head of the table. "Marcel," he said, "you must present your companion."

Unaware of the intrigue that was unfolding, Marcel stood and placed a hand on Karle's shoulder. "This is my young nephew Jacques, come to Paris for a visit. At a most inopportune time, I must say, but he would pay respects to his *grandmère* at my sister's insistence. I did not see fit to discourage him."

"Welcome, nephew of my great friend *le provoste*. I am delighted to know you, and honored that you would tear yourself away from your *grandmère* to sit at my table. But it seems to me that you may already know one of my other guests."

Karle looked nervously in de Chauliac's direction, then let his gaze travel all around the table. He felt himself falling under the curious scrutiny of the other guests, most notably the young man Chaucer. He struggled to maintain his composure while all waited for his response. Finally, he stammered out a denial. "N-no . . . but for a moment the gentleman put me in mind of someone." He turned back to Alejandro and said, "I apologize, sir, if my attention gave you cause to take offense."

Alejandro quickly shook his head no. He sat still and stiff, his eyes glued to the amber-haired rebel, the man who was supposed to be looking after his beloved Kate. *What lunacy is this?* he had thought when he heard this Marcel's false introduction. He himself looked around the table, and wondered if everyone there was some sort of imposter; he came quickly to the conclusion that it was as likely as not. When it came time for him to make known his own name to the late arrivals, he rose slightly and joined in the assumed deception. "Hernandez at your service, *messieurs.*"

Almost instantly, de Chauliac added an embellishment. "There is too much modesty in this room. This is *Doctor* Hernandez, to be accurate. My former student."

Marcel's eyebrows rose in interest. "Then you must be much in demand, sir; there are few doctors left in Paris. So many have perished. I have expended many hours in grievous worry over how our citizens will be provided for."

On this matter, the lad Chaucer had a word or two to say, and he leapt into the conversation enthusiastically. "My lord Lionel often mentions how his father decries the lack of physicians, and then further bemoans the excess of lawyers."

Marcel smiled. "Having been subjected to one too many lawyers myself, I can sympathize with the king's wariness of advocates. But physicians are a treasure."

"He has not come here for the purposes of treating patients, Etienne," de Chauliac said, "but rather, to learn. He has brought a fine medical tome for my consideration." He smiled sweetly in Alejandro's direction. "I am very grateful for the honor Dr. Hernandez has done me in seeking my opinion."

"Then I am even more impressed!" said Marcel. He turned back to Alejandro. "Do you realize, sir, that the French royal family often seeks the opinion of your teacher? And the holy fathers themselves, may the departed rest in peace."

This well-intended reminder of the irony of fate brought a bitter look to de Chauliac's face, which Marcel could not fail to notice. The provost's tenor changed in an instant. "Well, let me simply say that you are in fine and noble company."

By sheer force of will, Alejandro quieted his pounding heart so he could hear the words of his own answer. "Far more than my station would merit, I think."

Which statement prompted de Chauliac to recover. He said, "Again, I declare, you suffer from a marked excess of modesty, colleague. In my opinion, you are quite fit for service to a king."

"And what is your natural station, if I may be so bold to ask?"

After a brief moment, Alejandro answered Marcel as truthfully as he could. "I am a Spaniard."

"I took that from your name, sir. What of your family?"

Then he lied. "They are ordinary folk of Aragon."

"And yet you are a well-educated man."

The moment he took to formulate a plausible response felt too long to him. "The town was in need of a physician, and saw in me a fellow who could learn. And for a time, when my education was complete, I served them well."

"And now Paris is blessed by your presence. How long have you been in our fair city?"

"I have only just arrived."

"Then the people of your town must miss you greatly."

"One would hope."

"One is certain," de Chauliac said with a smile.

"What prompted you to leave? That is to say, what beyond the beauty of Paris, and the wisdom of your esteemed teacher?"

Alejandro could barely contain himself; he wanted nothing more than to get Karle alone long enough to find out what had happened to Kate. But he forced himself to be cordial. "Those were reasons enough," he said, "but if there was any other, I suppose that wanderlust could be blamed."

"The mandate of a young man," Marcel said. He gestured toward Karle. "Such as my nephew here. The elderly among us, and I refer to our host and myself, must be content to stay at home and see to our obligations. Though I am certain that young Jacques, by nature of his outstanding character, will look to his own responsibilities when the time comes."

De Chauliac took the rib with an amiable laugh, for he and Marcel were on quite intimate terms. Karle smiled wanly and made a simple nod. Alejandro could see that he was intent on playing the provincial simpleton. *Good*, he thought. *The less attention he attracts to himself, the happier I shall be.*

And then the girl danced again, and great platters of sumptuous food began to arrive: fragrant turnips and sautéed greens piled high around a steaming roast of beef, long loaves of bread, and thick slabs of creamy white butter. Flagons of dark red wine were set on the table and the gentlemen invited to pour for themselves, which they did without restraint. As soon as one flagon was empty, it was replaced by another, and in short order the mood was even more jovial than before.

"A handsome feast, is it not?" Chaucer whispered to Alejandro. "My lord Lionel will be sorely displeased that he was forced to miss it."

"One assumes your lord has had ample feasts, and thus acquired the condition that led to his unfortunate absence."

Chaucer cast a quick glance toward de Chauliac, and when he was satisfied that their host was otherwise engaged in conversation, he said to Alejandro, "Indeed. And de Chauliac says that he is far too young to be so afflicted. My lord complains that *Monsieur le Docteur* has no sympathy for his pain. He begs for a draft of laudanum to relieve it, but de Chauliac will not hear of it."

He refuses wisely, Alejandro was about to say, *for it will bind up Prince Lionel's insides like a bowlful of clay to the great aggravation of his gout.* But he held himself back from that statement, for an idea had suddenly come to mind. "Perhaps your lord would benefit from a second diagnosis," he said instead. "I would be delighted to render one, with de Chauliac's assent, of course."

Chaucer looked back at the arrogant Frenchman; even as a mere page, he understood from household whisperings that de Chauliac took himself a bit too seriously. He leaned closer to the Jew and said quietly, "Such a request would have to be handled delicately. With the most tender of words."

The lad had eagerly taken the bait, and Alejandro found himself admiring the page's adventurous nature and inquisitive spirit. He admonished himself not to squander the great opportunity before him, but to use it wisely and to his benefit. "You aspire to be a wordsmith, my friend; find the necessary words to bring your lord the relief he craves."

Chaucer took the challenge. "It is no sooner spoken than done," he said with a smile. "I will arrange it."

Alejandro returned the smile, and thought how delightful it would be to bind up the bowels of Isabella's younger brother. His efforts to keep the Plantagenet innards loose in England had been vastly unappreciated. But this time, what he did would not go unnoticed.

Alejandro's opportunity to speak with Guillaume Karle came only when dinner was finished and the groaning, overstuffed guests finally pushed themselves drunkenly away from the long table. He had waited with gut-grinding patience, his own goblet barely touched, for de Chauliac to be otherwise occupied. And though his guards would keep sharp eyes on his movements, they would not be alarmed if he spoke privately to another of the guests.

He watched with interest as de Chauliac took the alchemist Flamel by the arm and led him out of the room, up the stairs toward the part of the mansion where his own cell was situated. And he realized with a bit of alarm the likely purpose of their disappearance—de Chauliac would show this Flamel the manuscript. For the briefest moment, he felt a terrible temptation to follow, to hear what the alchemist would have to say about the writ of Abraham. But he could not waste the opportunity to speak to Karle while they were out of his French captor's scrutiny.

Marcel was occupied in a slightly drunken and very passionate argument with one of the other guests, leaving his "nephew" unattended. Alejandro took hold of his arm, none too gently, and steered him into the vestibule. The guards watched carefully, but did not interfere.

When he judged that they were out of earshot, he hissed, "What of her? *Speak.*"

"Calm yourself, Physician," Karle said, "and loose your grip! You will need to repair my arm if you squeeze any harder."

Alejandro unclenched his fingers. "You have back your arm, now speak. And speak plainly, for there may be little time."

Karle's voice was filled with urgency. He looked over Alejandro's shoulder repeatedly as he spoke. "She is completely well, I assure you. We have gone several times looking for you."

"To Rue des Rosiers? Beneath the sign of the *fromagerie?*"

"Exactly."

"So she remembered, then, after these many years."

"She did. Better than you, it would seem—for here you are, so close!" Karle said. "Why did you not come?"

Alejandro stared at him in disbelief. His face hardened into anger. "Can you not see that I am prisoner?" he whispered.

"I see no irons on you."

Alejandro inclined his head briefly toward the door, where the guards stood. "Human irons, he has me in. Do you think I would not come if it were possible for me to do so?"

Karle returned the angry look. "How am I to know what you will or will not do?"

"My daughter would know! Has she not told you of my complete devotion to her?"

"Many times. And she also speaks of her devotion to you. So you need not worry on that account."

Alejandro moved closer to Karle, his expression now even more menacing. "Is there an account on which I ought to worry?"

A slight hesitation, but long enough for Alejandro to notice. "Well?" he demanded.

"No. She is well, and happy."

"Happy? How can a maiden separated so long from her father be happy?"

Karle stammered, "W-well, perhaps she is not truly happy, but she seems content." He struggled for an explanation. "She has a female companion to keep her company, a maid in Marcel's house where—"

"You have taken her to Marcel's house?"

"Yes. And he has made us quite welcome—without prying into who she might be or why she is with me. I went there because there was no other safe roof in Paris under which to shelter her. And myself."

"A stable would be safer for her. Why, all manner of nobles will float in and out of there!"

Karle's eyes narrowed. He decided that the secrecy had gone on long enough. "I think it is time you tell me why it is that you fear showing her."

Alejandro backed away a bit. "She has not told you, then."

"Told me *what*?" Karle hissed in frustration.

But Alejandro remained silent, his expression stony and unreadable.

"When I return to Marcel's, I will ask her to reveal this secret to me."

"She will not."

Karle took hold of Alejandro's collar and pulled him to within a hand's breadth of his face. "Do not be so sure of that, Physician."

They locked in a stare, each hating the need that he had for the other. In the stark quiet of that moment, Alejandro heard the fall of feet on stone steps, and the rustle of robes. He looked over his shoulder to see de Chauliac and Flamel coming down the stairs, engaged in a deep discussion. He turned back to Karle and whispered, "There is no more time to talk. We must make plans to get me out of here. I am constantly guarded; there is no easy escape from this house."

"Then how—"

"I think I may have managed to arrange an outing."

De Chauliac was walking through the salon, his long crimson robe billowing elegantly behind him, the stout and red-faced alchemist at his side. The Frenchman smiled as he approached, and Alejandro knew there would be questions to answer when he reached them.

"There is a barred window on the top floor, facing west. That is where I am being held. I will drop you a letter. Come after dark tomorrow. Do not fail me, Karle, or—"

But he never had the chance to say what he would do in the event of Karle's failure, for de Chauliac was upon them with his portly companion.

"Such an intimate dialogue! Come now, confess to your acquaintance."

Karle nodded respectfully, then said, "There is none, sir, we are newly acquainted, but since the gentleman is a physician, and as my dear uncle Etienne has pointed out there are so few these days, well, I thought it wise to ask him about a certain ailment from which I suffer, one that may concern a woman."

"Ah!" de Chauliac said with a wave of his hand. "Such ailments are beastly. Say no more!"

"Happily, I need not, for the good doctor has given me what seems to be excellent advice."

"He is an excellent physician. You will do well to heed what he says. And may I add my personal advice as well?"

"Please do. I am eager for good advice on this matter."

De Chauliac smiled. "Then I would advise you to take care, young man, in choosing the sort of women you associate with."

Karle and Alejandro glanced briefly at each other, then Karle said, "In this case, sir, the maid chose me." And with a polite bow he departed their company.

It was a long moment before Alejandro recovered enough to realize that Flamel was speaking to him. He had to ask for a repetition of the alchemist's question. And then he had to think quickly for a proper answer to the question of how he had acquired the book.

"It was bought from an apothecary."

"Where, might I ask?"

"I do not recall, specifically. I was traveling at the time, and I did not always know the names of the villages I passed through. It was in the north, I think. No—wait; it may have been in the south." He shrugged apologetically. "I have a poor memory for such details."

Flamel glanced at de Chauliac, then turned back to Alejandro. His face glowed with uncontained excitement.

"I have been seeking this tome for a very long time. Within the circles of my craft there have been rumors of its existence, but no one has ever seen it. You have done the world a remarkable service by finding it. Tell me, did the apothecary say where *he* had gotten it from?"

"I did not ask the man, and he offered no explanation. I think it is safe to assume that he obtained it from a Jew. It may have been among the plunder of Strasbourgh. Or perhaps he bought it from some Jew who escaped."

"Few escaped, praise God."

"Only one would be required," Alejandro said bitterly.

And before the discourse could sour further, de Chauliac jumped in. "Your translation proceeds well, I see."

"Indeed, but there is much yet to be done."

Flamel said, "I saw from your writing that you have just begun the pages that give instructions for transmutation. It would be a great honor for me to know your progress as it is made. And perhaps I can be of assistance to you, for I understand the meaning of many of the symbols you will find in the manuscript."

"Why, that seems a wonderful idea!" de Chauliac said.

And Alejandro realized that there would be no choice, that it had been arranged while they were upstairs in his chamber. He wondered how de Chauliac had explained the bars on the windows. Or if the alchemist had even noticed them.

The party was ending, and one by one the guests took their leave. Karle had already followed Marcel through the door, leaving Alejandro with the gut-wrenching fear that he might never return. And the gross and unsavory alchemist had made effusive promises to return, much to the Jew's regret.

Now the page Geoffrey Chaucer was about to depart. Alejandro took him aside briefly and whispered, "Remember, you must speak with your lord. Tell him I am most anxious to be of help."

Chaucer winked his understanding of the conspiracy and said, "You shall hear from me soon. You may be confident of that."

And then the lad went to de Chauliac and pleaded for a note to excuse his long absence. He received it, in short order, and went happily on his way, a youth with all the possibilities of the world before him. Alejandro watched with wistful envy as he disappeared into the courtyard. His adventuresome spirit and eager mind reminded the captive Jew of his own younger, freer self before he had stumbled on his path.

The lad's love of English, however, was worrisome. But Alejandro could not concern himself with it now. And ultimately, he knew, such a youth would not be restrained, regardless of the world's opinion of his chosen language.

* * *

On the straw pallet of their small upstairs room, Kate trembled in Guillaume Karle's arms, and though the night was warm, she shivered in terror.

"But why can we not go now?"

"He said specifically tomorrow."

"De Chauliac!" she moaned plaintively. "Who would think it?"

He let out a frustrated sigh. "Were I to know their history, I might understand the meaning of their meeting, but I have not been made privy to the secrets of your past."

She shut her eyes tight and went silent.

"Kate, please, you must tell me these secrets. I am *dangerously* ignorant."

She opened her eyes and searched his. "He told you nothing, then?"

"No," Karle said, "but *he* asked me if *you* had told." He took her face gently into his two hands and looked deeply into her eyes. "I will not betray you," he promised. "My desire for you forbids it; and even without that, I am a man of honor. I would never be the cause of any harm coming to you, no matter the benefit to myself."

She turned her face away, but he brought it back again to his own. *"Please,"* he begged. "Do you fail to see that I love you? I *implore* you to trust me. If we are ever to make a life together, I must know who you are."

She removed his hands from her cheeks and pulled them gently down to her lap, then sat up straight and looked directly into his eyes. "I must have your promise that you will tell no one what I am about to reveal to you."

"You have just now had it. Never doubt my sincerity."

"Karle, this knowledge may not serve you well."

"I will take that risk."

She drew in a deep breath. "Should this become a burden, you must remember that I warned you. And that you accepted—"

"Yes! Accepted! For the love of the holy Virgin, go on!"

"Very well." She sighed wearily. "What do you know of the English royals?"

"No more than any ordinary man ought to know."

"You will soon know more than you ever cared to, I fear."

He seemed genuinely confused. "But what has that to do with you?"

"It has everything to do with me. You see, Karle, I am—I—"

And then choking back her tears, she stopped, unable to continue.

"Yes?" he said. "Tell me!"

She blurted it out; there was no other way. "I am not Père's child."

"Dear God!" he said. "You might as well say that the sky is blue! Any fool could see that in a glance. Now, whose child *are* you?"

"I . . . am . . . the daughter of King Edward."

An involuntary gasp escaped his lips. *"Mon dieu."* He crossed himself.

"My mother was a lady of Queen Philippa's household. Père was sent to Edward's Court during the Great Plague to serve as physician, by de Chauliac himself. That is how our lives first crossed."

Karle's jaw dropped in shock, and when he found himself again, he said, "A princess? *You are a princess of England?"*

"No! You do not understand! I am nothing. *Nothing.* A bastard, despised by all who had anything to do with me. I was taken from my mother at a very tender age and sent to the household of my sister Isabella, who is the true daughter of my father and his queen. I was little more than a slave to her; the only ones who were kind to me at all were Nurse, God bless her, and should she have departed this earth, heaven hold her. And my sister's lady, Adele! She was more a sister to me than Isabella. The queen, the king, all my royal brothers and sisters, they treated me like cold ashes from the hearth!"

"And what of your mother? Could she do nothing for you?"

"The queen forbade it. It was her vengeance against my mother for allowing herself to be bedded by the king, though how she might be expected to escape him, I cannot understand. And then when I was only seven, she was taken by the plague."

"So you told me. *Mon dieu,"* he repeated in amazement. "Truly, this is a most astonishing history. I never expected *anything* like this. . . ."

"What is most astonishing is that I am yet alive to tell it!" She hesitated a moment, then said, "And now I must demand another promise of confidence, or I cannot continue the tale."

"Again, you have it—but can there be anything more damning left to tell?"

"Perhaps you will think so, perhaps not." She caught in a breath, then blurted, "Père is a Jew."

Shocked silence was followed by a hushed, "That *cannot* be true. I would know it."

"How?"

"By his . . . *qualities* . . . he bears none of the characteristics of a Jew."

"He bears a scar. On his chest. He was branded with the circular mark."

And as he allowed his memory to redraw the images of that night in the cottage, he remembered wondering about the strange scar he had seen on the man's chest. But he had too many other competing thoughts to give the scar more than a cursory consideration at the time; men were dying, he himself was a hunted fugitive. "He turned away from me, the one time I saw him without a shirt. Now I understand why." Then after a puzzled moment, he said, "But how is it that de Chauliac came to send him to England, then?"

"De Chauliac did not know. Père hid his identity. He took the name of a dead companion, a soldier with whom he traveled out of Spain."

"Why?"

"Because he killed a bishop there."

"A *bishop*? And he yet walks about, untortured?"

"I swear it is true—and you must believe, Karle, he was well justified in what he did."

"But a bishop . . . truly, this is a burdensome sin."

"And he is burdened by the memory of it every day. The cursed cleric had ruined him and his family, all for the exhumation of a body, a man Père tried to treat for a terrible affliction, and he needed most desperately to understand why the man died. So he took the body out of the grave—"

"*Mon dieu!*" Karle groaned.

"Karle—you must try to understand—when one seeks knowledge as passionately as Père does, one is often forced to take chances. And for his acts, he has paid dearly. His family was forced out of Cervere, their goods confiscated—they had to make the journey out of Spain during the worst of the Death." She hung her head a bit. "He does not know if either his mother or father completed the journey—they were well on in age, and it was ten years ago."

"It is right and fitting that he should have paid dearly for these crimes."

Kate's cheeks were flushed with building anger, but she held it back, with much effort. "Père knows that he will be judged for these acts one day. But in his holy books, it says 'an eye for an eye,' and though he cannot be overtly devout he takes the words of his own prophets quite seriously."

A quiet moment passed, then Kate continued. "In Avignon, he sought to establish himself in medical practice, and await his family's arrival. But he was conscripted along with other physicians to be trained under de Chauliac. They were sent all over Europa to protect the health of the royal households, for the pope wanted to make mischief with royal marriages, and he could not do so were all the brides and grooms to perish before he got his hands on them. That is how Père came to be in England—otherwise, he would still be in Avignon. For many years he has hoped that his family was able to reach there, but he is afraid to return, lest he be recognized and captured. And despite his dearest hopes for them, he knows there is little chance that they survived both the plague and the journey from Spain."

Karle sighed in deep amazement. "How cruel the hand of fate can be. He thought Paris safe, and yet it was here that his greatest danger lay." He was thoughtful for a moment, then said, with a very grave expression, "It must have been terrible for you, all these years."

Kate's eyebrows furrowed. "Terrible? How do you mean?"

"You have traveled now for ten years as his daughter."

"And why," she said unhappily, "would this be terrible?"

"Bad enough that he should be a Jew, but also to be a robber of graves, a *murderer* . . . you have shown him remarkable devotion, consid—"

Without thinking, she reached out to strike him. He caught her hand before it hit his face, and held it tight. He saw the anger in her eyes, the wetness of tears about to flow, and he understood that she gave these considerations no weight. She loved the man as she would a true father.

After a few tense and motionless moments he whispered, "I'm sorry. I meant no disrespect." He kissed her clenched and trembling fist with apologetic tenderness. "I spoke too quickly, and from ignorance."

Kate yanked her hand away. Her cheeks were flushed, and when she finally spoke, her voice was dark. "Père is the finest man I have ever known. He is far more noble in spirit than the one who sired me. I have never wanted for one moment in his care. He has given me the gift of knowledge, of language and reading, and the ciphering of numbers—I know medicine, and hunting, and all of the skills one needs to survive! Few men can make such claims, let alone women. And never once did he try to force his beliefs on me. But I know that he longs for it, I can see it in his face sometimes; he has an emptiness about him that no man should have to endure."

Karle said, very quietly, "He has lost much."

"He has lost everything that matters to him, save me."

And when she spoke these words, Karle understood that he would, indeed, have to accept the father to have the daughter. "I swear that I shall do whatever is necessary to see that you are never separated again."

"You will have to make your peace with him, then, if we are to be together."

"Then peace it shall be."

* * *

But the mind of the man in question would give him no peace, for it still swirled with the evening's events. The nimble-minded young Chaucer, who might unwittingly be the key to his escape; the unexpected reunion with Karle; the thrilling news of Kate's safety, and Karle's troubling assertion that Kate had "chosen" him in some way. Of course there could be only one way in which a maid would choose a man—the very thought of it burned inside him and ate away at what little solace he had left.

It was all too confusing to comprehend, beyond the understanding of the simpleton he had come to believe himself to be. But understand it he must, for he was desperate to be out of de Chauliac's control. At least in the Spanish monastery, he remembered silently, it was certain that his captors wanted him dead. De Chauliac inflicted upon him the torture of gross uncertainty. He despised being an unwilling intellectual accomplice, a plaything of the mind. *And damn the man, he has an intellect that in better circumstances would make him the most welcome of companions.*

By the light of a single candle, he stared at Abraham's manuscript and wondered if he would ever feel the same about it again. This Flamel seemed to desire it like a man longs for a woman, as if by having it he could redeem himself from some great and disappointing failure. Now that the greasy alchemist had run through its pages and seen its secrets, Alejandro no longer felt like it was truly his own.

Fool! he chided himself. *It belongs to the people for whose guidance it was written.* Now it was his duty to see that it got to them.

Suddenly there was a soft knock, and in came de Chauliac himself. Gone were the formal robes of entertainment; the elegant Frenchman was now attired in a light robe of the finest indigo silk. Their eyes met, and for a moment Alejandro felt the stab of de Chauliac's searching and probing; the man was trying to look into his very soul, it seemed. He looked away, which forced de Chauliac to speak.

"It was a fine evening, was it not?"

"It was interesting, I will admit. But why in God's name did you invite the lord Lionel?"

"Why should my reason concern you?"

"But he might have come."

De Chauliac smiled. "I suppose it was the potential for danger that made me do it, to see how you would react. I admit that it was enjoyable, to see you squirm with fear of recognition. But it turned out well, did it not? You seem to have enjoyed the company of his young page. Lionel was but a child when you were there, and unconcerned with the doings of his elders." He grunted cynically. "He is *still* little more than a child. He certainly indulges himself childishly, to the point where he has managed to get himself afflicted with gout."

Alejandro sat up straighter. *Here is my chance to plant the next seed.* "I would like to examine him, then, if you think he will not know me."

De Chauliac's eyebrows raised in surprise. "Whatever for?"

"Because, as you have already said, he is too young to suffer from gout. Perhaps it is not gout that tortures him. Perhaps it is something else."

"You would doubt my diagnosis?"

Be careful what you say. Remember his pride and use it against him. "This war has brought many new forms of misery, afflictions that yet defy classification, and I have seen many of them. Royals do not remain untouched simply because they are royals. Once I learned from you, because yours was the greater breadth of knowledge. Is it not possible that now, you could learn from me?"

De Chauliac shifted uncomfortably. "I suppose it is possible. . . ."

"This young Chaucer says that his lord suffers from pain of the extremities, in particular one foot, but that you will not give him laudanum. I think this is the correct course of treatment, because it may bind him up, and you are wise to recognize that the body must be able to rid itself of all its foul humors and wastes if he is to recover. But if gout is not his curse, then he may be suffering needlessly from pain that you might cure. He would be forever in your debt."

The Frenchman was quiet and contemplative, but did not respond.

Finally, after a long and tortuous silence, he said, "You make a good point, Jew. Perhaps our combined wisdom will serve my prince better than mine alone."

Alejandro was quick to add, "We could then retire to another room to discuss our findings. If we come up with some other cause for his affliction, we will say that the discovery was yours alone."

De Chauliac took on a pained, hurt look. "I do not need such false accolades."

"No, of course you do not. What I meant is that I can ill afford the attention."

"Yes, of course," he said contemplatively. Then his look turned dark and threatening. "You will be very sorry if you try to escape."

"With the guards you have set upon me? How can one man overpower them?"

The Frenchman stared at him for a moment, as if he were trying to probe his mind. "I will consider it," he eventually said. And then with a swish of his silken robe, he rose up and walked to the door. Without looking back he whispered, "Sleep well, my friend," and then left, closing the door behind him, leaving his prisoner to wonder why, exactly, he had come in the first place.

Janie no longer assumed it was a benign presence on the other side of
the door when the bell sounded, as she had during another phase of her
life.

Was it a good thing, or a bad thing, this new caution of hers? What
would her friends say, if they could see her hovering near the peephole?

Michael and Caroline would discuss it between themselves before giving an opinion, which could not be predicted in advance. Bruce would
say *good*, right away. Tom would think about it for a while, finally con-
cluding *bad*. Kristina, now standing impatiently outside the door, would
not have an opinion beyond *open the door.*

"I got your message," the young woman said. "I assume you meant
you have something to show me."

"I do," Janie answered nervously. She motioned for the girl to enter,
but as Kristina passed through, Janie looked around outside, her eyes
darting from the sidewalk to the bushes to the driveway. Kristina stared at
her with genuine concern.

"Are you all right?"

"Oh, yeah, I guess—but it's taking me more time than I thought to
shake off the heebie-jeebies from the break-in. I hope it isn't too long
until I stop doing this," she said.

"Me too," Kristina said. She presented Janie with a brown paper bag.
"Here, maybe this will help."

Janie pulled an ice cream container out of the bag, and with a broad smile she said, "Oh, this will definitely improve my state of mind." Her door paranoia began to fade. "Now, let's see, what do we have here."

Janie held up the cardboard ice cream carton and read the label, and saw that the flavor was her own esoteric favorite, a gooey concoction of chocolate and butterscotch and nuts, and her grateful expression turned into a sharp stare.

Some magical coincidence, or . . .

"How did you know this is my favorite?"

The question brought a nervous little flutter of stammering from Kristina, but no specific answer.

"Look," Janie said, "you need to be a little more careful about flaunting all this minutiae you somehow seem to know about everybody. *I* can look beyond it, but someone else might be inclined to punch you out for being an arrogant little know-it-all."

Kristina looked stricken and started to gush an apology. "I didn't mean—"

Janie turned away so Kristina wouldn't see the little smile that had arisen on her face, or notice that she was trying to stifle laughter; she was developing a healthy respect for the girl's obvious competence, and rather liked her. But it was strangely satisfying to see her in a dithered state. Janie wanted to say the same thing to Kristina that her own mother had often said when she was too full of herself: Every time you look back over your shoulder, there's going to be someone smarter than you back there.

But I'm not her mother.

She set the container down on the counter and got out bowls and spoons. "Forget I said anything. Of course I assume you're all watching me. But this is a *wee* bit close." She patted the top of the ice cream container, now dripping its condensation on the kitchen counter. "I forgive you for knowing my favorite flavor *because* this is my favorite flavor, and I'm glad you were considerate enough to go out and find it." She laughed quietly as a memory came over her. "For the first three weeks after I left home for college I ate so much ice cream that I couldn't even look at it until I was about twenty-five. But since I started eating it again, I've never been able to get enough."

Kristina took off her light jacket and hung it over a kitchen chair. "And during that hiatus you were also a vegetarian."

Janie stared in complete disbelief—it had been only a few seconds since she'd complained about this very thing. *How quickly they forget!* The mother in her wanted to rise up, stern and corrective, but she kept her voice low and delivered a somewhat gentle lecture. "All right, if you don't stop this right now I'm going to have to ground you." She pointed toward a section of counter. "There are spoons in that drawer."

Janie found the scoop in its usual place and served for both of them. They sat down at the kitchen table and set their bowls on either side of Virtual Memorial. "I didn't hear from you all day, so I figured I'd better check in," Kristina said.

"I was a little busy today, and anyway I assumed you would be coming—I got your message from this afternoon. And you told me yesterday that you would check in tonight, don't you remember?"

Janie noticed immediately that Kristina seemed to stiffen. The girl didn't answer the query, but instead tossed back one of her own that had the feel of a counterpunch to it. "What were you doing that kept you so busy?" she demanded to know.

Janie tried to sound as casual as possible, though she was bothered by the shape the conversation seemed to be assuming. "I worked at the foundation in the morning, then I had a personal appointment, then I went for a hike with an old friend—"

"You like to hike?"

"Oh, you didn't know? Well, there's a refreshing change—and I'm not that crazy about it. But someone invited me."

You probably know who, she thought.

"And I—needed to blow off a little steam. And by the way, V.M. was with me all the time. And then this evening I went over some of the demographic evaluations." She paused. "And ran a genetic one."

That revelation changed the look on Kristina's face. "Did you find anything?" she asked.

Janie turned the computer's screen slightly toward Kristina so they both had a clear view. "Take a look," she said. "I'll let you decide that for yourself."

The display was full of report choices—charts, lists, rankings. She touched a spot on the screen and the whole thing turned into a well-labeled bar chart with an overview of all the data to date, showing the incidence of similarity. "We have this geographical spike here, but we knew about that, and I really think it's entirely coincidental, just a secondary result based on more important common factors. I think it's safe to say that there are more Jewish people living on the East Coast than there are in the Bible Belt." She touched one particular spike on the graph and the details of the data appeared in a side window. "And the major underlying common factor is still Camp Meir, and they were all there, as you can see from this line, in the same year, just before the first Outbreak of DR SAM."

There was a twinge of disappointment in Kristina's voice when she said, "We were sort of expecting all this, though."

"I know," Janie concurred. "None of this surprises me at all. And to tell you the truth, I don't think we're going to find much more than that in the demographic data. It feels like a great big dead end. A little something more might come up in the medical histories, since they aren't all complete yet, but I don't get the sense that anything earth-shattering is going to reveal itself. But we'll look, because I could be wrong. It's happened before."

She expected Kristina to laugh, but the girl's attention remained tightly focused on the screen. So Janie drew in a long breath, and continued. "However . . . here, I think we're looking in the right place." She touched the screen again, this time on the icon for the genetic evaluation. Another series of options appeared. "There are a few very interesting things that showed up."

Kristina's face seemed to tighten even more as she read the information on the screen. Unearned wrinkles appeared in her forehead as her eyes darted from line to line. "I always feel like I can't wait to see these genetic evaluations. Then I remember what they can mean." She looked at Janie with a worried expression. "I see a few cancers here." She let her own finger glide down the screen, checking file after file. "Here's colon cancer, and testicular, nothing so terrible yet, I guess . . ." She stopped, with her finger on one particular name. "Oh, shit. This kid's going to need a pancreas one of these days." She sighed in distress. "Well, maybe by the time this actuates, there will be a better treatment."

"Maybe we'll figure out how to grow the organs we need," Janie said in a wishful tone. "But look here—we've got a pending case of Lou Gehrig's disease." She sat back and looked at Kristina. "Do you have any idea if these boys or their families have been told of these potentialities?"

"I doubt it. Why would anyone think to look this stuff up in the first place, except insurance companies, I mean . . . and I don't know how we'd find out. But we can hardly walk up to a parent and say, 'Excuse me, has anyone told you yet that your son is going to die a slow and painful death in what should be the prime of his life, and that he'll end his days drooling and pissing on himself?' Especially since we obtained this genetic material in a rather questionable way."

In a deadly serious tone, Janie said, "None of these problems will matter much if they don't all recover from their more immediate problems. And while we're on that subject . . ." She brought up another page in the program. "Here's what I think might be the link. I found it in every one of them."

It was one particular gene on one particular chromosome, with a simple little flaw, a repetition of an adenine-thymine pair, plopped down in a place where it shouldn't have been plopped.

Kristina touched the screen in a few places and brought up a graphic illustration of the gene in question. "Hello, darling," she said, her expression revealing forbidden, guilty excitement. She touched the symbol that directed the computer to display its proper scientific title. The letters and numbers came up on the screen, and Kristina turned to Janie with an immensely satisfied expression on her face.

"I knew it," she said.

"Knew what?"

"That we'd find something like this."

Janie eyes narrowed; she stared at the young woman beside her. "Then why have I been doing all this searching and evaluating?"

"I didn't know we were specifically going to find this gene," Kristina said, "I just knew in my gut that we would find a gene. Somewhere. With something like this."

"Like what?"

Kristina pointed to the gene's name on the screen. The letters were red and underlined. "I guess I should explain. You haven't used this program before. We set it up to recognize certain things and report them back in different colors."

"Such as?"

"Well, the program looks for specific qualities in the genes as it reads them, ones that are of potential interest to us." She drew in a long breath through her nose, and pointed to the image on the screen with her finger. "This particular gene, the one you found in every one of these boys, has what could turn out to be a very interesting quality. It's patented."

"But I don't understand," Janie said, "you can't patent a native gene."

Kristina smiled. "I know."

"Then—then this gene . . ."

"Um-hm," Kristina said with a nod, "this gene is not native. It must have been introduced."

The disturbing revelation sent Janie straight back to the ice cream. Bowl in hand, curled up almost defensively on her couch opposite Kristina, she dipped out small mouthfuls and kept the spoon in her mouth each time until the ice cream melted. She stared out blankly, lost in thought, until the bowl was empty.

She tapped the spoon against the side of the bowl without realizing how annoying the sound was. Finally, Kristina reached out and took the spoon out of her hand.

Janie refocused and looked at her.

"Too bad there aren't pennies anymore," Kristina said, "or I'd offer you one for your thoughts."

With a cynical half-smile, Janie said, "These thoughts are probably worth a little more than that."

The young woman reached into the pocket of her jeans and pulled out a quarter, which she flipped once on her thumb. She tossed it across the coffee table to Janie. "Think out loud," she said.

"I don't like what I'm thinking. I feel like if I give voice to it, it'll become real."

"We wouldn't be seeing this thing if it wasn't already real. So speaking it isn't going to make any difference."

With a grim, firm-set look on her face, Janie said, "A gene can only be patented if it's been altered. So this particular gene had to have been removed from someone, altered, and then reintroduced to these boys. There's no other way it could have been done." She sighed deeply. "We have to find out who did this. But the really fun part"—she rubbed her forehead and closed her eyes—"is going to be figuring out how to fix it."

The list of variables seemed to be growing, not shrinking as Janie had expected it would. Each new bit of information, instead of resolving a problem, seemed to present another one. Needing to see it all in front of her, as soon as Kristina left Janie scrawled a list on a lavender-lined steno pad with red ink. It was messy, as her notes had been since medical school. *Alejandro was a physician,* she chided herself, *and he had beautiful handwriting.* She tried to relax her grip, and made a conscious effort to form her letters with long strokes and spidery flourishes as had her hero, even in his most desperate hours.

But it was still a mess, and she came to the conclusion that it was more a matter of what she'd written than how it had been applied to the paper:

Altered gene starts as a native gene. Whose? Patient Zero.

Native gene is changed. By whom? And why?

Altered gene is reproduced and presented for patent. Patent is granted—to whom? And for what potential use?

It had to have started somewhere. At some point in time, a child with this one genetic anomaly must have landed in the care of an orthopedic surgeon with a strong interest in genetics. The incident had to have been pre-Outbreak, back when patients could still sometimes choose who would give them care, and physicians could use innovative treatments without fear of being undermined or ostracized. Or financially ruined.

The whole situation smacked of research that had been left unfinished. Perhaps it had gone bad and was abandoned, and then was subsequently picked up by someone else with a different notion of what the outcome should be. In her mind's eye Janie saw the skeletal image of Abraham Prives's backbone after the break. It made her furious—the boy's spine looked like someone had taken a hammer to it, just pounded until there was no piece left larger than a dime. What a tragic, horrible mistake someone had made.

Because this had to have been a mistake, an originally well-intentioned attempt to do something beneficial that had somehow gone terribly wrong. There was simply no way that a decent human being involved in the care of another human being would allow this sort of thing to happen without reporting it.

And if it wasn't just an accident, but instead an intentional act, then when Janie figured out who'd done it, she was going to kick some very serious ass.

Do you know how much I love you? the e-mail message opened. *How much I want to be with you? What you mean to me? I sense that your life is filling up with distractions that will pull you away from me and from the things that are important to us. And though I know I have no right to tell you what to do, I beg you to consider what will happen to our life if you keep going down this road you've taken. I'm so afraid that you'll miss something important, some signal of impending doom or danger, and that you'll get hurt.*

Oh, Bruce, she thought sadly, *please don't do this now . . . please don't stand in my way.*

His message continued. *We need to talk about this, face-to-face, in Iceland.*

Iceland! she thought when she read it. *Oh, my God . . . how am I going to leave this work to go to Iceland?*

She typed out and queued up a frantic message to the travel agent—could the arrangements be changed, the trip delayed, perhaps by a week? Bruce's visa covered an entire month. Surely her own could be postponed to the end of that month . . . she would pay more, if that was necessary.

As that message was flying out, the little mailman appeared on the screen.

More? I just picked up the messages ten minutes ago.

It had no return address, no posted sender, no source information at all. It was a prime candidate for unread dumping.

She read it anyway.

Now would be a good time for you to back off.

The message was reply-ready, but address-blind, so if she replied, she would not know where her words were going, as she had not known when she'd answered Wargirl's first missive. But that incoming note had been friendly, and this new one clearly was not.

Stop, Bruce had said. *Go,* Tom had advised her. *Proceed with caution,* Caroline admonished. It was one big mental traffic light.

Janie saw only green.

I don't think so, she typed in the reply box. She touched the SEND icon.

Sandhaus would know; he was the answer man. He eschewed computers because he was one.

"What would be my best source for pre-Outbreak medical records?" Janie asked him.

"What specifically are you looking for?"

"A Patient Zero. He would be suffering from some sort of vertebral trauma."

John Sandhaus chuckled cynically. "Oh, yeah, that'll be easy to find." He thought for a moment. "NIH would be where I'd start. Use the foundation's spinal regeneration study as your excuse to get in."

It wouldn't be all that difficult to come up with a plausible reason for the retro-search, she realized. "And if I wanted to get information about physicians who'd died during the Outbreaks?"

"Janie. You have to ask? The AMA."

She was quiet for a moment. "I hate the AMA. They're the reason—"

"I know. I don't love them either, and thank God I don't have to do too much business with them. But if anyone will have physician records, it will be them. Just come up with a friendly-sounding reason for asking."

"The family of a woman who died of complications of osteoporosis wants to endow a chair with part of her estate, but they want to remain anonymous. So they've asked us at the foundation to look into it and come up with the name of an orthopedist, someone who might have gone on to really exciting things after the Outbreaks, if he, or maybe she, was still around."

"I'd be happy to send you a list, but it's likely to be rather long . . . that was a tough time for physicians."

"It was, wasn't it? But a lengthy list is fine, we're happy to do the necessary research as long as all the names are there. We'd hate to overlook someone inadvertently."

"Our records are very complete. And I'll be glad to get them to you. But I have a request for you—if you'd just be kind enough to send along the name of the final choice when the decision is made, that would be good."

"No problem. I'll be more than happy to let you know who I come up with."

"Great. We like to keep tabs on our members, even if they're no longer with us."

"Yes," Janie said bitterly, "I know you do." She gave the AMA's public relations officer her e-mail address at the foundation.

It came through less than an hour later, bearing a daunting number of promising and prominent orthopedists who'd been carried off by the nasty bacteria that ruled the new millennium, nearly four hundred physicians in all.

And these are just the ones who were still in the AMA then. The one she actually wanted might not even be on the list.

But, she reminded herself with painful cynicism, their records are very complete. She wondered what her own record in the AMA's files looked like, then decided that such speculation was not a productive use of mind space.

But the list before her was. By a repeated and logical process of elimination based on their specialties, locations, association memberships, and a few other factors, she refined the list to fifteen possible candidates for orthopedists.

But the issue of Patient Zero was not so easily resolved.

Was this what it was like in Europe after World War II, records all a mess, some people trying to reestablish identities, and others trying with equal desperation to wipe out their own? *Probably,* Janie thought. Much of what went on during DR SAM's rise to power remained undocumented because people had been far too busy trying to stay alive to worry about recording who had done what to whom and for what reason. Many people had simply disappeared into what had jokingly come to be called the Outbreak Void. Janie suspected that this void was really just ordinary life, under an assumed identity—life being lived by people who had, prior to all the confusion, been marginal, who'd marred their own futures to the point where they'd lost all hope of latching on to the American dream. What better way to start over again than to die as who you were and be reborn in the identity of someone much sounder? It would never all be unraveled.

Schools? Hospitals? Charitable organizations? All would be likely to have records, woefully incomplete, and much of what they did have would have been transferred to Big Dattie, but all of those records would be protected by privacy laws.

At least they were protected from entry by legitimate researchers.

We did it once before.

But it had proved a deadly thing to do; its tragic consequences would color the rest of her life with guilt, and those of Michael and Caroline, as well. Janie could not ask for their help again.

But to ask Sandhaus for help again was another thing entirely. And though he was the true Anti-Nerd, somewhere in his academic bag of forensic criminology tricks would be a vintage hacker, probably the one and only hacker who was not already in jail.

She was not disappointed. "Yeah, I know someone," he told her, "but he's a greedy little son of a bitch. Creepy too."

"How much?"

"Ten thousand credits, probably."

She paused before responding. "That's pretty steep."

John Sandhaus shrugged. "It's cheaper than a car."

"I'm not buying a car. I just want access to certain information."

"So get some deep pockets to pay."

Hesitation. Did he know somehow? He seemed to know everything, all the time. "I can't even ask until I know for sure what the real cost is going to be."

"Well, assuming you come up with the money, here's what you have to do. . . ."

It was like returning to the scene of a nightmare, one she'd played over and over in her mind, to her mind's great unhappiness. But there at one end of the chrome-and-wood counter at another dishearteningly similar computer bar was a man who had to be the one John Sandhaus had told her to contact. She picked him out by the tattoo of a cursor on his forearm.

Like some vamp in a B movie, Janie stared across the crowded room at the "gentleman," who looked like anything but, and flashed him an inviting smile. He looked her up and down with cool amusement as she approached him.

He had pocked skin and more wrinkles than were merited by his age, to judge from his remarkably buff physique. His hair was oily, slicked back in waves, and she expected to find a hand-rolled cigarette tucked brazenly behind one of his ears, because he smelled faintly of tobacco. The near-empty glass of what she took to be Scotch whiskey in his right hand explained the other smell. The overall effect of his contrived appearance was aging cool.

And now, she would have to try to be cool herself, a prospect she found quite annoying. "Hi," she said, gesturing toward the bar stool next to his. "Is this seat taken?"

He almost chuckled, and shook his head no.

As she slid onto the padded leather seat, Janie couldn't help but think, *This Mata Hari bit is just not going to work, I should just tell him what I want.*

But he was quite an agreeable fellow. "I was hoping you would decide to join me. May I buy you a drink?"

It surprised her to hear what she thought was a French accent, which accounted for the tobacco smell and the sailor-in-port charm.

"That would be very nice, thank you."

He made the slightest dip of his chin and miraculously the bartender appeared. Janie was impressed; it would have taken her ten minutes to get the *garçon*'s attention.

"What is your pleasure, *mademoiselle?*" the hacker said.

Oh, you sweet young thing, you just know how us old biddies melt when you call us "miss" . . . and in a few moments you're going to pay me some flowery compliment, like how good I smell.

"Pinot Noir, please," she said to the bartender, "if you have a good one open."

"Bring a bottle of your best," the Frenchman said. And when Janie tried to protest, he waved her to a stop. "It is my favorite. How did you know?"

He smiled beautifully. In contrast to the rest of his rough appearance, his teeth were straight and white, and incredibly healthy-looking. Janie thought they probably looked very dashing in the glass on the bedstand at night. She smiled inwardly, his potential hold on her now suddenly loosened by the thought of him toothless.

The bottle came, with two glasses. He tossed down the last of his

Scotch in one gulp and poured for both of them. He set one glass ceremoniously in front of her, then raised his own. "To what shall we toast?"

"To the Pinot grape, one of God's finest creations," she said. She clinked her glass gently against his, then brought it close to her face to savor the wine's bouquet. She closed her eyes in pleasure for a moment, then opened them again and took a slow sip of the clear red liquid.

"Ah . . . heaven," she said. "Now your turn. Make a toast."

"To my lovely companion." He leaned closer and sniffed the air around her delicately. "Who smells so wonderful."

By the end of the bottle she had him down to five thousand credits for half an hour of wandering through Big Dattie, a sum she could afford to pay on her own if Kristina's "agency" refused, a sum she would gladly pay if it would streamline her search to the degree she thought it might. "I just need to be guaranteed that it will completely anonymous. You can't use anyone's ID number."

"Of course not," he assured her, his plastic choppers flashing. "Not just anyone's."

She wondered what he meant by that, but couldn't bring herself to ask. She would find out soon enough. They set a time and place for a future meeting, which would take place after her return from Iceland. Janie went home, to work on that list of the things she didn't know.

D e Chauliac read the message on the parchment and then looked up at the boy who had delivered it. It was not the lad Chaucer, but a rather more doltish-looking young man, so the elegant Frenchman phrased his response as simply as possible, without the flowery effusions of affection and respect he might have entrusted to Lionel's more literate page. "Tell Prince Lionel that we shall attend to him this afternoon. And convey my great eagerness to see him."

The messenger bowed somewhat clumsily and left, and de Chauliac returned to the study. He wore a quizzical expression when he rejoined Alejandro, one that was colored with slight amusement. But when he spoke he sounded a bit annoyed. "Well, it seems that Prince Lionel had a spy in my household when we conspired to treat him together," he said. "He has just sent this request that we do so." He placed the parchment on the table.

Alejandro picked it up and read it, then looked up at de Chauliac, hoping that his expression would not betray his excitement.

"As you can see from the note, the page Chaucer was quite taken with you," de Chauliac said. "Now we are 'invited' to attend him at our earliest convenience."

His heart began to pound. *The lad had done it!* "Meaning, I assume, that we are commanded to appear immediately."

"Exactly," de Chauliac said. He raised his chin and looked down his long nose. "Really, colleague, one would think there was a conspiracy between you and this young man. Though I think I shall enjoy the practice of medicine with you, I am not entirely pleased to have you out there in view."

It was only with the greatest effort that Alejandro managed to quell a smile. "Shall I prepare myself, then, for this visit?"

"I suppose you should. I will lend you a proper mantle and cap."

"It would also be very helpful if I could have my bag."

"No," de Chauliac said instantly. "Certainly not."

"It would be detrimental to your reputation to bring a colleague who lacks implements."

De Chauliac's pride got the better of him again. "All right," he said. "You may have it. But you shall *not* have the knife."

They rode through the Paris streets more swiftly than they ought to have, considering the number of pedestrians they encountered. Alejandro was flanked on either side by his usual guards, who were both armed with short swords in fast scabbards. But he made the most of his freedom by taking in the sights and sounds all around him—he had stared far too long at the inside of de Chauliac's mansion, and handsome though it was, there was only so much to be seen. He did not realize how much his eyes had hungered for a glimpse of real life until he was once again surrounded by it.

Before leaving, de Chauliac had made a point of having the men show Alejandro just how sharp the guards' swords were and how quickly they might be drawn. "To put any notions of fleeing out of your head" were the Frenchman's stern words. But Alejandro did not allow this warning to dampen his spirits. He had no intention of trying to escape on this journey abroad, because he felt certain that if this outing went well enough he would have many more opportunities. Eventually, de Chauliac would let down his guard, and he would seize that opportunity. It would not come today, he was sure of it.

It was a great comfort to be astride a horse again, although he missed the familiar broadness of his usual mount's back. This one was smaller and had a slightly different gait, slower and more plodding, unlike the prancing almost skittish steps of his stallion. He could not predict how this horse would respond were he to slap the reins on its neck and dig his heels into its sides to make it run. Still, he was reassured by the presence of his leather bag, which had been strapped to the horse, behind where he sat. As they rode along, he felt it pressing up against the small of his back as it had for nearly a decade of traveling.

What was most grievously missing on this ride was the company of the child, now a woman, to which he had grown so accustomed.

The Dauphin, who would someday occupy the throne of France if all went according to the plan of his father, King Jean, had a manse far grander than the one in which de Chauliac resided. But when they went inside, Alejandro was put immediately in mind of Windsor Castle by the furnishings, which were more rudimentary than those in de Chauliac's home. Perhaps, he theorized, Prince Lionel's own furnishings might have been sent for his comfort, for how better to keep a royal hostage happy than to surround him with his own belongings.

Geoffrey Chaucer led them into the bedchamber, a large room with tall windows and ornate appointments. A massive bed with tall posts and a heavy canopy was situated against one wall; on either side of it were long tapestries in lush colors, depicting this or that saint, working one or another of the miracles that had led to canonization. On this bed, under a heap of fur, they found Prince Lionel, reclining in considerable discomfort. He moaned as he turned his head to face them.

At his side was Countess Elizabeth of Ulster, his wife. The surprisingly young woman wore a worried look and she was inordinately pale, even against the white veil that hung from her headdress. *But such is the fashion these days,* Alejandro reminded himself. No woman of royal station would allow herself to look as if she had been laboring in the hot sun. He remembered Adele's creamy ivory skin, and envisioned her raising up the hood on her cloak to keep the sun off her face, lest it color too greatly.

This Elizabeth was not much older than Adele had been, when Alejandro had loved her. And the color of her hair—so similar it made his heart ache.

The countess clutched one of her husband's hands in her own, as if she feared that he might slip away from her, and whispered a few words of what Alejandro thought would surely be comfort or solace. Then she patted his hand gently and rose up from the bedside.

When she stood up, the silk of her gown rustled. She put a hand demurely to her chest, touching the drape of her veil. "Oh!" she said as she crossed the room, "de Chauliac! I am so glad you have come! When Geoffrey told us that there were other diseases to be considered, I went faint with concern." She turned back to her prince and said, "Did I not, dearest?"

The prince groaned convincingly from under his fur coverlet, several times in quick succession.

When Alejandro heard the dramatic wailings, he thought, *Here is a man who loves his laudanum enough to allow his wife to feel distress over it.*

"You see?" Elizabeth said. "He suffers! You must bring him some relief."

De Chauliac went down on one knee and lowered his head in a bow, and Alejandro quickly did the same. *I had forgotten all their silly rituals,* he thought as he rose up again. He had not been forced to bow in nearly ten years. *I did not much like it then, and I like it less now.*

"Of course, when told of this grievous situation, we came straightaway," de Chauliac said.

"Dear de Chauliac," Elizabeth crooned. "You are most exceptionally loyal to us, and it has not gone unnoticed." Then she turned her attention to Alejandro. Her gaze settled on him first critically, as if simply for the purposes of appraisal, but it soon turned to something else: unmistakable interest, of a nature he could not exactly define. She moved a pace closer and held out her hand. "And this must be your colleague from Spain, the one young Geoffrey speaks so highly of. Welcome. We are most grateful for your attendance." Her eyes were full upon him, taking in the details. Her lips curled very slightly in a smile.

Though her frank and undisguised stare made him slightly uncomfortable, Alejandro stepped forward quite boldly and took hold of the hand she offered. He pressed it to his lips, lingering just a bit too long. The young woman blushed and put the other hand to her mouth. She drew in a little gasp of pleasure. "Is this a custom of your countrymen?" she said. "If so, I find it delightful. A sweet respite from my worries."

He detected the lilt he had heard in the voices of Irish people when she spoke to him in French; he found it far more pleasing to the ear than the guttural inflections the English seemed to put upon it. She wore a robe of soft green that complemented her fair coloring handsomely; its sleeves and bodice were decorated with entwined gold patterns in the Celtic mode.

She is only a few years older than Kate.

"Yes," he answered, "to kiss the hand is our custom. But a jealously guarded one—we employ it only when presented to the loveliest of ladies." He said it all with a flirtatious smile and a twinkle in his eye.

"Oh, *monsieur,* you shall make my blood boil, and then what?"

"Then I shall be delighted to treat you for that affliction," he said.

"And no doubt I would be well cared for." Still holding his hand, she turned her attention back to de Chauliac, who scowled with disapproval. "You shall bring your colleagues around to call on us, de Chauliac, without waiting for invitation. If this gentleman is representative of their quality, then we simply *must* have more of them."

Alejandro could almost see the blood rising in de Chauliac's neck. After a light squeeze, he gently drew his hand away from the countess's grasp. The Frenchman glared at him for a brief moment, then faced the countess again with a polite smile. "I shall try to do so, *madame,*" he said. "And now, shall we see to your husband?"

Prince Lionel had almost become an afterthought. "Yes, please do," she said. "I want him well and happy again."

"We shall do our best." He turned to Alejandro with a smile that might just as easily be taken for a sneer. "Colleague? What first?"

"The heart, I think," Alejandro said. He opened his bag and extracted a parchment, which he rolled into a tube. "You must unbutton your tunic, my lord," he said, "in order for me to hear its beating."

"What has the beating of my heart to do with the throbbing of my toe?" the prince asked.

"Much can be learned about the general health by listening to the flow of blood. Observation of the vital signs can be most useful in diagnosis."

He pulled back the coverlet, which was mink or marten and lined in the finest silk. He stopped for a moment before proceeding and looked to the countess. "Is it your custom to sleep under fur, *madame?*"

"On occasion, sir. With my husband ill, I thought it best to keep him warm."

"Ah," he said. "I see." Then after a brief pause, he added, "Before we proceed, if I may be so bold as to make first an observation."

"But of course," the countess said.

"And then a suggestion."

The countess nodded and said, "And if we find your suggestion useful, perhaps we shall follow it."

Perhaps, he thought. *Of course, in matters of instructing royals it will always be "perhaps."* He continued. "I have observed through careful study over the course of the Black Death that it originates in rats."

The countess was momentarily speechless, then said, "But what has this to do with our coverlets?"

"Well," Alejandro said, "though the fur is unquestionably lovelier, the animals from which it is taken are not unlike rats."

"Oh, dear God! This is a most unsavory discussion."

De Chauliac stepped forward, mouth open, ready to intercede.

"I am well aware of that, *madame,*" Alejandro said, "and for that I apologize, most humbly. It is not my intent to upset such a lovely lady as yourself. Only to protect."

"And how will I be protected by distancing myself from fur?"

"I do not know how it is that rats pass on the agent of plague. Perhaps it lies in the fur, somehow. It is, after all, the most outward part."

Elizabeth was quiet for a moment, her eyes examining the coverlet. When she looked back to Alejandro again, her lovely young face looked worried. "Do you truly believe this, sir?"

"With all my being."

She looked to de Chauliac, seeking his opinion on the matter. He hemmed and hawed, then finally said, "My colleague has had great success in dealing with the Death. He is an authority to be trusted. And I should add that I do not sleep with a fur myself."

"Well, then," Elizabeth said, "when my prince is well enough to part with it, we shall remove all our furs and store them until the temperature absolutely requires their use."

Alejandro gave her a grateful smile. "I am honored by your indulgence of my theories. Now, let me proceed with the heart."

He pressed his ear to the rolled parchment and held it against Lionel's chest. The beat of his heart was strong and steady. When he raised himself up again he offered the parchment to the Frenchman. "De Chauliac, will you have a turn?"

"I will," he said, and accepted the implement. He bent down and listened.

"Well, what say you?" Elizabeth demanded anxiously.

"Your husband has a vibrant heart, lady," Alejandro said. "It is my opinion that it is also quite large. This bodes very well for his health."

"I concur," de Chauliac said, not to be outdone. "The heart is very large. Very large, indeed."

"But what of my toe?" the Prince groaned.

It will also be large, Alejandro predicted silently. "Soon enough we will get to it," he said. "But first, we must examine your liver."

"My liver?"

"Indeed," de Chauliac said. "There may be an excess outpouring of bile, or a blockage, even, and such an imbalance could put great stress on the body, which might be manifested in the toe."

"Ah," the countess said, quite gravely. She whispered to Lionel, "You must allow this, beloved." She pulled down the fur coverlet and raised his nightshirt, revealing the royal manhood.

Which unlike the heart, and probably the toe, is not terribly large. Alejandro looked at de Chauliac and said, "You may examine the prince first, colleague."

"With pleasure. *Colleague.*" He palpated the prince's belly. "I detect no abnormalities," he said.

Alejandro did the same. "Nor I," he said. He pulled the nightshirt down and the coverlet up, to the obvious relief of the prince. "I think it best that we now proceed directly to the toe."

The prince obliged by sticking his foot out from under the coverlet, shoving it almost into Alejandro's face. When the rank smell hit his nostrils, the physician turned his head away for a moment. He met the blue eyes of Elizabeth of Ulster, which were fixed firmly and unabashedly on him. He smiled, took a breath, and turned back to the presented foot.

The toenails were far too long and unkempt, and the big toe was swollen and red. He looked up at the countess and said, "I was right. The toe is very large." Then, very soberly, he added, *"Madame,* I am sorry to inform you that I detect an accumulation of a foul humor in your husband's toe. Praise God we have found it now, for had it gone missed, the foot might have been lost."

There were gasps from the entire royal entourage, and quiet swears from de Chauliac. Holding back a smirk, Alejandro said to the Frenchman, "Please, colleague, I would have your opinion on this. I dare not make such a critical diagnosis without your sage counsel."

De Chauliac leaned forward and peered at Prince Lionel's ingrown toenail. He gave Alejandro a scathing look and said, almost under his breath, "Your diagnosis is correct."

They would have to clip the royal toenails. "Surgery is required."

More gasps, combined with whispered prayers. "Yes," de Chauliac said, his voice an angry whisper. "Surgery."

Alejandro smiled wickedly. "You brought your knife."

"And the laudanum," de Chauliac said with a sigh.

That afternoon, while Marie stole away for a *rendezvous* with her lover, Kate took over her work. And when she answered the bell, Marcel asked of Marie's whereabouts. "She is indisposed," she said, and for good effect, she added, "in a womanly manner."

It was always enough to dampen the most insistent male inquiry. "Well, then," Marcel said, "I suppose you will have to do. We require some refreshment, if you please."

She was prepared, for Marie had said, *He will require refreshment. He always does in the afternoon. So I have left a kettle of greens and some bread.* Kate ladled out generous portions of greens into two bowls, and carried them up the stairs.

Marcel and Karle were poring over maps and tracts and flattened parchments, applying ink lines liberally to mark gathering places and routes. "If we meet him here," Marcel said, pointing with the tip of his quill, "we will have the shortest route to where the forces supporting the king are likely to gather."

When she set Karle's bowl down, Kate looked over his shoulder and lingered for a moment, surveying the map before placing Marcel's bowl in front of him. "I see no routes of escape," she said.

Marcel stared up at her in annoyance and said, "Woman, remember your place. This is man's work. See to your own." He gestured toward the stairs. "There is more to serve, eh?"

"Bread and wine, for your pleasure," she said smartly. And when she brought the remainder of the refreshments, she leaned over Karle's shoulder again. And after a moment of silent scrutiny, she pointed to a spot on the map and said, "Here is better."

Marcel, who was far more affable when drunk, was not amused by her continued intrusion and scowled at Guillaume Karle. "See to your woman," he said. "She is making a pest of herself."

"I would hear her reasoning before dismissing her," he said quietly to Marcel.

Marcel looked suspiciously back and forth between the two of them. "Very well," he said. He gestured toward the map with his hand. "Give us your strategic opinion, *mademoiselle.*"

She smiled nervously, looked to Karle for confirmation, and when he nodded, she sat down on one of the benches. She touched the area north of Paris, a village called Compiègne, that Marcel had proposed as the meeting place for the battle to come. "There is but one road in here, and when you face your enemy on it, your only route out will be by the same road. Unless your forces scatter into the woods. But should they be forced to do so, you will lose the advantage of organization. You will become a divided troop of forest rebels. And if the king's commanders have decent skills of war, they will send a contingent through the woods and around your troops, so they can come up behind you and box you in. You will have no choice but to disperse." She let her eyes wander to a different place. "Here," she said, pointing to a town called Arlennes, "is a place where three roads converge. If the king wishes to surround you, he will have to divide his own troops to do so. He will not have the same advantage as in Compiègne."

Her eyes traveled further over the parchment, settling on a thin blue line. "Is this a river or a stream?"

She had Marcel's complete attention. "A river, I think," the provost said.

"Then it too can act as a road for escape, a route for supplies, a place for the horses to water. And before you go into battle, you must designate a place where your troops can re-form, for once the battle begins there will be chaos."

Marcel sat quietly for a few minutes, scanning the map, thinking about what she'd pointed out. "It seems," he finally said, "that Alexander the Great has come back in the form of this maiden. These notions of yours are very sensible," he said to Kate, "though I know not how a maiden should come up with such warrior wisdom. I think we should propose to Navarre that they be followed."

"The countess would have sent me sooner," Geoffrey Chaucer explained in the vestibule of de Chauliac's manse, "but she required assistance with her correspondence. That is, of course, my most critical service to her. She says that I always manage to make her seem a woman of great letters."

"No doubt she appreciates this," de Chauliac said.

"I believe so, sir, for she has me writing nearly day and night. But I find no reason to complain." He smiled broadly and said, "But now to my business. She did not wish to send anyone else on an errand of such importance."

He produced two small ivory boxes, both ornately carved with flowery images of saints and angels and crosses, one for de Chauliac and one for Alejandro. Chaucer handed each box to its intended recipient. "I am instructed to stay and see your reactions to these gifts, and then to report back to my lady with a description of your sentiments."

Which will no doubt be delivered in florid excess, Alejandro thought with amusement.

De Chauliac opened his gift first: it contained a fine quill with a sleeve of gold surrounding its shaft, and a small vial of *encre rouge.*

"She favors this rare color, sir, and hopes you will be pleased to have some."

"I am *most* delighted," de Chauliac said. "It will be a great addition to my medical works to have markings of red for accent. Please tell the countess that her gift is most generous and will be very useful. I shall begin to use it right away. Her largesse is—humbling."

Chaucer raised one eyebrow in amusement. "She would not have gifted you so had she not thought you deserving, sir." He turned to Alejandro and waited for him to open his box.

Alejandro expected something of a similar nature, perhaps a seal or a bookmark or, as de Chauliac had received, a quill, but instead he found a small gold ring with an *E* carved into it. To the right of the letter was a single emerald, and to its left a pearl. He took it carefully out of the box and held it up, and as he turned it in the light, the fire within the green stone sparkled. The gift's intent was clear.

But of course Queen Philippa has a champion, Adele had told him, and he loves her well, as she does him.

But what of her vows to Edward?

He will not mind her engaging in a bit of courtly love, as long as she is discreet, and he knows that she beds only with him. She and her admirer exchange gifts frequently to show their mutual admiration.

In his hand, he realized, was the signal of Elizabeth's desire for such admiration. From him. He slipped it onto his smallest finger and held out his hand to display it. De Chauliac's quill required no response save a hearty expression of gratitude. But a ring . . . it had a different meaning. The flirtatious countess was sending him a signal.

"Well?" Chaucer said.

"You must tell your lady that her kindness and generosity have left me speechless, as has her beauty."

"She will be very pleased to know that she has stolen your words. But she will want to have some back from you, I think." He leaned closer. "And should you see fit to send a gift of your own, she will not be offended, I assure you."

This was a very young man, Alejandro decided, to be the conduit for such an intrigue. He cast a glance in de Chauliac's direction and received back a withering glare. But he would not allow himself to be withered, nor would he let his lack of possessions hinder him in an exchange that might serve him very well.

"Have you a parchment that you might spare, colleague?" he said. "And a quill? I would write a few words of gratitude."

De Chauliac grunted unhappily. He clapped his hands together once and a servant appeared. De Chauliac stated his need and the servant returned in short order. He handed the pen and parchment to Alejandro, who offered them in turn to Chaucer. "Tell her that I cannot possibly match her generosity, so I shall not even try. But I offer her my most heartfelt sentiments of admiration."

"With your permission, good physician, I shall embellish your words so she will enjoy them all the more. They are a bit dry for my lady's taste. If you have no objection, that is."

"Do as you see fit, Chaucer. It is you who are the wordsmith, not I. I am only the admirer, with his tongue tied by the magnificence of the one he admires, who greatly benefits from your service." He smiled.

Chaucer set the parchment down on the table and bent over it. He thought for a moment, then grinned and began to scribble.

Cherished Elizabeth, fair as a goddess and likewise generous, take to your heart my deepest admiration. Let it burn as a candle in your breast and warm you. Until we meet again, I am your most loyal servant and admirer.

"And how does one write your name?"

He told him.

The page handed the parchment back for approval, and Alejandro read it.

"It is perhaps more direct than I would have written."

"Precisely, sir. That is what is required."

"You would know better than I, lad . . . and now, a gift." He reached back and untied the black leather cord that held his hair, then plucked a few hairs and tied them into it. He gave the tiny bundle to Chaucer. Then he took the parchment and tore it in half. "She will not appreciate the unfilled space, eh? So we shall remove it." He tucked the excess piece into the front of his mantle and gave Chaucer the part that had been written on.

"You are wise, sir; the countess would want to see it filled. I shall deliver these things right away," he said.

"How might she respond?" Alejandro asked.

"She will press it all into her bodice, I suspect, and hold it near to her heart."

De Chauliac was nearly groaning by the time the lad Chaucer slipped out the door again. He set upon Alejandro immediately. "You realize, Physician, that she will expect this flirtation you have started to continue."

"I see no harm in it; if it brings the lady pleasure, why not? And anyway, I did not start it. That was done by the lady herself."

"You cannot imagine the complexity of such liaisons! She will discover a new ailment for you to treat every day! Or she will persuade her husband to. It will become an untenable situation, completely unmanageable."

"You have only yourself to blame for this, de Chauliac."

"It was not I who plucked hairs from his head and sent them to her bosom."

"You must remember that if you had seen properly to Prince Lionel's toe, there would have been no need for me to go there in the first place."

"Do you denigrate how I administer healing? This Lionel is the worst sort of complainer. If I ran to his side every time he had the slightest ague, I should never leave his house." His eyebrows knitted in dark disapproval. "And you must remember who you are."

"And who am I?"

"A Jew. An unacceptable admirer, even for a countess of *Irish* origin."

"To her I am a Spaniard. A physician of great skills. And perhaps the lady wishes to have a physician in her house all the time."

"*Harumph,*" the Frenchman grunted. "Perhaps. But she does not wish for me. She wishes for you. And you are my prisoner."

"Then why not tell her that? Tell her also that I am a Jew. It matters not to me."

"Are you mad? It would be your ruination, and even worse, mine."

"Then you will have to escort me there when she calls for me, I suppose, and keep my inherited *vileness* to yourself."

Their pitched argument was interrupted by the arrival of Nicholas Flamel, who had come a bit earlier than was expected. The portly alchemist handed his cloak to the valet and scurried eagerly into the salon on his stubby legs, putting an end to whatever more might be said on the subject of the unsuitable flirtation. "Good evening," he said almost breathlessly as he bowed. "I am honored to be in such learned company once again."

De Chauliac hid his chagrin and offered Flamel a seat. "No," he said, "it is *we* who are honored. Am I not right, colleague?"

He will put his fat little greasy hands upon that fine manuscript, Alejandro thought unhappily. He nodded and forced a smile, saying nothing. Flamel would not have an expression of admiration from him until he was certain that the man was no threat to the precious words of Abraham.

"Well," Flamel said, rubbing those fat hands together, "shall we commence with the work?"

"Calm yourself, Flamel," de Chauliac said, "you have only just arrived."

"Colleague, you must allow the man his eagerness," Alejandro said. "Such work is very exciting."

"Indeed!" said Flamel.

"Well, then if you gentlemen will allow me," the Jew said, "I shall go upstairs and retrieve the manuscript." He stood and smoothed his clothing. "I suppose I ought to refresh myself a bit. So I may be a few minutes in returning. Will you mind?"

"See that you do not take too long," de Chauliac said, and when Flamel's face showed surprise at his harsh tone, he added, more sweetly, "since we should not keep Monsieur Flamel away from his poor deprived wife any longer than necessary tonight."

"I shall hurry."

He left the room, and the guards fell in behind him. Flamel watched as they all disappeared, then turned to de Chauliac and said, "Why does he always require an escort?"

The simple question caught de Chauliac unprepared. He cleared his throat nervously while he formulated a proper response. "He has the falling sickness," he whispered. "I dare not let him alone, or he will fall and injure himself."

Karle and Marcel labored over the letter to Charles of Navarre well past sunset, listing point by point the reasons why they believed it would be best to try to stage the battle at Arlennes. And then they enumerated the reasons why Compiègne would be a poor choice for the rebel troops to amass: no water, poor supply routes, no escape, the ease with which the forces of the Dauphin might surround them. When it was finally finished, Marcel rolled it and sealed it carefully. He set it on the table and said, "In the morning I shall call for a messenger." He gathered his robes around him and flopped down onto the pillowed bench, sending up a small cloud of dust as he settled himself in. "We accomplished much today, I think, far more than I'd hoped. With the unexpected help of your young lady. Has she a warrior father?"

One might easily describe her true sire as that, Karle thought with no small irony. But his answer was "A physician."

"Well, then her competence is all the more remarkable. I shall salute her with my best wine. In celebration of a plan well laid."

He reached out and was about to pull the bell cord, when Karle said, "Not for me, Marcel. I have promised to take the young lady out for a bit of air."

"The air is no better outside than in," he protested. "Come. Sit. Drink wine."

And as Kate appeared from the kitchen, he smiled and put an arm around her shoulder. "Perhaps later. This woman deserves to have what she wants, eh?"

They rushed through the dimly lit streets, dodging the piles of ordure and garbage that would not be banished until morning, and finally came to de Chauliac's manse. Karle took Kate by the hand and led her around the stately edifice until they reached the west side. They positioned themselves below a small window, assuming from its bars that it was the one in which Alejandro was being kept.

Karle cupped his hands and let out a soft coo that sounded like the hoot of an owl. A silhouette appeared in the window and looked down.

"Karle?" came faintly from the window.

"Yes!" Karle replied, his voice an urgent whisper. He put an arm around Kate and led her out of the shadows. "And look, I have brought Kate."

"Père!" she cried joyfully, "Oh, Père, are you well?"

They heard no answer. Instead they heard a *whizz* of air and the *thunk* of something landing at their feet. Karle bent down and picked it up. It was a piece of parchment crumpled around a small piece of wood. And then, from the window, "Come again tomorrow!"

And the silhouette disappeared.

"Your Freedom of Information Act application has been processed and approved. Please follow the instructions listed below to retrieve the requested documents. Check to make sure your ID chip is ready."

Janie stared down at her hand. And then she almost laughed at herself. *You can't see the chip, you idiot.*

Then why had she looked when they told her to have it ready? It occurred to her, with no small unhappiness, that she was becoming the robot they wanted her to become.

But right now, to get what she wanted, such behavior was required and there was no getting around it, no matter how distressing or distasteful it might seem. She was directed to go to a site in the GovNet, and there, upon presenting her ready identity, she found waiting for her the personnel records for the town of Burning Road and the county in which it was situated, for a period from two years before the Outbreaks to two years after. But then came the unexpected miracle—by searching in current voting records, she discovered that the part-time public health officer for the period in question was still very much alive.

They had died in droves, just like the physicians, mothers, and priests in Alejandro's fourteenth-century plague journal. To have survived DR SAM in an official medical capacity was akin to being part of a platoon on a mission and somehow the only one to return alive. Doubts always arose, followed closely by unspoken accusations. The woman in question no longer lived near the camp—*No surprise,* Janie thought, *she was probably hounded out of there*—but she'd moved to a place that was still less than an hour away from where Janie herself lived.

A drive out there would probably get her better information than a phone call or a letter. She considered her remaining gallonage; in all likelihood, it was not going to be enough to last the rest of the year.

So I'll walk when I need to go someplace, or take the bus. She sent the woman a message asking if she could come for a visit the next day.

I need to quit my job, she e-mailed Kristina. *It's starting to look a little fishy, all this time I'm taking off.*

"You can't," Kristina told her later. "You'll lose the authority you have from being on staff at the foundation."

Janie almost laughed. "What authority? I'm just a research associate."

"It worked with the AMA, didn't it?"

She was right, Janie realized, it had.

"What if you run into another situation where you need that position? And besides, your record for the time you've worked there has been exemplary, so no one's going to give you a hard time. You have just about the highest attendance percentage of anyone in your research department. And what do you care, anyway? You hate that job."

Of course, Kristina would know all these things.

"I do. But I still want to do it well. And it's getting harder, with these distractions."

The distractions were piling up, fast and deep, and becoming noticeable.

"You're going on vacation, I see on the schedule," Chet had remarked the day before when she flitted in and out of the office. It was the second comment he'd made in recent days about her increasingly frequent absences. "I know you do a lot of work outside the facility, but we do like to see you every now and then."

She was going to have to be careful because things were getting crazy again. She remembered how it felt from London, and dreaded its return. Maybe this trip to Iceland would actually end up doing her some good— it would force her to slow down, assess her situation, regather herself. "I'm completely up-to-date on my projects," she told Chet. "I'll make sure I leave everything in good shape. And anyway, I'll only be gone a few days."

"You have a week blocked out on the schedule."

"That was the original plan, but I don't think I'll be taking the whole thing."

Oh? his look said.

She shrugged. "It just doesn't feel like a good idea right now."

The Berkshire town was high in the hills and Janie watched her gas gauge with alarm as the Volvo whined upward slowly in second gear, consoled only by the fact that the trip home would largely be made on gravity.

It's half an hour to the nearest quart of milk, she thought. *What do people do out here, when they need to go out for—whatever?*

What they did was ride horses. She passed dozens of them on the narrow, twisting roads, almost hitting one or two. Most carried packs behind their riders, a few even pulled small carts. Janie dreamily envisioned carved signs for wainwrights and blacksmiths over open straw-floored storefronts on some old-fashioned Main Street. City laws would not permit it, but out in the hill towns, where bicycles were understandably out of the question, horses were figuring in daily life again. Fertilizer would no longer be a scarce commodity.

She saw only one or two other cars on the road, an old pickup truck grinding down the hill in what remained of its second gear, the other slowly making its way up behind her. It was one of those all-black Darth Vader four-wheel-drive monsters that Janie always imagined to be carrying mafiosi, of whatever sort might be in power at the time. She wondered, as she always did when there were tinted windows, who in the vehicle was so important that absolute privacy was required, and that the gas to run it was not a problem.

Maybe they're following me, she teased herself. A smile came to her lips. *Okay, catch me if you can.*

She slowed down and the car behind her slowed. When she increased her speed, Darth Vader did too and she began to feel a little nervous. She stopped varying her speed and just drove steadily. The black vehicle behind her did exactly as she did.

For a moment, she considered coming to a complete stop on the side of the road, but two things prevented her: It was a narrow road, a dangerous place to stop if one didn't need to, and she was, according to the landmarks, about to reach her destination. So she kept driving, and when she reached the right driveway the black vehicle sped on past her while she was still in midturn.

Once she was off the road, Janie sat in the car for a moment and thought about what had just transpired. She discovered, unhappily, that she was shaking; what had started out as a little joke with herself had turned into something way too real. She got out of the car and looked around for a few moments to calm herself. The setting was beautiful and secluded, and from the rustic appearance of the house, Janie had the feeling that her electronic sidekick would not be welcomed by the human who inhabited it. So she locked V.M. securely in the trunk of the Volvo.

But when she stepped inside, ushered in by a gracious and smiling Linda Horn, she found herself within an aerie of light and sound and perfect climate, with moist air and the smell of peat, and butterflies, hundreds of them all over the place, their colorful wings silently aflutter. They were perched on the lamps and books and knickknacks, but in greatest numbers on the amazing assortment of plants. It was as if a tropical wonderland had inexplicably relocated in the low mountains of western Massachusetts. Off in one corner of the great room, she saw a sleek new computer, its screen aglow.

"Oh, my," Janie said softly as she gazed around in awe. "This is just— wonderful. But how . . . ?"

"My husband is an energy engineer," Mrs. Horn answered. "He set the whole thing up for me."

"Does he hire out?"

Linda Horn smiled. "He's retired now. Sorry."

"Well, if he ever decides to come out of retirement, I'll be his first customer."

The woman laughed quietly and shook her head. "I don't think so," she said. "There's a line, believe me."

A small bright blue butterfly landed on Janie's shoulder. "I can understand why. What a haven you've created here."

"We've been working on it for a long time. We're members of a movement, of sorts. Of people who want to live like this."

Movement. It was a word from a previous generation, and it carried a certain weighty implication. "The participants must be awfully quiet."

"Oh, we are—but there are lots of families setting up situations like this and we all stay in touch." She nodded in the direction of the computer and smiled. "There are a number of people in this area who are rather heavily involved," Mrs. Horn said.

Janie gazed around, entranced by what she saw. "It must have been quite a challenge to get this all going. It's so—*perfect.*"

"The biggest problem was acquiring the land. You need at least a hundred acres to get a permit for the type of setup we have here. We bought this land a few acres at a time over the course of our entire marriage, otherwise we couldn't have done it. The solar collectors don't take all that much room, but the windmills require a lot of space and a certain kind of placement."

Still exploring with her eyes, Janie said, "I congratulate you. This is truly amazing. This is a type of living that's always appealed to me. But I never got even close to it. My life was just too—busy."

"It's never too late," Linda Horn said.

"Oh, I don't think anything like this is going to happen to me, at least not in the immediate future, anyway. But the reason I wanted to see you . . ."

She explained, slowly and carefully.

Linda's brow tightened and little lines appeared on it. "I was wondering when someone would start looking into that whole thing."

Janie nibbled quietly on a lemon crisp as Linda Horn related all the details of the incident at Camp Meir.

"They had lab tests showing *Giardia lamblia* in the bloodstream of some of the campers. And their water samples from the pond showed an infestation. But we never did find anything. We didn't do the blood tests."

Janie wondered why—it could be considered an oversight. "Any particular reason?"

"I worked for the town, but in a situation like that the county called the shots. They told me to accept the camp's tests as valid. Didn't want me to spend the money to replicate them. A few of the boys had the right symptoms. . . ."

"You wouldn't by any chance have kept the records from back then?"

"No. When the whole thing started, I had no inkling that it would all develop into something that smelled so fishy. But I remember it all pretty well. Largely because the camp's on-staff nurse refused to accept any assistance from our office when we offered—usually she welcomed our help. I mean—a camp full of teenage boys? Come on. It would have been mayhem if they all got sick at once. So it stuck out in my mind as an unusual reaction on her part. And we never were able to reproduce the results they had in their water tests. You probably remember that all the antibiotics were on their way out at the time—and we weren't allowed to authorize casual or prophylactic use—so we wanted to have solid evidence."

"But you never found anything in the local water."

"No. Well, wait a minute—that's not entirely true. We found one spot with a slightly elevated level of *Giardia*. But nothing that would cause a major health hazard, and certainly none of the water from that source was making it anywhere near the camp's water supply. They weren't using that pond for swimming or canoeing, either. We tested and tested, at a lot of different sites all around the area, but we never found anything more than that little trace."

"Interesting."

"Very. But even so, someone from the camp's insurer showed up one day at my office with a fistful of official-looking papers and explained how they were going to drag us into court immediately for keeping them from carrying out their *in loco parentis* duties toward the campers. They had most of the parents convinced that the threat was real."

"But you think it wasn't."

"It doesn't matter what I think. I can only go by what the water tests showed, and all but one of them were grossly negative."

"But you gave them the permit for the antibiotic anyway, so you must have—"

"I didn't really have any choice, Dr. Crowe. These people were quite assertive. The county and town were already suffering from fiscal difficulties—we were terribly understaffed, and sometimes my paychecks were delayed. It didn't seem like much of a sacrifice to give these campers a nearly useless medication if it would keep the town from being sued."

Janie was pensive while she sipped her tea.

"So," Linda finally said, "why are *you* looking into this? Does your foundation have an interest here?"

Janie set her teacup down before answering. "A lot of boys whose only connection to each other is the camp are getting sick, at the same time, with a similar rare condition."

"Which is?"

"At this point, I should probably tell you only that it's orthopedic, with neurological implications. I haven't sorted out the details completely just yet."

"Well," Linda said as she refreshed her own tea, "I for one am not at all surprised." She took in a long breath and gazed straight ahead as if she were trying to remember something. "I went out there on some other silly pretext on the day the treatments were being administered. I admit I was curious, and being the health officer I couldn't just be turned away and told to come back at a more convenient time. I saw a couple of the vials. The medication they were supposed to be giving those kids was metronidazole. In injectable solution it's almost perfectly clear with a slight golden tinge to it, and it comes in transparent rubber-topped vials.

There was only one company still manufacturing it at the time, and that's what its product looked like. Now there are none, by the way, if that's of any interest to you."

"It's not an effective medicine anymore."

"And it was on the way out then, which is another reason why I found the whole thing very odd. In any case, what they were injecting into these kids was being drawn from opaque white plastic containers, but I couldn't really get close enough to see what color the liquid in the syringes was. And instead of dropping the empties in a biosafe bag for disposal as would ordinarily have been done, they put them all into a plastic case with some sort of snap lid."

"So you didn't get the impression that they were being discarded, then."

"No. Not at all. In fact, it looked to me like they were accounting for every one of them." She looked directly into Janie's eyes. "I remember this weird, creepy feeling I had for the rest of the day. And something else—there were two men there, watching the whole thing. They looked ludicrously out of place. They were wearing suits. It was July, and well over ninety degrees."

"Any idea who they were?"

"None whatsoever. But everyone at camp wore those blue T-shirts. As it happened, I wore one too that day."

"So you blended in, then. I don't suppose you did that on purpose, did you?"

Linda made a little smile. "I had a bunch of those T-shirts. They were always giving them away." She shrugged. "That color looks good on me."

Janie stayed quiet as she mulled over Linda's revelations. There didn't seem to be much more to ask. It was so thoroughly pleasant in the house that she didn't want to leave. But it was time to move on.

"I was wondering," she said, hoping it would seem like an afterthought, "during the Outbreaks, how did you manage . . ."

"To stay alive?" Linda Horn smiled. "I hid."

As nonjudgmentally as possible, Janie said, "Ah . . . I see."

"Here," Linda added. "The place wasn't quite finished, but that didn't matter to us."

"So you and your husband had this place . . . to hide."

A little bittersweet smile of recollection came onto Linda's face. "We brought the entire town of Burning Road with us."

Janie stared at her. "The whole town?"

"It was a small town."

"Still," Janie said with uncertainty, looking around, "this house isn't all that big."

"We set up a campsite. The townspeople had some experience in that, after all. If you bother to look at the records, you'll see that the Outbreak death rate in Burning Road was zero for local residents. There were some squatters and out-of-towners who died—"

"But no one from the town?"

"No one. We all went back, a year later."

"I wasn't expecting a happy ending to that story."

"No one ever does."

"The people of the town were very lucky to have you. Well, here's hoping they won't be needing you in that capacity again."

"Oh, I don't know."

Janie stayed quiet for a moment, then sat back down again. "I think you might mean something by that remark, but I don't quite get it."

"I do. I was wondering if you had heard anything, that's all. About DR SAM coming back again. I've been reading things, hearing things."

It cannot come back, Janie thought. *It just can't.* "I read a small article in the paper a few days ago—in fact it was on the front page—but it wasn't being described as a comeback."

"Then they are keeping it quiet."

"When did you hear this . . . and where—"

"People in our movement—we behave like one big family, really, and when there's any kind of DR SAM news, it travels really fast. We're all starting to get a little nervous. There have been a couple of pop-ups on the West Coast in the last week or so."

"Dear God."

"And what's most troubling: we heard it was all over Mexico, and they aren't saying anything down there. Or doing a blasted thing to stop it."

"Well, they didn't before."

"And that's how the whole thing got out of hand."

"Okay, here she is again."

The sound of a car starting came through the speakers, then the crunch of gravel under the tires, and shortly after that, there was music. And then painful shrieking, as Janie tried, in her own unique way, to sing along to a recording of Maria Callas.

The listeners all winced. The volume was turned down. "She obviously just left it in the car when she went inside."

"I'd like to know why. Kristina, what do you think?"

The young woman looked around at the gathered group, whose eyes had all come to rest heavily on her. "I don't know," she said. "She's been very good about taking it with her. And she brought it along, she just didn't bring it into the house when she went inside."

"Curious. I wonder . . . do you think she suspects?"

Call me, the e-mail from the travel agent said. *I have some information for you.*

"I can change your return flight," the agent told her when they spoke a few minutes later, "but the outgoing flight is fixed. You have to enter on a certain date. That way they don't get too much of a pileup in immigration. Iceland's a small country—until the year before the first Outbreak the President's phone number was still listed in the directory."

"No kidding. Don't suppose I could get it now, and ask if she'd help me change my incoming flight?"

"Probably not," the woman said. "The problem is that they can't just call up a few immigration agents to come in for a little overtime. They don't have the manpower. So they try to pace the entries."

"Going out, though, I can pretty much get on whatever plane I want to."

"Yes. Whichever plane has room for you."

Then she read the rest of her mail. The next incoming message was another unfriendly one, much like the one she'd received just a few days earlier, which said that she ought to back off, though what she was supposed to avoid doing wasn't made clear.

I don't think so, she'd replied bravely.

Janie assumed it was from the same source. But this time it was a little more jarring than the first.

She didn't reply. She deleted the malevolent little blip from the mailbox as soon as she finished reading it.

Janie needed advice and company, so she was very grateful when Tom said yes to her last-minute offer of dinner.

"Ten minutes' notice and I'm here," he said when he met her at the restaurant. "Pretty pathetic, don't you think?"

She laughed. "I'm imagining that you canceled a date with the clone of Marilyn Monroe to meet me."

"I wish. But you *are* one of my most important clients. So if I did happen to have a date like that, I probably would have canceled it." He grinned.

"Now, *that's* pathetic."

"Oh, I don't think so." He cleared his throat with a nervous little cough. "So, when are you leaving? Soon, I imagine."

"Tomorrow, actually."

Tom looked away briefly, then said, "Well, I know you'll have a good time. But like I said yesterday, I'll miss you."

A silence followed as thoughts went unspoken on both sides of the table.

"So how long are you going to be gone?"

"I don't know yet. I have to arrive tomorrow, there's no choice on that. Apparently they schedule their entries pretty rigidly. But I can go back out again anytime there's room on a plane as long as I stay within the date limits of my visa."

"Which is how long?"

"I could stay for up to a month if I wanted to."

His face seemed to fall, just long enough for Janie to recognize the expression for what it was, though he seemed to be trying to hide it.

"I won't be staying that long, Tom. I don't think I'll be gone more than a few days. I'm way too involved in this other stuff right now. I don't really want to leave it at all. I feel pretty confused about it—and other things."

They stopped speaking and smiled mechanically when the waiter presented himself, and remained silent while he recited the specials. They ordered soup and salad for simplicity's sake. And as soon as the waiter was out of hearing range, Tom said, "This isn't just something mildly interesting to you anymore, is it, or a way to get relicensed?"

"No. I'm hardly even thinking about my license at this point. It's become much more than that."

"I get the feeling that you're actually enjoying it."

His understanding felt like a blessing. She leaned forward with a gleam in her eye and let the excitement come through in her voice. "Yes. I am. I can't tell you how much, and how everything else just seems very small and unimportant all of a sudden. I wish it was . . . cleaner, though. Things seem to be getting much more complicated in the last couple of days."

She told him about the second threatening message, and watched him as he considered what she'd told him. She couldn't avoid the thought that he was trying very hard not to show any reaction.

"I wonder if I should have someone look after my house while I'm gone."

"That might be a good idea. Do you know anyone who could do it?"

"I was thinking of asking this girl Kristina who's been—uh—for lack of a better word, *running* me."

"Interesting way to put it."

"Well, that's sort of what it feels like. I don't know what else to call it. It's like she's my spymaster."

"Bond has his M, you have your Kristina."

"There you go." She reached down and patted the briefcase that contained V.M. "And my fancy technological gizmo. I don't think I ought to be taking him to Iceland."

"You could just give it back to her and she could take it home with her."

"I suppose I could." Then she paused for a moment. "You know, I don't have the faintest idea where she lives."

He looked surprised. "You're kidding."

"I never had any reason to ask her. I've always reached her electronically. V.M. has a mail module with a preset route to her, but I don't have any way of unembedding the address. I've never called her on the telephone, even. But I assume she lives somewhere close by because she shows up on pretty short notice when I contact her."

"Maybe she's really some bizarre alien being and only corporates when she's with you. Maybe she reverts to a gaseous state the rest of the time, and hovers in the air, awaiting your summons," Tom said.

"Wouldn't that be a neat explanation? In the case of this particular girl, it doesn't sound all that far-fetched. She has some—oddities. And there was something I've been noticing in the last few days. Something really unusual in a young person."

"Which is?"

"She seems to have some difficulty with her memory."

"Really? That is unusual, I guess. What kind of difficulty?"

Janie noticed an unusual edge to Tom, a sudden stiffness that wasn't generally present in him. She wondered why. "Well," she said, "I would tell her something one minute, but the next, it was as if she hadn't heard me."

"Maybe she was distracted."

"I thought of that. She's quite distractable. But it's happened more than once. And I know she hears well enough."

"How can you be sure?"

"Tom. What did I do before the Outbreaks?"

"Oh. Right. Neurology."

"She shows all the classic signs of short-term memory problems. Long term, I don't see anything unusual. She calls up knowledge in impressive depth. But moment to moment she seems to be skipping a few beats. Twice yesterday there were funny little incidents, lapses almost."

"Maybe you should examine her. See what's going on."

"Maybe. But not yet."

"Why not?"

"I don't want her distracted."

"You don't want *her* distracted? From everything we've discussed, I got the impression that it's this Kristina handling *you*, not the other way around."

"Well, that's true, in terms of this project, or whatever you'd call it. This mission, maybe. But that's not what I'm talking about. She needs a different kind of handling, I think. She seems awfully lost sometimes, like she could use a little parenting."

After a reflective pause, he said, "Something I know very little about."

"Which I, for one, have always thought to be one of the Cosmic Troll's worst decrees. You would have been a great father."

Tom smiled down sadly at his plate, and Janie asked him, "Do you ever regret not having had children?"

"There are way too many things I regret." He looked up at her. "I would've needed a partner, and that just never seemed to work out. But the flip side is that I never had to go through losing a child. I watched a lot of people crumble a few years back. I don't know how well I would've done with that."

"I don't think that's something you can predict ahead of time."

"Maybe not."

"Imagine how the parents of these camp boys must feel now. Their sons all made it through the Outbreaks. They probably thought they were home free."

"Are you ever home free when you have kids?"

"No," she said quietly.

"I didn't think so."

Janie sat on the edge of her bed between the two items that were going to occupy the remainder of her night. Though both required her attention, she was simply sitting and thinking, ignoring her obligations.

"Sorry, guys," she said, as if her empty suitcase or Virtual Memorial could hear, or would understand. "I don't mean to neglect either of you, but he's a tough act to follow."

She finally heaved herself off the bed and went to her closet to begin the onerous task of figuring out what was just enough, and what would be too much to take to a country where the temperature was hard to predict from one day to the next. The travel agent had given her a book with guidelines and suggestions, which seemed too complicated to follow.

Fuck it, she thought, *I'll just pack everything I own. Let someone at the airport decide what I should leave home.* Once upon a time she could have taken what she wanted, for a price. But everything now had limits.

She came back to the bed with an armful of clothing, and set it down. Then she went to V.M. and typed in a few more additions to the growing list of what she wanted to search for in Big Dattie when she returned from Iceland. The list was growing longer at an alarming rate. But she had only thirty minutes to do the work and record what she'd done.

"Okay, that's all the attention I can give you tonight," she said to V.M. "But I promise to be better when I return. I'm going to give you back to your other parent while I'm gone."

One last thing to do. She needed to tell that other parent that she planned to take an excursion into Big Dattie, and she needed to try to get the mysterious "agency" to fund it.

She e-mailed Kristina. *Bring the leash,* she wrote, after everything else was conveyed. *It's your turn to walk the dog.*

K arle waited until they were safely ensconced in their small
chamber to read the letter Alejandro had tossed from his
barred window. He unwrapped the parchment from around
the piece of wood as Kate looked anxiously over his shoulder.

*I am healthy and well fed, though I grow wearier every minute of my
captivity. I am constantly guarded and cannot see any means of
escape from this house. The chamber in which I am kept is small but
properly appointed, though in comparison to the hovels we have
known this is luxury. But I will not allow myself to enjoy it while we
are still apart.*

*De Chauliac has become my shadow; he rarely lets me out of his
sight, follows my every step, if not in physical movement then with
his eyes, and his constant vigilance seems more a prison to me than
my bodily captivity in this house. But I am thinking of ways to get
myself out of here. I have begun a friendly flirtation with Elizabeth,
Countess of Ulster, who is the wife of Prince Lionel . . .*

"Dear God!" Kate gasped. "Lionel is my half-brother!"

*. . . with the cooperation of her page, a lad named Geoffrey Chau-
cer, who has brought me a gift from her and carried my message of*

thanks back with him. He is a spirited lad and fond of amusement; I believe I can entice him into a conspiracy for the sheer love of the intrigue. If I can arrange it, I will have him come to you with a message—I will have to conjure some way to convince him that it is part of my dalliance with the countess.

Parchment seems dear in this house, and de Chauliac grows suspicious when I request it, so if you can, toss back a message with one side blank—I will leave the window open, so you need only get it past the bars. Come late at night so we will not be discovered.

Kate, my beloved child, stay well and take care of yourself. I long to hold you in my arms again and to smother your sweet cheeks with kisses. Karle, take care to guard her. I am counting on you.

Kate held the letter to her face and cried. "Oh, Père . . . we must write back immediately."

"This drawing signifies the fire from heaven that breathes the spark of life into man and all beasts," Flamel said, "and this"—he pointed to a tri-lobed icon—"invokes the presence of the Father, the Son, and the Holy Ghost. They are shown here as the red stone, the white stone, and the *elixir vitae.*" His traced a finger along the drawing. "See how these rings join them together in divine union?"

"But how does this apply to the work of transmutation?" de Chauliac asked. "If it is just a recombination of the elements, why is all this necessary?"

"Ah," Flamel said, "it is not mere recombination, it is an act of creation. These first steps are perhaps the most important steps of all, for without heavenly sanction no man can do what falls naturally into God's realm. Anytime man attempts to engage in such an activity, he must first seek the approval of the Divine One Himself so as not to offend. Otherwise the process cannot be successful."

De Chauliac was fascinated. "And how does one know if such approval is granted?"

"God sends a sign, of course."

"Which is?"

"There is no way to predict—it is different every time. Each practitioner of the art of knowing must pray deliberately and continuously in order to discover what God wants of him, and when he comes to that sweet knowledge he will recognize the sign. A flash of fire, a change in the wind, the rising of the waters, the upheaval of the earth. These four elements have always been under God's control, and He can make them do His will. And so He will use them to make man understand his *own* power, and the work can begin. He can learn, through the guidance of God, how to catch the wind, claim the earth, light the fire, and harness the water. Then all things are possible."

There was silence around the table as each man gave private thought to what was before him. The flame of the candle flickered as de Chauliac carefully turned the seven pages of the first section of the manuscript— pages that already bore Alejandro's elegant scrawl. At the end of that folio, he came to an image, beautifully rendered in soft colors overlaid with gold, but its evil subject was not in keeping with its inviting appearance. Into the mouth of a vile and odious-looking serpent a virgin was disappearing, and her tiny painted face seemed alive with the pain and horror of her terrible fate.

"Colleague," de Chauliac said to Alejandro, "what words are these around this drawing?"

He had finished translating the page, but he had neglected the caption. He passed his eyes over the Hebrew writing. "One or two come quickly," he said, "but the rest will require study. I will need to sit and work at this in order to bring out the words."

"How long?"

"Only to translate this line? An hour or two, perhaps. But what is the sense of that, when there are two sections of the manuscript yet to be revealed, with images of their own?" He turned the pages of the second section forward until he came to the image of the same terrible serpent nailed to a cross. "What can this mean?" he said.

"I do not know," Flamel said reverently. He crossed himself and pushed his hands together, then muttered a quick prayer. "But God in His wisdom will reveal it in due time." He turned to Alejandro and said in a solemn voice, "He has chosen you as His instrument of revelation. I am certain of this. That is why He put this treasure in your hands."

"Praise God!" de Chauliac whispered. "This is an honor, colleague, a very great honor."

To free the words of an ancient Jew in order that Christians might use the wisdom they conferred, perhaps against those Jews? A tortuous honor, a burden! The serpent on that cross is me, he thought. *I will be the writhing betrayer of my people.*

Yet if not me, then someone else will do it, and I will lose all hope of controlling the destiny of these words. One or two, or ten, could be mistrans-

lated, so no formulae would work . . . until this tome falls into the hands of a Jew again and can be corrected.

Flamel's eyes gleamed with excitement. "And might you give me some hint of how long it will take for you to complete your work on the next two folios?"

"A fortnight, perhaps, or longer, considering how much is already done."

Flamel looked disappointed at first, but gradually his face brightened. "I have waited many years to find this treasure; it will not be my undoing to wait a bit more." Then his expression sobered. "I will use that time to prepare myself to go before God as a Creator, if He will have me. I shall begin to pray tonight."

It was perhaps Marcel's longest and most detailed letter to date, and when he finished reading it Charles of Navarre sat by the fire and contemplated its contents. That the Paris contingent had come to a decision about where to stage the uprising meant that there would be no more uncertainty. Karle would gather his forces over the next few weeks and outfit them to the best of his abilities, and then he would train them to behave like warriors, not the stinking, cowardly peasants that they were. He read it a second time, committing the important parts to memory, then tossed it into the fireplace. It hissed and shriveled and gave off an unholy stink.

"Marcel thinks it best to gather at Compiègne," he said to the Baron de Coucy. "And so we shall."

"The Countess Elizabeth requires your attendance," Chaucer said. "She is feeling inexplicably faint."

With a long sigh, de Chauliac replied, "Then I shall ride out within the hour."

"She would have Dr. Hernandez as well."

"I fear he is otherwise occupied in the work of translation at this time."

"The countess will be sore distressed to hear this, sir. But if it is impossible, then of course, she will simply have to understand." He reached into the pocket of his mantle and extracted a sealed parchment. "But would you be kind enough to give the good physician this note? It describes her symptoms. Perhaps you can confer prior to your departure, and carry with you his thoughts about her mysterious condition."

De Chauliac accepted the note. "Very well," he said. "I will give it to him immediately."

And as soon as Chaucer left, he slipped into his library and broke the wax seal.

"You see? I told you this would happen. We shall be required to visit these whining English every day to see to their false afflictions. There will be no time for your work."

Alejandro read the note, then looked at de Chauliac and smiled. "The work will wait." He closed the Abraham book carefully. "It will be there long after the countess and you and I have turned to dust. And in all fairness, colleague, these symptoms do not sound false to me. She writes, in descriptive terms and exceptional rhyme, I must say, of pallor, faintness, lack of appetite, shortness of breath, general unhappiness—these are the symptoms of lovesickness."

"Since when is love an affliction?"

"It has been so for all time, de Chauliac. It is an affliction of the soul and the spirit, rather than the body and the mind, though it manifests itself by weakness and general dyspepsia in the body and confusion in the brain. Have you never been in love?"

"Not to the point that it bends my body to its will."

Alejandro smiled cynically. "A pity. It should be required of all physicians to love at least once so they might know its symptoms from more dangerous maladies."

De Chauliac raised one eyebrow and sneered. "It *is* a dangerous malady, wisely avoided, I think."

"Only by those who would not know its sweetness. But we might debate this ad infinitum and never come to a conclusion. It afflicts women far more viciously than men, for some reason. You must explain this to her."

"I shall not."

"Why?"

"Because I do not believe one word of it."

"Oh, come now, colleague—be kind to her. If you cannot find such kindness in yourself, then you are not the superior physician I believed you to be. One must always be compassionate and have pity on those weaker than oneself, especially the ladies."

"You will not convince me."

"Then I shall have to leave my work and accompany you. Otherwise she will just send for me again because she will be dissatisfied with your efforts on her behalf. You will tell her that she suffers from malaise, and that the cure is rest. And the next day she will send for you again, with the same complaint."

De Chauliac looked terribly bothered, but finally agreed. "Come along, then. Let us be done with it."

They were ushered into her private chamber, in the middle of which stood a giant canopy bed with the curtains drawn on all four sides. The servant who led them in took hold of the bed curtain and rustled it, then said, "*Madame?*"

"*Oui?*" Her voice was weak and frail-sounding.

"The physicians have arrived."

There was a muffled sigh of relief. "Oh, praise God."

"Shall I pull back the curtain?"

"In a moment."

They heard the brief rustling of fabric, then the countess's voice. "You may open it now."

The servant pulled back the drape to reveal Elizabeth propped up against several pillows. Her hair was loose and she wore a thin silk shift tied at the neck. She placed one hand dramatically against her forehead and closed her eyes. "Oh, thank all the saints that you have come, at last!" she moaned. "I have spent this morning in misery. I simply do not have the wherewithal to raise myself up."

"Take comfort, lady," Alejandro said. He neared the bed and gestured toward its edge. "May I?"

"Please," she said, "seat yourself." She patted the bed with her hand.

He sat, and took hold of one of her hands. "You are clammy, dear Countess," he said.

"Another symptom! Oh, the distress! What can be ailing me?"

He patted her hand reassuringly. "We shall know what ails you shortly and prescribe the necessary treatment."

"Oh, that such treatment should exist."

De Chauliac cleared his throat impatiently and said, "Dear Countess, I believe you are in good hands with my colleague. I shall look in on Prince Lionel to determine the progress of his toe while Dr. Hernandez tends to you, which he will surely do quite magnificently. That is, of course, if the lady has no objection to receiving the attentions of only *one* physician."

Elizabeth raised her head up off the pillow and looked at de Chauliac, who waited quietly at the far side of the room. "You are so attentive to my husband, kind sir. How gratified he will be to know that your first thought was of him! Go, indeed—we will try to manage somehow without you."

Alejandro smirked at his colleague. *"Somehow,"* he said.

And as soon as the French physician had taken himself out of the room in a billow of robes, Alejandro turned his attention back to the countess. "Now, tell me again what your specific afflictions are."

She breathed out. "Oh, I am blighted by the most terrible lethargy. I lie in bed pining for I know not what, and I cannot seem to make myself rise up. My heart feels as if it has abandoned me entirely."

"Then I shall need first to examine your heart." And with a warm smile, he reached out and untied the bow at her neck. The shift fell open and revealed her delicate collarbone. He let his eyes wander over her white skin, and said, "You do not exaggerate. You are as pale as the finest pearl."

He took his rolling parchment out of his bag and pressed it against her chest, then listened for a moment. "I cannot seem to hear what I need to hear," he said, feigning dissatisfaction. "Sometimes it is best just to place the ear directly over the heart, and then it may be heard more fully." Then he looked directly into her eyes. "But I shall do so only if you would not be offended by such intimacy."

She quickly shook her head no, and then whispered, "Suddenly my cheeks feel warm. What can that mean?"

"In due time, we will know." He leaned over and put his ear against her chest.

She made a small gasp of pleasure and placed her hand on his head, twirling her fingers lightly through the waves of his black hair. And when he rose up again, he said, "Your heart has taken on a small flutter."

"Is this a terrible thing?"

"No affliction of the heart is ever wanted, but this is one, fortunately, that may be cured."

"Say you so?" she said.

"Do not fear, it is true. When I read your note I thought I knew what your condition might be."

She lowered her eyes, and smiled coyly. "Do you mean to keep me ignorant?"

"And aggravate your condition? It would be the furthest thing from my mind."

She leaned forward and took hold of his hand. "Tell me, then."

"It is my opinion, dear Countess, that your heart suffers from an excess of love."

"Oh," she said, "what a noble affliction . . . and what, dear Physician, is the cure?"

"You must take care to see that this excess finds regular release, and you must call for your physician whenever you feel the need."

There was a light tap on the door; they turned toward it and found de Chauliac standing there, looking terribly impatient. The Frenchman did not wait to be invited, but strolled in with his usual majestic determination. "I am pleased to report that by releasing the humor from your husband's toe, we have succeeded in diminishing his pain quite considerably. And the appendage seems to have shrunk a bit, almost to normal."

"By all the saints," Elizabeth said, "I am beginning to loathe the notion of returning to England. Where shall we ever find such marvelous physicians there? You must both stay and take your supper with my husband and me."

"You are feeling well enough to eat, Countess?" de Chauliac said, one eyebrow raised.

She smiled at Alejandro. "I am much improved, yes, enough to take a bite or two of nourishment."

"This is quite marvelous news. My colleague seems to have worked another of his miracles. But sadly, we must decline. There is work we are doing that must be attended to."

"Experiments?"

"Work that will lead to experimentation eventually, if all goes well."

"Oh, how exciting! I would hear all about this work."

"It is still very secret," de Chauliac said. "We dare not speak of our new theories. On our next visit, perhaps we will have made enough progress to report on it. But now, I'm afraid, we must actually *do* the work." He glared at Alejandro.

The Jew rose up from the bedside. "My colleague is right. We must depart." He leaned over and whispered, "Though I would stay and watch the progress of your improvement. But another time. This malady you suffer from is known on occasion to repeat itself. Send your page Chaucer, and I shall give you further advice on its course." He winked and straightened up again, and they departed.

They sat at the table in de Chauliac's salon, the cold greasy remains of their supper between them. De Chauliac, to Alejandro's amusement, had muttered his way through the meal, never directly addressing his captive.

Finally he looked up from his plate and nearly shouted, "You are engaging in an exceptionally vile deceit to encourage this flirtation, Canches."

"Ah," Alejandro said, "the cause of your annoyance finally reveals itself. You must take care not to let such things fester. It is very bad for the constitution. And in truth, I see no harm in what passes between me and the countess."

"No harm? This lady is the wife of a prince of England and a noblewoman of considerable stature herself! She stands to inherit the entirety of Ulster on her father's death. How can you think yourself a proper match for her?"

"Oh, come now, de Chauliac, no one is looking to a match, least of all the countess herself. She has already made a fine match, perhaps as good as any match she might have made. But that does not necessarily mean that the arrangement satisfies her completely. When I look upon Prince Lionel I see a man who would attract few women, save for the accident of his royal birth. He bears all the marks of a Plantagenet, but in him those qualities have expressed themselves in a rather uncomely form."

"They have a goodly number of children, so there must be some affection between them."

"There must always be affection between husbands and wives, if not for each other, then for their common end. But I am led to understand that among royals it often takes on a rather bland form. This lady is simply indulging in a little excitement."

"But you . . . you are . . ."

"A Jew, and therefore unsuitable even for a flirtation?"

"Yes!"

"She will not know unless you tell her. And I daresay it will do you as much damage as me should my 'deficiency' be revealed." He tossed down the remains of a goblet of wine and stood up. "Now, with your permission, keeper, I shall retire to my chamber and continue my work on the translation. Good Flamel seems ready to burst with impatience. He is probably on his knees right now as we argue, pouring his soul out to his God in the hopes of being found worthy. Who knows when that determination will be made? It may be quite soon, if he is as pious as he would have one think. I would not want to keep him waiting."

"As you like, Physician."

As he passed through the salon door, he turned back and said with a bitter smile, "Tell me again why you would keep me here with you—is it for the pleasant stimulation of my company?"

"Something akin to that."

Alejandro sighed. "I thought that was what you said." But that was no longer true. Now he was being kept until the secret of riches hidden in Abraham's manuscript had been revealed. It was time to start making mistakes.

Another leaf revealed itself that night, and the first small error was made. Alejandro translated the symbol for "green" to mean "red" but all else was flawless. *He will have no reason to suspect it is not correct,* he thought with an inward smile. As he was wiping the tip of his quill, a small missile sailed through the window and landed on his bed with a soft *whump*.

He rushed to his bars. It was a moment before his eyes adjusted, but he saw two figures in the darkness, and as his focus cleared he knew they were the ones he wanted to see.

"Wait while I read your words," he whispered incautiously.

He took his treasure to the candle and unwrapped it. One side, as he'd requested, was blank, and the other full of Kate's beautiful writing.

Marcel has made us welcome, though he knows not who I truly am, and Karle has not betrayed me to him, nor anyone else. I too am well, and we are well sheltered, especially from the prying eyes of those who might question us. Karle and Marcel spend all their time plotting for their revolution, and I have managed to be of some assistance where I might. And well I ought, for they would have made terrible mistakes of strategy had I not pointed out their follies.

Our journey to Paris was protracted, as you no doubt know. We were delayed by tasks that Karle said could not wait—and in truth, they could not. There were many women told of their widowhood, many messages left for warriors who would return, many calls to arms delivered. There was so much sickness and death, Père, and there was never a lack of horror to be seen.

In one farmhouse we found a man who had the cholera—I did as much for him as I could by recommending the dandelion, and the woman was with child, which was eating her flesh as it strove toward life. But in this house a more heinous thing had occurred—an older son had died of plague, not a month before we arrived. I questioned the woman, but she gave me little information; she would only say that the Death came and went, but always took someone. I asked her of rats, and she told me that the boy often hunted on his own and that he might have eaten one out of desperation to fill his belly. We

found his grave and I took one of his hands—may God forgive me—
for I know such flesh might one day be needed. It is wrapped and
safely stowed.

And so, he thought to himself, his heart incongruously full of pride
while his gut trembled in fear for her, *the daughter has become as the*
father, a robber of graves.

Had his own father felt the same pride and fear for him, when he was
Kate's age? He longed, with all his soul, to ask. And so he did, in a silent
prayer, whispered briefly. But there was no time to listen in his heart for
an answer. He returned to the letter with this thought: *May all who watch*
over mortals grant that these deeds shall not lead her as far astray as they
did me.

We must hasten to get you out of there, the letter continued, *for we*
need to leave Paris and go north again, and I will not let Karle leave
until you are freed. There is to be a battle between the forces of
Charles of Navarre and the supporters of the Dauphin, and Marcel
has negotiated with Navarre for Karle to lead a contingent of peas-
ants in support of Navarre, in return for concessions toward freedom
when the Dauphin is deposed. Though Karle and I agree that Na-
varre is a cruel beast, Marcel has made us believe that it is the only
way to accomplish our ends.

Take care in your dealings with Elizabeth, Père, for she is the wife
of my half-brother. Karle insists you will know this, but I must make
certain that you do by saying it in these lines. We fear for you if
Lionel learns who you are. Nevertheless, we await word from this
page of hers.

May God keep you safe, and send you to us soon.

He glanced out the window; the shadowy figures were close together.
Karle seemed to have an arm around Kate as if he were protecting her,
not for Alejandro's sake but for his own. With a long sigh, he went to his
table and scratched out a hasty reply:

Daughter, I am taking all due care to ensure that Elizabeth does not
learn my true identity—and it does not suit de Chauliac's purposes
right now to reveal it to her. My next missive to you will likely come
from Chaucer—I have set this in motion just today, but I cannot say
when it will happen. Soon, though, I am sure, for Elizabeth seems an

impatient sort. He will ask for Karle by the name of "Jacques," as they have been introduced.

I long to stand beside you once again. Perhaps then you will tell me why it is that your letter contains far more we's than I's. God-speed to you both.

chapter

22

Janie stared out the window as the airplane banked in preparation for landing. Sunlight gleamed on the water below, and she squinted to ward off the piercing reflections that, were she to stare long enough, would dapple her vision with floating blue spots. She wondered, as an attempt at self-distraction, if those were whitecaps glinting down below, or perhaps the tips of icebergs.

It would be only a few more minutes until they landed. She'd had a surprising slow build of excitement as she went through the beginnings of the journey, the check-in, the suiting up after they boarded, and now the anticipation of seeing Bruce again after so long was close to overwhelming. Though the flight was relatively short, she'd already read everything the screen on the seat-back in front of her had to offer, and the novel she'd brought for just that purpose couldn't seem to hold her attention. In near desperation she pressed the talk button on her headgear and said to the man seated next to her, "Looks choppy out there. Hey, do you think we flew over the *Titanic* site?"

The big, Nordic-looking man leaned forward slightly, his suit crinkling, and cast an uninterested glance out the window, then sat back again and shrugged. Without a word of comment, he returned to viewing his own screen.

She'd hoped for at least *"Yah shoor yoo betcha,"* which might have led to a pleasant, anesthetizing conversation with her Viking seatmate, a crosscultural exchange of viewpoints on how the surface of the sea ought to look. But it was not to be.

She'd been so ambivalent about this trip until now, when the strain between her and Bruce suddenly seemed all but forgotten, having been rendered insignificant by the knowledge that in only an hour or so she would actually reach out her hand and touch him.

Four months it's been. The airplane banked again and then straightened, and as they came in closer Janie could see the desolate black beaches of Iceland's southern shoreline. Off in the distance, rising up out of a flat expanse of water, implausibly close to the beach, were the tall columns of a geothermal plant, which looked far more deadly and ominous than it was. Clouds of steam dotted the otherwise crystal-clear air like runaway cotton balls, and as the plane came closer to the ground, Janie was charmed by the sudden appearance of the pastel-painted homes and businesses of Reykjavík.

One stowed bag was all Icelandic Air would allow her, so she'd layered herself, and when she got off the plane and out of the plastic flight suit she thought she must look like a walking laundry basket. She'd sweated inside the suit, and strands of hair were plastered to the side of her face. A quick glance around failed to reveal the bathroom for which she had a sudden and dire need, but until she went through customs there would be no stepping out of the line.

For once her bag was one of the first on the carousel, so she dragged it off and literally ran to the inspector's station, where her one electronic device, a telephone, scanned through without a hitch. Her visa was declared to be in perfect order, the hotel reservation confirmed, her passport stamped, so all that remained was to put her hand on the sensor and pass on through.

She reached out slowly, but pulled her hand back for a second or two as internal bells blared and paranoia ruled her.

Don't worry about it, Tom had told her. He'd been very adamant that she would be in no legal danger by going to Iceland. *England has no jurisdiction there. All they can do is record that you've been there and send you on through the gate. They can't detain you or arrest you or otherwise harass you in any manner.*

He'd seemed less forceful when he'd said, *Now just go and have a good time.*

She held her hand in front of the sensor. It flashed out a beam onto her palm, and in the blink of an eye the electronic gate clicked open. She hauled herself and her bag through, turned the corner, and saw Bruce. After one hard swallow, she ran to him.

* * *

The hotel was built almost entirely of concrete, easily had in Iceland unlike wood or metal, but in keeping with most of Reykjavik's buildings it was painted in a soft, cheerful color, in this case a lovely butter-yellow with rose-colored trim. The room they were shown to was similarly pleasant, with spare but deceptively comfortable furniture and few other adornments. It was on the iron-framed bed, painted Swedish blue, and under the soft blanket, woven in rainbow stripes of Icelandic wool, that Bruce and Janie knew each other in more than two dimensions for the first time in a third of a year.

When they awoke again at ten P.M. the sun was low in the sky but still visible. It hovered just over the horizon, threatening descent, and cast its thin, muted glow in nearly horizontal rays, creating subtle hazy shadows that seemed to stretch out to infinity. As she slipped into renewed consciousness, Janie let her eyes rest on Bruce's angular face and rediscovered things about it that she'd forgotten in the time since they'd last been with each other. The halo of curly hair—did it have a touch more gray than it had last time she'd seen him? The dark, lush lashes that rested so innocently, almost on his cheekbones, when his eyes were closed, and stole her breath away when those eyes were open. The one or two gray hairs in his eyebrows, a little scar just at the bottom of his lower lip. She touched it with the tip of one finger and he flinched slightly.

"I know you told me," she said, "but how did you get this?"

Though his eyes were still closed he smiled and said, "Learning to ski. Put my tooth right through it when I was a little kid."

"Ouch," she said softly. "Where?"

"I forget. Somewhere in New England."

"How old were you?"

He breathed deeply. His eyes fluttered open for a second, then closed again. His brows knitted together as if he were thinking very hard about an important question. "Eight, nine, maybe."

"Oh. Young to be skiing."

"Not in my family. My mother said we were all born with skis."

And trust funds, and a pedigree, Janie thought. It accounted for the uncanny grace with which he moved through the world.

He kissed her on the forehead with unstudied grace and rose up naked from the bed. Janie followed his easy movements with half-open eyes, admiring the silhouette he made against the balcony doors. A salty breeze came in when he opened the multipaned glass panel, bringing with it a slight ashy smell, a reminder that they would be sleeping that night in the foothills of a volcano.

He found his shirt from the pile on the floor and slipped it over his arms, then pulled on his pants and went out onto the balcony. And though she was exhausted from the journey and the time-zone change, Janie managed somehow to get up out of the soft, warm bed. She draped herself in the first rumpled garment her hand found and went out to join him in the night air. When she reached his side he wrapped his arms around her and drew her close, then kissed her on the cheek while the breeze blew her hair around in wispy threads.

"Oh, God, I can't believe you're here," he said. "This has been one of the longest days of my life."

"It has been long," Janie agreed. She hugged him closer and smiled. "But it's ending pretty well, don't you think?"

Kristina's day was ending badly. "I'm just not getting anywhere with finding the patent holder. I'm getting the distinct feeling that whoever did this left a deliberately confusing trail."

"You know what? That's been known to happen before when bad guys don't want to be discovered."

"What are we going to do, then? I'm stuck here. I need to know who the patent holder is, and then I need to find Patient Zero."

"There may not be a Patient Zero at all. And if there is, it's a statistical likelihood that he's dead."

Kristina pushed herself away from the computer. "I'm so confused," she said. She rubbed her eyes with one hand. "I thought everything would just fall into line. We could do all these backward traces and end up with someone to blame."

She looked away, and seemed to slip off somewhere until her companion brought her back with a little *ahem.*

"Oh," she said as she came around, "sorry. One of my ozone moments." She took in a long breath and said, "I was just thinking about Janie. I wish she'd brought V.M. with her. She might be talking to her friend about all this."

The man said nothing for a moment. "She hasn't seen him in how long?"

"I think she said four months."

"Then believe me, she is not talking to him about this quest of ours."

"The work is completely exhilarating. I barely even remember that I'm working at the foundation anymore. I haven't felt so alive in almost a year." Then quickly, she added, "I mean, except, when we've been together."

They sat on opposite sides of a small table, their hands intertwined over a partially consumed assortment of fruits and cheese. Bruce removed one of his hands from the tangle and picked up a cherry, which he teasingly held out by the stem to Janie. She stopped talking long enough to lean forward and suck the little red ball of sweetness into her mouth.

"I'm glad you clarified that," Bruce said.

"Sorry," she said. She swallowed, then leaned even closer. "Come here," she whispered.

He obliged. She slipped her cherry-flavored tongue between his lips and passed him the pit.

Kristina's companion gave her a pat on the shoulder. "Do you have any idea of what time it is? You must be exhausted."

"I'll be okay." She rubbed her forehead.

He was not convinced. "Go to bed. Right now. Use the extra bedroom upstairs."

"Will you get me up early in the morning?"

"Why? Are you going someplace?"

"No—but I want to get back to the work as soon as possible. I want to have a lot to show her when she comes home again."

"I see so much of Betsy in her, Bruce, I can't help it. They'd be about the same age now."

He pulled her closer under the bedclothes. "Does she look like what Betsy would look like?"

"I haven't done a projection of Betsy since we—used her in London. But she just reminds me of the type of young woman I think Betsy would be."

Bruce got up on one elbow and looked at Janie in the thin glow of the incomprehensibly still-visible sun. "And that would be?"

Janie sighed. "Full of life, enthusiastic, interested in everything, and so sweet."

"From what you've said, I don't get the feeling that this Kristina is particularly sweet."

"Oh, she is, in her own way," Janie said as she played with his chest hairs. "She has some very endearing qualities. Mixed in with the odd ones. But I like her more all the time."

They were quiet for a moment, listening to each other's breath. Janie began to drift into sleep. "I can't fight it anymore," she murmured. "I think I'm out of here."

"Go ahead."

Tom stared out his bedroom window and watched absentmindedly as bug after bug flung itself against the streetlight outside, to no apparent purpose. In the silence he heard the clock on his bedstand ticking, ticking, and ticking some more, and he glared over at its illuminated face, as if by doing so he could make it jump into the nearest toilet.

Three A.M. Most people in Massachusetts would be asleep in bed. Perhaps not those who live on some edge, and those who keep an eye on them while they skirt that edge. But in Iceland, people might already be awake.

And doing things.

With an aching heart he wondered why his life and hers had been so completely out of synch. He'd vowed to himself as he drove her to the airport for the three-week trip to Iceland that the second she set foot on the home soil again he would get down on one knee in front of her and beg, if necessary, for the privilege of sharing her life. He hadn't dreamed that another three weeks would make any difference.

"This is breathtaking," Bruce said. "What an incredible view."

"Amazing," Janie said, "truly amazing."

They held hands as they made their way carefully along the metal viewing platform at the peak of the climbing trail. They'd come up the side of the volcano slowly over the course of the morning, stopping now and then to rest, or to kiss when the mood came over them. The reward for their considerable effort was the starkly beautiful moonscape before them, a massive, glistening sheet of glacial ice.

The sun, as high as it ever got in Iceland, was still at an angle low enough to cause a nearly blinding glare. It bounced off the ice and cut right through their dark glasses. Janie shaded her eyes with one hand against its merciless attack. "I think this afternoon I'd like to do something inside," she said. "My eyes have really had it."

"I can think of at least one thing we could do inside."

She laughed aloud, and the sound echoed out over the ice sheet. So she lowered her voice and said, "Well, of course, that, but after that, I mean."

"Is there anything beyond that?"

"It might surprise you to know that there is. Actually, I had something in mind. The travel agent gave me a guidebook, and it had a listing for this place called the Arni Magnussun Institute—it's sort of a museum. They have a lot of old manuscripts there."

For a split second Janie thought she saw the tiniest flash of anger in his expression. But it disappeared almost instantly. He smiled and put an arm around her shoulders. "Can't get enough of those old manuscripts, can you?"

"No. I can't. Bring 'em on."

As they headed toward the downward trail, Bruce said, "We had our first date in a museum, as I recall."

"We did, indeed."

"Well, I guess we should go to this other one, then."

"We used to call these nooners when I was younger," he said softly as his hands moved from button to button down the front of her sweater. And as it dropped to the floor behind her, leaving just a lacy camisole and panties to be removed, he breathed softly into her ear, "But you know us boys—we had these silly ideas, like you had to hoot and brag when you got something in the middle of the day."

She moaned softly as his fingers found a nipple under her camisole. She moaned louder when his tongue found it. "By 'something,' " she whispered through her pleasure, "I assume you don't mean anything contagious."

"Well . . ."

His pants crumpled to a heap where he dropped them.

Now her breathing came deeper and slower. "Perhaps . . . you want to explain . . . this 'something.' "

"No," he moaned, "later would be better."

"Oh, Bruce," she said with a different kind of excitement, "take a look at this."

He came up behind her at a massive display case in the Arni Magnus-sun Institute and peered over her shoulder. He read the placard and then regarded the item being exhibited in the massive climate-controlled case.

"Hmm." He looked closer. "From the thirteenth century, it says."

"This is even older than Alejandro's journal."

He examined the case with only his eyes; he decided from the looks of it that the slightest touch would set off a flurry of assorted security responses, all unpleasant. "This thing is like a vault," he said. Then with an almost challenging tone in his voice, he said, "Will they put your journal in a case like this at the book depository?"

She shook her head no as she read the placard mounted on one side of the case. "Probably not. The other book with his handwriting is a lot older. I mean, the fact that there are two books with the same writing makes Alejandro's journal more valuable and a lot more interesting, at least to me, and probably to some scholars. But even still, I don't think the journal I brought from London will be considered to be in the same league."

"Maybe not in the United States, no. But in England, it might."

She gave him a surprised look. "It's not in England anymore. And no one there is even aware that it exists. At least as far as I know."

"They didn't get much of a chance."

She stared at him, perturbed.

"If it were back there and someone knew about it," he said, "it would probably become part of the literature. Certainly the literature of the healing arts."

She looked away for a moment, confused, and wondered precisely what it was that he was trying to intimate. Why did he always seem to want her to get rid of it?

"Do you think I should've left it there?" she asked.

"I don't know if I'd say that. I have my doubts occasionally about whether you should have it at all—I think that's what really bothers me. And I think the thing is trouble."

"In what way?"

"That's the problem," he said. "I'm not completely clear on it. But I'm still not sure you should be giving it to this book depository."

"It's in Hebrew. I think it's pretty appropriate for it to go there. It needs a home, Bruce."

"*Part* of it is in Hebrew. But most of it is French or English. And most of the techniques are from English folk medicine."

"*Some* of the techniques are English folk medicine. A lot of what's in there is Alejandro's, and we know for sure that he was a Spanish Jew. He learned a good deal of what he wrote down from this fellow de Chauliac in France."

"But it did spend the better part of its existence in England. I just think a case could be made that it belongs there."

"No. You're wrong. It doesn't belong in England any more than France. And it's not trouble, not at all. I've had many hours of pleasure looking through it. So has Caroline."

"I can recall a few very unpleasant hours that got spent with that journal open."

"They would've been a lot more unpleasant if we hadn't had it."

They began walking slowly toward another exhibit. Janie was shaken by the disagreement, and wanted desperately to get the matter behind them, to neutralize the negative influence of this inanimate object on their relationship, which seemed suddenly more fragile than she remembered from their last visit. She wondered silently if this was just the strain of separation showing, and if Bruce had picked the journal as something tangible to focus on in letting that strain reveal itself.

"Look," she said with more firmness than she actually felt, "I've got the journal now. I took the risk of bringing it out of hiding, so for the moment it's going to go where I want it to. Which is just where it is right now. At the depository."

He stopped and stood still. "Well," he said stiffly, "I guess I've been told."

Janie felt a little stunned by this sudden evidence of a gap in their understanding at a time when they ought to be reveling in each other's presence. A strong desire for everything to be all better again came over her. "Come on," she said softly, "let's not let this spoil our time here. If we really need to argue, we can probably find much better subject matter—something where one of us might even win. And I'm sure we will—another time. In fact I hope we'll have the luxury of many in-person arguments. But right now, we're on a time budget, so let's give it a rest and enjoy ourselves, okay?"

A few seconds passed, then he said, "Okay. You're right."

"My two favorite words from a man." She smiled, and hoped it was convincing. "Now will you let a pigheaded middle-aged woman buy you dinner? Please say yes. I'm hungry after all that bouncing around we did before."

The hard look on his face softened. "Me too. Let's go."

The smell was evident for blocks around, the fear-inspiring odor of wet, charred wood with a nauseating undertone of firefighting chemicals. Michael Rosow stood in front of the ruined house and shook his head sadly from side to side while Caroline cried beside him. He'd been in the station when the call came through from a neighbor, but by the time the fire crew had gotten there, it was already too late to save Janie's house. What remained of the home she'd once shared with her husband and daughter was little more than a dripping pile of rubble, with steam rising from the still-hot embers. Bits of floral-printed upholstery, miraculously unburned in what had once been the living room, were the only color to be seen in the blackened mess.

He rubbed Caroline's back as she sobbed into one hand. "When did she say she'd be home?" he asked softly.

"She wasn't sure. A few days, maybe."

"I think someone ought to call her."

Caroline wiped away tears and said, "Why? The house isn't going to get better if she comes back now."

"She'll want to know." He sighed heavily and pulled a phone out of his pocket. "I think we should let Tom do this."

Tom stood outside the immigration area in the international arrival area at Logan Airport, and tried to shove away the memory of what it had felt like the last time he'd come there to fetch Janie. This time, at least, he wouldn't be subjected to the same stunning blow. He'd been holding a bouquet of flowers when he came to fetch her after the trip to London, but when he'd read the message she sent out with another passenger he'd put the flowers on a nearby chair and simply left them there. Now he was empty-handed. It seemed a shame. At least the same could not be said for his heart.

As de Chauliac had predicted, and Alejandro had prayed for, the Countess Elizabeth's symptoms mysteriously returned the next morning. So they set out again to see to her, for de Chauliac would not renege on his promise of care to the king, no matter how silly the illness.

Alejandro rode alongside Geoffrey Chaucer, with the guards behind them. De Chauliac stayed a good distance back from the rest of the entourage, stewing and fretting and muttering his resentment of their trivial mission. Now and then the Jew looked back over his shoulder and gave the Frenchman an annoying smile, which only heightened de Chauliac's ire.

About halfway through the journey, Alejandro leaned over and spoke to Chaucer in low tones. "You love an intrigue, young Chaucer, am I right?"

"Do I wear this love so plainly, then?"

"Plain as the pocks on a whore's ass, I think," Alejandro said.

He was not accustomed to such talk, but the lad seemed to have an appreciation for the bawdy, and he wanted to create a brotherly sort of intimacy between them.

Chaucer laughed. "Not plain enough, then."

"Well, I will give you the chance to engage in an intrigue of the most sublime sort."

"Oh, do reveal it, sir!"

"Are you a loyal fellow, Chaucer, to your lord Lionel?"

" 'Tis to the Lady Elizabeth that my true allegiance belongs, though when my lord requires it, my assistance is always available."

"But were you to swear fealty, it would be to . . ."

"The countess, sir. It was through her household that I first came into service."

"She was astute in her choice of pages. You are a most able fellow. And clever."

"Your words are kind, Physician. But there is cleverness within me that has not escaped as yet. I long for the day when my service is complete and I may devote myself entirely to words."

And Alejandro was surprised to hear this admission. Their hopes were so similar. "You are a man of my own heart, I think."

"There may be truth in that. But tell me, Physician, what of this intrigue?"

"Ah! I nearly forgot. Do you remember Jacques, the nephew of *le provoste* Marcel?"

"I do. A rugged amber-haired fellow with a bit of a swagger. Were it not for the timely arrival of him and his uncle, my virtue might have been forever compromised."

Alejandro chuckled. "Your virtue will only be safe until the next time the opportunity for compromise presents itself, lad. As I recall, the opportunity presented itself in a comely package that night."

"Rather. But what of this Jacques, who was my unwitting savior?"

Alejandro gave Chaucer a conspiratorial grin. "He has promised to assist me."

"In what regard?"

"In arranging to meet a certain lady."

Chaucer's expression livened. "Might I know this lady, Physician?"

"Intimately, young page. Intimately."

He broke into a wide grin. "And will this lady want this meeting?"

"I had hoped you might tell me whether or not she did, in view of your intimacy with her."

"In my opinion, kind sir, all ladies would do well to desire a meeting with you, in view of your handsome presentation, your keen wit, and a certain, shall I say, seductive air that you have about you."

Seductive? Absurd!

But he took the observation well, and continued. "Your flattery is well noted. But you have not answered my question. I pray you do so, and directly."

He made a little shrug and said, "She would not be displeased. But wherein lies the difficulty in making these arrangements for yourself?"

Alejandro tilted his head backward. "De Chauliac. He is jealous of the time such meetings might take away from our work. And I daresay, he is as nosy as an elephant."

"An elephant! Have you seen one of these fine beasts?"

"Only in a book, I fear."

"But tell me what it looks like."

"Another time, Chaucer. There is a plot to be hatched and time is wasting."

"Ah, yes. Forgive me."

"The excitement of youth may always be forgiven. At any rate, I am guarded night and day by these two ruffians who follow us—de Chauliac has set them upon me to make sure I do not waste any time so we may get on with our work—"

"Which work, in its secrecy, gives rise to intrigue in and of itself, if I may say so."

"You may, and we shall address the nature of the work at another time. I am too preoccupied with the present intrigue. Now, de Chauliac's jealousy leaves me no chance to meet with this certain lady without undue observation."

"Are you certain that the jealousy is only for the work, and that de Chauliac is not jealous of you in some other way? Perhaps he does not wish you to see the countess because it rankles him in some place other than his intellect."

Alejandro stared at Chaucer for a moment.

"It was merely an observation, Physician, do not look so shocked. His eyes never leave you."

If he had noticed it, he had pushed it away, but Chaucer was right: de Chauliac did watch him more closely than was called for, even considering that he was a prisoner.

"And this is Paris, where God seems often to look the other way."

Alejandro shifted in his saddle. "God's discretion is a subject we will not properly address between here and Lionel's manse."

Chaucer laughed. "Too true. On to conspiring, then."

"Jacques has agreed to help me get away from de Chauliac, if only for a day, so that I may spend some time untethered with this lady we speak of. He is willing to come in disguise and abduct me. Your help is needed in seeing that he knows of my next sojourn to the lady's side. Which I hope to arrange today. Then, if you will, you can carry a message to him telling of the time. We will choose a good place on the route, when I might be around a corner and my guards still not yet turned. And if all goes well, it will happen swiftly, and I will meet the lady in question, in privacy at last."

"Simple enough, I think. But really, not that great an intrigue. An abduction in Paris these days," he mused, "is not the subject of which legends are made. So I will agree only if I may be there when this supposed 'abduction' takes place. I long to see such an event with my own eyes."

"Why?"

"The better to describe it later, sir. Who knows when the need might arise."

"You have just said it is not the sort of subject from which a legend might be born."

"Not unless I choose to make it such," the youth said with a confident smile. "I am fond of embellishment, and skilled at it too. Think of it, Physician . . . the fair countess, languishing in staid wedlock, swept off her feet by the handsome and exotic Spanish physician, a man of great mystery, who wins her heart with his gentle ministrations, an escape from bondage, perhaps a tragedy."

Alejandro thought Chaucer a curious young man at that moment, but smiled and laughed, for he was enjoying the subtle patina his participation had brought to what would otherwise simply be a dangerous escape attempt. "It all suits me well," Alejandro said, "except the tragedy part. There is a great poet in you, Chaucer. Do not let the page keep him at bay."

"Have no fear, Physician. The poet already rises." He laughed aloud and glanced briefly backward. "The look on de Chauliac's face will be worth something too, will it not?"

Alejandro winked. "Something, indeed."

"Now, let the rising poet guide you for a moment. You must be sure to flatter her. Tell her you must see her in the purest daylight in a garden, where she will be surrounded by like beauty, God's other fine handiwork."

Marcel grimaced as he read the scroll from Charles of Navarre. The further he read, the wider his eyes opened, and the more furious he seemed. When he had finished, he swore aloud and flung the parchment at Guillaume Karle, who read it for himself with similar reaction.

"We must convince him otherwise."

"Using what persuasion?" Marcel demanded.

"Another message, stronger entreaties, sounder logic, whatever it takes!" Karle flung the scroll back at Marcel. "But to meet at Compiègne is not to our advantage."

"Navarre sees no disadvantage in it."

"From his position, he would not. And in truth, his own forces stand little chance of harm from the king unless his armies show up with a far larger force than anticipated. Navarre's men are weaponed, mounted, and armored. Only the foot soldiers are at serious risk. But any forces I gather will have no such advantage, and must have the means of escape if they are not to be slaughtered."

"That is only if things do not go our way. If Navarre crushes the king's forces, then your troops will be in no danger at all."

"Save from Navarre."

"But he has already promised to ally himself with you. He has given his word to speak to your demands after the battle is won."

"I think perhaps we must ask him to speak to these demands before. I am suddenly less willing to pay my penny first."

Marcel heaved an unhappy sigh. "Much negotiation has gone into this, Karle. It is a delicate alliance, and must not be jeopardized by your short-of-the-candle doubts."

" 'Tis a fresh candle, when the terms are altered."

"This is not an alteration of the terms. Merely the strategy. You and Navarre will still join forces against the king. You will have your demands heard and answered when the battle is won. That the site of the battle changes has no bearing on that result."

"No? What if the battle is lost because of the difficulty of the site?"

"Navarre seems to have faith in Compiègne."

"I do not share his faith."

"Why? Because your young lady says it is not worthy?"

"We agreed that she was right in her thinking."

"And now, we hear from Navarre that he finds it flawed."

"Write back, Marcel, and tell him he is wrong."

Marcel stared quietly at Karle for a moment, considering the challenge. "No," he finally said, "I will not. He was quite firm in this response. Compiègne it will be. Whether it suits you or not."

Alejandro stood at Elizabeth's door and smiled warmly, with de Chauliac a pace behind him.

The countess sat up from her pillows and waved away her servants. "Oh, Chaucer, do wait yet," she said as the retinue was filing out. "I would have you escort de Chauliac to the nursery. Nurse says there are complaints aplenty among my children, and as long as *Monsieur le Docteur* is here, shall he not see to them?" She glanced around Alejandro and looked at the Frenchman who stood behind him. "Dear de Chauliac, will you mind? These little ones are so very precious to me."

It was a banishment, which de Chauliac accepted with his usual grace. But not with cheer: He did not smile when he said, "Of course, Countess, I shall see to them immediately."

With a complicitous grin to both the countess and Alejandro, Chaucer led de Chauliac away, and closed the door to the chamber. He nodded to the guards, who posted themselves against any escape attempt.

"At last, we are alone," Elizabeth said softly.

Alejandro wondered how a woman in such excellent health could force herself into a state of such pallor. "And none too soon," he said gently, "for you are alarmingly pale."

The countess took hold of his hands and pressed them to her heart. "Am I? I thought as much. I feel that I am pale inside and out." She let his hands slide out of hers and reached out to touch his cheek. "But you do not suffer from such debilitating fairness—look how fine and rich the color of your skin is."

Her hand came a bit too close to his neck, only inches above his still-visible brand. He took hold of her small hand and brought it to his lips, then kissed each finger gently in turn. And though it was all a ruse, this supposed passion he had developed for her, the act of pressing his mouth against her warm skin sent waves of confusing emotion through him. Warm flashes of pleasure, radiating out from his heart, reaching all the way to his fingertips. He found himself feeling slightly unsettled.

When he was finally able to stop he gazed into her eyes and said, "I know of no medical tome that speaks of fairness as an affliction. It is simply your Norman heritage that makes you so. And the will of God, may He be blessed for creating such a vision as you."

She moaned and swooned, and he flattered even more, and they carried on for some time in this giddy fashion, leading Alejandro to wonder where this talent for flirtation had hidden all his life, and why it came so fluently at this particular time. *Maybe it is just the absence of such pleasure from my life, for so very long.*

And it did bring him pleasure, for the countess was a beautiful and clever woman, obviously much in need of a man's attention. He liked her, enjoyed her wit, admired her intelligence.

And so he felt ashamed to be using her so. But use her he must. "I have a strong desire," he said longingly.

"Oh, tell me, what is this desire, and if it is in my power, I shall move heaven and earth to see it done."

"Happily, no such force shall be needed, for I only wish to see you in the light of day, in a garden, where your beauty can be surrounded by like beauty, God's other handiwork."

It was not precisely as Chaucer had instructed him, but the result seemed adequate. "A *rendezvous!*" she breathed. "Oh, what a marvelous idea. But how shall we accomplish this, with de Chauliac so jealous of your time. . . . It shall be no difficulty for me to get free, for the king allows me to travel about Paris at will, provided I am properly chaperoned. He knows I will not abandon my children. And my guards seem to know how to keep their distance. But yours . . ."

He smiled. ". . . may have their ears against the door, to spy on us," he reminded her.

She giggled, then said in a lower voice, "I forgot!"

"I think we should leave it to Chaucer to make the necessary arrangements," Alejandro whispered. "He is completely loyal to you, lady, never doubt it."

"I have not yet. I see no reason to begin."

Marie opened the door of Marcel's house to the spare young lad in page's attire, who smiled boyishly at her and said, *"Bonjour, ma jolie."*

Not *Miss,* or *Woman,* but *my pretty.* She smiled coquettishly and returned his greeting. *"Et à vous, jeune homme."*

"I would speak with you for a moment."

"Oui? Pourquoi?"

"Because it pleases me to look on your lovely face, and while I am speaking you will not go away, so I may continue to gaze on it. And may I also say, I am enticed by the sweetness of your voice."

She laughed. "And you shall hear more of it, when I call out for the person you *really* wish to see."

"Ah, then, I am caught. And I thought this dalliance to be proceeding so well. I am rejected, again. May I then speak with *Monsieur* Jacques, *s'il vous plaît?*" He nodded in the direction of the salon, where the pitch and tone of the voices was distinctly uncivilized. "That is, if he can be torn away."

Kate had warned her of the name. *"Entrez,"* she said, "and wait here. They are arguing their detestable politics in there, and I daresay he will be glad of the interruption. I shall fetch him." He had charmed her so that she forgot to inquire his name.

And as he waited alone in the small vestibule, Kate came up from the cellar kitchen to make her way up the stairs. She glanced at him, but seeing nothing recognizable in his face, passed by. But when she heard a quiet expression of astonishment, she turned and looked back. "Are you unwell, sir?"

"No, *mademoiselle*, just a bit taken aback."

"And why, might I inquire?"

"Because, although I am surely crazed to think it, you bear an uncanny resemblance to my patron, the lord Lionel. Why, you might be the prince's sister, so strong is the likeness."

She took a step backward as shock filled her face, which Chaucer misinterpreted as offense. He quickly added, "Though you are a far sight more beautiful than he. On you, it is comely; on him, well . . ."

She grabbed hold of the railing at the foot of the stairs to steady herself as Karle came out of the salon. When the Frenchman saw her unsteadiness, he rushed forward to support her.

"Kate!" he said. "What ails you?"

She took a deep breath before stammering, "Nothing, it is just . . . uh, this young gentleman has . . . mistaken me for someone else."

"Forgive me," Chaucer said in alarm, "it was just something I noticed as you passed, an uncanny similarity . . . of course it cannot be true, for my lord's sisters are all in England presently, and you are too young to be any of them, in any case."

Karle gave him a withering stare and the boy stopped speaking. "Dear Kate, let me help you. This is the youth Chaucer I told you about, come from the countess Elizabeth." He put an arm fully around the girl and held her up.

"Yes," Chaucer said, "and I beg to be excused. I did not mean to upset the . . . uh, your . . . uh . . ."

"My wife," he said, pulling her closer to him.

Kate's head whipped around in surprise.

"Ah! Your *wife*, stupid me . . . I am doubly ashamed." Then with a curious grin he whispered, "Your uncle failed to mention that you were married, in fact he seems to think that you are not."

"Well, here, young man, stands the proof." He looked nervously back over his shoulder toward the salon. "I may have neglected to mention it to Marcel."

"I fail to understand such neglect, sir. One would think you would want to keep the eyes of other gentlemen off a gem such as this wife of yours. You, good sir, are amply blessed."

"I am," Karle agreed. He turned to Kate with a smile. "Perhaps you will go upstairs, *chérie*, while Chaucer and I conduct our business."

"No, *chéri*," she countered, "I cannot bear to be apart from you! And I require your support yet to recover from this . . . shocking misidentification. So please, go on with your business, but ignore me. I shall be but a mouse. But wait—here is a better idea! Shall we all go upstairs together, where I can recover, and we can have a bit of privacy?"

It was agreed. Karle supported her as they climbed up the steep, narrow stairs to the tiny chamber. Chaucer followed.

Once inside, Karle closed the door. "Now, tell me of the plan."

"I am given to understand that the physician wishes for you to 'abduct' him, although since he will be a rather willing hostage I hardly see where it can be called an abduction. But I suppose if that is what he wishes de Chauliac to think, we can make it appear to be so. He wants you to disguise yourself somehow, but not so as to alarm the guards, or they will take too much notice of you."

He described the route that would be taken from de Chauliac's house to the manse where Lionel and Elizabeth resided, at the pleasure of the king, against his own safe return from Windsor. "The guards have grown complacent to this route. We take it often, for the physician and the countess have heightened their little romance to include almost daily assignations. When we round the corner I will fall back between Alejandro and the guards, and you will grab the reins of his horse and whisk him off. He will then proceed to the garden where the lady will be waiting for him."

"At what hour shall this all take place?" Karle asked.

"Precisely at the highest of the sun."

"And that is all? There is nothing more to this plan?"

"Should there be? Of course, the ending. How could I forget! I sometimes forget to finish things. It is a habit I must shed, and soon. Later he will return to de Chauliac's with stories of having been abducted and robbed of his goods, of being dazed in a gutter and awakening to strange surroundings, but that seems too obvious to require mention. He will make up a tale about the kindness of strangers who aided him in his hour of need, and de Chauliac will be none the wiser. Meanwhile, he and the countess will have enjoyed each other for a time, however tragically brief, without the watchful eyes of de Chauliac or Prince Lionel. I do not know who will be the more jealous."

But Kate and Karle knew beyond doubt which of those two about-to-be-cuckolded men would be the more angry by the time the day was through. It would be de Chauliac, by far.

* * *

"I have decided that it is not wise to further annoy Navarre by asking for a change in the site for the battle," Karle told *le Provoste*. "We have reviewed the maps again, and have decided that Compiègne will do. You need not contact him again."

Marcel set down his quill. "This is wise, Karle—I am very glad you have come to this decision. I have been avoiding that unsavory correspondence all day because I know not how to make it seem palatable to Navarre."

"Nothing will ever seem palatable to Navarre, save his own ends and pleasures."

"Nevertheless, it is a great relief to me that I am no longer required to be the deliverer of a message he might deem counter to his interests."

"So then my reasons for staying in Paris have run out."

"I suppose they have."

Karle took a long breath. "Then we will depart in the morning and make our way north. I will begin to gather my army. When we are assembled and prepared, we will inform Navarre."

Marcel stood. "You will not regret the alliance. Now, Godspeed, Karle, to you and those who may join you. You do the work that other men are afraid to do for themselves, yet cherish anyway."

They joined in a rough embrace and patted each other's back as if they were true uncle and nephew. "Now," Marcel said, "one last toast, and then I suspect you shall want to retire early. You've a long day ahead of you, I fear."

"Many long days, it would seem."

Marcel raised his goblet. "To *Jacques Bonhomme*. May his spirit rise."

They lay on the straw mat in the tiny chamber, knowing it might be the last of their nights of comfort, understanding that when Alejandro rejoined them things might be very different. They clung to each other in the fierce desperation of uncertainty, and spoke sweetnesses into each other's ears. "You called me wife," Kate whispered.

"I mean to call you that many more times," Karle said. "As soon as the chance presents itself, we shall speak to a priest."

"*Husband,*" she murmured. "It is a handsome word."

He kissed her first on each eye, then on the tip of her nose, then softly and deeply on the lips. "One hopes your *père* will think it seems so, as well."

* * *

It seemed to Alejandro that the obnoxious little Flamel could stay away for only a day or two, because here he was, just two nights since his last invasion, disrupting the work he claimed to need done so speedily.

"Not even the second section complete!"

"I am proceeding apace, Flamel. Do you think this sort of work can be rushed? It takes time and care, and you must be more patient."

"Ah," the little man said, smacking himself punitively on the forehead, "you will think me unlearned for not realizing this. I do, I do! It is simply that I have made my prayers, and God has accepted me for the work of creation, or so I am given to understand, and I am anxious to be about the work of knowing His secrets."

Alejandro set down his quill and gave him a mildly surprised look. "God has already made His sign to you?"

Flamel clasped his hands together and looked heavenward. "He has, may all the saints be blessed."

"You must be an exceptionally pious man for Him to have responded so quickly."

"He must believe me so, I suppose. I do admit, it was far quicker than I could possibly have hoped for."

"And might I know the nature of this sign?"

"Of course. I see no reason to hide it. It was a vision that came to me in a dream. It was terrible at first, but then I understood that God meant to impress me with its magnitude, so I paid strict attention. It started in a dungeon of some sort, a deep and airless place with very little light, and I was frightened to the very depths of my soul to be there. The only way in or out was a small door, and though I pleaded with my keepers to be released, they ignored me until one day the door opened, and I was brought forward into the light again, and my eyes could barely see from having lived so long in darkness. But God provided something for me to see, something wonderfully bright: a circle of light, red-hot and glowing, and as it advanced toward me it burst into the most beautiful flames . . ."

Alejandro did not listen to the rest of the alchemist's dream. Whatever was left to be told could only be the insignificant recollections of the one meant to deliver the sign. For in his heart of hearts, the physician knew that the sign was meant for him and him alone, and that it was time to leave Paris.

"I've never been upstairs in your house before."

"Not for lack of trying on my part."

Tom's flirtatious humor gave Janie the comforting sense that some small thing in the world was still the same. She followed with uncharacteristic meekness as he carried her bag down the long carpeted hallway of his second floor. He opened the door to his guest room and brought the bag inside, then set it on the bed, bellhop-style, and extended his hand as if for a tip.

She tried to laugh, but it came out sounding forced and insincere, and quickly melted into tears. Tom came up to her and put one arm around her shoulders, attempting to soothe her with reassurances that he knew would ring more pretty than true in her ears.

She sniffed ungracefully and said, "Why has my life turned to such a pile of shit all of a sudden?"

"Look," he said, "I know this may not be entirely comforting, but it could've been worse. Your valuables were out, at least, and you can rebuild, probably for less money—there are plenty of builders out there looking for work. I took your insurance policy out of the safe last night and went over it. You're covered for—"

"I know, I'm covered for everything. Which is good, because what I have left is either in your safe or right here in this bag." She put her hand down on the suitcase. "It's not just that . . . it's . . . oh . . ."

"What?" he asked gently.

She heaved a long sigh in and out, and after a few determined breaths, she seemed to recover a bit of resolve. "Never mind. I'm through with moaning for the day. Maybe for my life. I've got work to do." She lowered her gaze and said, "I never should have gone to Iceland."

Tom said nothing. They were both quiet for a few moments. Then Janie looked up at him with weary eyes. "I just want to thank you, Tom, so much . . . this is one of those times when I don't know what I would do without you."

"It's all right," he said, smiling. "I don't mind at all. I'm just afraid I'll get used to the company, though, and then what?"

"Look, if this doesn't feel right to you, I can stay with Michael and Caroline."

"No. Really. I was kidding. This will be much easier for you."

"You're right. Thank you. I hope someday I'll be able to do something this nice for you."

Tom was silent. He hoped the same.

"Look, there's just one more thing," Janie said. "Kristina was coming to my house for—I guess you'd call them 'meetings.' That's obviously not possible anymore. I need someplace where I can meet with her."

"She can come here, of course."

"I was thinking of your office, actually."

He seemed to stiffen when she said that. "Here would be better."

"You're sure? Tom, they burned my house down . . . where would we go if they burn yours down too?"

The "we" sounded musical and sweet to him, but he didn't comment on her use of it. "I don't know," he said. "Some tropical island, maybe. Barring that, some Utopian paradise. But we'd figure it out."

Chet cornered Janie when he saw her emerge from the elevator. It was as if he had been waiting for her, ready to pounce.

"Was that your house that got burned? I heard about it on the news. What happened, do they know?"

Not Welcome back, not Are you okay? not We're so sorry, take a few days off if you need them, but Give me the juicy details.

"Kerosene happened, or something like that. Everything's gone."

"Ooh. That's bad," the Monkey Man said.

And Janie thought she saw a momentary blanching, just the slightest little reaction to her revelation that the fire had been set. But he recovered quickly enough to make her think that it might have been her imagination, which was still in overdrive.

"My brother-in-law's a contractor," he said. "I'll tell him to give you a call."

Oy, she thought with annoyance. *Brother-in-law contractors.* Soon a flock of them would be swooping over the charred remains of her house like crows over carrion. "Do that, Chet. But tell him to wait a couple of weeks."

"You're not gonna hire someone right away, are you?"

"Not in the next few days, no. I have a lot of things to take care of first."

"Yeah, I'm sure you do. It's a good thing you're back. There's some catching up to do here too."

"Right," she said. She stepped around him and pointed toward her office. "I guess I'll get right to it, then."

One of Kristina's e-mails was on her office computer, reply-ready. After she answered all of her job-related correspondence, Janie sent her a quick note.

I'm back. Oh, boy am I back. We need to meet.

Half an hour later came the reply. *Hot dogs. After work.*

"I feel like I've been gone forever," Janie told the girl as she sat down next to her on the bench. "It's only been three days, but my God, what a mess I came back to."

Kristina held out the leather case that Virtual Memorial lived in. Janie accepted it happily and opened it up. "Hello, baby," she cooed. "Mommy's home."

"Dr. Crowe," Kristina said.

Janie looked up.

"Are you sure you're all right?"

"As all right as I can be under the circumstances, yes. Why?" She glanced down at herself, then looked back up again. "Am I oozing something?"

"No, but you're talking to a computer."

"A familiar computer, one of the few familiar things in my life right now. I feel like I just got my dog back from the vet." She closed the case. "I'll feed you later," she whispered. Then she turned back to Kristina. "So," she said in a voice full of anticipation, "tell me what happened while I was gone."

"Just about nothing."

"You're kidding—weren't you following up on the data I left for you?"

"Yes. I followed up on everything you found."

"So . . ."

"So there's nothing there. No patent holder. And I can't find Patient Zero anywhere."

Janie was quiet for a moment, then said, "That doesn't necessarily mean he doesn't exist. Or that we're not going to find out who he is. Or who did this."

"No. It doesn't. But unfortunately what it does mean is that we probably won't be able to work a fix, at least not quickly. We need the original gene segment."

"We can build one from scratch. From nucleotides and other little snippets of material."

"That'll take months. I don't think we have that much time."

While Janie watched, Kristina unwrapped a mint and popped it into her mouth. She tucked the wrapper into her pocket. "It's very frustrating, to come this far and then hit the wall like this."

"Can we get this segment from somewhere else? We know from your reconstruction what it's supposed to be, so we just need to find it. Someone out there is bound to have it."

"Yes, one of the hundred sixty million people in the United States. Maybe we should just call each one of them and ask."

It was a wall, but there were ways they could climb over it. Janie leaned closer and whispered, "Look, when I take my little walk inside Big Dattie I can do a thorough search for it."

Kristina seemed surprised. "Walk inside Big Dattie? When?"

"Soon," Janie said. "I sent you a message about it before I left."

"I don't—think so."

Janie considered Kristina's denial, and found herself feeling disturbed by it. But she was sympathetic too, for the girl was clearly having difficulties of some kind. She felt a great need to choose her next words carefully, to be firm yet gentle with the young woman. "Yes," she said after a moment of recollection, "I *did*. It was one of the last things I did before I went to Iceland. And when you came to pick up V.M. that night you said the money wouldn't be a problem. You ate a mint then too. I can remember the wrapper crinkling."

As Kristina whitened, Janie said, "Are *you* all right?"

"Yes," came the too-quick answer.

"The money won't be a problem, will it? Because if it is—"

"No. It won't." She pressed her palm against her forehead. "I'm sorry. I forgot. I've got so much going on in my head right now that I forget things sometimes."

"Kristina," Janie said softly, "I've been meaning to ask you about something. I've noticed—"

Kristina almost seemed to rise up off the bench. "There's nothing wrong with my memory."

So, Janie thought, *I was right.* And maybe Tom's suggestion that Janie examine Kristina was a good one.

She patted the girl lightly on the arm and said, "Relax. I was just going to say that I've noticed you seem to be under stress. And when we have a lot of stress in our lives, our memories can be affected. So let me take this opportunity to personally welcome you to the People Who Forget Things Club, of which I am a charter member, especially this week."

"I'm sorry," Kristina said quietly. "It seems like an awful lot all of a sudden, this project."

"It is an awful lot. It's very consuming, and it's probably just going to seem bigger as we get deeper into it. So let's just do a little bit at a time, and eventually it will all unfold. We'll just search for this segment we need instead of what I'd originally planned to do. We'll find it."

The young girl was rattled, uncertain. "How can you be so sure?"

"Because it has to be out there somewhere. It has to. And eventually, you and I will corner the little sucker."

A pleasant early evening breeze came up, and it blew Kristina's loose hair around her head like a feathery halo, though she herself didn't seem to notice it. She seemed lost and distant, sad in an undefinable way. Janie reached up with one hand, almost without thinking, and brushed a wayward strand out of Kristina's eyes. "I'm staying with my lawyer until I get settled someplace else," she said gently. "He knows a little bit about what's going on."

She expected a reaction, but got none, and she began to feel a little worried. "He said he doesn't mind if we meet at his place."

"That's good."

Janie wondered what she was thinking about. When the silence had gone on for too long, she added, "There was something else I wanted to tell you—I talked to that hacker again this afternoon. He said we could hook up anytime I'm ready. I want to do it as soon as possible, tonight even, if I can. So I should get the gene sequence from you right away."

"All right. I'll mail it to you as soon as I—as soon as possible." She stood up, nodded, and walked away.

* * *

The hacker assured her the bar would be a safe place to meet.

"No one will be looking over your shoulder," he said. "They are all much more interested in other things, eh?"

She looked around at the crowd of young, hungry-looking people. The hormone-thick air was warm and almost oppressive.

"I suppose so," she admitted. "So—how are you going to do this?"

"This is not something I should be telling you. A *gentilhomme* must have his secrets, I think."

He was playing up his French accent, using it to good effect. But Janie didn't let his dark European looks and facile ways influence her. "Of course you should be telling me. I'm paying you, aren't I? I want to know what I'm going to get nailed for if I get nailed."

"You will not be 'nailed,' " he said with a wink, "at least not in that way." He reached into his carrying case and pulled out a corneal scanner, the now defunct technology that had once been the only way to enter Big Dattie. "You are going to put one of your lovely blue eyes in front of this device, and it will let you enter. But it will not leave behind a record of who you are."

Janie was shocked—this was ancient history. She looked around nervously to see if anyone noticed her surprise. But as the hacker had predicted, no one was paying them any mind. Still, she wanted to say *Give me back my five grand, you faker, and then maybe I won't yank those plastic teeth out of your smarmy mouth and shove them up—*

But she was here, the money had changed hands already, and maybe, just maybe, this dinosaur technology could open the gate. She decided to wait and see what happened next.

The French hacker attached the scanner by a cord to the back of his computer, then slipped a disk into one of the side slots. He tapped the keyboard a few times and touched the screen, then touched it again, and after a brief pause touched it one more time. Then with a triumphant smile, he said, *"Voilà!* Step right up, *mademoiselle!"*

Very quietly, Janie said, "This can't possibly work. They took out all the corneal programming two years ago. Along with all the records of everyone's corneas."

"Ah," the Frenchman said with a grin, "but I have just reintroduced the program. I snuck it in; the database thinks it is just another data entry."

"You couldn't get your hands on that corneal program."

"You are right, of course. I am far too unsavory a character for anyone even to sell it to me. However," he said, still smiling, "I did not need to get my hands on it. You see, I was the one who originally wrote it."

A few minutes later, as promised, she was in. The hacker looked at his watch. "You have thirty minutes," he reminded her. *"Bon voyage."*

This time it felt like a wonderland. But Janie didn't allow herself to wander aimlessly—that would have been too much of a luxury. She entered the coding for the gene segment Kristina had mailed to her and told Big Dattie to find it. It would be a long search through millions of files, and Janie prayed it would yield something.

Fifteen precious minutes went by. She tapped her foot nervously and bit her nails nearly down to the quick as lines of code scrolled by in an unreadable blur on the screen before her. At the sixteen-minute mark a message came up on the screen.

SIX MATCHES FOUND

If they could get a tissue sample from one of the matches, they could isolate the required gene, replicate the hell out of it, and replace the altered gene in the afflicted boys. Even if they never managed to find out who'd been responsible for this travesty, they would still be able to correct it. Her heart began to race with the tantalizing thought that success in at least one part of their quest was so close at hand.

Display, she ordered.

Six names and six addresses came up on the screen. After each one of the entries was a big red boldface *D*.

Deceased.

She stared at the screen in disbelief. Her heart sank. She looked quickly through the *vitae* of the group: two adult men, one infant boy, three teenage boys. How could they all be dead?

Stupid question, horrifying answer: half of the population died. These people all happened to be in that half. It was not a statistical impossibility.

But it *was* deflating and discouraging. Janie wanted to cry. But in an establishment like the one she was in, that would be a signal to the closest loser to come over and attempt a consolation. So she squeezed her eyes closed until the tears resorbed, and got on with it.

Could one of these boys be dug up, if, by some cosmic grace, he'd been buried, not cremated? Maybe, but it was a real long shot. The wild and woolly DR SAM had loved the open invitation so often issued by young boys with their dirty hands and runny noses, and had eaten them up with gusto, from the inside out, liver first, then kidneys, then the diaphragm. . . .

But maybe one of them had died from some other cause, some less ghastly problem that didn't require cremation. There might be a body, somewhere, from which she could take the single cell she needed. But when she took a quick look in the files of each of the positives, she only confirmed what she already suspected—that the cause of death in all six, including the boys, had been massive, drug-resistant staph infection. There would be no body after all.

She tried a few things that might yield a donor, but all her attempts proved futile. All she could do in the time remaining was to search for the information she'd originally wanted, the inquiries she'd set aside in favor of the fruitless search she'd just made.

One by one, she entered the names of the fifteen orthopedists she'd gotten from the AMA. Then she asked the database to give her a list of gene alteration projects, past and present, that might have anything to do with bone tissue. Several came up, including two from the foundation.

She moved all these files into the holding area, then reached into her purse and pulled out a data storage disk. She tried to put it into the slot.

But the Frenchman's programming disk was still in there. *Well, well . . .* she thought to herself. *Another member of the People Who Forget Things Club.*

But this was a big item to forget, and a surprising notion slipped into her head. She astonished herself even further by acting on it. Apparently the computer god was looking over her shoulder, because by some miraculous accident the corneal program disk was not write-protected, and she was able to copy the data files directly onto it. When the disk finally stopped spinning, Janie removed it, shielding it from view with her hand as she did. She slipped in the blank one she'd brought with her, but left it partly exposed, and tucked the purloined disk back into her purse.

Her time was almost up. There was one more thing to do.

Find: Kristina Warger, she commanded.

Big Dattie was checking itself. *Good,* she thought, *there won't be too many matches. That'll make it easier.*

But to her astonished disappointment, there were no matches at all. Alternate suggestions were displayed—in this case, people who had similar names: Elena Warger, Frederick Warger, Harold Warger, Matilda Warger . . . and so on down the alphabet. But no Kristina. Deeply confused, she closed the program. And when the Frenchman came back a minute before the sign-off time, he smelled heavily of Scotch.

As she slipped off the stool, she said, "All done. It's been a pleasure doing business with you." She put out her hand, expecting him to shake it. Instead he pulled it to his face and kissed it dramatically. Janie froze and cringed, knowing that the plastic teeth were only a few millimeters from her skin. But she let him do it, for she did not wish to upset him in any way.

"The pleasure is all mine," he said. He glanced over at the computer, and seemed satisfied by what he saw. *"Au revoir, mademoiselle.* Perhaps we shall meet again."

"A bientôt, monsieur," she said. "Perhaps we shall." She smiled as warmly as she could, and got out.

It was the closest thing to a normal family setting that Janie had experienced in years. There were so many blended families now, where one parent with surviving children found another with whom to join forces, and a new unit was formed, sometimes more out of necessity than desire. Janie recalled all the self-help books with advice on how to structure new families born out of divorce; they were popular in the late nineties, at a time when many of her and her husband's friends were calling it quits and starting over again. Those books didn't have much validity now, when the primary issue was grief, not anger.

Tom was in the kitchen cooking, while Janie and Kristina worked on the computer doing something that felt oddly like homework. He had graciously allowed them to usurp his entire home office for the purposes of their work, but Janie didn't get the sense that he felt in any way intruded upon. He seemed almost eager for them to be there. She was surprised by how smoothly he and Kristina made each other's acquaintance; with herself and the girl, it had been a bit more rocky. But Tom seemed to understand Kristina really well. He'd had the benefit of Janie's prior comments, but that advance work wasn't adequate to explain their almost instant rapport. They seemed, quite simply, to have a sense of each other.

They were looking through the information for the orthopedists, trying to narrow it down to one or two likely choices, but they were getting nowhere fast. When they'd been at it for an hour, Kristina sat back in her chair and rubbed her forehead. "No Patient Zero, no orthopedist, no gene match."

"There *must* be somewhere else we can look for that match," Janie said. "We have to give this more thought. I know we're missing something terribly important. We have to go over what we know about these boys until something jumps out at us."

"They're mostly from New York. They're all the same age. They all went to this one particular camp."

"They're all of European Jewish ancestry."

"If there was something, anything we had from one of the matches that we could use to gather just a couple of cells," Kristina said, "a baby tooth or a snippet of hair, or sweat or a nail clipping, anything with a trace of DNA on it . . . God, what it's going to be like explaining this to their relatives, if there are any left—"

"Wait a minute," Janie said. "Say that again. In fewer words."

"We need something with a trace of DNA from one of them."

"Or from someone else with the right gene." She sat back in her chair, a slightly perplexed look on her face. "Oh, my God," she said quietly. "I don't believe what I'm thinking."

She pulled out her phone and punched in the code for the Hebrew Book Depository.

E lizabeth called her husband's manservant to her chamber early in the morning, and banished her own maids to the anteroom for the duration of his visit. It was an unusual invitation, for one who attended exclusively to a gentleman was seldom able to enter the realm of a lady, with its more feminine accoutrements and trimmings. And while he was honored to be summoned and intrigued by his surroundings, he could not imagine the nature of the countess's business with him.

"I shall be brief," she said, "lest idle tongues wag about the seemliness of a wife enclosing herself in her *chambre* with the servant of her husband . . . I have had a word of warning about Prince Lionel's health from de Chauliac, through my own physician, Dr. Hernandez."

When the valet showed grave concern, she said, "Oh, he is not in any immediate danger. But these two very wise and learned men have examined my husband many times, and they agree that if his gout is to be contained, and if he is to avoid the further buildup of the foul humor that caused so much agony to his poor dear toe, then certain steps must be taken."

"Name them, *madame*. I shall see to their implementation immediately."

"Good. I knew I could count on your assistance. And your discretion.

This difficulty with his health has deeply strained the cordiality of our marital union, and only his continued improvement will repair it. In any case, the first and most important thing is that he is to take more air. On this point they were quite vehement. To that end I have arranged for the groom to bring around his favorite horse, shortly before noon today. He shall bring one for you as well. You are to see that he has a good ride along the river, and that he stays out for at least two or three hours. I too am to take more air, but not of such great duration, say, perhaps an hour or only slightly more. So I shall go separately to a garden with one of my ladies, under escort, of course."

"*Madame,* he will surely object to your vulnerability."

"I will not be vulnerable. And he may not object. He is under his doctor's strictest orders, as am I. Now, I will give him this news myself, but I thought to tell you first so that you would not be surprised if he summoned you for the ride. The best hours of the day are the ones just after noon, according to our physicians. He must take a good fill of them. And make sure that one of his stoutest knights rides along with you, so there will be no chance of violence. It happens far too often these days in Paris."

In the morning, Kate took a tearful leave of Marie, who had become like a sister to her. They hugged each other tightly and whispered womanly affections, and promised to remember each other always. Then, as Marie watched her and Karle leave through the same cellar door they had first entered, she fingered the coin Kate had given her, the price of a sheet torn into strips and a few lengths of string, and thought that Kate was a sister even a princess might covet.

Burdened once again with all their possessions, their progress through the streets of Paris was slow but driven forward by purpose. When this day was through, if all went well, they would be outside the walls of the city and into the countryside in search of something to serve as their headquarters for planning the battle to come. Pace by pace, side by side, they went forward, newly pledged, full of both hope and trepidation.

Alejandro stuffed everything he could into the pockets and crannies of his clothing, so his bag could be empty enough that the Abraham manuscript might fit inside without attracting undue attention. He had struggled all night with the wisdom of trying to take it with him; it posed grave risks because of its size, its distinctive shape, and the weight of its unusual brass cover. The papyrus was so light as to be negligible. For all he knew, it might have no weight at all. He pondered that notion for a moment, and it was a welcome distraction to his other worries. After a few minutes of serious consideration, he came to the conclusion that no visible item could be without weight, and then continued his packing, firm in his belief that to leave it behind would be a sacrilege against Abraham and all who had gone before him.

About an hour before noon, the anticipated sound of the bell being rung could be heard throughout the house. A few moments later he heard de Chauliac's footsteps trudging up the stairs, weighted with the frustration of yet another unwanted and frivolous summons. The Frenchman entered his small room without bothering to knock, and sat down heavily on a chair.

"She is pale again. Can you not put some color into this woman's cheeks, that we may have a day of uninterrupted work?"

"There is only one sure way I know to do that, save having her pinch those cheeks with her own fingernails. And she will not take kindly to such advice. She will complain to the Dauphin. And while I will not suffer for her laments, you surely will, colleague."

"I rue the day that ever I invited that Chaucer to dine with us!"

"Oh, be charitable, de Chauliac. One may not slay the messenger."

"One would like to slay this particular messenger."

"Then the world would be cheated of a very clever young man."

"He is a page. The world would not miss him. But I miss the peace of my days most dreadfully. She would have us come immediately. Chaucer waits in the vestibule now, for us to attend him."

Alejandro wiped his quill and carefully closed the book. "Then I need only freshen up a bit, and we shall be off. Tell him I need but a moment."

De Chauliac rose up slowly, as if his bones ached, and for the first time, Alejandro noticed the lines in the Frenchman's forehead. "I shall await you in the vestibule." He disappeared down the dim hallway.

Quickly and quietly, Alejandro stuffed the manuscript into the bag, but it would not quite fit; the bottle of sulfur water would not fit into any of his pockets, and he had no place else to store it. So with great reluctance, he removed the bottle and hid it at the back of a deep drawer in the table. Then he shoved the manuscript into the bag and tied the closure. After one last look out the barred window, he left the room for what he prayed would be the last time.

* * *

Chaucer nodded slightly to him, tipping his head a bit to the right, and Alejandro knew that the message had been delivered and the plan agreed to.

The party of five left the courtyard of the manse shortly before noon and threaded its way through the foot traffic on horses. Their pace was slow, for it was marketing day, and though supplies were low and prices high many still came out just to see what might be had. Most went home disappointed. Alejandro did not mind their trudging pace, for his heart was beating wildly in anticipation of the events that would soon transpire. Chaucer seemed unbearably lighthearted. *But then,* Alejandro realized, *he thinks this is all a harmless plot in support of some romantic lover's tryst. He thinks that this is merely trickery to bring an exotic Spaniard and a noble-woman of the Green Island together in privacy.*

"You seem distracted, Physician," the lad said. "Are you nervous that the lady will not be there when you arrive?"

"Oh, no. I put my entire faith in her. I am only anxious about Jacques's part being played to perfection, for therein lies the key to the plan's success."

Chaucer chuckled. "I too should be worried, were I required to depend on a man with a young and luscious wife to keep him distracted from the task at hand."

Alejandro deliberately slowed his horse. "Wife?" he whispered, almost a hiss. "I know of no wife."

"Nor does his uncle," Chaucer confided. "He has kept it a secret from him, although I cannot see why. I saw her when I delivered your message. She is a comely young woman with golden hair and the bluest eyes, and for a moment or two I thought her to be the very image of my lord Lionel. I told her as much when we spoke, and she seemed somewhat offended."

Alejandro's horse was now nearly at a standstill; Chaucer pulled slightly ahead of him, against his better judgment, but he did not wish to give the guards cause for concern. "Do not slow your animal, Physician, or you shall ruin everything; pick up your pace now and go ahead of me, as we planned for you to do."

Through his sudden confusion, Alejandro managed to do as he was bidden, and in a moment he was once again slightly ahead of the page. He heard the boy say softly, "The meeting point is just ahead, around this corner."

Forgetting his unhappiness, Alejandro looked ahead, through the throngs of milling people, and saw several men who might be Karle. But it seemed impossible to tell which one was he. Alejandro knew he would simply have to wait until Karle revealed himself, then react as quickly as possible. His blood rushed faster through his veins and sweat began to form on his forehead. He scanned the crowd nervously. The sound of human voices and horse hooves clopping on the pavement, the clucking of fowls, the barking of dogs—it suddenly became a din, and it was only because it was shouted that he heard Karle's voice say, "Alejandro!"

He turned in the direction of the voice and saw a cripple, bound in bandages almost from head to toe, waving a white-wrapped crutch. But within a second or two the item was unwrapped and transformed into a sword. And then Karle took hold of the reins of his horse and was pulling him through the crowds, shoving the objecting masses aside, brandishing his sword over his head like the devil himself.

Chaucer set his horse horizontally in front of the guards and tried to look as confused as possible. He effectively blocked their way with his horse's nervous prancing, until finally one of them managed to charge past him and through the melee of shrieking citizens in pursuit of Alejandro. "Abduction!" the guard shouted. "Kidnap! *Stop them.* . . ."

He got close enough to Alejandro's horse to reach out and grab hold of the saddlebag, and for a moment or two the caravan of horses fronted by a seemingly mad cripple was suspended in equilibrium of motion. Karle pulled, but so did the guard. Finally Karle shouted, "Untie the bag!"

Alejandro stared at him. He turned and looked at the guard, who was groping about with his free hand, searching for the hilt of his sword.

It was a painful decision, but in the end, a clear one. It was life or learning. He chose to survive. With one quick pull on the leather cord that bound it, the saddlebag with its precious manuscript came free, and he and Karle were propelled forward, leaving the guard behind, clutching the bag, as the crowd closed around him.

Through back alleys and side streets barely wide enough to accommodate them, Karle pulled the frightened horse, and all who saw them pass stared in wonder at the sight of a cripple in ragged bandages running before the horse, while the traditional robes of a healer billowed out from behind the man who rode. And when Alejandro realized why people were staring, he threw off the outer garments, which only called attention to them and impeded their progress.

Finally, gasping for breath, Karle slowed his pace to a trot. He looked back and wheezed, "Just beyond the corner," and Alejandro nodded. And after the next turn, Karle opened a wooden gate and led the horse into the courtyard of a house whose overlord was away at the wars, a man who had wisely sent his wife and children south for the duration. And behind a tree, out of view of the street, waited Kate.

"Père!" she cried wildly as she emerged from her hiding place. She rushed over the stones of the courtyard and fell into Alejandro's arms as Guillaume Karle secured the gate.

And while he held her in his arms, every minute of her time with him passed through his mind, from the moment they set foot on the ship to France until his last sight of her behind the cottage where Karle had first encountered them. He finally let go, held her out at arm's length, and stared into her eyes. They were the same bright blue, though now they overflowed with tears of joy. He stroked her yellow hair, and felt it slip through his fingers as it had a thousand times before. He touched her cheek and felt its familiar glowing warmth. He looked her up and down, and as his own tears flowed, he said, "You are well. Thank God. Your God. My God. All gods who have ever been or ever will be." They embraced again, rocking in each other's arms, father and daughter at last reunited.

The horse secured, Karle flung away his wrapping rags and came up behind Kate, smiling, eager to shake the hand of his accomplice in escape. "All gods be praised indeed, Physician, we thought never to—"

And suddenly the amber-haired Frenchman found himself slammed against a wall, with the physician he had just rescued upon him like a bear and pummeling him savagely. Kate jumped on Alejandro's back and clawed at him, crying "Père! Dear God—oh, Karle, he does not know what he is doing—I fear he is insane from his ordeal."

And Alejandro was screaming, *"Wife, you call her wife, you fiend, they will call you newcomer in your Christian hell before I have done with you."*

Finally Kate forced herself between them, and when he saw her tender face, Alejandro's fist stopped in midair, short of her nose by no more than a few hairs' breadth. She reached up and took his hand and drew it to her face and kissed his bleeding knuckles, softly weeping as she whispered, "Père, oh, Père, what have they told you?"

"These rags turned out to be an uncannily wise investment," Kate said as she dabbed the blood from Guillaume Karle's face. She spit on the one she held in her hand and wiped his forehead tenderly. Karle stayed very still, wincing when she drew the rag over a long gash that had been delivered by Alejandro's raging fist. The imprint of Countess Elizabeth's ring was emblazoned red and raw on his cheek.

The Jew sat in a bewildered daze and watched quietly as Kate attended to the Christian man, the rogue into whose reluctant care she had been given, the rebel whose care she now saw to herself. *She behaves as if she were a wife,* Alejandro admitted to himself with a stab of almost killing pain.

And it had been only a short time, a matter of a few weeks at most—or had it even been less than that? No, more, surely—the truth was that he couldn't say precisely what the time had been since he last saw her. Long enough for her to learn to love this man, and for him to love her. Too long for him, the father, to have any right to say "Cleave to me still, daughter, for I am yet thy father and keeper." She had learned to keep herself, and she had learned to give herself away. He had not been there to stop her. And now, it seemed, it was too late.

Newly freed, unshadowed by de Chauliac for the first time in far too long, and all he could think to do was to kill the man who had rescued him for imagined offenses against his daughter, who seemed, by all accounts, more offended by his own behavior than by Karle's.

When Karle's wounds were seen to, Kate turned back to Alejandro and looked at his hands. "What can you have been thinking, Père? You almost ruined your hands. Your wonderful skilled hands."

He turned his vacant gaze in her direction and whispered, "I was envisioning my child in the arms of a ruffian."

"He is no ruffian, Père. You know that. Else why would you have put me with him at all?"

"You must understand, child, that to me all men who even look upon you are ruffians, beasts even, and can be nothing else."

She wiped the blood from his knuckles with unimaginable tenderness. "I am no longer a child, Père. Must I tell you that again? My childhood seems a thousand years ago. And you trusted Karle then, you must trust him now."

Must I? he asked himself. *Is that the only path open to me?* He wondered how he would phrase that question to her. Should he simply say, *"Will you choose one or the other of us? And if forced to choose, will you go to him, and abandon me?"*

He looked at her as she fussed over his fingers with all the skill and gentleness he had fostered in her. She no longer had the chubby, dimpled hands of a child but the slender strong hands of a woman. She glowed, radiating a kind of happiness and inner peace he had never noticed before. But then, he told himself, she had never loved a man in this manner before.

Now she clearly did. "He has cared well for you, then?"

"Better than you can imagine."
Better than I want to know.

When they had finally restored themselves to the appearance of ordinary citizens and roughly healed the wounds between them, they decided it would be best to leave Paris as soon as possible—before sunset, if it could be done.

"But there is a difficulty—I cannot retrieve my horse," Alejandro said. "I have nothing to redeem him with—de Chauliac has kept my gold."

"I have not spent much of the gold you gave me, Physician," Karle said. He dug in his pocket and pulled out the satchel, then thrust it forward eagerly, as if proof of his careful stewardship might improve him in Alejandro's eyes.

And indeed, it did. "Well done, Karle," he said as he counted the coins. "But what of your own horses?"

Karle went back to the steed Alejandro had ridden to freedom and inspected the large animal, running his hands down the horse's long neck, peering at his hooves and ankles. "This seems a decent animal, and de Chauliac's groom outfitted him well. He might carry two." He looked at Alejandro and said, "I say we retrieve your horse and leave the others. Kate can mount up with"—he was about to say *me,* but finished his sentence otherwise—"with one or the other of us. Then we will still have some coin left to see to other needs."

"A sensible plan," Alejandro said. He sighed deeply. "For the first time in my life, I find myself a poor man." He looked up at Kate and Karle and said, "I have always guarded my fortune as if I *were* poor, but the comfort of the fortune has always been there. Now it is not. I do not quite know how I should proceed." He turned to Kate and smiled apologetically. "I am sorry, daughter, I had always hoped to provide well for you."

"You did, Père. We will never be poor in knowledge."

"Nor shall we ever be able to *eat* it."

"Nor shall we *have* to, for we will never know deprivation that terrible. I am certain of it."

Karle interrupted them, and pointed toward the sky, where the sun was hovering above the rooftops, leaning toward disappearance. "It is the advice of *this* poor man that we get out of Paris before the sun goes down."

* * *

Geoffrey Chaucer stood before the furious Countess Elizabeth and protested his complete innocence. "I beseech you, *madame,* to believe me! I
was more duped by his wicked plan than you!" He was stooped in shame
and humiliation, very much the foolish young boy who had been well and
carefully used by a wicked and clever man of greater worldly experience.

Chaucer took his dressing-down in the countess's bedchamber, amid
the flurry of frantic housekeepers—for when the spurned Elizabeth had
returned, raging, from her failed rendezvous in the Dauphin's rose garden, she had ordered the immediate reversal of every change Alejandro
had suggested for the benefit of her health and that of her family. *Bring
back my ermine bedcover,* she had ordered the maid, *all fleas be damned! I
will not be reminded of him. And tell cook to prepare such rich foods as he
sees fit—we will not follow this revoltingly lean diet any longer.*

Somehow, in the middle of all that activity, Chaucer found the wherewithal to say to the countess, "I think his affection for you was genuine.
At least he told me that it was! But he needed to escape. And you provided him with a most convenient exit. I am sure he is very grateful."

Elizabeth turned away to hide the tears in her eyes. "You are kind,
young man. I hope you are right. Else I shall do my best to see that his
heart is ripped from his breast, one way or another."

The horse was thinner than he'd hoped to find it, but still a sturdy
animal. His feet had been seen to, and the equipment well serviced, so
Alejandro paid the man the agreed-upon sum and took back possession
of the animal. The transaction seriously depleted their remaining store of
gold—but they simply could not do with fewer than two horses.

He cooed familiar gentling words into the stallion's ears, hoping the
big animal would remember him, which he seemed to do. He mounted
and settled himself into the saddle, then leaned down and extended a
hand to Kate to pull her up behind him.

She did not reach out to take his hand, but looked instead toward the
other horse, on which Guillaume Karle had seated himself. Then she
looked back at Alejandro and said, "I think your horse looks a bit thin to
take two riders—let us fatten him up a bit first. I will ride with Karle."
And before he could protest, she was climbing up behind Guillaume
Karle and settling herself against his back as if she knew the nature of its
curves. She put her arms around the Frenchman's waist, a bit too tight,
and when she leaned her head against his shoulder it was a bit too gladly.

And as Alejandro followed Karle on the road north, his heart was in
his stomach. It was a bit too heavy for his chest.

The restaurant where Janie met Myra Ross in the morning occupied the entire top floor of an old warehouse on a side street of the main square.

Nicely dressed patrons faced off over pastel tablecloths and white china while black-and-white clad waiters floated from group to group with steaming pots of coffee. The yellow light of morning streamed in through floor-to-ceiling windows and the whole place was resplendent with the sounds and smells of breakfast.

None of which neutralized the low concerned buzz or the nervous expressions. Worry was in the air.

Janie came flying in, a little late, and found the curator already installed at a window table.

"You look a bit rattled, dear," Myra observed as Janie sat down.

"I am," she panted. When she was finally situated and her chair pulled in, she gave Myra a slightly perturbed look. "And I usually hate it when people call me *dear,*" she said, "but today, I have to admit, it sounds pretty damned good."

Myra smiled. "It's a generational habit, I assure you. So don't take it too personally. I'll try to remember to use it sparingly in your case." She took a sip of her water. "Now, I must say your invitation to breakfast was very unexpected." She leaned a little closer and said quietly, "You might want to give some thought to how you issue your summonses, though."

Janie was almost whispering, though she couldn't have said why. "I know. It was a little forceful, but please forgive me—things are a little out of whack for me right now." She took in a deep breath and began a recitation of her latest round of troubles. "Someone burned my house down—"

The curator clasped her hands together and said, "Dear God! That's just awful! Is it destroyed—completely?"

Janie nodded soberly. "And to make matters worse, it happened while I was away on a trip that meant a lot to me, and I had to come back early. I didn't get to finish the business I went to do."

"Well, in view of what happened, it was probably appropriate for you to return. I mean, your *home* . . ."

Janie made no comment. "Anyway, I'm a little leery about discussing much of anything over the phone right now. That's why I was so abrupt."

Myra reached out and gave one of Janie's hands a reassuring squeeze. "This is just such terrible news—but thank God you weren't home at the time. You might have *died.* To live through DR SAM and then die in a fire . . ."

"Yeah. Wouldn't that have been a kicker?"

"All your things must be gone—how can you just sit here so—calm, and normal? I would be absolutely beside myself."

"I'm not calm or normal. Not even close."

"And you're sure it wasn't an accident—someone actually meant to burn it?"

"It looks that way. Someone's been trying very hard to mess things up for me. In every part of my life."

"But—*why?*"

"Because of some work I'm doing that seems to be striking a nerve. Somewhere. I don't know where. Whoever is doing this seems to know just what I'm doing and when."

She glanced around nervously, a recently acquired habit that was beginning to disturb her. Myra did the same. When their eyes met again, Myra said, "You don't think you're being listened to or followed, do you?"

"Maybe. Funny little things seem to be happening to me all the time. Or maybe I'm just paranoid. I do know one thing, though—I'm about as confused as I've ever been."

The waiter appeared with coffee. Both Myra and Janie nodded at their cups. When they were refilled, the waiter departed.

"And then to top it all off, I've got these two men all of a sudden."

Myra's eyebrows went up immediately. "Two? Well. I don't think I can help you with that one."

"I don't know if anyone can."

"Oh, I'm sure someone out there knows how to handle two men, but I don't. One was enough for me. Too much, sometimes. Back when I had men, that is, I mean *a* man . . ."

She seemed to drift into a melancholy place for the briefest moment, and Janie politely waited until the wistful look dissipated before going on. "That situation will work itself out, one way or the other, I'm sure. And it's not why I asked to see you."

The curator jumped immediately to what she thought was the obvious. "Is there some problem with your journal?"

"No. Nothing's changed about that. But the journal does relate to why I asked you to meet me." She sighed wearily and closed her eyes for a moment. When she opened them, she said, "I'm in desperate need of some sanity, and this place is . . . special to me. The last time I took my mother to breakfast it was here."

"Then it must hold a lot of memories for you."

Janie glanced around again, this time absorbing the warmth of the place, and when she turned back to Myra she felt more balanced. "It does. You can't imagine how much I miss my mother. I was expecting to have her a lot longer than I did."

"I'm sorry," Myra said. "We've all gone through such terrible losses. When I look back on the last few years, I think I'm just very happy to be alive."

"I am too."

Menus arrived. A new waitress made suggestions and they chose quickly. "I have a favor to ask of you," Janie said when the waitress was gone.

Myra sat back in her chair. "Well, you have me curious now," she said. "But I did assume you were inviting me for some reason other than a great love of my company."

Janie managed a small laugh. "I knew this would make me feel better. Your candor is so . . . refreshing."

"That was very gracefully put, considering what you might have said. Please, go on."

Janie told her about Abraham Prives's strange affliction, and as much as she felt comfortable revealing about the mystery that surrounded it. And when the tale was finished, Myra sat in silence for a few minutes. Finally, she said, "This is very, very distressing."

"It is. And these are just the boys we know about."

"Oh, the poor dears, and their poor mothers."

"Yes. I personally know only one of the mothers, and she's being incredibly brave, but it has to be awful for her. I haven't asked the other—uh—personnel about how the other parents out there are doing, but I imagine it would not be a pretty report."

"No, it would not be. It would be full of expressions of disbelief. And horror."

"I suspect that's why I haven't wanted to hear it."

"Is there anything at all that can be done?"

"We do have people working on it—there's a young woman who's quite strong in genetics, an expert really, and she's spending all her time on this one problem."

"This is like Tay-Sachs all over again," Myra said.

"Worse, I think."

"This woman, the expert, is she a Jew?"

Kristina's heritage was not something Janie had ever even bothered to consider—there was so much else to think about regarding the strange young woman. "I've never asked her," she said. "Her last name is Warger. If I had to guess, I'd say her background was Celtic. Sandy hair, blue eyes, very tall and big-boned."

"No, it doesn't sound like she is, although these days you can't really tell anymore. When I was a girl things were different. We all knew who we were back then. But my point is, what I'm really interested in knowing is if she's any good."

Janie didn't quite know what to say. "There are always different benchmarks for 'good' in situations like this, but I can tell you that she's brilliant, and innovative, and a clear thinker. She has certain—quirks, but her work seems very thorough."

"Because something like this," Myra went on, "it requires the absolute best available."

"Therein lies the problem," Janie told her, "the one I need your help for. We're missing a piece of the puzzle, an important one. Einstein could be doing this work, and if he didn't have a certain material he'd fail."

"Is there a chance you might obtain whatever it is?"

"We've been trying. But we're not having any success."

"This is beginning to sound almost hopeless."

"I hate to admit, but that's exactly how it's starting to feel to me." Janie paused for a moment, as if to gather her thoughts, while in truth she was gathering courage. "Then she and I were working last night, racking our brains over how we were going to solve this problem, and an idea came to me. Actually, a couple of ideas."

She took a badly needed sip of water to refresh her mouth, which felt cottony and dry. "We're looking for a source for a certain small segment of one gene. From a donor—living or dead, it doesn't matter. The people most likely to carry this gene are Jews. We looked very thoroughly in . . . certain databases where we thought we might find it. But it wasn't available. Then it occurred to me that there are probably a lot of Jews in other countries who haven't registered their genetic material with any government. I imagine if I had the sort of motivation they might have, I'd do just about anything I could to avoid registering."

Myra's voice was flat, almost emotionless. "You're speaking of Holocaust survivors, and their families, of course."

"I am. They're mostly European Jews, which means there's a greater chance of finding someone, because that's what most of our boys are."

Myra sighed. "I know very little about genetics, but this much I do know because it has been a matter of great concern to some Jews who *are* knowledgeable." She made a little smile and said, "There are a good number of those people. You see, the population of European Jews was so decimated by the Holocaust, and then the Outbreaks, that the gene pool has shrunk, to a point where some say it's gotten dangerously narrow. Now, I don't know exactly what that means. Frankly, it's all very frightening to me because it's led to some disturbing discussions. There's been talk of testing potential mates, in an organized program of sorts, so that some of the enhanced genetic traits we suffer from won't be passed on to weaken us. Tay-Sachs, the propensity for ovarian and breast cancer— these things could destroy us far more effectively than Hitler ever dreamed."

"I haven't heard any of this," Janie said.

"And you won't. It's all been kept very quiet. And I trust you will keep it to yourself."

The look Myra gave her was a blunt, undisguised warning, and Janie was certain there was some force or mandate behind it of a kind that did not appreciate interference. She nodded in accord.

"On the one hand," Myra went on, "we have this very reasonable fear of opening ourselves up to tampering, and on the other we have a lot to lose if we don't tamper. So the debate rages. It started with scientists, but it's moved on to the rabbis and scholars, and it's a little stuck right now, I think. Some very wise people think we should do whatever we can to maintain and improve the quality of our population. Other equally wise people say we should let God do His work as He will."

"There are things to be said in favor of both approaches," Janie said philosophically. "Nature always finds a way to do what needs to be done, regardless of what we happen to think of that process. That's just how things are. You and I would be running out from under the feet of dinosaurs right now if things had gone just a little differently. And who's to say that it shouldn't be that way? The dinosaurs would have loved it."

"I am always running out from under the feet of one dinosaur or another," Myra said facetiously. "It's a condition of these times, I think."

"A universal condition," Janie said with a little chuckle. Then she became serious again. "But biodiversity is the key to survival for any species, and if the only way to create or maintain it is artificial introduction of beneficial genetic traits, or the removal of faults, then I support that."

Myra allowed Janie's declaration to hang in the air between them for a moment. "So do I, in theory," she finally said. "But I'm afraid that theory, noble as it is, won't get you very far with this search. The vast majority of former European Jews now live here if they don't live in Israel. I'm sure that most of them are in that 'certain database' you refer to. Nothing, not even sick children, will make the Israelis agree to let you look in their version of it. And forget about hacking—just don't even consider it. God Himself couldn't hack into that database, it's so secure."

Janie had no doubt that Myra was right. But it was disappointing, and she sighed deeply.

"I'm sorry if this upsets you, but all you need to do to understand why is to think about what happened the last time most of those people lined up to get their numbers," Myra said. She allowed that stark image to sink in, then added, "So you may want to consider your other idea more seriously."

Janie reflected on her suggestion, then shook her head. "Right now it seems almost stupid. I must have been feeling desperate when I dreamed it up."

"Go ahead. Desperate is something I understand."

She cleared her throat. "This is going to sound crazy."

"You would not be the first person who ever had a crazy notion."

"Okay. But please don't laugh. I—I want to test the journal. For old genetic material."

Myra's penciled eyebrows rose up in surprise. "Well," she said. "I'm not laughing, but it *is* sort of crazy."

"Alejandro was a European Jew, and it's entirely possible that he might have had the sequence we're looking for. He must have left something of himself on that journal."

"Well, it belongs to you—why don't you just take it and test it? You don't need my permission. Or my help, really."

"Actually, you're wrong. I do need your help. There's a long wait for sequencing unless there's an official reason to rush it. It's gotten . . . *busier* at Biopol all of a sudden."

They both knew why. And for a moment, they sat in silence with their thoughts. Then Janie said, "I can't explain this to anyone official without giving away an awful lot of information, some of which might inspire whoever it was that burned my house down to get even nastier."

"Shush," Myra said quickly, "don't say such things."

"I don't even want to think about them, but I have to. I have a good friend who's—in law enforcement, and he says that if the journal were involved in some kind of crime, anything that was found on it could be sequenced on police equipment. Right away, because it could be construed as evidence in a criminal investigation, which moves it into a different waiting line. All that would have to happen is for you to report a security breach to the police, then say the journal was touched by someone 'suspicious-looking.' They'll gather the evidence, and then this friend will give me whatever comes of it. I get what I need without tipping anyone off that I'm still looking into this. Simple."

"I don't think it's so simple. What if something happens to the journal?"

"Nothing's going to happen to it. They'll bring out the equipment and take their samples, very carefully, and it'll never leave the depository. And it's insured now, right?"

Myra paused, then said quietly, "Not for its full value."

"I thought you said you put a binder on it for two hundred fifty thousand dollars."

"We did. But the estimates of its value are starting to come in now. And they're a little higher than that amount."

Janie forced herself to fold her hands calmly in her lap. "Maybe you'd better tell me how much."

Myra set down her fork and looked Janie straight in the eye. "How does eight hundred thousand sound?"

"Oh, my God."

"And if you don't like that one, we just got another. For one point one million."

Janie nearly choked. "This is unbelievable."

"Well, you'd better believe it. These are expert opinions. And I do support what you're attempting to do here, so I'm willing to help you in this little adventure of yours in any way I can. I'd prefer it if you asked me for a different kind of help, but if you decide to do this—this *crazy* thing you're contemplating, which is your right, of course, then I think you'd better be very careful."

It was sound advice. "I will," Janie assured her.

At the end of the meal, as Janie commandeered the check, she said to Myra, "I want to thank you for joining me. I know the conversation wasn't entirely pleasant, but it was very helpful to me. It almost reminds me of the last time I was here with Mom."

"That's a lovely thing to say, dear." Then Myra looked away for a moment, and when she looked back again, her eyes were teary.

"And you were very lucky to have a nice place like this to be with her," she said quietly.

"I know," Janie said.

"Because I barely remember the last time I shared a meal with my mother. I was a very little girl. We were at Auschwitz." She recovered her composure and smiled wistfully, then dabbed at her lips with her napkin. "But one thing I do remember is that it wasn't this good."

Janie counted the rings anxiously. When Michael finally answered his phone she nearly assaulted him with questions.

"Slow down!" he said defensively. "It went well. The detective who answered the call said the lady was very professional and quite cooperative. Helpful, even. Civilians are usually just a pain in the buttocks."

"Well, I briefed her pretty carefully. I guess it must have worked." She hesitated for a moment and bit her lip nervously. "So. What did you get?"

"Rather a lot, I'm afraid."

"Oh, good! Wait—what do you mean *afraid*?"

"We got twenty-three complete human positives, and a bunch of incompletes, some of which may be partials of the complete ones. But they might also be separate individuals."

"Well, one of them has to be Alejandro."

"I'm sure you're right. Trouble is, which one?"

"You can start by eliminating all the females."

"I did that already. There are still seven males. But there's a problem." She hated that sinking feeling.

"My supervisor won't let me do seven complete sequences."

"Why not?"

"Because it was a property crime where no one was hurt. Genetic sequencing on that sort of violation has to take a number behind crimes against people. That's the usual policy. And I'm sorry to say, we're a little backlogged right now. All of a sudden we seem to have an awful lot of unidentifieds . . . more than we had yesterday."

Already? she found herself thinking. *It's way too soon for that.*

"DR SAM–type unidentifieds?"

Michael waited for a few seconds before answering, then quietly confirmed her fears. "Yes. That type."

A moment of silence passed.

Then Michael told her, "They're spreading the victims out over all the divisions, mine included." His tone of voice was flat and informational. "I assume that's to minimize the shock of the numbers while they do whatever it is they try to do about it."

His matter-of-fact recitation was no surprise to Janie. He'd cleaned up all sorts of Outbreak messes. But she felt cold nausea creeping into her own belly at the thought of what might be coming. When this had happened the first time, no one had known what to expect. Now they all did. She heard Bruce's advice, too harsh when it was given, now more appropriate, saying, *Get out, run, go anywhere to hide.*

But there was nowhere to hide.

And there was so much she had to do before she could make her escape. It made her mission seem all the more urgent, so she set aside her fears as best she could and concentrated. "Just give me the bottom line, Michael."

"It's slim, I'm sorry to say. She's agreed to let me do one complete sequencing for ID purposes, because of the journal's value. And because I told her there was a lot more genetic material from one particular individual than any other, and we thought it logical to assume that it would identify the perpetrator."

"Was there?"

"A bit more, but not enough to really say for sure that it was your chap. It could just as easily be from the gent who bound the book. He'd be all over it too."

After a few seconds' pause, Janie said, "Can you give me the information you got off the journal?"

"I think I can make a case that because you're the owner, you have a right to see the evidence."

"Good. Beam it all over, then."

"What are you going to do with it?"

"I'm not quite sure. But there might be something I can do to narrow it down, at least a little."

It was not something she liked requesting over the phone. In person would be far better.

He had to have left a mark on the older one, too, a fingerprint, a teardrop stain, anything would do.

"We have to stop meeting like this," Myra said with a smile when she greeted Janie in the reception area of the depository. "I hope everything came out as you expected it would. It was quite interesting around here earlier. I don't mind telling you the whole thing absolutely exhausted me—I was just about to leave for the day."

"I'm glad I caught you, then. I can't tell you how I appreciate what you did. I know you had to go to a lot of trouble."

"Actually, it wasn't as bad as I expected. I just took the journal out and laid it on top of a display case, then whacked the case with my elbow. It went off like a rocket, just like it was supposed to." She smiled. "Then I stood over in the corner and watched as all sorts of handsome young policemen swarmed over the area picking things up. That's probably what has me feeling so drained. But I survived the whole ordeal quite nicely."

"Well, that's good to hear. Especially since I need another little favor."

She explained her thinking.

But in this case, Myra was not so supportive. "Absolutely not. That manuscript is much too fragile for anything of the sort."

"All I need is a fingerprint. A tear. Any physical trace at all."

Firmly, "No."

"Myra, please, I just have to identify Alejandro, and if I could match something—"

Suddenly Myra's brow furrowed in concentration. Her expression intensified and she said, "Wait a minute—would a hair do?"

"A hair would be perfect, if it was the right one. I just need to see if I have the same two people in both books. Then I'll know it's him. It'll have to be him."

"Come with me."

Janie followed her to the same room where they'd done their previous examination of the journal. As she stood in the doorway and watched, Myra went to a refrigerated storage unit and passed her hand over its sensor. The door clicked open. Myra turned to Janie and said, "This will just take a second."

She closed herself inside the unit. Janie could not hear what she was doing beyond the door, because its thick insulation muted the sound. But as promised, Myra came out shortly. The door swung closed almost silently behind her and Janie heard the latch click.

Myra held in her hand a medium-sized plastic bag with a zip-type closure, and inside that bag were several smaller ones, each containing some minute archaeological treasure. "We found all this material when Abraham's manuscript first came to us."

Janie saw at least one hair. And there were flakes of papyrus, some stained.

"I'll want them back," Myra said. "As intact as possible."

Janie's eyes settled hungrily on the bag. "Of course," she said. "I'll be very careful."

"Now, I have no idea who these things came from, but one of them might be from your fellow Canches. And now you've got me curious too, so hurry up and do your work. I'm dying to know."

"Two," Michael said.

"Two?"

"Two of the same people show up in both of them. But one is very faint in the journal."

"Still, I can't count on that to be the determining factor . . . God, how am I going to tell?"

"Do you have any idea what this chap looked like?"

"He was described in the journal to a degree by the woman who had it after him."

"Then why don't you put both of these gents up on an imager? Take a look at them."

She was about to say, *I don't have an imager.* But then she remembered—Virtual Memorial did.

"Beam them over," she said.

It was a well-witnessed and thoroughly momentous event. Janie sat in Tom's loaned study—now temporarily a birthing room of sorts—and balanced Virtual Memorial on her lap with Kristina at her side and Tom looking over her shoulder. The first of two male human figures unfolded slowly on the screen before them as the image compiler did its work of clarifying, sharpening, and defining what it assumed the contributor of the rough genetic code would look like. The resulting apparitions would not be perfectly clear—a complete sequenced code was required for that, or to delineate other more specific traits—but they would show the general characteristics of the subjects.

"Do you think this will be enough?" Kristina asked.

"I hope so," Janie said quietly as she stared at the screen. "I don't know where we're going to go from here if it's not."

"Then there's that other small matter of whether or not the strip we need is going to be there."

Janie reached over and patted Kristina's arm. "I'm keeping a positive attitude."

The face of the first man was beginning to come into rough focus. When his naked image was complete, she looked it over carefully, with a kind of curiosity that was almost disturbing to her. She wanted to feel cold and clinical about the work before her, but instead she was nervous and excited, as if she were meeting a long lost brother for the first time. How deep would their kinship extend? There was no way to tell. It would just have to unfold.

The image that had appeared was of a man dark-complected and well formed, and his features were Mediterranean-looking, which was what she had expected to find in Alejandro's case. But unclothed, unbearded, uncircumcised, she simply could not say with any certainty that it was the man she wanted.

The second image was just as slow in building; cell by cell, it followed its predestined pathway from zygote to fetus to infant to childhood, and finally to adulthood, growing, reshaping and transforming itself in million-fold acceleration until the fully formed man appeared. He too was nicely shaped, but slimmer than his counterpart, an ectomorph to the other's mesomorph.

"What a marvel," Tom said as he watched from behind her. "It's like seeing someone born."

"But it pales in comparison to the real thing," Janie said.

After a slight pause, Tom said, "I'm sure you're right."

Janie looked up at him briefly, realized her gaffe, and wanted to apologize. His childlessness was a somewhat sore subject. But she continued. "Now, for the moment of truth." She put the two images up on a split screen and directed the imaging display program to zoom in on their faces.

"What are you doing?" Tom asked.

"Closing in," Kristina said as she watched.

Janie centered the zoom over the eyes and went closer, closer and closer, until finally she had nothing but eyes on each side of the screen.

Image One: brown eyes.

Image Two: blue.

"It's number one," she said, dropping the other from the screen.

It was not as clear as she would have liked, but it was there for her to see, finally, and it would have to do for now. There would be time later to get to know this man better.

"Hello, Alejandro," she said softly.

She looked over her shoulder at Tom; his eyes were full of excitement, reflecting perfectly what she herself felt, though understandably less deeply. She would not get the same reaction from Bruce when she told him; he would correctly point out how silly it all seemed, how compulsive and obsessed she was, how illogical her thinking had become. In an entire nation of DNA she couldn't find the little segment she needed. But in one ancient Jew she would. It was absurd.

But it was undeniably possible. He fit the profile perfectly.

"I need some answers," she said aloud to the brown-eyed man. "You always seem to have them."

T he abandoned stone longhouse with its thatched roof was plain and anonymous, and probably long forgotten by its previous occupants. It was set well off the road, so it was not overly visible, but it was near enough for convenience. It was sound and looked to be weatherproof, and it had everything they needed to headquarter a rebellion in the making. They found no decomposing bodies inside, nor any fresh graves in the near vicinity, so Karle and Alejandro assumed that the former tenants had either lost hope and left, or incurred the wrath of their overlord and were carried away. There was adequate room for the three of them and their two horses, and the stone walls were stout and would be impervious to arrows, should the rebellion ever be brought to their doorstep.

A stream ran nearby with clean-enough water for the horses, and the previous occupants had left behind cisterns into which the rain might fall, or in lack of rain, into which they could filter the water from the stream for their cooking and drinking needs. Not far away was a meadow where the horses might be grazed and trained, and where the peasants they intended to gather might be magically transformed from their base-metal selves into golden warriors to the cause of freedom. Small game was no more plentiful than in any other area, but it seemed adequate so they would not starve.

Kate and Alejandro set about a practiced routine of establishing themselves into a new home, for they had done it many times in their decade of wandering and they knew the rhythm and feel of settling in. Karle did as he was directed to do, for it was to his benefit that they chose this site and made these preparations. Try as he might, Alejandro could not convince his daughter to abandon Guillaume Karle, though there was sure and certain danger ahead if they stayed in his company. But stay they did, at Kate's insistence.

As was always their habit, they cleaned first, to remove the remnants of those who had been there before them. The father cut for the daughter a straight branch, and she herself gathered some straw, and with a thong of leather they tied the straw to the stick to fashion a simple broom. Kate promptly took it away from him, for she understood that sweeping was the work of women, while men saw to the things that required their greater strength. *Besides,* she had told him many times before, *you have not the innards to do it as well as a woman.*

Alejandro let his own tasks lie for a moment and watched as she swept the dirt floor smooth and made sure it was free of vermin, and as the dust rose up around her he lost himself in it and saw . . .

. . . *the tiny child who bravely worked the broom left behind in Mother Sarah's cottage, who wiped away the cobwebs, and when she was through with that silky but offensive stuff, attacked her own tears with her dirty little hand, a little girl who plumped the straw and carried in the armloads of faggots, who hurried to get things ready as he shivered and slumped and finally fell to the straw, in the grip of the Plague Maiden, and whether he rose again or not was up to the child entirely, and would be determined by the strength of her small will.*

She had done then what was needed, as she did now. And somehow, as they went about the work of providing for themselves, Guillaume Karle managed to slide himself into the old rhythm as if he had always been there, eventually usurping Alejandro's tasks like some young buck with velvet antlers bent on unseating the aging King of the Stags. Out, on Kate's banishment, went the dirt and dust and cobwebs, and in, on the back of the amber-haired Christian, came the faggots that would light their nights and cook their food and boil their water. And when Karle was done carrying faggots, the Frenchman cut great quantities of fresh straw for their bedding and carried it in bursting armloads into the longhouse. He piled it in a corner in a great heap.

When he judged the pile to be high enough, he said, "Where shall it be laid?"

They all stopped what they were doing. Kate and Karle looked at Alejandro, and Alejandro looked back and forth between them. The unspoken question hung in the air, awaiting settlement, as the sun glowed in the west on its way to sleep.

Finally Kate said, "Père, I would have a word with you." She glanced briefly at Karle, who nodded his head and then quietly stepped outside.

When they were alone, the daughter put a gentle hand on her father's arm. "He is a good man, Père. You could not have known how well you chose my protector."

Alejandro stroked her hair and smiled, a bit sadly. "I think it was not I who chose, daughter, but perhaps God."

"Then I hope you will understand that I wish to stand before God and take this man to husband."

"Will he take you to wife?"

"You must speak with him for that answer."

He did not wish to remove his hand from her hair; it felt clean and cool, and wonderfully familiar, as it had always felt since he had first taught her to brush it.

"Must I?" he said softly.

"Aye, Père. You must."

An unsavory notion settled in on him, that before him was a full-grown woman, and not the tiny child he had brought out of England. Under its troublesome weight, he understood what he would be required to do.

He took his hand away. "Karle," he shouted, loud enough to be heard outside.

Karle appeared in the doorway. He glanced quickly at Kate, who made a small smile and then quickly lowered her gaze.

The two men faced each other in silence for a moment, then Alejandro said, "My daughter says you would speak to me."

As de Chauliac looked around the now vacant room, he saw nothing except a neatly folded pile of courtier's clothing to indicate that a human being had recently occupied it. *He leaves no traces of himself anywhere, at least none that are visible.* No detritus, no pot of bodily wastes to be emptied. He had arrived spare, and departed just as spare, leaving in his wake only the one item that the guard had managed to yank away as he made his escape and his small fortune in gold.

But that was understandable; he had become a vagabond and had learned in the course of his wanderings to live by vagabond habits. And wisely, de Chauliac thought, for a Jew never knew when he would need to uproot himself. Best to be prepared.

But had he needed to take his spirit too? Could he not have left behind just a faint trace of the wonderfully curious character that was so irresistible and seductive? De Chauliac had the manuscript, and certainly there were leavings of the man within it. But now he would have only Flamel to share it with. And Flamel would not be pleased that the translation remained unfinished.

They found a priest an hour's ride north of Compiègne, an old, drunken, and very smelly friar who could barely recall the words of the ceremony he'd been commandeered to perform. Kate wore a garland of late-summer flowers in her golden hair, and Karle had brushed his clothing clean for the occasion and tied his own amber waves back into a string Alejandro gave him. They stood reverently before the ragged cleric and promised to be faithful unto each other until death did them part.

And then they returned to their new home, and Alejandro dutifully rearranged the straw. An unlucky pheasant, encountered on the ride back from the small church, served as their wedding feast, and they ate apples gathered from a tree on the other side of the meadow.

And as the sun made ready to fall again, Alejandro said, "Were we in Spain and celebrating your wedding properly, you would right now be receiving the bride gifts of your well-wishers and relatives. You would receive a feather bed from all of your grandparents, and candlesticks from your parents, and cloths and beaters and wax from your neighbors. All manner of useful things, big and small, to start your life together." He sighed. "But I am the sole relative, and the sole well-wisher, and I have none of these necessities to give you. So I will give you what I have."

He pulled the emerald-and-pearl ring he had received from the Countess Elizabeth off his finger and handed it to Kate. "Put it on your ring finger, that you may show with pride your marriage. You are a wife now, and you will be a fine one, I know it."

She accepted it and handed it to Karle, who slipped it onto her finger. Beaming, she reached out and embraced Alejandro.

He turned to Karle and said, "I have nothing that you may hold in your hands, Karle, but I will give you something that very few men have known, something I hope you will hold in your heart. I give you my respect. We are family now. You are a man of honor, and I think my daughter has made a fine choice."

And then he could say no more, lest he shame himself with tears on their day of joy. With a few simple words of good-night, he left them alone in the main part of the longhouse and went to where the horses were stabled. And as he climbed the ladder into the hayloft, he decided it was not so painful to lose a daughter like Kate, if one should in the same act gain a son like Karle.

After reading Marcel's latest scroll, and finding nothing in it that might compromise his own position, Charles of Navarre read it aloud to the Baron de Coucy.

"Today Karle left, once again accompanied by this mysterious maiden of his. She seems to have a pronounced influence on the man's thinking." Navarre looked up from the missive and smiled at Coucy. "Such is the way of the world," he said, "that we let women ride herd over us. Let us hope her influence is more hobbling than helpful."

He returned to the text. "It is their intent to ride north to the vicinity of Compiègne and begin the assembly of an army, though I use this word in the loosest possible manner. How many men can be brought together he could not estimate, nor can I, but it may be a substantial number. There is little else for these unfortunates to do, and if they are promised food and arms, I believe they will come."

Coucy interrupted. "How can such things be promised? Karle has not the means to purchase them."

"Some among them have arms of their own. Though it cannot be a substantial number."

"And what of mounts?"

"Those they have not eaten are skinny and worthless."

Coucy *hmphed,* and Navarre continued to read: "Though there are many factors weighing against him, I have come to know this Guillaume Karle. He has the one thing that *les Jacques* have lacked since the beginning of their uprising: the ability to lead them. He is an intelligent, inspiring man whose heart blazes for victory over what he considers to be his godless oppressors, and those of his countrymen. He has the most dangerous reason of all for doing what he does: his belief in the moral rightness of it. Make no mistake, many will follow him. Some will be zealots, as he is. Others will go because they have little left to lose, least of all their miserable lives. Still others will be in it for the reward they see waiting: fortune and land, to be stolen from the nobles they slaughter."

Coucy said, "It will not matter on the battlefield what their reasons might be. Once there, they will fight."

Navarre laid down the parchment. "Perhaps we ought to try to speak with Karle before we join forces against the Dauphin. There may need to be further understanding."

Coucy chuckled. "Further understanding about how he may keep his head?"

"Among other things," Navarre said. He handed the parchment to a page, and nodded in the direction of the fire.

In their few days of occupancy, the longhouse had become a serviceable abode, and it began to take on the feeling of a home. The young wife who now made her bed with her gallant new husband fairly glowed as she clucked like a hen over her roost, although thoughts of what lay ahead were never far from her heart. The man who had taken her to wife strutted like a lion over his domain, and made himself as useful as he could in view of the competence of his bride.

The new father-in-law held his tongue when it was appropriate to do so, and let it loose when he could not help himself. But all in all, they found their way together. With hard work and cleverness, they had managed to put together a few rough benches and a plank table, and though the newly hewn boards bore the flaws of Karle's inexperienced hands and oozed the dampness of green wood, when Alejandro sat at the table the bench did not come apart and the table did not rock unevenly. He could eat and think in motionless peace, which he considered a blessing.

It became their habit, as they sat together at their evening meal, to review their preparations, and under the light of a torch the list of the things that would be needed was studied and perused and reworked until all three of them could recite it from memory. Tools, weapons, oil and fat of any sort, scraps of leather, the simplest armor, especially that taken from slain nobles in the last battle. Horses, extra shoes, grain, dried beans, anything portable that might increase their chances of victory.

"We must beg our recruits to bring what they have of these items," Karle said, "and convince them to add them to the common lot."

"A man with two pocketfuls of beans will not give them to the cause," Kate said.

"But he may give one," Karle said, "and that will be a help. We must also seek the help of men with certain skills: grooms, carpenters, black-smiths . . ."

"If such tradesmen have not already been conscripted by Navarre."

"We will find them," Karle said, "I assure you. They are out there. And they are waiting for the opportunity to do some harm."

* * *

His prediction was correct: They were out there. As word of Karle's arrival spread through the countryside, men came from all directions, and the longhouse became *l'hôtel de ville* for a small city of warriors in the making. Karle took his natural place as their leader, the *roi des Jacques* that Navarre had so cleverly predicted he would become. And he did it, this former man of numbers, as if he were born to it. There seemed no limit to his ability to organize a war, nor to inspire the assembled malcontents to follow him into it.

Carpenters were put to use in making first bows, then arrows, and those who were otherwise idle were taught to strip away the bark from a long, straight branch and smooth off the joints where smaller branches had been cut away, then to implant a flake of sharp rock into the tip, and feather the green opposite end to give it balance. Leafy sections of the stripped branches were piled up to use as thatching for the roofs of the lean-tos that started to rise along the edge of the meadows. Latrines were dug, and a modicum of sanitation maintained, at Alejandro's insistence.

When birds were caught for food, their feathers were used on the arrows. All manner of viscera could be seen hanging to dry, twisted from the guts of small forest creatures into the strings that would carry those new arrows forward. Their pelts were dried and scraped to become protective padding for the shoulders of those who would be transformed into archers. Woodsmen carried their axes deep into the woods and came back dragging bundles of long, straight saplings, young trees that gave their flexible shafts to the making of spears.

Blacksmiths chipped the flint that was needed for points, and when metal could be gotten, these brawny, sweaty men formed it magically into sharp tips for spears. And finally, Alejandro had to take their own horses out of the stable area of the longhouse to make room for the growing store of weapons, rudimentary but serviceable implements of attack that should be sheltered from the weather until they were carried into battle. He tied a rag around the ankle of each horse, to mark them as his own, and sent them away to the meadow, where the scrawny lot that had been brought by some of the volunteer army were being grazed and trimmed and trained by skilled grooms who would no longer serve the nobility.

The ceiling of the longhouse became a hanging place for herbs and spices and leaves that had medicinal value, and pots boiled all day and through the night, brimming with the potions that would be needed to treat the wounded. Some of the volunteers had brought wives and children, and those that could not be sent home again were set to the task of gathering and spinning fibers, first to be twisted into ropes, and then if there was time, woven into bandages. Cotton simply could not be had, and so rough wild flax was pressed into service; the bandages that could be made from it were stiff and somewhat scratchy, but they softened to usability when water or oil was applied.

And in a locked metal box by the hearth, never too close to the flame to catch but always close enough to be warm, sat the hand of the plague child that Kate and Karle had exhumed before reaching Paris. She checked it now and then while no one else was looking, and watched with grisly fascination the progress of its desiccation, as the flesh shriveled and dried first to leather, then to something like clay, and finally into a grayish, greasy powder. Every time she opened the tin, she crossed herself against some unknown demon that she half-expected to rise out in an angry mist, and she was always careful to show it to Alejandro so that he might gauge its progress toward readiness. He would grimly nod and shake the can lightly from side to side, to see how much more of the flesh fell away each day. Finally, it was nothing but powder and sinewy bones. Alejandro separated out the bones and took them into the forest, where he dug a shallow hole and buried them again beneath a pile of rocks.

And when the weapons were finally assembled and the horses a bit plumper and better shod, and all the supplies to be had were gathered, the training began. From dawn until sunset, day after day, Karle rode through the meadow on his horse and watched as his lieutenants, chosen for skill and bravery from among the gathered, instructed raw recruits in the arts of war. Peasants thrust and parried and rolled away, then rose again, shot arrows into targets, and chucked spears at scarecrows from very long distances. They formed up and marched forward, their wooden swords held bravely toward the sky, then split into smaller troops, fell back, and regrouped for a charge. They charged and retreated, then charged a little farther and retreated a little less, then charged a little farther again. They became an army.

The lieutenants met nightly in the longhouse and were served thin stews and porridges by the women while they discussed the details of what training remained to be done. It was down to simple lessons now, for the work had been thorough and exhaustive. *They must never let a weapon lie unused on the ground by its fallen owner. A weapon down is a weapon free. It is no shame to retreat when by doing so an advantage might be gained for a later attack. They must water themselves as often as possible, for blood sport quickly drains a man of his liquid humors.* These and other such bits of wisdom were the last that could be given to the *Grande Armée des Jacques,* which started with one, grew to hundreds, and stood, at last, at thousands.

"And now a message must be sent," Guillaume Karle announced at one of their suppers. "We must tell Charles of Navarre that we are ready."

The sequencing is done, the message from Michael said. *I'm bringing the file and your original materials home.*

They drove to Michael and Caroline's house in Kristina's small, gas-friendly car. There was an unusual amount of traffic, both vehicular and human. Kristina was visibly distracted by the goings-on outside the car. She finally made a quiet but rather profound observation. "People are walking faster. They look scared, I think."

"I noticed that too," Janie said. "It's starting to scare *me* that everyone's rushing."

"I wonder where they think they're going to rush to."

"I wonder where *I'm* going to rush to. If it comes to that."

They were stopped at a traffic light. Dozens of people were hurrying across the street in front of them. Kristina turned to Janie and said, almost casually, "Do you actually think there's a chance that it won't?"

Janie stared at her for a few seconds. "I don't know how to respond to that, Kristina."

The light changed. With uncertainty still hanging in the air, Kristina drove on in silence. And when they arrived at Michael and Caroline's house, *Nowhere to run to, baby, nowhere to hide* was screaming through Janie's brain.

* * *

When Janie introduced them, Kristina stared at Caroline for a few seconds, a bit too intently for politeness, then turned to Janie with a look that said *Is this the one?*

Janie understood, and nodded very slightly. Caroline saw it all, comprehended, but added nothing beyond a little smile of her own. "Michael couldn't stay," she explained as she handed Janie the envelope. "You just missed him. He asked me to tell you he's swamped at work."

He would be in the front line when the time came, leading the charge. The worried look on Caroline's face betrayed her understanding of the danger he would be in.

Good Lord, Janie found herself thinking, *if anyone should be running and hiding . . .* "He'll be all right, Caroline," she said softly. "He knows what to do."

"I know. But it's hard." Her glance moved downward. "Especially right now."

"Any news?"

Caroline shook her head, but the look in her eyes said *Maybe.*

Janie sighed. It was love amid the ruins. "Well, keep me posted. I'm keeping my fingers crossed for you."

Caroline smiled and displayed her own crossed fingers. On one was a Band-Aid.

Janie reached out quickly and took hold of Caroline's hand. "What's that for?" she demanded sternly.

"A hangnail," Caroline answered. Then, a bit more nervously, she said, "And maybe you're overreacting just a little bit, *hmm*?"

"I want to take a look at it."

She tried to pull the hand away, but Janie would not give it up.

"Oh, really, Janie . . . this isn't necessary."

"Why don't you let me decide that?"

Back out in the kitchen, Janie unwrapped the finger and scrutinized it under a strong light. "Let me see the same one on the other hand," she said.

With a sigh, Caroline held the other finger out next to its mirror twin.

There was a visible hangnail, a tiny little tear in the flesh around Caroline's index finger cuticle. The area around it was swollen and colored. "How long has it been red?" Janie demanded sharply.

"Just since yesterday." Caroline was trying to sound casual and unconcerned, but was failing miserably. "I clipped a nail too close, I think."

"Plague can leave you vulnerable to infections for a very long time," she said to her friend. "I want you fastidious to the point of compulsiveness."

Caroline's forehead wrinkled into a pained, almost hurt expression. "I know that. You've told me plenty of times. And you know I'm careful."

"I just want to make sure you're careful *enough*," Janie said. "Although I'm not really sure that's possible."

As they stood together at the sink and scrubbed their hands with strong soap and steaming-hot water, Caroline said, "Good Lord. You need to lighten up. It's not plague, and it's not DR SAM."

Paper towels, immediately discarded. "Then what is it?"

"A hangnail," Caroline said. "Just a hangnail."

The atmosphere at the foundation was as rushed and uncertain as it was anywhere else. The in-and-out traffic was intense and noisy with a strong undercurrent of confusion, and security guards were stopping people who looked even slightly suspicious. The first thing Janie noticed as she entered the logjam at the main door was that they had the bacterial scanners operating again.

Janie waved her own hand over the ID sensor and passed through the scanner, reading clean, and then waited on the other side as Kristina followed her through the machine's archway. She saw the glint of Kristina's metal car keys in her right hand, and heard the metal detector sound. When the guards turned in Kristina's direction, the young woman smiled at them and made a little *oops* shrug of the shoulders. She held up the keys, and after a brief hesitation one of the guards waved her through.

Janie watched the whole scene with slight discomfort. *She's not in Big Dattie. She held her car keys in her implant hand as she passed through.* It was another notch on the tree trunk, but there wasn't time to examine what had just transpired. It would have to wait.

"We don't want to take too long," Janie said as she led Kristina down the stairs to one of the basement labs. "My supervisor is not very happy with me."

"Considering the way things are going, he's probably going to be a little busy now," Kristina said.

"You might be right, but still . . . we should get out of here as quickly as possible."

She had never traveled this corridor's length when such worries were in the air. As she looked up and around there was something strangely familiar about the walls and the ceilings and Janie found herself slipping into a memory of London, an occasion when a similar hallway had presented its terrifying self for passage and she had succumbed to its imagined horrors in much the same way.

No, she said to herself firmly. *Not now.*

She tried to resist the pull of it, but the vision grabbed on and clutched her mercilessly, and she couldn't get loose of it. As sweat beaded up on her forehead, she imagined herself in the corridor of what had once been a hospital, where dying Swine Flu patients and groaning World War I soldiers had reached out through a century to grab at her arms as she made her way through the shades of their presence.

Her step faltered slightly. She stopped and put a hand on the wall for support as the recollection forced its way through her.

Kristina noticed and moved to support her.

"Are you all right?" she said.

She was breathing deeply, concentrating on safety and goodness and white light, all things foreign to the vision. "I think so," Janie managed to say. "This place—it's *disturbing* all of a sudden."

"We can do this on V.M. if we have to," she said. "It'll take time, but—"

Janie shuddered and shook her head to clear it of the unwanted recall. "No," she said. "I don't think we can afford the delay."

Suddenly a technician came out of a side door and rushed past them with no acknowledgment, no greeting. He was wearing a full plastic face mask and long latex gloves, and the look in his eyes was frightened and focused. After watching the tech disappear into a turn in the corridor, Kristina looked at Janie and said, "No. I don't think we can."

The lab they slipped into at the end of the corridor was not writhing with ghosts, as the path they'd taken to reach it had seemed to be. When she closed the door behind them Janie felt calmer. She pushed away her fears as best she could and fed the data disk with Alejandro's genome into a slot at one of the workstations, and with a few tentative commands, set the search for the elusive DNA segment in motion. Kristina sat by her side and they waited in nervous, contemplative silence while the massive evaluation computer did its job.

Now and then a tempting similarity would be located and the screen would display two shaded vertical bands of DNA for the fractions of a second it took to analyze them further. The longer the image remained on the screen, Janie knew, the greater the points of similarity. And after a few minutes of rapid on and off, a pair of bands stayed on the screen, and stayed, and stayed.

Janie sat up and gripped Kristina's arm. "Look at this," she said.

Base pair by base pair, the nucleotides of the two similar strands were compared. Against all odds, against logic itself, the images remained where they were. The word *Match* flashed onto the screen in big white letters.

And a few seconds later, as Janie and Kristina were hugging each other in the joy of their success, celebrating the contribution of an ancient and long-dead wanderer to the lives of those who had come centuries after him, Chet Malin was trying to figure out how he ought to respond to the beep he'd heard on his computer. He tapped the screen and read the displayed message. He touched it again and looked at the details of where Janie was in the building and what she was doing.

"Time for a trip upstairs," he muttered unhappily.

Janie deleted the file containing Alejandro's genome from the drive where it had resided temporarily during the evaluation.

"I guess I know what I'll be doing this afternoon," Kristina said, taking the envelope from Janie's hand, "cooking up a batch of Alejandro soup. We're going to need a lot."

Wonder crept into Janie's mind about where Kristina would do this. "Do you have an adequate facility?" she asked.

"Yes. I have a complete lab."

Janie burned to know. "But—*where?*"

"I'd love to tell you," Kristina said with a wistful but slightly guilty glance in Janie's direction. "But I can't."

At last, Janie's patience petered out. "Why not, for God's sake? I've been in on everything else. I located this gene. I was the one who—"

"Please," Kristina said. "I know all that, and I can't begin to tell you how awed I am by what you've done. And I want to show you where I live and where I work, more than I can say, but it would put us—and you—in danger. If you were followed it would—"

"I'm not going to be followed."

"You already have been. More than once."

Janie stared back at the young woman, dumbfounded by the revelation. "*When?*"

"To the book depository."

After a hard swallow, she said, "No one could possibly learn anything about what we're doing from following me to that place."

"And to the camp nurse's house."

So I was right. "By whom?"

Indecision was all over Kristina's face. Finally, in near agony, she said, "I just can't tell you."

"Kristina," Janie said, "please . . . now you're starting to scare me. This is my safety we're talking about here. I don't understand why you have to keep this from me."

"You'll know soon enough" was all she would say. Then she seemed to pull back and stiffen, to sever the emotional link that their success had created. "Look, I'll drop you off at Tom's. I'll see you there later tonight. Please, Janie, be patient—you'll know everything soon enough. And I also need to tell you—now is a good time to be careful."

Now was seeming like a good time to be alone, at least for a little while. It hurt, being left out in the cold. "I think I'll take a walk," Janie said when her spinning head finally cleared. "That'll give you more time to go—*wherever* it is you're going. And there are a couple of things I need to take care of on the way. I mean, I *do* have other things to do."

What, precisely, was she doing? Waiting halfheartedly for Bruce, pouring the heart and soul she might otherwise have given to him into a project orchestrated by a clandestine group identified only as "we," and engaging in a dangerous flirtation with her lawyer.

Oh, yes, she reminded herself. Answering to and obeying a young woman less than half her age in matters of great importance.

It was time to start shutting things down.

She found Chet Malin in his office with his head in his hands. "I'm giving my notice," she said.

With uncharacteristic calm the Monkey Man said, "If you leave me in the lurch like this, I promise you'll never work in the genetic research industry again."

It was an absolutely absurd threat, in view of the state of things. "Chet, in a few more days, from the look of what's happening out there, the genetic research industry is going to take a little forced vacation. Along with just about every other industry, except the funeral business."

By the time Kristina reached Tom's house that night, Janie had forgiven her.

"The patent trail dies in both directions," Kristina said as they sat before V.M. "Backward, it disappears. Forward, I lose it in the Outbreak mess." Oozing frustration, she denuded a mint and popped it into her mouth. She crumpled the wrapper and tossed it toward a wastebasket. It bounced off the rim and landed on the floor, and Janie, ever the neat-nik, reached down to pick it up.

"So let's just forget the corporations for now and move on," Janie said. "We have other things to check out."

Kristina sat back in the chair and stared at her. "Such as?"

"Such as individuals. Genetic patents don't have to be owned by corporations, although most of them are. Maybe the owner is a single person, or a small group, with access to a lot of support." She tossed the
crumpled mint wrapper into the wastebasket. "I think we should go back
to our orthopedists."

"We didn't find anything there the first time."

Expect the unexpected, Alejandro had written. "Maybe we weren't looking in the right way. Look what we found today, and think about where
we found it. We've been looking for what we expect to find. And it's not
working. So let's look again, differently."

Kristina complained of a headache after another hour of fruitless computer work.

"Go home," Mother Janie said. "Do you want me to drive you?"

Why hadn't she found the courage simply to ask where Kristina hung
her bandana? Every time Janie summoned her Kristina showed up, so
home had to be relatively close.

But precisely where remained a mystery.

And why is it, she wondered, *that even when I don't contact her, she
knows when to come looking for me?*

"No. I'm fine to drive. Really."

Paranoia was hard at work in Janie's mind, offering up wild possibilities and fantastic scenarios to explain Kristina's Johnny-on-the-spot appearances. As she watched Kristina gather her things Janie considered an
injected microscopic transmitter, or radio waves infused into her sham-
poo, maybe communication chips masquerading as corn flakes. Pure science fiction, intriguing, but nonsense, every bit of it. It would have to be
something much more sophisticated than that.

But it would certainly be something. When all this was over, when
there was nothing dreadful looming just around the corner, she would
find the wherewithal to ask.

Still in front of her on the screen was the file for one of their orthopedists; at that particular moment a list of her significant publications was
displayed. *I'll work for a few more minutes,* she told herself, *then I'll go to
bed.* She was instructing V.M. to go another level down in the data when
she heard a light tap on the door.

She looked toward the sound and saw Tom leaning against the door
frame, looking relaxed and sporting his familiar wry smile, the same
quirky little grin she always saw in her mind's eye when she envisioned

her longtime friend in his absence. A pleasant little shudder of surprise went through her at the sight of him.

He had a bottle of wine and two glasses in his hands. "I was going to have a nightcap and I wondered if you might want one too. I had a nice red open, so I thought maybe . . ."

"I'd love some. But right now if you poured me a glass of beet juice I'd probably think it was the best thing ever bottled."

He came into the room and set the glasses down on the edge of the desk, then poured each one about half full. The wine was a beautiful dark color, almost opaque. "I think this will be a little better than beet juice." He picked up one of the glasses and raised it. "Well, cheers. Here's to, uh . . ."

Janie raised hers and said, "Figuring it all out."

Tom smiled in accord. "Whatever 'it' is."

"I'd settle for it being Orthopedist Zero."

He nodded toward the screen and said, "Getting anywhere?"

"I wish," she said. "I've rearranged this group every way I can think of. I've looked at each file individually, brought up the lists of their publications, the dates when they published, their awards, all of that happy horseshit, but I just don't see anything."

He pointed toward V.M. "May I?"

"Please. Maybe you'll see something I've missed."

She started to rise from the chair, but he stopped her, saying, "Stay there. You don't need to get up." He positioned himself behind her and put his hands on the back of her chair, then leaned forward over her shoulder. "This is fine," he said, "I can see from here."

He looked, and after a moment he reached around her, his arm brushing her shoulder as he touched the screen. The files sorted themselves once again. He looked closer, as if he were concentrating.

Janie remained quiet and absolutely still for what seemed like an eternity as Tom worked the screen display with small but effective touches, and she found herself wanting to be that screen, to have him touch her in some reactive place. *You cannot do this,* her conscience told her. Yet the distance between the two of them seemed to be shrinking down to almost nothing, unlike the distance between her and Bruce, which seemed to widen every day. She was a doorbell and Tom was leaning on the button, and the signal being sent so urgently was *Let me in, let me in.* She closed her eyes and tried to breathe deeply, hoping to drive off the sudden case of "I want" that had reared its demanding little head and was threatening to make her do things she might later regret.

But her attempt at self-suppression was a miserable failure. The current within her surged, seeking release, and as Tom drew his arm back again, Janie turned her face just slightly so the sleeve of his shirt stroked her cheek, and as his hand passed by her face, she reached up and grabbed it, and brought it to her lips. The circuit between them was completed.

When they passed the small room where Janie had been sleeping, she slipped inside the door and tried to draw him in, but he smiled and shook his head no, then pulled her farther along to his own lair. And when they entered, Janie had to stop and let go for a minute, to absorb the place where Tom made his bed and had his dreams, to understand, if she could, all the things it said about him. It all said spare, simple, well thought out. It was orderly and contained, and the hint of his scent was in the air.

On an oiled wood bureau there were photographs, people Janie remembered as his family. In the neat arrangement there was a space where one seemed to be missing. *A woman he doesn't want me to see?* she wondered.

There was a candle on the bedstand, and flowers in a vase. It was as if he had prepared—and the notion of it pleased her immensely. "You forgot the whipped cream." She smiled.

"Damn," he breathed as he pulled her closer, "and I wanted everything to be so perfect."

"What could be more perfect," she whispered to him later, as they lay wrapped around each other in the bed, "than having all this sweetness with your oldest, dearest friend?"

"Having it sooner," he answered.

God, Janie, I love you.

And I miss you. I hope everything about the house is getting worked out—tell Tom how much I appreciate his helping us like this. I guess you must be asleep—that's good, because I know I didn't let you get much sleep while you were here, and with everything you're going through, you need to take good care of yourself. I'm sad you had to leave early, but I know it couldn't be helped.

This will all be over soon, you'll see. We'll work it out. I just have a feeling that things are coming to a head.

The last sentence in his message felt like a slap across the face, a blow Bruce couldn't possibly even know he had delivered. She closed her eyes for a minute and remembered the night that had just passed, the warmth of being held close by someone she knew so thoroughly and trusted beyond any doubt, who touched her with enduring, patient love.

How had she not seen it before?

She opened her eyes again, and the message was still on the screen, staring back at her with its damnation.

Suddenly there were footsteps on the stairs and Janie heard the clink of a spoon against a ceramic cup. She closed the message from Bruce quickly and brought back the list of orthopedists. Tom came through the door bearing a tray. Her heart began to pound, and to distract herself she stared down at her hands, which had assumed a forced position in her lap and were pretending, unsuccessfully, not to tremble.

She was wrapped in Tom's bathrobe as she sat in Tom's home office, the morning after having slept in Tom's bed. With Tom.

The confusion was so overwhelming that she almost started to cry, but she contained her tears with a bite on her own lip. It was surprisingly painful, and she touched it with her finger to see if she'd drawn blood. To her relief the finger came away clean. But her conscience did not.

"Good morning," he said as he came in. He rested the edge of the tray on the desk and moved V.M. slightly to make way for the mugs he'd brought. All the while he was beaming, a beautiful morning-after smile. "Well," he said, "something else to admire. You're still a workaholic."

She found her way somehow to a small laugh. "I am. You find that admirable?"

He kissed her on the forehead. "I find everything about you admirable."

Those words sounded so good, so right as they fell on her ears. *But, oh, dear God,* she thought, *this is all so wrong.*

As he stood next to her, he looked down the list of names on the screen. "Find anything yet?"

"No."

Mug in hand, he sat down on an overstuffed chair a few feet away, the sort of chair someone would sit in to read while his significant other worked at her desk. A companion seat. Janie swiveled the modern desk chair around so she faced him. With a little twinge of jealousy, she wondered who else might have sat in that chair, if she and Tom ought to be trading positions. But he seemed very comfortable where he was, though it was his own study, in his own home.

"So," he said, "I guess we need to do some talking."

Janie reached out and took the remaining coffee mug off the desk. Its warmth was comforting in her hands. She gripped it, hoping the surface of the coffee wouldn't be rippled from her trembling. "I don't know why this had to happen now," she said quietly.

"Funny," Tom said, "I was just wondering why it didn't happen sooner. If I'd had the courage to tell you how I felt before you went to London, we wouldn't be having this conversation."

"Why didn't you? God, Tom, if I'd only known . . . I mean, I've always had this sort of peripheral love for you, even while I was married, and I never lost my feelings for you completely—but I guess I thought what we had was really just friendship." She shook her head and made an ironic little *hmph*. "Listen to me. *Just* friendship. As if that wasn't what it all comes down to in the end. Or should, anyway."

"I wouldn't argue with you about that."

"No, I know you wouldn't. But that's just what I mean—there's so much about us that's comfortable, that fits, and if I'd had any idea at all about how you feel, I wouldn't have let myself fall for Bruce. We could have started this when I got back from London, or maybe . . ."

She paused to fight off the impending deluge.

"Maybe what?"

"Maybe I wouldn't even have gone."

"Janie—of course you would have gone."

"Maybe not."

"You wouldn't have let that opportunity get by you. That it didn't turn out exactly as you'd planned is something you couldn't foresee or control. I've never seen you shrink away from a challenge. You would've gone with something to come back to, but you still would've gone. I understand that. I helped you set it up, remember? It was supposed to be a really good thing for you, and I would never let myself keep you away from something that was good for you."

"It's strange to hear you say that," she said quietly. "You're very much on the verge of doing that right now."

He set his coffee cup down on a table and leaned forward in the chair, his hands clasped together around his knees. "Am I? I don't get the sense that you're entirely sure about that."

After a long sigh, Janie said, "You're right. I'm not. You know me too well."

"And you know me. You know I don't do things like this lightly."

The silence that followed was nearly unendurable. "Look," Tom finally said, "I can back away if you want me to. But I have to tell you, it wouldn't be the road I'd choose to follow right now."

"Which road would you follow, then?"

"The one I'm on."

"And where do you think it's going to lead you?"

"Into your heart. I hope."

"It's getting pretty crowded in there."

"You'll do what you have to about that, Janie. I'm not going to try to convince you to abandon Bruce or come to me. That's something you'll decide, no matter what either of us does. I just want my chance, that's all."

"Look," she said after a moment, "maybe I should go to stay with Caroline, or even a hotel. That might make it easier for you and me to work this out."

"Do that for yourself if you want to, but not for me. I've been holding all this inside for so long, and now it's finally in the open, and it feels so good—I don't think I can just shut it off again. Anywhere you go, I'm still going to love you."

He got up out of the chair and came next to her. He rested one hand on her shoulder; the pressure was gentle and soothing. "I think you should stay here until you have a few more things straightened out in your life. You're almost done with this work you're doing with Kristina. It'll just be easier."

"I think I might feel like I was taking advantage."

He gave her a brave smile. "And here I was thinking it was me taking advantage of you. Just goes to show you how people can see things very differently no matter how well they know each other. But I should warn you," he said, his expression now a shameless grin, "that I plan to stand outside your bedroom door every night and whine like a puppy dog until you let me in."

And with that, he picked up the tray. "Back to reality, I guess."

"Reality's always there, isn't it?"

"It is," he said. "Gets nastier every day too." Then he nodded in the direction of the computer screen. "One of your orthopedists"—he balanced the tray with one hand and pointed to a long Eastern European–looking name with the other—"rings a bell. I think I might have known his son, back in my wild law school days."

Every little detail seemed worth following to her. She touched the screen repeatedly until the man's family information was displayed. A photograph of the man in question came up, and for a brief moment Janie wondered if she'd seen him somewhere before. But it wouldn't come clear to her.

"I don't see any mention of a lawyer son here," she said.

"I don't think he finished. He might have, later. I lost track. Happily. The guy was a jerk."

She smiled. "Then he would've been a good lawyer."

"Ha ha."

They had slipped out of intimacy, and Janie missed it immediately. As she watched Tom leave the room, a sense of terrible loneliness came over her. But there was no time to wallow in it. She set aside her own little misery and turned back to the confusing, mute reality before her, wishing it would speak up, and speak clearly, because inside Big Dattie the DR SAM clock was ticking.

N avarre and Coucy stood on the castle wall and watched as Karle's messenger rode off in the direction of Compiègne.

"The man has raised a fighting force," Charles said. The Navarrese king was subdued and worried-looking, not his usual fiery self. "An *army*. And if this lieutenant of his is any indication, a loyal army. Of men with some intelligence. This one was no dolt. There are likely to be more of the same."

"He hinted at thousands," the Baron de Coucy added in a sober voice. "How has he managed to do this?"

"Perhaps he has some secret ally."

"No one of consequence remains undeclared," Coucy countered.

"Then these thousands are indeed, as he said, all peasants."

"In which case, you have nothing to fear, my lord."

Navarre turned away from the wind. "He describes them as mounted troops with swords, foot archers, javelin throwers, and foot soldiers, just as we count ours."

Coucy said, "He exaggerates. What he says can be true only if he has managed to transform them, and I do not believe that there are adequate magicians for such a task at the moment." The baron tried to laugh, but the sound was unconvincing. "And swords—where will they find the materials, never mind the armorers? But perhaps he has an alchemist as an ally, making the necessary materials. Turning rocks into metal, no doubt."

"Do not underestimate this man," Navarre said. "It would be very unwise to do so. But you are right—he does exaggerate. What matters now is to find out how much. And to what end."

"One cannot know the mind of these peasants," Coucy commented.

"Perhaps to impress us? That is hardly to his advantage. He is supposed to be our ally. If the early reports of the Dauphin's troop counts are correct, we will need him. Karle knows this."

"And until we know for sure how many we face from the Dauphin, we must not offend him by sneering at his peasants. He has prepared them for an earnest charge, but he cannot think he will usurp you with his peasants when the battle against the Dauphin is done."

"With the numbers he claims," Navarre said soberly, "and if *we* are badly hit when we charge against the Dauphin, such a usurpation could be achieved. And since we are to lead the charge, *we* will be the worse hit, for certain."

He left the wall and walked across the stone decking and back into the room in which he had received Karle's lieutenant. "He is clever, this *roi des Jacques.* But we are clever too." He summoned his page. "You are to ride out to Compiègne this afternoon and deliver Karle a message. Tell him we will meet him there three days hence at dawn, and join our troops together for attack. We will bring our soldiers up behind his to form a phalanx. Since he has amassed such an outstanding force, it is only fair that they have the honor of striking against the Dauphin first."

The message set Karle's lieutenants to arguing almost instantly, the subject of their discord being the nature of their response to Navarre's message. All agreed that a reply was required; no two seemed to agree what it should be. So after an hour or so of heated discussion, Karle weighed what he had heard and made a decision.

He worked his way around the table, pointing at men and saying their names. "Tomorrow morning all of you shall go to visit Navarre and his puppet, Coucy. Go mounted on the best horses we have, carrying the finest swords we have, wearing the best armor we have purloined. Carry any standard you can find. Present yourselves as warriors. Tell him that it is my considered opinion that the most useful strategy would be for his troops and ours to intermix in the attack on the Dauphin. Tell him further that I believe this will confuse the Dauphin to the point where he will not know what to do. Say that we both know the Dauphin to be a man of weak will, and when faced with the dilemma we shall present him, he will lack the will to make an immediate, decisive attack. And that will be to our advantage."

Then more quietly, he added, "Do not tell him that when our joint attack on the Dauphin is done, while we are still dispersed among his men, while the lust for blood still runs within us, we will turn upon them. We will slaughter them. They will not expect it. We are peasants, after all. Would we do something so audacious as to attack the fighting force of a king?"

Enthusiastic cheers and shouts filled the longhouse. Watching and listening from the hearth, where she was boiling flax bandages, Kate felt a shiver of dread run through her.

She found Alejandro making his way slowly along the edge of the meadow, tending to the myriad of small injuries that happened during war-play, the blisters and splinters and sore ankles that might, if untended, lessen the effectiveness of the men who bore them. They had amassed a good store of boots, torn along the way from corpses, given by widows, though few fit their recipients as they ought, and Alejandro knew that the feet of Guillaume Karle's troops could well turn out to be like the heel of the Greek Achilles, the point of vulnerability that could bring them down. So he paid special attention to them, to see that none went to battle with bleeding, unbound sores.

"Ah, Kate," he said when he saw her approach.

She walked toward him, treading lightly on the grassy spots, her skirts lifted in one hand to avoid the mud, the other hand full of the familiar gray-white strips that had been her personal industry since settling into the longhouse. "I brought more bandages, Père. These are just now ready."

"You work miracles, child. How shall this war be won without you?"

She smiled and handed over the bundle. "I am not a child, Père. I am now a married woman. Yet I think I shall always have to remind you of this."

They worked alongside each other, and despite the grimness of their task and the horrors that surely lay ahead, Alejandro Canches knew more contentment in those moments than he had in many years. His daughter by his side, her happy situation with a fine man, the good work he did with his fingers and hands and mind, it was all the very stuff of contentment.

When the supply of bandages had been exhausted, Kate said to him, "Walk with me, Père. I would have some time alone with you."

These were the sweetest words he had heard all day. "It would be my pleasure, *Madame* Karle."

She laughed lightly as they walked through the forest behind the encampments. "It is such a good thing to have a name at last. I have never quite known what to say. Was I Plantagenet, or Hernandez, or Canches? Now I am Karle. 'Tis a very fine thing to say it aloud, without fear."

He put an arm around her shoulders. "You are happy, daughter?" He laughed softly. "You will please make note that I did not call you *child*."

"Happier than I thought possible, Père." She ran a hand across her forehead, brushing back a stray blond strand that had come free of her headpiece. "But I think that soon I will know even greater happiness."

He stopped walking and looked at her.

"My menses have ceased, Père."

He stared. "But you have only been married—"

She quickly put a hand to his lips. "We shall not speak of the duration of my marriage. There is much of it yet to come. That is all we need concern ourselves with right now."

He took her by the shoulders and looked into her eyes. "So you are certain of this."

"I cannot be sure quite yet, but my suspicions run strong."

"I do not know whether to curse God or thank Him."

"For my sake, you must thank Him. For the sake of this child's father, you must curse God for sending him into battle just now."

"Does Karle know?"

She shook her head as it dropped slightly. "I fear that such knowledge will distract him from the task at hand. Weaken his resolve. And though I would give God half of my life to have Guillaume abandon this battle and run with me to someplace safe, he is too much of a man to do it. So I have not told him."

He took her in his arms and embraced her. He rocked her back and forth, and shared her joy completely. *I am to be a* grandpère, he thought. *And the child will have a name.* He wished, achingly, that he could tell his own father.

When the six lieutenants set out the following morning, they looked like the bravest knights in their borrowed finery. Attired in the spoils of war, mounted on purloined steeds, brandishing polished weapons they could barely have lifted the month before, they rode up the hill to the Château de Coucy and delivered their proud news to Charles the Bad.

Navarre left them waiting in the courtyard for a while as he conferred with his underlords, principally the Baron de Coucy himself, who was barely more than a boy yet already had a reputation for the fierce savagery needed to run a protectorate as vast as the one he had inherited only a short time before. In comparison to their longhouse camp, the keep of the Château de Coucy was massive and fortified and almost luxurious in its appointments. Colorful flags flew everywhere, proclaiming both the wealth and influence of the owner. The hefty iron portcullis, were it not worked by pulleys, would have required a team of horses to raise it. It stood between the rest of the world and the inner keep, which was paved with flat stones and free of the mud that sucked at the ankles of horses and men all around the longhouse. The soldiers who practiced here had dry feet and full stomachs, and the might of the mightiest behind them. The lieutenants, as they waited, keenly felt the differences.

And when Navarre's answer came back a sneering no, it was accompanied by a request, almost a command, that Guillaume Karle himself appear before Navarre and Coucy to discuss the terms of their alliance, and that the appearance be the following morning, or the alliance would not go forward. They gave no answer, for none would speak for Karle without first conferring with the man himself. And as each man rode under the rising portcullis, back to the roads and fields of mud, he knew that their fate rode on Karle's answer.

They had taken to making their bed in the hayloft above the store of weapons, for there was no place else, save the deep forest, that would give them the privacy they hungered for, and Guillaume Karle did not wish to be so far away from the center of command with so much needing attention in the final hours of their preparation. And though the smell of oil and leather and fresh-smithed metal rose up to the loft and made Kate want to gag, she did not let it ruin the delight she felt in lying in the arms of her cherished husband.

That night they made love with tearful tenderness and consummate joy, for each one knew the unspoken truth: it might very well be the last time they lay together. Sometimes they writhed like lions, clutching at each other with near violence, and other times they lay in near stillness, with only the slightest movement, the simple fact of their joining enough to satisfy them. They whispered sweet promises to each other and shared their hopes of what they might establish in the world when it returned to sanity, after this battle was done.

And at the crowing of the cock, Alejandro found them asleep and peaceful. He gently shook Karle with one hand and whispered, "Karle, it is time to rise."

He had decided to meet Navarre. "Though the thought of it makes me nearly retch," he'd told Kate and Alejandro the night before, "not from fear, but from revulsion at the things he has done. I do not know how I shall speak with such a man without wanting to fall on him and slit his throat."

And Kate had argued, "How can we be sure he will not fall on you and slit your throat, even before you've had a chance to retch?"

"We cannot."

"Then do not go," she'd pleaded.

"I *must* go. I am the leader of this army. Navarre is the leader of that army. There is business to be done between us. Even such scum as Navarre knows that to slay the leader of an ally is to make enemies of his troops. We have troops enough to guarantee his defeat of the Dauphin. He cannot make us his enemies."

"Perhaps not yet," Alejandro had said.

To which Karle had replied, "Perhaps not ever. But if I do not go, we shall shame ourselves before him. He will slay us with ridicule. We have come too far to let that happen."

They sent all the lieutenants out into the encampment and began to prepare Karle for his encounter with Navarre. They stripped him of his peasant rags and washed him and combed him and scented him, then dressed him in the fine garments Alejandro had worn when he escaped from de Chauliac. From among the armor purloined by peasant rebels at Meaux from the nobles they had slain, they selected the best pieces. They strapped on a metal breastplate and scaled leg defenses, and as Kate tightened the buckle around each of her husband's calves and adjusted the drape of his shirt, Alejandro thought to himself how ironic it was that she, born to this sort of activity, should have come to it at last, in such a roundabout way.

"I have no helmet," he said when they were through.

"No matter," Kate said. "No one will take you for anything less than a prince."

He smiled and said, "Coming from a princess, I take that to be the truth."

"I will always tell you the truth, husband," she said, and she kissed him, her lips lingering on his cheek. He in turn pressed his lips upon her forehead, and then whispered a promise of eternal devotion. Alejandro turned away so they could not see the look of woe on his face.

Karle left the longhouse and mounted the horse that had been brought around for him, a big, sturdy black stallion with a lively step and a fiery eye. The animal too had been prepared: his mane plaited with strips of red and blue cloth, his back and flanks draped with a cream-colored, scalloped-edge cloth, emblazoned with a gold fleur-de-lis that had been set into a diamond of deep blue. Karle looked more a prince of the realm than *le roi des Jacques,* and his lieutenants cheered and shouted, *"Vive Karle! Vivent les Jacques!"* when he appeared before them.

He sat astride the horse and made an impassioned speech to those he had entrusted with command under him. It was a far cry from the street corner pleas he had made in the past, in villages and marketplaces. Those ragged calls to arms had been the seeds of the work that was now coming to full and fruitful bloom in Compiègne. "We are one battle away from realizing our dreams," he said. "One battle. And that will happen on the morrow. We will join with the forces of Charles of Navarre in fighting against the Dauphin, we for our reasons, Navarre for his. And though we will be temporary allies, our alliance will stop when the battle is won. I will present Navarre with our demands for self-governance. And if he fails to comply with these demands, we shall fight for them, if need be, to the last man."

There was somber silence after the last comment. Karle looked from man to man and said, "God willing, it shall not come to that."

"God willing," all murmured.

He urged the horse over to where Kate was standing next to Alejandro and reached down a hand to her. Beaming adoration, she reached up, and Alejandro hoisted her so she landed in the saddle in front of her husband, who wrapped one arm around her and rode off toward the meadow, his lieutenants close behind. They worked their way around the perimeter of their practice field, to the cheers and shouts of the motley army assembled there, waving and smiling, stirring all who saw them to rise up and beat the air with fists and swords and clubs and spears, and whatever other rudimentary implements they could lay quick hands upon. And when they came back to the longhouse again, Karle gave his final instructions.

"If I do not return tonight, then set out in the morning in the formation we had planned. For if I do not safely return, then you will know that our battle is with Navarre, not the Dauphin. Do whatever is needed to draw him out, and when his troops are exposed make your attack."

He kissed Kate one last time, then set her down next to Alejandro. He leaned over and said, "There was a time when you gave her into my care, saying, take care that no harm comes to my daughter. I proved myself worthy of the task. I ask you now, Physician, to see that no harm comes to my wife."

Their eyes locked, and Alejandro nodded. Karle turned his horse and rode off.

From his spot on the wall of the château, Charles of Navarre watched the tiny cloud of dust as it progressed on the westbound road. He had been waiting, none too patiently, for this rider, and he burned with curiosity to hear the man's report. If Guillaume Karle was going to respond to his request, he would cover the distance before noon. Navarre judged by the sun that the other rider would reach them before noon, but just barely. He was tempted to send out a groom with a fresher horse for the man, but decided against it.

All in due time, he assured himself. The pieces were coming together. He need only be patient.

But how he hated waiting, wondering what this spy would tell him. He stared at the cloud of dust and willed it to move faster, but it kept the same steady pace, a pace which was thunderous on the ground, but snail-like when viewed as God Himself might view it, from this lofty perch on the wall. Would the Dauphin's troops, as rumored, fall far short in number of the expected, thereby negating the necessity for an alliance with Karle? Or would his supporters rally sufficient strength that the Dauphin needed to be taken seriously?

The rider would tell. He had only to wait.

Kristina appeared later that morning and presented the results of her efforts for Janie's approval—a box full of small, well-padded packages, each one addressed to one of the field operatives.

"Essence of Alejandro," she said with a triumphant smile. "Ready to do battle. Enough to treat every one of the boys we know about. We'll have to send them by air freight."

"I can't believe you did this already," Janie said incredulously.

"I was up all night, slaving over a hot computer."

"Good work." Then, more tentatively, she added, "This was really fast. You're completely sure you got it right?"

"It's perfect. I promise."

Such conviction. "Well, then, let's get this stuff on its way, before—"

She'd been about to say *before it's too late,* but instead she finished the sentence with "before all the air shippers close." With a few touches on its directory screen, Janie had Tom's phone display numbers for all the air freight companies that serviced their area. She quickly called the nearest one.

But pickups had already been suspended there, so she hung up and called the next. Over and over, as she worked her way down the alphabetical list of haulers, she got the same lament: "We'll get it there, but you gotta get it here first." One had a plane on the tarmac, loaded and scheduled to go in two hours; it would be the last flight from western

Massachusetts to their distribution center, because the pilots were no longer all showing up to do their runs, and other areas were a priority. The pilot of this last flight would stay in the Midwest for reassignment, Janie was told; she would not be returning to her home base, because it would no longer be served.

And while Kristina raced to the airport, Janie e-mailed all the other operatives:

Expect a package, instructions to follow.

She ran her tongue over her teeth.

Could I have forgotten to brush them this morning? Janie wondered. She went upstairs to the bathroom and picked up the tube of toothpaste, which was rolled halfway. Before applying the paste to the brush, she held the tube in one hand for a moment, dwelling on two thoughts: first, that she and Tom were both bottom-tube rollers, not middle-tube squeezers. It could only be an omen. And second, how much she hated being without toothpaste.

It was one of those mundane necessities that would soon become difficult if not impossible to acquire. There were others, so Janie took her creaking Volvo out of Tom's garage, intending to gather up as many of those things as she could while order still prevailed.

The Holy Grail would always be gasoline, and at her usual station there was already a long line as people waited, anxious and jostling, to fill their tanks and cans and mayonnaise jars. For a moment Janie considered moving on, but she knew it would be the same situation in the next place she tried—it would be the same anywhere she went.

She gave an entire precious hour to the wait, resenting every minute of it, but the time simply had to be spent, and when it was finally her turn at the pump she passed her hand over the sensor and listened with relief to the sound of the liquid gold gurgling into her gas tank. As the numbers on the meter clicked steadily upward and the power to move from one place to another flowed into her vehicle, she remembered with excessive clarity how quickly it had become difficult to get around the last time. For months people walked everywhere, carried things, dragged things—until workers who knew how to extract oil from the earth and refine it into gasoline emerged from their caves and went back to their jobs. Fuel could be had back then for the right price; she'd heard of a few deals that were worked around rare car parts and obscure tools, occasionally even coffee. But you had to know someone, or you walked.

She gathered up batteries, candles, powdered milk, canned goods, bottled water, tampons—and the ultimate necessity—toilet paper. She managed to find a Swiss Army knife tucked behind a dusty rack in a hardware store—someone had dropped it long ago, and Janie was certain it was waiting just for her to come along in need. All the other knives had long since been sold. How long would it be before the shelves looked empty again—and when would the clerks disappear, leaving the stores dependent entirely on their electronics as if they were giant walk-in self-serves?

When would the electronics finally break down and the looting begin?

Automatic vending machines for protective face and hand gear had popped up like mushrooms after a rainstorm. They could be seen on street corners like preachers of doom and destruction, big green reminders of the impending slide toward mayhem. People rushed by them in haste, just to get past, because to stop and partake was to admit the unthinkable and accede to the inevitable. Janie stopped and looked, in sad dismay, but did not buy.

Her last stop was at a small grocery known for the fine quality of its offerings, to trade her credits for the fragrant roasted fruit of the coffee tree. A burlap bag of whole beans rested open on the counter, half-full and incredibly inviting. Janie knew beyond doubt that it would be shapeless and empty within the hour. She flashed the still-unmasked proprietor a look that pleaded *May I?* He nodded his permission solemnly, and Janie put her hand into the bag and scooped her fingers luxuriously through the remaining beans. She withdrew her hand with reluctance when another customer asked to do the same, and turned away to the fruit trays, which were usually filled to overflowing with colorful, succulent delights, but were now pitifully bare. Janie picked up the lone remaining lemon and squeezed it in her hand, long and hard enough so that her fingers would remember the cool feel of it. She brought it to her face and pressed it against the hollow of her cheekbone and closed her eyes for a moment as she imprinted the shape into her consciousness. Then she put the firm yellow fruit to her mouth and ran her teeth over the rind to set the flavor free. It was bitter, but so, so sweet, and she would miss it more than she could ever begin to say.

She allowed herself a few short moments to catch her breath when she got back, then went upstairs to Tom's guest room. She found Bruce at home and glad to hear from her, a feeling she knew would not last as their talk progressed.

"Things are getting crazy," she said to his image on V.M.'s screen. "I don't know what we should do, whether we should—"

"Whoa, wait a minute," he interrupted her. "I don't like the sound of this. I'm not sure I understand—what are you *talking* about, what we should do?"

"DR SAM," she said in surprise. "It's coming back again."

There was an interval of silence, then Bruce said firmly, "Not here."

Janie let that declaration settle in before responding. It seemed impossible that he wouldn't have heard. "You're sure?"

"No one's saying anything about it."

"No news bulletins, tightened security?"

"Nothing."

Janie was confused. "That's very strange," she said. "But maybe it's not happening there. Maybe it's only here."

"Well, if it is in England, they're keeping it under wraps. There hasn't been a peep."

They were both quiet; Janie knew that Bruce would be watching her face on his screen just as closely as she watched his on her side of the ocean. As she waited for one or the other of them to speak, she could almost hear her own heartbeat picking up.

"So what does this mean for us?" Bruce finally managed to say.

It took an immense effort to keep her voice steady and even. "That it's coming to the point where we have to move quickly, if we're going to. If this new wave of DR SAM really takes hold, we're not going to be able to travel at all."

"Janie—what do you mean by 'if' we're going to . . . when did 'if' come into this discussion? I thought it was just 'when.' Is there something you're not telling me?"

She was quiet for a moment. He was the first man she'd loved since her husband had died. They'd been through hell and back together in the brief time they'd been united, most of that journey made on faith alone. They were going to see each other through the rest of their lives.

But there was no more holding it back. "Oh, Bruce, I . . . I . . ."

The old-fashioned transmitter on V.M. was working just beautifully, on a frequency that no one bothered with anymore, and the conversation between Janie and Bruce came in crystal-clear, but as it unfolded the listeners began to regret that they'd heard it.

Kristina sighed and said, "I think I'm going to cry."

The man at her side nodded and shook his head. "Tom's going to want to listen to this when he gets here later."

"Maybe we should edit it before he does. I don't think he'd want to hear it all."

"Maybe not. But he's going to like the gist of it."

"I'm not sure she managed to convince him, though," Kristina said. "He seemed pretty determined."

"We could screw things up for him, and make it completely impossible for him to get here. Have Frenchie post something negative."

"No—that's too extreme. We don't want to make him miserable for the rest of his life, we just want to keep him where he is."

The man gave that notion a moment's consideration, then said, "You're probably right. And if we did do something, Tom would get on us for messing with the natural order of things."

"But that's what we do," Kristina said. "That's the whole point."

"No. *Restoring* the natural order is the whole point."

"It's still interference."

"Hey, it's like everything else—there are two sides. Good, productive interference, or bad, counterproductive interference."

"Okay," Kristina said. "Then I guess we do nothing. Things will just have to work themselves out."

"They always do, whether we like it or not," the man said.

Janie came downstairs after her call to Bruce feeling as if she had a double-ended axe balanced on the top of her head, and any way she leaned or turned would bring disaster. But she entered the kitchen to find the table set, wine poured, and Tom standing over the stove, stirring a pot of something that smelled savory and wonderful. In the shadow of doom and destruction, he had made dinner.

The axe melted away. She admired the scene for a moment, then said, "God, you'd make a wonderful wife."

"There's a good reason for that. I've been my own wife for a long time."

"It looks like you've learned a lot."

He transferred the tempting concoction from the pot to a platter and brought it to the table. "I live to learn," he said as he set it down.

"That's one of the things I've always loved about you."

They traded a quick and silent understanding that expressed itself as a mutual smile. "Make yourself comfortable," he said. "You look a little stressed out."

She settled herself at the table. "I am."

He sat down opposite her. "I am too."

"Then you wear it better than I do."

"I just don't let my emotions show as easily," he said. "That's not necessarily a good thing."

"So show them. I want to hear about the things that trouble you. You listen to my tales of woe all the time."

"That sounds dangerously like a commitment, you know."

She opened her mouth to say something, then thought better of it.

"Sorry," he said with a grin. "You know I'm just going to keep chipping away at your resolve." Then the grin faded. "I'll tell you what's troubling me. I did some digging around today, through a lot of old corporate filing papers. I found out something that sheds a little light on this whole thing that you and Kristina are working on."

It was not at all what she'd expected. She'd been prepared for tales of the new plague. She sat up straight and stared at him. "What is it?"

He reached into his shirt pocket and pulled out a folded two-page document, which he handed over the platter. "I think it started out as a reasonable genetic project. But I guess things didn't quite work out the way they'd planned."

"But lots of projects don't work out the way we anticipate," she said as she accepted his offering.

"This is a pretty extreme example."

As she read the papers, the furrows in her brow deepened. She looked up with disbelief all over her face. "You've got to be kidding."

"I'm not. It's all right there."

"Dear God," she said. She looked up at him with an expression of consummate surprise. "It all fits, doesn't it? The shattering, the calcium absorption blockage . . . No wonder we couldn't find the patent holder."

"You may still not find out who it is."

"But with this—"

"Janie, there may not be time. At least not now. What you did today— it was a good start in getting ready, but it's a scratch on the surface, you know that. We have to finish preparing."

Janie wore a stricken look as she said, "Jesus, Tom, how can we prepare for something that eats everything in its path?"

"We figure out a way to stay out of its path." He glanced at the wall clock, then pushed himself away from the table. "Want to take a ride?"

*   *   *

Bruce didn't particularly like the fact that the meeting was taking place in one of the dirtiest, smokiest pubs still operating in London. But he hadn't set the rendezvous place, the man he'd contacted had.

"Cash only," the man had said. All the way there he'd been nervous to be carrying such a large amount in negotiable bills. He'd grown so accustomed to simply pulling out a card. Cash was a burden, with its displacement, its germs, and its stealability.

His "date" was late, quite significantly, and he was just about to get up and leave when someone tapped him on the shoulder from behind.

He turned. He'd been expecting an unsavory-looking character in unkempt clothing, someone who smelled of alcohol and reeked of illegality. Someone far more marginal than the person who greeted him. Someone far more male.

"You're Merrill Jenkins?"

The petite, attractive, well-groomed woman smiled and said, "Oh, good heavens, no. I'm his assistant. I've been sent in to fetch you. Mr. Jenkins is waiting outside with a car. So if you'll follow me, please?"

Bruce gathered up his jacket and umbrella and followed the young lady out of the pub, to the envious stares of the other customers, who had a different notion of what might be transpiring. They assumed that Bruce would be paying this young woman to lavish certain attentions on him. What they didn't know was that he would instead be paying her employer, rather a bit more than he would've paid for the pleasure of the lady's company, to make all of his visa problems disappear.

Just what you'll need for overnight, he'd told her, saying they could come back tomorrow for the rest. She threw a few things into a knapsack he'd given her. Change of clothes, a sweater, a nightgown, a few toiletries . . .

Her shoes . . . the last remaining pair of a once proud collection. She'd taken them off earlier and put them under the bed in the guest room, just before talking with Bruce. But they were not visible in a quick glance, so she got down on her hands and knees and looked under the edge of the bedspread.

There they were. She reached in and pulled them out, and as she dragged them across the wood floor, she heard a crinkling sound.

Stuck between her two shoes was a mint wrapper.

She stared at it in her hand for a few seconds, then whispered, "Oh, my God . . ."

*   *   *

An ambulance passed them as they drove out of town in the early evening. They exchanged nervous glances as the flashing red lights appeared
over the crest of a small hill.

What was that wrapper doing under the bed in the guest room?

She searched her brain for an occasion when Kristina had been in that
room. She could not recall a single time—they had always worked in
Tom's home office. She felt confused and betrayed, and very tired.

The ambulance passed, and the lights disappeared behind them.
"Those things make me nervous all of a sudden," she said.

*They must have some sort of relationship I know nothing about, some-
thing they've hidden; no wonder they seemed so comfortable with each other
so quickly.*

"They should. We should all be nervous. About a lot of things."

And when the second ambulance passed them a few minutes later, she
whispered, "This is not a test."

"No. But we are all going to be tested."

He would not tell her where he was taking her. "I want it to be a
surprise," he said.

Janie wondered how she could be any more surprised than she already
was.

"Just please trust me," he said.

Oh, how I want to . . . but . . .

She picked up the small bag at her feet and placed it on her lap. She
clutched it protectively to her and said, "You know, this is just about all I
still have in the world. A few clothes back at your house, and the things I
put in your safe, but that's about it."

After a pause, Tom said, "Do you miss everything?"

It seemed a silly question to her. "I miss the familiarity of it all."

"I think things are going to feel a little unfamiliar for all of us for a
while. Until this cloud passes again."

"You make it sound like you're sure it will pass."

"Everything passes. Question is, when."

Please, oh, please, let this distrust pass, and quickly. She leaned back
against the headrest and closed her eyes as the car moved through the
thickening darkness. "There is something I'll miss," she said after a minute.

"What?"

"My garden. I've put a lot of years into making it my own. I'll miss it
next spring if I don't rebuild there."

"You probably won't."

She looked at him curiously. "What makes you think that?"

"I don't think you'll be able to, at least not next spring. If DR SAM comes back with even half the force it had last time, rebuilding your house will be the last thing you'll worry about."

"You're scaring me, Tom."

"I mean to."

Janie stayed quiet for a moment after that, then said, "I'd feel a lot better if you'd tell me where we're going."

"Almost there," he said. He pointed ahead to a road sign emerging from the darkness of the road.

The headlights lit it, made it glow. It said BURNING ROAD, 5 MILES.

Shocked and dumbfounded, Janie stared at the assembly of people who greeted her, some familiar, some unknown, at least by appearance. When she found her voice again, she whispered, "I don't get it. Did I just walk into *Atlas Shrugged*?"

John Sandhaus looked around the room, a huge grin on his face, then brought his gaze back to Janie again. "No architects, no robber barons." He glanced at Kristina. "You see any?"

"No," the girl said, "but now *I* don't get it."

"You wouldn't," Janie said. "You're too young. But you'll read the book someday. From the way things seem to be shaping up, I'm guessing you'll have time this winter." She shook her head in disbelief. "I am just so—*stunned* by this."

She looked from face to face: John Sandhaus, his wife, Cathy, their huddled children, hanging on their parents' legs. Kristina, looking youthfully eager. Linda Horn—the butterfly lady—serene and regal, and beside her a man Janie took to be her husband.

Another man who'd stayed off to one side now came forward and offered his hand. "Jason Davis," he said. "Former owner of this fair establishment."

"Former?"

All eyes went to Tom. "And still the owner of record, as far as the outside world is concerned," Tom said. He put a hand gently on Janie's shoulder. "Welcome to Camp Meir."

Janie looked back at Jason Davis again. "What would you have done if I'd said I wanted to come see this place when you asked?"

"I'd have made the arrangements," he said. "We can make it look pretty rustic when we want to."

The room they were in, which had obviously once been the central meeting hall, was anything but rustic. It had a peaked ceiling with skylights and quiet fans suspended from long supports. They were twirling rhythmically overhead, fluttering the leaves of the plants as if they'd been touched by a light and tender breeze. But all along the center ridge of the ceiling, and all along the edge where the walls met the sloped roof there were drapes, rolled and tied, no doubt part of some elaborate set that could be activated quickly to fool a surprise visitor. There were windows everywhere, separated by just enough wall to slide them into if necessary. The air had the same faultless climate that she'd experienced in Linda Horn's cabin in the woods, cooler than her skin and just perfectly moist.

She turned toward the former camp nurse. "No butterflies?"

"I really can't bring them until we're sure we won't be opening up wide anymore. But I will, when the time comes."

"Soon, I think," Janie said.

Linda made a simple nod of her head. Her voice was subdued. "I think you might be right."

Then Janie turned to Tom. "You keep surprising me."

"I'm not done yet."

"I believe you." She let her eyes wander around the room again, whispering, "Incredible," as she took in the cavernous space. "So," she said when her gaze came to rest on Tom again, "is this that utopian paradise you were talking about, where we'll all hide out to weather the coming plague?"

The question got a nervous little laugh from the assembled.

But Tom's answer was deadly serious. "Yes, in fact, it is."

I t was decided, after much pained and heated debate, that the entire army would assemble in the morning and go to the proposed meeting place, and wait there in the hope that Karle would show or that Navarre would lead his troops out. So the lieutenants went out to the meadow to speak to the soldiers, to tell them that Karle had not returned, to advise them that when the bugler next gave the call it would be well before dawn, and that they should be prepared to rise and take their last bits of food and water, and gather their weapons and armor for the short march to the Compiègne Road.

But Kate would not go to bed; she sat on a hill overlooking the road and waited in the darkness, listening for the pounding of his horse, the most precious sound she could hope to hear. She would not hear of abandoning her watch, and finally, in keeping with his promise to Karle, Alejandro took her by the arm and literally dragged her back to the longhouse.

There he wiped away her tears and held her in his arms until her sobbing finally stopped, and she fell asleep against his shoulder from sheer, draining exhaustion. And as her heart broke and her hopes dissipated, so did his. *Who knew this fathering would never end?* he thought as he cradled the woman-child against his breast, feeling every gnaw of her pain as if it were his own. Who could predict that the daughter, not even of his own blood, would forever own such a commanding piece of him?

Pieces of him were scattered all over Europa. He had left a piece in Cervere, his hometown in the starkly beautiful Aragon region of Spain. A good piece of his heart lay in England, with Adele, and in Avignon, where he had last seen Hernandez, and where he now hoped, against all reason, that his aging mother and father had found safety. A resentful piece of his mind rested in Paris, with the despised but admired de Chauliac, and would forever call to him against his will. And here, on his shoulder, was the girl who owned the biggest piece of all. The piece that could finally break him.

He closed his eyes, and propped against a mound of straw, he dozed, his arms tightly around his pregnant daughter, whose husband was now in the hands of a man who had proved himself in the past to resort to the most despicable sort of savagery to get what he wanted. He dreamed, in his half-sleep, of Carlos Alderón, but this time, instead of himself, the giant blacksmith was chasing Guillaume Karle.

The clarion called in what felt like an instant, and he jolted awake from his short sleep to find Kate still leaning against him. Carefully, he pulled himself away from her and laid her down on the straw. He stripped away his shirt and washed himself, and then dressed in his roughest, sturdiest clothes. He took one last look at the contents of his physician's bag, and found it wanting in fine implements, but in general adequate for the quick attention required by the wounds of war. He checked the pile of bandages and wished it were quadruple what it stood. He looked in every vessel and pot and cistern to see that they were full of clean, filtered water. He looked to the ceiling and made note of the herbs that would promote healing and diminish pain. He checked his supply of laudanum and sighed in deep worry. And when he was satisfied that the preparations were as complete as they could possibly be, he wet a cloth in clean water and wiped the crusted tears from his daughter's eyes, and as he did so she awakened.

Her first pained words were "Has he returned?" Alejandro put a gentle hand on her forehead and smoothed back her hair. He shook his head sadly. "No, daughter, he has not."

She said nothing, but rose up and went about her own brief toilette. On the stable side of the longhouse they heard the comings and goings of the troops as they took their simple arms from the store. Lieutenants and garrison leaders rode in and out and among the troops, instructing them how to line up, and how to shape those lines into fighting formations. Alejandro and Kate came out of the longhouse as the army was just beginning to move. As one of the lieutenants rode by, Alejandro stopped him and said, "If we come to battle, bring only those wounded who might be saved to the longhouse. We have not the space to take in a man who will only soak the straw with his blood and then expire."

The lieutenant nodded and said he would spread the word among his fellows, then he rode to the beginning of the formation to join his compatriots.

"We shall watch from the hill," Kate said, and before he could protest, she was drawing Alejandro along by the hand. If he closed his eyes, he could feel her hand grow smaller, and his own less rough, and the sound of marching was replaced by the sound of her childish laughter. But when he opened them again, the sights and sounds of impending war came crashing in, forcing his face into an involuntary grimace. They ran alongside the advancing troops, and separated from them only when they came to the path that led to the peak. They hurried through the cool damp woods until they came to the pinnacle, there to wait and watch.

And when finally assembled, Guillaume Karle's *armée des Jacques* was a breathtaking and awesome sight. One could not tell, on first glance, that they were little more than dressed-up paupers, for they held their heads high and their weapons ready and waved their ragged banners and shouted passionate slogans of war. At the head of the long phalanx were the riders with their lances, and behind them the spearsmen. Following the spears were the archers with their rough bows, and after that the men on foot who carried swords. They in turn were followed by those who had only clubs, or maces roughly fashioned, and at the tail end, their number greatest of all, were the men who had nothing but knives and their bare hands.

As the sun came over the treetops, it settled on this half-mile of humanity, who waited, in near silence, in trembling readiness, for their king to return.

Before the sun had completely cleared the tallest of the trees, the call came from one of the lookouts.

"Army approaching!"

A buzz of excitement started at the beginning of the rebel assembly and worked its way steadily backward until even the lowest clubman knew that Charles of Navarre was leading his troops in their direction.

And from their perch on the hill, Kate and Alejandro saw the army of Navarre coming down the road, but at its front was a separate party of six or seven men on horses. It seemed an eternity until the party came close enough for any detail to be seen. Alejandro cupped his hands around his eyes, but it did not do enough to sharpen his vision.

"I cannot see yet, Père!" Kate cried.

"Nor can I! They are still too far. But wait . . . something is happening, I think." He shaded his eyes more carefully. "The army itself is coming to a halt. The smaller party is moving forward still."

His vision had always been better than hers—a bit of difficulty in seeing things far away seemed to run in her bloodline, and it had touched her, though not as cruelly as some others. And so Alejandro remained quiet, saying nothing of his growing sense of dread. The flag of the Baron de Coucy was held high by a well-armored standard bearer, and behind him rode a young man whom Alejandro took to be the Baron himself. There were three other riders, all beautifully horsed and handsomely armed with swords and maces and spears. And amid them all was Guillaume Karle. They had given him a plumed helmet. Alejandro held his breath and watched.

But soon enough the troops themselves saw what Alejandro wished to keep from his daughter, and began to shout, "*Vive le roi des Jacques!*" She clung to his arm and begged for details. "*Tell* me, Père! Oh, curse my deficiency of vision!"

"They are saying Karle is among them, daughter," he whispered, "and I think it true."

She said not a word, but turned and ran down the hill, giving him no choice but to follow.

When they reached the head of the phalanx the lieutenants were waiting, their horses prancing nervously, and watching the small party as it slowly advanced. *Why do they not just ride forth boldly?* Alejandro wondered. The lieutenants seemed as confused as he, but wisely held their troops in readiness. Kate and Alejandro worked their way forward along the edge of the wood until they were in close range of the horse contingent of their own army, a position from which Kate could see for herself what happened ahead.

The party kept advancing, slowly, pace by pace. Kate turned back to Alejandro and said happily, "Oh, Père, it *is* Karle! My prayers have been answered, for they have brought him back to me!" Then she faced back toward the party again.

He put a hand on her shoulder; he could feel her trembling slightly. And then the riders stopped, all but Karle, and as they watched, breath held, the physician felt his daughter stiffen underneath his touch. He squinted for a better view; something was not right. Karle wobbled in the saddle, but his horse moved forward, almost of its own volition, as if Karle had no control of it. Alejandro drew in a breath and put his arms around Kate's waist, clasping his two hands together. His heartbeat accelerated until he could feel it in his temples. He watched; everyone watched.

Finally the confused animal stopped short, and Karle slumped forward. His hands seemed strangely fixed to a particular spot on the saddle. The plumed helmet came tumbling forward. It crashed to the ground and rolled around noisily, for there was nothing there to hold it on.

Kate screamed and wailed and tried to break free of her father's grip as the headless body of her husband was bucked around on the frightened horse, and only when several of Karle's lieutenants rode forward to restrain the animal, shielding her view of the horrible sight, did her knees finally buckle and give. She slumped to the ground, near fainting, so Alejandro picked her up in his arms and ran through the forest edge back toward the longhouse. He crashed through the woods, his vision blurred with tears, and as he ran toward shelter he heard the clarion ring and the rebels shriek, and the pounding of horses' hooves as Karle's *armée des Jacques* surged forward to avenge the cruel slaughter of their leader. And soon Navarre's troops could also be heard, responding to what both Navarre and Coucy would later claim was a direct attack against them though an alliance had been offered.

The din of battle became overwhelming as Navarre's mounted troops mixed in among the *Jacques* footsoldiers. Alejandro's throat burned with each gasping breath in his wild dash to bring Kate to safety. His chest ached, and his arms were seared with the pain of not being able to release a burden that was nearly beyond his strength; Kate was as tall as he, and it seemed to him as he hauled her forward that they might be of a weight. But his feet were miraculously sure and he finally reached the longhouse.

He sat her down on a bench and shook her face, none too gently, to rouse her. She opened her eyes and looked up into his with the most heart-rending expression of sorrow he had ever seen. She began to wail again, so he took her in his arms and held her to his chest, and tried to absorb her pain. Her body, though it was racked in sobs, felt as rigid as a corpse and would not yield to his embrace.

The sounds of the skirmish grew closer, and Alejandro knew that before long they would be deluged with wounded, bleeding men crying out for mercy, for some of whom the best mercy would be swift death.

He loosened his embrace of Kate and took her firmly by the shoulders. "Daughter," he said, "your grief is immense. I know this. But you can be a widow tomorrow. Right now you are needed as the midwife you were educated to be."

"Oh, Père, oh, Père," she sobbed, "he is gone . . . my husband is slain."

He spoke firmly, but with aching sympathy. "And he will never come back. From this moment forward that is your burden." Then he softened his voice. "Adele has not been with me for many years. And I still feel the sting of it. But I have you. We have each other. And soon we will have your child. And we must act now to be sure that your child has a world to grow in."

The grief never left her face and she was terribly dazed, but she valiantly wiped away her tears and stood up, and father and daughter held each other in what would be the last quiet moments of that day. And when they let go of each other, Alejandro went to the door of the longhouse and opened it. He looked outside, through the trees toward the road, and all the breath rushed out of him.

The piles of wounded were already two deep in the mud of the road beyond the longhouse; as they had wept inside, the wounded had either made their way back and collapsed, or were brought there and deposited. Their wails, once the door was open, could be heard clearly, and Alejandro looked back at Kate with a shake of his head. "We must treat them where they lie," he said.

They gathered up everything they could carry and made their way to the roadside, and one by one they began laying out the wounded in an orderly fashion, neat rows, one body close to the next. Some had already died, and those they carried to a clear spot beneath the trees, where they were just piled without regard for the proximity to the next body. Those who required immediate and extreme attention were laid in one row, those whose wounds would not kill them immediately were laid in another, and those whose wounds were beyond hope in yet another.

They started with those in most desperate need of care, and as each new victim came in Alejandro took a quick look to assess the wounds and ordered the man to be laid out in the appropriate row. Amputations, without laudanum, were done in mere seconds, and the wounds tied off with the piece of garment no longer needed after the removal of the limb. The severed limbs themselves were brought to the pile of bodies, lest their draining blood make the road into a river of red mud. Alejandro told Kate to go into the longhouse and bring out faggots enough to make a fire, and then to light it with a coal from the hearth, and when it was burning lustily they dug out red coals and used them to cauterize the bleeding limbs.

Alejandro took the sword of a fallen man and thrust it into the fire, withdrawing it only when it was glowing red. He attended to a hundred gut wounds by pressing the sword against the gaping holes, and thus stopped the bleeding and thwarted the putrefaction that would otherwise surely follow. After each use, he would thrust the sword into the fire again, to purify it. Often, the wounded wanted nothing more than for someone to pray for them. They sought only to die in company, not alone in the mud, trampled by horses' hooves and sneered at by the soldiers of Navarre. So Kate would kneel at the man's side and softly whisper, "Hail Mary, full of grace, the Lord is with thee," and it was laudanum for the souls as they departed to what peace lay on the other side.

The hours passed like minutes, and the wounded numbered more than a thousand, when Alejandro heard the insistent pounding of hooves from the forest on the west side of the road. He stood up from dressing a wound to see who was coming, for it was surely more than one rider. The riders were too far yet to see, but the fresh sound of the animals meant that they could not be friendly. The horses of *les Jacques* would all be exhausted by now, many surely fallen. He looked around for Kate, who he saw across the road, praying for yet another dying man.

"Kate!" he cried out.

She looked up from her patient.

"Take shelter in the longhouse! These riders are not ours. Go, *now!*"

"But, Père . . ."

"Now!"

She picked up her bloody skirt and dashed through the trees to the longhouse.

Just moments after she disappeared from view the Baron de Coucy and Charles of Navarre himself rode out of the forest. They led their horses through the rows of wounded, taking little care not to step on those already down, and headed straight for Alejandro.

"Are you the medicus?"

He stared straight ahead in silence.

"Are you the medicus? Karle told us of a wife." Getting no answer, Navarre glanced toward the longhouse and back again, and saw Alejandro's face tighten. "He said her father was a physician. Answer me, man, or I shall ride through these wounded with a vengeance."

Very quietly, Alejandro said, "I am."

Charles of Navarre jumped down off his horse. With the baron close by, his hand on his sword, the king of Navarre strode purposefully toward Alejandro. He pulled up his sleeve to expose a deep gash on his arm. "You will treat this wound, then. It is my sword arm, and I cannot be disfigured."

The wound was not so deep that Navarre stood to lose the arm, but Alejandro knew that it was causing the man considerable pain. He took the arm in his hands and examined it more closely. "The best treatment for this is cautery and stitching." He pointed toward the waning fire, which wanted more fuel. "You are welcome to plunge your arm into the fire to prevent putrefaction. Now, if you will leave me, there are dying men to be attended to."

He felt the tip of Coucy's sword under his chin. "His Majesty has requested that you treat his wound. These peasant swine will wait. And die, for all one cares. But the king will be treated."

"I must have your promise first. That you will not harm my daughter. Or me. I am sorely needed by these unfortunates."

Navarre sighed, almost casually. Alejandro knew it was costing him considerable self-control not to cry out. "I gave my promise already to Karle that I would not harm his wife. I don't suppose it will harm me to make the same promise for her father. Very well, you have my word on both counts." He extended the arm, and grimaced slightly. "Now, this wound, if you please."

"I have no laudanum."

"Laudanum be damned. I do not wish to have my wits dulled at my hour of greatest triumph. Just sew me up and I shall be on my way to celebrate my victory."

He looked around; there were no rebels who stood to die without immediate help. "Follow me," he said, and he led them through the woods.

When Kate saw the royal emblem on his mantle, her face became a twist of rage and anger, and she started to rush forward, until she saw the sword at Alejandro's back.

"We will treat the king's wound, and then he shall leave us," Alejandro said.

With visible difficulty, she stood back.

"You will bring thread and a needle. Plunge the needle into the fire."

He washed the wound with clean water and picked out the dirt introduced by the sword that had made the cut. He sutured it carefully and neatly, while Navarre dripped sweat onto his own mantle as he fought against the excruciating pain. Alejandro dressed the wound with herbs and tied a linen bandage around it. All this he did with the point of Coucy's sword pressed up against his liver.

And when it was done, he said, "After three days, remove the bandage and pour wine over the wound, white wine if you have, then wrap a fresh bandage around it. After a fortnight, you may cut out the thread. Be careful to remove all of it, or what remains inside the wound may fester and we will have done all this for naught. Rest this arm for a turn of the moon, so the freshly made skin will not tear. Your only disfigurement will be the marks of the sutures. And the scar, of course. But your arm will once again be a sword arm if you do what I tell you to do."

Navarre rolled down his sleeve and said, "Well done, Physician. You are fit to serve a king, I think." He turned to Kate. "Now, if the lady will come with us . . ."

"But what of your promise?" Alejandro hissed.

"I promised not to harm her," Navarre said with a smile. "But I did not promise not to take her. She is comely, and will suit me well, I think. I like a woman with fire, especially in my bed."

Kate rushed toward him shrieking, *"Murderer, betrayer!"*

Coucy caught her by the arm and twisted her around, and pressed his knife under her chin.

"Let her go," Alejandro begged, "take me instead, I can be of great use to you."

The distraction of his pleas gave Kate enough time to reach down into her stocking and pull out her own knife, and before Coucy knew it she spread her legs and cut right through her own skirt with the fine sharp instrument, the tip of which came to rest barely a finger's breadth from his manhood.

"You may kill me," she said, "but as you do, I will take all your future children with me. You must believe me when I tell you that I care not if I live or die right now."

Coucy believed her. He pulled his knife away from her chin and held it away, and she rushed away from him, into Alejandro's open arms.

As he went through the door, Coucy said, "A shame that Karle had to die. He never had the chance to savor your spirit. A pity."

"Murderer," she hissed after him, and then she collapsed.

The mint wrapper might as well have been a boulder, so immense was its presence in her pocket.

"Come with me," Kristina said. She took Janie's hand and pulled on it, as a child might. "I want to show you the lab."

Janie glanced quickly at Tom. He nodded and said, "I have some things to take care of. Go ahead."

At some cost, Janie was managing to keep her discomfort hidden, but as Kristina started to talk about what they would be seeing she found herself more willing. "There's a lab here?" she asked with genuine surprise.

"There's everything here. You won't believe this place. But you're going to love it."

Soon Janie found herself being led through the gathered people in the main room to an exterior door, and when they stepped outside the controlled climate into the night, the air felt foul and heavy in contrast to the light cleanliness of what she'd breathed within. It was just the sort of thick, wet air that minute floating things loved.

She stopped, midstep, and stood still.

It passes through the very air, and so invades the corpus . . .

Alejandro's words.

For a moment, she experienced a panic akin to being underwater, as if she were about to fill her lungs with something they were not intended to hold and could not survive. She took in as small a breath as she could and plunged forward after Kristina, her hasty steps crunching over the gravel path with uneven clumsiness. She did not release the half-breath until they were safely inside another building. As the door closed behind her again, shutting out the foulness, she expelled the air aloud to rid herself of the imagined contamination.

Kristina continued to be oblivious of it all—there was too much else to think about, and she gave herself over to it with youthful vibrance. She led the way down a softly lit passageway, chattering as she progressed about all the wonderful things they had yet to see. Janie struggled along behind her, feeling light-headed and balancing with one hand against the wall as she walked. Finally Kristina stopped in front of one particular door, and with obvious pride, she said, "Here it is."

The lights inside the room went on automatically when she opened the door, shedding a bright luminance that looked like filtered sunlight and caressed Janie back to a state of balance. She stored it against the darkness to come and stepped into the modern laboratory beyond the door.

She was flabbergasted by what she saw. She stood in the open doorway of the large white room as her eyes roamed from item to item, admiring the rich assortment of instruments and machines and computers contained therein. It was a playground worthy of even the most demanding researcher.

"This is . . . remarkable," she said with great reverence.

"I know. It's a wonderful place to work. This is where I extracted the DNA sequence."

On one counter there rested a cardboard box with its flaps opened out. Dribs of shredded excelsior revealed that it had yet to be unpacked, so Janie walked over and glanced inside. It was filled with unopened smaller boxes. Janie knew, by the corporate names printed on their sealed flaps, that each one would contain some wonder of technological manufacturing, perhaps an instrument or a gauge. Janie picked up one of the cartons and read the specifics of the contents, which turned out to be, not surprisingly, the best of that particular item that money could buy. She replaced it carefully with its companions and said, "You aren't even completely set up yet. I can't imagine what this lab will be like when you do get everything in place and working."

"It'll be unbelievable. I can't wait."

Janie shook her head slowly back and forth, an expression of her disbelief. "Remarkable," she said. "Wonderful. And I can see now why you managed to get that work done so quickly."

"Speaking of which," Kristina said, "there it is. I mean, *he* is. What's left, anyway." She nodded in the direction of a small ice chest on one of the workstations.

Janie went to the chest and opened it. Inside was a stoppered beaker with perhaps an inch of pale yellow-gold liquid in it. Janie picked up the beaker and regarded it for a moment, then set it back down in the ice chest. "You know," she said, "this is just the most amazing thing you've done here."

"*We've* done," Kristina corrected her. "If you hadn't come up with the original material, I couldn't have multiplied it."

After a long pause, Janie said, "I suppose you're right. It was a cooperative effort."

"The first of many, I hope."

Janie did not respond to Kristina's kind words in the way she imagined Kristina would want her to. She stayed almost expressionless when she said, "I have no doubt that you and I will have a lot of interaction to look forward to." Then she glanced downward, in slight sadness. "But I'm feeling very frustrated because I know these boys aren't going to get the rest of what they need. Not until everything calms down again. Some of them may not make it through the—the disruption, despite what we were able to do for them."

They both knew it was true; it was a very sobering thought. "There's not going to be much we can do about that. We've done what we had to do, what we could. At least now they'll have a chance. And that's what really matters, to me, anyway. The rest will be up to—whoever is out there to do it. But as soon as the serum takes, and the proper genetic string is absorbed, the danger of additional broken bones will really be reduced. And their surgeries will have a chance of being successful. And then, when the next wave is over, there'll be a place to start from."

"There may not be any 'whoevers' left out there. The 'whoevers' got hit pretty hard last time."

Kristina looked at her sadly. "I know. But that's out of our hands. Completely."

She left the lab feeling as if she'd had the stuffing knocked out of her, a feeling she knew she was going to have to get used to. She rejoined Tom in the cavernous main meeting room, and by the time he'd finished showing her around the complex it was nearly midnight.

"I'm almost speechless," she whispered as she walked by his side. "But there's something you need to consider . . . if people find out about this place, you're going to be inundated."

"That's why we've been so quiet about it. To the outside world it looks like just another summer camp."

"People will try to crash it. You know that."

"They'll have to get past an electronic fence. Linda Horn's husband was more than an energy engineer—he was a weapons expert when he served in the military. So now we have a slew of tranquilizer rifles, ready to go. One decent shot will drop an intruder in about six seconds."

"But even if you manage to keep it quiet, there'll be other people you want and need, and the population will grow—where are you going to put everyone?"

"We have six hundred acres here."

"Six hundred! Jesus, Tom, how did you get all this land?"

"The camp came with a good chunk of it, but I managed to round up the rest through what you might call quiet acquisition."

"Meaning?"

"Meaning that there are a few town clerks with very nice retirement accounts in the surrounding area. Every time someone got sick or died, or a piece of property went into probate, I'd get a call."

"And the money for all this came from . . . ?"

"I've settled a couple of pretty impressive lawsuits." He smiled and added, "Quietly."

"But six hundred acres—that's a small town!"

"Sometimes it feels like it."

"Should I be calling you Mr. Mayor?"

"No," he laughed. "Not me. I'm hoping the place never gets so big that we need a government. The meetings are already tricky enough."

"Well," she said, "you've only got yourself to blame for that, with Sandhaus here."

He let a moment pass, then said, "Actually, the most problematic one is Kristina. When we're making decisions as a group, she's always very vocal. I think it's her youthful notion that she can change the world—we all had it at one time or another. She's having hers in troubling times, though, so she gets pretty enthusiastic. Sometimes it takes a long time to explain things to her so she really understands."

Janie stopped walking and took firm hold of his arm. "I know you know her—beyond all this, I mean."

He looked her directly in the eye. "What makes you think that?"

Out came the mint wrapper. She held it in her open palm, and his eyes went straight to it.

"This," she said. "I found it under the bed in the guest room. It's like a fingerprint for her. She leaves them all over the place."

In the pause that followed, Janie saw Tom's expression soften and then sadden. He seemed to drift for a moment before he spoke. "You're right," he said, "I do."

And then he was quiet, leaving Janie to push for an explanation. "Care to elaborate?"

"I'd like to think about what I'm going to say before I get started with it. Right now I'll just tell you that I told her mother I would take care of her."

"Her mother—so Kristina's not, uh . . . your, uh . . ."

He gave her a hard look. "My, uh—*what*?"

"Girlfriend, I guess."

"Janie! How could you even think such a thing?"

"Well, you hid your relationship from me entirely—why would you do that unless there was something about it you didn't want me to know?"

"Okay, so I did hide it. But that doesn't mean it's what you seem to think it is."

After that stern declaration, Janie stayed quiet for a moment.

"Her mother is dead?" she finally said.

Tom sighed. "Yes."

"You knew her mother—well?"

"I did. Very well." He took Janie's hand in his own and started walking toward the main building. "It's getting late."

She decided not to press him further, and followed along. "I know. Very late. I don't know how I'm still awake. I must be running on adrenaline."

"If you're hungry I could make you something."

"No, thanks, you don't need to go to any trouble for me. And I think I'm too wired to eat, anyway. I need to wind down."

He slowed his pace, then came to a stop again on the path. Somehow in his presence the heavy outside air seemed less menacing. "Want some help?" he asked. "I'm pretty strung out myself." He pulled her closer and wrapped his arms around her, then whispered in her ear, "I have this big tub in my bathroom."

She hesitated, then said, "What will everyone else think?"

"Whatever they want to think. I'm not concerned about anyone else right now. Just you and me."

"What about Kristina? Tom, I know you're important to her . . . I don't want to upset her."

Tom laughed softly. "You won't."

* * *

Janie leaned her back against Tom's chest and rested her head on his shoulder, and together they let the warm water soothe away the gritty, insistent coat of trouble that seemed to have settled on everything around them.

She snuggled closer and in response he tightened his arms around her. "This must have been what it was like back then . . ." she whispered, "in Alejandro's time. During the Black Death. Everything fell apart then too. No one knew what was happening—it was total chaos."

"Oh, I think we know a little more about what's happening now than they did then."

"Well, we know what causes our plague."

"They didn't?"

"No one had a clue. Except Alejandro, of course. He figured out that it was associated with rats somehow. But no one would believe him, anyway."

"Did anyone believe the prophets of doom when they said we should shut everything down in this country a few years ago?"

"No. And I don't know if it would've made a difference. We can't do anything more about our plague than they could about theirs. Our controls are useless."

He dipped a sponge in the warm water and squeezed it out on Janie's arm. "You said the controls made a difference in England."

"When I first got there it felt like they did, and I thought it was different, like they'd survived DR SAM better. Everything was so orderly and no one was screaming about the government being too heavy-handed, or not heavy-handed enough, not like it was here. But it started to feel tight pretty fast. I was glad to get home."

"I remember."

She turned to the side slightly and slipped an arm around him. "I'm so sorry," she said.

"For what?"

"For what I brought you when you came to get me."

"Janie, you can't change that, and you didn't know."

"No, Tom, please, just hear what I have to say. Bruce was—so necessary for me. He came into my life at a time when I really needed someone like him. It was such a coincidence that I'd known him years before, but that was so brief, really, and he was so different then."

"There's nothing like an old flame," Tom said. He kissed her lightly on the top of her head. "I speak with some authority on this subject."

She sighed and snuggled closer. "I think that's what made it easy for me to connect with him—not that we were flames, but he was so familiar—and he was very willing. But when Caroline was finally well enough to go home, we talked things out and I thought we were going to go our separate ways. Then when I got on the plane, he was there and it made me feel so happy . . . I guess I just didn't think about what it really meant."

"And now what?"

"I don't know. It's been a year of long distance, we've seen each other three times in that period, but never any place where we could really spend good time together. Iceland was beautiful and wonderful, but we argued—over the stupidest things. And then I got called home . . . it's been one frustration after another."

"So what do you want to do?"

"I already did something. I told him not to come. At least not for a while—I think it would be better." She turned to face him. "And that would give you and me some time to try to figure things out."

He smiled and took her chin in his hand and pulled her face toward him. When Janie had pulled back from the deep, satisfying kiss, she spoke again. "What is it with us and catastrophes? We have the worst timing." She dripped water from the tip of her finger onto the skin of his chest, and watched the rivulets slide down between the hairs. "I suppose one thing works out about this timing, at least, although I feel incredibly guilty even saying it—Bruce won't be able to get in right now. They'll probably start shutting the airports down again from international flights."

Tom was quiet for a moment, then said, "He will if he leaves right away."

Janie separated herself from Tom's embrace and sat up in the tub. "What do you mean?"

"I got a message this afternoon, Janie. His visa came through."

Janie stared at the steaming mound of scrambled eggs with a mix of horror and revulsion. "You can't be serious," she said to Linda Horn.

"They caught that chicken," she said. "And these eggs are from our own henhouse. Organic, range-fed, one hundred percent unblemished."

Janie sat down at the table, still looking reluctant. "You're sure?"

"Watch."

Linda helped herself to a portion of eggs, then sat down next to Janie and began to eat them. "See? I eat them."

"You're a brave woman."

"No, I'm not. I just know they're okay. It wasn't the genetic change in the chicken itself that was a problem—and it's almost impossible to absorb an altered gene by eating it. But they weren't sure of that back then. The foundation people were frantic, because the work could be connected to them if an investigator was persistent enough, as you've been. What they did was supposed to be precautionary and though they didn't know it at the time, completely unnecessary. If they'd just left it all alone, no one would have been any wiser and all those boys would be fine. But they didn't. They tried to cover their tracks. And in doing so, they created a much bigger problem."

Janie watched Linda eat for a few seconds, then said, "You knew it was an agricultural gene, a chicken gene, for God's sake. Why didn't you just tell me? You might've saved me a lot of trouble."

Linda put down her fork and wiped her mouth with a napkin. "I'm sorry for your trouble," she said quietly. "We all are. We had no idea of the things that would happen to you. I'm just glad you weren't inside that house at the time."

"I am too."

"It had to look like someone just stumbled onto it—I wasn't kidding when I said I'd been waiting for someone to start looking into this. If any one of us had gone forward with this information, we might have uncovered our group. And that would've been a very bad thing. We have a lot of work to do yet."

"So you just kept putting things in my path, things for me to discover."

"We wouldn't have come to you with those things if you hadn't made the initial discovery on your own. We just kept feeding your curiosity. We were all starting to laugh about what an insatiable beast your curiosity is."

"To think all this happened so someone could extract the calcium out of eggshells more easily," Janie said sadly. "How incredibly inane. How trivial. One bird gets loose and dozens of boys are horribly affected." She looked up from her plate into Linda's eyes and said, "Where was God when all this was happening?"

"God only knows," Linda said simply.

After a quiet moment, Janie went on with her queries. "And the call from Jameson . . ."

"One of us, of course. But you could've just brushed it off. You didn't, though."

She smiled weakly. "It's a habit I might have to change."

They heard a door opening and turned to see Tom approaching from the far side of the main room. He got himself a cup of coffee and came to

the table. As he was pulling out his chair, Linda gave Janie a conspiratorial wink and got up to leave.

"Good morning," she said to Tom, then, "I'll see you later, I hope?" to
Janie.

"Don't know yet," Janie said. "There are some things I need to do
outside."

"Well, hurry back," she said. "We need you." Then she left Tom and
Janie alone at the table.

They traded glances, and after a few seconds of discomfort Janie said,
"Bruce wasn't there when I called. I left a message for him to contact me
right away."

"Oh, boy."

"I know. I can only hope he isn't already on his way. It would be like
him to do that—he likes to surprise me."

Tom drew in a long, worried breath, then expelled it slowly. "Well,
there isn't much we can do about it now. And over the next few days
what we can do will get less and less, I guarantee it." He sighed heavily
and handed over the front page he'd printed from a Net newspaper. The
headline read: MARTIAL LAW REINSTATED.

With a pained and frightened look on her face, Janie scanned the first
few lines of the article below it. She looked up at Tom, her brow tight and
said, "I don't really need to read it all. I know what it's going to say."

Tom nodded gravely. "Same as last time. The plague era begins.
Again."

"I guess it does. There's a lot to do. I don't know if I'll be able to do it
all today. It might take two."

"You can let it all go, and just stay here."

She looked him in the eye. "No, I can't."

He smiled sadly and squeezed her hand. "You have gasoline, I hope?"

"Close to a full tank."

"Good." He sat back in his chair and let out a sigh. "Well, then, I guess
I can't delay this any longer." He reached into one of his pockets and
handed her a small gun.

Janie actually recoiled at the sight of it. "Tom, this is nuts—I have no
idea what to do with that thing. Put it away, *please.*"

"No. I want you to take it."

"I can't. And even if I take it, I would never use it."

"Janie, it's already very dangerous out there. Carjackings, looting, it's
crazy. And it's only going to get crazier. I don't even want you to go back,
but if you have to I want you to be able to protect yourself."

Eventually, she took it. After a few minutes of instruction, she put it gingerly in the case next to Virtual Memorial. And as Tom drove back to town, back into the growing anarchy, Janie sent out messages to the operatives with detailed instructions for the administration of the serum. But she added something more, something she hadn't planned on adding the night before. *Stand by for additional communication, later today.*

She remembered where she'd seen the photo of that orthopedist.

It was midmorning when they pulled into the square. The street outside the foundation's main door was teeming with frantic people, all scurrying around with packages and bags, pulling children along behind them, weaving helter-skelter through the tight foot traffic. An area of sidewalk was cordoned off in green tape, and suited cops stood guard over someone who had fallen. Janie thought she saw Michael among them, judging by height and stance and movement, but she couldn't really be sure, because of the masks on the cops' faces.

They both stared in silent horror as the car glided slowly past. Tom said quietly, "Might have been a heart attack, or something like that."

"Might have. Probably not, though."

"Probably not."

Tom guided the car carefully through the sea of jaywalkers and brought it to a stop at the curb.

"Where do they all think they're going to go?" Janie wondered aloud.

"Wherever," Tom said quietly. "To their homes, or the homes of friends or relatives, most likely. Whatever seems safest."

As she watched from inside Tom's car, Janie took hold of his hand and gripped it like a lifeline. "God be with them all," she said. "I don't usually say things like that—but I guess now's as good a time as any."

"May something—anything—be with them all."

Tears came to Janie's eyes. Her own voice sounded shaky to her. "Last time no one knew what it would be like, but this time . . . oh, God, can we all make it through this?"

Tom reached out and brushed back a strand of her hair. "This time some people will be better prepared, you and me included. Try to think of it that way. And the ones who aren't, well . . . hopefully that unknown something *will* find a way to be with them."

After a quiet pause, he said, "You don't have to do this, you know. It can wait."

"I don't think it can, Tom."

"Okay," he said sadly. "Your call completely. Where will you go tonight, if you don't finish up today?"

"Michael and Caroline's. And if they're not home, I have a key. But I think they'll be there."

"Sure you don't want to come right out?"

"If I can, I will. But I need to see Caroline."

At that moment a green van passed by them with its lights flashing. They both followed it with their eyes. "Michael may have to be on duty," Tom said.

"Then Caroline and I will stay together." She paused, then said, "Look, Tom, I've been wanting to ask you since last night, but I was afraid—how much can I tell them? I mean, it would be good to bring them out—they could make a real contribution."

Tom's face took on yet another layer of worry. "Michael's a cop," he said. "Now that the old regulations are back in place, he might have to report us. It's possible that he could end up having to reveal the camp."

"He's already been involved in some of this pretty deeply, and he hasn't revealed anything yet. He gave me information on the coach's autopsy . . . he knows everything that happened in London, and he's never breathed a word of it."

"I know, but I just don't think—"

"Tom, Caroline is like a sister to me. She's the only family I have left."

"I'm sorry," he said finally. "But I can't decide without the others. The rest of the group will have to discuss it."

"Michael could be an incredible resource . . . and Caroline, I can't begin to tell you how—"

"Janie, please, I'd love to say yes, but I can't. Not without talking it over first. I'll do that tonight when I get back." Then he reached across the console that separated them and held her painfully close for a few short moments. "I love you," he whispered.

"I love you too."

"You be careful out there," he said.

"I will," she promised.

The air was close and hot in the wood-paneled elevator car. It was filled with worried-looking people, some of whom she recognized, none of whom bothered to greet her. "Every man for himself" was settling in, hard and fast.

When the door opened at the floor where Janie once worked, panic hung in the air like heavy weather, primed to drop its destructive load on anyone without protection—and no one even knew what the proper protection might be. Janie shoved her way out of the car as people clambered to get in. She found Chet Malin behind his desk, packing up his personal items and looking even more frazzled than she'd expected.

She sat down calmly in the chair opposite him.

"What are you doing here? I thought you'd be—"

"Gone? Scared off?" She chuckled bitterly. "I'm scared, all right. But not of you. Or the people upstairs. There isn't much more they can do to me beyond what they've already done."

He glanced around nervously as if someone might overhear them. "Look, Janie, get out of here. Can't you see what's happening? We have patients to move, wards to seal off, all sorts of shit to do. . . . Now, unless you've got a cure for DR SAM, you'd better leave."

He started to place a framed photograph in the box before him. Janie reached across the desk and took it out of his hand.

"You look a little like your father, I think," she said as she regarded it. When she'd satisfied herself that it was the orthopedist she sought, she handed it back. "I know about what happened, Chet."

He stared at her, and for a moment he looked frightened. But then the arrogance returned. "Yeah, well, things are getting hinky again," he sneered, "and no one will give a shit about a little genetic accident that happened years ago. Especially since it wasn't even a human genetic accident. It's all gonna get lost in the shuffle."

"And when the shuffle stops, Chet, then what? I have copies of the evidence. And there are a few others out there in obscure places, so if anything happens to me, anything *more,* that is . . ."

He looked around again. Beads of sweat started to form on his forehead. He wiped it on his rolled-up sleeve, adding another smear of grime. And then the full confession gushed out of him, as if he could not stop himself. "It was supposed to be just a little fire, just to scare you, not an inferno—but the guy got a little nuts on me, and the egg thing, Janie, you have to believe me, it was an accident, for God's sake. And we tried to fix it with a gene wash. We had something we thought might work. The *Giardia* thing was just a way to scare people into cooperating so we could give it to everyone. We thought it had worked, because nothing showed up till recently. But we tried, we really did . . . listen, Janie, my father— he was sick over this. That's what killed him—the stress of feeling like he was responsible for what happened."

"He *was* responsible, Chet. And you know what? It wasn't the original accident that caused the problem. It was your 'cure'—"

"Please! A bird got loose. A valuable bird with a patented gene, so we were keeping a pretty close eye on it."

"But birds will be birds, won't they? They have those annoying wings." She narrowed her eyes and glared at him. "And now you own part of that patent."

"Yeah, but—"

"So when everything gets normal again you stand to make some money on it."

"Yeah, I do. But that's got nothing to do with this."

"Someone who wasn't worried about losing that fortune would have come forward before now."

He started to say something, then stopped. He heaved a big sigh in and out and then stared down at his fingernails.

"You know, we used to call you Monkey Man, but I think Chicken Man is more appropriate."

He looked up. "Monkey Man?"

"Please don't tell me you didn't know."

"I didn't."

For some reason, she believed him. "Then you're dumber than I thought. Hopefully you'll be smart enough to do what I'm going to suggest." She told him about the replacement gene, the fix for the first "fix," and the vials of serum that had been sent out. "That's going to keep them from breaking any more bones. But it's not going to repair the bones that are already broken. So when you move all those study patients you have out there into isolated biosafe wards like you're doing now, you're going to have a few more patients than you planned on."

"I can't do that."

"You have the room, you have the money. Make it work. And do it today. Because if you don't I swear I will rise up out of the ashes of what's to come and kick your ass from here to Hong Kong."

"Janie, they will *never* let me do this upstairs. . . ."

"Then wave these pretty papers under their noses, Chet. There's also a police report about a dead basketball coach in there. With a little perseverance, I could establish a connection. The evidence is pretty compelling. I'll bet someone upstairs would love to know something about that."

He stared at her, horrified. "I had nothing to do with that, I swear."

"But your father was the guy who set all this in place. Someone I know happened to see a list I had on my computer, and he *remembered* the name. So you can wipe out all the evidence you want. People will always have memories, even if the machines don't."

I t was the coldest winter Alejandro could remember since they first came across the Channel, now more than a decade before. And though the winters they had known in France had not been especially kind, they were for the most part far milder than the one winter he had known in England, when it seemed to him that no birds or flowers would ever come again. But he had been warmed by the love of a woman that winter, and now it was he who tried, most times in vain, to warm his daughter. Sometimes he was successful, but only when she would agree to be warmed.

Miraculously, the child within her had managed to survive the horrors of the rise and fall of the *Jacquerie,* and as he watched her belly change from flat to slightly rounded to fully round and finally near pendulous, Alejandro marveled at how God always provided for those who could not provide for themselves. In the case of Kate and her forming child, however, God seemed to have provided the flesh from the girl's own bones, for she who had once been voluptuous and ripe was now thin and angular, giving every bit of what meager food she took in to the child of Guillaume Karle. Though she had not lost her beauty, something Alejandro thought near impossible anyway, the pregnancy had cost her the glow that once colored her cheeks. She was ghostly pale most days, unless she took some air, but that was often too tiring for one so terribly undernourished. She complained often of aching teeth, and Alejandro prayed daily that she would not give any of them up to the carriage of the babe. An apple once in a while, or, should God be so magnanimous, an onion with its miraculous qualities, would have taken care of the problem. But there were no such fruits to be had.

The unborn infant marched through her belly like a little soldier, and Alejandro never had any difficulty finding the babe's feet when he kicked into the thin skin of his mother. It gave Kate almost all the pleasure she knew to run her hands over the one thing, beyond her memories, that remained of her love for Guillaume Karle. And Alejandro thought it only fair that she should have some pleasure of her burden, for she had spent the first few months retching and heaving and trying to keep down what little food she had. There were no herbs to make the proper teas and potions to cure her pregnancy sickness, for they had all been spent on the wounded soldiers of the *Jacquerie,* or for other curative reasons, and when the last of the maimed were finally brought out of the longhouse, the earth had already given itself over to brown and there were no more herbs to be had. There would be none till spring, and by then, the child would be born. Alive, Alejandro hoped. He did not think he could bear to watch his daughter suffer another torment.

They had started that winter with two gold pieces, and he had thought for sure it would get them through. Two pieces of gold was enough to feed a large family for a year, or so he had been told, and so he wanted desperately to believe. With no one to tend the cattle and no one to harvest what little wheat had been sown, and no one to bring it to market, people paid outrageous prices for anything that could be found. There were likely no nobles going hungry, he thought, especially not Charles of Navarre or the Baron de Coucy.

But even they were expending their coinage at a faster rate than ever before, and their grumblings were whispered throughout the countryside, and brought into the longhouse by anyone who passed through it.

They were down to the last few *sous;* Alejandro knew that their only food until spring would be what he himself caught. But game was scarce, and with the ponds frozen it was a miserable, often impossible task to obtain fish. His dreams were full of golden loaves and steaming white fish and juicy red apples; his belly was full of grit and gristle and groans. And he would have been thankful for more of those, if only they could be found.

A few people came seeking treatment; he no longer bothered to try to hide the fact that he was a physician, for it was well known among the countryfolk what he had done for their wounded brothers, sons, and husbands, and legends of his compassionate deeds were told for miles. And he was the only physician left north of Paris, or so it seemed when the streams of *misérables* presented themselves. Often he could do nothing for these poor ones who suffered from the diseases of deprivation and came seeking some reason to hope; most times he sent them home with encouraging words and little else. Those who he could help were rarely able to pay him anything, though he gave his services without demand for payment. Sometimes they would bring a strip of dried meat, or a wormy apple, or a crust, for food was the only tender anyone cared about during the long winter of 1359. He was grateful for what was brought, and effusive in his thanks, but he gave most of it to Kate. The knocks on the door of the longhouse were no longer surprising to him, and he never bothered to wonder if the agents of King Edward had come at last to claim him. *Let them come,* he often thought with terrible bitterness, *if only they bring food.*

One cold and sunny morning in the late winter, when the air should have much warmer and the icicles much smaller, there came a knock on the door that was somehow different from the rest. The touch was firmer—there seemed to be some strength behind it. Peasants seeking his help always knocked meekly, knowing that what they were doing amounted to little more than begging. But this was not the knock of a beggar. And for the first time in many months, he reached for his knife before opening up.

Again, the knock came, this time even stronger, and Kate's face began to show alarm. *So close to her time,* he thought; *let it please not be a robber or a knight seeking even more plunder . . .*

Knife in hand, he slid back the wooden bolt and opened the door just a crack. A tall man in a riding cloak stood there, a mass of darkness against the gray-white of the snow. With the sun behind the stranger, and his vision blurred by malnutrition, Alejandro could not see the man's face.

"Physician?" he heard.

The voice was so familiar, but it did not register in the dullness of his mind.

Then came "Colleague?"

He nearly fainted.

You are not welcome here, Alejandro had said as he tried to slam the door.

But de Chauliac had shoved his shoulder against the wood and pushed his way inside, far outdoing his weakened colleague in both strength and will.

No, but I am needed.

And now the Frenchman watched in silent and guilty embarrassment as Alejandro wept over the food he had brought from Paris, and handed it to the pitifully thin and massively pregnant girl, who devoured every morsel as if she were a starving animal.

When he had taken his own fill, the Jew thought momentarily about attacking his caller and making an end of him, once and for all. But he had been wise enough to know that his strength would not permit it, and sane enough to understand the terrible loss it would be.

"How did you find me?" he only said.

"I have known where you are since the day you first came here. I had a spy among your soldiers. One of the guards you so heartily despised and so handily tricked. But you would not have noticed him; the man came and went discreetly among your thousands. And you were rather preoccupied, or so he said."

"And did he . . . ?"

"Perish in the battle? Nearly. But your daughter treated him, and he lived." He cast his glance in Kate's direction and nodded respectfully. "The man sends his most heartfelt thanks, and his promise that he shall never keep your father captive again."

This brought the faintest smile to her lips, and Alejandro's heart soared with the sight of it.

De Chauliac gestured in the direction of her belly. "Karle's child, I suppose."

Alejandro nodded.

"When shall her confinement be?"

"Soon, I think, though I cannot say exactly."

"Stand up, *madame*," de Chauliac said, "if you please."

She looked at Alejandro, who only raised his eyebrows in surprise. She stood.

"Turn to the side, that I may view the extent of your maternity. Hold your dress against your belly—I wish to see its curves."

She turned, revealing a rounded protuberance that bulged just over the top of her skinny thighs.

"The babe sits low," de Chauliac said.

"No wonder," Alejandro said, "for her belly has no flesh to hold it higher."

"Yes, but a babe only lets itself drift this low when it is ready to come forth. She will bring this child out in perhaps a week."

"From whence comes this knowledge of childbirth? I had thought you above mere midwifery."

"I am the royal midwife, or was when I had His Holiness's favor."

"Père," Kate said, "can this be true—can it be so soon in coming?"

"I think it so," de Chauliac said, without waiting for Alejandro's comment. "So you had best come back to Paris with me."

Alejandro looked at him with narrowed, suspicious eyes. "To be your prisoner again? Never."

De Chauliac stood up and glared down at Alejandro. "Fool," the Frenchman said, "you are a most bitter and unappreciative guest. And what little I want from your company you hoard to yourself, quite jealously. I care not if you stay or you go, if you do not see fit to share your learning with me. And when you are in my keeping, I am obliged to feed you. That is a dear thing to do, these days."

The diatribe was stunningly unexpected. Alejandro could only stare, dumbfounded, at the man who had delivered it. When he found his tongue again, he said, "Then why . . . ?"

"There is plague," he said, "in Paris. You are needed."

At last, he thought. Something he could bargain with. "And what of my gold?"

"I have it still. You shall have it back."

"And the manuscript of Abraham?"

De Chauliac hesitated. "It is with Flamel."

Alejandro raised himself up slightly, as if he were going to pounce. "You *gave* it to him?"

"He begged me for it."

"But he knows not what it means."

"He promised to find someone to finish the translation."

"And then he will do with that wisdom what he will! It will not be used toward the benefit of those it was intended for!"

De Chauliac sighed. "There is nothing that you or I can do about that. It fell into your hands quite by accident, and now, by similar accident, it has gone to Flamel. He is a good man at heart, though undeservedly pompous; he will do good work with it. And somehow this tome has found its way to safety through a very long journey before this without your stewardship. What makes you think it requires your protection?" He stood up and began to pace. "One begins to think that this manuscript has a will of its own. Or, if you would prefer to think of it another way, one might say it is under the influence of the will of God, and will end up where He wants it to."

Humbled, Alejandro was quiet for a long moment. "And you believe now what I told you about the cure for plague. Do you also believe what I told you of the rats?"

"I am not in a position *not* to believe. And I am oathbound to seek out *any* cure, for I gave my pledge to the Dauphin. You see, the patient we must treat is the young son of Prince Lionel and the Countess Elizabeth."

Alejandro swallowed hard. "I cannot go there."

"I believe you owe her this, colleague."

He lowered his head. Then quietly, he looked to Kate, silently asking her permission. She said yes with the tiniest movement of her eyes.

He turned his own eyes back to de Chauliac. "In the room, where I was captive . . ."

"Aye," de Chauliac said. "The maid found it. She would have got rid of the smelly stuff, but instead brought it to me. I have it still, in a bottle in my study."

"Then it has not dissipated."

"Perhaps some, I cannot say for sure. But it is still immensely foul, so whatever quality you treasure in it seems to have survived. I am glad now I did not dispose of it."

When they came out of the longhouse to depart, Alejandro saw two horses tied to the post, waiting unguarded. He turned to de Chauliac in surprise and said, "You rode out alone? With an extra horse?"

"There are no highwaymen about just now," de Chauliac explained.

"How can that be?"

"They are all dead, colleague. Slaughtered. Navarre and Coucy have dispatched anyone they even suspect of such activity. And of course, they have deemed that begging to feed one's family might qualify one as a highwayman. So I had little to fear."

Yet they left us alone, Alejandro thought, *in keeping with their promise to Karle. There is honor among monsters, it seems.* He whispered a brief word of thanks to the departed soul of Guillaume Karle, and wondered if the good man's spirit had found repose.

It had been too painful to speak of Karle, and so he had been remembered silently through the long winter. Though he never gave voice to his thoughts, Alejandro often wondered what his final hours had been like. Had he stood in defiance of his tormenters and taunted them as they had taunted him, knowing it would be his last opportunity? Or had he remained stoically silent as Navarre and Coucy went about the business of plotting his demise? It must have been a shock to Karle, Alejandro thought, to hear that his alliance was not needed, that the Dauphin had failed to raise the necessary troops, and that there would be no battle between Navarre and the French heir to the throne. Yet he managed to extract a solemn promise from Navarre, with enough passion that the scoundrel had honored it.

He had often wondered—had it been Karle who slashed Navarre's arm, thus earning his respect? The wound might have been a day old when he treated it.

These questions were revisited in his mind as they prepared for the journey to Paris. But he would never know the answers without confronting Navarre. And that was something he could only do when his body was not likely to betray him with weakness.

"Colleague?" de Chauliac said gently, when all was prepared. "Are you ready?"

"Aye" came the quiet reply.

They had nothing worth bringing save Alejandro's bag of implements and the tin of desiccated flesh that Kate had so carefully prepared when they first came to the longhouse. These items fit neatly into the saddlebag in which the food had been brought. It was pitiful to realize that all they had in the world could be crammed into the space once occupied by what now filled their bellies. So Alejandro tried not to think of it as they rode along—he concentrated instead on keeping a firm grip on Kate, who rode in front of him on the larger of the two mounts. At first he thought it would be a great burden on the horse, and he wanted to walk alongside, but de Chauliac convinced him without much difficulty that their combined weight could not be much more than his own. So, gratefully relieved of his guilt, he rode.

The roads were still frozen, and there were few tracks in the fresh snow, only lightly covered impressions of the tracks de Chauliac's horses had made on the ride out. The forest around them was eerily silent, for the game was mostly gone and the birds had not returned, and the snow muffled everything except the occasional crack of a branch that could bear no more ice. Along the side of the road, Alejandro saw now and then the unmistakable shape of a skull layered with a fresh film of snow, or a mound that could only be the remains of some poor man's body. Once, this road had been lined on either side with pyres, for when tinder could be found and the time taken, those who still had the strength to do so would set the dead aflame. Red flames leapt up, and a revolting stench filled every breath, searing the nostrils. If he closed his eyes he could hear once again the cries of the men who had died on the road to Compiègne, the screams of the wounded, the pounding of Navarre's mount's hooves as he rode in to be repaired with the vicious Coucy at his side.

They passed through the gate into Paris without incident, for de Chauliac had arranged ahead of time for their return. The streets were quiet and near deserted except for the wool-cloaked hour criers who called out the time to the occupants of tightly shuttered houses, wherein the fortunate who had fuel would be huddled together over meager meals. Shops were boarded or shuttered, cafés dark and quiet. And when they rode by Notre Dame, Alejandro saw no workmen on the scaffolding, nor did he hear any of the singing that made proximity to that bastion of Christian excess tolerable.

There were no pigeons in the courtyard.

At last! Eaten! he thought with no small glee.

Finally they crossed over the frozen Seine to de Chauliac's manse near the university. And when Alejandro stepped inside the heavy door, he felt true warmth for the first time in many months.

They were taken immediately to separate rooms, and in them found all the necessities of decent living—once again, de Chauliac had proved himself a worthy and considerate host. Clean water, fresh attire, brushes for the teeth, combs and ribbons for Kate's hair—everything was laid out with exquisite care. As Alejandro cleaned and dressed himself, his mind finally freed of the need to find ways of keeping his body alive, an unfamiliar emotion began to creep in, a sense of urgency and fear over the task he had been summoned to perform.

Could he do this again? The last time he had conquered plague it had been his own disease, and Kate had been as little as a whisper. She had done for him, by an expenditure of will, what he had not managed to do for Adele: she had forced him, in his delirium, to swallow the horrid potion that was his only hope for cure. She had held her small hands over his mouth and nose until he had no choice but to swallow or suffocate. And though death might have been welcome then, he had chosen to swallow. He had lived, and in the years since the girl had described that moment as one of the most difficult she had ever faced, more difficult even than watching her own mother succumb.

Should she go through that again, with her child so near due?

No, he thought decisively, *it cannot be allowed.*

So when they came together again in the vestibule, he told her that she must stay behind with de Chauliac.

"Père! Never!"

"De Chauliac, convince her of the folly of it. Tell her she must stay here with you."

"I would, colleague, but my words will mean little, for I do not intend to stay here myself."

*   *   *

They were ushered quietly through the château. Alejandro felt himself almost shrinking from the guilty familiarity of the place, and he dreaded his first encounter with the countess, for by rights, his first gesture toward her ought to be to fall to his knees and beg her forgiveness for the falseness of his love.

But had it been false? Not entirely. In another time or place, under different circumstances, they might have flourished in their little court-ship, for he found Elizabeth to be a pleasing companion, lively and jovial. She had a quick wit and keen intelligence, and the sound of her voice pleased him greatly. Moreover, he did not wish to hurt her.

But she was no Adele, and never would be.

His concern over their initial confrontation proved to be groundless, for the place seemed deserted. Few servants were about beyond the one who led them, and when they opened the door to the room where the small boy lay in his bed, the manservant turned quickly to depart. Alejandro caught him by the wrist and said, "There are things we will require to do this. You need not come inside, only leave them here, outside the door. Do not fail to answer the ring, or the child may suffer more, and I will be sure your mistress knows who failed her."

They tied cloth masks provided by de Chauliac around their faces, and entered, closing the door quickly behind them. The smell of plague assaulted them instantly, and the first thing Alejandro did was to throw open the windows to let in some breathable air. They found the boy lying under the mink coverlet in his sweaty nightclothes, soiled with his own excrement, for no one, including his mother, could come close enough to see to his care. His heart ached with sorrow for the boy, whose neck was swollen and dark and whose eyes were wide with fear. Surrounded by strangers, he would now be subjected to what would seem like cruel torture masked in the garb of a cure.

Alejandro stripped away the fur and bundled it into a corner, then pulled the bell and went to the door. The manservant came to the hall-way, but would not come near the door, though it was opened only a crack. "Bring fresh linens and nightclothes, and several large pitchers of clean water. And a new robe for the bed—but it must be wool, not fur. We will need a pot for boiling, and food for three days for all of us. Leave it all here, outside the door.

Back inside, as he waited for the items to be brought, Alejandro took de Chauliac aside. "You put yourself in grave danger by being here. Kate and I have both survived this. And I have never seen one who survived the first trial contract this pest again. So I am sure we will be safe. But you—you are vulnerable, I fear."

"Nevertheless, I shall remain here. I am oathbound."

"Curb your oath, Frenchman, or you will learn this cure, but you will not be able to deliver it after the learning."

With unbending determination, de Chauliac said, "I will stay."

"Then stand back, so you do not breathe the child's air humors. Then perhaps you will not be afflicted."

"But I must see this for myself . . . this is among the finest wisdom to be had in my lifetime."

Alejandro stared at him, and finally said, "It is nothing more than the wisdom of a crone. A woman."

"So you have said, colleague, but there must be more to it than that."

"De Chauliac," Alejandro said, "it is that alone. And you must never underestimate the power of a woman to do what needs to be done."

There was a task that Janie desperately wanted to see done waiting inside Jameson Memorial Hospital, but when she arrived there in her car one quick look told her that there was simply no getting near the facility in a vehicle. The parking lots were cordoned off to accommodate a fleet of vehicles that would have looked more at home in front of a military installation than a hospital. Cops in green suits were letting ambulances onto the driving areas of the hospital's grounds, but not private cars, so Janie parked her Volvo a few blocks away in a place that was sadly familiar from her pre-Outbreak life, a lot behind the school her daughter, Betsy, had once attended. After checking that the gas cap was indeed locked, she set out to walk the remaining distance to the glass and steel hospital.

Time was wasting. She knew she needed to finish this work and then leave, quickly, but she couldn't seem to make her feet move as fast as she wanted them to—like swamp weeds, old memories tangled around her ankles and brought her to a halt at the edge of the parking lot. She turned halfway and gazed back at the near-empty expanse of pavement that once held buses and minivans, and watched as a thin, dry breeze bent the green shafts of plantain that poked up, accusations of neglect, from between the cracks. She had once stood on the same spot and watched as hearses pulled out of that school lot in a long, continuous line, each one easing slowly over the same speed bumps she'd negotiated hundreds of times with a car full of laughing children, all destined for happy homes with loving parents, their natural place in a world that was as it ought to be.

An involuntary shudder ran through her; she stiffened as it made its cold way down her spine. She tore herself away from the pain and turned back toward the hospital, and as she neared it she saw post drivers on the roadside and huge rolls of chain link on a flatbed truck. It had taken only a day or two the first time around to rim the hospital completely with the metal barrier. *The turn of two sunsets,* Alejandro might have said if he were here. Jameson Memorial would soon be a fortress as formidable as any medieval castle the ancient physician had passed through on his journey across Europe, and far more deadly. It was just no place for a sick child to be, and the delivery of Alejandro's saving grace to Abraham Prives seemed reason enough to brave the gauntlet of halls and corners and stairwells required to reach him.

But when she came face-to-face with the newly erected security station and its shiny chrome and plastic scanner, her bravado felt thin and inadequate. The guards were suited in the familiar but dreaded green, and when she saw them together in a cluster Janie could not help but think of Heathrow Airport, where they'd been amassed along the mezzanine like sharpshooters over a barrel of fish, ready to take out anyone who misbehaved.

When she approached, one of them pointed to the ID sensor, so Janie stepped forward and ran her hand, palm up, under its laser reader. He handed her a face mask. She took it and slipped it on. No words were exchanged.

She was then directed by another series of hand signals to step forward and pass through the scanner itself. It would be at this point that she'd be taken, if a reason to do so surfaced, though no one knew quite yet where the retention centers were this time around. Within a few days, Janie knew that a frantic relative with political or financial influence would have pried the information out of some frazzled civil servant preparing to desert his post for the assumed safety of the hinterlands, one who no longer worried about the consequences of telling.

By the time any of this happened she would be ensconced in the foothills hideaway, out of harm's reach. Eventually, they would learn where people were being taken.

Not that knowing it would make a bit of difference.

The alarm did not ring, and Janie was waved through. She ran down the hallway, her footsteps echoing on the hard tile floor, and then flew up the stairs, bypassing entirely the elevator with its recycled air. The doors to all the rooms were closed, but none bore the deadly green tape yet, the fearful sign of quarantine. Still, there was an eerie sense of emptiness to the place, and when Janie reached Abraham's room, she went right in and closed the door quickly behind her.

Not that closing it would make a bit of difference.

She found Mrs. Prives at the bedside, precisely where she expected the woman would be, clutching her son's hand in what seemed an effort to preserve whatever spirit remained within him. When the mother saw Janie, an almost painful look of relief came over her face.

"Oh, thank God you're here, everyone seems to have just up and left."

Janie came bedside and put a hand on the distraught woman's shoulder, though she was sure that whatever comfort the touch might provide would seem small and insignificant. "It's getting crazy out there," she said, inclining her head toward the door. "DR SAM—"

"That much I know," the woman said abruptly.

There was a helpless sound to Mrs. Prives's voice that gave Janie a moment of pause.

"Has anyone come in to talk to you yet?"

"No. There doesn't seem to be anyone around at all. I'm starting to get really scared by all this—I just wish I knew something about what's going on here."

"I think anyone who could leave already has," Janie said. "And I can't blame anyone for going home. I'm going, uh, *home* myself as soon as I finish up here."

"But who's going to take care of Abraham now, if everyone's gone?" Her voice was almost pleading.

"That's why I'm here," Janie said. "He'll be taken care of, I promise."

She opened her bag and took out the small vial she'd brought with her.

Mrs. Prives followed the vial with worried eyes. "What's that?" she asked nervously.

Janie said the simplest thing she could think of in the hope that it would suffice. "This is a gene wash, from a donor we found after some protracted searching. There's a snippet of DNA in there that will replace a damaged strip in Abraham's genes. The damage happened a long time ago. This isn't going to repair the break he already has, but it will keep Abraham from breaking any more bones, at least from shattering them. Now, the break he already has will require surgery—"

"Oh, dear God," Mrs. Prives moaned. "But—the contamination—will it be safe to do it, now that . . ."

"Where it'll be done, there will be a sterile environment," Janie reassured her. "But please, I need you to listen to me now," she said. "I won't be available to you after today. I've made some arrangements for Abraham. This afternoon someone from the foundation will come to transport him to their medical facility. It'll be a special ward that he's going to, where there are other boys with similar problems, and they'll all be receiving treatment for shattered bones—starting with the same gene wash. And after that takes effect, surgery to repair the shattering. Then followup therapy."

She checked the drip rate of the liquid. Wanting it to go faster, she opened the valve a bit. "No one here will know anything about it. But with what's going on outside, they won't try to stop you or get in your way when you take him out of here. So just go with your son and get him settled in. I don't know if you'll be able to stay with him during his treatment, but I assure you that he will be well cared for, and that everything possible will be done to correct the damage to his vertebrae and his spine."

"What are the chances that . . . that . . ."

Janie didn't wait for Mrs. Prives to conquer her fear of completing the question. She went ahead and answered it, as frankly as possible. "He may not play soccer again," she said, "but there's a very good chance that he'll walk."

Still fighting off the tears, Mrs. Prives put a hand over her mouth. She looked at Abraham, then back at Janie, who smiled and said, "You can cry now. It's okay."

And as the mother burst into sobs of relief, Janie leaned over and patted her gently on the arm. "Good luck, Mrs. Prives," she said quietly. "I really hope that you and everyone you love will make it through." She straightened and looked around the room, then at Abraham. There was nothing more she could or should do.

"Now I have to go to some of the people I love." She turned and left.

But before she escaped the growing madness to go to Caroline's house, Janie had one more thing left to do. She wove her car carefully through the thickening traffic with her doors locked and her windows fully up. It was hot in the car, because air-conditioning sucked up too much gas, and she knew she wouldn't be getting any more in the foreseeable future. She was sweating, and she felt drained by both heat and anxiety. But soon, when all of this was behind her, she knew she would be cool and dry, and if God was good, safe.

She passed the tall buildings of the university and headed for the south end of the campus to the book depository. There were only two cars in the parking area. One, she assumed, had to belong to Myra Ross.

Inside the starkly modern facility she found no chaos, no panic, just immense quiet and the same filtered, almost holy light that she'd admired in this building on her other visits. And before she got to her business, she stopped and stood in the shaft of a skylight's beam to let the illumination wash through her. She leaned her head back and closed her eyes, and let the light transfuse her with energy. When she opened her eyes again, Myra Ross was standing in front of her.

"They told me you'd come," she said.

"You know what's going on out there?"

Myra shook her head slowly and made a wistful smile. "It's hard to miss," she said, "if you have your eyes open."

"We all missed it before."

"We won't again," Myra said sadly. "So. I think I may know why you've come, but tell me anyway, just so I can see if dreams actually do come true."

"And the dream you're referring to, what would that be?"

"That you'll leave the journal here."

Janie looked down, almost in shame. "I can't. I'm going away from here for a while. For—the duration. I want to take the journal with me."

Myra sighed and gazed off to one side. "I thought you might. And I understand why, I really do." She glanced back up at Janie again. "I don't even fault you. But I'd like to ask you to reconsider. It's very safe here. Even if we're forced to close, this facility is like a fortress, it's designed to withstand an assault, even one with heavy weapons. So there's no reason to worry, really."

"It's not that. I know it will be fine. I have the feeling if it came to that, you'd be right there at the door with a machine gun, keeping the bad guys at bay."

Myra let out a small chuckle and inclined her head slightly. "I've kept a whole slew of bad guys at bay before in other times and places, and I'm not so old yet that I couldn't do it again."

Janie thought briefly of the gun nestled next to Virtual Memorial. "I'm sorry," she said, "I want the journal with me. It's become so important to me, like those things from my old life that I managed to save from the fire. I can't stand the notion of being separated from it."

"All right, I'll get it, then." Myra started to take a step, then stalled and said, "You're sure about this?"

Janie nodded.

"Well," she said, "wait here. I'll be back shortly."

In less than a minute she returned with a carefully padded envelope, secured with a string.

"You really were expecting me," Janie said.

"Yes, I was."

Janie looked into Myra's eyes. She saw no visible fear, but plenty of determination and resolve. "I hope we'll meet again when this is over."

"I do too, dear."

"Do you have someplace to go?"

"I'll stay here, of course. I have everything I need, and I'll be doing something I care about. Where else would I go?"

"Yes, where else," Janie said quietly.

"And yourself? Will you be safe? You're welcome to be here, there's plenty of room."

"Thank you. But I have good arrangements. I'll be—out of town," she said. "Some friends have a safe place, out in the country."

"Well, good-bye, then."

"Good-bye."

They reached out and hugged each other. Then Janie turned and started toward the door.

"Dr. Crowe."

She stopped and looked back. "Yes?"

"I feel like I should be saying 'And there goes my daughter, the doctor . . .' Please, go with God."

"I will. And you."

She left Myra with the depository's treasures, and departed with one of her own, one of the few that remained.

It was the best of news, but the worst of times to be hearing it.

"Oh, my God, Caroline, it's wonderful, but *now* . . ."

"I know," she said. There was an edge of worry in Caroline's voice but it was being drowned out by happiness. She wanted this badly. "It's so ironic—we've been trying so hard, and Michael is just so thrilled, and now all the rest of this happens."

"Life always finds a way," Janie said. "Even in bad situations." She put a hand on Caroline's shoulder. "And this is going to be bad, I think."

Caroline looked off into some undefined distance, thinking her private thoughts about the world her child would come into. "I know," she said softly. "Michael says it's happening very fast. He's overwhelmed again. Already." When she glanced up again her face showed both sadness and fear. "They all are, he says."

Janie suddenly felt a need to think happier thoughts. The first one that came to mind was a question, the one she would have asked anyway, under more certain circumstances. "So—how long have you known?"

It seemed to please Caroline that she wanted to know. "Since last night. I thought I had my period yesterday, but it was just some spotting and it stopped completely. So I took a test. And it was positive!"

"You're absolutely certain."

"Yes. No doubt."

Janie put a hand on Caroline's still-flat belly. "Pregnant. My God."

"It seems crazy to even talk like this right now—but you'll be Aunt Janie. And I'll be *Mom*." Her eyes gleamed, full of the future. "I was beginning to lose hope, I mean, after London . . ."

"Hey," Janie said reassuringly, "one thing you should have learned in London is that there's always hope. Always. I mean, you came back from the precipice. You were halfway over. And now look at you. Pregnant." She let herself smile with complete abandon. "It's terrific, just terrific. Now, since I'm probably the only doctor you're going to be seeing for a while, maybe you should tell me how you're feeling."

"Wonderful. Perfect. Fantastic."

The hormones, Janie thought. "You were limping a little when I came in earlier. How's the toe?"

"It's a little sore today, but other than that I feel terrific."

"You're probably holding a little water—it might be making your feet swell. Now, you know about all the things you have to be careful of now, no alcohol, no cats."

Don't leave your house, lock all the doors and windows . . .

But if they could come with her to the camp, it wouldn't be an issue.

"I know," Caroline said. And then, as if she'd read Janie's mind, she added, "If I have to stay in this house the whole time I'm pregnant, I will. Then I won't need any maternity clothes—I'll just wallow around in Michael's big old shirts."

She was quiet for a moment, then added, "Look, Janie, I want you to come and live with us. We'll all be safe here."

Janie was desperate to tell her about Burning Road, about Bruce, about what she'd found with Tom and how it had changed everything. But she held it all back somehow and let Caroline go on.

"I just think we can get through," Caroline said after a hesitation, "whatever comes. We've weathered this sort of thing before, you and I, and we did fine, just fine."

Janie tried not to show her confusion. She reached out and hugged Caroline with sisterly warmth and affection. Inside, she was pure turmoil.

The sound was breaking up on the cellular phone.

"Tom—" She held the phone out and gave it a few taps. "God, what a time for the phone to go hinky on me." She raised her voice. "Can you hear me?"

The response came through in crackling little spurts. "Barely. Can you switch to V.M.?"

"Yeah."

A few minutes later they were face-to-face on their computer screens. "You don't suppose they're already abandoning the utilities, do you?" Janie said.

"If you were a utility worker, would you be hanging around right now? I wouldn't. I'd be gone."

"I guess I would, too. God, Tom, this is all happening very fast. Too fast."

"People remember, Janie. And no one who can avoid it is going to get caught short again." He paused for a moment, then said, "I've been worried about you, wondering if everything went okay today."

"As okay as it could go, I guess. I downloaded from the satellite just before I called you, and there was a lot of good news—confirmations that all but eight of the boys are under way to the foundation."

"What did you do to Malin?"

"Not enough. I want to nail his smarmy ass to the wall and use it for crossbow practice."

"But this may be all you get. And you got what those boys needed. You'll find a way to deal with him once this is over." He *hmphed*. "If he's still alive."

"You're assuming we'll be alive, Tom."

His voice never wavered when he said, "I know we will. And you have more important things that need your attention now."

He was right. It was unsatisfying, and it all felt unfinished. But there was no more time. "I got the journal," she said quietly.

There was relief in his voice. "Good. Because I want you to come out to Burning Road tonight. I don't like what I'm hearing from the other operatives."

"What about Caroline and Michael?"

He was quiet for a few seconds. "Janie, we decided."

Line in the sand, she thought as she blurted, "I'm not coming without them, Tom."

"Please, don't be like this."

"Like what—loyal? A good and caring friend? Isn't that what you've been to me? I would do the same if it were you out here. Or Sandhaus, or Kristina."

"All right," he said after a minute's pause. "I'll try again."

"I'll be waiting."

Janie didn't like the look of Caroline's toe, and the hangnail remained unhealed.

"Have you been soaking these?" she said.

"Yes," Caroline assured her.

Then why are they not healing?

Michael came home a short while later. He headed directly to the sink, where he scrubbed his hands and face vigorously in a futile effort to remove the grim coating of horror that was settling on his skin, a little thicker with each new case of DR SAM he was forced to handle.

Janie followed him there. "Have you suited up yet?"

As he rubbed the towel on his hands and face he said, "They just made it mandatory."

"You look exhausted," Janie said.

"I am. We've got a new one coming in about every half hour."

The numbers had been worse last time at the height of it all. But it was early yet. "Anyone started looking for the local source?"

"We haven't really had time. Been too busy taking care of the victims."

"So it could be anywhere."

"Yes."

Was it some bathroom floor, some old doorknob that hadn't been replaced with a foot pedal yet? The font of holy water in a church?

Everything was suspect, absolutely everything.

"Has Caroline been out in the last few days?"

"She has," he said. "She went out yesterday afternoon for the pregnancy test."

"Do you happen to remember what she was wearing on her feet?"

"Sandals, I think. Her toe was bothering her. That's what she wears all the time, though. Why?"

So the toe had been exposed.

I have to tell him, she decided. But just as she opened her mouth, she was summoned by the insistent electronic voice of V.M.

"Don't leave," she said. "I need to talk to you." She left him at the kitchen sink and went to his study, where V.M. sat on the desk. She sat down in front of it and touched the screen. Tom's face came into view.

"We worked out a compromise," he said. "With conditions. They can come if they agree."

Janie caught in a happy breath. "Oh, Tom, thank you."

"You better listen before you get too excited. Michael has to bring his suit and all the rest of his paraphernalia. And he can't notify anyone at Biopol that he's taking off."

Janie was quiet for a moment. "That'll be the end of his service as a cop. You know that. That's a pretty stiff entry fee."

"Janie," Tom said wearily, his face finally showing the strain, "we all pay a fee of some kind. Some are worse than others. But we all pay."

After disconnecting, she spent a few moments in quiet thought in the study. Then she got up and headed for the kitchen. "Michael . . ."

"They've kept it pretty quiet," Michael said. "No one at Biopol has said anything about a group like that."

"They've been very careful. They—I guess I should be saying 'we' now—have a dedicated satellite for communications, and a system of computers with the operatives out in the field—which essentially means anything outside the camp now. They all report in on a regular basis."

Michael remained stiffly silent while Janie explained what was required of him.

"I'm getting the feeling that they view me as some kind of prize catch," he said. "I suppose I ought to be flattered."

"What I think we should all be right now is grateful."

"Good heavens—for having my career ruined?"

"For having your life saved," Janie said.

He knew she was right. Eventually biocops suffered the same fate as medical workers. Continued exposure, protected or not, took its toll.

"Look, Michael, there's another reason why I think you ought to go with me. I examined Caroline's toe a little while ago, and I don't like how it looks. There's an infection there. She also has an infection of some sort in one of her fingers. I don't know what it is."

Alarm spread over Michael's face. "It was all right this morning—I saw the toe when she was washing it."

"Well, that may have been the case this morning, but it's not all right now. Look, do you think you can convince her to go, without telling her what I've told you? I don't want to scare her until I know for sure."

"But if it's DR SAM, they won't want her in the camp."

She knew he was right. She was in a tortured state of denial over just that notion. "Let me worry about that," she said. "She's obviously fighting off whatever is there—she feels a little warm, and that's actually a good sign. Some people claim the immune system is somewhat heightened during pregnancy, and it makes sense. But we need to move quickly. I don't need to tell you it could be only a matter of hours before—"

"No, you don't." He got up and paced around the study for a few minutes, one hand rubbing his chin, deep in thought. "I'll be an outlaw if we do this, you know. It might be worth it if I thought Caroline would be okay, but you don't seem to be giving out guarantees."

She hung her head and was quiet for a few seconds. "We're all going to be outlaws. I'm not going to be able to work as a physician for a very long time, if ever again. And there are no guarantees that *any* of us will be okay."

Without thinking, Michael glanced in the direction of the kitchen, where Caroline was still sitting at the table.

"You don't have to do this, you know," Janie said. "You can decide to stay on the outside."

"And lose my wife? Our child? When someone finds out, they'll take her away. And I know what happens to those people who get taken away."

"It may just be her toe acting up. Simple as that. And if it is DR SAM, well, my guess is—"

She wanted to say, "that it's being contained by something." But it seemed too wild an utterance. She said instead, "—she could beat it."

"Less than two percent do that."

"She lived through bubonic plague, Michael. She's very tough. And she didn't have anywhere near as much reason to live then as she does now."

He sighed in weary resignation. "I'll go speak with her, then."

Janie glanced at the wall clock. "Better make it fast."

He started through the study door.

"And Michael," Janie said.

The expression he wore when he turned back to her was pure grief.

"Don't say anything about her toe—please—not yet."

The last thing Janie did before they departed was to bandage Caroline's finger and toe in an impermeable biosafe dressing. The last thing Michael did, when all else was ready, when all his equipment was loaded in the back of Janie's Volvo like the pile of tribute it had suddenly become, was to climb into his suit.

Never know but what it might come in handy on the drive.

As he was closing the door to the house, his helmet still tucked under one arm, he took a last look around at the things he and Caroline had amassed in their short but happy marriage. He realized, with a vague sense of shame, how superfluous it all seemed when the bell was about to start tolling again.

W hat de Chauliac saw as he watched a demonstration of the greatest new wisdom of his lifetime was not the sure-handed work of a master scientist, but instead the frantic, uncertain-looking ministrations of a bone-thin Jew to a small frightened boy, a child who suffered gravely from an affliction that was far more likely to claim him than not. At his side was a young woman, a widow well before twenty, whose suffering had already been boundless and stood only to worsen. And though the child they tended to would call the young woman "Aunt" under different circumstances, these two had no familial obligation to see the terrified lad through his trial by pest. The Frenchman knew that Alejandro's guilt over deceiving the young countess could not possibly be reason enough to do what he now did for her ailing son. It could only be the incomprehensible honor of the man, the love he had for his art, and his desire to do it well. With care and tenderness, he and his daughter washed and cleaned and gave comfort to the child, even as they forced the terrible grayish slurry into his mouth, a cure prescribed by the wisdom of an old woman who had taught the physician how to do what needed to be done.

He watched in amazement, from the far corner to which Alejandro had banished him for his own safety, as father and daughter worked side by side without apparent regard for their own well-being, often through long periods of sleeplessness. They mixed their disagreeable potion to certain specific proportions—two knuckles of the powdered dried flesh to a cupped hand of the mysterious water. At precise times, without deviation, they administered the doses, grimacing through the child's screams of objection as they forced the swill into his mouth.

And in the times when the boy's pain seemed under control and he lay quiet, the physician sat at the bedside and told him stories, tales given to him by a long-dead companion who had seen much glory in war, of charging horses and jousts and fierce swordsmanship—things this very little boy would one day be called upon to do, were he to survive.

The girl will make a fine mother, de Chauliac observed to himself. And with a growing sense of respect for the Jew who had so tormented his thoughts over the years, he admitted to himself that the girl had been well raised. It was yet another thing the man did superbly.

When the boy's fever finally broke and his buboes began to shrink, de Chauliac found himself filled with strange and unfamiliar joy. Not the sense of triumph he usually knew when conquering a fierce malady, but a simple happiness to know that the child would live to cling to his mother and follow his father, and deep pride in the way this enigmatic wanderer practiced his beloved art. He was, for once, humbled.

"Père," Alejandro heard.

He came awake in the chair by the boy's bed, and saw Kate standing over him.

"My belly wants to heave."

His senses came alive almost instantly. He stood up, and made her take his place in the chair. "Has your water flowed?"

"I—I do not know," she said nervously as she sat back. "I was asleep, by the hearth, but my skirts are wet, so I think it must have." And then she doubled forward, clutching at herself. *"Ugh,"* she moaned. "Another heave . . . I feel it deep in my bowels."

He had no idea what to do, so he went to the far corner and woke de Chauliac.

"The babe," he said when the Frenchman was awake enough to understand.

"It is coming?"

"Aye."

The Frenchman stood and adjusted his robes around him quickly so he might walk. Disregarding any danger to himself, he went to the bedside where Kate was still sitting in the chair.

"Describe your pain, *madame,*" he ordered.

"It begins in the very pit of my bowels and spreads around my belly until I feel as though the whole of my innards will be expelled," she said as she clutched her own abdomen. She looked helplessly at Alejandro and said, "This must be the pain of hell, Père, I am sure of it."

Alejandro rushed forward to comfort her. "You shall never know that pain," he said defiantly.

"We will take her to my manse. Quickly, before she can no longer travel."

Alejandro turned and looked at the child on the bed, then faced de Chauliac again. "But the boy—"

"You can remain here with him. The girl will go with me. She cannot bring the child forth here—there is plague in this room, to which a new infant must not be exposed."

"No," Kate cried when she heard the proposal, "I beg you, Père, do not leave my side . . . I have no sister or mother to help me, I have only you."

Alejandro gave de Chauliac a fierce look of resolve. "I will not leave."

They both turned toward the long moan that poured desperately from Kate's mouth. They watched with horror as she stood suddenly and raised up her skirt. A long streak of blood was pouring down her leg, staining her stocking as it flowed into the top of her leather shoe. Alejandro saw the knife she always kept there, the very knife that she had pressed against the Baron de Coucy when he tried to abduct her. It seemed so small, and yet she'd saved her own life with it.

Now the blood of that life poured out of her, and Alejandro felt his own bowels wanting to heave at the terrifying sight of it.

"*Mon dieu*," de Chauliac whispered. "She will have to have the babe here, then." He ran to the bell and pulled it, then went to the door and looked anxiously for the servant.

"Please summon the countess," he said when the man appeared. "It is a matter of much urgency."

"The boy . . . ?"

"Just summon her!"

And a few moments later, Countess Elizabeth herself appeared. She stayed well down the hallway; the first thing she said was, "What of my son?"

"Praise God and the Spaniard, he will live."

The countess crossed herself dramatically. Mouthing prayers, she clasped her hands together and looked heavenward.

"But you also have this girl to thank," de Chauliac said. "She stood over him and cleaned him. Had she not been there for him, he would have suffered terribly. And now she has need of a clean place to bring forth her own child."

"Let her bring it forth in there," Elizabeth said stiffly. "She is surrounded by physicians, is she not?"

"Countess, the babe cannot be born into a plague room . . . I myself should not be there, but out of loyalty to you I felt that I must."

"She should have considered that before she went in there. And now she should be thankful that I will allow her even that space." She turned and was about to run off, when Alejandro came to the door. He carried her son in his arms.

"Countess, please," he said.

She continued to depart, with heavy steps.

"Elizabeth."

And at the sound of her name, her shoulders slumped a bit. She stopped and turned back slowly, her head slightly bowed.

"Look at your son," Alejandro said. "He lives." He held the child out, and the pale, weak boy reached toward his mother.

She glanced briefly at Alejandro. Her green eyes flashed anger and the pain of betrayal. But she would not look at the boy he carried in his arms.

"Come," Alejandro said, "take him. He craves his mother's arms."

Finally, she looked up. And when she saw her child, she began to weep. She rushed forward and took the boy into her arms. "He is so pale," she cried.

"But in time his color will return," Alejandro said. "He will thrive again, I know it, because I have seen to him, taken care of him, given of myself to bring him back to you." He pushed the door open slightly. "Now look within, and see how *my* child suffers. Will you make it possible for her to be brought back to me?"

Elizabeth peered hesitantly beyond the door and saw Kate wiping at the blood on her legs with a cloth that was nearing full red, with de Chauliac at her side, holding her steady. The countess blanched and whispered a prayer, then looked at Alejandro fearfully. "It cannot help but go hard when there is that much blood." She peered back inside the room again.

"Then *please,* help—"

But she interrupted him by raising a hand. For a moment she stared at Kate, and as she did, her expression seemed to harden. "By the grace of God," she said as her eyes examined the bleeding girl, "Chaucer is right." She looked back at Alejandro, her face full of accusations. "This daughter of yours bears a most uncanny resemblance to my husband."

Alejandro made a nervous little smile, but inside him his bowels were once again churning. "It is nothing more than a coincidence, *madame*. But her mother was English, so it is only to be expected that she should bear some of that look, with regard to the coloring, especially."

He was explaining as fast as he could, but Elizabeth would hear none of it.

"She bears none of your looks," she said suspiciously, "But she could be my lord's twin, were she a man."

"But clearly, by her condition, you can see that she is *not* a man. She is having a most womanly difficulty right now, and you can make her way easier, if only you will. *Please,*" he begged. "Put these unimportant notions of resemblance aside. It is coincidence, it means nothing. *Help* me now, as I have helped you. She cannot be taken out of here. It is too late. We must have another room."

When the countess looked back at him, her eyes were still full of anger and hurt for the way he had abandoned her. "I do not understand why you came back to torment me."

"It was not my intent to torment you." He reached toward her, tentatively, and when she did not move away he boldly touched her cheek. The skin was soft beneath his fingers, and something within him stirred. "I came to save your son," he said. "By virtue of the affection I bear you, though you are well justified if you do not believe me. I owe you that."

"You owe me that and more," she said, her eyes filling with tears.

"I know. And I am sorry, truly I am. May God grant that this work of healing I have done for your child will help you to understand that. But we must speak of these things at another time, I beg your indulgence, for now my daughter needs my help."

Finally the countess relented. She called for another servant, to whom she handed off the child. The servant scurried away with the little boy in her arms. Elizabeth turned back to Alejandro. "Follow me," she said. "You may have my maid's room."

She led them up a narrow flight of stairs to the third floor of the château. Alejandro carried Kate, though it took all of his strength, and de Chauliac tried to help, but the passageway was too slim to accommodate both of them at the same time. So they struggled, each one taking a turn as needed, until the stairs were conquered.

The room she brought them to was much like the one Alejandro had occupied in de Chauliac's house, with a sloped ceiling, more corners than the laws of geometry would seem to allow, and one small window. The furnishing consisted only of a narrow bed, a table, and a simple chair. The ever present cross with the image of the bleeding savior was affixed to one wall, probably the maid's most prized possession. He laid Kate on the bed of straw and started to remove her clothing.

"I will send my women with the necessities," Elizabeth said quietly, and with one last mournful look into his eyes she disappeared down the stairs.

The promised women arrived in short order with linens and swaddling and water. One stout *femme* carried in a wooden birthing chair that she had hauled up the stairs by herself, but one look at Kate told her that the chair would not be useful. She set it aside, and shoved her way in between Alejandro and de Chauliac.

She spoke in an accent that betrayed her as an Irishwoman, a native of her mistress's homeland. "My lady says you gentlemen are physicians."

They both nodded.

The woman laughed aloud. "Then you'll be useless in the birthing of a child. You'd best stand aside."

And to de Chauliac's protestations of competence, she said, "Has either of you yet looked between her legs?"

Stunned silence was followed by rapid declarations of propriety.

The Irishwoman shook her head in disgust through their stammered explanation. "Simpletons," she said. "You must look to see what needs doing." And when Kate next moaned out in a wave of pain, the woman leaned forward and stroked her belly. She cooed reassuring words at the panting girl. Then she turned back to the gawking observers.

"Stay and watch if ye like, and mayhaps ye'll larn somethin' of use."

They relegated themselves to one corner of the room like useless drones while the women hovered around the bed like a buzzing swarm of bees, their Irish queen at the center of it all. The sturdy redhead was a force quite magic, who with little more than the cajoling motion of her hands was drawing the child into the world stroke by well-placed stroke.

She urged Kate gently toward release. "That's right, lady," the Irishwoman said, "now bear down as if ye were going to fill the pot."

"But I shall soil the bed," Kate moaned.

"No, ye shan't" was the reply, "but ye'll think ye are. It cannot be helped, that feeling. It means the child is near, and crossing your bowels in its passage. And never you mind if you do soil the bed. 'Tis part and parcel. The countess can well afford a new one."

Comforted by these reassurances, Kate set about the task of delivering her child with more determination. She pushed and cried and strained and moaned, and finally in another gush of blood a head popped through.

"Now do that again, lady, and make womankind proud!"

With a groan that seemed to rise up from the very center of her soul, Kate bore down with all the strength she could find. And with that final push, the child was freed, and lay on the straw between her legs. The Irishwoman reached inside her and pulled out the steaming afterbirth, then leaned over and bit through the cord with her own teeth. She wrapped the organ in a cloth and handed it to one of her helpers. "Boil it till it is brown," she said, "then bring it back while it is still hot."

She held up the child by the feet and gave it a good whack on the buttocks. The child began to cry.

The woman wiped the infant and wrapped him in swaddling, then laid him in Kate's arms. "A fine son you have, lady. And fair. He's colored just like ye are."

Alejandro stepped closer, and gazed in stuporous awe at the child he would henceforth call Grandson. Though only moments old, this babe was the very image of Guillaume Karle. But the Irishwoman was right; he would have the coloring of his Plantagenet grandsire, and his half-Plantagenet mother. And even in his mother's thin arms he looked so perfect and sound, a marvel of nature, a miracle brought forth by God's wish that humankind know another hour on Earth. He ached to feel the child in his own arms. So he said gently, "Daughter, may I hold your son?"

"Yes," she whispered. And as she watched the child rise away from her, into her father's embrace, she said softly, "Oh, Père, I have a son . . . if only Karle could be here to see him, to hold him."

"I shall hold him so he thinks it is his own father," he assured her.

De Chauliac, left behind in the corner, now stepped forward and looked over Alejandro's shoulder. "He seems a handsome lad," the Frenchman observed with his customary distance. "But I cannot see him well. Bring him here, to the light of the window. I would see the details to know that he is sound."

But the light had moved away to the other side of the château, and there was little improvement near the window.

"Take the babe out into the hall and carry him to the west window," the Irishwoman advised. "There will be light aplenty there. I have work to do on the lady, and she will want privacy for it."

"May I, then?" he said to Kate.

"Go. But bring him back soon."

With slow and careful steps, for he carried a load far more precious than all the gold he had seen in his life, Alejandro took the child out of the room, and headed down the long hallway, then around a corner to the window the Irishwoman had spoken of. De Chauliac followed for a few paces, then stopped and said haltingly, "You will know well enough yourself if the babe is sound. Perhaps I should . . . leave now."

Alejandro turned around. "No," he protested, "stay, unless you have a reason to depart."

"But I am not needed here."

The Jew said to him, "Necessity is not always the binding between men."

"It has always been so between us, colleague."

"Not at this moment." He motioned with his head toward the window, with its greater light. "Come," he said, "and regard my grandson. For once, let there be something good between us."

They stayed there admiring the child, waiting for the midwife to announce that Kate's womanly parts had been properly seen to, and that the infant should be returned to taste his first milk and know the arms of his mother again. But time passed and the light began to fade, and soon they began to worry.

"I begin to wonder if something is amiss," Alejandro said.

"I shall go ask," de Chauliac offered.

But the Irishwoman would not let him in the room. "She bled a bit, but I have packed her birth parts in the proper herbs, and it seems to have stopped now. But she wants total rest and should not be moved for the moment."

"Then what shall we do?" Alejandro asked nervously when de Chauliac returned with this news. "The countess will not want me here a minute longer than necessary. And she will want my daughter moved."

"Surely she will not object to Kate staying," de Chauliac said. "This woman may be angry at you, but she is not a monster. There is a kind and gentle heart beating in her breast. She will allow her to stay and recover. I shall insist."

"I am loath to leave her behind," the Jew said. "I gave her up once, and it came to no—"

He stopped speaking because he heard footsteps coming up the stairs. Heavy, masculine footsteps, not the dainty tread of the countess and her ladies. And voices—the deep sounds of men with firm purpose. His heart pounding, he slipped around the corner and leaned against the wall, clutching the child to his breast. He glanced at de Chauliac, his eyes full of fear.

The voices and footsteps reached the top of the stairs, and de Chauliac leaned out around the corner just enough to catch a quick look at the arrivals. He swore under his breath and hid himself back behind the corner again.

"It is Lionel himself. And . . . and . . ."

"And *who?*"

". . . and Charles of Navarre, I fear."

"Elizabeth!" Alejandro hissed. He leaned against the wall and closed his eyes. "She will have her revenge on me." He clutched the baby closer to himself. "She must have sent word to him as soon as we arrived—and the fiend has been biding his time, until the boy was cured. Well, he shall bide the rest of it in hell."

He tried to shove the child into de Chauliac's arms, but the Frenchman would not take the wrapped and helpless thing. Instead he grabbed Alejandro and restrained him from the madness he was thinking to do. He whispered urgently, *"No!* Do not go out there!"

"But I would kill this rogue . . ."

"Do you forget that you carry the grandson of the king of England in your arms?"

He *had* forgotten. He looked down at the child, *his* grandson, and God curse anyone who tried to separate him from either the child or his mother.

They heard voices from the small room. "I have come to claim this nephew of mine, in the name of my father," Lionel said with great conviction, "and to speak with my long-lost sister."

Alejandro's heart was pounding in his throat.

"Where is the child?" they heard.

"The physicians took him away," the Irishwoman said. "I know not where. Perhaps they went down the stairs before you came up."

Good, kind woman! he said silently, blessing her.

"The Jew physician, or the French one?"

"I know not which," the Irishwoman said. "I took neither of them to be Jews," she added. "But both might be, for all I know."

De Chauliac put a hand on Alejandro's arm and said quietly, "You must take the child and go."

"But I cannot leave her behind . . ."

"Her fate is out of your hands. I will return to the room—I have nothing to fear from these men—I know too many of their secret deficiencies. I will distract them while you make your escape with the child."

"But Kate . . ." he moaned.

"Save her child," de Chauliac said, "or lose both. It is your choice. But if you go I will try to look after her, I promise."

"But what can you do?"

"I know not yet," the Frenchman said, "but whatever is in my power, I shall do it. You have my solemn promise, by the great affection and respect I bear you."

Alejandro looked into his former mentor's eyes, and saw a friend. He would not have believed it a fortnight earlier, but he believed de Chauliac's promises now.

"Go," de Chauliac said, "run to my manse, take a good horse, and leave Paris. Your bag of gold is in my study, behind the book of Greek works I lent you."

Where could he go? Where, in the dark world, was safety to be found?

"Are there Jews yet in Avignon?" he asked.

"Aye," de Chauliac said. "Clement's edicts have left a strong mark. There is a flourishing ghetto there. You will be welcomed."

Alejandro's mind raced with details that begged to be spoken before he left. "Then I shall go there. Where there are Jews, one can always find a rebbe. Send a message to me through him."

"As soon as it is safe to do so, I shall." He embraced the frightened Alejandro and the infant together in his long arms. "Godspeed, colleague. And may He grant that we meet again, in better times."

Then the tall Frenchman let go and slipped around the corner. He stole quietly down the hallway. Alejandro stuck his head out from behind the wall and watched as de Chauliac entered the small room and closed the door behind him. The sound of men's voices, rising in distress and agitation, came through the door as Alejandro slunk along the hall and down the stairs. Clutching the baby, he slipped down the main staircase of the château and out the door, into the cold dark Paris night.

Janie made her way out of the real world in the sweet grip of one of her fondest fantasies, a dream that had gone unfulfilled until that moment, when the end of the real world seemed too much a possibility. With a cop in the car, she finally had carte blanche to put her foot to the floor and drive as she always wanted to—like some maniac roadrunner with the wind at its tail. Not that the road cops of western Massachusetts would be bothering with speeders that night—they had more pressing duties to see to, obligations more urgent than pulling over an ancient Volvo pushed to the limit on its last journey before retirement. The venerable car would spend its dotage nestled under a camouflage tarp in the New England woods, its gas tank drained, as an archaic symbol of how the world used to seem: dependable, sturdy, eternal. Janie reminded herself as the trees whizzed by that there was a Maria Callas disk still in the player, and that she should remember to remove it before she put the car out to pasture.

Wouldn't want to disappear from the face of the earth without that.

Oh, God, is there anything else I forgot? There must be.

Brights blaring, almost thirty miles over the posted speed limit, she careened down the narrow country highway toward her life's next phase with Michael in the front passenger seat and Caroline in the back. It was gulp-and-tremble time, *What are we going to do?* time, when "Take to the woods" seemed the best answer from a short list of bad choices.

They passed darkened houses, cars abandoned on the side of the road, pairs of red eyes peering out from the underbrush. They were less than twenty miles from safety when a little girl of maybe seven or eight showed up suddenly in the headlamps. When they first caught a glimpse of her she was sitting on a boulder by the side of the road, unkempt and thin as a rail, but as soon as she saw them, she started to jump up and down frantically on the rock and wave her skinny arms. Her movements were mechanical, as if someone behind her had pushed a button to get her started.

So Janie passed her. But even in the darkness, she had seen the vacant, desperate Outbreak look on the child's face, and it tore at her heart. She slowed the car and glanced into her rearview mirror.

She looked at her fellow fugitives. "What should we do here?" she whispered.

"Keep driving," Michael said sternly from the passenger seat.

"But she's a child," Caroline said, "and it's the middle of the night, for God's sake." She leaned forward and put a hand on the back of the driver's seat. "Janie, pull over—we can't just leave her there."

Janie glanced back over her shoulder. She saw the starkly white bandage on Caroline's finger and remembered what lay before them still, how very long this night would be.

But it's a child. She guided the car toward the shoulder, pulled off the road, and killed the engine. The silence seemed huge.

"What are we going to do with her?" Michael said finally. "We can't take her with us."

"She might have wandered from her house," Janie said.

"So we'll just take her back there and then just be on our way." Caroline turned to her husband, her eyes pleading. "Michael . . . some day our child might need someone's help."

"Look," he said gently, "this could be a trap of some sort."

But Caroline would not be swayed. "Who would put a little girl on the side of the road in the middle of the night? Who could *do* a thing like that? She must be lost. Please, Michael—we have to help her."

His voice was full of reservation. "Back it up a little."

Janie turned the engine back on and put the Volvo in reverse, and the car whined backward; when the child came in sight again, Janie brought it to a full stop. Michael peered out into the darkness indecisively for a moment, his eyes trying to pierce the cover of the roadside brush. "Lock the doors," he told them. "Don't open them until I get back."

He got out of the car, put on his helmet, and headed back toward the little girl.

As instructed, Janie pressed the lock handle down and heard its reassuring *thunk*. As she watched in the mirror, she could see Michael in the illumination of the backup lights, neon green from head to toe. The child shrank away from him, so he crouched down to her level.

Janie watched carefully as the child pointed into the woods along the side of the road, and when Michael looked in that direction and nodded she felt somehow relieved, as if Caroline had been right about what the child needed from them. He put out his big green hand and the child took it, and together they disappeared into the brush.

"He's taking her somewhere," Janie said as her eyes scanned the mirror image.

But then she realized that Michael was no longer visible, and he could therefore no longer see the car.

We are all so paranoid, she said to herself, *there is nothing to be afraid of here.* And the idea that they'd overreacted, that this was just a little girl in trouble, was very liberating. She turned to Caroline in the backseat. "She probably just lives a—"

She heard Caroline's cry before the crunch of the safety glass assaulted her ears. She shrieked and turned toward the noise and saw the head of a small wood axe moving, in slow motion as if through water, toward the already cracked window. The flat, blunt end of the metal was pointed forward, but its menace seemed just as sharp as the opposite side when it whizzed toward her. A pair of large hands were wrapped around the wood handle, and beyond that, on the edge of the darkness, was the shadowed and desperate face of a man, only partly visible.

She leaned inward over the stick shift, away from the blow, and as Caroline screamed Janie thrust her arm back into the rear seat for the bag that held V.M. She hauled it forward with one mighty yank as the axe head connected with the glass again. Through some miracle of karma her hand found the gun Tom had given her, and she wrapped her fingers hard around the textured grip with unspeakable gratitude, then pivoted in one sharp motion back toward the window and pointed the gun directly at the shadow man, the sighting point trembling along with her hand as she attempted to aim it.

He had the axe drawn back again, ready to deliver what would probably be the final blow required to break the window completely.

Then he would drag them from the car, render them— .

. . . motionless . . .

—and leave them on the side of the road while he made his escape with their functioning vehicle, almost full of gasoline.

Their eyes locked for a moment. A clear understanding of what was about to take place passed between them, and everything else stopped. Somewhere in the woods behind this clean-cut thirtyish man there was probably a woman hiding, perhaps with another child or even two. There might be frightened, elderly parents waiting for him down the road a piece, hanging on assurances that their son would come and take them away to some place where things were better. He was only doing what any responsible man might do when forced to revert to the natural state, the condition where the first priority was to keep the genes intact long enough to pass them on.

But it was still unforgivable. A question flashed into Janie's numbed brain: Would this man have enough adaptive intelligence to realize that she would blow his head off so Caroline could pass on *her* genes? Would he depart in an act of genetic self-preservation, understanding that she would kill him if she had to? In these freeze-frame seconds of the confrontation, there was no way to tell. On Main Street, Janie would have taken him for an office worker, a newspaper reporter, someone's next-door neighbor. But here, now, in his eyes, she saw something almost feral, something way out of control.

Those eyes widened even further as he brought the axe forward. Janie had a brief inner-sight glimpse of a young, dark-haired Myra Ross with her weapon pointed in the face of a turbaned enemy who meant to relieve her of her life if she did not find the *chutzpah* to take his first.

She pulled the trigger.

What remained of the cracked glass blew out, and the man tumbled backward into the night. As soon as she saw he was down, Janie's eyes went straight to the mirror and she saw Michael rushing out of the woods, the child struggling against his grasp as he attempted to pull her along. Finally, the little girl broke free and disappeared into the night as Michael raced back toward the car. Janie flipped up the locks, and as soon as Michael was in she sped away, showering the fallen body with sand and pebbles as her wheels spun hard on the shoulder.

Caroline was sobbing, and Janie trembled almost violently as she pushed the groaning car to a speed she hadn't thought it would ever achieve again. Michael looked back through the rear window and screamed obscenities into the night, his fist clenched in anger. She realized, as the distance from the body on the side of the road increased, that she, a physician and healer, had never even considered getting out of the car to see if there was anything she could do for the man. And even beyond her horror at what she had done to him, that notion brought deep and instant shame.

The gun, minus one bullet, was on the floor just below Janie's seat, within easy reach, where it would remain until she no longer needed its selective advantage.

There was nothing subtle or quiet about their entry into the camp, though it was well into the wee hours when they finally rang the bell at the gate to the courtyard. Tom was waiting outside the main building. He answered the ring by swinging the gate wide open, and then he slammed it firmly shut once the car was through, without regard for the noise it made to do so. And as Caroline and Michael looked on in astonishment, he and Janie rushed toward each other in the courtyard and fell into an almost desperate embrace.

"The gun," she cried, "Oh, Tom, that gun, thank God you gave it to me, but I shot a man, and I think I may have killed him."

"I know, I know," he said as he cradled her, "Please, Janie, you can't blame—"

She pulled back in surprise. "You *know*? How could you know—it just happened an hour ago."

"V.M.," he admitted. "There's a transmitter."

Of course there was. It made perfect sense. And she no longer cared. She was already too fractured to let indignity have any room in her heart. "I didn't even try to help him, Tom, I just left him there. . . ."

"Stop," he hushed her. "Do you think you're the only one who's gone through something like that? There are a million stories just like that one. You have to leave it out there, it doesn't belong in here."

She clung to him fiercely. When they finally pulled apart, Janie whispered, "There's a problem," so only he could hear. "I need Kristina."

Then to his questioning look, she said, "It's important, Tom."

"I'll get her, then." He gestured with his head toward Michael and Caroline. "But why don't you bring them inside and we'll get—"

"No," she said quickly. "Not yet."

His look was all piercing accusation. "Janie—is there some reason they shouldn't come in?"

She bit her lower lip to keep herself from crying again. "There may be. That's why I need Kristina."

She stared through the eyepiece at the worst beast in the recorded history of microbiology, a single-celled fire-breathing dragon that all the knights and dames of the biochemical round table had tried to slay in the years since its first appearance, without even a hint of success. So even though she'd been a mere child when drug-resistant *Staphylococcus aureus mexicalis* made its terrifying debut, Kristina recognized DR SAM in her microscope the moment she saw it. She looked up from the eyepiece and nodded at Janie, who leaned, her face full of horror and shame, against the door frame outside the hastily arranged isolation room off the lab, the bare white room in which Caroline was weeping behind the locked door.

Michael stood on the opposite side of the door frame, his face pinched and tight from shock. Left to his own devices, he would have disregarded all the sensible precautions he followed so religiously in his work every day and clawed his way through the door with his bare fingernails. When they'd first closed the door that now separated him from his wife, Tom and John Sandhaus had had to hold him back. As soon as they let go, he tried to attack the steel panel with pounding fists, cursing everything and everyone he could imagine.

An emergency meeting was called. The discussion was heated and often painful, but accord was reached. There was talk of containment, of necessary evil, and of heartless resolve to do what was needed.

"I think you need to come look at this," Kristina said quietly after a few minutes of looking in the microscope. Her eyes went to Michael for a few seconds, then came back to Janie again.

Janie rose up wearily from the chair and moved across the small lab, one leaden step after another, thinking that what Kristina had to show her would surely be worse than she anticipated, that the bacteria were multiplying, thriving, arrogantly resisting everything that could be thrown in their murderous path.

Why, she asked herself desperately, *did I think this was something I could fix?*

They would all die, right there in their "safe" place, when DR SAM got loose, which it certainly would because it always did, sooner or later.

She pressed her own face against the eyepiece of the microscope at Kristina's urging and gazed down at the slide of cells scraped from Caroline's semiamputated toe. There was another slide, waiting to deliver its own news, with cells taken from her hangnail.

They'll be swarming and swimming around and dividing, and just having a big old party—

But they weren't doing any of those things—instead, they were engaged in the bacterial equivalent of gasping for breath.

"Sweet Jesus," she said in a whisper. She looked up at Kristina. "What is *this*?"

"I don't know. But take a look at the other one."

They flipped out the toe slide, clamped in the finger slide. The view was virtually identical.

"Something is making them—shrivel up," Kristina said. "I can't even begin to think what—usually they just eat everything they come in contact with and then find a new meal ticket." She looked back into the eyepiece again. "Is she taking medication of any kind?"

"Not that I'm aware of."

When she looked up again, Kristina's face was full of taut excitement and hopeful disbelief. "Either that or she has a strain of DR SAM that's mutated to a self-destructive state."

"It usually goes the other way—that's how DR SAM became DR SAM in the first place. Mutated to invincibility. I've never heard of any bacterium taking itself out of the picture."

"Neither have I."

"But DR SAM has always had this knack for doing things we don't expect it to do," Janie said.

Expect the unexpected, Alejandro whispered in her ear.

She was thinking aloud now. "Maybe there's something we wouldn't expect going on here."

Kristina looked at her. "What wouldn't we expect? I don't even know where to start thinking about that."

Janie began listing the possibilities. "Like we said, we wouldn't expect the bacteria to mutate for negative traits. So they're probably not doing that."

"That's not it, though."

"I know." She pressed one hand against her forehead as if it would help her to think more clearly. "We wouldn't expect all of them to die at once, even if there were an effective antibiotic."

"Well, they are, but that's not it. Damn." She looked back into the microscope. "Come on," the girl whispered, "speak to us."

And while her young cohort was thus absorbed, Janie glanced away— sometimes just to look at something else was enough of a stimulus to set an idea or a realization in motion. She looked back toward the room where Caroline was being held and saw Michael leaning against the door with his hands and forehead pressed flat on the painted surface, as if he might be able to reach right through it.

Such terrible pain for anyone to go through, she thought with sympathy. She pitied him for the uncertainty he was going through, and recalled for a moment the hours that she and Bruce had spent hovered over Caroline, before Michael even knew her. *He would have collapsed if he'd seen her when she had plague.*

She had plague. . . .

"Kristina," she said softly.

The girl looked up from the microscope.

"She had plague."

"What?" Kristina said.

"Caroline had plague. She survived it."

"Well, I know," the girl started to say, "but—"

And then Janie's meaning became clear to her. "Oh, my God. People who survived plague have a natural resistance to HIV."

"Yes, they do. The viral docking ports get blocked."

"So why couldn't something similar happen with DR SAM?"

"It could," Janie whispered. "If the docking ports were similar." She looked back into the microscope again, then pulled away from the eye-piece, a look of intense concentration on her face. Muttering to herself, she adjusted the focus and enlarged the magnification. "Okay, I've got a view of them." She looked up at Kristina and nodded toward V.M., which was sitting on a nearby counter. "In the imaging program—can you bring up one of the stock images of HIV at the same level of depth as these bacteria are?"

"Sure," Kristina said. She started tapping keys immediately. She brought V.M. closer as it searched for the proper image and drew it on the screen.

They both looked back and forth a few times. "What do you think?" Janie said after a few glances.

"I think there's reason to think that what we're seeing is plague-based resistance to DR SAM. Genetic in nature," Kristina said with quiet excite-ment. "It actually makes complete sense, *total* sense, that a person who'd had plague could be resistant to DR SAM. But—why hasn't anyone thought of this before? Or noticed a pattern?"

"Do you know anyone other than Caroline who's survived plague? I"—*Alejandro,* Janie thought in midsentence. *That little girl.*—"don't."

"There can't be many," Kristina said.

"We'll have to find out how many there are, then test them."

"Yes—but we'll have to get inside Big Dattie."

In the bag where V.M. was usually stored, Janie still had the corneal identification program she had lifted from the French hacker. Big Dattie would be one of the last government services to break down—the mili-tary and Biopol depended heavily on it. "I know how we can do it," she said.

"You're joking."

"I'm not."

"But—this is incredible—think what this means! We can find a way to deal with DR SAM by isolating the gene that affords resistance, then we can do a gene wash, just like we did for those boys."

Kristina took on the pulsing glow that was proprietary to young people in the act of discovery. "Oh, this is so huge, I've got to go find my fath—"

She stopped and went completely silent.

For a few stunned seconds, Kristina and Janie just stared at each other. A silent understanding was passed, and Janie was flooded with unexpected relief. Finally, when she felt she could breathe again, she said quietly, "How about if I tell him?"

Tom was contrite, almost dazed when Janie confronted him.

"Why did you keep this a secret from me? A beautiful child like she must have been, and now such a wonderful young woman—oh, Tom, it must have been torture to keep this to yourself. I would love to have known her when she was little."

"I don't know how I did it. There just never seemed to be a right time to tell you."

"You never married her mother."

He hesitated a moment, then said, "I didn't love her mother."

"But you love Kristina . . ."

"My God, of course I did, do, she's my daughter. And I've always been there for her when she needed something, always taken care of her."

So kind and steady and calm . . . Janie had no doubt that he'd been a wonderful father. But it was still a huge, weighty burden. "It's like you had this secret life all these years and I didn't know anything about it. I thought I knew—"

"We were both in college. We weren't in regular contact back then."

Something stirred in her, a thought about the timing of it all, but in the confusion of the moment she let it pass. "Good grief, Tom, I hate to tell you what I was thinking."

"What were you thinking?"

"Well, that there was something—romantic—"

"Janie, please. The difference in our ages alone . . . how could you think that of me?"

"I don't know. I'm not sure I really did. I didn't want to believe it. But I do know that you should be very proud—she's a remarkable young woman. Wise beyond her years . . . I just keep wanting to ask her where she comes up with some of the stuff she says."

With pensive, almost wistful sadness, Tom said, "She is remarkable. In more ways than I can even begin to tell you."

But you will tell me, eventually, because whatever it is about your daughter that distinguishes her so dramatically is something you had a hand in. Secrets like that always wanted to get out, to be set free. It was time, Janie believed, to start that process of unburdening.

"She's not in Big Dattie, Tom."

He looked into her eyes.

"I know."

"But just about everyone her age is in there."

"I, uh, had someone take her out, in . . ."

He looked away again. "When . . ."

He couldn't seem to finish the sentence.

"Tom," she said, very gently, "I'm not sure I understand—you can have people taken out?"

He nodded slowly. "Once upon a time."

"How?"

"It was all money."

"But that kind of money . . ."

"A couple of big lawsuits, settled very quietly, remember? I mean huge."

Janie let him sit with his thoughts for a few moments. Memories overtook him. And eventually, he shared them with her.

She was stupefied. "But I didn't know that was being done then. Oh, my God, Tom—she's got to be one of the very first."

"The very, I think," he said. "The very."

Life will always find a way, even in the worst of times, and during the plague winter that followed the closing of Camp Meir's doors to the outside world, a child was born to Michael and Caroline, a beautiful little daughter with her mother's red-gold hair. They named her Sarah, after the ancient crone whose wisdom, recorded so carefully by Alejandro Canches more than six centuries earlier, had held the key to her mother's survival in the new millennium. Her middle name was Jane, after the woman who was there to receive her when she finally struggled, wailing her protests, in blessed perfection from the womb of her mother.

And every time Janie Crowe saw the baby at Caroline's breast, so safe and unaware, surrounded by the love of her parents and protected by the vigilance of an entire devoted community, she couldn't help but think of all the babies born on the outside that winter, into the dark cold pain that she knew must exist out there. She often wondered, with a heart full of fear for her species, what the desperate mothers of those babies would sacrifice to see that their offspring survived. Anything they had, most likely, would be given without a second thought; such was the nature of motherhood in the wild. In that dreadful plague winter, it would not be much.

But life always finds a way, she reminded herself during the long nights, as wind-driven snow and ice worked their furious rage on the stark New England landscape. Some of those babies would survive, as they had during DR SAM's first reign of terror—that much could be claimed with reasonable certainty. What those babies would grow into, however, could not be predicted.

Now and then some poor soul would stumble witlessly upon the camp's electronic fence and rattle it, only to wake up later a good distance away with a sore arm and a fuzzy head. Occasionally there would be a hoofprint left in the snow, or sled tracks to account for the unexpected relocation. Janie ventured outside when the cold was not too brutal and the wind not too biting, to walk on the camp's grounds and think her private thoughts. Most often on these winter strolls she found herself dwelling on the anonymous man whose life she had taken in the desperate effort to preserve her own and Caroline's. She'd been accountable for many a human being in her work as a physician, and there had been occasions when her act, or her failure to act, had tipped the scale of life and death one way or the other. But in all of those cases, Mother Nature had brought the ailing patient to her already damaged and she had used her gifts to work the best outcome.

But not so with Anonyman, as she had begun to call him in her own mind. Killing him had been a choice, and Janie had to believe that she had chosen wisely, or it would be impossible to go on. Giving him a name had not made it easier to shed the weight of her guilt. He raged through her sleep as vividly as she imagined Carlos Alderón had slouched through the sleep of Alejandro Canches, and she found herself seeking comfort in the pages of the ancient physician's journal more and more frequently as spring approached.

News from the outside was sparse and irregular. Every few days Virtual Memorial would light up and scream *incoming, incoming, incoming,* and everyone would gather around in eager anticipation of some word of improvement. The news was never entirely good or entirely bad. Minnesota reported in most frequently, for the hearty Scandanavian plainsfolk who lived there were already building communities again.

Janie knew why the death rate there was lower than in anyplace else. And so did everyone else in Camp Meir. Especially Caroline.

She'd survived plague.

The bridge's white expanse was just as he remembered it from a decade before, when he'd stood in its center with Eduardo Hernandez and looked down at the blackened bodies that floated in the fouled waters of the Rhone, bodies with tortured expressions and swollen necks, all crying out through their masks of death to be laid to rest. But there were not enough living to collect them, not enough graves to accept them, not enough priests to mutter over them. The feelings of that day came back to him like the glancing blow of a mace, heavy and stultifying, and he stopped his horse, as he and Hernandez had done so long ago.

He'd been terrified then, and he was terrified now, but it was a different sort of fear that held him in its grip on this gray day. On his first crossing of the bridge, he'd been afraid of life away from his protective family, frightened of the journey, uncertain of what lay ahead. He hadn't known if he was man enough to face the road ahead of him, but he'd found that he was. And in the time between his first passage over the bridge and the one he made now, he'd come to know that inner man far more intimately than he'd ever thought possible, than he'd ever really *wanted* to know him. He longed for the naivete of that first passage, for his youthful ignorance, because now what lay ahead of him was clear: that portion of his life in which he would miss, and long for, the daughter whose child he had strapped to his chest.

Ah, Hernandez, he mused in thoughtful silence, *my dear companion, how I have missed you!* How innocent they had both been when they first crossed that bridge. *I knew nothing of life, nothing at all, and you, with all your worldly experience, could not even imagine what awaited me.*

If only they had stayed on the other side—might Hernandez be alive today? Could such an adventurer as that great Spaniard have lived through the decade that followed his untimely death?

Half of everyone had died, he remembered.

But look down from your Christian heaven, my friend, and take note of how well you instructed me! I have lived, against the very will of God!

I have made another friend, you know, though I did not recognize his affection for me until it was nearly too late to enjoy it. And he has helped me on my journey, as you did, though he did not have to give up his soul to do so.

The child moved against his chest.

And yes, I nearly forgot, I have a daughter. I stole her from a king. She taught me that there is much to love in this world, if only one looks . . . and she has presented me with this fine grandson, though I am still such a young man!

But sadly, she has never brought him to her breast . . .

He opened the top of the swaddling and looked into the pinched pink face of the stirring infant. "You know nothing of what lies before you, little man," he whispered, "but I swear on the life of your mother that I will do what I can to keep you safe." He rubbed the child's back, and in a few minutes the baby settled down again. He kneed his mount gently in the side, and the beast began to move forward, with slow, sure steps.

"We shall find you a suitable wet nurse as soon as we are on the other side." He looked back at the nanny goat who trotted behind the horse at the end of a tether, her full teats swaying as she scurried along. The animal looked immensely unhappy and bleated in a most disturbing manner. He had paid the princely sum of two gold pieces for the aggravating beast, but she had provided warm milk to nourish the child and for that Alejandro would have paid ten times the sum. "Then when a proper nurse is found, we shall put this annoying nanny out to her reward at pasture, with our undying gratitude for her good service."

The papal palace still dominated the vista, its white spires striving heavenward toward that ethereal place all Christians believed lay beyond the miserable bonds of life. He looked up and imagined the new pope, whose name he did not know, and did not care to know, ensconced in his private tower, surrounded by advisors and sages, though Alejandro could not imagine that any of them could be so shrewd as de Chauliac had been on behalf of his patron Clement. The current ambassador to the Christian God would be firmly seated in the glorious might of the Church, with its unending reach and limitless mandate. He could disrupt the lives of Avignon's Jews, and many more, by scribbling a few words on a parchment scroll and pressing his seal into a bit of heated red wax on its surface—and despite the suffering he could cause with such a simple act, he need never give it another thought. Would this one turn out to be as unfathomably considerate as Clement had been, against all advice, when de Chauliac served him? He would find out in short order.

The streets of Avignon were far cleaner than he remembered them to be. "Ah, young Guillaume," he said to the baby, "you cannot imagine the filth of this place before! It shines now in comparison." And it was true; he saw no rats, and very little garbage.

He found himself in a large, open square. He did not remember it from his first time in Avignon, but unlike Paris, which suffered under the pall of a war, Avignon had prospered quietly under the protective wing of the Church, and the means to beautify it had been found. The wide expanse of cobblestone was aflutter with the despised pigeons, who swooped down to poke through the occasional droppings of the horses, and alive with pedestrians. Goat still in tow, he scanned the plaza, looking for some sign that there was a natural route one ought to take. But people were walking in all directions, and nothing inspired him.

The baby began to stir again, this time more vigorously, and he would not be comforted. So Alejandro got down off the horse and led the animal to the edge of the square, where he tethered it to a tree. He untied the goat and bent down next to her. Her milk sac was nearly full; it would be time to empty her, anyway. He massaged the sac with one hand, while patting Guillaume's tiny back with the other, and soon her milk began to flow. "Here comes your dinner, little one," he said, and he set a small pail from his pack underneath her. Slowly and patiently he filled the pail, for to rush would sour the milk or spook the goat, and neither was a desirable result.

Then he sat down on a stone wall and placed the child in his lap. He dipped the corner of a small white rag in the warm milk, and laid it gently on the child's lip. The tiny baby sucked lustily and made quick work of draining the rag. He did this over and over until the child was satisfied, and then he dipped his own finger in the milk and offered it, so the infant might know the warmth of flesh between his lips. "When we have found you a nurse, you must know what to do," he cooed. "She will not come with rags for teats."

All he had done in the time since he had left Paris, it seemed to him,

was ride and feed the child, and change his swaddling when it was required. When he was not doing any of those things, he would try to sleep.
But it felt to him that he had closed his lids no more than a few hours
altogether. *Imagine,* he thought to himself, *being a woman alone with an
infant . . . how would one survive?* More often than not in such cases, he
knew, neither the mother nor the child lived.

But this would be the last time this child would eat his dinner from a
bit of fabric, for if all went according to his plan, he would find a temple,
and there seek a Jewess who would take pity on them and offer herself in
hired service as a nurse.

When the child was cleaned and swaddled and back on his chest again,
he retied the goat to the horse. He walked out into the square and
stopped the first intelligent-looking passerby.

"Please, sir," he said, "where might I find the section of town where
Jews live?"

The man stared suspiciously at him. He held out a scroll that he
himself had written in Hebrew. "I am owed a debt, and I must collect it."

The man looked at the scroll with disdain, then turned and pointed in
a southerly direction. "That way," he said, and he started to walk away.

"What street should I seek?" Alejandro called after him.

"Rue des Juifs," the man said.

It was, like Rue des Rosiers, a dark and narrow street, thoroughly unlovely
but clean and uncluttered and alive with familiarity. And on the door
frames he saw not the leftover traces of mezuzahs, but the symbols themselves. He got down off the horse and led the animal along, and as he
worked his way down the street he reached out and touched each one.

He went two or three blocks, attracting vague but not unfriendly stares
from those he passed. This would be a tight-knit community, where the
denizens all knew each other, where everyone knew his place. As watch-
fulness, his constant companion for a decade, slowly ebbed out of him, he
felt oddly light and uncontained. And though his attire was completely
European, he was not immediately taken for an outsider. Cautious nods
of greeting were given to him as he proceeded, toward what he did not
know, and he found himself smiling and nodding back with genuine
friendliness and a complete lack of suspicion.

And suddenly, as if God Himself had led him there, he found himself
in front of a small building that could only be a temple. He brought the
horse and goat to a halt and stood there for a moment regarding the neat
facade.

"Well, young Guillaume," he said, "I believe this is where we wish to be."

There was no place to tether the animals so he stopped a passing youngster and offered a *sou* for their temporary care. The boy happily accepted, and when handed the rein, stood there gravely, the pride of a working man on his small face.

Clutching the baby firmly to his chest, Alejandro bent over and entered through the small door. The floor was sand, to soften sound for those who would meditate deeply on the wonders of God. And there at the front of the small room were two old men, doing just that. Their heads moved rhythmically in a bobbing sort of motion while their lips poured out a steady stream of worship. It was the classic stance of a devout Jew at prayer, something he had seen many thousands of times in his youth. But the eyes of the man who had been across Europa noticed something he had not observed as a youth.

How curious this practice looks.

One, Alejandro assumed by his attire, was a rebbe, likely the leader of this congregation and the greater community itself. The other seemed to have no special significance beyond his obvious devotion. So deep was the concentration of these two men that they did not notice him.

Surely the rebbe will know of a nurse, he thought. And when he spoke aloud, the Hebrew rolled off his tongue with uncanny fluidity.

"*Shalom,* Rebbe," he said quietly.

The rebbe turned slowly and faced him. "*Shalom,* my son."

"Might I ask you a question? I am a traveler in need of advice."

"If I can be—"

But his words were cut short by a sudden moan from the other elderly worshiper, who turned around and now stood facing the tall intruder. On uncertain feet, he took a few steps forward through the sand. He steadied himself by placing a hand on the wood railing and squinted through the dim light at the new visitor. And then, in a trembling, shaky voice, he whispered, "Alejandro?"

Alejandro thought for a moment that God had commanded him to give up his tongue; he could not make it move. All spit deserted him. But somehow, in his shock, he managed to utter the one word that needed to be said.

"Father?"

The old man started to teeter, so he rushed forward to support him. And then, with the child still against his chest, he took the old man into his trembling arms as hot tears of joy streamed uncontrollably down his cheeks.

* * *

The baby Guillaume Karle screamed inconsolably as he did what the sons of Jews had done for centuries before him: he gave up a bit of his manhood to God, and received in return God's promise to remember him. And though the child was not the blood son of Alejandro, the rebbe had decided that it would accomplish nothing to hold this shortcoming against him. *He is just a baby,* the wise man said. *We shall teach him how to be a good Jew.*

And when the brief ceremony was over, Alejandro brought Guillaume to a woman nearby, a young widow with a child of her own newly weaned, but plenty of milk left to service Kate's infant son.

"Ah, Leah," Alejandro said with a smile as he handed the child to her, "what wonders you have worked. See how he thrives in your care!"

She bounced the child gently in her arms and felt his warm weight against her. Alejandro noticed the ease with which the woman carried him, almost as if the child had been born her own.

"He seems made of hunger," Leah said. "But I think he is content. He sleeps well enough."

And Alejandro found himself thinking that even at the babe's tender age, a man recognizes welcoming arms. . . .

He traded one last smile with the striking young widow as the rebbe approached them. With a shy glance, she left, Guillaume clutched to her breast.

"A letter has come for you," the old man said. He produced a scroll from the sleeve of his robe and held it out.

So soon? he thought as he took it. He noticed that his hands were trembling.

De Chauliac's fine hand was firm and clear on the parchment. The strokes, in keeping with the man, were bold and well formed. He had added flourishes in Elizabeth's red ink, an unmistakable sign of his esteem. He could only hope that the news contained in the letter would be as fair as the hand that conveyed it. He took a deep breath and read.

> *My dear colleague,*
> *I hope this news finds both you and your grandson safe and in good health.*
> *They, by which I mean Prince Lionel and the lady Elizabeth, have taken Kate into their household, naturally against the girl's own will. She has yet to recover completely from her labors in bringing the infant forth, but the Irishwoman stays at her side and does good work on her behalf. I have looked in on her three times since you left.*

She was nearly delirious with fear for the first day, and suffered a fever, until I assured her privately that your escape was accomplished.

Young Chaucer is beside himself with grief over your circumstances—though I know not why! He seems to feel some vague complicity, undeserved, in my opinion. The boy has taken your position to great heart and has made himself nearly my accomplice. Through him I know that there is talk of returning Kate to England, though when this shall occur has not yet been decided. She is not a hostage of the Dauphin, as are Lionel and his entire Court, and may be brought out of France at Edward's discretion. I dare not think what Edward Plantagenet's pleasure will be in this matter.

If you send word of yourself and the child, I will see that it gets to her—Chaucer has sworn he will assist me in this. No doubt your daughter is as eager to know your fate as you are hers, and it may speed her recovery to have a message.

As for myself, I am praying, and will continue to pray, for good fortune to bless you. I would welcome a word now and then; indeed, I crave it. Do not deny me.

We shall meet again, I am certain of it.

Your faithful servant,
Guy de Chauliac

He wrote back, telling de Chauliac all that he could of his journey south and of the unexpected joy he had found at its end. He told of the child's progress and growth, that the news might be conveyed to Kate and strengthen her spirit for the trials that were surely ahead of her.

Slowly, Alejandro found a place for himself and his grandson among the Jews of Avignon. But Avram Canches was slow to welcome the fair, blue-eyed child his son had brought out of the north.

"I shall not have a son of my own, Father. You must accept him."

"You do not know what God has in store for you, Alejandro. There are many good women here who would accept you, despite the foreign child . . . indeed, this Leah who suckles the babe lacks a husband, and she would be a worthy match for you."

"She is a fine woman. A good mother. I would be honored to have her, were it not for . . ."

"For what?"

He sighed deeply before he told his father that he had loved once, and he would not love again.

"What does this love matter?" the old man wanted to know. "A good woman is a good woman, and you are a fine man. Far finer than I dared dream when you were taken away from me. You need only open yourself to the will of God, and I am certain you will know contentment, as I did with your mother, may she rest in peace. In time you will learn to love a woman, if you are of a mind to. I know of these things, you must listen to me."

"I loved one woman, Father, and I am not of a mind to love another."

"But you will leave nothing behind, no legacy, no son to carry on after you, to pray for your soul."

"So be it. I shall leave my work behind me. It will be legacy enough."

"Then sadly the name of Canches will come to an end. When your flesh passes, the world will never again know the flesh of our flesh . . ."

"So be it," Alejandro said finally. "If God sees fit for the flesh of a Canches to be brought into the world, He will surely find the means to do so. Without our help."

epilogue

The two women sat in wood rocking chairs on the wide-planked open porch that rimmed Camp Meir's main building, listening to the surrounding forest as their chairs creaked back and forth.

Janie relaxed her head against the chair's padded backrest and sighed in true contentment. She closed her eyes for a moment and let the earth-sounds resonate within her. The rhythm of the creaking was calming, almost soporific.

She opened her eyes and smiled at Kristina. "Makes you believe in God, doesn't it?"

"I do, anyway."

Janie was not surprised.

"Kristina," she said curiously, "There's been something I've been meaning to ask you. How does it feel, I mean internally, to be—" She struggled for an acceptable way to ask, and settled on "like you are?"

"Do you mean, does it feel different?"

"Yes."

A few creaks passed, then the young woman said, "Why are you asking?"

"Well, I think I need to know. Don't you? So I can explain to this one." She patted her belly.

Kristina looked off pensively into the early autumn night. Crickets chirped noisily. The fluttering of bat wings could be heard faintly from the tree canopy. "I guess you do," she finally agreed. "But I'm not sure I can really answer your question. I've always been this way, at least as far back as I remember."

Alejandro's journal rested on what remained of Janie's lap. Her massively swollen belly lay heavily on the top of her thighs. The child within her had settled down into the birth canal at last and might be born any day. And though the September night was cool and pleasant, Janie was feeling way too old, at least physically, to be pregnant. She shifted slightly to adjust the pressure and said, "How far back is that?"

Kristina reached out her hand and placed it on the center of Janie's protruding abdomen. Ignoring Janie's question completely, she said, "My father is just so happy about this."

The question would wait. "I am too. I can't think of anyone who could be a better father for this baby. I mean, Tom understands completely. But we are a little old to be parents. When he starts crawling all over the place and climbing on things, I think we'll be depending on you for a lot of help."

"I don't mind," the girl said happily. "I never had a brother."

They rocked quietly in the evening air, enjoying each other's company. The unborn child kicked, and Kristina drew her hand away with a small gasp of pleasure. She and Janie both laughed.

It was a matter of pure joy to her, except for the occasional moments when she worried about being able to care for a baby.

"I'll have to wash diapers, Tom."

"I'll wash them too, you know. We'll get used to it."

"But what if I don't make enough milk? Women my age—"

"Do you honestly think Caroline wouldn't be a wet nurse if he needed one? And if that doesn't work out, we have the goats. Or the cows."

"I don't know if I remember any lullabies."

"You'll remember them. Or you'll make up new ones."

"Well, at least we have stories to tell him . . ."

"That we do."

"Did you guys finally settle on the name?" Kristina said.

As if there could be any question about what the baby boy would be called. "Yeah," Janie said with a little chuckle. "We're going to call him Bigfoot. For the way he wanders around my stomach."

"No, I mean seriously . . ."

"Yes. We did." Janie Crowe grinned broadly. "It'll be Alex."

ABOUT THE AUTHOR

Ann Benson lives in Amherst, Massachusetts, with her family. Readers may e-mail her at ptales@crocker.com or visit her Web site at www.plaguetales.com.